A COUNTRY GROWN UNREAL

A Country Grown Unreal

Robert Turley

Writers Club Press

San Jose New York Lincoln Shanghai

A Country Grown Unreal

Writers Club Press
an imprint of iUniverse, Inc.

For information address:
iUniverse, Inc.
5220 S. 16th St., Suite 200
Lincoln, NE 68512
www.iuniverse.com

ISBN: 0-595-22689-2

Printed in the United States of America

Contents

▼

BOOK II

BOOK III

BOOK V

EPILOGUE

Prologue

CHAPTER I

▼

1905

"Mama, one of those old men in our courtyard tried to kiss me when I came in just now."

Her mother stiffened. "He didn't…he didn't…?" The idea was too frightful to think of, let alone put into words. She had been tranquil, brushing her eldest daughter's hair quite mechanically and staring unseeing through the dense lace curtains at the anaemic winter sunshine outside.

"Of course not. I could see the lice jumping about in his beard." Sonia laughed. "I kicked his shin, but he still crossed me and blessed me. He didn't seem to mind at all. Perhaps he really is a holy man."

"Where was Pyotr Alexeivich? Didn't he come through the gates with you?"

"He couldn't. He was afraid to leave his car. There are so many rough-looking people in the streets. Everyone says this is the beginning of the Revolution. Anyway, we were quite safe really. We only had to run from the gates to the door."

Her mother's voice harshened with a guilt she would never acknowledge to anyone in words. "Where's your sister? Is Marie all right?"

Sonia laughed. "Dearest, you must know by now, nobody will ever try to kiss poor Marie like that. She's upstairs now tidying her room I expect, like she always does directly she comes home. She'll be down soon. Then she'll tell you I must have led the old man on, otherwise he wouldn't have tried to touch me. It was all my fault. Everything always is my fault according to Marie."

"And did you encourage him, Sonia?"

"Mama! Of course not. I spoke to him as I came by; I always do. Have you ever thought how absolutely ghastly it must be, not to have a roof over your head this weather?"

Her Mother chose not to argue and began once more brushing Dorothea's hair. Sonia sat on the sofa, watching and panting slightly. She longed for something remarkable to happen; secretly she longed for the Revolution. "You've heard, I'm sure," she said, "everybody's talking about it. The little yellow monkeys will be in Moscow within the month. They're already this side of Kazan. They burned down the Cathedral there and murdered everybody while they slept in their beds."

"Don't talk such horrible nonsense, child!"

"And don't make up rumours like that," her elder sister chided.

"Nonsense or not, Dorothea, it's what everybody says. There's another thing, too. Tomorrow! The girls at the Smolny are going to break down the gates to get out if they have to. They're coming to the Nevsky to watch the procession. It won't be as exciting as little yellow monkeys coming down the street, but almost. The people from the Putilov works are marching to the Winter Palace." She began to giggle. "They're bringing a petition to the Tsar. Only he won't be there. He's already in Tsarskoe Selo. Isn't that typical?"

"Sonia! Mind what you're saying."

"But it's true. He's already left. I know because some of my friends' parents have gone with him."

"That's enough!" Her Mother put down the brush and abandoned Dorothea who, thank God, she thought, had never been any trouble to her like Sonia.

Dorothea shook her hair free. In spite of Sonia's irritating determination always to be the centre of attention, she remained her favourite sister; she had been from the day she was born.

Her Mother said, wearily, "Listen to me, Sonia! Whatever happens tomorrow will have nothing at all to do with us. It's not the first time we've seen this sort of thing and I don't suppose it will be the last. It's nothing to do with this Revolution you're always talking about. It's just some Anarchist or Communist agitator stirring up the people and..."

"Oh no, Mama, I'm sorry, that's not right. It's a priest this time...someone from near the factory, I believe..."

"Don't interrupt me, child! What you have to understand is that if you continue to talk the way you do, you'll find yourself in serious trouble. None of you young people see the risks you run. That's up to you, of course. But I won't let you get your Father and the younger ones into trouble with your silly talk."

"No, Mama." Sonia looked chastened. Her Mother turned to Dorothea once more, but Sonia held her attention. "It doesn't matter who's leading them. Anna Vyrubova's new friend would have been much better. He works miracles, they say."

"God forgive you, child!"

"Sonushka, stop! That's blasphemy." Dorothea was unusually angry. Ever since Sonia came in Dorothea had successfully kept the words in the room at a distance, out of her consciousness. Today, she had her own dreams to dream. Tonight there was to be a party; the very first party in her honour.

"But he can, Dora," Sonia persisted. "There's a girl in my class whose Mother knows him well. She and some other ladies go to his flat regularly and she says..."

"That's enough, girl! In future you will have nothing to do with anyone whose Mother keeps that sort of company! Who is she?"

"I forget her name. She's only just come. Her father's one of those new people who own all the factories and everything and they're frightfully rich," Sonia said derisively. She turned to Dorothea. "Dora, darling, you'll look wonderful tonight. Every man in the room will fall in love with you."

That was undoubtedly bound to turn out to be the truth.

Dorothea's glowing black hair, marine-green eyes and olive, pink-blushed skin was just like her mother's, but otherwise unique in the family. And tonight she was being exhibited in front of some of Saint Petersburg's most eligible young men to be admired and fallen in love with. And, of course, they would fall in love with her...all of them. They knew why they had been invited. They would be carried away directly they saw her standing with her parents, in line to receive them.

Such daydreams! Dorothea wanted to be left alone to dream them over and over again. This would be her first grown-up birthday party. Nobody but grown-ups had been invited. No need for nursemaids to be chattering in the hall. No galoshes and tiny fur coats steaming in the boiler-room.

"Darling..." Sonia rushed across the room to hug her, "I could easily hate you, if I didn't love you as much as I do."

They both knew Sonia was talking nonsense. She herself was the prettiest of the sisters. Her hair was ash-blond, her skin creamy and her eyes naturally humorous and unflinching grey. The sisters looked at each other, laughing together silently, in their hearts.

"Good afternoon, Mama."

Marie stood in the doorway. She returned her Mother's vague, impersonal smile. She was no beauty, certainly. She had dark, colourless hair scraped back to expose an unnecessarily high forehead and too much dismal, sallow skin. Regrettably she needed to wear pince-nez because of severe myopia. She was fifteen and already realised, without acrimony, that her sisters were destined to make brilliant marriages. She saw her own future either as a nun or a Governess in some provincial middle-class family somewhere in central Russia. Which should it be? Marie frequently prayed over her choices.

Sonia pointedly ignored her younger sister's arrival. "On the way home Pyotr Alexeivich said this war with the Japanese is all wrong. People are too tired and hungry to go on any more. That's why there's all this trouble on the railways and in the factories."

"Pyotr Alexeivich has no business talking to young girls like that."

"Somebody has to say it," Sonia said flippantly. "Anyway, wasn't he a darling to fetch us from school in his new motor?"

"It was terrible," Marie said, only now advancing into the room. "So noisy and dirty." She wrinkled her distinctive nose.

"It was certainly noisy," Sonia admitted. "Everyone we passed on the Liteiny stopped and stared. And when we turned into the Nevsky an old lady outside Ponovsky's antique shop was so amazed, she fell into a heap of snow."

"It wasn't funny," Marie said sharply. "At least Pyotr Alexeivich wanted to stop and offer her a lift. He didn't because you threatened to make a scene if he did."

"She was all right. She got up and walked away."

"That's enough, girls! Dorothea, you must rest before your party. And you two—stop bickering."

Sonia flounced towards the door, but didn't leave before a parting shot. "I hope you'll remember, Mama, I don't want a party when I'm eighteen. It's a nauseating idea. Women don't have to be paraded to be married these days; there are so many clubs and societies they can belong to instead of surrendering their freedom to a man."

"Sonia...!"

"And this one will be a particularly ghastly party, I know. Pyotr Alexeivich will moon over Dorothea all night. People in love really are quite awful, aren't they?

Dorothea laughed; perhaps she agreed. She left the room arm-in-arm with Sonia before her sister could say anything else to shock her mother.

Only Marie was left. She asked diffidently, "Mama, where's Papa?"

"At his club. Did you want him for something special?"

"No. It's getting dark, though. It's not safe for him to be out so late."

Her Mother tried to generate some warmth in her smile. "He'll be all right, my dear. He'll come home in a cab."

Later, alone in her room, she watched the oncoming night and snowflakes drifting down to the icy crust of the canal beneath her window. Marie was right to be afraid. No one was safe since the war. There were bombings and shootings every day but it was a sudden disappearance she feared most. This was a bad time to be known as a Liberal, and her husband was at a meeting of the Cadets.

It wasn't only the police who kidnapped people. Other organisations were taking the law into their own hands. The Russian Orthodox Committee had hung a vile, rabble-rousing poster on the gate that very morning.

Roman Catholics, Priests, Poles and Jews were now trying to introduce Serfdom into Russia. They assisted the Japanese in the War and sent large sums to help them. They had not given a farthing to the Russian Red Cross. The Tsar said privately that if only he could get rid of the Jews and the Poles, he would divide large tracts of the Crown Lands among the peasants.

She twisted the grubby paper in her fingers and prayed for her husband to come home soon.

"Mama! I knocked twice but you didn't hear me. What's the matter?"

Eduard, the elder of her sons stood at the open door. His sharply structured face, so like his father's when they had first met, never ceased to thrill her.

"Nothing's wrong, my dear. Did you want something?"

"Two cart-loads of little orange trees have just arrived from Princess Surotkina's Estate."

"Oh, no! What is the woman thinking of! They're no use now. They're much too late."

"They're all potted, ready to be arranged round the house," he said soothingly. "They look very nice. And Mama," he reproved her gently, something no one else in the family dared to do, "imagine the trouble she must have had getting them here at all. The railways are in such a mess since the War."

"You're right, you're right, Eduard. You always are. And when she arrives tonight she won't be pleased to see them withering in a frozen courtyard." She turned and laughed. "Come along, my boy! We'll organise everybody into helping."

Within minutes potted plants were being carried backwards and forwards up and down all over the house. Family and servants worked together. There were collisions, spurts of ill-temper, apologies and laughter. During all the confusion, the Master returned.

He was middle-aged, tall, thin, silver-haired and slightly stooped. Everyone was relieved to see him, but Eduard greeted him with particular warmth.

"May I speak with you, Father?"

"Of course, my boy. Come into the study." He noticed Eduard's use of "Father" instead of "Papa" and concluded this was to be a serious discussion. They walked companionably up the wide staircase. Eduard made certain the door was closed before he spoke.

"Father, please tell me what's happening. After all, I have to look after Mama and my sisters when you're not in the house. I'm fifteen. I'm old enough to be told about things."

"I don't know what's happening, Son. Nobody does."

"Will there be a Revolution?"

His father shrugged. "I'll tell you everything I can. From reports I get at the office, the country is on its knees…though you mustn't let anyone outside this house hear you say that. People have lost their stomach for the War. I think sometimes, it's only His Majesty who still believes we can win."

"That's only because the Ministers are frightened to tell him the truth. The boys at the Lyceum say there'll be a Revolution this time for sure. And when it comes, it's essential that people of our sort control it."

His Father smiled fondly at this expression of youthful certainty. "We may be too late already. We should have acted sooner."

"If you really believed that, why do you still risk meeting your friends—as you did this afternoon, for instance?"

His Father's smile grew fonder. Eduard's awareness of his responsibilities for his Mother and his Sisters was splendid. It wasn't easy to remember that he was still only fifteen. His student uniform strained across his broadening shoulders, his hands were clenched in their eagerness for action.

"We must go carefully, son. We want Democracy. The Cadets want an elected Parliament, not a Revolution we can't control. And if anybody outside this house asks you, that's all you must say—that and nothing more."

Later he tried to speak more openly to his wife, but she had little patience just then.

"I'm tired, my darling. I've a lot on my mind. And whatever you're hinting at will happen outside our house and, please God, sometime after tonight. All we should be worrying about now is Dorothea's party."

"My dearest darling, even you can't afford to ignore what's happening in the country. These next few days could well mean the end for all of us."

Her shoulders shook irritably. "I've faced worse than this, remember. I don't know why everybody's making such a fuss. There's plenty of work since the War and plenty of food, if only the peasants weren't too lazy to grow it or too greedy to sell it. Nobody seems to have any sympathy for the Tsar. That new little boy has the most terrible disease, they say."

"They also say the Tsar's an alcoholic, and that he isn't the Father of the Tsarevich…nor of some of the girls."

"That's disgusting! I never thought I should hear you talking like that...you of all people. Oh...Oh, my dear one..." She sounded on the verge of tears. Instead of crying, however, she took him firmly into her arms because she could never bear to be angry with him for long. "Come along now, don't think about it any more. We have to change. Tonight we'll think of Dorothea's party. There'll be plenty of time to worry about everything else tomorrow."

And that's the way it seemed. At nine o'clock the orchestra began the first waltz of the evening, a popular piece by Johann Strauss. The family stood in line at the top of the staircase: Dorothea in purist white, her Mother in black and silver, her Father in the sash and medals of his grade of nobility and rank as a Director of the State Bank.

Guests ascended the staircase as they were announced. None expected to stand for a long talk until Princess Surotkina struggled up, feathers in her dyed black hair, her body imprisoned in a gown of brightest emerald. She leaned heavily on her ebony, silver-topped stick, her hands trembling with age and anxiety.

"My dear friend, I'm so worried. We must talk. I need your help. There's nobody else I can turn to."

He kissed her hand and whispered encouragingly, "Of course, Princess. A little later, I promise."

The Surotkins suffered badly when the serfs were liberated. Her brothers' gambling had destroyed almost all the family's collateral. The serfs the Princess believed she owned were long-since pledged by her brothers to their various creditors. She let them go, with the land they worked, but the compensation she believed was her due went elsewhere. She had no one to advise her then. Now, her brothers were permanently banished to the country where, being penniless, they could do no harm. She lived in the capital tormented by nightmares of poverty. She had sworn never to sell the Crimean estate as long as she lived. She kept it in memory of her dear Papa who had shot himself there in an alcoholic frenzy when she was fifteen. Her hostess, who now kissed her cheek so tenderly, was the Princess's dearest friend. They sat together on various charities.

Dorothea's mother was a woman who was easy to love. In the few years she'd lived in Saint Petersburg she'd become a great success in society. Men found her handsome (some even lusted after her) and envied her husband. Their wives liked her too, although she was an enigma. She spoke Russian with the slightest Polish accent and French, Italian and German with ease. She never mentioned any other members of her family and parried enquiries as to where she had been born; she had lived in so many places during her lifetime, she said, she couldn't now remember. In other circumstances, on account of her mystery, society might have consigned her to the demi-monde, but she was too well married for that.

While her parents unclenched themselves from Princess Surotkina, Dorothea was monopolised by Prince Krimovsky, writing his arrangements on her dance programme. Dorothea and Pyotr Alexeivich Krimovsky knew each other well. He had drunk a little too much before coming to the party and she was easily annoyed by him in his present mood.

Without either of them being consulted, hopes for their united future had been canvassed in both families. The Krimovsky Estates were in the Kaluga Province and valuable. Pyotr Alexeivich, the eldest son, having half-heartedly achieved a failure in the field chosen for him—diplomacy—was now charting an even less distinguished course in Agriculture, while feeling that the Marine was his only true métier. He was tall and thin with tow-coloured hair. He cherished a conviction that he would look his best in naval uniform. His only notable feature was a deep-set mouth, an almost perfect circle that snapped food like a fly-catching plant.

Behind the Prince a dark young man with a prominent black moustache, making him look like a southern bandit, hovered to pay his respects. He was a stranger. His dress was foreign. Dorothea held out her hand and Pyotr Alexeivich announced eagerly, "Dorothea Pavlovna, this is a new and very dear friend of mine, Monsieur Georges Costello. I implore you on my knees, be kind to him! He has been living with we benighted barbarians for only two weeks and knows no one but me in the whole of Saint Petersburg…poor devil! However…"

Dorothea interrupted his flow and Pyotr looked annoyed. "Monsieur Costello, how kind of you to come to my party. You are most welcome."

The young man shook the hand she offered; he was most definitely a stranger. He had an open-air complexion not often to be seen among the young men in Saint Petersburg drawing rooms. "The pleasure is mine, Mademoiselle." She was disappointed. It was only a platitude when she'd hoped for something more exciting. But she forgave him because he uttered it with difficulty and in an unrecognisable accent.

Pyotr burst in once more. "Since Georges came into my office the Minister is overwhelmed by my new-found speed and efficiency." He laughed. "When he's had a chance to practise his Russian, he'll be even quicker and more efficient, won't you Georges? And you'd like to practise with some attractive young ladies, wouldn't you, old fellow?" Pyotr Alexeivich leered.

Costello looked embarrassed though he may not have understood all the words.

Dorothea rushed to relieve him. "What a lovely idea, Pyotr Alexeivich. You must come to see us often, Monsieur. My sisters and I will be delighted. Perhaps you would be more comfortable if we spoke something other than Russian this evening?"

"No, no, no!" Krimovsky became petulant, realising he had lost the game. "He has to practice. He must learn our own beautiful Russian. From some points of view my sympathy is with the Nationalists. It shouldn't be always we Russians who must learn foreign languages as though our own language was no more than a succession of prehistoric grunts. If foreigners are so ignorant that…"

Dorothea ignored him. "Tell me. What is your language, Monsieur?"

"French. I was born in the north of Quebec Province in Canada where we pride ourselves on continuing to talk seventeenth-century French."

"In Canada." Dorothea adopted the right tone of surprise. She had been well-taught by her Mother the skill of putting visitors at their ease. "How interesting. What is it like there?"

"Very much like here, Mademoiselle." he laughed. "Bears and birches, fir trees and snow. In winter, Montréal is as crowded as Saint Petersburg, with all the sleighs carrying beautiful ladies. In the North we have frost that never thaws beyond a finger's depth. And in summer—ah! you should see my home in summer. Such flowers. They bloom over night like magic; a special blessing for the North because we live in the cold and dark so many months in the year."

"You make it sound very wonderful and very close."

"Of course it's very close," Krimovsky said sarcastically. "Dear Dorothea Pavlovna, you have only to walk from Saint Petersburg to the North Pole to shake hands with a Canadian any time you like." Dorothea laughed uncertainly and Costello took advantage of his difficulty in Russian to say nothing.

"That's why he's here," Krimovsky continued, unstoppable. "Because Canada and Russia are so alike…except that Canadians are cleverer than us. Costello is an agronomist. He's paid by our progressive government to show us muddle heads how to grow crops in the Virgin Lands. Directly after Easter he's being put onto a barge and sent down the Volga. I warn you, you must teach him Russian very quickly, my dear, before the Tartars get hold of him and ruin his accent for ever."

Dorothea was angry but had no time to reply. A straight-backed Hussar approached to take her into the Mazurka. The music rang and rattled through the room. Young people formed lines and leapt forward like thoroughbreds at the starting gate.

Dorothea's Mother, sitting comfortably on a sofa with Princess Surotkina beside her, smiled complacently. Everything was going well.

The Princess, by contrast, watched everything absently, breathing prayers in old Slavonic. She interspersed her ritual with pleas to her hostess.

"His Excellency won't forget me, will he? I must talk to him."

"Don't worry, my dear. Does he ever forget you?"

"Oh, I know, I know. He's a dear man." She sighed painfully. "But everybody says there's going to be a Revolution. That God should let me live so long to see such a thing!" She crossed herself vigorously and her friend would undoubtedly have said something well thought-out to relax her, but at that moment, someone across the room caught her attention.

She patted the old lady's hand and moved away through her guests to greet someone very special whom she hadn't expected to see. He was tall and thin like her husband, balding and with an empty sleeve tucked into his pocket. His complexion was fair but roughened by years spent out of doors in extreme climates. This was her husband's elder brother and she hugged and kissed him delightedly.

"How wonderful! But why didn't you let us know you were in Saint Petersburg? Now...let us find that brother of yours. Oh my dear..." she hugged him again. "I am so very, very happy to see you. And just when we're having a little party for Dorothea, too."

"Of course, it's her birthday. Why else should I have come all this way?" He laughed a dry, thin laugh, like ice cracking on a frozen pond.

The Ballroom of the Rastrelli palace at the corner of Nevsky Prospect and Fontanka flashed with light; light reflected from uniforms, sashes and medals of the various civil and military grades worn by the men; light reflected from the jewelry and glittering gowns of the ladies; gowns from Warsaw and Paris, the only places to buy gowns at that time. She guided her prize guest slowly through the crowd, being sure he recognised or was aware of every celebrity there. Her ambition was almost satisfied, but not completely. When it was Sonia's turn, she was determined the Grand Duchesses should be among the guests...if there were no Revolution before then, of course. "Where are you staying, my dear? You surely didn't change on the train? Why not come straight here from the station?"

"I have a room at the Moskovskaya."

"Oh, my dear." Her voice held the deepest reproach.

"I hadn't the slightest idea how long it would take me to get here, you see…hours?…days? nor even when there might be a train. I can't tell you what things are like at home…strikes, arson, murder…"

"Not tonight, chér ami, please. Tonight we think about nothing in the world except our darling Dorothea."

Her husband was in his study when they arrived, speaking earnestly into Princess Surotkina's ear trumpet. He heartily embraced his brother. "This is my brother, Princess," he said a little irritably because he didn't want the moment spoiled. "Princess Surotkina is anxious about this Revolution business, Brother. You don't think it will come to anything, do you? Can you help me put her mind at rest?"

His wife slipped out of the room saying she was neglecting her other guests. She practically carried Princess Surotkina with her. She was determined not to have tonight spoiled by politics. At the top of the stairs Igor, the Tartar footman she'd hired because he was beautiful, announced supper and shepherded dancers downstairs.

A flutter of excitement took her and held her. Tonight might easily settle Dorothea's future. Pyotr Alexeivich would marry her instantly if she'd have him. It would be a good match, too. The Krimovsky Estates were in Kaluga Province and that was a draw-back. Kaluga peasants were notoriously dishonest. The young couple wouldn't have to live there, of course. And Pyotr could never be described as good looking but he had a kind heart. There was plenty of time, though. Dorothea was only just eighteen. No need to rush things.

Upstairs, drinking vodka together and inevitably talking politics, the Brothers ignored the remainder of the Ball.

"Things at home…in all the Provinces…terrible! The police are too frightened to leave their barracks after dark and since the War there are no spare troops to back them up. In the usual Russian way everything will be all right in the end, I suppose. At least our own people recognise we house them well and pay them well."

"Housing and pay are no longer the issues, Brother…not in the cities, anyway, and the cities are the breeding grounds for all this discontent. It's freedom they want—though God only knows what they think that will be like. In the morning I'll take you to see some of our factories…if we can get through, that is. Those places…they're like prisons…too new, too big. And they're not properly managed…Russia's never needed managers before, so we've nobody skilled to do the job. We employ experienced foreigners when we can get them, but there aren't enough of them who are willing to come. The result is, we've hundreds of workers on our hands in badly run factories. And because nobody's ever thought of providing proper housing for them, they're herded into dormitories: men with men, women with women, girls and children together and married couples with strips of blanket hung between their beds to give them privacy. Pigs wouldn't eat the food we give them. Vodka's their curse and their only consolation. They live like animals, and we're surprised they behave like animals." He shrugged and poured more vodka.

"I shall have to get home as soon as I can tomorrow. I only risked coming at all for Dorothea's sake."

Nobody wanted to risk being away from home for very long. Throughout the house lights were already dimming, guests stood in groups awaiting their carriages. Their hostess went from one to another greedily accepting their thanks and congratulations. All the time she was watching Dorothea and Pyotr. Satisfied, she saw them go together into the small family parlour. That was satisfactory, and she trusted Dorothea not to commit herself over hastily.

Had she been in the parlour with them, she would have been disappointed. There was no talk of marriage. Dorothea was giggling.

"It's true, I tell you, Petka. Any of the girls at the Smolny will tell you the same. This monk person is one of Anna Vyroubova's lovers and Madame Anna herself has been the Empress's lover for ages."

"Dorothea!" Pyotr's pale skin turned quite red.

"They say the monk often stays in Madame Anna's house at Tsarskoe Selo, though he's the filthiest creature in the world and smells like a sewer. They don't know how she can bear to have him near her. And she's not the only one, either. Lots of society women go to his flat for tea and cakes while he tells them his queer ideas about religion. You have to sin before you can be forgiven, you see, and...and..." She could hardly carry on for laughing, "...and he organises the sinning right then and there around the tea table. Can't you just imagine it?"

"Dorothea! Stop it! You don't know what you're saying."

"This is 1905, darling, the twentieth century. Don't be such an old fuddy-duddy."

He grunted.

"The monk knows Grand Duke Nicholas now. They met when the Grand Duke's little dog was ill and..."

"That's certainly a lie," he broke in. "The Grand Duke would never have anything smaller than a Saluki or a Samoyed."

"Do be quiet, Petka darling. Saluki, Samoyed, Chihuahuau...what does it matter? The dog was ill. The monk cured the dog. The Grand Duke was grateful and now he's one of the monk's most devoted followers. He'll obviously introduce him to the Tsar quite soon and they'll be best friends in no time, too."

Pyotr Alexeivich took her hand. "Dora dear," he pleaded, will you stop your silly chatter and let us talk seriously?"

"Seriously?"

"About the War."

"No! No, Petka! No War tonight when I've had such a gloriously wonderful time. Darling, I'm young. I'm still only eighteen. I want life to be exciting and romantic a little longer. Don't spoil it for me. I don't want to be reminded of horrid things like War and Revolution."

He paled. "I see. I'm sorry I'm boring you."

"Don't be silly, of course you're not. But everything has always been special between the two of us...such fun. We've always shut out the rest of the world. You've been such a wonderful comrade, my dear. That's what I want. I want you to be my dear, dear comrade for ever."

He replied very slowly. "That's truly everything you want from me? Comradeship? Is that really all?"

"Oh, my dear, don't look like that. Sit with me and tell me what you wanted to say. Something serious, you said. Only remember…it has to be nice as well. Serious and nice." She pulled him down beside her and muzzled her cheek against his neck. But he was enclosed, withdrawn.

"I've taken a Commission in the Foot Guards. I'm going east next week."

"Oh! But you mustn't!" She screamed and writhed away. "The Foot Guards! It's madness. You mustn't."

"We're growing up, you and I. Time is cruel, perhaps, but we can't go on forever avoiding whatever's unpleasant."

"You don't have to go. People say the War's nearly over…we can't hold out much longer."

"And when I come back, perhaps," he began diffidently.

"No! No, Pyotr, I won't think about that. I don't want to…I can't. I'll never know whether you will come back and I can't stand it."

He stood at her side but seemingly she had nothing more to say. Neither had he. He left the room slowly, bowing to her Mother as he passed her on the landing.

When he was gone, Dorothea rushed to her room. Her Mother followed, perplexed. She held her daughter close while she sobbed. She couldn't believe her instincts had been so wrong.

At last she got the girl quieted and rang for her maid to put her to bed. She went downstairs in wintry disappointment and loneliness. Everything had gone to waste; not only tonight, but all the years of struggle that preceded it. And the struggle wasn't over yet. Tonight had been a triumph but it hadn't begun anything…hadn't ended anything. Nothing ever had a beginning, nor an end. And her happy, optimistic husband would never understand that, not if they lived together through all eternity.

At the foot of the stairs the hall was emptying and her brother-in-law was approached her uncertainly. Her husband, she saw, was leaving the house surrounded by a group of silent men in grey overcoats.

"Those men?" she queried wearily.

"They're taking him away."

"Oh, no! They can't want him for more business at this time of night."

"Not business, exactly, though I'm sure it's nothing to worry about."

"Worry? Why should I worry? Who were those men?"

"Security Police! You must be very brave."

"Security Police? They need his advice about something, then. Your Brother has a great deal of influence. Though you may not realise just how much living in the country as you do."

"You must be very brave, my dear."

"Why? What are you talking about?" Suddenly she leaned heavily against him, her eyes frozen, her voice hardly audible.

"You mean…they've really taken him away?"

"Enquiries, they say. We must hope he'll be back before morning." He held her arm to steady her and stop her falling to the floor.

"Go to bed, my dear. That would be best. I'll go to Police Head-quarters. There must be someone there who remembers me from the old days."

"Yes…yes," she said uncertainly. "But what is it they say he's done?"

"Treason."

"Oh, no," she breathed. "Oh, my God, no!"

She suddenly felt very old. A whole lifetime destroyed in minutes. She would never be young again.

With tremendous effort she dragged herself up to her sitting room and dragged the heavy curtains apart. The house grew cold but she stood by the window all night. In the greyness of dawn she heard a growing hum of voices. Men and women in felt boots, sack cloth over their shoulders, were assembling on the pavement of the Nevsky laughing and talking with holiday cheerfulness as though something wonderful would happen very soon.

BOOK I

▼

1881

Loff and Paul returned into an uneasy atmosphere when the old Baron died. Snowdrifts had delayed them. When they arrived they found that Margarethe, grim-faced now as the portrait of her mother, had done everything that was to be done. The old man's grave was marked by a heap of snow under a fir tree on the Estate.

"You should have let us know sooner, Margarethe," Paul said unsteadily. He wore the green tunic of a Captain in the Preobrazhensky Guards and was not quite sober.

"We were cut off."

Paul looked to his Brother for support, but the new Baron said nothing. He was in his thirties, a tall gaunt man in civil service uniform. He had a soft blond beard, his eyes gimlet sharp like his mother's.

"We should have been here," Paul persisted pointlessly.

"I'm sure Margarethe did all she could," Loff said softly. "It wasn't easy for her, shut up here with him at the end, I'm sure."

"It wasn't," Margarethe snapped. Her face was flushed and her black woolen dress, tight as slave-shackles at her neck and wrists, swirled angrily as she left the room. She slammed the door.

Paul looked sheepish. "Sorry about that," he said, without much meaning. "We have to talk about what's to be done, Loff. God knows,

I was never meant to be a farmer. Neither were you. But one of us has to stay. It takes a man to deal with peasants nowadays."

"A man like Father?"

"He was harsh at times I grant you, but he knew how to keep them quiet." He reached for the brandy at his elbow. "I still feel winded after the shock," he excused himself.

"Don't worry, Paul. Stay with your Regiment."

"Well…you are the new Baron of course." Paul was unable to hide his relief. "What about your work in Saint Petersburg? You're a national hero after the way you handled the Narodnik trials. You're certain to be Minister of Justice after that."

Loff shrugged. "In some places I'm hated as the tool of a vindictive government. Even people of our class wish they had only been sent into exile. Some of those youngsters came from good families."

"Hanging was no more than they deserved in my opinion."

"You think hearing you say that lets me sleep easier?"

"They were scum. Remember, Loff, our poor old Russia wouldn't survive if it weren't for people like you and me."

"What the hell are you talking about Paul? What has Russia to do with us?"

"Everything! Good God man! You and I can call ourselves Balts, Estonians, Germans…whatever we like. At heart we're Russian because there's nothing else for us to be, nowhere else for us to go."

"You never see those youngsters like I do, their faces as close to me as yours is now. Those faces haunt me when I go home at night. So do the faces of the policemen and Cossacks who guard them. Brutes! They've starved, beaten, and raped them for long enough before they drag them into my court. It's a rotten system. I'm sick to death of it."

Paul shrugged complacently. "Natural justice, or whatever you call it, governs everything. Nothing changes so nothing really matters, I suppose."

"There you make your biggest mistake, Paul. Things will change one day. And it will be a terrible time when they do."

Paul took another drink. His conscience wasn't yet quite easy about the Estate. It was Loff's inheritance, of course, not his. "We could hire a bailiff. Find someone who really knows what he's doing."

"And Margarethe?"

"Buy her an apartment...Reval, Saint Petersburg. Good heavens! She might even get married. A widower, maybe, someone with children who needs looking after. She'll have a dowry many men would jump at."

"She'd never agree to being sold off like that. Anyway, the question doesn't arise."

Paul's freedom was confirmed! "So long as you know what you're doing, Brother."

Margarethe accepted the idea of Loff's return with her usual restraint. "I shall continue to look after things in the house. There will be more time now that Father's gone. I shall do what I've wanted to do for years: start a school. An Estonian school," she emphasized. "We must do something to stop this criminal Russianisation."

Paul was unimpressed. "She won't get any pupils," he told Loff later. "Peasants want their children out in the fields as soon as they can walk. What's the use of reading and writing when you lead their sort of life?"

Undeterred by her brothers' skepticism and when the local tracks had turned to rivulets of ochre slime, Margarethe tucked her skirts into her waistband and, leaning crazily on a stick, negotiated unseen hazards in the muddy depths. She visited all the huts in all the villages, concentrating on the women. She knew that in this man's world, that was the way to get things started: stimulate the women and leave the women to stimulate the men.

Secretly, Paul admired her. She understood the value of discipline and except for being the wrong sex, would have made a good soldier. Discipline was everything. Fräulein Baumberg and Herr Trott had instilled in them that everyone was heading for the lash of God's rope-end on Judgment Day. From earliest childhood they were accustomed to seeing peasants tied to the wooden cross-frame outside the Church, stripped to the waist, their backs raw. That was Paul's experience of natural justice. In Margarethe's school, she said, there would be no beatings. Her pupils would learn discipline, but justice as well. She was looking to the future, dreaming of the time when the Baron would no longer have to sleep with a pistol under his pillow.

Paul tried to dissuade her as gently as he could. "How old are you, Margarethe? Twenty-four? Twenty-five? Haven't you ever wanted to be like other girls…live in Reval or Saint Petersburg? Enjoy yourself? Get married?"

"Since you went away, Paul, you've no idea what my life has been: nursing peasants through their fevers, binding half-severed limbs, splinting fractures, cleaning filth and stink day after day. Then Father had his stroke. I had no time to think of anything but my Duty to him and I dare say it will be the same with Loff. What chance will I ever have to live in Reval or Saint Petersburg or get married?"

Paul flinched. "How you must have made the poor man suffer," he said before he could hold the words back.

"What do you know about it? After that first stroke he never left his room. He called for me day and night. Night after night I read to him till dawn because he was terrified of dying alone in the dark. I fed him, cleaned him. And didn't the people around here enjoy seeing me do it. Life for me, Paul, has been like life for one of Loff's condemned prisoners in exile: no parole, no reprieve, no hope."

"I'm sorry. I'm really sorry."

"It doesn't matter to me whether or not you're sorry. I did my Duty. And that's a comfort to look back on."

"Loff will be married one of these days. He'll have daughters. He'll never need you to sacrifice yourself for him."

"We shall see. Whatever happens, I shall be here for him when he needs me, just as I was for Father."

CHAPTER 2

▼

1881

When the roads cleared, Loff went to Saint Petersburg to resign. He was back in time for spring sowing and spent his days riding the fields. Paul amused himself as the mood took him, enjoying a long, lazy, trouble-free holiday. At last orders came; he was to rejoin his Regiment.

"In Warsaw, Brother."

"So they are expecting trouble there, then."

"There's been a little unrest recently I gather. Nothing too serious. Not that you'd expect anything at all, after the way we put them down in '63..."

"There's a new generation since '63, Paul. They're raiding post offices all over the country; collecting subscriptions, they call it, the young devils!"

"Jews are at the bottom of it!" Margarethe snarled. "It's always the Jews. They're God's curse on the human race."

"And there are millions of them in Poland, God knows," Paul laughed. "But if He meant them as a curse on the human race, why did He dump them all on us in Poland, I wonder?"

"Their wings are being clipped at the moment. They're being shifted out of their villages by the cartload and into ghettos in the cities. Is that why they want you in Warsaw, do you think, Paul, to keep an eye on them when they get there?"

"We have police for that sort of work, surely," Margarethe burst out. "They can't order the Preobrazhensky to have anything to do with that. Myself...I can't see why they don't go somewhere else of their own accord. Surely they must know by now we don't want them here."

"They know that well enough," Loff reassured her with half a smile. "When I was in Saint Petersburg, rumours about them were running all over the city like fleas. There are new laws; Jews are being turned out of gymnasia wholesale, and they're only allowed into universities on a quota system. Incidentally, Margarethe, children of poor parents will no longer be allowed into gymnasia at all, no matter who pays their fees. So you won't get young Jaan Tsekis into Reval now, I'm afraid."

Margarethe threw down her knife and fork in a fury, but Loff was still thinking about the Jews. "They're going to America by the boatload. And those who remain..." he almost spluttered with amusement, "They're opening factories, I'm told. God only knows where they're getting the money from."

"The West of course," Margarethe thundered. "They've always believed in the West they could undermine us with their money. But they won't! Wealth here is land. Always was and always will be. We gather our harvest in the fields as God intended. In the West they believe money is a harvest they can reap in their exchanges."

"Talking of money, Shmuel Litvak has looked after Father's accounts for years. I'll keep him on, of course, though he might have to move his hut if the Government orders us to make a ghetto for Jewish villagers. I won't let them take him away to a city. Have we any other Jews, Margarethe?"

"Nobody will bother about a God-forsaken place like this," Paul assured him. "And don't worry about your school, Margarethe. Whatever the regulations in Saint Petersburg, local officials will always be too lazy to enforce them."

"Not necessarily. Now we have a new Tsar. A new Tsar, a new harvest of bureaucrats, reaped in the corridors of the Winter Palace." Loff laughed but only briefly. "Don't build hopes on what Paul says, Margarethe. You won't be allowed to build your school. No child, anywhere in the Empire, will be allowed to learn anything blasphemous, scientific or nationalistic. Everything has to be pure Russian. And that's the word of our new God—Constantine Petrovich Pobedonostsev, Head of our Holy Tsar's Holy Orthodox Synod...and Head of just about everything else, so far as I can see."

"What the stupid man doesn't realize," Paul added gaily as though it were all a game, "is that peasants aren't bothered by Petersburg regulations. The brighter ones run off to the towns. They get themselves educated in ways Constantine Petrovich has never imagined. They rely on the factory paymaster instead of the four seasons for their food. It follows naturally: if they don't need the seasons, they don't need God, and if they don't need Him, they don't need His self-appointed representatives on Earth—and that includes the President of His Majesty's Holy Synod."

"Our Lord Jesus Christ told us to give to Caesar whatever belongs to him, and to God whatever belongs to Him," Loff mused. "We've got everything the wrong way round. I believe we must be the most confused people on Earth."

CHAPTER 3

▼

1881/1882

A fortnight later Prince Krasnov, a product of the Emperor's newly reaped harvest and appointed Governor for the region, wrote saying he would visit the Estate on his first official tour. Margarethe narrowed her lips and drove her maids into a frenzy of cleaning and cooking.

"Krasnov? Krasnov?" she muttered. "We don't know that family, do we Brother? Who is he? Why is he here?"

Village children were rounded up, scrubbed, rehearsed and bullied into clean shirts and skirts before the unknown Prince arrived. To them, Fräulein von Hagen's fuss was incomprehensible. A visit by Almighty God might have stirred their torpor. An inspection by a Government Officer? Phoo! In the Russian Empire Government officers were as numerous as grains of sand on the Baltic dunes.

Loff was fatalistic, Margarethe furious, Paul bored and wasting time before he left for Warsaw. It was between seasons in the social calendar. Sleigh rides and dances in over-heated drawing rooms were over; picnics and swimming parties not due to begin. It was a desultory period, worse this year because of the men's reluctance to leave their women unattended. Since the assassination of the unlamented Tsar Liberator the future wasn't certain any more.

On the Sunday night before Orthodox Easter Margarethe lay in her bed, curtained against draughts, reading her Bible. She was surprised to

hear late horsemen approaching, jumbled shouts and whinnying animals. She wrapped a shawl around her and went to Fräulein Baumberg's room. Together, they ran down the stairs to meet the heavy
knocking at the door. Loff and Paul were in the hall persuading four
terrified footmen to open the door. Margarethe was relieved to see that
Loff was carrying his Father's revolver. "Don't open the door Loff!" she
screamed.

"Open up, damn you!" the Baron roared at the footmen.

The frightened men drew the bolts. Half a dozen figures stood
beneath the porte-cochere, hatted and cloaked, their faces muffled.
Horses stamped and shifted their weight in the courtyard.

"Baron von Hagen?" The leader spoke Russian with a Petersburg
accent but rolled his 'r's with a curious intensity.

"I am Baron von Hagen."

"I apologise for this disturbance, your Excellency. Captain Paul von
Hagen is staying with you, I believe."

"Yes." Paul stepped forward.

The man held out a paper. Paul read it and Margarethe saw his
shoulders stiffen as he crumpled it into a ball. "In just a moment," he
said. "Please wait." He turned to Loff. "I have to go with these gentlemen, Brother...official business. May I take a horse?"

"Of course, but..."

"I'm sorry Brother...No time to explain."

"Have Valiant saddled," Loff ordered as Paul ran up to dress. He
was down in a moment, uniformed, cloaked and muffled like the rest.
Valiant was led from the stable and Paul jumped into the saddle. "It's
for Russia, Brother," he called as the animal reared under the shock of
his sudden weight.

The house stood on a slight rise a mile or so inland from the Baltic
shore, stone-built and three-storied, with colonnades to the curving
wings each side of the main door. The courtyard was sheltered from
the weather on all sides but one.

Outside this protection the wind seared Paul's cheeks as the troop rode at a trot across meadowland with copses of birch and elm. Beyond the grassland the track went through a dark chaos of birch and fir whose fallen cones crackled under the animals' tread. Two miles on, they entered the peasants' land, and the muddy village street, frozen to steel-like greyness.

The villagers roused themselves, apprehensive, but stayed hidden. Dogs barked. There was no other sound. The Commander halted with Paul beside him. Paul could imagine what was happening in the huts, the hasty pulling-on of clothes, the suppressing of children's' cries.

"This is the main village, your Excellency?"

"Yes. There are others, of course, and some small settlements along the coast. The people here are the best types. There's some interbreeding in the others."

"The Pastor...Priest...whatever you have..."

"Pastor Vikkers. We're all Lutheran here."

"A schoolmaster...?"

"There is no school."

"You!" The Commander summoned a trooper. "His Excellency will guide you to the Pastor's house. Bring him!"

As a mark of his superiority Pastor Vikkers lived at the end of the village, slightly away from his flock. While Paul was riding there he heard a shot followed by a confusion of shouts and screams. More shots followed closely. Screaming. Doors banged. Terrified horses whinnied hysterically. Paul looked back. Several huts were already ablaze.

Pastor Vikkers was outside his house running round in crazy circles. The trooper hoisted him, shivering, on to his saddlebow and carried him to the village. When they arrived, the dogs no longer barked. Some had been shot and lay in the street; the rest had fled. Flames from burning huts threw eccentric patterns across faces frozen into fright. Troopers added to the mayhem by firing at the stars and throwing fresh brands on to turf roofs. The peasants were cowed to silence; there was only an occasional sob as someone's home collapsed in a cascade of orange sparks. Terrified babies unable to find suck, wailed in the unaccustomed cold of the night air.

The Commander looked scornfully at the cowering Pastor. "Well, my man, you'll probably be able to understand better than these…these animals. Translate for me and explain what I say." He straightened in his saddle and surveyed the peasants shaking in the street. "We are patriots. We honour His Majesty and love the Empire. We will not see everything destroyed by anarchists and Jews…nor by Estonians, either!"

The Pastor translated in a trembling voice as well as his scanty Russian allowed.

"We're prepared to make good Russians of you, even if you are Estonians. Though, of course, you're not all Estonians, are you? There must be some Jews. Come on! Where are the Jews?"

No one moved. He pointed at the Pastor. "You, there, Priest, Pastor, whatever you are. Where are the Jews?"

The Pastor, his chin dripping with the spittle of terror, touched a man, pulled him to the front and urged him to his knees.

"He looks like a Jew. Give him a cut or two. You can always tell a Jew by the way he screams."

A trooper dismounted, took a whip from his belt and laid it across the man's shoulders. A woman in the crowd cried.

The Commander looked pleased. "Strip him! He can't feel it through those rags."

Two troopers jumped to the ground, tore off the man's jacket and shirt and pinioned his arms.

"That's better! Now give him fifty…across the chest."

The crowd gasped as the man was spread-eagled on the ground face up. The man screamed as the lash rose and fell tearing the hairy skin, laying the spare flesh open to the rib cage and incising the nipples. The woman continued screaming after the victim was silent. Paul turned away sickened.

The Commander laughed. "That's the way! Where are you, you Jews and Catholics? Come out like honest brothers and we'll let your friend go."

There was no response save for the woman's demented howling.

"You! You there, on the ground! Tell us who are the Jews and Catholics and you can go."

The man said nothing. His body recoiled with every blow, but lifelessly now. Who could guess whether or not he still breathed?

The Commander shouted: "Listen you people, you Lutherans. It'll be your turn next if you don't help us! Jews and Catholics are plotting to steal your land. The Little Father is trying to stop them, but he doesn't know who they all are. That's why you must help him. You have to give him their names."

The villagers shuffled. Nobody spoke except the Pastor who stammered something but his Russian was mangled with fear, his voice tentative and cracked. "Your Honour, there are no Catholics here," he managed at last.

"You fools! I'll teach you! You scum! Make a fool of me, would you? Drive them off! Burn them all out!"

"What shall we do with this one, your Honour?" one of the troopers shouted.

"Tie him up on the cross-frame till he rots. That'll teach them to hide Jews!"

"Your Honour..." The Pastor was crying now with cold and shock, and with self-disgust too, perhaps. "He was the only Jew in the village, your Honour. We have no Catholics."

"He's dead," someone called.

The troopers drove the villagers away, the cracking of their whips growing fainter. The Commander looked at Paul. "Why didn't they say, Captain? If that's the truth, why didn't they say?"

"Your Honour," the Pastor broke in, unable to be silent now he'd found his voice. "They didn't understand. None of them speaks Russian. I...they didn't understand what I tried to tell them...they were too shocked."

A woman fought her way back through the troopers to kneel beside the man lying on the ground. Suddenly she leapt up. "You monster! Look what you did!" she screamed in Yiddish. "You're a devil from hell!" She flung herself at the Commander's horse. He didn't understand the words, but her meaning was clear. She tore at his breeches and tried to bite through his leather boots. He reined free. There was a shot—the very last that night. The woman fell dead.

"She was his wife, Your Honour," the Pastor babbled, making his words sound like an apology.

CHAPTER 4

▼

1882

The Baron and Margarethe passed a sleepless night trying not to imagine what was happening in the village. At dawn an unnatural glow against the heavy clouds meant they could avoid the truth no longer. Paul reached home in the early hours, his face black with smoke and sweat.

"It's all over," he blustered shamefacedly. "You won't have any more trouble with them."

"Is anything left?" Loff asked dully.

Paul shrugged. "We must make examples of terrorists. That's imperative."

"There are no terrorists here, only peasants. Margarethe, pour us all some brandy, please. Now you, Paul…listen to me! I've spent my life dealing with terrorists, young people who'd spent half their lives abroad because for one reason or another the Government refused them any education here in Russia. Naturally they came back with dangerous ideas and a determination to change things. They congregate in the cities to write their pamphlets, hold their meetings, throw their bombs. You won't find any of them out here among their beloved peasants, breaking their backs working the land."

Paul gulped his brandy, his excuse to say nothing.

"Who were those men last night?"

"'The Sons of Russia.' You must have heard of us. The Tsar's a member."

"Out with you last night, was he?"

"You should join us, Loff. We have to stop what's happening. Revolution will mean the end of everything."

"It could mean independence. Think of that, Paul—an independent Estonia."

"That wouldn't do us any good. We Germans are only a minority here. The Estonians will want everything for themselves."

"They'll need us for a long time yet, though. They're nowhere near being able to govern themselves."

"It won't take long after all the well-meaning Margarethes have taught them to read and write. Their leaders will appear when the time comes."

"We'll teach them to read their Bibles Paul, nothing else. We'll make them into better Lutherans."

"My poor Margarethe, it won't stop at Bibles. What about newspapers…history books? How will you stop them reading about the French Revolution?"

"Nothing will be allowed into the village that isn't right for them to know about."

"They won't be staying in the village; Loff's already told you that. They'll go to the towns and join the Revolutionaries; it's inevitable. And they'll be very different men if ever they come back here again."

"Well, I'm going to bed," she said suddenly, as though that settled everything and proved that she was right. The house was chill as a mausoleum in the early morning and Loff and Paul soon followed her.

A little later and before Paul gave any sign of being awake, Loff got up and called for his horse. He rode towards the village and long before he was out of the tangled forest could smell the foetid stench of wet charred wood. The street, beginning to thaw, was littered with dead dogs, and domestic wreckage. Men, women and children drifted aimlessly, hungry and thirsty. Directly they saw him they clustered waiting to be told what to do. Outside the church, tied to the cross-frame, Shmuel Litvak drooped unseeing over his lifeless wife lying at his feet.

Pastor Vikkers elbowed through the crowd. "He's dead, your Excellency," he said and it might have been an explanation or an apology.

"Yes."

"Your brother was one of them, your Excellency."

"These two must be buried."

"They're Jews, your Excellency." The Pastor was shocked at the idea of having to handle such carrion.

"Bury them!"

"If your Excellency insists."

The Baron rose in his saddle. "You! You people! Clear up this mess. Repair what you can; rebuild what you have to. I will see to it that you have all you need."

They stared at him with shock-glazed eyes.

"I shall go back to the house to tell the Frau Barönin what has happened. She will bring you food. We will help you." His voice choked on his own inadequacy. He knew the only thing they wanted was for this not to have happened at all. But what else could he say? He knew they hated him, blamed him for not preventing their calamity. For generations their forebears had looked to the von Hagens to see them through bad times, feed them in famine, punish their enemies and dower their daughters. Now...the Herr Baron's own Brother had been one of their spoilers. They would never forget...never forgive.

Riding home he saw a flicker of white among the birches. Someone was running without direction, confused. He dismounted and ran too. Twigs snapped noisily but it didn't matter. This was no hunt, merely a chase. He quickly caught the fugitive: Shmuel Litvak's thirteen-year-old daughter, Channah. Her terror made her an easy quarry. He took her by the arms but she collapsed at his feet.

"What are you doing here, child? Where are you going?"

She lay on the ground gasping, fear-crazed.

"Don't be afraid, Channah. I shan't hurt you. You know me well enough. Come, my dear. You can't stay here."

He lifted her and half-carried, half-dragged her to his horse. Her body shuddered painfully in his arms, and he knew he couldn't comfort her. But he had to try. "I know, I know," he soothed. "You're safe now. The Frau Baronin will take care of you. Be calm, my poor child, be calm." When they reached his horse, she collapsed against its warm flank. He lifted her, whimpering, to the saddlebow and took her home. She moaned softly all the way.

Margarethe, disapproving of having to put a Jew between von Hagen sheets, nevertheless saw the girl to bed. Then she and Fräulein Baumberg worked all day in the village organising relief and making hysterical women and children as relieved as they could. She encouraged them to pray and to thank God that this was the beginning of spring, not winter.

Loff stayed in his study for the remainder of the day, lonely, impotent. Paul too, stayed in the house, but the brothers avoided each other.

Prince Krasnov and his wife arrived late afternoon. They travelled in three coaches with six footmen for protection, one valet and two lady's maids. The Princess had been delighted by the countryside she'd seen, she said, and couldn't hide her *frisson* of excitement over the chaos she'd seen in the village. She had highly rouged cheeks, artificially red lips and teeth going black. Loff immediately judged her to be evil. Paul, with the experience of a soldier, recognised her as the type of woman bored soldiers posted to far-away barracks were attracted to.

"Such devastation, *mon chèr Baron. Épouvantable!* I must help. Indeed, you must allow me! *Je dois tout faire que possible.*" She chattered excitedly in bad French with a disgraceful accent.

"My sister is doing all that can be done, Princess," Loff told her stiffly. "Doubtless you met her on your way...?"

"*Mais oui,* we met a most worthy young person *avéc sa fidèle compagne,*" she gushed. "Do not give us a thought *chèr ami.* We shall be altogether *comme il faut, n'ést pas?*"

She continued cascading words all the way to her room. Her husband, by contrast, was taciturn. He accepted Loff's offer of brandy and accompanied him to the study. Loff's dislike was instantaneous. The way he rolled his 'r's identified him as the commander of the previous night's affair though it was never mentioned between them. They were excessively polite.

When he was free of them at last, Loff spent another sleepless night wishing his father were alive and that everything could be as it was. His life in Saint Petersburg had been all he could wish. He valued his reputation as Prosecutor and was secretly flattered by the women attracted to him because of his aloofness, the chill of his impartiality and his power. He maintained a box at the Ballet, of course, and Society speculated on which of the pretty little dancers he was keeping. He was to be seen at every concert, every opera first night. After his cheerless childhood warm relationships were not easy for him to make. For him, life as a distant public official was perfection. He could know and be known without ever having to be intimate.

He prosecuted political offenders, but by the time their cases creaked across his Court, like a hold-up of trams along the Nevsky, they were academic, the suspects hardly more than burned-out names. He sent some to be hanged, some to exile, some to be eaten by disease in the slimy fundament of the Peter and Paul Fortress. But the problem was recurring and always the same.

In that life, wearing his official uniform, he himself was above suspicion. That was changed now, when he was entitled only to the garb of a country gentleman. Like everyone else he was regarded as a potential threat to the Autocracy. Krasnov, he was aware, was sent to intimidate and spy on him. The burning of the village last night was meant as a warning to Baltic landlords, as well as to their Estonian peasants.

The future was black. To seek support, he recalled the dedication of his forebears. The Teutonic Knights had come to free the land from barbarity and paganism. Now, it seemed, this same land needed another kind of protection: the protection of men like Krasnov. But Loff could never reconcile himself to that. He was still restless at dawn, scheming to send his sister and Fräulein to unchanging safety within the German Empire for a year or two.

CHAPTER 5

▼

1882

Paul had been introduced to the "Sons of Russia" as to an esoteric club enjoying a little sport from time to time. He was asked by fellow officers to join and he was not the man to say no to anybody.

"You can't stand by while Jews and Anarchists destroy the Empire, old man. And nobody gets hurt...not really hurt, you know. We just keep it in their minds that we know what they're up to."

He underwent the initiation without soul-searching—it was just another Mess rag. His eyes were bound, his breast bound in quasi-Masonic mode. There was a lot of laughter and a lot of vodka. Before it was all over Paul collapsed to his knees and his friend, Sergei Ouroussoff, also on his knees, muttered across the table:

"You're a good fellow, Paul. Isn't he boys? Three cheers for von Hagen!" There was no response. Their companions were already unconscious and, with a giggle, Ouroussoff joined them in insensibility.

Paul was quite young when he realised the advantages of becoming everyone's idea of a good fellow. He decided on it when he grew old enough to realise he could never please his father. It was the old Baron's habit to find fault with everybody and everything.

Loff was living in Saint Petersburg when Paul became aware of the problem. The jury system had been introduced in Russian courts by then and the old man studied all the newspapers for details of his son's successes. Then, Loff was transferred to the secret courts prosecuting in political cases and his name no longer appeared in the press, neither was it mentioned at home. The Baron ignored him from then on, as though he were a disgrace to the family. Paul thenceforward determined that he would not only do his Duty, but that he would be publicly acknowledged to be doing it.

Margarethe too, fell short of the Baron's expectations. Whatever pertained to the running of the household was her responsibility; if the jam were too sweet, the beer too sour, the linen too coarse or the bread too heavy (and it always was), it was Margarethe the Baron abused.

"You disappoint me, daughter."

"I'm sorry, Father."

"You tolerate laziness among the servants. It is your Duty to see they do their work properly. Make them afraid of you. They'll work then. Understand?"

Paul escaped to the Military Academy as soon as he could. "Remember who you are and what you are, boy!" his Father barked while the sleigh waited in the courtyard to take him away.

"Yes, sir."

"Do your Duty. Don't ever give me cause to regret I sired you."

"No, sir."

"There have been von Hagens on this land for six hundred years. Don't forget."

The old man held out a hand. Paul kissed it.

"Goodbye, Father."

Outside the study door he embraced Margarethe and kissed her vigorously. She stiffened. "I'll come back a hero," he laughed.

He ran into the courtyard and jumped into the sleigh. Ants, the grizzled coachman who had long since forgotten how old he was, put his whip to the horses' quarters and the bells began to ring. Paul shouted with the relief of freedom. His lungs would have burst, otherwise. Ants looked over his shoulder and laughed with him.

While the runners hissed over the snow, and the hoof-beats were muffled by the soft, sweet-smelling whiteness, Paul decided never to come home again. The Estate had been well enough when he was a boy, running and fighting with the village boys. Later, his education separated him from his village friends. He took more notice of their fathers, tied to the cross-frame and beaten raw on his father's orders. He realised his playmates must eventually take their places on that frame, perhaps on Loff's orders or even on his own.

Saint Petersburg enraptured him. The city sparkled. He loved the snow in its streets, the ice in its rivers and canals, the frosty facades of its rainbow palaces, its church spires piercing a blueness that to him was heavenly, its avenues and statues.

In winter days were short, nights long and starlit. Lights from palace windows softened the milky whiteness of the snow in the streets to the colour of rich cream. Theatres and ballrooms blazed with uniforms and jewelled gowns. Sleighbells performed a symphony in the streets. Ladies on their morning drives rode like little pink-cheeked fairies, half-lying in their sleighs, wrapped in mink or sables and peeping from under layers of bright wool.

For Ensign von Hagen it was a world undreamed-of. In the Preobrazhensky Barracks on Saltikova-Shchedrina Street he was soon accepted as a thoroughly good fellow. The Preobrazhensky was one of the oldest regiments in the Imperial army. It was a privilege to belong. Still only in his teens, Paul was dazzling in his uniform. He was already a fine rider and the ladies who timed their morning drives to pass the Preobrazhensky Platz while the cadets were exercising pointed him out to each other as they passed with meaningful smiles. Besides, he shot well, could hold his liquor, dance superbly and play cards with good-natured disinterest as to the result. He settled his debts and was never mean-minded with a brother-officer was in financial difficulties. The ladies in the *maisons de plaisir* on the islands welcomed him with rapture.

It was a good time to be a soldier. The Crimean War ended a stulti-fied period in military development. Now there was a glorious ripening of new militarism. France, after centuries as the European colossus was reduced to nothingness by Germany. Though Count Bismarck might strut, it was obvious to everyone that it was the German Army that had given birth to the new Europe. Paul von Hagen and his brother officers longed for it to be Russia's turn next.

Russia's turn began to come in mid-decade. Paul was promoted Lieutenant. Away in the Balkans, Christians in Bosnia and Herzegov-ina rebelled against the Turks. The movement spread to Bulgaria. The Sultan sent in his *Bashi-Bazooks* and twelve thousand Christians died horrible deaths.

"It's a damned shame," the Russian officers said.

"Barbarous."

"We have to do something about it."

"The Bulgarians are Slave and Orthodox like us. They're our broth-ers."

War looked inevitable through 1875 and 1876. Excitement for glory among young officers was hardly containable. Paul wrote to his brother in the autumn:

"We are all more shocked than I can tell you. The Turks have surren-dered any right they might have had to be treated as a civilised race. They should be driven out of Europe and back into the deserts of Ana-tolia to live like the jackals they are. And we're the boys to drive them there, I promise you.

"Our only fear is that the Preobrazhensky will be held back in Saint Petersburg to keep the ladies happy (delightful though that is) instead of going down to teach Ali Baba the lesson he deserves. If anyone has to stay in Petersburg, it should be the Pavlovsky. You really can't take seriously a regiment whose men used to be selected for the shape of their noses! We met up with some of those snub-noses on Vasil'yevsky Island the other night. I was with my friend Ouroussoff and a few oth-ers when some of the Pavlovsky came in and made utter bores of

themselves. We wouldn't stand for it. We gave them what for, I can tell you. One of them had the nerve to run out and fetch a police patrol. We very soon put them straight, as well. Ouroussoff got a cut over his left eye and two of their chaps were taken to hospital. But that will only help them to remember in future. They have to give way when the Preobrazhensky are about!"

His Christmas letter was in much the same mood.

"The Serbian and the Montenegrins did their best but they were only a few miserable tribesmen, after all. Everyone knew the Turks would beat them. It's disgusting that we weren't there to help out. It would have turned out very differently if we had been, I can tell you. Everyone's hoping the Emperor will make his move in the spring. He has to. It's the only way."

The longed-for orders came in March and the Regiment quitted Saint Petersburg for Odessa. Paul had never travelled so far south before. Other officers played cards on the way, but Paul was insensible to everything but the view outside the carriage windows. So much space, and no trees.

"Von Hagen! Make your bid!"

"Oh...er...I'm sorry."

"Are you playing or not?"

"Leave him alone. He's in a dream."

"He's in love again, most probably."

"Don't bother to deal him in."

"Come on, Paul, what are you staring at?"

"There's nothing to see out there."

"Only smiles and miles of nothing," someone laughed.

This landscape without firs and birches, green and gently rolling, was at first as empty as a wilderness. Yet there was the promise of something besides, something secret. When the locomotive stopped at villages to take on wood and water, Paul wandered along the track in waist-high feather grass, wild red tulips, anenomes and blue-grey sage. In places the ground was honeycombed by susliks. Cranes flew north and larks rose from under his feet to almost beyond his vision, filling the empty landscape with their song. For days the train continued its blundering jog across the Steppe. Mammoth-like creatures, heavy enough to splinter any car they bumped into, rushed pell-mell to avoid its noisy menace. Antelope stopped to watch with quiet wonderment, then skipped off on their dainty feet in a dream-world ballet.

At last they steamed in to Odessa. The city was built on a bluff overlooking the sapphire waters of the Black Sea. It was already warm there and people appeared to have abandoned their houses to live in its streets.

Paul passed time riding along the beach or struggling on foot through alleyways where Turkish vendors clutched for his custom as he passed. Sure-footed tribesmen from the Caucasus swung their robes round them proudly as they passed. And there were whole streets of Jews, unlike any he had seen before. Saint Petersburg Jews were unostentatious; Odessa Jews were not. They grew their hair in locks and wore long gabardine topcoats in spite of the heat. Men wore broad-brimmed black hats trimmed with red fox. The women, he was told, wore wigs. They danced and sang their way to holy ecstasy, and their wooden Synagogues trembled with the strain of their extremities of worship. And there were Russians too: Middle-class, dark-suited men, in with their tight-laced wives from their Ukrainian Estates, parading the Promenade where the municipal band played in its filigree kiosk.

At last Paul's wish came true: War was declared. The Romanians proclaimed independence and opened their frontier to Russian troops. Paul boarded a troop ship—normally engaged in the grain trade—for the voyage across the reedy mouths of the Danube to Constanta. From there he travelled in medium comfort in a troop train to Bucharest and from there, in considerably less comfort south to Zimnitsa, for the ferry across the River.

In normal times Zimnitsa was a village with a Customs Post in the shadow of a Turkish fort. Now it was an Amy camp, a confusion of men and supplies, with barges racing each other across to the Bulgarian side. Other barges, competing in futile swiftness, came back. They brought cargoes of men, muddy and bloody with shocked faces, heaving and groaning on stretchers or hobbling on makeshift crutches.

On both sides, the flies were indiscriminately contaminating everything and driving everyone mad.

An Army at war never sleeps. At all hours of the day and night, men ride back and forth, shout orders, obey orders, grumble, swear, scream with pain. Here on the complacent Danube, these sounds men made raped the silence and the smell of unwashed and rotting bodies, of sweating horses, blood and putrefaction joined the air.

On the Bulgarian side, men marched long miles in the burning June sun as far as Plevna. There they pitched their tents and there they stayed. The glory of Russia was checked outside a tiny town tantalisingly close and teasingly out of reach. The Turks were skilfully dug in and there was no way round. Shells whistled from side to side and the heavy stink of cordite rasped men's chests. Trees and rocks flew skywards taking men with them. The lucky ones lay safe behind boulders, their rifles trained on unseen enemies. Riders made sorties. They rode out shining in their confidence and rode back chastened. Tomorrow, please God, they would still be alive to shine again.

Paul had no idea what was happening. He couldn't follow what they had in mind (if anything) those staff officers who planned. Company 'A' to parade at this hour, Company 'Y' at that. Count Milyutin headed the War Office in Saint Petersburg. How could he possibly know what has happening here at Plevna? Had he any idea how many men were killed wholesale in the shelling or picked off one by one by snipers? Did he know about the shortage of vodka, even in the Officers' Mess? Had anyone told him how much the natives charged for their local brew, how filthy were the whores, how maggot-ridden the food?

"Holy Christ, it's hot!"

"Got any tobacco?"

"No."

"What wouldn't I give for a night on the Islands!"

"Remember Masha? The one with breasts like water melons?"

"Do you think they know we're still here?"

"Take your filthy arse somewhere else, Brother. You stink."

"These bloody lice."

"Down boy! Here comes another!"

Their little piece of ground heaves.

"Christ! Ivan, are you all right"

"No, of course he's not bloody all right. Look at him!"

"Jesus!"

"Bastards!"

"Look at his neck."

"It took the poor bugger's head bloody nearly off."

"Take him away! We can't sit looking at him all day."

They stayed at Plevna from the sweating time to the freezing time. Winter was cheerless torture. Typhus killed more of the men than did the Turks.

In December at last, someone in Saint Petersburg or, maybe it was someone here in Plevna—it didn't matter which—gave the order to move. The men woke at dawn, their blankets wet with thawing breath. Their boots were hardened with frost and half-a-dozen more of them had died of typhus during the night. A fresh-faced Colonel galloped up.

"Company 'A' to attack here, Company 'B' there! Battery 'O' to lay down a barrage here, Battery 'P' there!"

The men roused, cracked lice and shivered in the uniforms they'd slept in all these months. Nobody knew what was happening least of all the men who galloped around the rocks, sabres swinging, screaming curses and victory oaths, defying bullets that hit some and spared others until they realised with Satanic joy they were in the mean streets of Plevna.

There was still a long way to go. They had to march south all the way through Bulgaria where villagers cheered their Slav Liberators and threw them flowers and fruit. Hirsute priests swung censers and smiled hairy smiles. Baggy-trousered Turks hung from trees like ripened, fly-blown fruit.

It was a glorious progress they made, fording rivers, breasting mountains, roistering through villages. They crossed from Bulgaria into Turkey. Constantinople was their goal. Soon…soon, now. They halted ten miles away. The domes and minarets of Byzantium were visible in the misty distance, but they had stopped!

"What the hell are we waiting here for?"

"Why don't they let us finish the bastards off?"

"The English fleet's anchored at Constantinople."

"What's that got to do with it?"

"I don't know."

"They don't want us in the Straits."

"It's their way to India they're worried about."

"What's bloody India got to do with it?"

"Getting into Constantinople's all I want. They can keep their India."

"You're after getting into those harems, Brother. I know what you want."

"Oh Christ! Couldn't I use a woman, though."

"Breasts as soft as silk and large and round as water-melons, they do say."

Day after day, they sat there and it was like Plevna all over again: the killing impersonal and relentless, though not quite so ruthless, perhaps.

"Holy Christ, but it's cold."

"Got any tobacco?"

"No."

"What wouldn't I give for a night on the islands?"

"Do they know we're still here, do you think?

In March the Russian and Turkish Governments signed a Treaty at San Stefano. No one asked the men what they thought about it.

"Where's San Stefano?"

"How the bloody hell should I know?"

"Can we go home now, then?"

"Bulgaria's getting it's own king and we're getting chunks of Turkey down in the Caucasus."

"Can we go home?"

"Do you think they know we're still here?"

Paul and the Preobrazhensky were among the first back in Saint Petersburg. In the Capital they heard the full story. All Europe was meeting in Berlin to rob Russia of her victory.

Revolutionaries placarded the streets: "*It is for Russians to free Bulgaria then to free ourselves, Comrades.*" The police tore down the posters and chased anyone they saw putting them up. The general public were unconcerned. The War and its outcome had little to do with them. Vera Zasulich shot General Trepov, head of Saint Petersburg's police, in protest against cruelty to political prisoners at 25 Shlapernaya Street—one of the buildings Loff von Hagen used to interrogate his prisoners in the old days. Zasulich was tried and acquitted. The Army was shocked. It was about that time Paul joined "The Sons of Russia."

Soured by memories and dilemmas that doing his Duty laid him open to, Paul was sleepless the whole of his last night at home longing for dawn and to be able to leave for Warsaw. There, at least, the Regiment around him would make everything easier. They might find themselves coercing a few Poles and Jews but at least they would do it like gentlemen. Krasnov, sleeping with his wife in another room of the house was one of the rotten parts of a thoroughly rotten system. He would surely go like the rest of them, when the time came.

CHAPTER 6

▼

1882

Dear Loff,

Warsaw is beautiful, but too far from the sea for my taste. It's full of narrow twisting streets and none of the long straight avenues we have in Petersburg. And there are no weather vanes and storks to speak of, not like Reval. Our barracks are across the river from the main city in a suburb called Praga.

We're busy most of the time, drilling and parading. We ride across the Poniatouski Bridge and into the town every day to let the Poles and the Jews know we're here and that they can't expect to get away with anything.

When we come into direct contact with the Poles, we are polite on both sides but not over-friendly. They invite us to their houses sometimes, but we take care to avoid politics in our conversation, of course. We rub along quite well enough so long as we play by the first rule of the game: don't say or do anything to upset them.

Tell Margarethe I can get her some nice lace here if she would like some.

Your affectionate brother,

Paul von Hagen

CHAPTER 7

▼

1882

Life in the barracks was heavy with sameness, and Warsaw quickly lost its novelty for Paul and the rest of the Preobrazhensky. Here there was none of the merriment of the Petersburg Islands, no gypsies to entertain. True, a few admirers—ladies with parasols, children with nursemaids, watching them ride over the Bridge and up the incline to the roughly cobbled Old Town Square. They waved but didn't cheer. This was an occupation force, and they knew it.

The troops fell into melancholy. Their function was either to fight or to display. At present, they displayed, but like a band of actors playing every night to empty houses. The feelings of an army can be easily hurt.

Wherever they are, though, soldiers find consolation in girls to make love to, bars and cafes eager for their custom. Paul and Captain Ouroussoff found comfort in a beamed, smoke-darkened tavern in Brewery Street. The proprietor, big-bellied and damp-skinned Pan Koblinski, offered music and pretty girls, grossly overcharging for champagne and making a huge profit while doing so.

Each of the Preobrazhensky officers "adopted" a special young lady, naturally. Paul was becoming the butt of his friends' humour for not having one for himself. Their jests were good-natured; they understood. He wasn't Russian, of course, but that was no excuse. They must educate him in Russian ways.

"There's a pretty little one over there, Paul."

"Shall I call her over?"

"Thanks, but I'd rather you didn't."

"Oh, come on, old man, have some fun! Here! I say, Mademoiselle!"

The girl had just finished singing a song about a young man in an apple orchard. Every apple he picks, attracted by its sweet scent and blushing skin, reminds him of his sweetheart. Alas, in every one of the apples there lurks a worm, and the young man is sad because his sweetheart flirts with other young men in the village.

The audience enjoyed the performance. Her voice was in no way remarkable, but Paul surmised that she was employed on account of her looks. She was petite and exquisitely formed, with ravishing black hair and a blush of pink to her subtle, olive complexion. She approached their table reluctantly. Ouroussoff stood up, kissed her hand and clicked his heels with extravagant politeness.

"Ouroussoff, Mademoiselle, Captain Sergei Antonovich. My friends called me Seriozha. This is my comrade, Captain Paul von Hagen, who very much wishes to meet you. We are officers of the Preobrazhensky." He drew her gently into a seat.

"We very much enjoyed your singing, my dear. Will you honour us by taking a glass of champagne?"

Ouroussoff called to a hovering waiter, while Paul studied the girl. She was no more than sixteen, he guessed.

Sergei insisted on opening the wine himself and, deliberately, as it seemed, spilt some. He thrust a napkin at Paul to dab the girl's dress. It was a pretty dress, ice-blue silk with a pattern of peacocks woven into it with delicate silver thread. Paul began to feel hot and was finding it difficult to breathe.

In a moment they were joined by Sergei's special friend, Clementine, a confident contralto. She enjoyed herself with Sergei, by turns patronising and possessive. Paul's girl left to sing again and disappeared immediately afterwards. They didn't see her any more that night.

The next morning, riding at the head of his Company across the Poniatowski Bridge, Paul saw her standing among the thin crowd. She wore a plain black skirt, white blouse, scarlet necktie, and a straw hat enlivened by scarlet ribbon. She could, he thought, have been a pastor's daughter from Estonia—Germany, even. He saluted her smartly, but she became confused and hurried away. That night at the Kabaret, he reminded her of their meeting.

"I...I had to go to Praga. By chance, we were passing at the same time," she stammered guiltily.

Her vulnerability appealed to him.

"That was lucky for me," he said. "I was very happy to see you." The excitement he had felt last night repeated itself.

She blushed but said nothing.

"I don't even know your name, Mademoiselle."

"Leonore...my name is Leonore," she told him, with strange insistence.

"And do you remember mine?"

"Captain von Hagen," she told him timidly, and rose. "Now I must sing."

"That isn't necessary. Pan Koblinski will understand."

He looked across to where the proprietor sat at the much-scored desk checking chits and writing bills. Of course, he would add a percentage to the Captain's bill, but he nodded and blinked his eyes.

"There! You see? You're excused." She said nothing. "Leonore, don't be afraid of me. I mean you no harm, I swear it."

He paused, hoping she understood his sincerity, and changed the subject. "Do you like working here?"

"No, but they are good to me. I must earn a living."

"Your parents?"

"They're dead."

"I'm sorry."

She shrugged and looked across the room towards Sergei, sprawled with a group of friends at a nearby table. "Your friend is very happy tonight, I think."

Sergei's group, with their young ladies, laughed too loudly, Paul thought. Poles at other tables watched them with marked distaste. Ouroussoff raised his eyebrows to invite Paul over. Paul shook his head.

After that he visited the Kabaret Doma almost every night, and it was accepted that Leonore would spend the evening with him. Several times on Sundays, when the weather was good, he took her driving out of the city and along the river.

She would tell him nothing about herself, and he wouldn't press her. He treated her with extravagant care, like the most delicate bone china. His anxieties on her account kept his own desire in check, though there was always the shadow over their happiness that the report would be ordered back to Russia. Perhaps she feared that, too, though she gave him no sign that there was any blight on her happiness. His moments of greatest pleasure were when they met; of greatest desolation when they parted. On the days they didn't meet, he could only dampen down his growing lust with an equally strongly growing sense of guardianship.

CHAPTER 8

▼

1882

25 Sept. '82

My dear Loff,

I am alive and well, writing because you have heard of the trouble we've been having.

Young hooligans started demonstrating about ten days ago, after Mass at St. John's Church in Swientojanska Street. You may not know it, but St. John's is special to us because it contains the tombs of the Dukes of Mazovia. And, you'll remember, it was a Duke of Mazovia who invited those long-dead von Hagens to Estonia all those years ago.

The important part is, the Church was full of university students. The priest said afterwards they were astonished to see so many young people there. After Mass, they hung about in the street outside and...until you've been here, you can't imagine how hot-headed these young Poles can be...they started shouting slogans and jostling passers-by. Then...it must have been planned...they ran all over town, nothing could stop them, breaking shop windows, stoning banks and attacking the houses of anyone they suspected of being Jewish or pro-Russian.

We were called because the police couldn't control them. Frustrated at not being able to do any real damage anywhere else, they wracked through the Old Town again and into the Jewish quarter. There was no stopping them there. By the time we arrived, they'd already set fire to some of the buildings. Jews—men, women and children—were running everywhere, scared half to death, under a hail of stones, clubs and bullets. Our Colonel decided it would be best to contain the riot—at least, to keep it away from other parts of the city—so we circled the ghetto and stopped anyone going in or coming out.

The rioting lasted three days. Jews barricaded themselves in their shops and houses as best as they could. But the rioters fired anything that would burn, and Jews, with their clothes flaming, threw themselves out of windows and off rooftops. Those who weren't killed when they fell were clubbed to death as they lay on the ground. Thank God, most of the poor devils were already unconscious!

The students must have got arms from somewhere. So must the workers, who came out on a sympathetic strike. They tore up paving stones for barricades and let us have it, of course. But we moved in, and God knows how many died in the crossfire and confusion after that.

This isn't the kind of thing I thought I would be involved in when I joined the Army, Loff. At least the War against the Turks was clean, fought for a purpose, or so we believed. Here in Warsaw...I can think of nothing like it except that raid on our village...remember? That was bad enough, but this was even worse.

Loff, where in God's name are we going? I'll always be before anyone in doing my duty to His Majesty. But this slaughter of civilians...so many women and children among them...burning them to death in their own homes...that's no work for the Preobrazhensky. We can't be accused of starting the fires, but neither did we try to put them out, God help us!

In great confusion, I am,

Paul von Hagen

CHAPTER 9

▼

1882

After the riots, the Preobrazhensky were confined to barracks as a conciliatory measure. Civil police used spies and informers to hunt down students and, at the same time, anyone else wanted out of the way. The terror lasted several weeks, but the agony of it lasted longer. Dead bodies were cleared off the pavements, even in the ghetto, and trouble was taken to board up some of the burned-out buildings. But clearing the wreckage wasn't enough; normal existence was dessicated for years to come.

It was some time before Paul and Sergei could go back to the Doma. Pan Koblinski was still head and welcomed them with shining relief. Business had suffered badly.

"What times we live in, your Excellencies. What times! How good to see you again. Tadzio! Champagne for the gentlemen! On the house, your Excellencies. How good it is to see you. What times! What times!" He pointed to his boarded-up windows.

Clementine joined them directly, cheerful as ever. Sergei kissed her and told her fulsomely how much he had missed her.

"Me you, too," she laughed in her broken Russian. "We thought you would never come back. Such goings on! We watched it all from upstairs. Who could sleep in those days? We were stranded. We couldn't get out. There was no food. We daren't go into the street. If I ever have to face another of Pan Koblinski's smoked sausages, I'll die; where does he get them, do you think?" She laughed again and complacently sipped champagne.

With all the unconcern he could muster, Paul asked:

"Where's Leonore?"

Clementine gave him a long look and sounded evasive. "I'm sure I don't know, Captain."

"Isn't she here?"

"I really don't know."

"What do you mean, you don't know? Wasn't she with you during the riots?"

"No. No, Captain, she went home."

"Home? How could you let her go out in all that? Where's her home?"

"You had better ask Pan Koblinski, Captain."

"I'm asking you, my girl!" Paul seized her wrist. "Believe me, Mademoiselle, I'm serious."

"Here, I say, steady on, old chap," Ouroussoff cautioned nervously.

"Well," the girl began and stopped, watching him with genuine surprise. "I shouldn't be saying anything, but...you really don't know, do you?"

"What don't I know? What's happened to her?"

"It's the God's truth I'm telling you, we've heard nothing about her for weeks. I don't suppose we ever will."

"Why do you say that? She's supposed to be a friend of yours."

"Please, Captain...Pan Koblinski said not say anything. He was afraid you'd get him into trouble." She rubbed her wrist and winced as the blood flowed back. "I said you surely must have known, but Pan Koblinski said to keep quiet, just in case."

"Enough! I don't understand any of this. What are you talking about? What's happened?"

"She can pass...that's why Pan Koblinski gave her the job. Her name's not Leonore, Captain. It's Leah! She's a Jew!"

Paul gritted his teeth with shock and fought for control. He stamped across the floor to the cash desk without another word. Koblinski was more than usually ingratiating.

"Of course, if your Excellency found the girl amusing, there was no harm done. I never expect any of you young gentlemen to take a serious interest in my young ladies. They're pretty, that's why they're here. And...we're all men of the world, aren't we?" He smiled, but Paul's gaze wouldn't be deflected. He went out seconds later, pocketing a scrap of paper. Ouroussoff caught him up at the door. "You can't go out alone at this time of night, old man, not in that uniform."

"I'll be all right."

"At least wait until morning. I'll come with you."

"I'll have to chance it. I must get away...I must think."

He walked across the Square and down to the Vistula, relishing the cold early autumn night. Nobody else was venturing out. He walked alone beneath the stars, feeling like a horse in quicksand. Why had they lied to him? More shameful that he had not known without being told. Jews were different—everyone knew that—their skins swarthy and none-too-clean, noses out of proportion to the rest of their features. They mangled Russian in a peculiar sing-song. They wouldn't eat the same food as everyone else. How could he not have known?

It was a joke. Sergei had known all along. That's why he called her over in the first place, to make him look foolish. But that...that was nothing. This was not foolishness, risking himself in streets like this, worrying about her at this time of night. It wasn't important! What the hell did it matter? He was a Balt, a Lutheran, an officer in a prize regiment, conditioned since birth to be an anti-Semite. She was only a café girl on her way to being a whore, probably.

He stood on the bridge and closed his eyes so tightly the lids ached. When he opened them, the blackness was tinged with purple and grey as blood recharged them. But the feeling of colour altered nothing. The reality of his situation wasn't the same, even worse, colder than ever as a new horror jangled his consciousness. She was a Jew. She might well be dead by now, killed on his own orders, perhaps, in all that confusion. No one could tell in the rush and the crush of it who was left alive at the end, innocent or guilty. Anything had been possible while he led his men almost unseen through the chaos of Zamenhofa, Sienna, Chloda or Leszno, indiscriminately chasing rioting students and terrified Jews.

He gripped the balustrade to steady himself. He would have to resign his Commission. He couldn't continue doing his duty—not with a semblance of sympathy in his heart for anyone on the other side of the line. Jews would always be on the other side. They always had been. Nothing would change that now. In any case, Warsaw sickened him. Duty meant killing his country's enemies, and the killing was only justified when the enemy were trained soldiers, too. He could never again raise a weapon against women and children, not even Jews.

The girl was a Jew, and he knew all about them. They cheated peasants in their stores and taverns, loaned money at exorbitant interest and did dirty, secret things in their Synagogues, drinking the blood of kidnapped Christian children. Leonore, or whatever she called herself, was one of them! Knowing her had taught him their greatest crime of all, something so horrible it was never mentioned aloud: witchcraft!

They knew magic! For a while she had held him captive in her darkness. It was the only excuse he had for maintaining any self-respect at all. Now, thank God, he understood. He had joined the "Sons of Russia" in ignorance and had doubted them after what happened in his village. He would never question them again!

Sergei and the others would quite soon be crossing the bridge on their way back to the barracks, he remembered. He couldn't be seen. He walked back towards the Square and turned into a dark lane parallel to the river. On both sides of him were wooden houses leaning crazily forward, like drunks in a bar. There were no lights from the houses and only one lamp in the street. As he passed under it, a girl emerged from the gloom.

"Hello, Captain." She sounded hopeless and weary, but still attempted the lilt of seduction. "You want company, your Excellency? I'll give you a good time, darling."

How thin she was. Her red dress was gathered baggily 'round her waist, her pale skin all the paler in contrast with her crudely painted cheeks. She shifted her tippet to reveal the scanty swelling of her breasts. She took his hand in hers and guided it to her bosom. Hardly knowing what he did, he grasped her naked nipple and squeezed it hard. With his other hand, he pinched her cheek, viciously. She screamed, surprised. He released her, disgusted at his urge to make someone share his hurt. He pushed her aside.

"Don't go away, darling...please. I'll give you a good time," she begged.

He felt a heavy hand on his shoulder and heard a man's voice soft yet menacing. "That sort of thing costs extra, your Honour, a lot extra. You don't have to worry. She'll do it. She'll do anything you say. But you'll have to pay. She's a good girl. She'll give you a good time. Come on, I'll show you where."

Paul was revolted by the nauseating strength of the man's perfume. He didn't reply. He was confused. The man took the pause between them to be significant. The girl stood under the light, showing no interest in either of them. Paul suddenly struck at the man's sneering smile, and his blow was parried by an iron-hard arm. The man chuck- led. He danced to one side, and Paul was unprepared for the blow to the nape of his neck that brought him to the ground, unconscious.

Paul lay for some hours in the gutter, unconscious. When he awoke, first light was breaking over the city. He shivered, and his head throbbed. His tunic was damp, and his cap lay beside him on the muddy ground. He got unsteadily to his feet and felt in his pockets. The pimp had left nothing except a crumpled piece of paper of no apparent value to anyone: Leonore's address. Paul's urge to see her was now greater than ever...just to see her, to be sure she was alive.

He limped to the barracks and changed his uniform in time for parade. When that was over, he haggled with several cabdrivers before anyone would consider taking him into the ghetto.

The route lay through streets of dismal tenements, many ruined; the centre of Warsaw's clothing industry. On the top floors lived the Jews who worked at cramped benches in the fetid basements. In spite of the turmoil, their trade was flourishing. The fashion was for Saint Petersburg ladies to have their day frocks and evening gowns made in Warsaw.

Paul told the driver to wait for him at Leonore's address, but the man refused. He insisted on being paid and drove away immediately. Paul looked around. There were few people in the streets, and those few kept their eyes to the ground as they passed. For them, a Russian uniform meant only trouble.

Leonore's building was as shabby as its neighbours, the open doorway emitting its inner stink. Little light from outside disturbed the interior dejection and Paul climbed slowly up the curving stone stairway, deeper into an atmosphere of boiled chicken, garlic, urine, and *gefilte* fish. His hand strayed to the banister rail, and he quickly drew it back, sticky with accretion of old unknown substances. On the third landing, he traced the number of a door and knocked. Light footsteps retreated in a rush, and after a pause, the door slowly opened.

"Leonore!"

"Captain!"

"Thank God you're safe."

"How did you find me? You must go away, please."

"I've got to talk to you."

She tried to close the door, but his foot jammed it open.

"I can't. Not here."

"Where, then? I won't go until you tell me."

A woman somewhere in the flat shouted something in Yiddish. Two very small children crept giggling, hand in hand, towards the door to grasp Leonore's skirt.

"When, Leonore? Tell me, or I'll stand here all afternoon if I have to."

"I don't know. Tomorrow, perhaps. Why did you come!"

"Tell me where...when?"

"The Saxon Garden. Tomorrow. Three o'clock, by the ruins. Now please, Captain...please go."

"That is my cousin's flat," she told him the next day. The Saxon Garden was almost empty in the autumn drizzle. The air was raw. "She could just about accept that I had to sing at the Doma, we needed the money, she could never tolerate a Russian officer started coming to the flat, though. She'd think...well, you know what she'd think. So would everybody else. I couldn't bear to disgrace her like that. She and her husband have been very good to my sisters and me. They took us in when our parents were murdered."

"Your parents were murdered? You mentioned that the last night we met. What happened?"

She shrugged. "It was during the pogrom after the last Tsar was killed. They blamed the Jews, of course; they always do. The Cossacks came to Warsaw to keep order. When they left, you came."

"Tell me what happened to them...your parents."

"I don't want to talk about it."

"Please, Leonore, I must know."

Her face grew tight as if she was groping to remember events as painlessly as possible. "I don't know why they picked our flat that day. Two of my sisters and I were upstairs with friends. We heard them on the landing below...they were drunk and swearing horribly in Russian. We were terrified they'd come to rape us. They banged at doors downstairs. When they went to our door, we heard my father open it and ask what they wanted. I couldn't make out any of the words after that. It was all shouting and awful screaming. My sister wanted to go down, but I kept her with me, as quiet as I could. We expected them to come to us next, but they didn't. We heard them leave and go out into the street. Then we went down and found them…my other two sisters and two little brothers with my parents—all dead."

"What can I say?"

"What is there to say? It happened." She pulled back her shoulders, as though putting it all behind her. "My cousins are good people, Captain. They don't have much money, but they took us in. My sisters have work in a dress factory. I could sing a little, so I got that job at the Doma. I earn a little more than they do, even though Pan Koblinski didn't pay me as much as the other girls. He was taking a risk having me there at all. He doesn't want me back now."

"What will you do?"

"My cousin's expecting another baby. She'll need help. After that…Oh, I'll find something."

"No! Listen!" He put his hand on her arm. "There must be something else we can do. I must think…work it out."

She sighed, looking up at the slate sky through the leafless lindens. "It's lovely here," she said. "The air smells delicious in the rain. I used to come here often. People didn't use to take any notice of you. Nobody shouted *Zhyd!* It's as though everyone comes here to be happy, and they're willing to let other people be happy, too." She laughed gently. "I'll bring the little ones whenever I can."

"No! Leonore! That's not good enough. You must let me take care of you." He spoke with a surprising firmness for which he knew he had no right.

She drew away sharply, "No!"

"You can't go on living in that place. We might have more riots! I'll want to know you're somewhere safe. And I swear I'll never bother you. You'll never have to see me at all if you don't want to."

That was the first of many circular conversations, either in the Saxon Garden or walking along the river in the hardening frost.

"I'll never leave my sisters. They're young. It's my duty to look after them."

"We'll find a flat big enough for all of you."

"No!" she said for the thousandth time, though there was a wavering in her voice.

One day in the garden, fresh snow lay on the eighteenth-century ruins, and everything dazzled the eye.

"I've been talking about you to Ouroussoff," he told her. "He agrees with me."

She shrugged, irritated. "I have to think about my sisters."

"I'm thinking about them, too."

"You don't understand. They must live like Jews. Our parents died for that. If we stopped being Jews, we would betray their memory."

He wasn't listening. "Ouroussoff agrees with me. He understands about that; we both do."

It wasn't true. "You're the last chap I'd expect to be so stupid, Paul," Ouroussoff said, exasperated. "You're a romantic idiot."

"She can't stay in that place, Sergei. You haven't seen it."

"That's where she belongs; it's what she's used to. Take her away from there, and what will happen when we go, or..." he grinned "...more likely, when you get tired of her?"

Opposition turned Paul's urge into an unmanageable obsession. His father had taught him never to accept "no" from a woman, nor from any inferior person. Not to be able to persuade Leonore would be humiliation, or a blow to the von Hagen pride, as well as a disappointment.

Leonore nursed her cousin through puerperal fever, tended the baby, cleaned the flat, washed clothes, shopped and cooked for the family. There was no time for anything and at last, exhausted, she gave up the struggle like a landed salmon. Having fought long, valiantly and beautifully, she surrendered. Paul was overjoyed.

In glorious spring weather, he moved the three of them into a flat in Praga with five sunny rooms looking across the river to the Old City.

He started all three at a nearby Ursuline convent. They studied French, Russian, drawing, needlework, sketching, and music. They were sharp, eager students all of them. Paul kept to his promise: they remained Jews. Their landlord didn't forget, either. Having three young Jewesses living in his flat could have meant trouble. He accepted them because Paul was a Russian officer and didn't argue about the rent. He felt he needed to know what went on there, however, so he hired a maid who would watch carefully and report back. She was surly, she squinted, and she served them gracelessly. She was also illiterate, a fact the landlord had carefully taken into account. She would be unable to write scandal to her relatives in the country. She was also well-enough paid not to risk losing her job by spreading gossip among the neighbours.

Ouroussoff and Clementine occasionally came to dine *en famille*, scornful and wondering by turns. "I don't know where you think all this will end, Paul. There has to be a break eventually."

"I know. But they're so happy. Let them enjoy it while they can. And…" he added hopefully but without conviction. "I'll think of something when the time comes."

CHAPTER 10

▼

1883

"Dear Loff,

Everything is calm here now, though we expect another rising eventually. We've taught them a sound lesson this time, but they're so hot-headed, so obstinate, peace can't last. For the most part we keep out of the public eye, except when we put on splendid ceremonial parades to entertain them. (And to remind them that we're still here and that they'd better not forget the fact!!!)

My men are becoming restless. They no longer enjoy being here; it would be wisest to send them home and bring out another regiment. I am well..."

Margarethe threw the letter aside impatiently. "I'll read it later, brother. I told Pastor Vikkers to be ready to operate school at eight o'clock. You'll come too, I hope."

"No, Margarethe!" Loff replied. "I've told you so many times it's illegal to open a school before you have permission from Synod."

"This is our own land, Baron. We must not allow Prince Krasnov—
nor any like him—to think we're afraid of them."

"Fear doesn't enter into it. Krasnov administers the Law just now,
so it's essential for people like us—people with our country's real interests at heart—to obey Imperial Law in every possible way. That's our
sacred duty."

"Yours, perhaps. Not mine. My duty is to my own country, my own
home…not to the one you're trying to drag me into. *Hie stehe ich. Ich
kann nicht anders. Gott hilf mir!* Remember, brother? Or are you allowing all these bureaucrats to turn you into an Orthodox and a Russian?"

She left, closing the door noisily. He sighed, not for the first time,
for the old days in Saint Petersburg. Everything had been so much easier then. Outside, he could hear Margarethe calling out to Channah
Litvak.

Channah was another of his dilemmas. He had kept her in his house
since the night the village was burned. At one time he had contemplated settling her with one of the families in his villages; but he knew
no one would accept her, however much he paid. He could have sent
her away, of course, to Wilno, perhaps. But that was too far, and she
was too vulnerable. He knew no one there, or how Jews handled such
matters. Gossips on the estate were speculating on their relationship,
naturally, but after a week or two, that didn't seem to matter.

"I don't know what he sees in her, I'm sure."

"They do say she's put the *Fräulein Baronin*'s nose out of joint."

"Do you wonder? Taking her to live in the house and her a Jew and
everything."

"Do you…do you think there's anything…well, you know what I
mean…anything like that between them?"

"What does that matter? Personally, I shouldn't grudge the Baron
his little bit of fun. There's never been too much of that in his family, I
reckon."

"I shouldn't put anything past her, cunning little bitch."

"Too kind-hearted for his own good is the poor *Herr Baron.*"
"I can't imagine what he sees in her."

He kept the girl in his house in order to care for her. Though that wasn't the whole truth, perhaps. She was fascinating. Candlelight made her hair glow like a golden sunset. Her ignorance of any life beyond the village enchanted him; he saw the world afresh through her eyes. He taught her Russian because it would be useful for her future. Her studies were his reason for keeping her when Margarethe demanded he send her away. His blood-warming whenever he thought of her was important, too.

She moved silently through the house, never the first to speak. The Baron was her comfort, and whatever they said in the village, her thoughts of him were innocent. Jews only ever fell in love with Jews, and there were many other Jews somewhere in the world. Her father had told her so. But how she might get to them, she didn't know.

Margarethe hated her but didn't turn her out. Her brother wanted her, and obedience to her brother was her duty. She exercised her frustrations by working like a servant and was enthusiastically assisted by Fräulein Baumberg. A companion now, no longer a governess, the aging Fräulein was enjoying life too much to risk offence.

Sometimes, because the Baron insisted, Channah ate with them. Mostly, though, at mealtimes she excused herself, pleading something urgent to do elsewhere. Loff shrugged—he was shrugging a lot these days—and promised he would think tomorrow of a different arrangement...some way to make her feel more comfortable.

He took up Paul's letter from the table where Margarethe had thrown it.

"...I am well. Life still has compensations, though I shall never forget what happened during the riots. I still have nightmares about that. We should never have been involved. It had nothing to do with soldiering.

The news is that our boys have been doing splendidly on the Afghan border. I tell you frankly, brother, I'd have given anything to be there with them, giving those Afghans and Turkmen what-for, instead of shooting down Jews here in Warsaw. Jews are white and European like us, after all.

My friend Ouroussoff thinks I'm mad when I say things like that. In fact, there isn't very much at all that he and I see eye-to-eye about these days. I say shooting down women and children is no part of a soldier's duty. Ouroussoff says a soldier's duty is to carry out orders, whatever they are! I don't understand him anymore. In fact, I believe I don't understand very much about anything or anybody anymore.

I hope you and Margarethe are both well,

Your affectionate brother,

Paul von Hagen"

The Baron thought it best if his brother applied for home leave. A spell in the country would do him good. He would write later in the day. Meanwhile, he called for Valiant. He felt compelled to see what was happening at Margarethe's school.

Valiant chose his own pace to the village, and Loff wasn't inclined to hurry him. The ground was soft. Beyond the forest, peasants were cheerfully ploughing fresh wrinkles across the face of their fields. In the village, around the well opposite the church and in the shadow of the cross-frame, laughing women drew water, infatuated by the promise of the moment. The hardest part of the year was over. The sun shone, water was plentiful, the mosquitoes would soon be buzzing about them, and so would the men. They looked quickly at the Baron, then away again, simpering and giggling.

Loff could pass the cross-frame now without seeing Channah's father hanging there. He sat for a while, thinking only of Channah. He longed to gather her into his arms, to fondle her blossoming young body, to kiss her milky thighs clouded in glowing chestnut mist.

Sudden laughter from the women at the well brought him back to reality. He flicked the reins. Valiant snorted and continued on his way.

Originally, the huts had been built pell-mell, as and when they were needed. Former Barons had no interest in how their walking merchandise housed itself. Since the fire, Loff had taken stricter control. He supplied finance, timber, fuel, and food to keep the settlement alive. Now the houses were rebuilt in an orderly street, each family having access to water and to the church.

Had his generosity changed the villagers' feelings for him? Doubtful. Estonians hated their German landlords. Pastor Vikkers appeared never to think it necessary to instill in them any sort of feelings except hatred toward the German.

Beside the Germans, there were one or two other things God hadn't arranged as well as he might: flood, drought, Cossack raids, and pestilence. Otherwise, everything was reasonably satisfactory.

Life awakened each spring. Man ploughed and sowed, and the earth conceived. At summer's end the soil gave birth, and man endured the pains of its labour, the reaping, stacking, sweating, and threshing, and the storing of the harvest in wind-chinked barns. After that there was spinning, carpentry, logging, and metal-work to be seen to. When the days were dark man rested, following God's preemption for the Seventh Day.

The women round the well this morning were probably mothers of boys and girls starting at Margarethe's school. On the whole, they were looking pleased. *Die Frau Barönin* had explained the advantages of education. They didn't wholly understand but were willing to try it. Their husbands were indifferent until they themselves promised to see to the bird-scaring, the water-drawing, the gathering of kindling, the fruit-and berry-picking, as well as their own tasks; looking after the poultry, herding, milking, helping on the vegetable plot and doing everything else that needed to be done.

A short way out of the village, the Baron turned off on a grassy track. The barn Margarethe had chosen for her school stood ahead of him, painted iron red. The mutter of children's voice ceased immedi-

ately when they saw him enter. They were learning Martin Luther's
Kleine Katechismus by heart and were delighted for this diversion.

Pastor Vikkers shuffled forward. "Say good morning to the *Herr
Baron*, children."

They greeted him with a sing-song "Good morning, *Herr Baron*."

He waved absent-mindedly. Pastor Vikkers said: "We are making
sure we know our Catechism, your Excellency. Would your Excellency
like to hear us?"

"That won't be necessary." Loff spoke German so that the children
would not understand. "Tell them to sit down, Pastor. There are
benches?"

"Yes, yes. Sit down, children."

Margarethe came forward to receive her brother like a visiting dele-
gation.

"Each morning, the children will have an hour's religious instruction. They will then divide. Fräulein Baumberg will take the older
ones, Channah Litvak the others."

"Margarethe, by giving them religious instruction you'll be commit-
ting a very serious offence. You know that, don't you?"

"Fräulein Baumberg, Channah Litvak! Will you begin, please?"

She afforded each of her assistants a brittle smile; when she turned
again to her brother, her face might have been set in granite. "They will
never know if no one tells them, brother."

The teacher attempted to focus the children's minds on mathemat-
ics.

"One two is two, two twos are four, three twos are six…"

The children repeated the words without thought of their meaning.
In the fields and if they ever got hold of money, they knew quite well
the difference between two and four, the difference between a littler of
two pigs and a litter of twelve.

"You each have ten fingers and ten toes," Fräulein Bäumberg told
them. Silly old woman! They already knew that. They used them all
the time—for counting! They scraped their feet, stifled a yawn or two

and wondered how long it would be before they were free to run outside. The novelty of school hadn't lasted long. They had already com-
prehended a basic argument in child philosophy: whether or not
thumbs counted as fingers.

What were *der Herr Baron* and *Fräu Barönin* arguing about? It was
so boring, having to sit here reciting things, instead of being out in the
sunshine scaring birds. That was a good job; two of you at opposite
ends of a field, rushing to meet in the middle with rattles and voices
going full-blast, while flocks of blackbirds, starlings or rooks rose complaining and unfed. That was real learning—a lesson in power. Just as
it was power to stalk downwind of a rabbit and kill it suddenly and
silently with a catapult at fifty paces. It was best of all to drowse
through sunny afternoons when nature rested and there was nothing to
do but talk.

"My father was out fishing when this shark came along and turned
his boat over."

"Oh, yes…? Where was that?"

"At sea, of course."

"I know that, stupid. What sea?"

"The Baltic."

"Liar! There aren't any sharks in the Baltic."

"That's all you know."

"My father says…"

"Your father. What does he know about it?"

"At least he's not a liar like your father."

"My father's not a liar."

"Oh, yes he is."

"You take that back."

"Shan't."

"You take it back or I'll make you."

"You and who else?"

So on and on until the inevitable, delightful outcome when, like puppies, they come together in rough contact on the dusty ground, rolling over in a heaving, grunting spray of arms and legs.

"All right! All right! All right! Get off!"

"You take it back."

"I take it back."

Take what back? It doesn't matter. Two boys lie sweating on the warm earth, staring at the sky, panting and giggling. It's good to be alive, though they can't put the feeling into words. For them life is neither good nor bad; simply a series of incidents, some good others not so good. Scaring birds is one of the most enjoyable, while being in this stuffy old schoolroom…

The children drift into private dreams, the teachers teach regardless, and Loff and Margarethe continue their whispered debate. No one hears horses approaching. The visitors, when they enter, are a police Captain and four constables. They form a stiff line inside the door. The Captain approaches the Baron, an uncomfortable amalgam of authority and respect.

"Seven twos are fourteen, eight twos are sixteen…pay attention, that boy!"

"May I ask what is happening here, your Excellency?"

"The *Fräu Barönin* is organising a school for the children."

"May I see your authority, *Fräu Barönin*?"

"We've always had the right to teach the children on this Estate, Captain. It's traditional. We need no authority."

"The law is changed, *Barönin*. You must now have written authority from the Governor."

"I wrote to the Governor. He lacked the courtesy to reply."

"If no authority has been granted, your Excellency…Go home, children. You are not permitted to be here. Go home!"

"This is preposterous."

The Captain saluted smartly and walked out, followed by his men and, joyously, by the children.

"I shall go to Reval…to Saint Petersburg!" Margarethe called after him. "Who is spying on us? Why did you come today? How can we maintain respect when you deliberately humiliate us?"

The next day, a priest arrived in the village. He was Father Tikhon, a Russian Orthodox priest with specks of porridge in his beard, dirty chipped fingernails and a perceptive odour about him of garlic and pickled herring. His bags were heavy with cheap icons and tawdry Communion plate. He came on foot, sweating, hungry and dirty as any zealous pilgrim.

"I understand there is a disused schoolroom here," he told the Baron, smiling.

"Temporarily, at least. So…for the moment…we shall have it as our church. I have the Governor's authority. We are establishing an Orthodox Parish here." His eyes mocked her beneath his bushy brows.

"There are no Orthodox here," the Baron said. "I don't want to appear inhospitable, Father, but an Orthodox Church can serve no useful purpose."

The priest continued to smile and sucked the ends of his straggling mustache. "Perhaps if you would be good enough to have someone show me to this…er…disused schoolroom, your Excellency?"

"Get Ants to show him the way, sister. If he has authority…" the Baron shrugged.

"You'll get nowhere if you don't know Estonian," Margarethe told him triumphantly as she ushered him out.

Afterwards, she rounded on her brother.

"I have no alternative. They have the power to take what they want. We must be patient until this nervousness blows over."

That night he lay sleepless and called his valet to fetch Channah from her bed. She came, pale and trembling in her nightgown, a shawl over her shoulders, her eyes anxious.

"Are you ill, *Herr baron*?"

"Read to me, Channah."

"What shall I read, your Excellency?"

"I don't mind. Here, take this."

The book was Goethe's *Wilhelm Meisters Lehrjahr*, and he lay for a long time, enthralled by the language and the gentleness of her voice.

"*Kennst du das Land, wo die Zitronen bluhn?*

"*Im dunkeln Laub, die Gold Orangen gluhn...*"

"*Knowest thou the land where the lemon-trees bloom?*" he interrupted, translating the words into Russian, unsure whether or not she understood.

"*Knowest thou the land where the lemon-trees bloom?*

In the dark foliage the gold oranges glow;

A soft wind hovers from the sky,

The myrtle is still and the laurel stands too—

Does thou know it well?

There! There!

I would go with thee, O my beloved with thee..."

She listened to him, her eyes downcast, not understanding his mood. He looked at her, long and silently. Then he said: "The great Goethe also said 'the last and greatest art is to limit and isolate oneself.' Do you understand what he meant, child?"

"No...I don't think I do, your Excellency."

"No matter. No matter. You will understand when you are older, like me."

He kept silent until she was forced to speak. "Does the *Herr Baron* wish me to continue?"

He paused and gave way to reason. "No...no thank you, Channah."

"Can I do anything else for your Excellency?"

"No, child. I'm sorry I disturbed you. Go back to bed."

"Goodnight, your Excellency." She replaced the book and left the room softly. He followed her departure with a deep, dry, frustrated sob.

If only it were possible to live Goethe's words...to isolate oneself...to take one's love too...But that could never be. His duty enslaved him here forever, watching the new society spread around him like a cancer that would eat away all his life's purposes until, finally, it killed his necessity for living.

CHAPTER II

▼

1884

Loff rode the Estate from morning 'til night to avoid his sister's careless reproaches. The Governor didn't reply to her letter. She positively refused Loff's suggestion that she should go for a holiday in Berlin with their neighbours, the von Aschenbauers. Uncertainty in the district was strengthening. There was no winter entertaining at all that year. Government spies were said to be everywhere, and landlords could no longer be sure of themselves, nor of each other.

The only person obviously unaffected by this unease was Father Tikhon. He arranged the schoolroom to look like a church, piled boxes to make a makeshift Altar and curtained it off into a Sanctuary. Around the walls he hung his Icons and over all, created an atmosphere of candlegrease, incense and mystery.

For most of his visitors, the core of the mystery lay in a corner close to the door, behind a raggedly hung baize curtain. This was where he lived and slept, and from whence came continual replenishment to the aroma of garlic and pickled herring that mingled with the incense. Beyond all this, he had a seemingly inexhaustible supply of gingerbread and apples to give to the children. He was growing daily more popular with them. The Orthodox Cathedral, as the children called it, was an Aladdin's Cave, altogether unlike anything they were used to in Pastor Vikker's neat Lutheran place of worship.

Physically, the Father was hugely built, with a barrel chest descending to a manly acreage of belly. His voice was harmonious. His hands, when the children leapt into them, were warm and secure. They loved him, though none had yet found the courage to creep into his Church for a Service. Their curiousity was strong enough; Orthodoxy promised to be an exotic entertainment.

Everyone in the village agreed that the Father was a good fellow, and that it was a shame he was a widower. Besides the esoteric pleasures he could bring to married life, he could run faster than anyone else, never tired of playing with the children, drank vodka day and night without obvious effect and, when women met him in the woods, his cassock tucked into his belt, his hairy legs mudstained, he never hesitated surrendering his kindling to them and set off to collect another load for himself. One afternoon the children found him outside his church making a kite. The open fields on the Baltic shore were excellent for kite flying, and from then on he was the Pied Piper of the village. He surprised them all by the speed at which he picked up simple Estonian.

The day the Emigration Officer came, he was surrounded by children and sitting outside his church stretching coloured paper over slivers of birch to make yet another kite. He immediately organised the children to fetch their parents, while he took the visitors into the church for vodka. The first that Baron von Hagen heard of this was from Channah, when she returned from a visit to a sick old woman in the village.

"There's to be a meeting at the Church this afternoon, your Excellency. Everyone must go."

"What's it about, Channah?"

"Nobody knows, your Excellency."

"Thank you for telling me."

"They said I wasn't to, *Herr Baron*. They said I should tell the servants, but I wasn't to say anything to you."

Early afternoon, as though by chance, Baron von Hagen rode by the schoolroom. Peasants with their wives were crowded round looking interested, while an Emigration Officer addressed them from a platform contrived from benches originally intended to seat young scholars.

"Conversions will be arranged," he was telling. "Father Tikhon will see to that. And only Converted Orthodox will be accepted...no Lutherans, Jews, or anyone like that." The speaker pointed and bowed politely in Father Tikhon's direction. Father Tikhon returned the bow, grinning.

"From Saint Petersburg you will travel south, commune by commune. There will be a land grant for everyone...good black land. Grows everything in the blink of an eye...corn, cucumbers, watermelons, sunflowers, rye...anything you are to plant. Waiting for you like a virgin, legs outstretched, it is. No more broken backs digging up rocks. No more standing up to your arses in freezing bog water. No more mosquitoes. Hey! Here! Listen to this! No more landlords!" He laughed excitably.

"Will someone tell me what's going on here?" The Baron's tone was menacing. Valiant reared nervously at this unusual tone of voice and threatened to come down on Father Tikhon's shoulders.

The Emigration Officer turned, opened his arms with a flourish and bowed like a traveling actor. "And who might you be, my good sir?"

"I am Baron von Hagen."

The man jumped to attention and maladroitly attempted to click his heels. His eyes opened with surprise, his mouth with simulated pain. Several times he attempted the salute, but could produce no sound. The peasants roared and called each other's attention to his antics.

"A Recruitment Campaign, your Excellency," he explained, abandoning all further attempt at military finesse. "His Majesty needs peasants on the Virgin Lands in the South. A land grant to anyone who converts, and a money subsidy, as well." He turned to the peasants once more, a huckster bidding for their trade. "Free travel all the way, free accommodation, free seed for the first year..."

"Get out of here!" von Hagen roared.

"Government authority, your Excellency. I have the paper here somewhere."

He fumbled in his pockets, his perplexity raising another laugh before he produced a much-crumpled piece of paper. The Baron disdained to take it. He knew there was nothing he could do to stop the charade…not even if every peasant on the entire Estate decided to leave on the instant.

The Officer jumped down and sat at a table loaded with heavy registers.

"Now, brothers, who's first? Who's a real pioneer? Who wants to be top of the list?"

There was much horseplay among the audience, with people playing the part of reluctant bridegrooms. Nobody reached the table, though, and it was obvious none of them wanted their name on the list. The Emigration Officer looked comically regretful and rode away at the end of the afternoon, contriving even to make his horse look dejected.

Father Tikhon calmly rearranged his benches inside the church. The villagers dispersed, feeling cheated because the Emigration Officer hadn't offered vodka. The Baron returned home, and everything was normal again.

In other areas, the campaign was more successful. Plots went to weeds, villages declined to disrepair. The cost of hired labour rose; profits from owning land fell drastically.

Before Easter, another official arrived—another Recruiting Officer. This one presented himself directly to the Baron with military punctiliousness. He was mustering men for the Imperial Army. He was polite but determined to carry away twenty-four able-bodied young men. Their service would last for twenty-five years.

"My Warrant, your Excellency. I am authorised to request a billet for me and my men—two days, I think, shouldn't be more than three."

"You and your officers will stay in my house, of course. Billets for your men will be arranged in the village."

"Thank you, your Excellency. And may I leave it to you to call a general meeting for tomorrow morning? All able-bodied men between seventeen and forty must attend. According to our records, your quota hasn't been filled for ten years."

The Baron left the room trembling with anger and sick with the frustration of being unable to turn the man and his troop lock, stock and barrel off his land.

CHAPTER 12

▼

1884

"We're going home, Paul! Isn't that wonderful?" Ouroussoff rushed jubilantly into the Doma. Clementine pouted. Paul felt Leonore's fingers stiffen in his. "The Seyonevsky are coming in, some of our chaps will have to stay for the takeover. Then it's off we go!"

"Seriozha!" Clementine slapped his wrist playfully. "You should not be happy to be leaving me. You are very cruel man. You take me with you, darling?"

"You know perfectly well I can't do that," he grinned. "I'll give you a spanking good present before I do, though. Seyonevsky aren't bad. Not to our standard, but better than the Ismailovsky and far, far better than the Pavlovsky."

She laughed. Regiments had come and gone before. Leonore looked fixedly at the gipsy orchestra. When it was time to go home, she chose to walk over the Bridge. Paul watched apprehensively for a tearful scene. He had had no time to prepare for it and wouldn't know how to control it. He cursed Sergei for blurting it out like that.

They walked slowly, as though stretching their time together. She said sadly: "Don't be sad, Paul. I knew it would have to end sometime."

"I would have given anything for you not to hear it like that. Ouroussoff's a fool."

"Don't let it spoil the little time we have left." She stopped and pulled him closer to her. "I'll never forget. So many, many kindnesses. And to my sisters, as well. They'll be sorry if you have to go very soon not to say goodbye to you. But I think it best if you don't come to the flat anymore. It will only upset them if you do."

"Of course I'll be coming to the flat! I'll stay for the handover, naturally. We'll have lots of time to work something out."

"I'd rather we said goodbye now, Paul, here on the Bridge, before I have time to think and it begins to hurt too much."

He replied with sharp despair. "At least you'll allow me to see you safely home tonight...?"

She didn't argue.

They were almost across the Bridge before she spoke again. "You must not be unhappy, Captain. You've been so kind to my sisters and me. We love you for it. But we are still Jews, you know. We're not brought up to expect that happiness will last forever."

"But...what will you do when...when I finally have to go?"

"Oh, we'll survive. Thanks to you, we're not still the ignorant girls we were a year ago. We'll be able to find well-paid work, I'm sure."

At the door of her building, she turned and faced him. Her eyes glittered with unshed tears. He tried to take her hand, but she drew away into the shadows of the vestibule.

"This can't be the end. You must help me to make arrangements and of course you'll stay until we decide what to do. Do you understand? Leonore! Are you listening to me?"

"Yes, yes, but...I can't talk now. Please, Paul, let me go."

He walked back to barracks, struggling to invent the man he had always thought himself to be. But he no longer controlled his situation. Before the riots, Leonore had been just another pretty thing. He adopted her, as his trophy, because that was the custom among officers. Now, realising it, day by day, she had become much more than that. He couldn't bear to see how difficult this was making his life.

At the barracks, he was irritated when Ouroussoff's door opened as he passed.

"I say, old man, you're not sleepy, are you?"

"As a matter of fact, Sergei…"

"Come on! Time to celebrate! We're going home. Just one…a Cognac."

The door stood open; Paul couldn't avoid going in.

"I say, old man, you're looking pretty green. Are you all right?"

"Yes."

"This is only a makeshift, you know. We'll have a real celebration tomorrow. We'll get the girls together at the Doma. Here! What about that little redhead on the Island? Ha-ha! We'll be back in time for the winter season. Warsaw is all right. There are plenty of worse places, but…"

"I'm sorry, Sergei. I think perhaps I don't feel too good after all."

"Oh, my God!" Ouroussoff's eyes widened, and he suddenly understood.

"You and Leonore! That's it, isn't it?"

"I don't want to talk about it."

"Sit down and have a drink, man! This mess had best be cleared up here and now."

"I shall stay for the handover while we work things out."

"No, no, no, old man! Worst thing you can possibly do. A clean break; that's best. And as soon as possible. Best all 'round."

"That's what Leonore wants."

"There you are, then." Ouroussoff's eyes glowed with relief. "Sensible little thing, your Leonore. You're lucky, old man. Some girls wouldn't take it so sensibly. I always said you're taking a hell of a risk, setting her up in that flat."

"She's still only a child, Sergei. And she has her sisters to think of."

"You can thank God she is only a child! Any girl more worldly-wise wouldn't let you off so lightly. Clementine will raise a real rumpus if I don't give her what she thinks she's worth."

"Leonore isn't like that."

"Of course not. But when you've had time to think about it, you'll realise how lucky you are. After all, you've given her a good time...lots of presents...all that sort of thing. She'll be all right."

Next afternoon, Paul hurried to Praga as soon as he could. The squinting maid opened the door and announced with vicious satisfaction that Leonore was ill and couldn't possibly see him.

"What's wrong with her?"

"She's very sick, I think," the woman told him, without much interest.

"Have you fetched a doctor?"

"The young lady won't have a doctor."

"Nonsense! Send for one immediately. I'll call again later."

She bobbed an insolent curtsey and closed the door. When he returned, Rachel and Ida were home from school.

"We don't know, Captain," Rachel told him anxiously. "We weren't here when the doctor came, and that woman doesn't understand anything. But Leonore's very bad; really, she is. She's crying all the time, and sometimes I think she doesn't even know who we are."

Paul called for the maid, who looked at everything in the room except him. "I'm sure I don't know, your Honour. I'm not a nurse. You can't expect me to look after the young lady. I don't know what it is. I might catch something myself."

"Which doctor did you call?"

"Doctor Zbygniew from Jablonski Avenue."

He took Ida into his arms and pressed her tear-smudged cheek against his own. "You are not to worry, little one. What would Leonore say if she heard you making such a fuss? Come along now...dry those tears. Rachel!"

"Yes, Captain."

"Take good care of Ida while I'm away. You're the grown-up one now. I'm relying on you."

"Is Leah going to die?"

"Of course not. I'll go and talk to the doctor right away."

At the doctor's house, he had to strut and shout before the servants would agree to disturb their master at his dinner.

"*Une crise de nerfs,*" the doctor said, wiping his full pink lips daintily on the napkin he had brought with him from the table.

"What does that mean?"

The doctor shrugged. "With girls that age, who knows? She is over-wrought, over-excited…"

"Is she in any danger?"

"My dear young sir, who can tell? There is always the possibility of a relapse into brain fever." He said it as though the prospect were hugely exciting.

"Brain fever!"

"With a strict regime, you know…plenty of rest, a healthy diet…we should have nothing to worry about."

"What caused it?"

"A sudden shock, an emotional crisis. As I say, with young ladies of that age…" He sighed. "Fads and fancies, my dear Captain, fads and fancies. Who can tell what it is that causes such affairs?"

They were standing in the hallway, the doctor glancing pointedly at his dining room door from time to time. Paul stood, undecided. The doctor put out a friendly hand and gently maneuvered him out of the house.

"Tell the young lady I will call again tomorrow. Now, goodnight, my dear sir, goodnight."

Jablonski Avenue was a string of newly built middle-class villas behind high iron railings. Paul stood looking up and down, forlorn, but he recalled himself quite soon. As a soldier, action was his only response to any emergency. He ran to the Ursuline Convent and beat on the wooden doors rising high above him into a sinister darkness. Anyone entering or leaving the building used a small wicket gate in one of the doors. Achieving no response to his knocking, he noticed a chain beside the wicket and pulled it forcefully. He pulled again. A grill in the gate squeaked back. He saw no face, only a flash of starched whiteness reflecting the light of a candle.

"Yes?" The voice was suspicious.

"I must see the Mother Superior, please."

"At this time of night?" There was no mistaking the shock in her voice.

"It's very urgent."

"Quite impossible."

"Please! You must let me in."

"I shall do no such thing."

"Sister, my name is von Hagen…Paul von Hagen. I'm a Captain in the Preobrazhensky. It's about one your pupils, Leonore Goldfarb."

"I know the child."

"She is very ill."

"We shall pray for her."

"Sister, I need someone to take care of her. Please help me."

"At this time of night? Quite impossible."

"There must be one of the Sisters you could send."

"We're a teaching Order, Captain. We know nothing of nursing."

"Another Order, then. Tell me where I should go."

"Captain, there are some aspects to the girl's background…her way of life. Perhaps you could find a woman at the public hospital who will help. We'll pray for the child. God bless you, Captain."

The grill snapped shut like the woman's tight lips. The whiteness was gone.

Paul could now think only of Ouroussoff. He found a cab to take him to the barracks. Ouroussoff had already left for his celebration at the Doma. Paul followed.

"My dear fellow, whatever is the matter?" Ouroussoff was already a little drunk and amused by Paul's distress.

"Leonore's very ill."

His friend's handsome face broke into a skeptical smile. "Really, old man!"

"It's true. Dr. Zbygniew says it's a nervous attack—might even turn to brain fever."

"And who, pray, is Dr. Zbygniew?"

"Her doctor. I've just been to see him."

"Well, old boy, so long as she's in good hands, there's no need to worry. Wouldn't you say so, Clementine?"

"She must be looked after. I can't trust the maid and her sisters are too young," Paul muttered.

"My dear Paul…here! Have some champagne. You're making altogether too much fuss. It's simple. Leonore's upset because you're going away. And, indeed, why shouldn't she be? You've been very good to her."

"Why won't you understand? She has to be nursed. I've been to the Convent…"

"Trust me! A good night's sleep, and she'll be as right as rain in the morning."

"Seriozha, do stop!" Clementine broke in angrily. "Can't you see how worried he is?"

"But there's no need. Isn't that what I'm trying to tell him, if only he'd listen."

"The Sister said I might find someone at the public hospital."

"You'll never get a Sister of Mercy in the circumstances, and you know what some of those lay nurses can be like."

"Then for God's sake, what shall I do?"

"Have another drink, old boy, and we'll think of something."

Ouroussoff refilled their glasses and tried to look concerned. He failed. Clementine showed her annoyance further by pushing her drink away.

"I'll come with you. Captain." She laughed self-consciously. "I know what you're thinking, but why should I work in a place like this?

Nine brothers and sisters, all younger than me! I know a lot about nursing, believe me."

"Clementine! Clementine, would you really?"

She stood up. Ouroussoff demanded pathetically, "What about our party?"

"Share the champagne with Pan Koblinski, my dear. It won't cost you much. He doesn't serve good champagne unless he really has to."

She laughed and ran after Paul.

CHAPTER 13

▼

1884

The Recruiting Officer sat behind a trestle table, struggling to keep his papers from blowing away in the boisterous breeze. The house servants filed passed him, giving their names. Captain Tuschchenko listed them and sat back waiting for the men from the villages. No one came. The Baron was requested to receive his complaint. Ants confirmed that he had spread the news of the muster.

"They're stupid if they think they can get away with it," Tuschchenko ranted.

A second order was issued. The muster was to be outside the Lutheran Church in the morning. Ants was sent once more to spread the message, accompanied this time by Captain Tuschchenko's Escort.

The Baron shut himself in his study, Margarethe, hurried to find him there.

"You'll do something to stop this, brother...?"

"There's nothing I can do, Margarethe. It's the law."

"But they look to you for protection."

"Anyone chosen for service has to go. We have to fill our quota."

"It's Prince Krasnov! He's pursuing us out of spite."

"Don't blame him, my dear. He administers the law, he doesn't make it."

"It's obvious instead of helping us keep the peace, the Government is determined to destroy whatever influence we still have. It's madness. We know the peasants. Nobody manages them like us. Why doesn't someone tell the Tsar the truth?"

Late that afternoon, Ants and the Escort were back. Captain Tuschchenko once more knocked at the Baron's door.

"My men say they can find no males of military age…not in any of the villages. Young boys, old men…women. But none of the fellows we're after."

"Really, Captain, I can't see what you expect me to do. None of them want to be sent away for twenty-five years. It's natural they'll escape if they can."

The following morning, with Margarethe's strongly voiced disapproval, the Baron rode out side-by-side with the Captain. They still found no men of the right age in any of the villages. Tuschchenko ordered his men to search the huts. Women ran out screaming, children in their arms.

Household possessions were piled in a heap in the roadway. First the furniture, then the huts were set alight. This second burning was really serious; this was the beginning of winter.

The Baron tried to explain as reasonably as he could. "This officer has His Majesty's Warrant. It is the law. All men of military age must register."

The women looked at him with spite in their eyes and said nothing.

"We know your men are in the woods. Send them word. If they don't come back, worse will happen."

Next morning, the Baron and the Captain rode out again. The troops' hoofbeats were muffled by the snow, and the men were forbidden to talk among themselves. Any quarry they flushed should have been taken unawares. Tuschchenko was sweating pleasurably with the excitement of the hunt. He had chased deserters before. Hounds make the kill more certain, but their baying robbed the pursuit of its most exciting element: surprise. To come upon a man and take him when he least expected it, that was the thrill.

Soon after they entered the woods they found their first fugitive, a seventeen year-old lad with fair, curly hair and intense blue eyes. He lay hidden beneath the overhang of a boulder until they were almost upon him. Then his nerve gave way. He broke cover and plunged down the slope towards a frozen stream at the bottom.

"There! Sergeant! Get him!" The Sergeant spurred his horse and made off through the trees. The Baron, watching, held his breath, excited in spite of himself. He recognised the boy. He was Jaan Tsekis, the protégé Margarethe had planned to send to the Agricultural Institute in Reval. Now that an Imperial edict had made that impossible, his future was sure enough as one of His Majesty's conscripts.

From the stream, they heard the sharp crack of a whip and a single cry. Minutes later the Sergeant returned, the boy following at a rope's end, his wrists tied and a trickle of blood on his forehead.

"What have we here, then? A very pretty specimen, isn't he? We'll soon make a man of you, darling! Keep your eyes open, men, the rest can't be far away! Don't walk him like that, Sergeant! Make him run a little! It'll do him good, warm him up…"

They discovered no more fugitives. Jaan was locked in the Church until Tuschchenko finished breakfast, following it with a glass or two of vodka.

The Baron began, tentatively, "The boy you have in the Church…that Jaan…"

"Your Excellency?"

"He was married only last Sunday."

"Yes, your Excellency?"

"He probably came back to the village because he couldn't bear being away from his wife. We were all young once. We know how it is."

"Yes, Excellency?"

The Baron frowned. He said no more. He was too proud to ask a favour he knew would be refused.

Outside the Church, Jaan was stripped to the waist, tied to the crossframe and lashed by one of the Escort. Greta, his new wife, looked on silently, comforted by womenfolk. When they took him down, the soldiers splashed vodka on his wounds and gave him some to drink.

"No hard feelings, brother," said one. "It's all in a lifetime."

"Come on, brother, let's have you here," said another, who forced him to kneel and dry-shaved his blond curls.

"It's all to be borne, little brother, the good and the bad of it. There are plenty more girls. Don't give up heart. God willing, you'll see it's not so bad."

Father Tikhon came out of the crowd carrying a water jug. He threw the contents over Jaan's shaved head and made the Sign of the Cross.

"There! You're a good Orthodox now. We'll call you Ivan Ivanovich."

The men of the Escort loosely tied the boy's hands, and he was locked in the Church until they were ready to leave.

Captain Tuschchenko said, "Your quota, *Herr Baron,* it's nowhere near met, you know."

The Baron shrugged. The Captain spoke with a heavy Ukrainian accent, and the Baron was grateful. No one in the village could possibly understand what he said, and no one would ever know the extent of his own humiliation.

Tuschchenko sighed, as though deeply unhappy. "Very well." He spoke uncertain Estonian. "If your men won't register, at least we'll have the names of the women and children. Sergeant."

The Sergeant marshalled the women already there, while some of the Escort rode away to fetch women from the other villages. The Sergeant was jocular. "Come along now, my darlings, my pretty birds," he urged.

"You won't mind doing your duty for the Little Father, will you?" His grin was lewd. He nudged one woman in the ribs and gently squeezed the breast of another. He was a fine, upright, soldier-looking man. The women responded to his attentions with shrieks of appreciative laughter.

"Come along! Come along! Everyone has something to offer...haven't you, my kitten?" He swung a woman almost off her feet and kissed her passionately as she lay in his arms. She giggled and made a show of pushing him away, but not too seriously. One by one, all the females filed past and received his attentions while he registered their names.

"Marya."

"Olga."

"Zelda."

"Katryn."

"Two children, your Honour, one boy one girl."

"Three children, your Honour, two girls and a boy."

"Four sons, your Honour."

"No children, your Honour."

"See me after parade, little chicken. We'll soon put that right."

The day ended in a holiday atmosphere. The Escort drank vodka and encouraged the women to do the same. Father Tikhon sang folk songs, and couples disappeared behind huts. The Baron couldn't believe what he saw. A Satumalian madness had overtaken his people. Even Jaan's wife was persuaded to take vodka to help her through this terrible day. She was now dancing a crazy jig with Father Tikhon.

The Baron went home disgusted. Later, Tuschchenko came to request the loan of a farm wagon and a team.

"You'll need a driver?"

"Thank you, your Excellency, my men will see to that part of it. Naturally, if there's any damage, the Government will pay."

The wagon returned to the courtyard after two hours, and the night was filled with screams. What he saw from his window sent the Baron running outside. The wagon was loaded with boys, each with his hands tied behind his back.

Mothers followed, screaming, biting, scratching, trying to reach the captives. Immediately when they saw him, they turned to the Baron for help. The Escort laughed and playfully held them off.

"Your Excellency! Your Excellency! For the love of Jesus, help us…"

"Make them give us back our boys."

"That Father Tikhon's a devil. He's worse than any of them."

"My man will kill me if I let him take the boy."

"We thought if we gave them a good time they'd leave us alone and go somewhere else, your Excellency."

"What you plan to do is unforgivable. Captain. Release those children immediately!"

"I have to meet the quota, your Excellency."

"But not with children. What you're doing is illegal now for anyone except Jews."

"They'll grow, your Excellency. A few years in the orphanage, and they'll be old enough. And we'll circumcise them if it will make you feel better."

A woman suddenly broke through the cordon and lunged at this face. A trickle of blood ran over his beard.

"Chase these bloody bitches out of it! Get rid of them! Here! You!"

The soldiers took their whips to the women they'd enjoyed so short a time before and drove them from the courtyard. The children continued to wail.

"Get ready to move out!"

Father Tikhon, sitting beside the driver, slipped down from the wagon and plucked the Recruiting Officer's sleeve. "Well? What is it?"

"The conversions, your Honour. They won't be yours 'til that's done."

"Very well. Father. Get water from the house. And be quick. You can't name them all…we'll do that later."

Father Tikhon slipped away. The Baron was aghast. "You can't baptize them like that. In the sight of God, they're baptised already."

"Can't have too much of a good thing, eh, your Excellency? We'll shave them later. Where's that damned priest?"

Father Tikhon came out carrying a large basin of water. He flung it at the children, and they screamed louder with the shock of it.

Tuschchenko saluted smartly. "I have to thank you for your hospitality, your Excellency."

"You'll burn in hell for what you're doing tonight."

"Goodnight, your Excellency. I am only obeying orders…that's my duty, you see."

Father Tikhon and the Baron remained together in the courtyard as Margarethe walked slowly out to join them. She had seen everything from inside the house.

"Your Excellency," Father Tikhon began, but the Baron turned away from him. Margarethe took his arm. She led him back into the house with unaccustomed gentleness.

CHAPTER 14

▼

1884

Leonore's family was barely surviving. Her mind resisted every feeble attempt at bringing the nightmare to order. Horror flowed over her emotionally, restless and dangerous as a river of white water.

Sometimes she lay in her narrow cot in Zamenhofa Street, smelling the smells of the place. While she watched, her dear brothers and sisters played around her bed and made no noise while they did so. Noise only began when they began screaming. The door was opened without warning and an assault by boots. Informal men, perhaps as long grey overcoats seized the children. Leonore joined the screams with theirs and left her bed. For a moment, she was allowed to take the children in her arms. They faded away from her like mist, as did the intruders. Tearfully, she left the flat and stumbled down the staircase to the parents. They never came up the stairs to see her these days, never sent her a message by one of the children. It was as though they thought she was already dead. She felt them looking for her, though they didn't see her.

The shop was narrow and freshly white painted, cold and unwelcoming. There was nothing to sell there; the place was full as always of parents constantly quarrelling.

Leonore stood watching them and turned away, unaware of why she had come down to visit them. She should have known it wouldn't be worth it. No words ever passed.

She climbed the dirty staircase, back to her bed, a shiny brass bed under a white lace couvlat with flimsy curtains hanging all the way round. Visitors had come to see her, though she didn't know who they were, nor why they came. A young man, gentle-voiced, sat beside her bed holding her hand. Strangely enough, except for the briefest of glimpses, she could hardly be sure he existed. Sometimes he appeared to be in some kind of uniform, at other times not. The young woman who was with him—they appeared to be with each other though not together—was plump, noisy and cheerful. She chattered with no expectation of a reply, laughed a good deal, sang songs that were somehow familiar.

She closed her eyes determinedly, as she thought, and everybody went away, the children with the soldiers, her parents, this couple. All that was left was the pain—the pain that was over her, under her, all round her; the pain of being not quite dead. It carried her forward reluctantly as though she was a tiny leaf on the restless white water.

The patient relaxed. So did Doctor Zbygniew. He called at the house cheerfully now, resting his plump hands together replying, though not asserting, that his Leonore was saved, it was a miracle and it was all due to him.

CHAPTER 15

▼

1884

The Semonyevsky were installed in the Praga barracks, and Paul was no longer needed in Warsaw; he cheerfully he went back to Petersburg.

In Saint Petersburg, he went immediately to his Colonel's office and applied for leave. He said his reason was "personal" and refused any other. The Colonel said he wouldn't be writing that. "A lengthy absence will have an adverse effect upon your career, von Hagen. You understand that, don't you? You'll lose seniority."

"Yes, sir."

Colonel Denisovitch-Komarevsky leaned back in his chair, his stubby peasant fingers drumming a military-style tattoo on the desk with his silver letter-opener. He was squat and square, risen from the ranks by fighting unconventional battles against Chinese regulars and Mongolian tribesmen across the deserts, plains and rivers of the Far East borderlands. His unconventional approach to discipline endeared him to rankers, though he never inspired much affection among his aristocratic officers.

"Listen to me, von Hagen! I regard you as one of the best officers I have. I don't like to see you putting a promising career at risk. Think about it. Come and see me again in a month."

"I can't wait that long, sir I must leave right now."

"Damn it, Captain! At least you can tell me what's wrong. What is it? Woman trouble? Money? I'll do what ever I can to help."

"I'm sorry, sir. I must have the time."

"I've heard talk about you, von Hagen; you and that little Jewish singer you've been living with in Warsaw."

Paul said nothing. He stared at the cucumber fingers drumming on the desk.

"You can't possibly marry her, you know. The Regiment would never allow it."

Paul was still, silent, embarrassed. He had been expecting an outburst of loud-voiced temper. This reasonableness unnerved him.

"Very well. Lieutenant. Three months! I give you three months. By then, whatever this...this personal business is, have it settled and you'll be back on duty...without fail...no excuses!"

Paul returned to Warsaw the same day. He took a room near Leonore's flat and sat with her every day while she dozed and wondered where he could be. His landlady had an oversized bust and a voice like a baritone with laryngitis. Black Jack was her favourite adornment, and she smiled incessantly.

She was afraid of him and consequently made too much of a fuss of him, as though by good grace and gratitude he wouldn't harm her. His comings and goings were irregular—always a reason for suspicion—though his manner was never anything but gentle. But would a young Russian gentleman, and he was not only a gentleman, be living alone in Warsaw at a time like this? Above all, why had he chosen her flat out of all the rest? His comings and goings were definitely irregular. She reviewed her friends and acquaintances, their backgrounds and political opinions. She could find nothing dangerous in any of them. Her friends warned her to be careful. Undoubtedly he was a Secret Policeman here on a special mission. They came, these friends, less frequently, to drink coffee and play cards. She persisted in liking him, nevertheless. He was the perfect lodger, and her efforts to ingratiate herself to him never ceased. She succeeded only in boring him.

"Your Honour can surely eat a little more," she coaxed from behind his chair. "My late husband...did I tell you he was a Civil Servant?...had a really healthy appetite. You are like him in so many ways."

"Your Honour has such beautiful linen," she told him another time. "I was quite appalled when I saw how that girl was ironing it. You should have told me. I will do it myself in future. My dear late husband would never let anybody touch his linen but me."

She went even further when serving his breakfast one morning, when she said: "You're out so much, Your Honour, and—I'm not prying, heaven forbid!—and it's your work, of course, I realise that, but if you're a student or anything like that...oh! Please, don't misunderstand me." She wished she had never started and that he would say something. "I'm not implying that you're one of those revolutionary students who belong to underground cells or anything like that." Of course, he couldn't be! No revolutionary ever wore linen like his, she was sure. "They all deserve to be rounded up and sent to prison; that's where they belong. What I meant to say, your Honour, is that I want you to be comfortable here, and you're welcome to use the entire apartment any time you please. I mean," she continued with a more confident laugh, now that she saw her way out of the wood, "you mustn't feel that you have no choice but to sit in your room or go out, you know." She sighed. "You remind me so much of my poor dear husband. He was such a home-lover."

When his three months were up, Paul reluctantly reported back to Colonel Denisovitch-Komarevsky. Spring was well started when he left Warsaw, but winter held its firm grip on Saint Petersburg. He found a room away from the centre of the city and avoided everyone he knew, even Sergei Ouroussoff. They didn't meet until after his final interview with the Colonel.

"It's all over, Sergei. I've resigned."

Ouroussoff paled and stared wide-eyed.

"I had no option. The Colonel was at pains to point that out."

"You're mad! For God's sake, why?"

"I'm hoping to be married. In the Colonel's opinion, the lady is an unacceptable choice for the Preobrazhensky. He's a bachelor, of course."

"Leonore?"

"Certainly."

"You bloody fool!"

"Sergei, you have me at a disadvantage. I'm no longer an officer; I have forfeited the privilege of fighting you. But I shall be forced to hit you if you talk like that."

"Oh Paul...my poor, poor Paul!" Sergei was silent, fumbling for a thought. Suddenly, he looked cheerful. "But you really are a fool. Go and tell the Colonel you don't have to resign. You can't marry a Jew, obviously. But she can convert. When she's a Christian, there won't be a problem."

"She'll still be a Jewish shop-keeper's daughter. Odd, isn't it? The Army will accept almost anyone to lead it...look at our own beloved Colonel. But an officer like me, his wife must be beyond social reproach."

"I really can't believe this." Sergei shook his head hopelessly. "I know! We'll get a genealogist to work on it. Jews can never be sure of their antecedents. We'll dig up some gentile ancestors...middle-class...provincial...and all conveniently dead, of course."

"No! Listen, Sergei! Jew or no, if Leonore marries me I shall be the proudest, happiest man on earth. Understand that! What the Army thinks...what anybody thinks won't be important."

"*If* she marries you? You mean she hasn't said yes?"

"I haven't asked her. I have to wait until she's better."

"You're throwing away everything on a gamble." Sergei sat down, thoroughly shocked. "Not that there's any doubt about that. She'll marry you. She'll jump at the chance."

"Sergei, you're my best friend, and I'd like it if you understood. But if you can't it, it will make no difference. She has to be well before I ask her. And…this is most important…she must know that I'm free. She mustn't be inhibited by my career, nor my family."

CHAPTER 16

▼

1884

Margarethe raged through the house, more angry than usual. "It isn't as though I have ever given her the slightest reason to suppose I like her, even remotely."

"She likes you, though, my dear, that's obvious," Loff said soothingly.

"I don't want her to like me! She had no right! The friendship of a woman like that isn't at all acceptable."

"At all events, you can't refuse if she wants to come. They are the new influentials. In times like these, we have to be grateful for their friendship…make the most of it. The Prince may only be what he says he is: the local administrator. On the other hand, he could be somebody much more dangerous."

Margarethe's lips tightened. The letter had come from Princess Krasnova that morning, recalling happy memories of her previous visit and expressing a determination to repeat the delightful experience with her *plus chere Madame la Baronne de Hagen. Monsieur le Prince* having business in the area, the Princess would avail herself of the pleasure, etc., etc., etc.

"It may be for the best," the Baron continued. "We'll give a Ball…make everything as normal as possible…ask our Blomberg cousins, the Aschenbauers, all our neighbours…"

"Surely it isn't necessary to go to that much trouble, not for the Krasnovs."

"It's not only for the Krasnovs, sister. We've all drifted apart during the troubles. It's as though we are living in railway stations, sitting on our luggage, waiting for trains to go to different places. But we're not going anywhere. We've arrived. We may as well face that fact, unpack and get back to normal. If that means giving a ball for the Krasnovs..."

Margarethe shrugged impatiently. She didn't understand that kind of talk.

Ants carried invitations to everyone in the district, deer and partridges were slaughtered, fish hooked, piroshki stuffed with cabbage or mushrooms, beetroot, salt fish, dried bilberries, cheese, and sour cream.

Suckling pigs were dressed. Floors were sanded and polished until they were hazardous to walk on, chandeliers lowered and shined, silver polished. Anyone on the Estate capable of playing an instrument was rehearsed for the dancing.

In all this activity, Margarethe found time to write to Paul at the barracks in Warsaw:

"We expect the Krasnovs for a visit—not my idea, I assure you. Loff insists we give a party for them.

I hope you will join us. You got on well enough with them when they were here last time, as I remember. You still have duties to your brother and me as well as to the Army, you know.

A further reason for your coming home is that I need confidential advice about our brother. He takes little interest in the running of the Estate. Nor will he exert himself to obtain permission for me to open a school. He rides every day but that, I believe, is merely his excuse for being alone and avoiding his responsibilities.

This sudden enthusiasm to give a Ball for the Krasnovs is another
example of taking the line of least resistance. He doesn't understand
that we remain independent in the face of everything.

He won't listen to me. You must come home and talk to him.

Your affectionate sister,

Margarethe von Hagen."

Margarethe's letter followed the Preobrazhensky from Warsaw to
Saint Petersburg and was redirected from there to his address in Praga.
That took a long time, and Margarethe was furious that he ignored her
letter and didn't come home for the Ball.

The other guests arrived early on the appointed afternoon to give
the young ladies time to rest before the night's excitement. They lay on
beds upstairs while their prospective partners drifted through the
reception rooms and in and out of the courtyard, smoking and being
generally bored. At any other time they would have talked politics;
everybody had an opinion about who should be the new Marshall—an
election first postponed, then delayed again, now definitely timed for a
few weeks hence. Today, however, the presence of Prince Krasnov pro-
hibited free expression. They only muttered gloomy monosyllables
until it was time for dinner and the ladies reappeared.

The dancing was a success. The village musicians had been drilled to
play with gusto, a gusto equaled by the abandon by Princess Krasnova.
She danced every dance, whether she knew the steps or not: the proces-
sional *Polonaise*, a series of *Mazurkas* in which she somehow managed
to lose her partner in the sets and ended each time with somebody
else's, and the *Kolomyika*, a peasant dance requiring wild cries from
time to time. She danced—not always in time with the music but with
wholehearted recklessness. Halfway through the third she collapsed
glowing and giggling into the arms of her partner, agitating the air
about her with her fan.

"*Comme je suis nicodeme!*" she gasped, while her unfortunate partner assured her she was not a Silly Billy and helped her to a chair. Her husband, taciturn and sweating in his high-buttoned tunic, declined to dance. He stood at one of the windows with vodka constantly in his reach, glaring at her.

"Such a delightful entertainment. *Comme j'adore les fetes campagne?*"

Margarethe was not happy to hear her Ball so criticised as...bucolic. Even herself, she did not dance, perhaps because none of her guests dared ask her. She moved among them in a gown of darkest grey as though absolving everyone like Pope Joan. Channah, always in black, hovered close by. Nobody asked her to dance. They all knew who she was and speculated upon what she was. Fräulein Bäumberg didn't appear.   Having   appointed   herself   Margarethe's   lieutenant-behind-the-scenes in the kitchen, she stayed behind-the-scenes and made the servants' lives a misery.

The next day, Princess Krasnova rose late, brimming with happy chatter about the Ball. It had all, of course, been *merveilleux, adorable, campagnard*, such a delightful change from the formal entertainments she and her husband were bound to attend in the course of their duties. How tastefully *Madame la Baronne* had arranged everything. How she herself relished the joy of simple country fellowship.

Margarethe sat with her over glasses of tea, the samovar hissing like a serpent between them. The Princess asked pointed questions about each of the guests and, from talking about people who had been there, passed on to the others—one in particular—who had not.

"My brother has his military duties," Margarethe said stiffly. "His Regiment is in Warsaw."

"Oh, but no…" The Princess put a hand to her mouth and lowered her eyes in an exaggerated gesture of dismay. They sat for a moment, the two of them, in screaming silence.

"But what?" Margarethe demanded.

"My dear, you must excuse me, I…"

"Princess, you obviously wish to tell me something. What is it?"

"My dear, how embarrassing! But I was certain you knew."

"Has something happened to my brother?"

"My dear...it is hardly my place to tell you, but since you insist: the Preobrazhensky has returned to Petersburg, but Captain von Hagen has resigned his Commission."

"Impossible!"

"*Chere amie*, we could hardly believe it ourselves. *Quelle catastrophe*, a young man of such promise. Colonel Denisovitch-Komarevsky is a close friend of my husband's...that's how we came to know about it, you see. He had no doubt your brother would have been appointed General some day. He employed every conceivable argument to persuade him to remain with the Regiment, I do assure you."

"My brother would never have resigned his Commission without...He would have discussed it with the Baron first. He knows his Duty."

"My husband's intelligence, *Madame*, is invariably to be relied upon. *Naturellement*, as it was a matter concerning *votre frere*, my husband made *les enquetes particulieres*. There is no doubt, *ma pauvrette*, *rien du tout*! And he said not a word to the Baron? How I wish now that I had said nothing also. I am so very, very sorry to have distressed you."

Margarethe was incensed, but kept her voice as calm as possible.

"This...er...this interesting rumour. Princess. Did your husband's informant give any reason as to why he should take this extraordinary step?"

Princess Krasnova fluttered her eyelids and looked deeply into her glass, her eyes transparent as the tears they shed. She gave the impression that she could say more if only she dared.

"Not another word," she said firmly. "I have already said too much...*tout-a-fait de trop*!"

During the Krasnovs' visit, the Baron spent as much time as he could in his study with the door firmly closed. Margarethe went to him as soon as she could. Channah was reading to him.

"I must speak with you, brother!"

"Of course."

"Alone, please." She looked pointedly at Channah.

Channah leapt from her chair blushing, dropping the book in her embarrassment. "Excuse me, your Excellency, of course, I will go."

Margarethe waited for the door to close before picking up the fallen book.

"Pierre Loti! *The Romance of Spahi*," she read contemptuously. "I can't understand why you keep that girl with you all the time, brother, reading such trash."

"Channah is learning French."

"Better let me have her. I could teach her something useful! However," she interrupted herself, "that's not important. The Princess has news of Paul. He's no longer in Warsaw."

"Ah, the Regiment's moved back to Saint Petersburg."

"Paul's no longer with the Regiment. He has resigned."

"I don't believe it."

"The Princess assures me it's true. She's a fool but she's not an imbecile. She knows we can check easily enough."

"There must be some reasonable explanation."

"Of course there's an explanation, brother, though how it can possibly be reasonable…"

"She didn't tell you?"

"That's the satisfaction in malicious gossip. Always hold back whatever's most important."

He stood up heavily, like a very old man, she thought, and shuffled uncertainly to the window. "There must be a reason…there must be…" he said, as though reassuring himself.

"To humiliate us like this! To leave us to hear it from that woman!"

He sighed. "You must try not to mind too much, sister."

"Shall I tell her you want to see her?"

He stared out of the window, silent.

"Brother!"

"Er?"

"Shall I tell the Princess you want to see her?"

"No...er...no, thank you. Tell Channah I'd like her to come back, will you?"

Margarethe left the room defeated. She didn't bother to find Channah. She went to her own room and wrote to Paul, instead.

"I presume you will have received my last letter by now. The Krasnovs are still here and she, poisonous creature, derived much pleasure from telling me you have resigned. I can imagine no sensible reason for your having done such a thing.

Of course, my feelings are unimportant. I am only your sister and therefore have no cause for complaint. I must tell you, however, that this news has caused your brother extreme distress.

As I told you last time I wrote, I am deeply unhappy about Loff's state of health, and this further aggravation will do him no good at all. I must insist, therefore, that you write immediately, giving a satisfactory explanation for your conduct.

Your deeply troubled sister,

Margarethe von Hagen"

CHAPTER 17

▼

1884

Doctor Zbygniew ponderously admitted that Leonore's recovery was now beyond doubt, although she remained pale and listless. Clementine, who never ceased to take her nursing duties seriously, banned Paul from spending all and every day in the apartment.

"You must let her rest more, Captain. She's exhausted, poor love. We must keep her as quiet as possible."

Paul reluctantly obeyed. Leonore commented listlessly on his long absences. "Did you send him away, Clementine, or doesn't he want to see me any more?"

"I sent him away," Clementine laughed. "He understands you need to rest."

"And he has his duties in the Army, of course. I can't remember very much, but he spent a lot of time here when I was ill, didn't he?"

"He'll come to see you every day, but I've told him he mustn't stay so long, that's all."

Sitting by her window some days later, Leonore saw him coming along the street and turned to Clementine in surprise. "It's Paul, Clementine. I didn't realise till now, but he's always in civilian clothes these days. Why doesn't he wear his uniform any more?"

"He hasn't any duties for the moment darling. His Regiment has gone back to Saint Petersburg. Paul stayed because...well, he'll tell you all about that better than I can when he gets here."

Leonore's face clouded. "Oh! Oh yes, I think I remember...A long time ago, Sergei told us they were going back...at the Doma, didn't he? He was pleased."

Clementine heard Paul's knock with relief. "There he is. You can ask him all about it yourself."

Leonore didn't ask. She was afraid of hearing something that would pain her. He noticed nothing out of the ordinary. They barely spoke at all these days. He acknowledged silence to weakness. They sat together by her window, watching the glory of the Warsaw early summer. Paul took her hand in his and gazed adoringly at the marbled skin drawn tightly across her cheekbones, at her dark, sunken eyes.

"Darling," he began gently, "you ought to go away, now."

She turned slowly to look at him, not wanting to hear him say anything more. It was better if she said it herself. "Oh yes, yes, of course, we must leave here. Now that I'm better, I'll ask my cousin if..."

"No, listen my love, you must stay here as long as you want, but I have spoken to my landlady and she has a little house in the country. We can have it for as long as we want. It's on the river, not far out of town. It will be lovely. Clementine will go with you, naturally; she needs a holiday, too. We can find a girl from the village to look after you both."

It took some moments before she could think sufficiently to answer. Then she said, "My sisters?"

"I've thought about them. They can board at the Convent for a few weeks."

"They won't like it if I send them away."

"It will be good for them to stay with the other girls, and they can come to see you every weekend."

Summer was well advanced when Leonore and Clementine went to the apricot-painted cottage by the river. It glowed warm in the afternoon sunshine, shielded from the road in a cloud of pink and white apple blossom. The Vistula flowed nearby in broad, quiet curves. Paul ate supper with them and prepared to return to town directly afterwards.

"Will you be coming tomorrow, Captain?" Clementine asked.

"No. I have to go home to see my brother. I don't know how long our business will take, but I'll be back as soon as I can. I'll write regularly, and I'll arrange with my landlady to have the girls brought out every weekend. See that Leonore has everything she wants."

"How long shall I be staying here?" Leonore asked disinterestedly.

"As long as you like, my dear. Why not stay all summer?"

"You had better go to bed now, darling," Clementine told her. "You must be tired after the journey."

"Yes." She turned with her hand on the door. "You've been very kind, Paul."

"I'll see you soon."

"Of course. I understand." She left the room without smiling and Clementine and Paul looked at each other meaningfully.

"She looks so hurt, doesn't she?" he said.

Clementine shrugged but had nothing to say.

"She's so distant. I don't know whether she wants me here or not. She's beginning to remember, I think. When she remembers everything, she'll know it was I who made her ill. Perhaps she knows already. Maybe she blames me."

"I don't think..." Clementine began, but he interrupted her.

"I have to talk to her, Clementine...but not until she's stronger and I've settled a few things at home. I can't say anything else just now."

She followed him into the hall and handed him his hat and stick. He said: "I'm very fond of her. You do believe that, don't you?"

She didn't reply until he stood outside on the veranda, the first summer moths fluttering in the lamplight. "She loves you very much. Captain. It's causing her such pain."

"Goodnight," was all he said before the carriage clattered away up the track towards the main road.

When he was gone, Clementine stood breathing in the scent of the evening. Moonlight made the apple blossom glow like gossamer froth around her.

Leonore's strength returned quickly in the country air; all the quicker, Clementine was sure, because Paul no longer came to visit her. Neither was there any word from him, in spite of his promise to write. Leonore showed no disappointment; perhaps in her heart, she had never expected to see him again. She and Clementine spent their days apparently untroubled, wandering the fields and through the apple trees, their dresses and parasols adorned with fallen blossom like confetti. On weekends, Rachel and Ida came out to stay.

They lived this idyll for two weeks. Then Leonore asked suddenly:

"Will that girl be able to find us a carriage, Clementine?"

"I expect so, darling. You'd like a drive, would you?"

"No. I'm going back to Warsaw."

"I can't let you do that. The Captain would never forgive me. He expects to find you here and thoroughly better when he comes back..."

"Clementine...tell me honestly. Will he be back?"

"Of course. He said so, didn't he? Why should you think he wouldn't?"

"I don't know...I don't know. But I can't stay here any longer. And we mustn't go back to that flat, either. The girls and I will go to my cousin's until I can arrange for somewhere else."

"So you shall, dear, if you want to, but later, when you're well again. You mustn't worry about all that just now. Come on, let's go for another little walk."

Leonore didn't move from her chair. She began to cry quietly.

"Clementine, you're so good to me. You do so much. I know you think I'm ungrateful, but…"

"Of course I don't think you're ungrateful."

"…I can't help it. I'm so unhappy."

Clementine knelt by her and held her hands. "I know, darling, I know. You've been very ill. You're still terribly weak."

"I don't know what to do."

"Of course you don't…not yet. But you will. Get strong first and you'll know what to do when you're better."

"I don't think I'll ever be better again."

"It's silly to say that."

"If only everything would stop going round in my head."

"It's the Captain, isn't it?"

Leonore gulped. "I have to fetch the girls from that Convent and settle in with my cousins before he gets back. This…being here…that flat, too…it's all been so terribly wrong. I've behaved like a…like a…"

"No, you haven't! Stop it! Don't you dare say that."

"I can't bear it any longer. I must get away and forget all about it."

"You love him very much, don't you? Why won't you say it? You'll feel so much better if you do."

"But I don't. I don't love him. It's not true. I don't, I really don't! I mustn't."

CHAPTER 18

▼

1884

Channah was crossing the hall when Paul reached Wirsberg, a little after daybreak. The bleary-eyed footman at the door called a hostler to care for the cab.

"Captain!"

He turned to the figure descending the stairs.

"How are you, Channah? It is Channah, isn't it? It's so long since I was here."

"We'd no idea you were coming, your Excellency. I'll tell *die Frau Baronin.*"

"That will do later."

"I'll fetch you something, then. Tea? Brandy?"

"Nothing, thank you. I'll wait for breakfast. Tell me about my brother."

Her shoulders stiffened and her face went blank. "Your Excellency?"

He smiled encouragingly. "When she writes, my sister tells me how well you look after him."

"I read to him; no more than that. With all the servants here, he has no need for anything else."

There was silence between them as ugly as a dropped stitch in a novice's knitting.

"Will you tell me nothing, then?"

"What exactly does your Excellency want to know?"

"My sister tells me he's ill."

"He isn't ill."

"What, then?"

"I think…" she paused and went on, dull-voiced. "Your Excellency. It isn't my place to speak of these things."

"Come now, Channah. Can't you see I need your help? I haven't been here since…"

"I remember when you were last here, your Excellency," she interrupted, and her voice hardened. "I lived in the village in those days." He knew she hadn't forgiven him.

"Channah!" He said her name with determination but broke off feeling lame. He didn't wish to bully. "Would an apology help?" He was willing for anything, but couldn't bring himself to it. He tried to question her again about Loff. "Won't you tell me more about my brother? You say he isn't ill, but…"

"He isn't ill. I think he is not happy; that's all."

Happy! Paul listened to the sound of the word as though he had never heard it before, certainly not here under the eye of Erica von Hagen.

Paul met Loff at breakfast, and he was shocked by Loff's pallor and sunken, lackluster eyes. They ate like peasants: goat's cheese, black bread and skimmed milk. Paul could hardly swallow any of it, and Loff ate very little, he noticed. Margarethe apologised with scarcely hidden irony for this prison house routine.

"We should have had something more suitable had we known you were coming, brother. You eat more extravagantly than this in your officers' mess, I'm sure."

"It's all right, Margarethe."

"Your sudden arrival gave me no chance to arrange anything else."

"It's all right, Margarethe," he repeated, sounding touchy in spite of himself. She smiled. She was pleased because of it.

"My decision was unavoidably sudden."

"Obviously. That must be the way things are with you young officers. Duty here, duty there! We understood you didn't ever have time to write us a note, didn't we, Loff?"

The Baron refused to raise his eyes from an editorial in the week-old *Konigsberger Tageblatt*. He left the table as soon as he could, saying he had to ride to the village. He obviously wanted to go alone, leaving Paul with no excuse for refusing Margarethe's invitation into her sitting room.

"You'll be surprised not to see *Fräulein Bäumberg* still with us, Paul."

"Yes," he said, wondering whether it was a question or a statement. He had never once, for years, given the Governess a thought.

"She left only a week or two ago."

"I understood she was staying with you permanently as your companion."

"One companion in the family is sufficient, I think. Financially, this is not the best of times for us. It would have been inexcusable extravagance to retain her here now that we have your brother's Jew to keep. And since Loff won't hear of sending her away..." She shrugged. "I must be frank. When I last wrote, I expected you home long before this."

"A lot has been happening."

"So I imagine. But you must discuss all that with Loff. Before you do, however, I think you should be aware of how things are."

"Loff seemed somewhat distracted at breakfast, I thought; no more than that."

"He is obsessed! Obsessed by that girl! He's given up everything else. He no longer has a social life. He does nothing on the Estate. I do my best, but I can't do everything. The money we have won't last forever. Land isn't worth what it was. If this is the way he wants to go, he should bring in a steward who will know how to make a profit."

"I understand it's difficult for you."

"We're still here! That's the important thing. We're still here and shall continue to be here, whatever the Government does. You must talk to Loff, brother. And you must stay until we can convince him that something must be done. I'm relying on you. Whatever else has happened, you're still a member of this family, and it's your duty to help me."

Afterwards, he wandered through the house, wondering how soon he could tell them what he had come to tell them and then leave. He went from room to room, examining the evidences of his childhood, astonished at how little significance any of it now held. Worse, he couldn't feel guilty.

At the evening meal, hardly more palatable than breakfast, Channah ate with them and was embarrassed because she knew she was being used as a shield. She ate practically nothing. Neither did Margarethe, furious because the girl was there. Paul gave up trying to make conversation, and as soon as she could, Channah excused herself and left.

The Baron tried to keep her there. "Stay with us, Channah," he said, a note of pleading in his voice.

"Channah has lots to do elsewhere," Margarethe told him sharply. When the girl had gone, she turned on him.

"Really, brother, we have to talk. Heaven only knows when we shall have another opportunity. If nothing else, Paul at least owes us an explanation for leaving the Army."

Paul recoiled, red-faced. "You know about that!"

Loff said quietly: "You must understand, Margarethe, Paul sees the old ways are changing. He is very sensibly making a new future for himself."

"I hope you realise, Paul, you're the talk of the neighbourhood. Princess Krasnova delights in telling everyone you've resigned your Commission, implying you did so under a cloud."

"He'll tell us about it in his own good time, Margarethe."

"I want him to tell us now! He owes us that. There's been too much scandal talk already."

"Then I can't see that it any more matters."

"I'm going to be married," Paul blurted.

"So that's what she meant," Margarethe said, bitter triumph in her voice.

"I told you, Loff...I knew she was keeping something back...the most important part. This...this whoever it is you propose marrying...it isn't anybody of whom we're likely to know or approve, of course. That's why you have to leave the Army."

"Yes."

"Is it too much to ask her name?"

"Leonore."

"A foreigner? Leonore who?"

"Goldfarb."

"My God!" Margarethe paled and leapt to her feet. The candles spluttered in this sudden excitement. "So that's it!" she triumphed, knowing in her heart that hers was a Pyrrhic victory.

"Of course, I shan't expect to bring her here. I imagine we'll live abroad."

"It's as simple as that, is it? You'll turn your back on your family, your career, the Estate, your Duty...? You'll run abroad to live with your Jew? Oh! God in heaven! Whatever did this family do to be cursed a second time by that evil race?"

"Margarethe! Try to understand. I've not been living at all, all these years, only existing. We all have. People like us have been brought up to believe that we're superior—intelligent, cultured. We're taught to look down on everyone without a 'von' before their name as some kind of lower animal. But we're all the same animals. We really are all the same, except that in many ways they're better off than us. We're caged, and they are not. We're shackled by all the false values of our past. They're escaped. They are free."

"Nonsense!

"It's worse than that, even." Paul too was shouting now. "We know that if we don't conform to what we've been taught, we won't survive. But we're not worth survival on those terms. To go on living only in the past is to be living in a grave."

"And marrying a Jew will set you free?" she sneered. "Very well. Live abroad…wherever you like. But you'll never escape the past. It's been lived by too many for too long. You'll never alter it. And you'll be running away from all the privileges you've known since the day you were born, the privileges you haven't earned. They were given you because you're a von Hagen, because you were supposed to perform certain duties. You will cut your own lifeline if you do this thing, Paul. You won't survive."

"The lady, too, has responsibilities—duties, as you prefer to call them. She is of a time much older than ours. She is an orphan. She is a Jew and deserves respect for that. Her parents were murdered in a pogrom. She nearly lost her own life in the Warsaw riots."

"Nothing you say will make any difference, she's a Jew."

"For years she's struggled to care for two younger sisters. She's had no help except from her Faith that tells her she too has ancestors who must not be betrayed. She too has a duty."

"Very well."

He was calmer now, and she tried to control her anger too.

"Our society, Paul, is a series of interlocking pieces. You, Loff, the Aschenbauers, the Blombergs, the people who live in the village. We're all connected; we all depend on each other. Take away one single piece, the entire structure is weakened. That's what you're doing. You are destroying us."

Loff suddenly lifted his eyes. "Paul's right, Margarethe. The structure's broken already. We don't realise it, that's all. We Balts have lived too long like fleas on the Russian bear's back. Now the shaggy old creature is shaking us off. 'Autocracy, Nationality, Orthodoxy:' that's what the Tsar demands. Like it or not, that's our future, sister, however much we shut our eyes to it. Our pride in what our ancestors did for this country hundreds of years ago isn't relevant any more."

"I don't see what any of that has to do with Paul and his Jew."

"Why shouldn't he marry a Jew if he wants to? I can't argue with him, but you've seen what's happened here: an Orthodox priest in a village where everyone is Lutheran; land grants to entice our peasants away; little boys kidnapped for the Army. They've broken up our structure; they'll get rid of us all in time. Paul sees we're an anachronism. He's leaving the dross behind, venturing out into the future."

Margarethe's lips quivered; her body shook painfully. She could no longer control the pain. She rushed from the room, nearly in tears, determined neither of them should ever see to what they had reduced her.

CHAPTER 19

▼

1884

Leonore and Clementine were cooling in the orchard when Paul arrived.

He had traveled from Haapsalu on slow, cross-country trains, tormented by unforeseen delays and missed connections. He had ridden out here from Warsaw on a hired hack, sweating and grubby, his cravat awry, his moustache untrimmed, his coat creased and dust-powdered. He looked as though he hadn't slept for days. His agitation startled them both.

"I must talk to you, Leonore! Clementine, will you see to the horse?"

"What?"

"It's simple enough!" He was in no mood to argue. "Rub him down, water him, tether him where he can get at some grass!"

Clementine looked doubtful. She had never before been ordered to attend to a horse. More importantly, she was concerned about leaving Leonore alone with him.

Leonore reassured her. "It's all right, Clementine. Go along."

Directly she had gone, Paul dropped to the grass beside Leonore; she looked blooming after her rest in the country. "How are you?" he asked, trembling as though overcome by the wonderment of seeing her as she really was for this very first time.

"I'm quite well, thank you." She had dreaded this moment. Now it had come, she was relieved.

He put his hand lightly under her arm and drew her slowly to her feet. He was calm, too, now. "You know I love you very much, don't you?" he asked, looking everywhere but at her while he led her towards the river. She drew her arm away and walked slightly ahead of him to emphasise her detachment.

"Leonore!"

"Don't touch me, Paul…please."

"I want you to marry me. I'm not saying this very well, I know. I don't know how I ought to say it. All I know is that I want you to be my wife. I want us to spend the rest of our lives together."

She stopped suddenly, her shoulders hunched with the pain he was causing. "That isn't possible."

"I've resigned my Commission. I've told my brother. I'm free…at last. Now it's just the two of us who matter. Leonore, my darling, please, I beg of you, say yes."

She shuddered impatiently. "You've told everybody what you want to do, to find out whether they approve or not. That's not putting things right."

"We'll go away as soon as we're married…somewhere where nobody knows us." Above all, she was implacable.

"You've put nothing right with me. You've made all these arrangements, but…"

He stood still, surprised, smarting as though she'd lashed his face. "But you must see, surely, I had to be free before I asked you."

"How could you? Without telling me! Don't you see what you've done? Of course you're free. Paul, you always were. What about me? Do I have any choice? Can I still say no?"

"You knew we could never marry while I was in the Regiment."

"Just leaving the Regiment doesn't alter anything. You're still Paul von Hagen; I'm still a Jew."

"Darling, darling, darling...I love you...I want you for my wife. What can anything else matter...who you are, who I am..."

"You've made me responsible for the rest of your life. It isn't fair. Can't you see? You should have asked me first."

"We'll be responsible for whatever happens to each other. Perhaps...perhaps," he suggested tentatively, very quietly, "you could even convert. It's happened before."

For a moment he thought she would hit him. "You've arranged that, too, have you?"

"We worship the same God. We take our customs from the same Book. I'm not asking you to become a heathen, after all."

"No! Only because you see me as a heathen already. We're not a handful of different sects like you Christians, fighting all the time. You've only taken out parts of the Book, whatever suited you. But we're different. But we're a race apart. We are chosen. Can't you understand? We've kept ourselves pure all these years, living the law because that's what He chose us to do for him. We truly are His Chosen People. He is at the centre of our lives, day and night, waking and sleeping. And you Christians can't stand for it. That's why you pretend to believe we murdered God. That's why you've beaten, burned, murdered us through the centuries, forced us into ghettoes, treated us worse than you treat your animals." She was crying unrestrainedly.

"You'll be free of all that when you become Christian."

"I don't want to be free of all that," she screamed. "That's who I am...that's me. That's my past and I don't want to get away from it." She sank to the grass, sobbing, "Oh Paul, if only you'd gone back to Saint Petersburg with Sergei and the others."

"I couldn't. I didn't realise it then, but I already loved you too much to leave you. And I'll never leave you now, Leonore. Whether you marry me or not, I'll always be there. You'll never know, when you turn a corner, whether or not I'll be waiting for you."

"I don't know...I don't know, Paul, you must give me time. I have to talk to my sisters."

"Leonore…"

"And all the dead ones down the years; I have to think of them."

He knelt beside her. "Darling, we must both think of what's gone before, but don't let the past poison the future. I'd give my heart's blood to wipe away your suffering…the suffering of all your people…but I can't. Their fate is already written on the page and we can only remember them with love. The future can still be ours. We can go on together for their sakes as well as our own, showing everyone that things can change; they don't have to go on forever in the same old hateful, bloody way. Darling…I'd give my life for you, you must know that."

CHAPTER 20

▼

1884/1885

The idea of conversion terrified Leonore: the dishonesty. She knew that whatever the ceremony, whatever the vows, she would remain a Jew; there was a brand-mark on her heart. Her children, when she had them, would be Jews, although the Orthodox among the tribe would never accept their mixed blood. Therein lay her terror. With Christians it was different. Whatever Paul was now, whatever he became, he would always be a Christian. But what of her family? They would find themselves equally unacceptable. Treated always with suspicion, never with respect.

And her dead parents? Was this all she could offer them, a placeless daughter and her placeless children? Like all the other Jews through the centuries, they too had refused to betray the Covenant. "Next year at Jerusalem," they would tell each other at the Seder and sound convincing. No Jew believed it would be next year, nor in a human lifespan, even. It was the Jewish destiny. They had been promised and were content to have the details in the hands of God. How could it ever be possible to turn her back on all of that? It would not, of course; her duty to the past and to the future forbade it.

It was the present, a maelstrom of sexual desire and open doors that tormented her. She was determined there was nothing Paul could say to dissuade her from taking the girls back with her to Zamenhofa Street.

There would be a sense of resolution in helping cousin Esther, struggling, starving and growing then with the effort of bringing up a family she could not afford.

Every morning when she closed the door on Mordechai, her round-shouldered cousin clung close to wall as he shuffled along the street to work, his eyes lidded but alive to everybody and every danger. Every morning she knew she might never see him again. There was for sure the danger of a police raid and a sudden disappearance. He worked in a press shop. On the ground floor, they printed a licensed Hebrew news-sheet and Holy books, whose beauty was their pride. Mordechai had nothing to do with any of that, though. He worked in the basement, proof-reading and printing Socialist tracts, on a rebellious hand press, and came home at night flushed with the efforts of the day.

Neither Esther nor Mordechai were overwhelming in their welcome. It was their duty to take her in; she was their kin, even though they would never forgive her for singing in a cafe for *goyim* and having a relationship with a Russian officer. Most dreadful of all was having the girls taught by Roman Catholic nuns…Roman Catholics! The sect most virulent in the persecution of the Jews.

"It's time you were married, Leah," Ester told Leonore every day, and it was a statement of practical fact. "You're not getting any younger, and Mordechai and I can't do anything for you; you know that. You need a man while you're young enough for him not to make too much fuss about a dowry. And you have Rachel and Ida to think about."

Mordechai had a colleague in the print shop—a man in his forties, a widower with young children. Leah had only to say the word, and Mordechai would invite him home for the Sabbath meal. They would owe nothing to any intermediary and in no time at all she could be respectable once more, as Froi Gershom.

"You'd be lucky not to do any worse," Ester persisted. "Your father—may he rest in peace—left you nothing. Everybody knows you've been living with that Russian. That hasn't improved your chances. Reb Gershom may not be every young girl's dream, but in your position you can't afford dreams. Just remember that out of snow you cannot make cheesecake!"

Rachel and Ida constantly attacked her on the subject too, but from a different point of view. Rachel was working in a sweatshop learning to be a machinist. Ida was hired out for several hours a day to the disagreeable wife of a neighbouring Kosher butcher as a nurse-maid-skivvy. Both found it impossible to settle down after their life in the flat at Praga.

"You're not being fair, you know, Leah."

"You can't expect us to live like this forever when you only have to marry the Captain to change everything."

"You're our big sister. It's your duty to look after us."

"Sister Agnes used to say my needlework was the neatest she'd ever seen. She said I should learn to make beautiful dresses for great ladies. What would she say if she saw the work I have to do now?"

"And that butcher's wife is really awful. She smells. I'm not spending my life cleaning up other peoples' babies, so you needn't think I am."

"And we certainly won't come and live with you if you marry that dirty old Reb Gershom."

"No, that's right, we won't. He smells, too. We'll run away."

Leonore sympathised with them, but Paul's loving her and her loving Paul—she admitted it now that it was impossible for anything to come of it—wouldn't be enough. Every Friday at sunset it was most forcibly brought to her. Esther lit the candles and fanned their light through the room after a day of cleaning, shopping, cooking, restraining the excitement of the children. They gave the little ones whatever jobs they could manage to do because it was important for everyone to make a contribution to the celebration. In late afternoon, the children were bathed. Mordechai would go to the bathhouse and on his way to Schul. Directly, he came in and blessed his children. Those of them able to remember the words joined in his serenade to Esther:

> *"Who can find a virtuous woman for her price is far beyond rubies; the heart of her husband doth safely trust in her so that he shall have no need of spoil. She will do him good and not evil all the days of her life."*

The wine waited to be poured. Two loaves of fresh bread lay on their platter. Mordechai recited the *Kiddush Hayom*, sipped from the cup and passed it round. After ritually washing his hands, he broke the bread that Esther had baked and glazed and sprinkled with poppy seeds that morning. While he passed the pieces round, he reminded his family that the loaves were symbolic of the number two, which has special significance. "Two" evokes all of life's irreversible pairings—space and infinity, time and eternity, work and rest, the six days of the week and this special day, when all families come together in loving, holiday mood.

The mystery gave way to more noisy celebration when the children saw the steaming chicken soup and the boiled fish—the best meal they knew all week. They ate, they sang songs, they told stories, repeated week after week but always enjoyed as though heard for the first time that night. At *Birkat Hamazon*, the children were tired enough to go to bed without argument. The magic was over for the time being, but, please God, they would all be spared for one more week to enjoy it again next Sabbath.

In the autumn, with winter only a week or two away, Esther and Mordechai became more pressing. Mordechai threatened to bring Reb Gershom home, whatever Leah said. Esther warned him Leah was too willful to be pushed into anything. Goodness only knew what sort of a scandal there might be if he did that. The girls were pressing, too. Life in the cramped flat was unbearable. The marriage became such an issue, the cousins no longer talked to each other. Esther's dark-eyed offspring sat mystified through the Sabbath meals now dutifully mouthing the responses but with no joy. There was only half-hearted singing and threadbare jokes.

Wednesday afternoons Leah walked into town, futilely window-shopping along Marszalowska Street before going to the Saxon Garden. Paul was there, waiting for her by the ruins whatever the weather.

Feeling like a leper, she continued to survive the winter. The following spring she could bear it no longer and told him "yes." Their arguments were ended.

He moved them back to the apartment in Praga and the girls resumed their lessons with the Ursulines. Before they could marry, Leonore would have to convert. Paul wrote his brother asking him to discuss the problem with Pastor Vikkers. Margarethe wrote back immediately:

"Your letter astonished us! You may be determined upon this disastrous marriage, but neither your brother nor I have the slightest intention of colluding in your folly. Neither would we allow any kind of ceremony on the Estate. That would result in our family being held to even further shame and ridicule.

Margarethe von Hagen.

P.S. If, in spite of what I say, you are so obstinate and foolhardy as to return home, bringing that woman with you, I suggest you apply for Father Tikhon's help. As things are nowadays, he will count it as a great victory if he has the chance to admit you into the Orthodox Church. The Government too would be happy I dare say, but your former friends here could only regard your action as black treachery and out-and-out madness!"

Leonore read the letter and said nothing; what was there to say? Paul said lightly: "Don't worry, darling, my sister will forgive us. Life hasn't been good to her. Margarethe hasn't..." Suddenly he stopped, aware of the disdain in her eyes. After all, what were Margarethe von Hagen's difficulties compared to Leah Goldfarb's? "At least Margarethe, bless her, has solved our problem," he laughed. "We'll both convert, my darling. You won't be a Jew and I won't be a Lutheran. We'll go tomorrow...together...St. John's on Swietojanska Street. The Romans won't turn us away. We can both make a completely new start."

CHAPTER 21

▼

1885

Saint John the Baptist's Day, the 24 June 1885:

'Leah' for nearly the last time and 'Goldfarb' for nearly the last time, Leonore stood at the window of Esther's flat looking down at the crowd on Zamenhofa Street. Today was her wedding day. She had no fear, no excitement, only weariness.

What she saw in the street was the same as always, yet it had a strange glamour for her now that she was no longer part of it. This morning she was looking at the all-too-familiar like a stranger seeing it for the first time.

She watched horse-drawn carts laden with meat or fish followed by swarms of flies. They jockeyed for position with small handcarts, piled high with vegetables, undistinguished junk or cheap clothes on the way from workshop to distribution point. Wood carts were pushed by young men, shirt collars open to the scanty breeze, heads ritually covered, prayer curls hanging limp with sweat. The carts squeaked over the cobbles.

On the narrow pavements, a congestion of women pushed their passage, some struggling with heavy baskets, others impeding them, standing in groups, gossiping. Men of affairs, gabardines flapping below their knees in the sweltering heat, in closely buttoned shirts, badly shined shoes and round black hats, clutched briefcases to their breasts, in haste for their next appointment. Moving lightly among them were youngsters, girls not sure of their own development and status in society; confined in their puberty to non-committal blushes and smiles. There were boys, for whom pubescence meant an explosion into manhood, an eager acceptance of whatever happened next. They moved quickest through the crowd, calling to one another in coarse Yiddish, relishing the expected, the long familiar patter.

All this, Leonore was about to relinquish. She would never know it in the future, but she had known it in the past and was grateful for that, at least.

With time to spare she left the flat with Rachel and Ida on either arm. She had refused Paul's insistence on a cab. They walked to Swietojanska Street, every step a pilgrimage for Leonore. Inside the church she, Leah Goldfarb, Jew, and Paul von Hagen, Lutheran, made Communion and were married as Roman Catholics. She trembled with fear or because even in midsummer, the church was like an icehouse.

Sergei Ouroussoff, still skeptical, came from Saint Petersburg to stand by Paul. Clementine was there for Leonore, and, whatever she might have been expecting, Sergei didn't look at her once. Rachel and Ida were chaperoned by Ursuline nuns.

Beyond this handful of intimates there were curious spectators, some in church, some loitering outside in the street. The wedding of an Estonian aristocrat with a ghetto Jew was a sensation and the priests of Saint John's made what capital out of it they could.

As he walked out of the church with his bride Paul caught his breath, amazed and overjoyed to see Loff sitting stiffly against a pillar in one of the hindmost pews. He made no sign. Outside he and Leonore stood a moment waiting for Loff to catch them up. He didn't come. Paul went back into the church, but Loff had already left by another exit. He was saddened because Loff hadn't stayed to shake hands and wish him well. It was a foretaste of what the future was going to be like.

He stood quiet a moment, then, for Leonore's sake, he rejoined her, smiling happily.

Book II

CHAPTER I

▼

1885

The wagon lits arriving at Venice was signal for the performance to begin. The guides behaved as though this was a second 'Rape of the Sabine Women' but this time without the blood. Guides flung open carriage doors. Porters and gondoliers seized passengers and their luggage. Urgency was all. To hold was to have. To have was to profit. No time for argument! Bargains were negotiated later in quiet, secret places, where the traveler was captive and no other dog could snatch away the bone.

Paul and Leonore were won by a cheerful, curly haired gondolier, stout as a tenor. He rode the choppy waters of the Grand Canal with theatrical vigour. The journey was a revelation. The restlessness of the Canal, the turgid quiet of its offshoots, the breeze against their faces bringing with it mixed essence of sea and sewage. This was always to be Venice, the shouts of passing boatmen, for the two of them.

Water lapped with sensuous sounds against bridges, landing steps and palace walls. As they shot out from the Canal into the Lagoon, lamps were already being lit on gondolas and quays.

The Gondolier took them to an expensive hotel on the Riva degli Schiavoni, putting them ashore among workmen pushing on to pompous little steamboats going home. Crewmen on shabby tramps, swarthy and swearing in a dozen languages, spat contemptuously at all the excitement and flicked cigarette ends into the water.

At least once every twenty-four hours Leonore and Paul watched this scene from their balcony. Later, Venetian families would be taking their evening *passeggiare,* as far as the public gardens in the one direction and the Piazza San Marco in the other. Around the corner, at the cafes bordering the Piazza, Venetians and visitors together sat sweating through selections from Verdi, gossiping, caressing noisy children and, when opportunity offered, flirting. Pigeons rose when the Mori struck the hours on the Torre dell' Orologio, so thick together it looked as if the paving stones themselves were taking flight.

In the daytime when Venetians were working, visitors took over the city. They buzzed everywhere like bees in a flower garden, gaily boarding steamers for the off-shore sights, or shopping along the Merceria. At the Rialto Bridge gondolas waited to take them to luncheon. Afterwards they agreed to visit a hundred other sights before they finally went home…but tomorrow perhaps. This afternoon they rested in rooms tightly shuttered against the sun. Later they dined, chattered through Verdi at the Fenice, paraded the Piazza, and gossiped, flirting…

Leonore loved every moment. She walked every inch of it arm-in-arm with Paul. She was enraptured by sun-starved alleyways, narrow hump-backed bridges, and hidden squares. Grubby children played singing games round ancient leaden wellheads, watched by mildewed churches, greening stones, and a general air of lovely unheeded decay.

With Paul, every day meant fresh happiness. But there was no moment so precious as when, his impassioned love-making spent, she lay in his arms, head on his shoulder rising and falling gently in time with his breast as he slept.

One day he took her to the shrine of Sant'Antonio at Padua.

"When we were children, Loff and I used to tease Margarethe. We called on Saint Anthony whenever we lost anything, but she hated that.

It was superstition and we were good Lutherans. He took a coin and threw it backwards into the gloom. "There, my darling, where did that go? Shall we see if we can get it back?" He lowered his voice and chanted:

"*St. Antonine de Padoue*
Rends-moi ce que j'ai perdu..."

She shrank against him, the cold inside the church gripping her. A cracked voice spoke unexpectedly at her elbow.

"Signora?"

An old woman, bent like a chair after years of planting rice, held out a coin in her monstrously distorted fingers.

Paul laughed and exchanged the coin for a banknote and a few words of thanks. The woman shuffled into the darkness, cackling. This is the way she made a living these days.

"You see, my darling? I told you He finds everything. Now you're a Catholic, you must call on Him too. He'll do it for anyone but Lutherans."

"We've seen it now, Paul. Let's go back. I'm cold."

On the drive back she was unaccustomedly quiet. What she dreaded had begun, refleshing the skeleton of his past.

On their balcony after dinner he was disturbed by her continued silence.

"What is it, darling? Please tell me."

"Mosquitoes."

"You've never minded them before."

"Well, I do tonight! I must go in!"

"It isn't only mosquitoes is it." He followed her. "What have I done to spoil it for you?"

"I'm a little tired and...we can't live like this for ever, Paul. Life can't be all holiday. We have to think of settling down, making a home. The idea of drifting for the rest of our lives frightens me."

They left Venice the following week. As soon as she saw it, she decided to stay in Florence. Paul rented a villa on the via Ugo Foscolo, up a hill outside the Porta Romana. It was sufficiently secluded but accessible to the city and the acquaintances Leonore hoped would make Paul's life interesting once more.

Venice was one land of dream, Florence, adorned by its necklet of green hills and with the sparkling Arno flowing through its centre, was another. Venice was a fading courtesan, Florence a plump and welcoming matron. The galleries and churches were incomparable and the cost of living attractive to interesting expatriates. Some came for the cities, some for cheap living; yet others were political exiles, some were subsidised by families wishing to keep them away from home for a variety of private reasons.

It was easy in this society to make friends. Seeing a person two or three times among the grotesques in the Boboli Gardens, strolling across the Piazza della Signoria or haggling with local leather workers in Sta. Croce and the jewelers on the Ponte Vecchio was enough for gentlemen to raise hats and ladies to exchange pleasantries.

Paul and Leonore were welcomed everywhere. His constant attention to her was a novelty in a cynical society. Callers were soon driving up the hill to visit them. Later they would compare notes.

"From Russia?"

"Even better than that, my dear…Estonia!"

"Estonia? How romantic!"

"And so much in love. You have only to see the two of them together. My husband declares that whatever they say, they can't possibly be married. The Captain would never be so attentive if they were."

"My dear! How wicked of him!"

The Contessa di Beltrano and Madame Ottilie d'Orangeville were old friends and understood each other perfectly.

"He's taken her to live on Ugo Foscolo to keep her all to himself, I suppose."

"We won't allow it, my dear. I shall give a party for them. I shall invite everyone."

"They do say she's a Jew."

"Nonsense! They both go to Mass at Sta. Maria Novella every Sunday. My maid assures me. Not that it would make the slightest difference to me if she were. In fact, I would find it rather piquant. Just imagine…he found her starving in a ghetto somewhere…"

"More likely she's an Estonian Princess. If they have them there."

"And he, a member of the Tsar's personal bodyguard! Such a scandal when he married her! They daren't go back. If ever they do, they'll be sent straight to Siberia."

Leonore was pregnant. Paul's face wore a permanent smile and he took more care of her than ever. He said "From now on I think it will be best if I go walking alone, my darling. You should stay here and rest."

Leonore laughed. "It's quite normal for a woman to be pregnant. I'm not ill."

"Even so…"

"Walking through the galleries can't do me any harm."

"No, Leonore! Allow me to know best. Stay here and I'll bring you back something beautiful every day."

People talked about the pregnancy as people always do.

"She'll have to watch her weight afterwards. Jews spread so, when they have children."

"I don't know why you should say that."

"It's the truth."

"And I really do not see why you should keep insisting she's a Jew."

"That's what she is. And conversion doesn't alter the fact."

"My dear Ottolie…"

"She's a Christian Jew now instead of a Jewish Jew, that's the difference."

Paul wasn't conscious of the gossip but Leonore knew everything they didn't say to her face.

She longed to share their conviction that Jesus Christ was the Messiah, that Bread and Wine could be miraculously transformed by a priest into His Body and His Blood. But, for her, it was unbelievable.

They were in the garden breakfasting beside her favourite wisteria when Paul suddenly announced that he would be going out alone. The shock gave her courage to mention some of the doubts developing in her mind for the future.

"I believe we should leave Florence."

"Not before the baby arrives surely. Afterwards we can go anywhere you say. Where would you like?"

She hesitated, feeling foolish. She wanted him to take her home, but knew he never would. He couldn't take her to Estonia and would never go anywhere near Zamenhofa Street again.

He prompted her playfully. "I liked Odessa very much when I was there. Not a bad climate.

"I'm serious, Paul."

"So am I. You're over-anxious, my darling. It's natural; it's your time. But we have to think about the baby. She comes before anything else."

It was the first time he'd mentioned a sex for the child. It must mean he wanted a girl and she would fail if she didn't give him one. It was another anxiety for her but he left the house smiling, unnoticing.

He walked briskly into town, having instructed their stout, hirsute house-keeper to be sure the Signora wanted for nothing while he was away. For Leonore it was the beginning of spending much time alone. She didn't mind. She had perceived the pointlessness of Florentine society. She genuinely preferred to sit in her garden reading and speculating about the baby.

At last Paul had expressed his expectation of the baby's sex. But had he any idea of what a baby really was? Did he ever think of it as growing out of his dream into solid reality? She had the advantage. She could already feel it moving restlessly within her. It impressed itself upon her as a living being, sometimes quite uncomfortably. Paul seemed to have no idea beyond its being a golden glow, swaddled in white, never changing, an abstract joy for ever.

In Sta. Croce Paul hoped to find a piece of leather work that would please her. Wandering into the Bardi Chapel he met an acquaintance, Michael Atherton, heir to a wealthy New England gas-mantel manufacturer. He was with a young companion he'd found...some said bought...in Naples. He was now spending money educating and grooming the boy, though nobody understood why. His hands dangled below the sleeves of his white linen jacket, his neck was long and red like a turkey's rising about his high starched collar. His greasy black hair defied all his efforts to train it.

Among his acquaintance, there were those who believed Atherton's father willing to pay anything to get him home again and those who believed him equally willing to pay to keep him away for ever. After Christmas, Atherton said he would continue Memo's education, but in Morocco. This morning they were paying attention to the Giotto frescoes.

"Giotto de Bardone, twelve sixty-six to thirteen thirty-seven," Atherton's humourless voice intoned from his guidebook. "The founder of Modern Art. He abandoned the flat, Italo-Byzantine form to give his figures Solidity and Naturalism." He shut the book and stared at Memo unable to see in the young man's face any sign of comprehension. "In other words," Atherton continued tartly, "he was the first painter of the Renaissance, the first to paint Round Solid Figures."

He caught sight of Paul with gratitude perhaps, and came forward with outstretched hand. "I was explaining to Memo here that Giotto was the Father of Modern Art, Captain." He employed the most elaborate convolutions of an expensively acquired Boston accent and often spoke in capital letters for emphasis.

Paul simulated interest; Memo's eyes remained glazed.

"Before Giotto everything was Flat," Atherton continued. "After Giotto everything was...well...er...Round."

Memo stared unseeing at The Apparition at Arles, Saint Francis unexpectedly appearing to his followers, hands raised in blessing, Stigmata dripping blood. The painting was eloquent; the young man mute.

"Alone today?" Atherton asked.

"My wife needs rest just now."

The American nodded sagely. He cleared his throat to catch Memo's attention and linked arms with Paul. "Shall we go next door? The Peruzzi Chapel has the frescoes of Saint John the Baptist and Saint John the Evangelist, so much more colourful that these Franciscans."

The Chapels were narrow, deep and high-roofed, the frescoes in crowded rows on each side. Atherton pushed Memo ahead. Paul said, "You must come to lunch one day soon, Atherton. My wife's a little bored just now and you have a gift for amusing her."

At the entrance to the Chapel, Memo stood poised like a painter. The floor space ahead was occupied by a sad-faced woman making a life-sized copy of The Dance of Salome—a night scene of solemn revelry in a red and gold pavilion, the Saint's head resting on a platter like a roasted joint in a pool of gravy.

Recognising the painter, Atherton became excited. "Here, I say! Do you two know each other? Oh, but you must! My Dear Madame, would it be too dreadful of us to interrupt you? I do so want you to meet a friend of mine and a countryman of yours too, I believe."

She looked up and Paul judged her to be less than forty, though her skin had a lifeless pallor and her hair, just visible beneath her headscarf was faded brown. There was, nevertheless, a sparkle in her eyes when she laid aside her brush and mahlstick.

"This is Madame Kholchevskaya," Atherton said. "And she's brilliant, my dear chap. Madame Kholchevskaya, this is my good friend Captain von Hagen."

She took Paul's hand in a firm grip. "You are from Russia too, Captain?"

"Estonia."

"Ah! I am Ukrainian…Kharkhov."

"This really is most fortunate. I'm delighted you should know each other. Madame has painted Memo. Full length. A wonderful piece."

Memo, unable to follow the conversation since it was in French, looked up sharply when he heard his own name.

"I had a fancy to have the dear boy painted as Narcissus," Atherton giggled; "Naked beside the pool, you know, gazing with adoration at his own reflection. But what have we here, Madame? Another triumph! Have you a buyer? It's a little larger than any purpose I have at the moment, but if it doesn't already belong to somebody else I must have it."

"It's a commission, Mr. Atherton." When she laughed, there was rich humour in her voice, and the animation in her eyes made her attractive, Paul thought. "Some incredibly rich Russians returning home at the end of the week will be taking it with them."

"And then you mustn't forget you're making a small copy of Memo's portrait, you know." He turned to Paul. "I'm shipping the original home right away. The small one I'll keep by me."

They chatted easily while wandering tourists stared, envying their air of belonging. Then Atherton left with Memo and Paul and the painter were alone. He liked the assurance he saw in her work, though he could not understand anyone commissioning such a thing and suspected she hadn't told Atherton the truth.

"These people really are immensely rich, Captain," she assured him. Officially they're peasants but they've made an enormous fortune out of vodka, I believe."

He grinned. "Even so..."

"No, Captain, don't say a word," she warned him lightly.

"They give me my living, rich peasants and the Mr. Atherton's of this world. Oh!" She blushed. "That sounds terrible. I really don't patronise all my patrons, I promise you," and she laughed gently at the pun.

"Do you think you might patronise me, if I were to patronise you?"

"Captain!" Her surprise was genuine.

"I mean it. I have a wonderful idea. You must paint my wife. She is pregnant and very, very beautiful."

"But...I couldn't...I mean...you don't know my work. You would have to see my portfolio."

"That isn't strictly necessary, but we'd love to see it anyway. Bring something to the Villa for us both to see. I like your humour, Madame, and I know you'll love my wife."

There was nothing more to say. Lydmilla Fyuodorovna agreed to lunch at Villa Belleguardo next day and when Paul told Leonore she was highly amused.

"It will be the most awful waste of money. Pregnant women are never really at their best. To say they are is absolute nonsense, something other people tell them to make them feel less like freaks."

"I want you painted in your green velvet gown."

"Paul, we bought that in Warsaw for the winter. I shall suffocate in this heat."

"You'll only need to wear it while she gets the feel of the material...the gathering of the folds of it."

"My darling Paul, whatever pleases you, but..."

"And your hair! We'll have it drawn back off your face and piled high behind. You really are so beautiful just now, just like a Flemish Saint."

Lydmilla Fyuodorovna started the painting ten days later and Paul left on a short trip to Arezzo and Assisi.

CHAPTER 2

▼

1886

Villa Belleguardo
Via Ugo Foscolo, Firenze
21 January 1886

My dear Brother and Sister,

Wonderful news! You have a niece! At half an hour before midnight, Leonore gave birth to a beautiful baby girl with soft black hair, the palest of pink cheeks, violet eyes and the two most adorable dimples you can possibly imagine. I thank God my wife and daughter are both well.

We are calling the little one Dorothea. That is a good German name (Father, God Bless Him! would have approved) and, besides that, Leonore is drawn to that Saint. You know the story of course. Her executioner taunted her to produce flowers and fruit from the Heavenly Garden and she made a small child appear, carrying a basket filled with everything he could possibly desire. The miracle so affected the executioner he became a Christian himself and was martyred in his turn, poor chap!

I trust you are both well. It's so long since we had any news of you.

Leonore would, I know, be very happy if you could find it in your hearts to write a note.

Your affectionate and very happy brother,

Paul von Hagen.

Warsaw
January 1886

Dearest Leonore,

Your letter arrived this morning! My darling, I'm so happy for you both! And, of course, it goes without saying that she must be quite the most extraordinarily beautiful, marvelous, and unique child that ever was.

Thank God for her, my dear, even if she isn't quite everything you say and turns out, eventually, to be no more and no less human than the rest of us.

How I wish you would come home so that I could see her for myself. But I can well understand why you remain in Italy. How lovely it must be to live without our terrible Warsaw weather.

I am still working at the Doma, and we often talk of you. Pan Koblinski is fatter and more fussy than ever—always anxious to make an extra ruble or two that one, my dear! And the officers of the Semonyevsky are quite nice but—oh dear—not nearly as nice as the Preobrazhensky, tell the Captain.

However, there's no point in brooding on the past when, in fact, there's someone very important in the present! He's an official with the railways...but more of all that when there's more to tell.

For the moment, my fondest good wishes to the Captain, a million kisses to your little Dorothea and...to you my darling, the warmest love in the world. Write again soon.

Your faithful, loving friend,

Clementine Bielska.

Warsaw
January 1886

Dear Leah,

We were pleased to hear your little one arrived safely—God be praised. We rejoice that you are both well.

It is very kind of you to send us the money.

Mordechai and the children join in sending good wishes.

There is nothing more to say at present.

Your cousin,

Esther Levy

Convent of the Ursuline Sisters
Warsaw
January 1886

Dearest Leonore and Dearest Captain,

It really is horrid of you to have a baby in Italy and not bring her home immediately for us to see! We can't feel we have a niece at all—nor even a sister—while you are so far away. Please, please, PLEASE, dearest Leonore and dearest Captain, come home soon. We are dying to see you.

School is all right. Sister Agnes is as sweet as ever. We had a lovely time when the girls had their Christmas holidays. Aren't we lucky to be allowed all the Jewish ones as well?

PLEASE, PLEASE, PLEASE COME HOME SOON!

Your very loving Sisters,

Rachel and Ida Goldfarb.

Wirsberg

Dear Paul,

Thank you for your letter. Of course we are pleased that you have such a beautiful daughter and that she and your wife are well.

It is a long time since you heard from me, I know. That is only because there has been no news to give you.

Your affectionate brother,

Loff van Hagen.

CHAPTER 3

▼

1887

Cecile von Aschenbauer and Margarethe von Hagen were best friends. They didn't like each other much—hardly at all in fact. But they were of an age and grew up on neighbouring estates. They were expected to share similar tastes in everything. Privately, Cecile despised Margarethe for her sallow skin, thin uncharitable lips and deplorable dress sense. Margarethe made no attempt to improve her looks. Cecile didn't understand that at all. In return, Margarethe abhorred Cecile's hedonism—so foreign to Lutheranism—her obsession with whatever was a la mode in Saint Petersburg or Berlin at the time. She also had a ridiculous habit of fainting on the slightest excuse whenever there was a handsome young gentleman nearby to catch her.

Delighted with a friend she considered to be in such unflattering contrast to herself, Cecile invited Margarethe to every von Aschenbauer party—to their winter assemblies, summer picnics on the Estate, Baltic cruises and spring and autumn shopping trips to Saint Petersburg and Berlin. Since the death of the old Baron von Hagen, Margarethe had refused these treats—so regularly that Cecile's mother considered crossing her off the guest list.

"Mama, you mustn't! Poor darling Margarethe would be so terribly upset if she were no longer included among our friends."

"She never comes." In her youth the Countess had been every bit as pretty as her daughter, but the years had brought plumpness, wrinkles, faded hair and darkened teeth. Only the eyes remained unchanged, clear and blue yet restless as though searching for her mislaid charms. "She hasn't been to see us since I don't know when. I'm sure I don't know what's gone wrong between the two of you."

"Nothing's wrong, Mama. Margarethe's life has altered since the old Baron died, that's all."

"It must be easier now. The young Baron isn't dependent on her."

"He's far worse than his father, I believe."

"I shall have to have a word with him. Your father said only the other day he'd have to contact him…something to do with prospecting for shale oil, I understand. Papa thinks it would be sensible to have prospectors go over the two Estates as a joint unit."

"How thoroughly boring."

"That's not a proper attitude, darling. Most of what interests men, you'll find, is thoroughly boring. But it will do you no good whatever to let them know you think so."

"All right, Mama." Cecile sighed. This was an opinion she'd heard many times before. "We'll ask Margarethe and the Baron together. But from all accounts he goes nowhere nowadays without that mistress he lives with."

"Cecile!"

"That's probably why Margarethe doesn't want to go anywhere either; she's too embarrassed."

"I don't know what you're talking about."

"Of course you do. Everybody knows about Baron von Hagen's Jewish mistress. She's hardly more than a schoolgirl, they say."

"Oh! Oh! I think I'm going to faint. Cecile, ring for someone! Quickly!" The guest list dropped to the floor, the Countess collapsed carefully into a chair. Smiling, Cecile rang the bell.

"There's no need to faint, you know. You can't pretend you're the only person in the whole country who doesn't know about it. And unpleasant truths don't cease to exist simply because the Countess von Aschenbauer closes her eyes to them."

The Countess groaned and fluttered her handkerchief. Her darling Cecile was shockingly outrageous sometimes.

The invitation reached Estate Wirsberg two days later, as Margarethe and Loff were finishing luncheon. Channah, who had eaten with them, scuttled away as soon as she could and Margarethe asked with heavy irony, "I suppose we may now speak German again, brother?"

He stared at her with sad grey eyes ignoring the jibe. "I have bad news for you Margarethe. I read it in that bundle of Petersburgskiye Vodomosti that came yesterday. All the schools in Estonia are being put under the control of the Ministry in Saint Petersburg. You'll never get permission to start your own here now."

"Yes, well...!" Margarethe straightened her immaculately starched white cuffs that didn't in the least need straightening. "If we are to be kept busy teaching Channah Litvak French, perhaps there wouldn't be time to teach anybody else anything anyway."

"Margarethe..." His reproval was soft and sad. "Surely it's no hardship to let her practice French with us while we're eating."

The reasonableness of his argument made her suddenly furious. "Yes! Yes, it is," she shouted, unrestrained. "A great hardship! It's a hardship to have her eating at the same table; living in the same house!"

"Think what you are saying, sister."

"Do you imagine I don't know what you're doing, the pair of you? Everyone knows! All our friends...everyone! And I don't know what to do. First Paul, now you! I can only thank God that Father never lived to see this day."

She collapsed over the table and Loff moved quickly to comfort her. "Margarethe. My poor, poor Margarethe. There, there now," he whispered, lifting her dry cold hand in his. "Come, come, Sister, it's all right, it's all right."

"I can't bear it, I can't bear it. I don't know what to do," she sobbed. "I can't go on...I can't go on."

Gradually she regained control and crouched over the table, staring at him with tormented red eyes.

"About Channah," he told her slowly, "it isn't at all what you're thinking. Indeed, you must be very ill my poor Sister, even to imagine such a thing."

She wiped her eyes vigorously and her tone became more normal. "Very well, I believe you." She said it grudgingly and then, with more determination, "But it isn't good for her to be here. You must send her away."

"No! We owe her sanctuary."

"Sanctuary!"

"Our Brother, God forgive him, took part in murdering her parents."

"How dare you! What a wicked thing to say!"

"It was a wicked thing he did. He went out with Prince Krasnov and the others but did he try to stop them?"

"How could he? He told you himself, even the Tsar belongs."

"This Tsar's capable of everything that's abominable."

"For God's sake, Brother!" She looked at him with dry, clear eyes, but he could see there was fear there. She was, after all, his little sister and he knew that she loved him in spite of everything. He wanted to put his arms round her to comfort her, but she would shrink from him, he knew.

"The Litvaks and all the rest used to think of themselves as our people," he argued reasonably. "Naturally, they looked to Paul to save them that night. He did nothing. They can't forget that and neither can I. We have to make amends. We must at least care for Channah because she's an orphan, a Jew...We have to protect, teach her everything we can until she's able to manage alone."

"You can look after her. You don't have to keep her in the house. There are Jews in Reval she could stay with. They'd do anything you told them, so long as you pay, of course."

"I'm doing what I believe is right...right for Paul, for all of us. I must keep her here...safe."

"Very well. You're the head of the family."

"Yes," he told her shortly. He could tell she was recovered now by the contempt in her voice. "Yes, well..." He left the room abruptly, fearing to say any more. Margarethe went to her own room and wrote immediately to Cecile.

Estate Wirsberg, April

Dearest Cecile,

Your invitation arrived at an opportune moment. My remaining at home is impossible and had I not heard from you today, I should have written asking if I might come to stay until my poor brother regains his senses.

You will understand that I do not wish in a letter to go too deeply into detail. Simply believe me when I tell you that your invitation has rescued me from painful embarrassment and earns you my sincerest gratitude.

Believe me, dearest Cecile, I am your most devoted and grateful friend.

Margarethe von Hagen.

P.S. Doubtless my brother will respond to your invitation on his own behalf.

The courier had only recently left with the mail when Loff asked Margarethe into his study. He was sitting by the window, his elbows on his writing table, his fingertips a pyramid supporting his chin. He rose and led her to a chair beside his own and they sat silently watching the afternoon sunshine sparkling on the distant sea.

"One thing we must agree upon," he began at last, as though continuing their previous conversation, "because it is, for us, an inescapable truth. The world is changing with frightening speed. If we don't cling to the instincts, we know to be good we have nothing. Above all, we must trust each other, believe without question all the good we know of each other, grasp it and never let go. Chaos is coming."

Outside the window she watched village boys running out of the wood and across the meadow. Startled redwings rose from the blue-green grass and circled, spitting angrily, "Tsyb! Tsyb! Tsyb!" Delighted to have disturbed them, the boys waved their arms and jumped and shouted in unrestrained glee. When the birds flew away, the boys ran back to the trees, waiting for them to come back to be frightened again.

"I shall go away, Brother."

"Ah." His shoulders sank.

"I shall stay with the Aschenbauers for a while."

"How long?"

"I don't know."

"You must do what you consider best, naturally. Always remember this is your home though."

CHAPTER 4

▼

1887

The garden of the Villa Belleguardo throbbed with heat. The sky was a heavy blue-grey—the kind of sky, so Florentines said, when the summer sun was at its most dangerous. The garden was nevertheless too tempting for anyone to want to be indoors. It had Mediterranean richness—yellow broom, cream magnolias, scarlet cannas, creamy-white hibiscus, purple wisteria and orange honeysuckle. The party sat in the shade of the chestnuts and hornbeams watching giant horseflies play tag. In the branches above, golden orioles watched and waited to pounce. Green lizards on the arthritic twists of olive branches were too lazy to move more than their eyelids. A spotted snake eased itself gently through a bed of wild strawberries and cicadas, those ever-present, changeless inheritors of the seasons, the soul of southern gardens, chirped.

Tables and chairs were arranged for guests whose only object in coming to the Villa these days was, of course, to see the beautiful baby. Dorothea herself, unconscious of the attention her devotees paid, lay shaded and sleeping in a high-wheeled bassinet, rocked gently by Augustina.

Augustina was the housekeeper's niece, appointed as nursemaid through her Aunt Carmella's influence. As soon as Dorothea was born Augustina magically appeared, and she was good, Leonore found.

Leonore nursed the child herself. Paul was surprised, embarrassed and frankly, shocked. This wasn't the way things were done in his world. He had imagined the doctor would select a suitable wet-nurse and when the child was weaned they would hire a well-qualified nursemaid until she was old enough for a governess. They would get the nurse-maid from an agency perhaps; they would fetch one from England, perhaps. All the best families in Petersburg had English governesses these days.

Leonore listened patiently but was adamant. For the moment, Augustina was the only help she needed, and Paul had no option but to come to terms with her quaint insistence. Secretly he was physically repelled by it. The idea of his beautiful Leonore as milk-cow revolted him. Though…was she still his beautiful Leonore. Since her confine-ment he wasn't permitted to see her naked body. He wasn't allowed into the room when she was suckling the child. Leonore now shared her bedroom with Dorothea and Augustina. He slept alone at the other end of the house so as not to be disturbed at night by the child's cries.

Today's gathering was to say goodbye to Atherton and Memo, about to set off on their North African tour. Their four-month delay in leaving Florence was caused by always having one more party to attend before they left. Now, at last, they were off; except that Atherton was beginning to fear they had delayed too long and Morocco would now be unbearably hot. Did not Captain von Hagen think a visit to some-where in northern Europe would be more agreeable at this time of year?

Paul glanced at Memo. Like most Italians he was inordinately fond of children and, possibly a little fond of Augustina too. He sat cross-legged on the carpet, close to the bassinet and as close as he could to the nursemaid. Paul reckoned with some amusement that Ather-ton's best plan would be to take the boy away as soon as possible, tem-perature and destination being of little account.

"My dear man, Africa at this time of year would be absolute insan-ity!" The Countessa di Beltrano opened her fan, flourished it and glared around the garden as though discovering in its beauty reasons for accusation.

"How one longs to be away from this heat. Even in our beloved Florence it is too much," signed Ottolie d'Orangeville, her voice exhausted.

"Nonsense, Ottolie! Where else should one be?" The Contessa turned to Leonore. "You, my dear, know so much more of those parts than we ignorant southerners. Where should they go? Poland…? Saint Petersburg…? Berlin? Your own Estonia, perhaps."

Leonore smiled. Paul broke in hastily. "None of those. Everyone there goes to the country to escape the heat in the summer."

"There! You see, Ottolie? Stay here!" The Contessa advised triumphantly.

"There's always Scandinavia of course," Madame d'Orangeville offered tentatively.

The Contessa squawked. "Why not the North Pole, one may as well ask! The Esquimaux, I'm sure, are an enchanting race and their food…all that blubber, my dear! You may go there if you wish! Captain! You know so much about everything, you can tell us I am sure, do Polar Bears make good pets?"

She looked around, expecting the others to be amused. On the whole they were not. Her irritation increased. She continued: "For myself, I shall be content to remain without moving from Florence for the rest of my life, winter and summer, summer and winter. And I think," she continued glancing significantly at Memo, "I know someone else who would be equally happy to do so."

Everybody looked at the young man and his neck turned redder than usual. He began, quite visibly and, the Contessa thought, disgustingly, to sweat. But her tormenting was not yet over.

"What is your name, young man?" She spoke to him patronisingly, in the simplest Italian. "I know they call you Memo, but no baby was ever carried into a Christian church to be given a name like that."

"Gugielmo, Contessa," he mumbled, and everyone laughed and said 'how nice' to cover his embarrassment.

"Gugielmo," the Contessa repeated, savouring the word like fine wine. "A beautiful name, my dear. Such a shame not to use it. Mr. Atherton!" She turned abruptly, accusingly, and Paul saw Atherton shudder. "There are many customs you and your compatriots have brought to us from America of which I thoroughly approve. Shortening Christian names is not, however, one of them." She turned to Paul, "Perhaps we Europeans are too set in our ways, Captain, but we can quite well effect change when we feel it to be necessary, can we not? Only recently we have re-made Italy! Re-made Italy, Mr. Atherton! Though one could have wished Signore Garibaldi had chosen a more tasteful shade of red for the shirts of his followers. The French..." she sighed in deference to Madame d'Orangeville, "we can only hope poor France will be feeling better very soon. Myself, I have great hopes of General Boulanger. They say he sits a horse magnificently and in his uniform, with his golden beard he is a very splendid looking man. His mother was Welsh, I hear. Extraordinary!"

Atherton gathered courage to defend his countrymen though he was not sure of the charge he had to answer. Everyone else was wishing everyone else would be quiet. It was too hot to argue.

"Really, Countess, you must not blame us for everything that goes wrong in Europe. There are still some things we have to put right in the United States itself."

"I have no doubt of it. Democracy, my dear Mr. Atherton—or your American form of it—all these short-cuts to overcome the natural differences which must exist in any healthy society...they won't get you there if, indeed, Democracy is where you want to go."

"I do assure you Contessa..."

"You are a people dangerously addicted to extremes. In the matter of names now, you either use a great many, the majority of which appear not to be at all Biblical, or you shorten them to an artificial expletive like...like Memo, for example!" She pounced on the idea like a sea-gull breasting a tide-race. "The young man has a perfectly natural and acceptable name. Why not use it?" She dismissed him abruptly. "Signora von Hagen, I trust we shall not lose you for the summer?"

"We've made no plans, Contessa. With the baby, of course…"

"Fiesole is particularly beautiful at this time of year," Madame d'Orangeville murmured dreamily, "if Florence grows too hot for the baby. There are still villas available in Fiesole I believe, and there's so much to be said for living a la campagne in the summer time, don't you agree?"

"Ottolie! You sound like a house-agent's tout accosting tourists at the Central Station."

The conversation brought to mind a problem Paul and Leonore were taking pains to ignore. Before Dorothea's birth Leonore was longing to leave Florence. Now nothing—not even Paul—held any interest; only the child.

They were both aware of the chasm between them. Leonore blamed herself. To herself she admitted a horrible fact: she no longer wanted him. His power to make her blood swirl through her veins was gone. It seemed to her he obstinately refused to understand what it meant to her to be a mother.

He wandered the town alone. He spent weeks away on trips to Volterra and the Etruscan hill sites. He went even further afield to Sienna, Rome and Naples. He brought her presents. He raved about the beauties of Capri and the thrill of climbing Vesuvius. He visited the Coliseum by moonlight and longed for her to be with him. He told her of longing to hold her hand through the brokenness of the Forum, to giggle with her, perhaps, at the monstrous magnificence of Saint Peter's.

None of it meant anything to her.

She welcomed him with a tranquil smile but with no joy.

Their distancing began before Dorothea came. Leonore experienced disturbed nights and Paul suggested, innocently enough, she might be more comfortable if he slept in another room. She agreed because she knew she was bloated and ugly. She understood that he didn't want to be near her now. But she cried herself to sleep for many nights never-theless.

After the birth she surprised herself by not wanting him back. Yet she resented his not being there. Now, his own need for undisturbed rest was the accepted reason. He would be disturbed when she fed the baby, or when the baby cried and had to be changed. She suspected it would be best to turn their bedroom into a nursery with Leonore occu-pying the huge, empire-style bed with its lion claw feet, Dorothea in a cot immediately next to her and Augustina dozing on a narrow couch by the window.

Paul felt himself reduced to being a stranger in his own house and resented his daughter.

"Of course things have had to change, my darling," Leonore assured him when he attempted to tell her of his feelings. "We're nearly an old married couple now. We have a family! And we're going to have a much bigger family, aren't we? Oh Paul, darling, I do so want lots and lots of babies." How this could possibly occur in their present circum-stances, she didn't specify.

Walking solitary one morning along the Lugarno below the Ponte Vecchio, Paul thought he glimpsed Lydmilla Fyodorovna, a half-famil-iar figure entirely in black, crouching on a portable stool at a portable easel. The quay was crowded with artists making water-colours and small oils of the Bridge. He ambled among them, curious to see the standard of work tourists tolerated. Eventually he stood looking at her work, admiring the forcefulness of the drawing. Finally, certain it must be her, he spoke.

"Lydmilla Fyodorovna! Is it you?"

She looked up obviously pleased. "Captain von Hagen! How are you? And your wife? Does the little one do well? I heard you have a daughter."

"Yes, yes, thank you, they are both well…very well, thank God! But what are you doing here?"

She laughed. "It isn't every day I meet rich Russians with grandiose tastes, nor generous husbands willing to pay too much for portraits of their wives in green velvet."

"That portrait is a great joy to us."

"When I have nothing to do, I paint Florence. The owners of the Trattoria San Matteo on the Piazza San Giovanni—do you know it?— allow me to hang my pictures. Lots of interesting Russians go there, incidentally. And I know the people who run the Pensione Iacopetti too. Wealthy English and American families stay there...very respectable. They see my paintings hanging in the rooms and sometimes buy them."

He stood twisting his hat in his hands, embarrassed. He knew he didn't want to associate her with the other painters producing such stale work—views so often repeated they were sad and soulless.

"I haven't had a major commission since I painted your wife. These...these are very trite, perhaps, no?"

"On the contrary."

"I do what I can. People coming to Florence—English and Americans in particular—have expectations of what they will see. When they get here, they naturally see only what they expected. When they go home, they want to take with them pictures of imagined memories. Reality would be too great a disappointment."

"And you have that much patience; with all your talent, you have the patience to pander to their dreams?"

"All artists pander to dreams my friend; their own or someone else's. If you have a talent for pandering to other peoples' dreams, you will make a living. If not..." she shrugged and gave him a trusted smile.

He invited her to lunch but she refused. She lived in a narrow street near the University and had to get back to prepare lunch for her husband, she said.

"Of course, of course...some other time," he said, not knowing whether the excuse was genuine. He watched while she cleaned her brushes, scraped her pallet, recapped her tubes and folded the stool and easel.

"That view—the Pone Vecchio—I should like to have it."

She glanced at him quite seriously before smiling. "Indeed you shall not! Oh no, Captain! That is not at all the sort of thing you would like to have. Come now! Be honest!"

"Forgive me, Lydmilla Fyuodorovna. If I've offended you, I am truly sorry."

"Oh, no! No, my dearest man! Of course you haven't. You touch me very much. You're very kind."

She stooped to pick up her belongings but he forestalled her and they walked together towards the Trinity Bridge.

"If you truly want a picture of the Pone Vecchio, I'll paint you one...a special one. Of yes, you may pay me for it. But this will be a picture I shall be proud, not ashamed for you to have. Will that satisfy you?"

They walked together through the crowded city centre to the Piazza San Marco where she stopped and thanked him for carrying her things.

"But...surely I can take you to your door."

"No! No, really! It's only a step from here. I can manage."

He appreciated there could be reasons for her not wanting him to know where she lived. Yet he persisted.

"I can manage from here, Captain," she told him again quite firmly.

"But...I'll have no idea of where you live," he complained.

"No...no you won't," she agreed. "But I know where you live," and her words seemed to have a meaning he didn't understand.

After that he walked along the Lugarno every day. She was not always there, but when she was he stopped and they talked. When the painting was finished, he had no further excuse for these meetings. But by then he felt he had no need of one.

CHAPTER 5

▼

1887

The letter from Loff was a surprise.

Estate Wirsberg
July 1887

My dear Paul,

The more things change here, the more I think of you and your family all, unfortunately, so far away.

Had you been here during the past few months you could better appreciate what I have to say. Without going into great detail, I will put the matter as succinctly as I can.

This Estate, in common with most large properties is rapidly approaching the point where it will no longer be financially viable. For me this is of little consequence. I have no intention of marrying and when I die I hope I shall leave behind me no financial obligations. You will inherit the title, of course, and your wife will naturally become 'Baroness.' Did you ever see that as a possibility when you married? It is time to remind ourselves, I think, that you and your family will always be von Hagens.

The two of you and your child are the only link between our past and our future. Perhaps, deep in my heart I might wish that your choice of a wife had fallen elsewhere, but I have long-since ceased to make judgments; I have not the right. I am happy for you that Leonore makes you a good wife and that you have a beautiful child.

Your sister is well and will be staying with the von Aschenbauers for the rest of the summer. Think kindly of her, Paul. She loves us both very much, and she loves the past too—a little too much, I fear.

At the moment I am alone here. I am truly fortunate in having Channah to look after my welfare.

Think over carefully what I say; I need ideas. Obviously, we must begin to think of our old home as a commercial proposition.

Your affectionate Brother,

Loff von Hagen.

Leonore was feeding Dorothea when the letter arrived, and Paul judged that it was not necessary she should see it immediately. She was enjoying her life with Dorothea too much for him to wish to spoil it, even though he felt himself abandoned and was angry because of it. Perhaps this was the time to think about rebuilding his own life—to become active once more in the world outside the Villa Belleguardo, the world he had been so happy to turn his back on during the days of his deepest love.

He walked rapidly into town. On the via Tornabuoni he entered a café and ordered coffee, seeking any acquaintance with whom it would be good to compare the present unfavourably with the past. No one came. He sat at a table reading Loff's letter over and over.

He was shocked. Not since his father's death had he ever thought of himself as Loff's heir. In his younger days his comfort was that he was the second son and carried few family obligations. Older now, he still considered himself temperamentally unfitted to shoulder the obligations of six hundred years of family history. Loff had no right to be writing like that! His duty, as the eldest son, was to marry a well-bred Lutheran wife capable of giving him heirs. He refused to allow of any other vision for the future.

He left the café in a panic, dizzy and needing air. Unbidden, the thought of Lydmilla Fyodorovna came into his mind. His special friend! His only friend here in Florence; a comrade, another Seriozha! He struck out to find her but, surprisingly, she was not painting on the quay. Instead, she was standing at the foot of the Ponte Vecchio as though wondering whether or not to cross.

"Lydmilla Fyodorovna!"

"Captain!" She smiled warmly and held out her hand.

"You're not working?"

She laughed. "No. Today I have a holiday for myself."

He stepped back, disappointed. "I suppose you're busy."

"Not at all. Today I am a tourist like all the other tourists. I wander."

"Then," his face relaxed, "perhaps we might wander together?"

She inclined her head. He caught her arm. "Not here. Too crowded. Your husband?"

"It's all right. Today it is all right. I am on holiday."

"Come along we'll find a carriage. We'll drive to Fiesoli for lunch."

In the carriage hoping not to sound too desperate, he told her how glad he was to have found her, how much he needed to talk, how lonely, how miserable he was. She listened gravely and patted his hand. He was calmed by her calm. Gradually while the carriage climbed the leafy hill he came to know the reality of her importance to him. In truth they barely knew each other. She had allowed him nothing more than to carry her painting equipment. On rainy days she would ride in a cab, but however bad the weather, she insisted they part at San Marco.

After Leonore's portrait in the green velvet dress was finished, she allowed no further visits to the Villa. Neither, when they parted on the Piazzest Marco would she definitely agree time and place for another meeting. Had she been younger, her coyness would have exasperated him. But now, he would tolerate almost any idiosyncrasy. Indeed, lying alone in his bed at night, wanting Leonore to be with him, but with the cries of Dorothea drifting along the corridor he contemplated whether he might be falling in love with her.

That was nonsense. He was no more than intrigued by the mystery of her. To go further, to know her secrets, might rob him of joy in her. A disillusioned married man needed the reassurance that he could still maintain, succeed in the hunt. He recognised that victory could render him desolate, futureless at the brink of middle age.

Today his mind was innocent of these unwelcome thoughts. He sat close to her, the horse taking the steeper ascent, the driver motionless, perhaps asleep. Sunshine dipped into the carriage, in and out like a bucket in a well. Paul watched her every moment. She said nothing and her face told him nothing.

At Fiesole he held back while she chose the restaurant, their food and the wine with a self-mocking air of make-believe experience. They ate on a vine-draped verandah overlooking Florence while their driver now snoozed on his box. He had already eaten well, of course, having cunningly guided them to his cousin's restaurant. The horse dozed to snoring and snuffling into his nose-bag.

After they'd eaten they climbed further up the hill, through woods to a tiny river feeding a shallow pond. They sat there together. Paul rested on a Cyprus, she rested against Paul. The scent of the pines heightened his desire for her, his need to possess her completely, body and soul. But only when the time was right. His desire was containable; this afternoon it made him happy and there was none of the crushing urgency that accompanied his earliest feelings for Leonore.

She took off her hat and loosened her hair. He gently stroked her neck. Cradled against him she told him about her life: her home in Kharkhov, the Art School where she'd met Volodya, their involvement in student politics, their escape from the town while the secret police were on their way to them. Her parents paid for the journey but insisted on their being married before they left Russia. They never pretended to love one another. They were nothing more than comrades.

They came to Florence after Volodya developed tuberculosis. They should have gone to the mountains but there were no tourists in the mountains to buy Lydmilla's paintings. She painted views of the city, and Volodya translated pamphlets from the West to be smuggled into Russia. Between them they survived, but only just.

Now Paul understood everything—her insistence that he never come to their room, her refusal to come to the Villa. He understood all and forgave all. His desire for her was fiercer than ever.

He knew their bodies were so close, she must be aware of how she affected him. He shifted and told her frankly why. Her response was to press herself more closely against him.

"We are all victims, my dear," she told him softly. "You, I, my poor Volodya, Lenore—even your little Dorothea—we are all victims because of who we are, where we come from. Russia takes us all as base metal and tempers us into what it wants us to be. If we crack in the furnace or snap under the hammer, it discards us—throws us away as useless, hopeless, rootless. All over the world, wherever you go, you will find wandering Russians. We are a part of a great diaspora, searching for our own lost souls until we no longer have the courage to continue our pilgrimage."

"Things are changing," he told her, not altogether convincingly. "My Brother tells me. In some ways the country now is unrecognisable…unreal."

"Will they have changed enough to save your little Dorothea, do you think?"

"I must believe so. It would be too terrible, otherwise. Sometimes I dream…"

"Dreams!" she broke in angrily. "What good are dreams? What must we do, Paul, my dear, what can we do? You say things are changing, but…"

"No, no, you are right! It will never be enough until the changes are of our making not theirs. Everything that happens to us is engineered by the Government, for the Government. They're grinding us down—

landowners, peasants, factory workers—down and down, deeper and deeper. Nothing can possibly change until we change the Government."

"Pooh!" she said, her enthusiasm seeming to evaporate. "Nothing changes quicker than our Government. The Emperor's favourites fall like autumn leaves."

"Not the favourites," he panted, "the system! Lydmilla Fyodorovna, we have to change the system."

She caught her breath and drew slightly away. "The Autocracy?"

"Of course! Everybody! Everything! It's all rotten; rank and rotten! Get rid of it. None of it is any good any more. None of it's worth saving. We must make a new world, a world where there is fresh air to breathe if we are to survive. We have to take everything into our own hands, stand up and look into each other's faces and see ourselves as worth-while human beings. We must love ourselves. We must learn to love ourselves, Lydmilla. To love ourselves, to respect ourselves is the only way."

He stopped suddenly, his face alight with happiness as though the future had come to pass already. She breathed heavily because of his fire. She slowly slipped away and lay on her back in the long grass as though in a dream. He looked down on her and loved her. Conscious of what was happening, surrendering, he felt her arms drawing him down into the grass.

CHAPTER 6

▼

1887

Countess von Aschenbauer was relieved when Loff declined the invitation to the Ball she proposed giving in town, at her house on the Domberg. He might have arrived there with his Jewish concubine—everybody agreed he was becoming very peculiar these days. Then what would people have said of the Countess herself, particularly? Proprieties counted for less in the country, though, and if he brought her to her usual summer party people would accept it as another of his idiosyncrasies. Of course, he would take Channah with him; there was no doubt about that in the Baron's mind. This was no mere social occasion. He had business needing to be discussed with the Count.

For Russians, industrial revolution was quickening. 'Economy' was now the Count's favourite word, but the Countess knew nothing about that and didn't want to. Economy, economy, economy! He said it all the time and each time it seemed to mean something different. Very soon now she expected him to say he couldn't afford the shopping trip she and Cille de Daporetee planned to Bohmin in the autumn. He was all ready to say they should be buying. But Russian made…?

She would think about that later, when she had the time. At that moment she had guests to welcome and she hurried into the hall to welcome them.

Baron von Hagen's carriage stopped and the Baron got out. He bowed to his waiting host, then turned to hand out the passenger.

"I knew you would have no objection to my bringing Fräulein Litvak with me, Margarethe deserted me, I have to have her with me all the time."

The Count advanced smiling. He couldn't understand why women made such a fuss about these things. He looked long at Channah. He liked what he saw. Pretty little thing! Von Hagen was a lucky devil. "My dear Fräulein..." He held her hand longer than needful, tucked her arm into his own and gently coaxed her up the steps to where the Countess was waiting. "Ah, there you are, my dear," he said cheerfully. "Here's the good Baron and look...he's brought Fräulein Litvak to visit us. Now...isn't that charming of him?"

The Countess moved forward, "Charming indeed. Come in, my dear, and welcome."

Margarethe lagged behind while Cecile and the Countess, one on either arm, took Channah up to the third floor landing. "I know all about young girls and the way they go on," the Countess told her. "Chatter, chatter, chatter, all day and all night. So I've put you into the room next to our dear Margarethe. There's a communicating door between your rooms. You'll look after Fräulein Litvak, won't you, Margarethe? You'll be nice and close to each other so you can chatter, chatter, chatter, as much as you like."

She left them smiling and fretting and when her mother had gone Cecile favoured her dearest friend with an ironic smile. Margarethe pleaded a headache to be alone. Directly she could she wrote to her Aunt Johann von Blomberg in Koenigsburg.

Spanskoi
July 1887

My dear Aunt Johanna,

I write to beg you a very great favour. There is nothing but treachery and betrayal all around me and I am seeking a refuge. I am staying at the moment with…I thought they were my friends…the von Aschen-bauers. But only today they have received as guests my brother and his young Jewish…I'm sorry I don't know what to call her. She has driven me from my home. Now she is driving me from my friend's house, Countess von Aschenbauer…I would never have believed it possible…received her like an honoured guest, she must have known how much she was hurting me.

Dear Aunty, could you grant me the security of a room in your house in Koenigsburg until this madness has passed and Russia has found the truth again? The principle entertainment for the ladies here at the moment is to read Tarot cards and orthodox priests encourage them in their four superstitions. Some who are supposedly God-fearing Luther-ans indulge in these blasphemous, so-called magical rites.

Among the men the talk is all of sordid money-making and of how they may profit from all the new industries. They will even associate in terms of equality with the new Jewish factory owners if they see in it franchise benefit for themselves.

I am, dear Aunt,

Your deeply troubled niece though,

And affectionately,

Your loving Margarethe von Hagen.

CHAPTER 7

▼

1887

Carmella handed Paul the letter. He looked at it, first casually, then with a deeper more careful interest. It came from Estonia, though in an unknown hand. He laid it on the table and stared at it. Was this the unwanted news he'd been fearing ever since Dorothea was born? News of his brother's illness and the necessity for his own return to the Baltic? He looked across the table to where Leonore was sitting and was ashamed of his thoughts.

"What is it dear?" Leonore asked. She watched him place it upon the table and glance at the back of the envelope for a clue to the sender.

"That's odd," he said, "It looks as if it's already been opened." He handed it to her but she gasped and turned pale and wouldn't take it.

"You know what it means, don't you Paul? God knows why, but they suspect you of something. You're under surveillance."

"My darling, what a fantastic idea. Probably some greedy post office official thought there may have been some money in it."

The shutters were closed against the afternoon sun.

"You know it's more than that."

"Well, they're wasting their time. I haven't done anything." He took up the envelope with an air of bravado but she wasn't reassured by the look on his face. "It's from Loff. But he didn't write himself."

"They can't be after him, surely."

"What does it say? There were edges of anxiety and anger in her voice. He wasn't taking the opening of the letter seriously. She was a Jew. She knew better.

Estate Wirsberg
August 1887

My dear Brother,

Channah is my secretary now. Valiant threw me a week ago. I badly broke my left elbow and my arm in several places. It was no fault of the horse. I was riding home through the wood one evening, lost in a world of business problems, taking no notice of what might be happening. The next thing I knew, the horse was rearing and I was in pain and lying on the ground. Unfortunately, the good old creature stamped on my arm. We examined the poor creature later; there was a nasty wound in his foot caused, I would guess, by a sharpened stone launched by a catapult. As you yourself know, all the boys round here are experts with catapults; we were ourselves. Any of the boys...or the men, for that matter...could be the culprit.

I haven't troubled you with details of our difficulties, particularly since I received no reply to my last letter. But we have severe labour troubles here. Peasants have been unable to settle. Those that stay work their own plots and will only come to us for outrageous wages. I was addressing a meeting at the Church that afternoon and left them in no doubt that local landowners would not be blackmailed. If they refused to behave themselves, I'd get Krasnov to send in guards.

I am bothering you over this only to warn you that your allowance may have to be slightly reduced. The situation is worsened because Margarethe has chosen to live with Aunt Johanna in Koenigsburg. You will agree, I am sure, that I cannot allow her to be dependent on the charity of relatives.

I trust Leonore and Dorothea are both well,

Your affectionate brother,

Loff von Hagen.

After he finished reading out the letter, the room seemed quiet except for ordinary sounds that adopted menace: the busy buzzing of a fly and the chirping of birds in the garden. In another part of the house Dorothea cried and Paul was surprised because Leonore didn't leave him immediately to attend to her. When she spoke, Leonore's voice was harsh, strangled. This was a simulation of the moment he had dreaded ever since her marriage.

"Will you write today? Ask him to come to us to convalesce."

"Things sound bad there. I must go to him. When I'm sure what has to be done, I'll send for you and the baby."

"No!" She half rose in her chair. "No Paul, you mustn't. You must never go there again."

"Darling, don't be so dramatic!"

"You don't know, Paul. You don't even know who wrote that letter. Your brother tells you it was Channah, but...well, you just don't know, do you? It could have been anyone working for the Information Department. It may simply be a trap, and they'll be waiting for you directly the train crosses the frontier."

He laughed, not at all sympathetically.

"Believe me! They have their spies all over the world. Why not here? Who do we know in Florence, Paul? Who do we really know...who they are, where they came from...only what they tell us." She wanted to throw her arms around him and to tell him she loved him. But she couldn't. There was something between them.

He stuffed the letter into his pocket. She was near hysteria, and he'd no idea how to control the situation. "I'm going into town, my dear. I'll find Lydmilla Fyodorovna and tell her I'm going away. She can keep you company while I'm away. You'd like that, wouldn't you?"

He couldn't find the painter along the path nor anywhere else. In despair he went, at last, to the café she'd told him about, the Matteo. The man behind the counter was spade-bearded, with black hair and a harsh profound voice. He refused to tell Paul Madame Khelchestaya's address but promised to pass on a letter if he wrote one.

My dear Comrade,

My brother has had a riding accident; I must leave for Estonia unexpectedly. Leonore is staying in Florence; would you do me the favour of going to see her from time to time; she'll be lonely.

My brother's letter, quite personal and harmless I do assure you, seems to have been opened on the way here. You will know, better than anyone in Florence, the fact of our being objects of interest to the Authorities has upset her very much.

I shall be taking the Rome-Vienna Express tomorrow afternoon.

My very warmest and good wishes dear Comrade,

Paul von Hagen.

P.S. By visiting my wife while I'm away, I assure you, you will not compromise yourself.

P.P.S. Leonore knows nothing of our wonderful lunch at Fiestola.

When he reached home again, he found that, under Leonore's instructions, Carmella and Augustine had re-arranged the sleeping arrangements. He was now restored to the big double bed with the lion's claw feet. When the time came, he climbed in diffidently, and they lay together side-by-side, rigid with embarrassment. At last she whispered, so softly he barely heard her:

"I love you Paul. I love you very much. Please forgive me."

He turned to her, took her into his arms and their lovemaking was ecstatic. Next afternoon he still had the glow of it on him when he leaned out of the compartment window watching his wife's figure slowly disappear in the veil of steam that drifted across the station.

He settled into his corner and thought seriously for a while before opening his newspaper. Of course, what he must do was quite clear: Loff had Channah to look after him. His duty was to get off the train at Bologna and return to Leonore.

But he didn't. At Bologna his determination wavered and his duty became less clear, confused. Leonore would be safe enough in Florence. She had friends there, including Lydmilla Kholdeskaye to take care of her. But Loff…how was he supposed to manage the Estate with only a young Jewish girl to help?

The train was beginning to gather speed when the compartment door was abruptly opened and a heavy-looking suitcase landed on the floor at his feet. At considerable risk, a round, red-faced man in a commonly cut brown suit, dropped himself in after it.

"Excuse me Signore, I was nearly too late." He giggled self-consciously. "May I join you?"

The train by now was traveling at considerable speed, too fast for Paul to refuse and jump out. The man looked meaningfully at his suitcase. "That is very heavy, Signore. I do not think I can lift it to the rack. May I leave it on the floor?"

Paul nodded his head, but made no verbal reply, hoping that would indicate his disinclination for conversation. The man smiled widely, took off his Tyrolean style felt hat and fanned himself. His head was round like his body, his iron-grey hair close-cropped. Suddenly he stopped, fanning, noted the hat neatly on the seat beside him and searched his pockets like a distracted squirrel. He found what he sought. He handed Paul a grubby oblong card.

Arturo Martinelli
Roma
Corso D'Italia 17

Purveyor of Exquisite Religions Statues and Holy Pictures

Paul read the card. The little man slid on to his feet and bowed low until a sudden lurch of the train bolted him ridiculously onto Paul's lap. "That is I, Signore; I am Arturo Martinelli, and here in the case I have my little ones. Excuse me." He turned the case on to its side and opened the lid. Its contents made Paul shudder—a row of carmine-cheeked plaster men in pale blue robes with expressionless blue eyes and meticulously symmetrical beards and moustaches, like a box of candied fruits. Worst of all was the smell—heavy, stale incense with something added, smelling acrid that unexpectedly assaulted his eyes and nostrils. The shock of it sent him reeling backwards until he stopped in the far corner of the compartment, his eyes closed, his mind turning over and over like a madly revolving Ferris wheel.

"Captain! Captain von Hagen! Are you all right?"

Paul opened his eyes slowly and stared unsteadily at the man with the suitcase, aware that something important was happening, not understanding what it was. When his mind settled, he recognised the close-trimmed, coarse-featured face opposite.

Colonel Denisovitch-Komarevsky. Yet how could it be? The Colonel was a trueborn Russian peasant. The man to sell Roman Catholic statues? He tried to stand but the man's grip on his arm was surprisingly firm.

"Relax Captain." The man's voice was sickeningly calm. "Underneath these I have more for you to see?"

"No! I don't want to see them."

The man shrugged. "Very well."

"How do you know my name?"

"You are Captain von Hagen, are you not? You see, I know everything about you. You resigned your Commission to marry a Jew." The forefinger of the man's right hand swung backwards and forwards like a pendulum. "However, we must talk about all that another time." He pulled down a window and leaned out. Paul gulped in the night air. "Ah yes, I thought we were slowing. I see lights ahead. Belzano! Though you Balts, I am sure call it Bazen." He smiled at the rather stupid salesmen once more. "I leave you here. You, I imagine, are traveling to Vienna?"

Paul nodded involuntarily. The train stopped. He stepped hastily across the man's case to leave the compartment. The man looked deflated as though disappointed that this was not to be a long drawn out farewell. But Paul needed to be away from him and into the fresh air as quickly as possible.

CHAPTER 8

▼

1887

It was a wet afternoon when Sister Agnes brought Rachel and Ida to meet Paul at the station in Warsaw. To look their prettiest, both girls wore unsuitable white summer frocks and hats trimmed with lace. Rachel covered her frock with a mackintosh; Ida by an umbrella, little more than a sunshade. She hopped from leg to leg, eager to be the first to see him. When she saw him she rushed forward, clasping him and covering his face with a shower of wet kisses.

"Darling Captain! How lovely to see you! Doesn't he look marvelous, Rachel. Where's Leah? And the baby?" She grimaced with genuine disappointment. "Do we have to wait until she's quite grown up before we're allowed to see her?"

Sister Agnes, smiling, gently reproved her for making a fuss. Rachel offered no kiss but gave him her hand with dignity.

"Welcome to Warsaw, Captain. It's good to see you again."

They went in a cab along Jerozolemskie Avenue to the Hotel Bristol. The afternoon orchestra was languidly rendering a Dibrazynski Romance against the high-pitched chatter of women eating pastries and critically eyeing each other's hats. Paul had their coffee and pastries taken upstairs to his suite. Ida's eyes widened when she saw the opulence of it; red plush chairs, polished mahogany. She ran from piece to piece admiring, feeling, smelling, testing for softness. "Oh how marvelous. Like a palace! Oh, Captain, it must be wonderful to live in a room like this. Is it like this in Italy?"

A waiter served them. When she saw the pastries, even Ida was momentarily awed into silence. "Sister Agnes," she said at last. "Could Sister Cook come here for some lessons?"

"Pastries like these only make you fat," Rachel told her sharply.

"I don't care. Enjoy! They taste so good. Sister Agnes, aren't they wonderful?" Her lips were already rimmed with cream.

"I really think you'd better not have any more, dear," the Nun said mildly. "We have to take care of our looks, don't we?"

"Fiddlesticks! Whether I eat one or a dozen won't alter the way I look. Fat or thin, I may as well please myself. Isn't that right, Captain?"

"I don't know what you mean. How do you look?"

"Like a Jew, of course." She laughed mischievously.

"Ida!" Rachel flushed furiously, but Ida only laughed louder and took another pastry.

"I'm supposed to say 'Semitic'," she told Paul confidentially. "At the Convent, they don't like us to say we're Jews. It upsets the parents; of the other girls."

"Ignore her, Captain," Rachel said. "She's always trying to shock."

"It's true," Ida persisted, red-faced but still laughing. "It's different for Rachel, Captain. She doesn't look at all like me, does she? Neither does Leonore. They could quite easily pass for Lutherans. Well...Leah is, of course, now she's married to you. But look at me. I look just like our poor Papa, may he rest in peace!" She shrugged impatiently. "But I want to learn all about the baby. Does she walk yet? Does she talk? Does she look like Leah or is she pretty like me?" She threw her arms around Paul's neck and nuzzled against him, covering his cravat with fresh cream.

"You're suffocating me, you little wretch," he laughed, pushing her gently away. "Let me go into the bedroom. There's a letter from Leonore in my briefcase. That will tell you everything."

The case was on the bureau by the window. He rifled through his papers but the letter from Leah and the pictures she'd sent weren't there. He turned to his suitcase and searched.

In a panic he pulled everything on to the bed. He could hardly believe it but someone had searched his luggage and stolen his papers. He went slowly back into the sitting room.

"I'm sorry, my dears, I must have forgotten to bring it."

"Oh, Captain! How could you!"

"Ida, by quiet!"

"Rachel's right, Ida," Sister Agnes said. "His Excellency has more important things to think about. In any case," she rose, "it's time we were getting back."

"Nothing's more important than Leah's baby!" Ida's voice trembled.

"Yes, yes," Paul said, relieved. "I didn't realise it was so late. They'll get you a cab downstairs, Sister."

"Come along now, Ida! Say goodbye like a good girl."

"I'll write to Leonore tonight," Paul told her. "She'll send you another letter."

"I shall be writing to her myself," Ida told him, and it sounded like a threat.

"I'd rather you didn't...not for a day or two."

"It's all right, Captain, she won't," Rachel assured him.

"Oh! Oh! You! Prison couldn't be worse than this."

Paul didn't argue. "I'll see you tomorrow when I come to talk to Mother Superior. You might tell her, Sister Agnes, I shall expect her to see me tomorrow morning."

He dined alone before going to the Doma. The café, smoke-stained and noisy as ever, was crowded with officers of the Semonyevsky. Pan Koblinski recognised him and waddled out from behind his grill to greet him delightedly.

"Your Excellency! How good to see you again! What a surprise! Welcome! Welcome! Tadzio! Champagne for His Excellency! A little gesture to express my delight at seeing you, Your Excellency. And your good wife? She is in Warsaw with you?"

"No. She's at home with our daughter."

"Your daughter! You have a daughter! God bless her!"

"Captain!"

Paul turned and experienced the real warmth of homecoming when Clementine Bielska gathered him to her.

"How marvelous. How is Leonore? Isn't she with you? I want to know all about the baby. Come! Sit down! Tell me everything!"

The orchestra played a Czardas. Paul smiled at Clementine over the rim of his glass. She smiled back, understanding. They were intimate, warm, family together, their glances tacitly acknowledging fellowship in conspiracy.

"It goes well?"

"It goes very well. And you?"

"Very well for me also." She laughed. "There is someone. Perhaps if you are still in Warsaw tomorrow you will meet him. His name is Alexander Schimanski. He works for the Railways. He's terribly clever...speaks Russian, German and some French besides Polish. He's an engineering supervisor. It's a very important job."

"You must both come to the Bristol. We'll have dinner together and talk about everything."

"Lovely." She became serious. "He really is very clever, you know. They've already asked him to go to Moscow to take over one of the locomotive yards there. Tell me all about Leonore, though. I'm very angry. She hasn't written in ages."

"She's very busy. She nurses Dorothea herself. Though why on earth she feels she must..."

Clementine laughed again and this time he sensed that he was the butt of her amusement. "Men are wonderful. Sasha's exactly the same. None of you know anything about anything, do you?"

"Not about that sort of thing, certainly. It isn't our affair."

"No, my dear. You have nothing at all to do with any of that. Is she a good baby?"

"Leonore doesn't have any trouble. She wrote and told you all about it, actually."

"Wonderful."

"The trouble is…the strangest thing, Clementine, I've lost the letter…the one she wrote her sisters."

"You lost it? Where?"

"I put the letters into my briefcase in Florence. When I looked for them this afternoon, they were gone. Something odd is happening. The last letter we had from my brother—that's the reason for this trip, actually; he's had a bad accident—was opened before we received it. Leonore thinks we're under surveillance, but that's absurd."

"Are you sure?"

"There's no possible reason."

"They don't need a reason."

"That's what Leonore says."

"Someone searched your bag after you left Florence."

"Impossible! I had it with me all the time." He suddenly stopped.

"And…?

"Oh, no! That's absurd."

"What?"

"A man selling religious statues. I left my bag in the compartment when I got off the train to eat at Bozen. He wasn't coming any further. I left the compartment while he was still collecting his things together." His stomach churned. He looked at Clementine with haunted, empty eyes and was shocked to see that hers were equally dead.

"Captain…" she hesitated. "Captain, I was telling you about my friend Sasha."

"Yes?"

"Captain, I think…oh dear! I really don't know how to say this. Sasha's quite young. He really is brilliant and his parents have no influence. I told you the railways want him to go to Moscow, didn't I?"

"Yes?"

"Perhaps it would be better if we didn't meet again…just for a little while."

"Oh!"

"I'm sorry, my dear, but you know how it goes. If they see me with you and then me with him…Once you're on their books, it's like dropping a pebble in a pond—the ripples go on and on. Everyone's drawn in; anyone they can in any way at all associate with you."

"Yes, yes, I see." The room heaved round him—after only a single glass of champagne?"

"You do understand, don't you?" She was pleading. "I have to be careful for Sasha's sake. And…maybe I shouldn't see Rachel and Ida at the Convent any more. They're getting on well enough and Ida is so fond of Sister Agnes."

"Yes! Yes, all right! I understand. Goodbye, Clementine." He left the table. Pan Koblinski came forward fussily to say goodbye. Paul ignored him and stumbled out, slamming the door behind him. Koblinski turned angrily to Clementine as she followed him towards the door.

"What have you done?" he spat at her. "Why is he angry?"

"They are watching him," she whispered.

"Ah!" Koblinski's eyebrows rose, his face relaxed. "Ah yes, of course," he said and returned to his desk.

CHAPTER 9

▼

1887

Paul went to the Convent early next day.

"Mother Superior, Ida said something yesterday that didn't please me."

"Indeed, Captain?" The Nun sat at a polished desk, polished like glass, on which stood two glass ink wells, one for red, one for black, a blotter and a tray of neatly arranged pens. On the wall, a sterile Christ hanging on His Cross, reminded him uncomfortably of his mother's portrait at Estate Wirsberg.

"Ida is not an easy child," she continued. "Rachel is different. She is obedient, assiduous, and intelligent. There is hardly any difference between her and any of our Catholic young ladies. She shows a strong inclination towards further study. The Sisters' agree with me that she should enter a training college for young women teachers when she leaves here."

"Reverend Mother, it was about...."

"Ida, on the other hand," she ploughed on, forcefully ignoring him, "we were prepared to keep here..."

"Were prepared?"

"Of course, until we received specific instructions otherwise. But if I am to be frank, Captain, I strongly recommend that you have her trained elsewhere for a trade of some description—dressmaking, perhaps?"

CHAPTER 10

▼

1888

Ulitsa Adowska 39
Moscow

My own Leonore,

You share your good news with me, so I must share mine with you.
My darling friend, Sasha and I are married. He has been promoted
overseer in the yards at the Byelorussia Station here. It's a very impor-
tant job. He is responsible for all the long-distance international
expresses to Smolensk, Minsk, Brest, Warsaw, Berlin and Paris. Sasha
says it's a job that carries with it an important patriotic duty. Other
trains from other countries run over the same rails. It mustn't only be
the Russian trains that are always breaking down! Sasha takes his
work very, very seriously, I can promise you.

We've found a dear little flat in a wonderful old building close to the
Arbar and, just along the street, there's the most exciting market
you've ever seen. You can buy just about everything there. And we
need just about everything, too! All we bought from Warsaw was an
enormous wine cooler, a wedding present from old Pan Koblinski
(and something he'd been wanting to get rid of for a long time, I don't
doubt). It takes up a lot of room but it doesn't go far towards furnish-

ing a flat that doesn't even have a bed; so I am grateful to be close to places where I can buy whatever we need. Oh, how I wish you were here, darling. We could have so much fun together, choosing everything.

Fortunately, things are reasonably cheap here—cheaper than they are in Warsaw. But most of the people seem poor—poorer even than our Polish Jews, I think. Sasha says his men live on rye bread, buckwheat porridge, cabbage and salted cucumbers—if they're lucky. Never any meat or fish, though. And they don't drink vodka because they can't afford it. All they have is kvas—that's a kind of weak beer they make out of fermenting rye bread, some way or another; I really don't understand, and it tastes awful, Sasha says. I've never had any of course. Champagne—even that awful stuff we used to drink at the Doma—spoils your taste for anything else, my dear.

Sasha took me into the yards once because I wanted to see where he worked, and I've been worried about him ever since. I hate the thought of his going into that place every day. The locomotives and the carriages are huge. I never before realized just how big they are...and how noisy and dangerous. But it's his being with those workmen that really worries me. Leonore, you've never, in all your life, seen such creatures: hairy, dirty, smelly and with the most terrible eyes. They stare at you all the time, but they don't seem to see you. Their eyes don't register anything. Sasha says he likes them very much and gets on well with them. But I'm not happy. They're more like animals than human beings. There are only or two who are different— more like us, if you know what I mean. Sasha says he doesn't know anything about them yet, and it isn't good policy to ask questions. Perhaps they're illegals. Who knows?

None of our Warsaw friends wanted us to come here, and I must admit I miss them all very much. My life can be very lonely, sometimes. Sasha is always away in the yards, and there isn't any of the gaiety there used to be at the old Doma. But my Sasha has his future to think about, and for a little while, it seems, his future is in Moscow.

I love you, my darling Leonore. I love you, and I long to embrace you and your dear little girl...and the dear, dear Captain, of course. Remember me, my dear and write to me soon.

Your sincerest friend,

Clementine Kondrakina.

Leonore read the letter many times. She had a passionate longing to write back immediately to comfort her friend. But she was afraid. The roughness of the glue on the envelope held her back. She was frozen into panic and wished that Paul were here to shoulder her fear. There was no one she could tell; she knew of no one in Florence would understand. She knew nothing of the personal lives of the Russians who were coaching Rachel and Ida and didn't dare be rash with strangers. Her fear was adversely affected by indecision: should she write to tell Paul, or would that merely distract him from more important business; indeed, would it be safe to trust her fears to the post?

Her terror was heightened by the arrival of a second letter. This one was addressed to Paul from Estonia, and it also bore a telltale line of rough glue along the seal. She opened Paul's letter, hardly understood its contents and locked them both safely away.

CHAPTER 11

▼

1888

Baron von Hagen was satisfied by the way his Russians settled in at Estate Wirsberg, though he was reluctant to admit it. Their smooth absorption into village life was largely due to the ministrations, secular and religious, of Father Tikhon. He was the Russians' link with familiar things; their guide and counselor. Baron von Hagen issued instructions. Father Tikhon translated and softened them. It was, therefore, the priest they credited with everything that was good: the long, warm, comfortable barrack they were allowed to build for themselves where each man enjoyed privacy far beyond anything found in the huts of the Estonian peasants. It was Father Tikhon who, having at first superintended and translated for the men the collection of wages in the Baron's office, gradually took over the collection himself. It saved the Baron time. The priest distributed the money among the men as it was due and they trusted him in that as in everything else. On his own initiative he held back a proportion of each man's pay to cover living expenses. He bargained with the Estonians for everything the Russians needed. The Estonians were content to trust him, too. They had found him invariably fair, his hairy lips always smiling, his dirty hands ever ready to assist Estonians equally with Russians. Unconsciously, the trust in which both sides held him communicated itself between the groups themselves. Whenever the Baron passed the Russian barrack after sunset, he would hear the men laughing, talking, and singing folk songs—Estonian as well as Russian. And Father Tikhon's rumbling bass was always prominent among them.

Socially, each group kept itself apart from the other. The Estonians drank in their tavern, the Russians in their barrack. There were no drunken fights and, so far as was known, no objectionable fornication. The coming of winter, however, threatened this inter-racial equilibrium. The shale beds were already too compacted with frost for digging to continue with the primitive tools that were all they had until money arrived from abroad. If the men were left without occupation during the long cold months, there could well be trouble. The problem was pointed out to him by Channah who, the Baron registered with a mixture of amusement and approval, took an active interest in the running of the Estate directly she heard it was to be placed on a commercial footing.

"What will your Russians do through the winter, your Excellency? Has Father Tikhon made any suggestions?"

"What my Russians do this winter is not Father Tikhon's affair," he told her testily. "But you do have a point, Channah. Oh! They'll keep themselves occupied like the local men, I dare say."

"Excuse me, your Excellency. The local men hunt. These Russians are from a long-settled agricultural district. They gave up going after anything bigger than rabbits generations ago. Local men repair their tools. The Russians have no need to sharpen scythes and repair harrows and ploughs; they have no plots."

"Of course not. They're here to work the shale. They've no need to grow their own food. They earn quite enough to buy whatever they want."

"But you can't leave them idle, your Excellency. Without women-folk and with no work to keep them occupied…"

He suddenly laughed, partly because of her unlooked-for knowledge of the world and partly because he cared for her very tenderly. "You have an idea, my clever little Channah. I can see quite well that you have an idea."

"If your Excellency permits…" she began diffidently.

"Come along, my dear one, tell me what you've decided."

"You could put the Russians to lumbering. They could cut down trees in the forests reserved for your use only…"

"The villagers have plenty of wood already, child. We don't need more." He was disappointed.

"No, your Excellency. To sell commercially. They can cut the trees in your forests, drag them over a snow road to the mills at Haapsalu and then put them on a coastal steamer to Reval, Riga, St. Petersburg, even…wherever there's a market we can undercut."

He stared at her, amazed. "We could even buy our own ship…"

Book III

CHAPTER I

▼

1888

Holiday euphoria held the hearts of everyone at the Villa Belleguardo captive in its golden cords for several weeks; everyone's except Dorothea's, that is. She inexplicably viewed her father with unshakeable suspicion, as though he were a wild animal everyone assured her was tame, but whom she could never totally trust.

Paul ignored his daughter's diffidence. He bellowed and blew and pounced on her like a jolly hairy giant and her fear of him slowly changed to irritation and then to anger. Paul's chief concern was Leonore's health and comfort during her pregnancy, though this second pregnancy differed from the first in that he was not relegated to a separate bedroom. This second child was to be a shared experience. He seldom thought of Paris or his brother's schemes. Nothing outside the Villa Belleguardo was of any importance at this moment. But he was most attentive to Rachel and Ida because he knew that was a way of pleasing Leonore. She was happy enough to remain resting in the Villa while he showed them the glories of Florence; its churches, its galleries, its parks. The girls were enchanted by everything he showed them but, most of all, they were enchanted by their handsome brother-in-law.

Winter rapidly eased itself into spring. The wind was still chill but the change of season was eagerly celebrated by the city's old men, who came out to lean like lizards against the comfort of sun-warmed walls.

After the damp, paralyzing cold of Warsaw, Rachel and Ida found in Florence a sort of heaven. As the weeks passed and her womb grew heavier, Leonore relished her sisters' freedom and happiness. She was surprised and a little uncomprehending when Paul called for the foreclosure on this Lotus-land existence of delicious indulgence.

"We have to think seriously about the girls, Leonore," he said, while Leonore was concentrating on her account books. "We must arrange for them to do something."

She licked an ink stain on her finger and smiled encouragingly. "Now what more could they possibly do, darling? They're always busy at something."

"They should be doing something useful."

"They don't have time to do anything you'd call useful. And it's all your own fault. Darling, you're giving them such a wonderful time. And what better can young people do than to enjoy themselves while they have the opportunity? They are so grateful to you, and so am I."

"I've loved it too. But it's time to think seriously about their education."

"You don't want to put them with the nuns again...not after Warsaw...?"

"No, darling, not with nuns."

"Anyway, it's not really necessary, is it?" she coaxed. "Their Italian is coming along so well. They practice with Carmella and Augustina all the time."

"That's just the point, darling, I don't want them talking like Carmella and Augustina."

She noticed the use of the personal possessive and it pleased her. "You've been wonderful," she said, smiling, "taking them everywhere and showing them everything. And it will be easier from now on. The tourists will be back soon. They already know some of our friends. There'll be lots of parties for them to go to...oh, darling! They'll have a marvelous time. And they'll hate it so much if you send them back to school."

"I don't know about the parties. They're neither old enough nor educated enough to come out yet."

She pouted but there was laughter in her eyes. "Paul, darling, don't be an old grouch! They don't have to 'come out'. No one ever did in my family. We were considered 'out' the moment we were born."

He hesitated. "I suppose I'd better tell you…though I wasn't going to, just yet. Darling, what passes for adequate in Florence won't do for…we won't be here much longer. They have to learn French. We're moving to Paris."

"Paris!"

"Dammit! I didn't intend telling you until after the little one came."

"Paris!" She repeated it so that it sounded like an echo. "That's marvelous. Why Paul? When?"

"Estate business. You needn't bother your head about it. Just don't argue about the girls. We have to prepare them. I know best, I promise you."

She gulped. "Of course, Paul dear."

"I'll have to take advice, of course. A cadet school doesn't teach you much about that sort of thing." He laughed.

"No dear." She was happy to agree with anything he said, happy because he was sounding so proprietary about her sisters. "We could I suppose," she offered tentatively, "ask the Contessa or Signora d'Orangeville, perhaps."

Paul shook his head. "I wouldn't trust them."

"Who, then?"

"Someone much more practical. What would you think of Lydmilla Fyodorovna?"

"I feel so guilty about her. She was very kind to me while you were away. Since I said you were coming home she hasn't been anywhere near."

"I'll talk to her then, shall I?"

"You know where to find her?" she asked with sudden sharpness. "She wouldn't give me her address. There was always an excuse, whenever I asked."

"Never mind. I'll find her."

When he awoke next day, the morning was brisk and clear. Shining through the closed shutters, the sun fell across their bed in zebra stripes. Beside him, Leonore snuggled closer and crooned a sleepy good morning. He turned and gathered her gently into his arms. She opened her eyes and her smile told him all he needed to know. She pressed against him. He responded happily and they made gentle love, almost passionless and selflessly generous.

He left the Villa directly after breakfast while Leonore closed her door firmly against her sisters, in order to write to Clementine Bielska.

Villa Belleguardo,
Florence, March 1888

Dearest Clementine,

I am so happy and I feel I must write to tell you about it at once! First of all, though, dearest, I must beg you not to be worried about receiving a letter from me. For months now, we haven't had any reason to believe that the police are still interested in us. And, in any case, we are very respectable persons, Paul and I, but I will tell you about that in a moment.

First, my dear, I must tell you that I miss you more than I can say. I miss you when I'm sad and need your sympathy. I miss you even more when I'm happy, like I am today, and want to share my happiness with you. Believe me, it's always you I want to share it with. There never can be anyone else in my life quite like you.

Now, my dear, I have some very, very good news. I'm pregnant and I know I shall give my darling Paul the son he longs for, though he never says a word about it. The little one will be born in June. Unless you write and tell me not to, I shall let you know all about it when the time comes.

My next news is almost more important than that, and only someone who knows me as you do can possibly understand why I say that. Paul has just returned from a long visit to Estonia — the Baron has been very ill. Paul told me the details — he doesn't want me to worry my head about it (isn't that sweet?) but it's something to do with plans they have for the Estate and Paul is going to raise the necessary capital in Paris. I thank God this will be the end of the restless life we've been leading here in Florence. This is something I would never admit to anyone else. I don't know how to express my joy that we will be going to live in Paris. We shan't move until after the baby is born, of course. Paul has arrangements to make before we do but, Clementine...oh, my dearest Clementine, won't it be wonderful?

And what else do I have to tell you? Something equally marvelous. Paul brought Rachel and Ida back with him. They think Florence is heaven. Paul has been taking them everywhere and showing them everything. Now he is arranging for them to learn French and every-thing else for the move to Paris. Oh, my dear, dear friend...I am so happy. We are living like a family again, but it's a family not quite complete.

My dear, my heart aches for you. I want you with me. Apart from that I don't know what to say. It's so long since I had any news. I know nothing at all about you. But you must know you will always have my best wishes, don't you? I pray that you are well and happy; your young man also. Does he still have great success in his profession? And do you still go to the Doma I wonder? It all seems so long ago now but, believe me, I shall never ever forget any of your many kind-nesses to me when I was ill.

Your ever loving friend,

Leonore von Hagen."

While Leonore wrote her letter, Paul enjoyed the freshness of the morning. He walked energetically along the Lungarno with elastic steps. His eyes searched the street and every doorway, titillating his eagerness to see her by taunting himself that there was no chance that she would be there. She could not be there this morning; it was too cold for her to be sitting and painting. He would have to leave a mes-sage with Spadebeard at the Cafe San Matteo.

He continued in cheerful hopefulness, nevertheless and, at last, he saw her. She was sitting on her low sketching stool, a little below the Ponte Vecchio, working on an impression of the Ponte di Santa Trinita in the glory of the morning sunshine. He stopped a yard or so off, afraid to go forward yet reluctant to turn away. His topcoat suddenly felt too heavy and his legs in danger of collapse. Nonetheless he savoured these moments, watching her. She was the first to speak.

"At last, my dear," she said, sensing him without turning round. "I hoped you would come to me."

"How are you?" He hated himself for sounding lame.

"I've seen you on the Lungarno and across the bridge many times...with Leonore's sisters."

"I didn't see you," he mumbled unconvincingly.

"It doesn't matter...not in the least." There was lightness in her voice that told him she meant it. He came forward and for the first time looked at her face to face.

"I knew you'd understand."

"Of course, my friend. Between us everything is understood, n'est ce pas? But tell me about Leonore. Is she still well?"

"Very well."

"Paul...Paul dear...when the baby comes, you will be very gentle with her, won't you?"

"Of course. You know me so well. Do you think I wouldn't be?"

"She wants so much to give you a son."

He stared at her in unbelief.

"If it's a little girl, you must seem to be very, very happy about it. You mustn't let her think you're disappointed."

He raised his arms as though to embrace her, but let them drop. "Oh, my dear, dear friend, how good you are."

She gave him a gentle smile and concentrated on her palette once more.

"Don't work any more today. I want to be with you. I want to talk," he said.

She shivered and looked towards the bridge. "All right. It's cold here. And I can't do any more to this today; the sun's already too high."

"We'll go to the San Matteo."

"We can't talk there…too many ears."

"You know somewhere else?"

She laughed. "Florence is full of places."

They went in a cab to the Hotel Olympia by the railway bridge across the Viale Fratelli Rosselli. They were greeted enthusiastically by an elderly Russian woman who gathered Lydmilla Fyodorovna into her arms, kissed her cheeks and crossed her forehead. She smiled broadly at Paul and curtsied before urging them to follow her to a bedroom on the first floor. "I bring you coffee right away," she said in basic Italian. Directly the door closed behind her they moved towards each other and embraced.

CHAPTER 2

▼

1888

Margarethe sat quietly fuming in her room. How dare Cecile assume she had no future other than a bovine existence at Estate Wirsberg, slaving to satisfy the ambitions of the von Aschenbauer family? She was heatedly composing in her mind a suitable reply to the letter when there was a commanding rap at the door. Frau von Blomberg came in.

"We are about to dine, Margarethe."

Margarethe was suddenly amused. This personal summons, so unusual, so unexpected, must surely be curiosity-inspired. She didn't reply immediately.

"Did you hear what I said, Margarethe? Your uncle is waiting." The old lady's eyes flashed round the room, seeking the mysterious letter.

"Very well, Aunt. I won't be a moment."

Her aunt's going was reluctant. When the door closed, Margarethe moved to the mirror and patted her hair, although it needed no attention. It was her face she was looking at, pale-skinned, thin-lipped with sharp grey eyes and recent telltale lines at the mouth. Her usual black dress with its narrow fillet of white around the throat accentuated the stark bloodlessness of her appearance. For some moments she stared as at an old acquaintance, accepting what she saw without criticism.

As she stood there, cold seeped into the room as it had already seeped into her life. She could never go home; Loff would never part with Channah. She saw no cure for his madness, nor for Paul's. But what was her own alternative? To remain here, her aunt's unofficial, unpaid companion, shutting her ears to the old lady's diatribes and her uncle's scant witticisms, visiting the Refuge and serving coffee to visitors, feeling all the while the need to apologise for her existence. The prospect sounded no trumpets of enthusiasm in her soul.

For an instant she experienced quite unaccustomed self-pity and was frightened to the very centre of her being. "It isn't fair," she muttered, yet even as she said it she knew it was possible to change her life. All around her, society was shuddering, shaking, rocking and cleaving in the stresses of a new renaissance. This time the renaissance was significant for women as well as for men. Kinder, Kuche, Kirke was no longer the only way. Many other gates were opening, and one she knew was already ajar for her.

She told them in the heavy silence that passed for companionship when the von Blombergs were alone. They were sitting with their coffee after their Spartan military meal. Uncle Otto rustled the pages of his newspaper. Aunt Johanna worked at a cluster of blowsy pink cabbage roses stretched across her embroidery frame. Margarethe's words pierced this resounding quiet like pistol shots.

"I am going to be married, Aunt."

Her uncle's paper rustled calmly; he clearly wasn't listening. Her aunt was. The penetration of her needle was resisted as though it had hit a slab of concrete among those roses.

"Really?" The needle recommenced its progress. "You do, I suppose, intend telling us the name of your prospective bridegroom?"

"It's Pastor Behrendorf."

The old lady laid her frame aside. "Pastor Behrendorf has actually asked you to marry him?"

"Yes, Aunt."

"And what did you say?"

"He asked whether he might speak to my uncle."

"Did he indeed! And what did you say?"

"I said I wasn't sure."

"No, well, one needs to be sure, of course." She nodded with grave understanding before asking in a sharper tone:

"And when did you and the Pastor find time for all of this?"

"About a month ago. We..."

"A month ago! A whole month and you've said nothing? That was hardly honest, Margarethe."

"I wasn't sure. I needed to think."

"And your letter this afternoon settled the question?"

"No, not exactly."

The old lady looked disappointed and continued probing. "Where did this interesting conversation take place, may I ask?"

"At the Refuge. Or, rather, on the way home one afternoon. It was one of the days you had a headache and I went alone. Pastor Behrendorf escorted me home. He proposed in the carriage as we were crossing the Pregel Bridge."

"But you were not sure then and now, suddenly, you are."

"Yes."

The old lady snorted. "Herr Oberst!" The drawing room seemed suddenly to have stretched to parade ground size. "Do you hear, Sir? Pastor Behrendorf wishes to speak to you about your niece."

"Eh? What does the fellow want?" The Oberst spoke from behind his paper.

"He wants to marry her."

"Good God!" He put aside his newspaper, evidently irritated. "Tell him to talk to her brother. He's the fellow he ought to talk to."

"No!" Margarethe's voice was determined. "Nothing I do now concerns my brother. Nor will it ever."

Her uncle stared, then demanded with a rough-toned curiosity, "Do you want to marry him?"

"Yes."

"There you are, then, there's nothing more to be said." He took up his newspaper but his wife wasn't yet ready to allow him to read.

"Indeed!" she snapped. "There's still a great deal to be said. It isn't at all a suitable match. Oh, I agree, on the surface he seems a decent enough person, though rather old. But he's been here less than a year and we know nothing at all about him."

"I know all I need, Aunt."

"What do you know? His family background? Connections? You are being foolish, Margarethe. The von Hagens have never been in the habit of marrying just anybody, you know."

"I'm doing the right thing, Aunt. I've prayed about it."

"That's as may be. I am not satisfied. And people will talk."

"People need know nothing about it. We shall be going away."

"Indeed!"

"We shall be married in Hamburg. Pastor Behrendorf has an old college friend with a church there."

"You won't like Hamburg at all. We were posted there…when was it now?…fifteen, sixteen years ago? I didn't care for it."

"We're not staying in Hamburg. We're going to Africa."

"Africa!" The old lady screamed.

"Africa!" the old gentleman echoed. "What do you want to go there for?"

"You can't Margarethe, you can't! You've no idea what it's like."

"We are going to Cameroon," Margarethe continued imperturbably. "The steamship will take us from Hamburg to Fernando Po and we shall cross from there to the mainland with a local trader."

"You seem to have worked out every detail."

"You have had many of your headaches lately, Aunt. The Pastor and I have had many opportunities to talk."

The old lady flushed and said nothing. The Herr Oberst demanded irritably, "What the devil does the fellow want to go to Africa for?"

"He has been accepted by the Lutheran Missionary Society. He feels it is his duty. There is still slavery there…unspeakable secret societies…poor creatures wallowing in sin because no one has ever shown them the light."

"Damn all that! What does Africa matter? The East! That's where he should be going. Do your missionising in the Polish provinces…Russia! The East is what counts these days…it always has. That's where you'll find the real heathen, though none of you will admit it because they've got white faces. You can't trust the Slavs; everybody knows that. They're sub-human."

"Uncle, Pastor Behrendorf says we Germans also have a duty to block the British in Africa. They're over-running everywhere and shutting us out."

"Huh!" The Herr Oberst took up his newspaper and straightened it noisily, having no interest in German expansion anywhere but in Eastern Europe.

"I know you will be there as the Pastor's wife, Margarethe, but what exactly do you expect you will be doing?" her Aunt asked quite mildly.

Margarethe unconsciously straightened her shoulders. "I shall assist the Pastor in every way I possibly can, Aunt. And I'll do all I can to educate the women and, particularly, the children. I can teach them hygiene. And I shall start a school. They will have to learn German if they are to improve their condition. The Pastor has already begun to compose a German dictionary for them and I shall help him with that."

"If anybody's taking Africa seriously," her uncle barked, "it's troops and guns we should be sending there, not missionaries and dictionaries. We only went in there because the place had fallen into anarchy…everybody fighting everybody else. Now they're fighting us…and not without British help, I assure you. It won't be a picnic, I can promise you that…not for that Pastor of yours, nor for you."

"Oh Margarethe, my poor, poor Margarethe, haven't you been happy with us? Why must you do this? Is it some kind of martyrdom you're looking for?"

"Martyrdom?" Margarethe clasped her hands until her knuckles showed white and let out a short, bitter laugh. "My whole life has been martyrdom, Aunt. I never chose it and it's made me old and sour beyond my years. But I've always tried to do what I saw as my duty and it's too late to change the habit of a lifetime."

CHAPTER 3

▼

1888

Sonia Eudora was born in June, an unattractive, jaundiced baby with red-rimmed eyes, a nose that needed constant attention and a whimper that only ceased on the few occasions she slept. She disappointed her mother but her father was extravagantly pleased with her. Dorothea was healthily curious. She crept softly to the cot, staring at the baby with wide, solemn eyes. As though testing a new substance that might be dangerous, she would poke Sonia's cheek or stomach with a tentative finger. Strangely, the baby responded, turning her head and momentarily ceasing her moans. Carmella and Augustina laughed and clapped their hands. They raised these demonstrations of sibling affection into minor miracles. Dorothea enjoyed their approval and took more interest than ever in her small sister. As a result, the adults made a fuss of her and said how sweet she was. Dorothea was delighted to have found so easy a way of attracting attention and pleasing everybody.

Rachel and Ida took less interest in the little one than Leonore reckoned they should. They weren't behaving at all as young Jewish women were expected to when there was a baby in the family. But they had been in Florence long enough then, to be self-consciously aware of developing into the young ladies their beloved brother-in-law desired them to be. They had little time for anything else.

Lydmilla Fyodorovna had found teachers for them: she herself took them three times a week for drawing and art appreciation in the Pitti; twice a week they went to a dancing master who pivoted on a cane when he was giving a demonstration and made them laugh a lot; a dapper young man with polished black hair and a neatly clipped goatee taught them French with an exaggerated accent; a bulky, lumpy lady took them to visit churches and promised, every week, that next time she would take them to the Piazza della Signoria to see the copy of the naked David; and a formidable lady with a limp and a working knowledge of no language other than Russian schooled them in deportment. All these were Russian, of course, exiled from their homeland for a variety of political crimes their set regarded as heroic. Paul and Leonore trusted their friend's judgment. They were too much concerned with their own affairs to make detailed enquiries.

Leonore clutched at the life of the newborn weakling with desperation. She was gratified by Paul's obvious affection for the child and encouraged Dorothea's interest.

Paul and Lydmilla Fyodorovna met regularly once a week for reports on Rachel's and Ida's progress. These meetings, generally at the Hotel Olympia, brought new depths to their intimacy. As the weeks passed, they spoke less of the girls and more of the world in which they lived, and the circumstances that, in various ways, constrained their lives. He became anxious because she looked ill, her skin pale, her eyes hollow. The strain of looking after her dying husband was too much for her. He offered her money but she denied her problems and laughed his assistance aside. He was frustrated. His anxiety on her behalf grew until one day in early autumn; she met him with a lighter step and a brighter eye.

"Volodya has gone to the mountains," she panted, breathless with happiness.

He stared at her, incredulous.

"I couldn't tell you before, I didn't know. It was all so quick." Her voice broke, and she began to weep with happiness.

"Try to calm down, my dear. Tell me what's happened."

"I can't believe it. All my friends…the people who are coaching Rachel and Ida…they've put aside what you've been paying them month-by-month. And they've had collections at the San Matteo and a couple of other places where Russians go. There was enough for Volodya to go to the mountains…at least for the winter. Aren't people wonderful?"

He agreed that they were but couldn't squash the stirrings of jealousy because she would never accept help from him. "Yes, people are wonderful," he said without meaning it. "But I'd already offered. And I've no doubt I could have afforded it better than any of them."

"Yes, yes of course you could, my dear. But don't you see…? It…it had to happen like this." She laughed. "We're all Russians. It's the Russian way."

"I know it," he said, and took her into his arms before sending the old woman out for champagne.

That evening, the atmosphere in the Villa Belleguardo was particularly cheerful, without any great effort on Paul's part. Rachel and Ida sat slightly apart, giggling together. They were learning enough about life to flutter their eyelids at the young men who openly admired them when they walked across the Piazza Santa Maria Novella. The Contessa and Madame d'Orangeville sat by Leonore, admiring the baby and laughing at Dorothea's performance. They laughed even louder when Paul took Sonia out of her cot and Dorothea angrily pummeled his legs to punish him for daring to touch her baby.

With tears of laughter still shining on her cheeks Leonore suddenly said:

"Now that her husband's gone to the mountains, we can't let Lydmilla Fyodorovna go on living alone in town, Paul. She should move in with us. There's plenty of room. And we owe her so much."

Paul looked askance and nodded non-committally. Leonore took his nod for agreement. "I'll write to her before I go to bed, and you can deliver it in the morning, darling," she said.

CHAPTER 4

▼

1888

The first sharp wind of the season was blowing out of Siberia, through the forests and across the meadows of Baron Loff's estate in Estonia. Window shutters rattled, fires burned erratically with sudden bursts of undisciplined flame as the draught caught them. The Baron's footsteps crackled as he walked through the early morning grass. In the village, the women watched slyly as the men blew on their hands for warmth and their blood rose as they contemplated the delights of the short days and long nights ahead.

The Baron was in his dining room, straight-backed, square-shouldered as ever, his empty sleeve tucked neatly into his jacket pocket. His golden hair and beard had lost their colour with the loss of his arm and his face was deep-rutted. His grey eyes were cheerless, contemplating a distance farther off than ever they had before.

Channah Litvak sat across the table. She still dressed entirely in black and moved as silently as ever. She had, though, acquired greater confidence since Margarethe had left the house and since the Baron had surrendered the secrecy of his early lust for her and had taken her to his bed.

Discretion he would have considered beneath his dignity. The house servants knew about the affair but dared say nothing outright now that Channah was the undisputed mistress of the Estate. They gossiped in the tavern, nevertheless, and whenever Channah went to the village alone she was spat at and insulted. The village women called her "filthy Jew" and "His Excellency's whore." The men eyed her lasciviously. She never told the Baron about any of this. It was no more and no less than she expected. She was content to be what she was.

The Baron threw a letter across the table. "She's mad," he grunted. "And she's given us no return address, of course."

Channah recognised Margarethe's well-drilled Gothic script:

Dear Brother,

This is to inform you that I am married. My husband and I have been undergoing instruction with the Lutheran Missionary Society and we shall be leaving for Cameroon at the end of the week. Henceforth will you discontinue sending my allowance to Aunt Johanna and send it instead to Frau Pastor Behrendorf, Lutheran Missionary Society, Dresdener Allee, Berlin. They will know exactly where I am.

I pray God to keep you from further error and endow you with His wisdom.

Frau Pastor Behrendorf.

Channah moved around the table to stand with her hand on the shoulder of the man she always called 'Your Excellency', even when they were making love. She never called him anything else because he never told her to.

"I'm very sorry," was all she could say.

"Don't be."

"If I had left, the Frau Baron would still be here."

"Perhaps. But I needed you, Channah. My sister needs misery to make her life bearable; I need you. We von Hagens inherited acid in our veins, not good red blood. You have nothing to regret."

"It's not right to say things like that, your Excellency. You're good and kind and so is the Captain."

"My brother! Humph! I often wonder who it was sired my brother."

Later that morning the tranquility of the house was disturbed by the arrival of a hasty carriage and the irascible voice of Count von Aschenbauer ordering a footman out of his way. He exploded into the room unannounced and apoplectic with anger.

"What the devil have you done now, von Hagen? Who are all those men?"

"What men?"

"A whole host of them coming this way. You'd better be prepared. They passed my place and, naturally, we stopped them and examined their passports. They say they're coming here. I've got them locked up in a barn."

"Ah!"

"You know about them?"

"Channah, my dear, the Count looks cold. Perhaps he'd like some schnapps…"

"Damn your schnapps, sir! Who are those ruffians? Answer me that."

Channah left the room smiling, but with her habitual silent calm.

"Miners I hope," the Baron said.

"Miners! And what the devil are miners doing here, sir?"

"They're going to mine my shale."

"What the devil! Where did you get them?"

"Kaluga Province."

"Kaluga province!"

"They're landless peasants and they're willing to work."

"Dear God, man! Don't you know what sort of reputation Kaluga peasants have? You can't trust a single one of them as far as a horse's tail."

Channah returned with the schnapps. The Count gulped his down and held out his glass for another. After the third in silent succession, his mood began to mellow. He almost laughed.

"Landless peasants! From Kaluga! Witch-worshipping hea- then...that's what you've got there, my friend. Miners, indeed!

"They were hand picked."

"Hand picked!" This time he gave into his amusement and laughed outright. "And who hand picked them?"

"Prince Krimovsky."

"Krimovsky? Do I know him?"

"He's a friend of mine from the Petersburg days. His Estate's in Kaluga Province, near Kirov."

"Huh! Landless peasants! What d'you expect them to know about mining?" He laughed again. More schnapps and he was beginning to see the whole thing as a stupendous joke.

"I've got a foreman coming from the Donetz."

"The Ruhr or the Saar...that's where the best miners come from, my friend."

"They'd cost me a lot more than these."

Von Aschenbauer exploded into raucous laughter again. "Of course they would. They are real miners. These you've got...God only knows! My dear friend, I always thought you were a Balt. But you're not. You're a Russian at heart. You throw money away. You try to save it in one direction only to throw it away in another. Exactly like a Russian." He collapsed into a chair, grinning at his own acuity. He held out a foot. "Come, Fräulein Litvak. Make an old man comfortable. Help me off with my boots."

The Baron rose immediately. "Boris will do that," he said. "Go and fetch him, Channah. And then I'm sure you must have something else to do."

Channah left the room. For a moment the Count looked dubious before deciding no insult was intended. Boris came in, presented his rear end to the Count and was literally booted away—twice. The Count let out a long sigh of satisfaction and helped himself to another drink. His cheeks were remarkably red in contrast to the Baron's pallid features.

"Well, well," he said, "you know best what you should do with your own money." He said it as though following a distant train of thought.

Von Hagen looked disinterested. It was not his custom to discuss money matters. "You must stay for lunch," he said, recognising that it was already the Count's intention to do so. "Meanwhile, you must excuse me while I find someone to bring you some more schnapps."

After their meal, at which Channah did not attend, the Count appeared partially drunk or partially sober, depending upon how well he was known by his interlocutor. His words were only slightly slurred but he adopted an air of confidentiality the Baron found distasteful. He leaned his chest against the table and gazed over-sincerely and over-long into his host's eyes.

"Do you ever think about the future, my friend?"

"Not often. Why?"

"You should, you know, you should. Damned problematic, the future. Always has been, always will be. You should think about it, you know."

"I find thinking about each day as it comes about as much as I can manage.

"That's all very well, but it's the future, you see. That's what you've got to think about. Look at it this way. I think about the future all the time. I have to. My brothers were all killed at various places with the army…damned fools! There's no one else…only my wife, my daughter and me. That's what I've got to think about—the future, you see."

The Baron didn't even nod to show he understood. He sighed, bored.

"What I have to think about it is what happens to Spasskoye when I go. My wife's hopeless, you know. Hasn't a brain in her head, to tell you the truth. And my daughter thinks she knows everything but she doesn't, you know. Just like her mother. Hopeless, the pair of them."

"I think perhaps this conversation has gone far enough, Count," the Baron warned, pushing his chair away from the table.

"No, no! Don't move! We have to sort it out sometime."

The Baron stood up and walked to the window. He looked out steadily, without seeing anything he saw. The Count spluttered on behind him.

"Cecile could always get married, of course. She could go off to Berlin or Petersburg and get herself a husband any time she wants. One of those fellows with a curl on his forehead, a moustache on his lip and a very narrow waist. Gamble the place away in no time. You won't…err…you won't mention this conversation to my wife, of course."

"I will not."

"Nervous. Very nervous woman. Quite hysterical at times."

The Baron turned around and faced his visitor. "My dear Count, we are old friends…very old friends, but…"

"That's just the point, you see. That's why we have to talk. The last time they attacked you it cost you your arm. Next time it could well be your life. You're in a worse situation than I am."

The Baron sighed again. "What is it you want to tell me, Count?"

"Me?" The Count looked as surprised as a puppet. "I don't want to tell you anything, my dear friend. I'm just saying you ought to be thinking about the future. Look! Look at it this way! Suppose that scallywag had killed you when he brought you off your horse. What would have happened to this place then?"

"My brother…" the Baron began.

"Your brother's no good at all. Forgive me old fellow, but you know what I say is the truth. He doesn't know anything about managing the Estate. He's too tainted with western ideas. And your peasants would never accept his wife as the new Frau Baroness. Your sister…"

"My sister doesn't have to be considered. I had a letter from her today. She's married."

"Good God! Who to? Anyone we know?"

"No. He's a Lutheran pastor. They're going out to Cameroon as missionaries."

"Good God!" This time the Count's surprise was entirely genuine. He was silent, but only for a moment. "Well, then, don't you see what I'm saying? You must think about the future, man! You've got responsibilities. You see what I mean?"

"No, I'm afraid I don't."

"The eldest son of the eldest son. You have to produce a boy, don't you see? Someone you can bring up and train to take over when you go."

"I see." It was said with frigid calm.

"Of course, we all understand and we make no judgments about the Litvak girl."

"That's enough."

"You have to face facts, old fellow. Fräulein Litvak's like your brother's wife...she'd never be accepted. But there is someone else, not so very far away, who'd have you like a shot, given the chance. Pretty...rich...she'd bring her own Estate with her..."

"Count von Aschenbauer!" The Baron stood rigid with fury, his knuckles clasped white. "This is no subject for a conversation between gentlemen, sir!" He turned abruptly. "I'll send Boris to help with your boots," he barked as he left the room.

Later, Ants was sent with the wagon to fetch the men released from the Spaskoye barn while Channah took the caleche to Pastor Vikkers' house. He was instructed to arrange for all householders in the village to meet with the Baron by the cross frame outside the church at sundown. When the time came, Father Tikhon stood, hairy and grinning, among them. As though by magic he had already heard of the arrival of the men from the Donetz. He was very happy. After all this time, playing with the village children and making himself agreeable to the adults, he now had the nucleus of a congregation. Close to him, though she had no reason but curiosity for being there, stood a woman alone. None of the villagers would stand shoulder to shoulder with her; she was thoroughly isolated in the little crowd. She wore her scarf pulled high over her face until only her eyes were visible as though to hide her identity. But the villagers knew very well who she was; they called her Father Tikhon's whore and warned their children never to go near her. With the natural sympathy of the outsider for the outsider, Channah Litvak was the only person in the area to give any sign that Father Tikhon's whore existed as a human being. She would often drive along the grass track to Father Tikhon's church to give the woman a parcel of food from the Baron's kitchen. She knew it was a purposeless gesture; the foolish woman hated her even more for these generous advances. She immediately gave every gift to her lover and felt satisfying revenge when she'd done so.

The purpose of the assembly by the cross frame was to arrange the billeting of the Russians among the villagers. The foreman was allotted to Pastor Vikkers' house to distinguish his seniority. The rest were distributed among reluctant peasants who hadn't any common language with their obligatory guests. This was the moment at which Father Tikhon at last assumed official status in the village. He had Christ's injunction to "suffer the little children" in mind, perhaps. Not only had the good Baron gratuitously presented him with a flock; that flock was childlike in its ignorance that he comfortably transposed into innocence. He danced from group to group, telling them in Russian what the Barton was explaining to the villagers in Estonian. The lanky, broad-shouldered Russians in stinking sheepskins, with lustrous bovine eyes, matted beards and hair hanging to their shoulders, clustered to him as though their futures depended on it. The Baron addressed his Estonians abstractedly, his mind on other things. For the moment, he was glad to have his instructions so easily, speedily transmitted.

The next day, selected villagers were to take the strangers into the forest to cut timber for their hut—one long shed to accommodate them all. After that, they would need more timber to prop the mine at the spot the Barton and the foreman would decide. After that, the villagers were delighted to hear, what the Russians did would no longer be a concern of theirs. They could resume their own pattern of life, and the two groups could remain as distant from each other as they wished.

It was later, in the quiet of his own home, that the Baron's mind strayed into abstractions he had put aside earlier. While discussing the plan to bring in Russian workers to mine the shale, neither of the von Hagen brothers considered their future immigrants as less malleable than their own Estonian peasants. The newcomers would be told what to do. They would establish a routine. They would work as little as possible for the money they were paid. Eventually they would learn sufficient Estonian to socialise with the local peasants in the tavern and become an accepted part of the community. There would be some drunkenness, naturally, a few fights, some fornication; nothing more serious. There was no stealing among the peasants of Estate Wirsberg; nobody had anything worth stealing. So long as the Baron and his foreman maintained discipline among the Russians as it was maintained among the native peasants, what could go wrong?

It was the sudden, energetic appearance of Father Tikhon at this afternoon's meeting that caused the Baron's present disquiet. Father Tikhon, without converts, still playing big brother to the village boys, had no more significance than any other village eccentric. Neither von Hagen imagined he might become a focal point in their plans; that he might create out of a few, lonely, confused foreign peasants a group that could cohere, achieve confidence and independence. It would be possible for them to do so because the village contained what dark people most needed: a leader whom by instinct and tradition they would without question love, trust, admire and obey.

How to checkmate Father Tikhon and his dangerous potential? The Baron considered the slight possibility—their relationship had always been amiable enough—that the problem might be sympathetically understood by Prince Krasnov. He had power enough locally to get the priest officially removed. From an official viewpoint, doubtless, Father Tikhon's sojourn in Wirsberg had been a failure; he had made conversions to the Orthodox Church, he had taught none of the villagers Russian; and he had not, apparently, extended the range of village loyalty beyond what they owed to the von Hagen family. The Tsar was still as remote to them as the Angel Gabriel. The villagers of Estate Wirsberg were typical targets for Petersburg's policy of Russianisation, Orthodoxy and Autocracy. Clearly, Father Tikhon was a failure. Prince Krasnov must, inevitably, recognise Father Tikhon's culpability and, in the line of duty, petition to have the priest transferred. Another would come—eventually. But it could take months for him to arrive and by then, the Baron determined, his Russians would be thoroughly disciplined according to his own ordinances.

Nevertheless, he would write to Paul and inform him that they had a changed social situation on their hands.

CHAPTER 5

▼

1888

The paddle steamer "Kronprinz" was having a rough passage through the North Sea and, according to the more sadistic-minded members of the crew, worse was to be expected in the Bay of Biscay. Margarethe loathed every member of the crew she'd so far met, including the Captain, a coarse-tongued man with gold teeth and filthy fingernails. He showed the Pastor no respect and that in Margarethe's view, was almost a cardinal sin.

Tonight, while the boat rocked and wrenched her, she knelt in her coarse calico nightgown, her hands clutching the bunk for support, her bible open on the rough blanket under which, should the Lord be willing, she might eventually sleep.

In the bunk behind her, the Pastor was already asleep, his breathing as regular as the squeak of the lamp, swinging over her head. She had already discovered that her husband could sleep in any circumstances, but not with her in the accepted sense of the term.

On their arrival in Hamburg for the marriage, he had taken a room for them each in a cheap hotel near the docks. Immediately after the ceremony they had taken the first train to Berlin. At the Missionary Training School he had elected to sleep in the unmarried men's' dormitory and she slept with the single women. On the "Kronprinz" she looked at the two narrow bunks in the cabin to which they were assigned and mused on what would happen later. Her husband had everything rehearsed. They undressed, back to back, at either end of the footway between the bunks. This maneuver, more complicated and therefore lengthy on her side than on his, triumphantly completed in modesty, she was motioned to kneel by her bunk. He then pleaded with the Lord in his own, especially aggressive tone of voice, with which she was already too familiar. Tonight, he was tired after traveling and the Lord's audience was therefore short. He was required to keep them clean in this cankerous world, until He saw fit to take them to Himself; to prosper their endeavours on His behalf in the virgin fields and forests of the African Continent; and to keep the pair of them free from all carnal and licentious tendencies. They both then stood up. He placed his hands roughly on her shoulders and scratched her cheek with his lips. "The Kiss Of Peace," he said shortly and climbed into his bunk.

Tonight she knelt, thin from the Training School diet and seasickness, green-featured and desolate. This, she acknowledged to herself, was her duty—to love, to honour and to obey the arid stick of a man she now called 'husband'; to suffer the tortures of this sea voyage which were to her an undreamed of, ghastly initiation; and to lay down her life, if necessary poisoned by snakes, eaten by crocodiles, sacrificed horribly by natives, wracked by fever if that were His will. This was her duty. All was her duty."

Significantly, her Bible lay open on her bunk at the Book of Job. She opened her eyes to it and mouthed the words silently, so as not to waken the Pastor.

"When I lay down, I say: when shall I arise and the night be gone?, and I am full of tossing to and fro until the dawning of the day.

My flesh is clothed with worms and clods of dust; my skin is broken and become loathsome.

My days are swifter than a weaver's shuttle and spent without hope."

She shuddered. She shuddered partly on account of the meaning of the words she saw before her; she shuddered partly on account of the reality of her own situation. "God help me! Dear God, Give me strength!" She muttered the words noiselessly before closing the Book and climbing into her bunk.

Prone, she lay with her empty stomach grinding agonizingly with nausea and watching the swing of the lamp above her. She closed her eyes tightly; she closed her hands into fists; she forced rigidity into the muscles of her arms and legs. "Stand still and consider the wondrous works of God," she urged herself.

CHAPTER 6

▼

1888

Sonia was tiny enough still to need breast-feeding when Paul first went to Paris. Leonore accepted the idea of his departure with equanimity. She loved him to distraction and felt a flush of excitement whenever he came into the room. But suckling her child brought her a calmness she knew in no other circumstances. She and Paul lived as husband and wife and joyously shared the large bed with the lion's-claw feet. But the children were now a major part of her life. She tended Sonia hour after hour, devoting much more time to this little one than ever she had to Dorothea. Under this constant tenderness Sonia flourished. Her face acquired a healthy colour, her flesh grew dimpled. Augustina watched with silent jealousy. She was hardly allowed to touch the baby and, these days, was rejected unmercifully by Dorothea who now felt quite grown up. She and her mother did everything together that Sonia could possibly need, and her possessive feelings for the little one grew stronger day by day.

Over and beyond this involvement with her daughters, Leonore watched with immeasurable happiness the flowering of her sisters. Rachel and Ida were daily becoming more sophisticated and by now quite outpaced herself. She knew it without envy. They were developing exactly as her darling Paul and her dearest Luyshka desired. They posed with ease as well-bred young ladies, Ida as well as Rachel in spite of her Semitic looks. In them, Leonore found absolution for turning her back on her parents' traditions, for marrying 'out' and for turning her back on the old faith.

Moving away from Zamenhofa Street had opened doors onto a wider world—a wider world that, itself, was changing every moment. Suddenly, the future belonged to anyone who had courage and strength to create it for themselves. There was even talk of a secular state for Jews somewhere in Africa, not even in the Promised Land. Leonore had made her choice. She accepted the new world gladly; accepted it for herself, for her children and for her sisters. She daily acquired new confidence about the life she imagined she would be living when she and Paul moved their home to Paris.

So she accepted Paul's news that he was going away and couldn't tell her when he would be back, with cheerful understanding. Her mood didn't change when he told her, a little breathlessly, that Lydmilla Fyodorovna would be traveling with him.

They made the arrangement during one of their meetings at the Hotel Olympia. She greeted him when he arrived with unusual exciting news and told him she had decided to leave Florence.

"It's for my poor Volodya you see," she explained. "He is so much better now he's living in the mountains. But it's very expensive to keep him there and I can't earn enough here. He must stay in the sanatorium if there's to be any hope of his getting better, so if I'm to make enough to keep him there, I have to try my luck somewhere else."

"Where?" He was relieved. He had come this afternoon with the self-same method and was glad not to be seen as the first to sever their relationship.

"Somewhere just as popular with American and English tourists as Florence, but where the ones go who have more money to spend. Oh, my dear, dear friend, I shall miss you so much," she added coming forward and kissing him chastely on the lips. "I can't possibly bring him back to that room now," she went on immediately. "It would kill him."

"You don't have to do that. We've both said there's room for you at the Villa."

"I know, I know. You're wonderfully kind. But the Sanatorium is best, and I need the money to keep him there."

"Anyway, it's an extraordinary coincidence you should be going away. That's what I came to tell you today. I'm going away myself."

"No!" She laughed but there was a glint of suspicion in her eyes and he noticed it, faint though it was.

"Really, it's a genuine business trip." He laughed too, but his laugh and hers hadn't the same motivation.

"Where will you go?"

"Paris."

She caught her breath in surprise. "Now that really is extraordinary," she said. "Oh, my dear friend, it's destiny. I'm going to Paris myself." She laughed and he laughed and again they laughed for different reasons. He had already told her that he would be going to Paris eventually. His laugh now held a note of triumph. His need for her was not so naked as hers for him.

They moved closer. He clasped her and swung her round and round until she begged him to stop.

"My own dear Lydmilla Fyodorovna," he panted when they'd settled, out of breath, on the edge of the bed. "What else can we do? As you say, this is destiny. We must go together."

Leonore was not in the least disturbed. From her parents' example she had seen what a perfect marriage was like. She and Paul had a perfect marriage. Perfect marriages held no place for infidelity. Indeed, she was pleased that Paul would have a sensible companion. He had been away from her before, but only into places that were familiar to both of them. Paris was strange and not a little frightening. From newspapers she had some idea of its size and of the numbers crowing its streets. The magnificence of its shops and carriages, she knew, was unchallenged anywhere in the world. Its theatres were brilliant, the beauty of its women unequalled. Paris, the chosen goal of hundreds of refugees from her own homeland had no rival. Above all, it made no distinction between Jew and Gentile. It was the golden Elysium where gaiety and glamour, beauty and intelligence dwelt forever in happy union.

"I shall miss you both so much Luyshka dear," she said on one of Lydmilla Fyuodorovna's frequent visits. "I'm glad you're going together. Nonetheless, I wish you weren't away at the same time. When Paul was with his brother, your visits meant so much to me."

"I know, I know. But it must be so, for my poor Volodya's sake."

"And you'll be there to take care of him," Leonore smiled. "Send him back safely."

Her friend smiled and squeezed her hand.

"And you'll write to me? Tell me what you're both doing?"

"My dear, I don't suppose, once we step off the train, we'll ever see each other. Paul will spend all his time with stuffy businessmen. I shall be working, too. They say there are more painters along the Boulevard St. Germain than anywhere in the world. And you can't move in Montmartre for tripping over their easels."

"You'll write to me about the fashions, though. You must promise to write and tell me all about the fashions!"

Once the announcement was made, the pace of their life quickened in a round of farewell parties.

"I know one often meets with Russians who have made spectacular mesalliances," the Contessa di Beltrano mused.

"Where else would one meet them, other than here in Florence," Ottolie d'Orangeville remarked.

"It is certainly unusual for them ever to be married," the Contessa continued.

"Indeed, dear," Ottolie d'Orangeville agreed. "But here in Florence…" She left the thought inconclusive. "In Paris, on the other hand…"

"Ah yes, Paris!" The Contessa breathed the word with a serpentine hiss. "Your own dear Paris is quite different of course, Ottolie. Paris could present the marriage of our young friends with many problems."

"Perhaps there are problems already, dear, and that's why he's apparently chosen to go without his wife."

"One hears such stories about that Left Bank of yours, Ottolie. But artists, harlots and pimps will hardly loan him money, which is the reason he's going there in the first place, so everybody says."

"He'll be meeting bankers and financiers, of course. But…there are twenty-four hours in each day, my dear."

"And he won't be spending every one of them plotting to find a fortune."

"Indeed not."

"The circumstances are all there to place a great strain on that marriage." The Contessa said it with purring satisfaction. "Such a pity. Whatever happens will happen in Paris instead of here in Florence."

"Oh, it may happen here even yet." Madame d'Orangeville moved closer for confidentially. "I hear he won't be traveling alone."

"Oh?"

"That Russian painter woman, whatever her name is…the one who's always there with dear Leonore whenever he's away…she's off to Paris too, they say. By the very same train, probably. It's almost too much of a coincidence, don't you think."

Leonore pleaded the children as her excuse for not going to the station when Paul left. She said goodbye to him quite cheerfully at the Villa. Paul met Lydmilla Fyodorovna at the steps of their railway carriage. She was a tousled figure in a mud-brown tussore costume and carrying a battered cardboard suitcase. A miscellany of further objects was tied to her portable easel. The sight of her made Paul laugh. She laughed too, not quite knowing why but feeling excited like a child going on holiday. By the time the train pulled out they were very happy together.

In Paris, Paul took rooms for them at the Hotel St. Petersburg in the rue Carmartin, close to the Madeleine and the Opera. It was a respectable establishment in one of the better parts of the town, notable enough for Paul's prestige, but not ostentatious. It was the class of hotel he need not be ashamed of when registering his arrival at the Russian Embassy. Lydmilla Fyodorovna protested that she couldn't afford to stay there, but Paul swept her arguments aside.

He called at the Embassy the following morning, though Lydmilla Fyuodorovna begged for a day or two sightseeing incognito first. Inside the building he was directed by a footman in a bottle-green frock-coat into an eighteenth-century salon elaborately decorated with gold leaf foliage across the ceiling and forbidding, naked female statues around the walls. He bowed and shook hands with a disinterested Councilor who respectfully promised whatever assistance he required while in Paris. He signed his name in the visitors' book and explained his business. The Councilor gave him names of people who might be of use, as well as an invitation to an ambassadorial reception later in the week.

Paul left well-pleased but still disturbed at Lydmilla Fyuodorovna's refusal to go to the Embassy with him. All Russian citizens were required to do so.

"I can't possibly, Paul."

"I really don't see why not."

"You know perfectly well! Volodya and I were activists. We were lucky to get out of Russia alive."

"But...This is Paris, my dear. You're quite safe here."

"We're not safe anywhere. Paul! Try to understand! When Volodya and I left Russia, we were wanted enemies of the State. Our names are on their list and they never forget...wherever you are...they never stop chasing you."

"Aren't you being a little over-dramatic, my dear?" he said, and sounded more patronising than he'd intended. "This is Paris...capital of the civilised world, not some fly-blown provincial Russian city."

She stamped her foot in a spasm of temper. "They take you from Paris. They take you wherever you are. But you'll never understand that. You can't. You pretend you're a liberal because you left the Army to marry a Jewess. But you're not. You are what you were born, Paul you'll never change. Well...go on! Go to your Embassy. Tell them about me if that's what you feel you have to do. I'm too tired to care any more. Just go to your Embassy and leave me alone."

He was happy on the way back to the hotel, and sorry that he'd upset her. He bought her some flowers. She was right, of course. She'd always lived on the other side of life. He went eagerly to her room. But she was gone. There was no note, no address where she might be found; only a pile of notes in scornful part-payment for her previous night's lodging.

CHAPTER 7

▼

1889

Paul's arrival in Paris was expedient. Paul needed money; Paris had money to spare. Peasants all over France were bringing out gold they'd hidden until it was no longer in danger of being requisitioned to pay reparations after the Franco-Prussian war. They were making it available at fair rates of interest. It was easy to find among them the menu people among whom stockholding was the new craze. To invest in the Wirsberg Shale Mining Company inspired dreams of the profits made by investors in the Suez Canal Company before the war.

Paris was throbbing with expectations. Next year would be the Centenary of the Revolution. There would be a Great Exhibition that would out-rival all Great Exhibitions anywhere in the world. Monsieur Eiffel was laying foundations for his Tower on the banks of the Seine—the Tower that would be the tallest building in the world, the planet's Eighth Wonder, in fact. And Buffalo Bill would be bringing his "Wild West Show" for everyone to see.

The names supplied by the disinterested young man in the Russian Embassy were surprisingly useful—particularly that of Henri de Cronach, the Paris representative of a Franco-German family of Jewish bankers. He was a small, precise man of sixty or so, with a halo of silver hair that looked as though he polished it every day. He spoke in staccato sentences and showed great interest in Paul when they met at the ambassador's reception. Perhaps he was intrigued that anyone should expect to be able to raise money for an industrial project anywhere so unlikely as Estonia.

"Put money in. Right project? Take money out! Put money in. Wrong project? Disaster!" he barked.

"This certainly won't be a disaster, Monsieur," Paul assured him easily. "Russia is beginning to move. She's acquiring new techniques...building factories...She's starting out on a new road."

"Good! Good!" The little man almost danced his excitement. "France too! Here too! It's a new world. You know Boulanger?"

"No, Monsieur."

"Must meet him. Man of the moment. New Napoleon."

"He sounds very interesting. I'd like to meet him," Paul said with rising curiosity.

"Charlatan, of course. All great men are. Ex-Army! Tripoli! Algiers! Paris! Commune! Great womaniser...wife, mistress...Too good looking, of course. Welsh Mother, I believe."

"Could I meet him?"

"I'll take you to the Chamber...introduce you."

"Thanks." Paul sounded as pleased as he could though he was more concerned with pleasing his host than with meeting this new political fireball.

"He'll teach you, young man. Clever. Very clever. All things to all men. Important for success in every field. Royalists, Republicans, Socialists...they all love him. Ridiculous. Everyone needs a symbol, though." It was said with an air almost of exasperation. "Some men follow a flag, some a drum beat, others a man. He's the flag, the drumbeat, the hero all in one. All France needs him. Man of the hour for everyone. Revenge! That's what it's all about. Vengeance for the lost provinces."

"I've seen the Strasbourg monument on the Place de la Concorde. You can hardly see it for fresh funeral wreaths but...it's almost ten years ago now. Won't they ever forget?"

"They mustn't. Shame and hatred unite them. People need to feel united. That's Boulanger's strength. He helps them to feel united. Come and see me in my office, young man."

With de Cronach's good will the loan was easily arranged. Russia was France's safeguard against another attack by Germany. Whose money it was that eventually arrived for Loff in the St. Petersburg State Bank, Paul didn't know. He was certain, though, that none of it came from de Cronach's own pocket.

The success of his financial mission raised Paul's spirits and encouraged his enjoyment of the city's mood. Boulanger excitement was everywhere. There were processions of the General's supporters through the major streets, Boulanger placards on every available wall space. These placards were covered, as soon as they appeared, by the posters of his opponents. These, in turn, were recovered by the Boulanger protagonists. If any length of wall space remained uncovered, the reason was probably that bill-posters of dissenting factions were fighting in the streets too fiercely to carry out their official purpose.

All this amused Paul greatly. He wandered the city streets and wrote three times a week to tell Leonore how much he loved her. On fine days he scoured the Left Bank and the Place du Tertre, hoping to see Lydmilla Fyodorovna, but he never did. He visited Les Halles and drank scalding coffee at six in the morning, savouring the freshness of the produce that would feed Paris for another day. He admired "La Gioconda" and the Venus de Milo in the Louvre. He had a heavy attack of conscience after he'd taken off a day to drive to Versailles. And all the time he wished Leonore were with him and felt that his reactions and emotions were only semi-valid because she wasn't there to make them complete.

In three weeks, thanks to Henri de Cronach's collaboration, Paul was ready to go home. Before he left he went to the rue de la Paix to buy the sumptuous present he felt Leonore deserved. Should it be jewellery?…some very expensive perfume?…lace?…a gown? Indeed, why shouldn't it be all of these? He stood in the street in the winter sunshine while carriages rolled by, their horses strutting nobly, their drivers and postillions straight-backed, their women passengers splendid and beautiful in pink gowns. Pink was the colour of Boulangism and anybody with a claim to being fashionable that year.

The magnetism of the passing show decided for Paul what he should buy: a pink gown, some pink perfume—Leonore used so little that anything would please her—and a string of pink pearls. When he explained to the pretty vendeuse that he required a necklace of unblemished pink pearls, she called the proprietor who approached him almost on hands and knees. Whatever Monsieur required, naturally. Monsieur would be more comfortable seated in an inner room. Monsieur would take coffee. At such short notice and for such a requirement, Monsieur would be patient while colleagues were contacted, perhaps…?

A chilly afternoon was wasting into darkness when the deal was struck and it was arranged for the pearls to join the perfume and the gown in Paul's room at the Hotel St. Petersburg. After much hand-shaking and good wishes and entreaties that he would call again, Paul stepped into the gas-lit street and was immediately overcome by another cascade of overwhelming friendliness.

"It is! It can't be! But it is! What joy! Oh, Monsieur! How extraordinary! How extraordinary that we two should meet again, and here in Paris. It is! My dear Monsieur, you really must not tell me that it isn't! My friend! It is my friend from the Vienna Express, isn't it?"

Paul involuntarily shuddered. He recognised the man immediately.

"You do not remember me, Monsieur…" The man shook his head in playful reproach.

Paul squared his shoulders. "But of course…of course I remember you. It's…" he paused, embarrassed.

"Arturo Martinelli," the man encouraged him. "And I have been in your debt…"

"My debt…?"

"But of course. I have been in your debt ever since that so delightful journey we shared on the Vienna Express from Bologna to Bolzano— Bol-za-no," he repeated, smiling. "Oh, my dear Monsieur, you must not tell me that you do not remember."

"No, of course not, I remember now," Paul assured him. "It was, as I recall, an eventful journey."

"You were good enough to admire my little ones," Martinelli told him gratefully. "But…you must allow me to offer you an aperitif, my dear friend. Excuse me, I don't have the honour…"

"Von Hagen," Paul told him shortly.

"Ah! Monsieur von Hagen. Yes, of course. The gentleman who speaks most excellent German, yet not quite like a German, eh?" He laughed and took Paul familiarly by the arm. Paul tried to move away but found himself firmly held.

Over drinks, Martinelli talked expansively. Business was good. "For you also, Monsieur?" he asked shyly.

"Yes." Paul determined to be non-committal. But even among the jostling evening crowds on the rue de la Paix, in an atmosphere so rational as that of Paris, this man could influence his self-control.

"The agreement between the Vatican and the French Government," Martinelli continued, "there is a fresh interest in everything religious. And there is Boulanger, of course."

"So everyone tells me."

"But of course. He offers the stability that allows men to think beyond their day-to-day requirements…to contemplate whatever might follow in the life to come." Martinelli snapped his fingers at a passing waiter to bring more drinks and looked self-satisfied as though he himself could be responsible for the Boulanger phenomenon. "Every nation should have its Boulanger, monsieur von Hagen. The French love him because he promises them everything…everything for everybody. And…" with a little laugh," and because he is so beautiful, of course…a gold-bearded hero on a black horse riding the course at

Longhamps while the crowd went wild with approval." Suddenly he began to sing some phrases of a pro-Boulanger music-hall song:

"Pour marcher vers le Rhin,
Pour marcher vers le Rhin,
Parais nous t'attendrons,
A General Revanche."

"Always revenge on the Germans, you see, Monsieur. But the Germans do not sleep. They have their own General…the Count von Bismarck, eh? You admire him I think?"

"It would be impossible not to. Within a decade he has created of Germany the strongest state in Europe."

"And France and Russia tremble, do they not? They draw close like children for the warmth of protection. They begin to talk together very tenderly. They begin to trade. Indeed…" He sniggered, "very soon, perhaps, I shall be taking my little ones to Russia. Very soon France and Russia will sign an alliance against the Germans, I think. After that, the Russians will look upon Roman Catholics more kindly."

His excitement quickly ebbed and he leaned back in his chair, his hands upon the table, the epitome of quiet satisfaction. Paul shuffled restlessly, despising himself for not being able to stand up and walk away. Martinelli put a restraining hand on his arm.

"But maybe it will not be like that." He shook his head. "Oh, no! Maybe it will not be like that at all."

"Oh?" Paul grunted in semi-encouragement, unwilling to admit that he could be interested in whatever the salesman had to say next.

"What if Boulanger succeeds?" He tapped his nose and winked.

"What happens then?" Paul asked in spite of himself.

"Suppose," the man began, leaning towards Paul and sipping his drink, "suppose Boulanger succeeds and becomes the French Bismarck?" He paused dramatically, enigmatically.

"Well? What happens then?" Paul demanded testily.

The Italian shrugged, kissed the tips of his fingers and released them to the air. "Poof to the alliance! Strong France will not then need weak Russia. What will you do, Monsieur?"

Paul shook his head as though to clear it.

"How to make Russia strong, Eh? How to make her strong like Germany and France? Who is to do it? Today that is impossible. The autocracy, the bureaucracy! Oh no, Monsieur! Everything must change, I think. Russia also must have her Bismarck, her Boulanger, do you not agree?"

Paul glared at him. "You misunderstand the situation," he protested. "Of course there must be changes, but…"

"Exactly," Martinelli agreed with enthusiasm. "You are a man of the world, Monsieur. We both understand these things. You and I…We understand each other."

Paul found his hand being grasped and wrung. He shuddered and rose from his seat.

"But you cannot go yet, Monsieur," Martinelli argued. "We have only just begun a very interesting talk, don't you agree?"

"Of course it's been delightful" Paul lied, recovering himself. "But I have an engagement for later."

"Ah!" Martinelli smiled knowingly and tapped his nose again. "At Maxim's, perhaps?"

Paul grinned stupidly because he didn't know how else to respond.

"Always when we meet our conversations are fascinating, Monsieur," Martinelli assured him. "There is no greater pleasure than speculating upon the affairs of the world, eh?…the past, the present, the future. We were talking just now of Russia, my friend. Now there is a field for speculation, eh? There is a need for a Boulanger, as we both agree." He laughed again, stood and wrung Paul's hand continually, and releasing him with the greatest show of reluctance.

CHAPTER 8

▼

1889

Prince Krasnov sent Government Inspector Schlepkov to enquire into the death of Father Tikhon's whore. Fyodor Antonovitch was an official with an enormous spiked moustache and an ego to match. He stayed in the Baron's house and Channah looked after him. The Baron, so far as he possibly could, remained locked in his study. The deceased had been a woman of no importance whatsoever and the Baron had certainly not reported her death to the authorities on her own account. Death was not unfamiliar. People died in their beds, in the fields, in the town, in the river, by act of God or human revenge. In this case the circumstances were unusual. Seldom were any of these murders the result of frenzied murder, the corpses stabbed thirty-seven times and hidden in snowdrifts where they might have been expected to rot during the spring thaw.

The Committee of Enquiry, the Inspector, the Baron and a scribe, sat at a baze-covered table in the hall of the Manor House. Father Tikhon was their first witness, looking remarkably unconcerned by the loss of the woman they called his whore.

"Well now, your Honour," he boomed in reply to Schlepkov's query as to why he hadn't reported the woman's disappearance, "may I correct your Honour? In the village they called her 'my woman'...'my whore'..." He laughed as though this was a very good joke indeed.

"But that was village gossip, your Honour…all prejudice. Of course she wasn't my whore," he grumbled like a deeply wronged man. "I took her in for charity's sake. But she came and went. She wasn't regular in her habits. She came and went just as she wanted. I never knew. When she was here, I took her in out of Christian charity. I asked nothing in return." He finished sanctimoniously and crossed his hands over his ample stomach.

"When was the last time you saw her?"

The priest shrugged. "In winter, all days are the same," he said.

"Was she with you recently?"

"Who knows? A week ago…a month, perhaps."

"Tell me then!" Schlepkov adopted a more business-like address; the time for showing sympathy to this deeply wronged Samaritan was over. "You minister to the Russians in the village?"

Father Tikhon briefly closed his eyes and inclined his head; this was obviously another of his crosses.

"They're all good communicants?"

"They come regularly to the Liturgy."

"And to Confession?"

"Yes…?" Father Tikhon's eyes glittered with suspicion under his bushy eyebrows.

"And…?" Shlepkov persisted.

"And…?" the priest repeated.

"Someone has told you something about this woman, perhaps?"

The priest straightened his shoulders and managed to look shocked and reproving at the same time. "Your Honour! The confidentiality of the Confessional!" He crossed himself as though the very thought of it was damnation.

"Come man! Don't play games with me! You either tell me now, or I'll have you taken somewhere they'll make you talk!"

"But your Honour…" The priest crossed himself once more and held out his hands as though ready to embrace his martyrdom.

"Think, man! I'm not talking about your usual run of peccadilloes…drunkenness, swearing pornographic fantasies…This is a government matter. Has anyone told you anything about the woman's death?"

Father Tikhon paused long enough for the Government Inspector to believe he would be hearing what he wanted to hear. Then he fell on his knees. "Your Honour, I swear no one has said anything. And if I go to my grave this instant…" he crossed himself, "I can say no more."

"Huh! Perhaps you killed her yourself, then."

"Oh, no! No, no, no, your Honour. I swear it before God. I never touched her." He crossed himself hysterically and swayed on his knees with fear. Schlepkov sneered and dismissed him with menacing looks and threats that he would not be forgotten.

Pastor Vikkers's examination began with trembling and stuttering and the possibility that he would fall on the floor in a faint at any moment. In comparison with Father Tikhon he was conspicuously anxious to assist the authorities; though everything he said was a nearly tearful plea for belief in what was hardly relevant and could never be proved.

"She was a bad woman, your Honour. Everybody called her Father Tikhon's whore; your Honour should excuse me. Everybody in the village knew what she was. She disgusted everyone."

"Everyone felt so strongly, did they?"

"My people, certainly, your Honour. Everybody knew her since she was she was a child. She was born here."

"She was a good Lutheran girl, your Honour. Her mother was dead already, but it broke her father's heart when she went off to live with that man."

"He swears she didn't live with him."

"Of course." The timid Pastor was gaining confidence. "That man, your Honour, he is…" Vikkers blushed. "He is like that, you know."

"Like what?"

"Women! There are always scandals about women. He won't leave anyone alone."

"The women in your flock, Pastor?"

"He mesmerises them...they can't help themselves. The good God only knows what sort of magic he has. Those Orthodox priests, you know..." He suddenly realised that Schlepkov must be Orthodox, stopped and looked exceedingly embarrassed. Schlepkov ignored the implications.

"We are all poor sinners, in need of Christ's redemption, your Honour," Vikkers offered by way of apology.

"Come man! Come to the point! This is no petty village scandal we're investigating. This woman was shockingly murdered and we're here to find out who did it and why. You still say she lived with Father Tikhon?"

"She was mad, your Honour."

"In your opinion, Pastor. I want facts."

"Truly, your Honour, she was mad. It happened years ago."

"What happened years ago?"

The Pastor turned to the Baron. "You remember, Herr Baron. It happened years ago. A Recruiting Officer came to take away recruits for the army. The woman was just married. They beat her husband unmercifully and took him away. She never heard from him again and she never recovered from the shock of it."

"She was Greta?" the Baron asked, astounded.

"She lost her mind, your Honour. She wandered in the woods for months and God alone knew how she lived. The following winter she went to Father Tikhon and he took her in. I'd tried to hold her myself, but she wouldn't stay. Father Tikhon had no association with her past...wasn't involved in her memories. Perhaps that's why she went to him."

"I remember. I remember now. She was a pretty little thing," the Baron said.

"And now she's horribly dead," Schlepkov said. "Who did it, Pastor?"

"Who can tell, your Honour?"

"One of your people?"

"Certainly not!" The Pastor's firmness was quite unaccustomed. "Excuse me, your Honour. I meant…no, I'm sure none of my men would have done such a thing. It was a Russian." His voice rose now he'd crossed the bounds of discretion. "Excuse me, Herr Baron, but you should never have brought them here. They did it. One of them did it. They're no better than animals and God only knows what they'll do next."

Schlepkov dismissed the Pastor. The Baron was embarrassed after the outburst and feeling a modicum of guilt because of what Vikkers said about the folly of bringing in Russian labourers. He glanced self-consciously, at Schlepkov but the Inspector was taking no notice. He was gazing unseeing at something in the far away distance. He turned to the Baron. "Tell me, Herr Baron…if all the men in the village had such good cause to hate Father Tikhon, why didn't they murder him instead of his whore?"

CHAPTER 9

▼

1889

Paul read the letter from his brother when he returned to Florence. He was in a mood of such euphoric optimism after his success in Paris, however, that he didn't regard the news of the murder nor the tell-tail trail of censor's glue as serious. Leonore responded to his enthusiasm and set about arranging affairs at the Villa with joyous haste. They were ready to leave for Paris immediately after the New Year.

Their departure resembled a triumph of ancient times. They were greeted at the station by an assembly of excited friends, all elbowing to kiss Leonore goodbye and shake farewell with the Captain. Ottolie d'Orangeville and the Contessa di Beltrano staggered beneath the masses of flowers they'd brought.

As always at departures, this bonhomie quickly became a strain to maintain and everyone was relieved when the guard blew his whistle. Augustina crossed herself vigorously and the train drew out. No one could have been more surprised than Augustina herself, to arrive in Paris next evening without having been raped on the way.

They left the Gare de Lyon in a shabby four-wheeler drawn by a disconsolate horse, followed in another cab by Augustina, suspicious of everybody and everything, and with their luggage packed tightly around her. In a very few minutes, crossing the Place de la Bastille towards the rue St. Antoine, they were accosted and halted by a riotous crowd. An untidy swarm of young men and women rushed at them out of the mist. Leonore began to tremble, threw herself into the corner of the carriage and held her children close to her. "Oh God help us all. What do they want," she moaned. "Paul, what is it? What do they want?"

Paul took a risk and let down the window. "What is it?" he shouted. "What's the fuss about, driver?"

"Boulangists, Monsieur. He's been elected Deputy for Paris. It's a triumph. He'll get Alsace and Lorraine back for us."

A young man at the front of the crowd grasped the door handle and thrust his face up to Paul's. "Are you for the General, Monsieur?"

"I don't know. My wife is exhausted. Let us pass, please."

"You don't know! Everyone knows whether or not they're for the General."

The driver interposed. "They've only just arrived, Comrade. Can't you hear the gentleman's a foreigner?"

"Where's he from?" It was a less friendly, female voice.

"I picked him up minutes go at the Gare de Lyon," the driver explained.

"Are they boches?" the woman screamed at no one in particular.

"You'll have to get down," someone else shouted.

"No!" Paul protested. "You've no right. Let us pass, please!"

"Germans come in at the Gare de l'Est," the driver argued. "Didn't I just tell you I picked the gentleman up at the Gare de Lyon?"

Paul glanced back into the carriage. Leonore was still clutching the children in the corner, pale faced and with a light film of moisture on her upper lip. He feared she would faint. The children were crying.

"For mercy's sake, what do they want?" she moaned. "Get us away from here, Paul. Don't argue with them."

The driver turned to face his passengers. "Maybe the Comrades would appreciate a token of good will, Monsieur...a little something to drink the General's health, perhaps?"

Paul instantly reached for his purse and ostentatiously drew out several pieces of gold. The leader of the mob, understanding the significance of the gesture, turned triumphantly to his followers. "Vive le monsieur etranger!" he shouted. "Vive le General!" The cry was echoed from the back of the crowd.

Paul reached down with the money and the young man stretched up to take it. Instead of simply taking the money, however, he opened the door of the carriage, grabbed Paul by the wrist and pulled him down on to the roadway.

"My wife," Paul objected lamely, taken by surprise.

"Vive la revolution, eh Monsieur! Come with us! These are magnificent moments in the history of France. We'll collect the General and carry him shoulder high to the Elysee. We have our man of destiny at last. Vive la revolution!"

"Vive la revolution," echoed behind him. But all Paul was conscious of was Leonore's terrified face at the open carriage door.

The crowd was beginning to move away, its excitement growing. The young man who still held Paul by the arm began to follow it, dragging his prisoner with him. Leonore screamed, adding to the general din. The crowd moved slowly as though unsure of the direction it should take. It continued making a great deal of noise—too much for anyone to hear the contingent of Garde Republicaine galloping down the Boulevard Beaumarchais.

The first riders reached the edge of the mob and laid about them with their sabres, some flattened others not. The youngsters screamed, wavered, broke and dribbled away in every direction. The man released Paul's arm in his surprise, turned and dropped Paul's coins in the filth at his feet.

The Square quickly emptied. The Garde pursued the fleeing rioters towards the River. No one was left save for a dozen or so bodies lying motionless, face down in the filth. When police arrived to remove these cadavers, they would find Paul's gold pieces scattered among them.

In the silence that followed, Paul could hear Leonore sobbing, but went first to the second carriage. Augustina sat there, her eyes tight-closed, her body rigid, whimpering. Paul touched her and she screamed in terror.

"It's all right, it's all right, Augustina," he assured her. "They've gone. You're quite safe now."

She opened her eyes and looked at him as though she'd never seen him before. "I want to go home, Signore," she said while her eyes focused. "Now! This very minute! I want to go home!"

Paul's temper snapped. "Be quiet, you silly girl," he shouted. "Stay there! Do as you're told!"

He went to Leonore. She was calmer and he hoped to divert her with the news that Augustina and their luggage were safe. She paid no attention.

"I can't stay here, Paul. I won't. It's a terrible place. Take me back!"

"There, there, my dear." Paul tried to soothe her as the carriage rolled forward. "I'm with you. You're quite safe. You're tired. It will all be different tomorrow."

Next day the city was remarkably quiet and the government had maintained authority. Rumours abounded but there was general agreement; there would be no revolution just then. General Boulanger had refused to be carried in triumph to the Elysee Palace. Those who still believed in him claimed that he had overcome the clamour of his most riotous supporters by refusing to act unconstitutionally. His enemies put it about that it was because he preferred to spend the night at home with his mistress.

CHAPTER 10

▼

1889

At night, holding Channah in his arm, her head on his shoulder, Loff von Hagen was more and more keenly haunted by his responsibility for Greta's death. He had done nothing to help her when Jaan was taken away. He had been too concerned to save his face in front of the peasants, leaving what would happen to happen. Now, his meager comfort was that Jaan would never ever come back to the village and would never know what had eventually happened to the girl he'd loved and married when they were both so young. The Army kept recruits serving as far from home as possible. That wasn't difficult. There were always petty rebellious outbreaks along the frontiers of the Empire, a landmass reaching from Germany in Europe to China in eastern-most Asia.

Greta was dead now, lying in an unhallowed grave in the woods, close to where some monster had desecrated her body. Pastor Vikkers refused to have anything to do with her committal. Father Tikhon recited some prayers in a language the corpse could never have understood while she was alive, and only the Baron, seemingly, left the place with sadness and regret in his heart.

It was over and nothing would ever be the same again. The Russians resumed their snow-clearing next day, but their road was ruined when a sudden thaw set in. The sum of their labour melted to slush and there were no more jokes, no more horseplay. Generally, relations between Russians and Estonians changed too. Toleration was a thing of the past. There were daily scuffles. Channah was kept busy with her medicine bag and pressed the Baron to send for the gendarmerie to re-establish order. The Baron was reluctant to bring in anyone from the outside.

"We've never needed outside help at Wirsberg," he argued sadly. "My Father and Grandfather would have gone out there with a whip and kept order with their two bare hands."

No helpful reply had come from his letter to Paul. There were several excited notes from Paris telling him how much money was being deposited in the company account at St. Petersburg, but no helpful advice about how to manage affairs at the Estate. It didn't do. The Baron needed to share his burden and for the first time since he'd known her, he found Channah's unquestioning adoration insufficient for his purpose. He was sensible, at bottom to know he didn't need practical advice; he needed punishment, he needed like a flagellant to expiate his guilt. Reluctantly, desperately, he wrote to Margarethe.

"Dear Sister,

You ignored my last two letters. I never thought, when you went to Africa, that you intended to have no further contact with your home and family. Perhaps you are very busy and I am being unjust. Perhaps it is difficult for you to send and receive letters. But if that is not the case, I beg you to write to me and give me your news.

The news from here is that I am fit and although I know you will not particularly like to hear it...Channah looks after me very well. You must remember, Sister, that without Channah I should have nobody. Paul and his family are living in Paris, but more of that later. Everything must go into order, in its proper context.

The beginning of the context is that everything I hear; everything I see about me has grown strangely unreal since you went away. I feel I am living in a dream, in a country foreign and quite unlike the one we knew in our childhood. Perhaps this nightmare began when our father died and I came back from St. Petersburg to run the Estate. Perhaps it started later, when Paul married his Jewish wife. Or maybe I was responsible when I took Channah to live in our house. You were always mistaken about our relationship at that time, you know. Maybe you were responsible yourself, and it started when you left...your going away and getting married destroyed our past.

But I can't believe that. I honestly cannot believe that we ourselves have been in any way responsible for what has happened, though we—that is, I—cannot avoid much of the responsibility for the many mistakes I have made. More likely it was all inevitable; the new times that are flooding over us; the burning of the village in which a member of our family colluded, the imposition upon us of the Krasnovs, government refusal to allow you to open your school, the establishment of an orthodox parish here, army recruitment...

Sister, do you remember your young protégé Jaan? You wanted to send him to the gymnasium in Reval but they stopped you. Instead, they hunted him like an animal in the woods, beat him unmercifully and kidnapped him for the army. God knows where he is now, whether he's alive or dead. Nobody ever heard from him again. And do you remember his young wife Greta? They had only been married a couple of days before they took him away. She lost her mind and never regained her sanity, they tell me. Some say she became Father Tikhon's mistress, some that she wandered the forests like a wild thing. Channah has always tried to be kind to her. A few days ago they found her body buried in a snowdrift and horribly mutilated.

This, in its way, is a saga of my own feeble attempt to dissociate myself from everything that's happened. What did I do while it was happening? Nothing. What could I have done? I honestly do not know. What should I do now? My dear sister, you always considered me weak and ineffective. I have lain awake night after night thinking of our Father and what he might have done in the circumstances. But of course, these particular circumstances never arose during his lifetime. If they had, could his strength, his firmness, his obstinacy have changed anything? I think not. Nothing, now, this is directly of our making. We are living through a tumultuous time in history and we are overtaken by its torrent.

Of course, life goes on and we must respond to its demands as best we can. The cost of labour here rises outrageously. If we are not to be reduced to poverty like many of our neighbours, we must find alterna-

tive ways to make money. To deal with all these difficulties, Paul and I have turned the Estate into a limited company; we are mining shale, establishing trade in our amber deposits along the coast and we intend building shallow-bottomed ships for the Baltic trade. Believe me, Sister, when all this becomes profitable you will benefit, too. Meanwhile, Paul and his family have moved from Florence to Paris to raise capital for our various enterprises.

But there is an obverse to every coin, as you must have discovered for yourself. Our new enterprises need labour and so, I have imported dispossessed peasants from Russia. For a time all went well. But the discovery of Greta's corpse was a catalyst. Our Estonians, certain none of themselves would have done such a thing, blame the Russians. The Russians despise the Estonians for remaining peasants when there are so many other things to be done, so many other ways of making more money. There is more to it than that, of course: the difference of race and religion, the absence of their own women among the Russians. There are fights every day. I have had to write to Prince Krasnov requesting him to send a gendarme to keep order in the village.

So you can see how far, since our Father's death I have abdicated my God-given authority. Right from the start, I know you saw that something like this was bound to happen. The only real difference between we two was that you blamed me entirely, whereas I am certain I was only in part culpable.

You will be wondering, sister, why I am writing to you at such length about all of this. The answer to that is simple. I know nobody likely to understand. Is that a compliment to you, do you think? It is meant to be. I know that you will understand because, all along, whatever our differences, you and I shared respect for tradition and love of the Estate, and that you always tried, as I have tried, to do your Duty.

I pray for your health and welfare wherever you are. Think of me kindly, sometimes.

Your affectionate brother,

Loff von Hagen."

Officers at the Missionary Headquarters in Berlin were not over-punctilious about forwarding personal mail to their field-workers.

It was difficult enough to find volunteers to go out; they didn't want their few volunteers distracted or disturbed by news from home. It took nearly a year for Loff's letter to get to Margarethe. She read it carefully and cried. She cried for Loff. She cried for the passing of the old ways. She cried for herself.

Her husband was away on a circuit of pastoral visits to distant villages. She had no one to share her thoughts. She went outside and sat, still, straight and statuesque on the verandah of the hut in which she dwelt in celibacy. Her husband, when he was at home, occupied a separate building. She rubbed her hand across her eyes, impatient. She must write something comforting to Loff in return. That was her duty now. But what comfort could there be? There was no comfort for Job until Our Lord bequeathed it; Loff must be patient for His time, too. Her eye caught the movement of a brown and green snake slithering into the shade of a nearby acacia. She didn't recognise the species and would have to have it identified. She kept notes on everything she saw. Next her attention was taken by the litheness of her assistant, running towards her out of the woods. The girl wore nothing but loincloth beads. Margarethe felt a flick of anger. For how much longer would she have to fight for the general acceptance of shirts, skirts and trousers—at least among those of the Pastor's flock living closest to the Mission centre? Her husband was no help to her in this. He gloried in the nakedness of his children, as he called them; he quoted Rousseau to her and worshipped their Garden of Eden innocence. Thank God, the Serpent had not yet appeared among them. Please God, with His help, Pastor Behrendorf would direct all his energy towards making sure that it never did.

The girl almost collapsed into Margarethe's lap. Her excitement made her almost incomprehensible. She forgot what little German she knew and babbled breathlessly in her own tongue. Eventually Margarethe understood that one of the women in a nearby village was having a baby that was strangling in its own umbilical cord. Local women would do nothing. It was a curse of their old gods, they said. What must be, must be, for the good of all their sakes; otherwise the curse would reflect upon the whole village. Margarethe jumped out of her chair, clutched at her medicine bag and, in spite of the heat and humidity, kept pace with the naked girl into the woods. The child was already dead when she reached it, the mother dull-eyed showing no emotion. Three hags, naked as when they were born, leapt upon their white mother to tell her of the curse, that there was nothing to be done, that even the white mother's God could have done nothing. Margarethe hardly understood the words. She simply stood over the apathetic mother and blazed away at the women in a transport of fury. When she was done, she felt tired and hopeless. She walked slowly home. And Loff never received a reply to his letter.

CHAPTER 11

▼

1889

Rachel and Ida were enchanted by Paris. In Florence, after their tours with Paul, they were sure they had seen everything in the world worth seeing. Here in Paris they realised that they hadn't. Isabel Chronach took them under her wing directly she met them. They fell under her spell too. She was petite, pretty and ebullient, much younger than her didactic little husband. She had two daughters herself, Esther and Eugenie, of about the same age. The four of them were inseparable and the Chronach girls were the first real friends they'd made since leaving Warsaw—separate attachments approved of and encouraged by Paul and Leonore (whom, incidentally, they now never called Leah!).

Together, the four girls wandered the Louvre and attended the Opera to hear "La Traviata" which left them in rapturous tears. They mingled with the popular crowd at the Theatre Guignol on the Champs Elysees and they fantasy-shopped along the rue de la Paix. (In fact they had more fun in the Grands Magasins du Bon Marche in the rue de Sevres where objects of their desire were cheap enough to be bought.) They scrambled in the rush for tickets to the Great Exhibition (where they astonished Esther and Eugenie by using their linguistic skills to help confused enquirers—Polish, Russian, German, Italian, French and Yiddish), and they attended the Exhibition at least once a week because it was advertised as a never-to-be-repeated experience.

They climbed the Eiffel Tower and went three times to the Wild West Show where they coughed in the dust raised by the wagons and shrieked and ducked at every pistol shot. It was a wonderful year, and they swore to be best friends for as long as they lived.

Leonore, on the other hand, was not content, even though she was starting her third pregnancy and in other circumstances would have been delighted. She could go to the rue de la Paix like her sisters and could actually afford to make her purchases there; but spending money never brought her pleasure. Visits to the Great Exhibition were exhausting. She had no desire to mount Monsieur Eiffel's Tower.

Paul had rented a large, pleasant flat for them near the Bois. Isabel Chronach helped Leonore to find suitable servants, most importantly a replacement for Augustina. Paul returned home cheerful every evening and more often than not insisted on taking her to dinner at some fashionable restaurant. Henri Chronach was introducing him to influential contacts on the Bourse. Paul's personality was naturally friendly and he easily became popular. Money began flowing between Paris and Wirsberg; sufficient money for Loff to arrange all the little difficulties he'd written about. Soon there would be dividends.

Isabel Chronach was Leonore's constant companion now, and the limit of her social life. Isabel had a vivid but practical imagination. She understood what life in the East had been like for Leonore, living constantly on the edge of catastrophe. She understood that the riot the night Leonore arrived in Paris had tarnished the city forever in her thoughts. The fear was the worse here than in Warsaw because in Paris she was alone; she lacked the assurance of community that Zamenhofa Street had always afforded her even in the very worst times.

Besides the happiness of his success in the business world, Paul was delighted by Leonore's pregnancy. He knew the pleasure she had taken in her first two babies, and was sure she felt the same about this one. He therefore considered himself justified by tacitly ignoring her desire to go back to Florence. It was essential for him to remain in Paris, in touch with sources of finance. Leonore, at the moment, was nervous and tense because this was the beginning of her pregnancy. She would understand the necessity of their remaining in Paris; she would understand and bow to this, as she bowed to all Paul's necessities. In his enthusiasm, he didn't see that the excitement of his success as a financier was, for her, an estrangement. Even his looks, she felt, had changed. He looked to her now even younger than he did when she first knew him as a Captain in the Preobrazhensky. He was noisy as he moved about the flat. He spoke too loudly and laughed a lot. He frequently interrupted her while she was speaking to explain to her what it was she was trying to say. His lovemaking became fierce, perfunctory, impersonal, almost coarse. She sensed that instead of loving her body, now he merely used it. For nights on end he slept in his own room instead of sharing hers. She suspected that he had a mistress and was being regularly unfaithful to her. She did not resent any of this. It was Paris. Paris was evil, a disease attacking them both in separate ways.

Deep down she had an insistent belief that only Lydmilla Fyodorovna was wise enough to reconcile her several confusions.

"We must find her Paul." she persisted. "We owe her that much loyalty at least."

"She obviously doesn't want to be found so we should leave her alone. That's where loyalty lies."

"How can you tell she wouldn't have been in touch long before this if only she'd known where we are?"

"They would give her our address at the Embassy."

"She was frightened to go to the Embassy. You told me so yourself."

"Dammit! That was ages ago!" He almost shouted. "She was tired and hysterical. We'd only just got off the train."

She ignored his outburst with an assumed dignity. "Where's her husband's Sanatorium?"

"I've no idea. She was always ridiculously secretive about things like that."

"I think she was always terrified. Well," she said finally, "if you won't do anything I'll have to find her myself."

He laughed and took her into his arms. "My own sweet darling, how on earth do you think you can do that?"

"Isabel will help and the girls are always roaming about."

"You won't be able to count on the girls much longer."

"Why?" She was instantly defensive. "I won't let you send them away."

"Listen, my dear, come over here. Sit down and listen to me. Things are good for us here. Chronach has introduced me to all sorts of useful people on the Bourse and I'm getting Loff all the capital he needs. And..." He was silent overlong, smiling secretly and smugly, "I've made one or two very profitable investments myself, I must admit. We're a lot better off now than when we first came here. Believe me, my dear, it's good for us here."

"What has this to do with the girls?"

She was angry because he thought money was of interest to her.

He continued with a slight sigh at having to explain everything in such detail. "It's good for us here. We're staying. And it's time the girls began making their own lives. Chronach can get Rachel a place with Maison Bertrande—one of the best couturiers in town, as you very well know. And there's a place for Ida's artistic skills out in St. Cloud. It'll be in competition with the Sevres Porcelain factory and it's to be called Frere Jacques—though it's largely financed by Chronach himself, I imagine. Anyway, he's willing to give our Ida a chance as probationary designer. It's a wonderful opportunity. Everything will be done by hand and you'll soon see the name Frere Jacques on the rue de la Paix, I've no doubt. There's Rachel and our little Ida on their way to making names for themselves."

"They must make up their own minds," she said shortly, unimpressed. So long as they stayed with her she didn't care what they did. She didn't care about Paul; she didn't even much care about the baby growing in her womb. Her obsession just now was to find Lydmilla Fyodorovna. Her need of Paul's friend was desperate.

Isabel was delighted, like a child offered the puzzles, excitements and surprises of a treasure hunt.

"But my dear, we shall search the length and breadth of every street in Paris," she urged, prepared to start at that very moment. "We shall surely find this elusive Russian for you."

"I'm sure I don't quite know how."

"Tomorrow morning we shall set out early and search along the Boulevard St. Germain…from end to end."

"That's a very long street," Leonore objected diffidently.

"Exercise will be good for the baby, my dear. And, of course, I don't intend that we walk all the way. We'll take the carriage, naturally."

"You think there's the slightest chance we will meet her on the street?"

"No, no, no!" Isabel trilled with delight, "You do not understand how practical I am. No, my darling, we shall ride in the carriage but we shall stop at every bistro, every cafe, every brasserie along the way."

Leonore was overwhelmed by what her boasting to Paul had begun. She now only wished to withdraw. "It would be too much of a coincidence, our all being there at the same time," she protested wearily.

"Of course, we don't expect to meet her in the flesh. But we ask. We ask every patron, every waiter, every likely looking customer. This is Paris, my dear, where everyone is interested in everyone, you know. And…" she clapped her hands gleefully, "we shall offer everyone a little money if they can tell us anything to help. How simple it all is, my precious. We shall very quickly discover your elusive Russian friend."

Isabel's optimism was not substantiated. During the remainder of summer and through autumn, Leonore grew to know Paris very well; all its central Boulevards and many of its side streets. She would arrive home after her search, too tired to go out to eat with Paul if he asked her. He didn't complain. He was happy that she had an interest, eventually, centered on Paris. The search spread wider and wider, long after

Leonore had any hope of its success. But she held to it as a terrier holds to a bone, not knowing what else to do if she were to let it go.

At the beginning of winter Paul declared that this fruitless hunting must stop. Leonore's pregnancy was far advanced; the physical and mental strain on her was inevitably too much. Leonore accepted the veto sullenly and ignored it directly he left the house. They were far enough estranged by now for her to do that. She rejected his authority over her, just as she rejected his authority over her child. She thought of it as hers alone…a relationship between mother and child only, something in which Paul was in no way concerned. He had forfeited his rights.

Her searches with Isabel continued and in October they reached Montmartre. This was demonstrably an area in which Lydmilla Fyodorovna might be living, but Isabel had delayed going there for as long as possible because it was an unsuitable area for ladies to visit without an escort. Many artists had moved into studios on the Buttee where they were surrounded by various houses of entertainment—theatres, music halls, cafes chansons…many of doubtful reputation. Risky nights there attracted a stream of bohemian tourists until local working men were going elsewhere for their regular consummations.

Leonore and Isabel went there on a cold morning. Winter was beginning. Rain drizzled in the air and the cobbles were covered with a coating of treacherous rime. Isabel ordered their coachman, Jean-Louis, to make their enquiries in this area while they themselves remained withdrawn into the corners of the carriage, out of sight of passers-by. Thus they had enquired all along the Boulevard de Clichy and the Boulevard Rochechouart. Isabel then decided they must visit the Place du Tertre, and Jean-Louis would continue to make enquiries along the way.

The carriage was halted in a narrow, busy street. Pedestrians collided, clashed, slipped and swore on the crowded pavements. Carriages and carts creaked and groaned by, the horses' flanks and nostrils steaming in the cold dampness. Jean-Louis had gone to enquire in several cafes in the vicinity and Leonore and Isabel sat silent waiting his return. Leonore's thoughts were not happy ones. She admitted now that she would never find Lydmilla Fyodorovna, however long they searched. She admitted too, that she could no longer ignore Paul's instructions. She was tired and heavy with the child and needing to rest much of the time. Isabel appeared to be sensitive to her mood and said nothing.

Unexpectedly they were jolted out of this silent serenity. The driver of a dray that had drawn up ahead of them, let slip a cask of wine. It crashed onto the pavement and split. Its contents gushed noisily down the hill and there was a chorus of loud, excited comment from bystanders. Isabel's horse, aware that Jean-Louis was not on his box, took fright, reared and snapped his trace. Feeling free, he uttered a bray that was nearly a scream and ran off, causing confusion and curses among the traffic further up the hill. The carriage, upended by the horse, came down in good order but had shed its brake in the eruption. It slid backwards down the hill and hit a lamppost with a bone-breaking shudder.

Both Leonore and Isabel were too surprised and shocked to utter a single cry. Isabel was first to regain control and her immediate thought was for Leonore.

"Are you all right, my darling?" Her whisper was quite audible, despite the rising chorus of comment from the gathering crowd.

Leonore moaned. She meant to convey assurance but the effort of speech was too much. Isabel experienced a moment of panic. She had no idea what to do but knew, right or wrong, that she had to do something. She was struggling with the lock when the door was suddenly opened and a cultivated male voice enquired for their welfare.

"Yes, yes," Isabel assured him. "I'm quite all right but I'm anxious about my friend. You see, she is…she is not in a condition for this kind of occurrence."

"One moment, Madame." The man, she'd hardly looked at his face, turned away and spoke sharply to someone near at hand. "Cognac! Quickly!"

A sip of the cognac and Leonore partially recovered her awareness. Consciousness flowed over her like the waves of the sea and Isabel and the stranger had gently to ease her from the carriage and into the nearest cafe. The patronne summed up Leonore's situation by magical feminine intuition and led them through the cafe and into a private room behind the counter. They laid her on a sofa and she held Isabel's had in a vise-like clutch. The helpful gentleman stood a little way off, embarrassed and apparently useless.

Jean-Louis returned, amazed and shocked by what had happened. Isabel ordered him to find a cab to take them home, but the gentleman intervened.

"I insist you allow me, Madame. We shall take my carriage. I was following you up the hill." He fetched a neat little case from his pocket and handed her his card in well-manicured fingers. "It would be better, Madame, if your driver were to calm your horse and see to the repairs on your carriage."

Isabel glanced at the card. "Raoul Versagne," she read. "You are really very kind, Monsieur Versagne, but really, we mustn't bother you further."

He seemed to make his podgy little body taller and raised his eyebrows until they came to two points above his sharp brown eyes. "It was my good fortune to be here when this unfortunate accident happened, Madame. And, if I were to speak frankly…" he paused.

"Yes, Monsieur?"

"I am shocked to find two ladies driving in this area even at this time of day without an escort. Your driver should never have left you alone."

"He was temporarily absent on my instructions, Monsieur."

"Ah…" It wasn't exactly a question but seemed, nonetheless, to demand further explanation.

"Madame here, is searching for a friend who has become lost somewhere in Paris."

"Ah…" Again, the same inquisitive inflexion.

"A Russian lady. A painter."

"Ah, A Russian. A painter!" Versagne said it as though the lady's nationality and profession explained everything. "Perhaps I may help in this affair also, Madame. There are several Russians among my acquaintance. Why…" he smiled expansively, "I may even know the lady myself."

Isabel returned his smile. "That would indeed be remarkable," she agreed, feeling somehow uncomfortable. "The lady's name is Kholchevskaya…Lydmilla Fyodorovna."

"Kholchevskaya!" The man scribbled the name on a small, leather-backed tablet, seeming to taste each syllable as he did so. He shrugged. "Unfortunately I do not know the lady myself, but I shall make enquiries." Then he put two fingers to his lips in an unexpected gesture. "Of course, Madame, I shall be very discrete," he murmured.

At home, at last, Leonore was put directly to bed. Dorothea and Sonia, excited by this wonderfully unexpected return, rushed into the room and broke into a squall of screaming and stamping when their nursemaid rushed them out again. Rachel and Ida, coming home later, were confused and frightened by their sister's descent into unexpected sickness. She lay fully dressed on her bed, her hair dampened down against her forehead, her lips bloodless, her limbs twitching uncontrollably. She would barely speak to them and they crept away silently, distressed. Leonore's only comfort was in holding tightly to Isabel's hand as she panted to fight off some silent nightmare.

She lay there many hours and the autumn light was failing but she refused to have any lamps lit in the room. Her breathing became more laboured and Isabel forced her fingers free in order to leave the room. She ordered a maid to send for the doctor and returned immediately. Left alone, even momentarily, had brought Leonore to her senses. For the first time since the accident she appeared to recognise her surroundings and addressed Isabel by name. Her voice was low and uncertain.

"It is beginning, Isabel."

"I know, darling. I've sent for the doctor."

"It must be a boy."

"You mustn't worry, my darling. Everything will be quite all right."

Leonore tried to rise and Isabel urged her gently back on to the bed. "I want him back," she moaned.

"Hush, my darling. You mustn't distress yourself about anything at all," Isabel told her, embarrassed and longing for Paul to arrive.

"I want him back. If I give him a son, he'll come back to me, won't he? Won't he, Isabel?"

"You haven't lost him, my dear. He loves you very much. He'll love you whether it's a boy or a girl. Be calm, darling. You must be calm."

It seemed a lifetime before the doctor arrived and Leonore was prepared for the birth. Marie arrived at half-past three the following morning. She hovered between life and death for several moments and was energetically slapped into life by a doctor who had little patience with irresolution on the part of any of his patients.

Paul didn't know of the birth of his third daughter until he arrived at the Bourse at ten o'clock that morning. Nobody could find him before that.

CHAPTER 12

▼

1890

Marie was loved demonstratively. Paul and Leonore could never pass without picking her up, dandling her or tickling her; they had to express to each other their impartiality as to her sex. Dorothea was genuinely fascinated, though not as fascinated as she'd been by Sonia. She now accepted new babies as an unremarkable feature of family life. She now displayed both children with the gravity of a connoisseur exhibiting her priceless collection. Visitors laughed and said how charming she was, which pleased her very much.

The new baby was lethargic, seldom crying and almost never laughing. She was the first of Leonore's children to be put to a wet nurse—a carpenter's wife from St. Denis who came to live in the house to suckle her. From the moment she was born, Leonore abandoned her search for Lydmilla Fyodorovna as though anxiety for her Russian friend had been a singular craving of her pregnancy. Afterwards, during the long, quiet, comfortable days, her thoughts were all of Paul. To give him a son was all she had wanted. Her certainty that Marie would have been a boy was all she remembered from the days before the birth. She lay, her body lax, her mind tense, concentrating all her might on recapturing strength to become pregnant again as soon as possible.

The first regular, exuberant interruption to this quiet reverie was Rachel's arrival home from Maison Bertrande. She was coping with life aggressively. Without taking off her outdoor things she would fling herself onto the bed, seething with the aggravations of the day. This time it was the forewoman, Madame Roseanne, who had been "absolutely awful."

"What did she do then, darling?" Leonore asked patiently.

"The mannequin was dreadfully annoyed too. I could tell from the way she kept looking at me."

"Why was the mannequin annoyed? What happened?"

"It's not fair, the way Madame Roseanne kept her standing about like that for absolutely hours and hours. I wouldn't have done it if I'd been her."

"But you're not a model, my dear. I suppose she knows what to expect...it's all part of her job."

"Of course I'm not a model. Though I'd be just as good at it as Hortense; better, probably. And anyway, Madame Roseanne keeps me standing around for absolutely hours and hours as well."

"Oh?"

"Holding pins and ribbons and things in case they're needed. She snaps at me if I so much as shift from one foot to the other; says I'm spoiling her concentration. And this afternoon I could see she had all the material tucked up at the back of the skirt. I told her so, but she wouldn't take any notice. She's much too grand to take advice. She went on dithering and mumbling about the skirt, pulling it one way and the other and not putting it right at all. I could still see what was wrong so I told her again." She stopped to take an angry breath. "And then, would you believe it, she actually said: 'Be quiet, Mademoiselle! I know exactly what I'm doing'"

"Perhaps she did, dear."

"No she didn't! When she'd finished at the front, she came round to the back and shook out the material a bit. But it still looked absolutely awful. And she finished by saying to nobody in particular, 'There! That's very nice!'"

Ida's life at the pottery was different. On her first day there she had fallen in love with Monsieur Leon, one of the senior designers. Monsieur Leon had golden hair, a golden moustache and a golden beard. His cheeks were pink, his eyes an indescribably beautiful blue. He had broad, pale hands, with supple fingers and his fingernails were scraped white. His clothes smelt faintly of musk and tobacco and his voice was like a warm shawl. Ida's feelings for him were intensely romantic but naively asexual. He was her knight on a white charger.

Half an hour after her arrival that first day, Monsieur Laurent, another designer, had told a tasteless joke about Jews. Then, as though noticing Ida for the first time, drew attention to his teasing by being apologetically embarrassed and saying he hoped she wasn't Jewish herself. Ida's eyes had filled with tears because she didn't know how to return the young man's rudeness. Monsieur Leon had stepped forward immediately, however, and firmly reproved Monsieur Laurent, shaming him in front of everyone in the studio. Thereafter, Ida went to sleep every night with Monsieur Leon's face a beautiful fantasy before her heavy eyelids.

Leonore was careful not to let Ida see how deeply she was shocked, but she told Isabel about it on her next visit. This was blatant anti-Semitism—the new word for it. But this, also, was Paris, the most cosmopolitan city in the world. In spite of liberal appearances, she wondered, how deep was this prejudice in French life?

"Everyone knows the French are the most narrow-minded race in the whole world, darling. Don't worry about it."

"I can't help worrying about it. You've never lived in a ghetto, Isabel. I'm shocked. I never thought we'd have to worry about this sort of thing in France."

"Darling, you must know what Chauvinism means. The French invented the man; they invented the feeling. Tell me honestly, have you ever heard a Frenchman genuinely praise anything or anybody from anywhere else? They don't. It's impossible for the poor dears."

"Why Jews? We do them no harm."

"Darling! You haven't been reading the right newspapers. Don't you know about Edward Dumont? He's a gutter journalist always writing about the Jewish menace. According to him you and I, my love, are a plot." She laughed. Leonore didn't want to hear any more, but Isabel persisted. "The French are Roman Catholics and they all claim to be good ones in spite of the immoral lives most of them lead. Being Catholic doesn't prejudice them in our favour, certainly. And they're Chauvinists. They were badly beaten in 1870 and someone has to pay for that!" Seeing the shadows on Leonore's face she hugged her warmly. "I'm sorry, darling. We're quite safe; you mustn't worry any more about it, darling. We're perfectly safe here so long as we have lots of money."

"And you're really not frightened yourself, Isabel? You're not just trying to make me feel better?"

"I don't worry about it at all, darling."

That wasn't altogether true. She often discussed with her husband the prejudice to which he was subject in his business dealings. She frequently suggested changing their name to something French but he always refused. In spite of what people said, everyone on the Bourse agreed that the name Chronach stood for trustworthiness on all the money exchanges of Europe.

Leonore feebly relied upon Paul to allay her fears. There were dramatic changes in their relationship since Marie was born. Paul came home more regularly and sometimes stayed at home for long periods during the day. There was never a night he slept anywhere but in his own bed. He was lightly amused by Ida's infatuation and didn't take the rest of the teasing seriously.

"These things happen," was all he said. "Our little Ida isn't the one to let it trouble her. She'll be all right so long as Monsieur Leon takes care of her."

"You don't understand, Paul. This is the way it starts. You've no idea what it can lead to."

"I know quite well what it can lead to," he told her quite roughly.

She knew Paul was having problems in his business and was reluctant to bother him. Since 1870 the French had been searching for insurance against further German aggression. Now there were friendly grunts from an almost bankrupt Russia, and a government loan was launched between Paris and St. Petersburg. The Bourse lurched into a new direction. Paul's pool of private investors became shallow, his private speculations less dependable. He bought less and spent more time calculating most favourable times to sell. The flow of new money to the credit of the Wirsberg Company diminished to a trickle.

On the other hand, outside of the Bourse, a new enthusiasm was taking over the town. The pink of Boulangism faded from the fashion plates; now, everything had to be a la russe. Ladies' fashions, (though nothing too outré of course, my dear), restaurants, cabarets, all took on tinges of Muscovy. Everyone was reading Turgenev and even Tolstoy; "War and Peace" was somehow reconciling everybody to the retreat from Moscow, which had, after all, been a very long time ago. Gipsy orchestras and balalaika bands were the latest sensation. It was all delightfully inconsequential, the ever-quickening carousel that was Parisian life.

Paul and Leonore were dining out again in fashionable restaurants, one of their favourite being the Cafe Orlov at the top end of the Champs Elysees. It was the latest place to see and be seen. For Paul and Leonore it had a special significance; much of the music there they had enjoyed together long ago at the Doma in Warsaw.

"Wouldn't Clementine love this, Paul? I haven't written to her for ages. I really must. How I'd love to see her again."

They chatted happily of their days in Warsaw and even spoke affectionately of Pan Koblinski. Afterwards, they walked arm-in-arm homewards round the Arc de Triomph. They were wandering carelessly, each fantasizing about their arrival home when they heard her, a woman's voice, low and soft, hardly above a whisper against the sound of passing traffic.

"Paul! Leonore!"

They stopped and were about to turn when she urged them on.

"Don't stop! Keep walking!"

"It's Lydmilla," Leonore breathed, but Paul was aware of it without being told. The unlooked-for reminiscence of old excitements burned in his blood.

"They mustn't see us talking together."

"Who mustn't?"

"Please keep walking! Paul, I need your help."

"I don't understand."

"You must be patient, Leonore, I beg you. May I come to your apartment later, when I can be sure it's safe?"

"Of course, but…"

"Not now. There's no time."

She was suddenly silent and they sensed that she'd gone. The street sounds that had been suspended while they talked roared back. Leonore turned round. She was gone. They walked silently now; the mood of the night had changed. They felt a menace they didn't understand.

She arrived before they could convince themselves their meeting had been a dream. She was pale, tired, much thinner than when they'd last seen her. She wore shabby black from head to foot, her spiky fingers browned with nicotine. She refused brandy and would accept coffee only if Leonore went to the kitchen to make it herself; no one else must know she was in the house. While Leonore was away she gave Paul a wry, conspiratorial smile, but was silent. When the coffee came, she drank two bowls, one after the other, nearly boiling.

"It's very simple," she said suddenly answering their unspoken question. "One of the waiters at the Cafe Orlov is a friend of mine. He sent me a message to tell me you were there. Such a chance! I so badly needed to see you."

"You could have come any time. You could easily have found out where we lived."

"Always so practical, my dear Paul. Of course I knew where you lived. It wasn't wise to come. Now...I'm desperate. When Mikhail told me you were at the Orlov tonight, I had to take the chance."

"Whenever you need help, you should always come to us first, my dear," Leonore told her reproachfully. "We're old friends."

Lydmilla Fyodorovna ignored her. Her shoulders slumped and her voice was thick. "My dears! What a horrible betrayal! Obscene!" She fumbled nervously in her bag, found a cigarette, lit it and inhaled deeply. "Hideous! What a hell we are living in!"

"Lydmilla Fyodorovna," Paul began earnestly, "you must..."

"But you do not know. How could you? Tomorrow it will be in all your newspapers, of course. They will be so proud to let the whole world know"

"Know what?"

"La belle France! Kropotkin and the others! She has taken them all! Everybody! Arrested by French police on orders from the Okhrana! They've lived in Paris for years and now, because of money—this new agreement with the Russian government—the French are arresting and deporting all the Russian revolutionaries in the country." She paused, looking at them intently. They offered no reaction.

"You know what it means, of course," she continued in a false, matter-of-fact tone. "You know what will happen when they get to Russia: the icy slime of the Peter and Paul until they're shot or an animal existence in Siberia for the rest of their lives." Her breath rasped in her throat.

"This Kropotkin," Paul asked, "he's the Prince Kropotkin I've heard about is he...the anarchist?"

"There is nothing to be done," she moaned, ignoring him. "He and the others are surely all taken by now."

"And you, my dear?" Leonore asked shyly. "You were one of them?"

Lydmilla Fyodorovna tried to laugh, but her laugh sounded like a death rattle. "I'm not important. What happens to me doesn't matter. It's only the others who count."

"This Kropotkin…" Paul began again.

"He is a man," Lydmilla Fyodorovna declaimed with dramatic energy. "He should never have come here."

"Your lover?" Leonore enquired softly.

"That is not important. It is the man who is important. He is working for the new Russia. Soon we shall all be grateful to him."

"The new Russia?" Paul intended it as an innocent enquiry, but she turned on him like an angry vixen.

"You see, Paul von Hagen? You see what you and your kind have done?"

"I?" He drew back as though avoiding a blow.

"You and your greed! You people who live for nothing but money. Man was born to live on the harvest of his labour in the fields, not on the kind of harvest you gather in the money markets and the slavery you impose on your fellow men. Where is the dignity in that? You and your kind have perverted the purpose of human existence. Kropotkin is working to purify humanity once more."

"You, too, are working for that?"

"I have told you, I am not important. I am the least of them. I simply look to see what needs to be done, and I do it."

"Here in Paris?"

"In Moscow, of course. There's no harm in my telling you now. I have a comrade among the workers at the Byolorussia Station there. I am a courier. I take him money, literature…whatever he needs to keep the movement alive. Now…it is finished!"

"Lydmilla…" Leonore was about to speak when she felt Paul's restraining hand on her arm and knew she should say no more.

"You want to send for a policeman, Leonore? You want me to go back to Russia with Kropotkin and the others?" she asked sarcastically.

"Of course not, my dear. I was about to ask after your husband."

"He's dead." It was said without feeling. She stared at Leonore with her cold grey eyes, trying to provoke her into saying more, but Leonore remained silent. "For him, there was never enough money," she continued spitefully. "I had to bring him to Paris last winter. He died, of course, after a few weeks."

"I'm sorry."

"Don't be. People die all the time," Lydmilla assured her, lighting another cigarette. "They die of cold, of starvation, of disease. Most sad of all, my dear, and once you have seen it you never forget, they die of despair while they are still alive."

These words introduced a heavy, unyielding silence into the room. Lydmilla Fyodorovna stared into the empty fireplace with half-closed eyes. Paul stood to one side, studying the greying hair of one who was once so significant in his life, and whom he would now give anything never to have met.

It was Leonore who brought them back to reality. She stood up, clasped her friend's head in both her hands and held it close to her bosom.

"O Luyshka," she said, "my dear, dear Luyshka. I love you. I do, most truly love you; and some time soon, when we are together with nothing to do, I'll tell you how I searched all over Paris for you in the months before my baby was born. I needed you then, so very, very much."

"Meanwhile," Paul broke in coldly, "you said you wanted our help, Lydmilla Fyodorovna. How can that be?"

"Money!"

"Money?" He sounded uncomfortable, sensing this to be the beginning of blackmail?

"There is a man in London I must see if anything is to be saved. But they will be watching the ports for anyone like me who's slipped through their net. I need to be able to stay in a safe place for a few days. Then I must have clothes...decent clothes such as a middle-aged governess would wear, perhaps. Certainly, I'd never get a mile out of Paris looking like this. And then there is the traveling. I must pay for respectable accommodation on the boat, you understand."

She looked up at him and he saw fleetingly, a glimmer of her old attractiveness. There was a smile at the corners of her mouth; he knew she was laughing at herself as well as at him, and he no longer feared her.

"Of course," he said quietly. "You must tell me how much you'll need. And you'll surely agree to stay here as an old friend for one night, at least."

"No, no, I dare not." She stood up, refreshed, recovered and looking younger than when she arrived.

"Where shall I bring the money, then?"

"Tomorrow morning, the cafe Orlov. My friend Mikhail will be there. He will contact you and you will tell him that your wife lost a comb while you were dining there last night. He will tell you that he found the comb and gave it to his Aunt Kara. Then you will give him the money."

It was simple enough, though thinking about it left Paul and Leonore little time for sleeping during the rest of the night. He rose early to be at the bank as soon as the doors opened. She remained in her bedroom, refusing to see even her children until he returned.

Afterwards, Paul gave every impression of having forgotten the incident. There was no word from Lydmilla Fyodorovna; they didn't know if she were still in France or in England. For Leonore, however, confidence in the security of life in France had been shaken once more. She was conscious of growing anti-Semitism all round her. Their correspondence from home continued to be clumsily opened. For her it now had even more sinister significance. Paul tried to make it a joke. Was the Tsar more secure upon his throne for knowing of the feuding between Pastor Vikkers and Father Tikhon? Were the foundations of the Russian Empire safer because it was known that the third great love of Sergei Ourourroff's life had abandoned him for an Admiral in the Black Sea Fleet? The tampering, the prying, the disgusting peeking of prurient civil servants in St. Petersburg had become so alien to their life in Paris as to have forfeited significance. After Lydmilla Fyuodorovna's nocturnal visit, the menace returned. If the Russian government could spirit back Kropotkin, it could claw back the von Hagens if it so wanted.

Leonore kept her fears secret so Paul could say nothing to comfort her. He worried, though, about her reluctance to leave the house alone. He recognised that the only peace she knew was at night, when they were together.

Weeks later he lunched with Henri Chronach at the Club du Bourse. In his usual blunt way, came straight to his point.

"Your wife, von Hagen! Isabel tells me she's ill. No more than the usual women's stuff, probably, though Isabel thinks it might be. Look here, my boy, buy her some new clothes! Take her south for the winter. Cannes will put the trouble right, whatever it is."

Paul hesitated. His relationship with Chronach had never been intimate. "It's more than that," he said at last and, talking to Chronach, he surprised himself by the detailed diagnosis he was able to make of Leonore's fears. Chronach sat nodding and grunting to signify how much he understood. When Paul was finished, he cleared his throat and ordered more Armagnac. "Do as I say. Take her to Cannes first, my boy. And when she's quite better, leave France altogether."

"Leave France?"

"Berlin!"

"Berlin? There are no financial transactions between Berlin and St. Petersburg now—not since the French loan."

"Nonsense!"

"What would I do there?"

"Do what you do here. Buy and sell in the money market."

"Even in the present political climate?"

"Damn the political climate! People with money are always ready to deal across the line, even in wartime. Russia is developing fast. You know that, yourself. There's nothing so interesting to foreign investors as a country that's developing. Go to Berlin! The Germans are civilised. You can deal from there with German entrepreneurs already in

Russia...Serbia...Turkey...the Balkans. You'll do well, my boy, believe me. I'll introduce you to my German cousins. But take your wife to Cannes first."

CHAPTER 13

▼

1891

"I believe you should begin to think seriously about him, my dear. With poor Fermatov you made a wise choice. You'd known him for years; you knew where his interests lay. But now he's gone, poor man, and you cannot go on trying to manage everything alone."

Loff looked at her resignedly. "And you really think that Stepan Stepanovich could be the likely answer?"

Channah nodded. "He knows the Estate well. He knows the people—the Estonians as well as the Russians."

"He's a peasant."

He was a peasant, she had to agree. And because he was a peasant and she was a Jew, he treated her like dirt whenever they met. But she could still put Loff's interests before her own. "He was a peasant when you first brought him here, certainly...a complete peasant. But you chose him because he was different and you gave him some authority over the others. Physically he's able to control them. Obviously he's the most intelligent among them."

"Too intelligent I sometimes think," Loff sighed. "And his accent! It isn't quite right, you know."

She almost laughed but restrained herself. How quickly he was growing old, how early, unfortunately, set in his ways of thought. "Isn't it a little late to be worrying about his accent? My dear, the truth of the matter is that you are working yourself to death and you cannot go on like you are forever. Stepan Stepanovich knows more about the diggings than anyone. He's excellent for supervising the lumbering. And what's more important, the men respect him. They'll do anything he tells them to. In times like this, when everybody's so restless, you might find it very useful to have someone like him on your side."

"He's too different from the others, I sometimes think. He could be a secret agent."

This time she couldn't restrain her laughter. "You're not serious, surely! You really think they'd employ a peasant to spy on you? Now Father Tikhon...! When you said we had to be careful of him, I thoroughly agreed with you. But Stepan Stepanovich...!"

He paused and when she said no more, he prompted her. "And now, isn't it about time you told me the truth?"

"The truth?" She sounded as innocent as she could.

"Isn't this some kind of a romantic plot of yours?"

"Well..." She sounded embarrassed. "I hear in the village that he wants to get married."

"And you are welcome to improve his prospects. Well, I don't mind. There's nothing to stop him. There are enough young unmarried girls in Russian Town."

"He wants to marry an Estonian."

"Good God!"

"They tell me it's Marika Haava he's set his heart on."

"A bit young for him, isn't she?"

"That doesn't matter if they both feel the same way. We know that."

He cleared his throat noisily. "Why doesn't he get on with it, then? What's to stop him? I'll give him her dowry, he knows that."

"Pastor Vikkers is stopping them."

"Doddery old fool!"

"He insists Stepan converts."

"And Stepan won't."

"If Marika becomes Orthodox, the Pastor will be losing another member of his flock. Numbers are his justification. They keep tallies in Saint Petersburg."

"Rot! Why won't Stepan convert, if he loves the girl? He can't think very much of her if he won't do a little thing like that. Has anyone spoken to Father Tikhon about it?"

"Father Tikhon doesn't say anything. But he doesn't have to, does he? He sits in that old barn of his and smiles. He knows he'll win in the end."

"Damned fools, the lot of them! Never mind. I'll ride over to the village in the morning and sort it out with Marika's parents."

"No, you can do better than that, my dear. Announce publicly that Stepan is to be your new first assistant. The Haavas won't resist the social status that will concede to their daughter and ultimately to themselves as her parents. They'll push the girl into Father Tikhon's church soon enough, I promise you."

Channah was right, of course. Channah was always right, Loff reflected.

CHAPTER 14

▼

1891

VON HAGEN: On February 24th at the Rottenburg
Nursing Home, Spandauer Damm, to Leonore (nee
Goldfarb) formerly of Warsaw and to Captain Paul
von Hagen, formerly of Estate Wirsberg, Estland, and
the Imperial Preobrazhensky Regiment, St. Petersburg
now of Charlottenburg, Hoffgarten Strasse 56, a son
Eduard Loff, a brother for Dorothea Frederika, Sonia
Elizaveta and Marie Margarethe.

The child was genuine, but the notice appearing in the Berlin newspapers two days after his birth was to advertise rather than inform; Berliners were to know that the von Hagens had arrived. They came to
Berlin on Henri Chronach's advice. There had been a slackening off of
French private investment in Russian enterprises since the government
loans. Cronach concluded Paul could reap a new harvest in Germany.
He was right. Berlin was bursting, it seemed, with Jews anxious to
assist the growing Jewish-owned industries in Russia, Germans were
eager to put their money into Russo-German concerns that promised
good returns. Besides, Paul had private, pressing reasons for leaving
Paris. The collapse of de Lesseps's Panama Canal Company hit him

hard. Many people lost money in that crazy scheme; and Paul lost more than he could conveniently afford. Edward Drumont, of course, was behind the fall and writing of the collapse as a Jewish plot. De Lesseps was arrested and convicted. Paris was no longer the Bourse for entrepreneurs laying out money far from home, far from the confines of close inspection.

So the family moved almost overnight to Berlin and Leonore arrived as she had in Paris heavy with child, and desiring above all else to give her husband the son for which she was convinced he longed.

She loved Berlin from the moment she got off the train. She recognised, on the instant, an east European city. The breeze that rustled the branches in the Tiergarten had come from somewhere beyond her own Warsaw. The rigid rows of six-story workers' flats east and north of Alexander Platz brought back the human courage and stoicism of people in Zamenhofa Street. There were Jews; many Jews east of Alexander Platz, the men as distinctive as Warsaw Jews in their kaftans and prayer curls. They passed on the pavements unremarked. For the most part, people talked neutrally about Jews. Assimilated Jews controlled commerce and the press. They featured in the theatre, art galleries and concert halls. They led in law, medicine and metaphysical scholarship, so beloved of German students. Germans acknowledged that Jews had stamped their imprint on German culture in the western world. Mixed marriages were common.

It was exciting for Leonore to have her baby delivered in a Jewish nursing home by Jewish doctors, to be attended by Jewish nurses. With the child at her breast, she lay basking in a warming, indulgent fantasy that she owed to Berlin and the security she felt there, the first boy, the heir, she could give her beloved husband.

Eduard Loff von Hagen was a beautifully formed, blue-eyed, blonde little boy whose tiny fists continually clasped the air around him as though, from his very first breath, he was eagerly grasping at life. Paul prized him from the moment he saw him and wrote the same day to his brother and to Serge Ouroussoff that he was now "a father." Dorothea was less sure of her feelings to begin with. Before she'd ever seen her brother naked she sensed that here was something different. She was uneasy. This was a little boy, they said, and she was accustomed to little girls. She eventually bent her neck to the block and accepted him as an addition to her "collection."

Eduard was, fortunately, a good-tempered, unassuming baby. He watched Dorothea with his sharp blue eyes, trying to copy her actions and the sounds she made, learning all the while. When the children were taken out in a group, walking in the Schlossgarten, passers-by turned and remarked what a beautiful family they were—a richtige deutsche!

Paul had rented a delightful, three-story stone house off the Schlosse Strasse. It stood directly on the street with brief steps leading up to its pretty green front door, and tubs of flowers were arranged in the balconies on every floor. It was a respectable, neat, flat-fronted house, looking like an illustration from a child's storybook where black-frocked, white-capped and aproned maids might be expected to be peeping from the windows at any time. It was barely a mile from Schloss Charlottenberg, a baroque palace built in the seventeenth century for Queen Sophie-Charlotte. It was designed to house some of her courtiers. By the time the von Hagens arrived the new villas in the Grunwald were perhaps "smarter," but Charlottenburg satisfied the standards of well-to-do bourgeois Berliners.

Paul's letter to his brother brought an immediate reply: Channah and I arriving Berlin Tuesday. Telegrams from Rachel and Ida came next day: "Coming to see you very soon." Within a week the house was bursting with congratulatory von Hagens and Goldfarbs.

Dorothea received them all and ruled their visit like a tiny Queen. No new baby, she was determined, should outshine her. She took scant notice of the naturally retiring Channah, but set about captivating her new uncle.

"Why do you put your sleeve into your pocket like that uncle Loff?"

"Because I haven't got an arm to put into it."

"Why?"

"Because I only have one arm."

"Why?"

"I lost the other one."

"Where?"

"I don't know."

"Why?"

"I can't remember where I put it."

He laughed and she giggled. How wonderful it was to find a grown-up who actually forgot where they'd put things and made mistakes. Rachel and Ida, she concluded, were an irritating distraction. Family visits were fun but she would prefer not to have two many family visiting at the same time. Apart from anything else there were too many secret conferences going on behind closed doors—doors explicitly closed against her.

"You can't expect me to spend the rest of my life painting plates, Leonore; not with all this going on."

News had reached the outside world that all Jews—the ones who couldn't afford the bribes to be allowed to stay—were being expelled from Moscow, Kharkhov and Saint Petersburg in the middle of winter. Fearful that this meant government-manipulated pogroms—similar to the ones the police had winked at in the 1880's—Jews who could leave were getting out in greater numbers than ever. Only the very poorest stayed—the very poorest and the traditionalists who feared a further extension of the diaspora would encourage secularism. They feared America, but Ida did not.

"It's a new world over there, Leah! Can't you understand? A new world for Jews as well as everyone else."

"I know, my darling. But you're too young and it's so far away."

"You understand what I'm saying, don't you, Paul? There's a great statue in the harbour there; they call it Liberty."

"I know my dear, but Leonore's right. You're..."

"There was a woman called Emma Lazarus. She's dead now, but she organised relief for Russian Jews in New York years ago. They'll need all the help they can get now, that's why I have to go."

"No, darling, you're much too young," Leonore repeated somewhat helplessly.

"Of course you would say that because you know it's something I want to do. But you don't think I'm too young to stay and earn my living in Paris while you two are in Berlin."

"We asked you to come with us, sweetheart."

"That isn't the point! Paris or New York—it doesn't matter. Where will you be the moment I need you?"

"You're not making this easy for any of us, Ida."

"It isn't easy for them is it? Can you imagine what it must be like…turned out of your home with nothing more than you can carry with you…in the middle of winter? That's what they're doing to them. Oh, Leonore! Leonore, darling! Do try to understand. That woman I was telling you about—she called America "The Golden Door." Don't you see? Everyone who can…we've got to keep that door open for them."

"Even if we said you could go," Paul put in, trying to sound logically masculine and conclusive, "What will you do when you get there?"

"I can teach."

"You don't know any English."

"I've been learning. And if I can't teach I can cook soup."

Leonore look defeated. "This isn't a spur-of-the-moment decision, then?" You're going, whatever happens, whatever we say."

Paul was anxious that the sisters' emotions shouldn't betray them into a serious quarrel. "And what does Monsieur Leon say about it?" he asked smiling.

"It's nothing to do with him. Leah, you might as well know I've joined the Zionists."

Once more, Paul attempted to avoid harsh words. "What does that mean, Ida? You're a vegetarian? You go everywhere by bicycle? You believe the earth is flat?"

She withered him with a look. "I wouldn't expect you to understand," she told him scathingly.

"Ida! How dare you speak to Paul like that!"

"Explain it to us, Ida."

"You don't need to. I know all about it. I can't imagine what kind of people you've been mixing with in Paris…"

"Zion's in Palestine, isn't it?" Paul asked quietly. "Tell me about it, Ida."

She smiled and took his hand. "It's the great hill at Jerusalem, Paul. It symbolises the Promised Land—the land God gave the Jews when Moses took them out of Egypt."

"Years ago it was to be in Africa, according to the politicians. Now it's in New York, I suppose."

"Oh Leah, how can you talk like that…after all you've been through. It doesn't matter where it is. We've got to get those poor people out of Russia; that's the important thing."

"Even if we allowed you to go, Ida, we can't afford to help you."

"I don't want your money. I've enough of my own."

"Enough to pay your way across the Atlantic and set yourself up in New York, my dear?"

"It won't cost much. I shall go steerage. Everybody does."

"You certainly will not! Tell her, Paul! If you go at all, you'll go like any other respectable young woman.

Paul smiled secretly. How long would it be, he wondered, before they all went to the Hamburg Station to wave his dear little Ida off to America.

"What about Rachel? Is she going too?"

Ida laughed. "You know Rachel. There's money in fashion and that's where she'll stay."

Loff and Channah stayed until after Ida had left for America and Rachel for Paris. Channah and Leonore enjoyed each other, and could laugh together over Cecile von Aschenbauer's attempts to trap Loff into marriage. Loff was wrapped up in the squirming little creature he called "the little Baron." To gain open access to him, however, he needed a special relationship with Dorothea. He scarcely left the house without her. They took daily walks through the woods and round the lakes of the Schloss, she running along beside him in a green velvet bonnet and coat, in high-buttoned shoes.

"Uncle Loff, will you please tell Papa I want a puppy."

He took her to the Egyptian Museum but it didn't impress her. He took her in the tram along the Spandauer Damm and that impressed her very much.

"What shall we do today, my little one?"

"The tram, Uncle Loff! The tram, the tram, the tram!

There were ice creams in the Tiergarten at the end of the ride and toys to be bought for "the little Baron" at Wertheims or one of the many shops along Kurfurstendamm. He bought his nephew nothing of which his niece disapproved. The Baron's greatest regret was not being able to take all the children back to the Estate.

"So far as I'm concerned, Brother" Paul laughed, the blasé father of the four, "you could take them all tomorrow. I'm afraid Leonore wouldn't be too happy about it, though."

With the security of the von Hagen established, the brothers were closer than they'd ever been.

"Why don't you come home, Paul? It's time. That little one...he should be rolling about in the earth that's going to him one day...the way we did. Berlin's no place to bring up a von Hagen, no matter how German we like to believe we are."

Paul turned the conversation clumsily. "How are you getting on with your Russians, by the way?"

"Well enough, I suppose. Old Tikhon pretends to help, though he doesn't do much. We still have the same old brawls, ever since we found Greta's body."

"They only needed an excuse," Paul told him lightly.

"Everybody's horrified. It was a terrible shock for everyone...and they all think one of the others did it. It was monstrous. And if I'd taken proper care of her it probably wouldn't have happened."

"My dear Loff, what on earth could you have done? She...well...every village has one or two. Interbreeding, you know."

"And what about us? Von Hagens have married von Blombergs, von Aschenbauers and second or third cousins for generations. Do you know, in Petersburg they call Victoria of England, the Grandmother of Europe. There's hardly a single royal house that isn't related to her one way or another. How is all that going to end, do you think?"

"Not in wholesale murder, I hope. Everything's moving at top speed...except for royalty..."

"And even they will be thrown off the carousel eventually."

"Why don't any of them think of finding brides in China or Japan, I wonder?"

"Probably because the Chinese and the Japanese wouldn't have them."

"It's a strange thing, you know..." Loff sounded serious. "None of our girls in the village have wanted to marry any of my Russians. There are scandals from time to time; they certainly aren't monks. But they never intermarry."

"The religious gulf?"

"That can be bridged, as you and I well know."

"The Russians prefer their own, obviously."

"Then why not send for them? They can afford it by now. Letters go backwards and forward all the time. Tikhon writes from our end. I've no idea what's in them, of course."

"Hire a Russian clerk, then. You could afford one. He could handle your correspondence with St. Petersburg and write for the village."

"I am thinking about taking on someone else, as a matter of fact. He'll be waiting to see when I get back to the Estate. He wouldn't be just a clerk, though."

"Another of your Russians, of course."

"A fellow student. Prince Fermatov. Semyon Semyonovitch. He'd already read for a degree in marine engineering when I first met him. Then he came north to read law—not very seriously, I must admit."

"How will he help?"

"I met him again when I was last in St. Petersburg. He's working for the Ministry of Marine but wants a change. He has some good ideas. For instance, he says we could boost our profit several hundred percent if we had our amber carved at home before sending it south. He could contract some carvers and engravers he knows from his Odessa days. We'd have to make it worth their while to move up to us, of course. We'll do that, of course, and set them up in a workshop in Reval. We'll sell our own finished pipe stems, cigarette holders, small jewelry—that sort of thing."

"I accept your judgment, naturally."

"You'll have to meet him. You'll be impressed. He knows what we should do about opening a yard at Khotla-Jarve to build our Baltic barges. And he'll be another voice in the district to counteract Tikhon's influence with their workers."

"You certainly seem to have thought of everything, Brother."

"You know I tried to get rid of Tikhon, don't you? After the murder business I wrote to Krasnov to have him removed. He behaved disgracefully over burying the poor girl. Nothing happened, of course."

"You know...we can at least speak frankly to each other, can't we, Brother? No matter how much care we must take with other people."

Loff looked startled, a hint of fear in his eyes, perhaps. "I should hope so."

"You know..." Paul repeated, searching for the right words, "everything we get from you or anyone else over there...it's all opened before we get it. You realise that, don't you?"

His brother laughed. "Good heavens! That happens all the time...to everyone I know. The secret is, never put anything on paper you wouldn't want to answer for afterwards. You'd never commit yourself to anything incriminating, I'm sure."

"It isn't a joke, Loff."

"No, of course it isn't."

"We shouldn't have to tolerate it. There must be some way to stop it."

"Now that's the kind of thing you must never put on paper, Paul. I think you've lived abroad too long. You should come home—for a short while, at least leave this lotus land and get to grips again with what we in the real world have to live!"

CHAPTER 15

▼

1891

Loff's real world was waiting for him when he and Channah reached Estate Wirsberg. Prince Fermatov greeted him warmly but had depressing news not published in Russian newspapers available in Berlin: total failure of the previous year's harvest in the central provinces. Together with hunger came cholera, long accepted by peasants with dull-eyed Christian resignation; did not their faith, after all, assure them that after passing through this temporal vale of tears, the meek shall inherit the earth? Today, this resignation was no longer absolute. Many had already migrated from the countryside into the towns. Hunger and cholera flourished among these new factory-workers and slum-dwellers in the nauseous mushrooming cities. Traditional fatalism was eroded and God's inevitabilities were being met with a new, frightening militancy.

"They write to tell me of a new impatience among the men in the docks and shipyards at Odessa," Fermatov said. "They can't afford to feed their families. They're a raging whirlpool of discontent, angry, frustrated, going round and round, but they don't know what to do. We must pray they won't find a leader who'll show them."

"There must be something more practical we can do than that," Loff mumbled.

"I know, old friend." Fermatov's eyes searched the room suspiciously, hastily like a fugitive.

Loff understood. "We're both too old," he sighed. "Whatever is done must be done by the young. God knows they've tried often enough in the past, poor devils. They've tried and they've failed. The system is too strong. It's broken them. It breaks us all."

Next day the district considered that the Baron had been allowed enough time to settle in again. His first visitor was Father Tikhon. The priest insinuated his black-robed body round the study door, all twinkles, bows and smiles, to offer an official welcome. He stood by the Baron's desk rubbing his grubby hands together like a dog wagging its tail in ecstatic joyfulness at the reunion.

"My dear Baron," he grinned, the hairs on his face appearing to bristle with happiness, "how good it is to see you home again—safely, thank God!—after all these weeks," His voice resonated with pleasure, making the room almost echo like a cavern. "And you have a nephew, God be praised! How is his little Excellency? There was such a party here when the news reached us—such a party, your Excellency. Music and dancing all night. And vodka flowing like the Volga—God be praised!—immeasurable, eternal." His voice and his eyes softened in blissful recollection, then he added tartly: "Good Russian vodka too. Not like the Swedish rubbish they usually drink round here."

Loff bowed acknowledgment and looked away. Since the discovery of Greta's dead body he could hardly tolerate the priest's presence in the same room. The supreme torture was knowing that they were equally to blame for the young woman's miserable life and terrible death. "That's...er...that's very good," he forced himself to mutter.

"And my Russian workmen...that is," the priest gave a cunning, self-deprecatory smile," "...that is your Russian workmen of course, your Honour, subscribed to buy an icon to hang above the little master's bed. They asked me how to go about it since nothing like it is available in these parts—and I told them a Holy Virgin and Child would be most suitable, don't you agree? I advised them to go to Jaroslavl where I personally know artists who are..."

"What is it you want, Father? Why have you come to see me?"

"...so I arranged—I knew you would have approved, your Honour—for the foreman to take the money and go to Jaroslavl himself to make the choice. He is a good, religious man, a true believer..." He paused for a reply, then hurried on as the Baron testily rose from his chair. "It will cost your Honour nothing, of course—not one single kopek. He is traveling on foot except—God save them!—for the kindness of any passing carter who stops to take him up. He should be back in three to four weeks, perhaps."

Loff relaxed into his chair. He had no intention of accepting the icon, but dared not say so outright, since the whole village had somehow found out that he'd sent secretly to Vilna for a Menorah for Channah to celebrate Hanukah; one of his many awkward tendernesses towards her. The ensuing pause didn't in the least embarrass Father Tikhon.

"There is another matter we should discuss, your Honour." The Baron stiffened. Discussion implied equality and, notwithstanding their mutual guilt, he was not prepared to allow it.

"Perhaps you have already heard, your Honour, there is famine and an outbreak of disease."

"So I have heard."

"Your Russians here are apprehensive. They are living in a land of milk and honey," he laughed unctuously, "but rough boys though they are, they still have human feelings, thank God! They naturally feel sympathy and anxiety for suffering ones at home."

Both remained silent for several moments, trading stare for stare.

"It was in my mind that if your Excellency were to organise some relief—wagon-loads of wheat, rye, potatoes, perhaps, to go down to Kaluga, the gesture would generate great gratitude and loyalty among our boys. They would..."

The Baron struck the desk-top with his fist. "I pay them amply for their gratitude and loyalty. If they're not satisfied, they must go elsewhere. Whatever we have stored here is for our own people. Whatever we have in excess of that will be sold on the open market as usual. That is all, Father."

Father Tikhon's shoulders visibly hunched. He was almost at the door when the Baron called him back. "I hope you haven't mentioned your idea to anyone else, Father Tikhon. If you have, I advise you to undeceive them immediately. And tell them to be grateful they're here and not in Kaluga themselves."

This opportunity to humiliate the priest was good for his pride but he had still not recovered his temper when Count von Aschenbauer and Cecile came to welcome and congratulate him. Although he knew it would annoy them both, he insisted on Prince Fermatov and Channah Litvak joining them. Surprisingly, the Count appeared delighted as well as relieved to make a new acquaintance. Cecile gave her attention entirely to the Baron, keeping her back, all the while, turned towards Channah.

"How long will your brother remain in Berlin, dear Baron?" she gushed and babbled on effusively without waiting for any answer. "What a positively splendid city, don't you think? Oh, of course, I know some people argue that St. Petersburg is more beautiful, and they are right, of course, but Berlin is so...so...dignified. Did you ever see anything more noble than the Brandenburger Tor? And the new Reichstag building...? I declare neither classical Greece nor Rome produced anything to compare with it. And the shops, my dear..." She stopped at last breathless, fatigued by the strength of her own enthusiasm.

"My brother and his wife will be living there permanently, I believe..."

"Wonderful," she thrilled, hovering for a further opening.

"They have a pretty little house near Schloss Charlottenburg. They're very happy there."

"Charlottenburg!" she nearly screamed. "But you must tell them, dear Baron, Charlottenburg won't do at all. My friends have all moved into the Grunwald. That's the place to live nowadays. No! Don't bother! I'll tell them myself. Mama and I will be going to see the little one very soon now."

Then her body drooped unexpectedly with a sudden thought. She looked desolate. "How we shall miss darling Margarethe. How she used to love her little jaunts with us. Why on earth did you ever allow her to go to Africa with that man, Baron?"

"Margarethe is a grown woman, free to make her own choices, Fräulein."

"She should never have gone," she persisted. "You should have stopped her somehow, Baron, you really should. It only needed for us all to make one or two little re-arrangements and she could have come back here and gone on as though nothing had happened. I wrote while she was still with your Aunt in Koenigsburg to tell her so."

He felt the ground trembling beneath his feet and refused to ask her what these re-arrangements might have been. Instead: "You might even see little Eduard Loff before you go to Berlin," he said. "I'm hoping my brother and his wife will bring him here very soon now."

"But how marvelous! Papa..."

The Count was already looking towards them, as though listening for a neutral topic of conversation in order to join in.

"Do you think that's altogether wise, my dear friend?"

"Eh?"

"I believe they'd be safer in Berlin at the moment; that's why I'm encouraging Cecile and her mother to go. These hotheads of ours, you never know where they'll turn up next...anywhere from Warsaw to Kazan and beyond, perhaps. The Countess is very alarmed. She wouldn't even risk coming here today. She's determined none of us can sleep safely in our beds any more."

"I'm sure she doesn't have to worry about anything here, Count," the Baron told him kindly. "All those troubles are a long way away."

"But they're not, you see. The effects are already with us. This famine's sending the price of bread sky high, even in Reval. Peasants who have food to spare sell it for as much as they possibly can, and at today's prices they soon find themselves with all their profits gone and they're among the hungry themselves. You've been away, my dear fellow. You don't know what's been happening." He crossed the room and came to clutch the Baron's arm distractedly. "Strikes in the Russian factories mean there's less for people who still have any money to buy; and people who still have any money must put it into something...for the bartering that will be necessary when things get even worse. The people are frightened and when they're frightened, they're dangerous...it's been the same for ever."

"Mama's perfectly right," Cecile put in briskly. "We should all be safer in Berlin."

"Perhaps you might," the Baron retorted almost belligerently. "But I trust my people. They'd never turn on a von Hagen...never. And my brother must bring his family here, whatever's happening elsewhere. Our people deserve it. Tikhon tells me they had a great party when they heard the news. They've a right to see their new little Baron as soon as possible."

"Their new little Baron...?" Cecile repeated his words slowly and softly.

He turned to her, smiling gently. "Of course, my dear. After all, his father will follow me and he'll follow his father. He's the next Baron von Hagen but one."

"But..." She made an ineffectual gesture with her hands. He was looking directly at her, but she knew he wasn't seeing her at all. She turned to her father.

"My dear fellow," he protested jovially, "a man can't possibly talk like that—not at your age. You'll marry in time, believe me. You'll have sons of your own, a fellow like you." He remembered suddenly that Channah was in the room and in spite of all his efforts not to do so, found himself turning towards her. She was staring straight ahead, her cheeks flaming. "That is...I mean...the rest of your life, you know..." he finished lamely.

All trace of a smile faded from the Baron's eyes. He moved swiftly to stand close to Channah and although their bodies didn't touch, everyone in the room knew he was making a public declaration. "After me there's Paul and after Paul, little Eduard Loff. It's settled and the thought of it makes me very happy."

The Count smiled foolishly, utterly lost. Cecile made a great effort to recover and her voice was as brittle as her smile. "I'm certain it does, Baron," she said firmly. "And we shall certainly visit the little one in Berlin if Mama and I don't go to St. Petersburg instead. Papa! We really must be home before dark, you know. For my mama's sake. You do understand, don't you, Baron?"

Channah left the room with them and Loff didn't see her for the rest of the day. When the time came, he went to his bed—alone for the first time in many months—and lay wide-eyed, staring up at the patterns his mind created in the darkness. Hours might have passed before she opened the door quietly, without knocking. His body was suffused with warmth as he sensed her standing close to his bed.

"Thank God you've come," he breathed. "Get into bed with me, Channah."

"No, your Excellency. Not any more."

He sat up vigorously. "Why not? Where's the light? Fetch me a damned lamp!"

"You told everyone."

"What?"

"Today. The Count. Now, after what you said, everyone knows."

"Everyone's known since we began, you silly girl. Go along, now! Light the lamp or come to bed in the dark and let us get some sleep."

"They didn't know. They gossiped but they didn't know for sure. Now you've told them—everybody. Channah Litvak is my whore, you said."

"No, Channah! No!" He struggled out of bed and his one arm flailed the empty darkness in an effort to touch her.

"I never minded what they said about me. I love you, your Excellency. I think I loved you from the moment you caught me in the woods that day. They all called me your whore, but I didn't mind that. I didn't mind what any of them said."

"I never heard anyone say anything of that sort about you," he lied.

"So long as you didn't say it yourself I didn't mind. But today...when you as good as told them you would never marry and then came to stand beside me to let them know I was the reason..."

"Can't you understand? Didn't you know Fräulein von Aschenbauer has been waiting for me to marry her since...for years, now."

"I knew it. You were very cruel to her today, as well."

"Don't waste your sympathy on her." He sounded as bitter as he felt. "There was nothing romantic about her. She saw marriage to me as a way of getting our Estate into von Aschenbauer hands. They've been after it for years."

"That doesn't matter. You should never have told her like that."

"I really don't understand why you're going on like this, Channah. Now! Get into bed and we'll talk about it in the morning."

"It was unbelievably cruel of you to humiliate her like that, in front of everybody. Just as it was cruel of you to let Fräulein von Hagen leave here the way she did. You could have kept her at home. All she wanted was for you to send me away. That's what Fräulein von Aschenbauer meant when she talked about re-arrangements."

"My sister was looking for some sort of life before it all finally passed her by."

"And it was cruel of you to brand me like that...to stand beside me and tell the world I'm the woman you take to your bed every night. You used me as a shield against Fräulein von Aschenbauer."

"Nonsense! It wasn't like that at all."

"Of course it was. You're a man, your Excellency. That makes you more powerful than your sister or Fräulein von Aschenbauer or me.

Besides being a man, you're a Baron, too. That makes you even more powerful. You believe you can say and do whatever you wish. But you shouldn't, you know. It's...it's beastly! And that's why the powerful are hated everywhere. That's why we'll bring you down, your Excellency...we'll bring you down before the end of time!"

CHAPTER 16

▼

1891

The von Hagens were ambling through the Tiergarten one summer Sunday when Paul unexpectedly met Arturo Martinelli again. It was after morning Mass at St. Hedwig's-Kathedrale. Now they were on their way to Dorothea's Sunday treat—a trip on one of the little steamboats flitting back and forth with butterfly busyness on the River Spree.

The first time Dorothea saw the river and the boats, she had persuaded her beloved Sonia that the crowds, the gay noisiness, the steamer-crews with their yo-ho-ho exhibitions of nautical skill and the traditional German bands umpah-pahing in the stern were, for her too, an unmissable treat. Marie hated it. Eduard Loff lay in his nurse's arms trying to seize the Florentine cameo brooch that Dorothea had given her and that held close her confining jabot.

Paul accepted it all with amused ease; he was by now, he had decided, an ideal family man. Leonore watched the crowds and, particularly her family, assessing their approving looks towards her family, with an assured smile. In Berlin, for the first time since her marriage, she realised true self-confidence. In part, that was brought about by the birth of her boy, the little one her brother-in-law promised would be a Baron one day. In part it was because she deeply understood and approved the life-style of the friends she was making. In Florence people were rootless; in Paris they were louche. Here in Berlin they showed kindness, coupled with conformity to social rules such as she had been taught to admire by her parents in Warsaw. There was anti-Semitism in Berlin of course; there was anti-Semitism everywhere. In Berlin, she found, it was not so offensively obvious as in Paris. And—this was also very important for her—running a home was comparatively easy here. Prussian-bred housemaids did exactly as they were told and did it thoroughly!

These were Leonore's thoughts as she walked, holding her husband's arm, among the crowds in the Tiergarten. They didn't talk together. Society had decided that respectable conversation between husbands and wives could only possibly be domestic and should be reserved for the proper place. Conversation between couples in the Park gave quite the wrong impression to people who didn't know them! Decorum was to be maintained at all times, the gentleman to raise his hat, the lady to incline her head and smile as friends passed. Paul and Leonore did a lot of that; they were getting to be known and liked by many people. Women found Paul charming, men considered him trustworthy. Members of both sexes admired Leonore in her conservative, dark dresses. They approved of her rounding, modest figure altogether suitable for a woman of her age. She could, they told each other, have been taken for a German herself—if one hadn't known, of course. At home, her domestic staff liked her well enough and, behind her back, called her dumpy.

She was watching the river, entranced by the tiny rainbows created by water dripping from the air-bourne oars of an inexpert rower when she heard Paul say:

"My dear, may I present Signore Martinelli?"

"She looked and saw a podgy man, no taller than herself, with a round head shaven close, the sun glistening through defiantly refulgent stubble.

"The Signore and I are old friends aren't we, Martinelli?"

Paul said in a tone Leonore didn't understand.

"Gnadige Frau, his Excellency does me too much honour," the man remarked in faultless German.

Leonore smiled, then suddenly squinted at him through her lashes, as though struck by short-sightedness.

"Come now, Martinelli," Paul laughed, though there was no humour in the sound. "We had that interesting train ride together to…"

"Bo-zen" the little man broke in excitedly. "Your Bo-zen, my Bol-za-no" he laughed. "How could one possibly forget?"

"Indeed! And that little talk we had on the rue de la Paix…"

"And now my little ones have brought me to Berlin and I am so fortunate as to meet you again, Your Excellency."

"I know you too, don't I, mein Herr?" Leonore put in abruptly. "I wasn't on that train and I wasn't in the rue de la Paix, but…"

"No, no, no, Gnadige Frau," he assured her hastily. "Believe me…had I had that pleasure it would have been impossible for me ever to forget."

They parted soon after at Dorothea's non-too-subtle insistence. Martinelli expressed most fervent wishes that they might meet next time he brought his "little ones" to Berlin. He stood on the riverbank, watching them and waving his straw hat in farewell, as the little steamboat chugged them away.

"Paul," she began, because once they were on the boat social constraints were loosened, "who was that man?"

"Just…just someone I met. He's not important. It doesn't matter."

"But Paul, I'm sure I know him too, from somewhere."

"Where?"

"That's the point. I can't remember. But I'm certain I know him."

When they arrived home in Charlottenburg in the late afternoon, they found the inside of the house in chaos. Cupboard doors and drawers were open, their contents spilled on the floor. The locks on Leonore's escritoire and Paul's desk had been forced, papers scattered everywhere. Even the children's' toy boxes had been plundered. The children screamed, Leonore nearly fainted. Paul uttered a quiet "damm!" and ran down to the basement calling for Ulrika. He found her at last, up in her attic bedroom, kneeling and shaking behind her bed. It took some little time for the police to arrive.

"Not very wise, your Excellency, if I may say so, leaving the house empty and unprotected like that."

"This is Berlin, Herr Kommissar. On Sundays my family and I expect to be able to leave the house in safety for most of the day. For us, after Church, Sunday is a holiday." The Lieutenant made a moue of envy. "We like to give our staff a little holiday on that day too. They take it in turns for one of them to stay behind."

"And today?"

"It was Ulrika's turn."

"And we shall get no help from Ulrika until she decides to come to her senses."

"That child is very badly frightened, Herr Kommissar."

"Yes," the policeman muttered, unconvinced.

"Where does she say she was when this happened?"

"In my wife's bedroom, examining the clothes and jewels she found there."

"And you believe her?"

"She wouldn't lie to me, I'm sure. Young girls are interested in that sort of thing, you know."

"Huh! And you're quite convinced she didn't come down to let in whoever ransacked the house?"

"They broke a window to get in. She didn't hear a thing until they came upstairs and then she ran up to the attic, terrorised."

The easiest thing in the world, your Excellency. Break a window. It makes a fake break-in look authentic, you see."

The door opened slowly and Leonore came in, looking pale.

"Paul…"

"Go back and rest, my dear," he urged her gently. "We're almost finished here…there's nothing more for you to worry about…really."

"No, of course not," the Lieutenant agreed. "Unfortunately, even here in Berlin, mein Herr"—he looked meaningfully at Paul as though this was a little joke between them, "we can't avoid having some of the wrong type of people, even here. And summer Sundays, you know...in districts like this...they know most of the houses are likely to be almost empty...Take more care in future, that's all I can say. Of course, we'll make enquiries. Meanwhile, I'll take that young girl along with me. She'll soon cool down when she sees the inside of a police cell."

"No!" Leonore rose from her chair and appealed to Paul. "You must stop him. Ulrika's a good girl. She'd never have anything to do with..."

"I know lots of good girls, Gnadige Frau, believe me. You'd be surprised at the kind of things they get up to," he told her complacently

"Paul!" Leonore said again, urgently.

Paul sighed. "Ulrika had nothing to do with it, Herr Kommissar."

"You sound very sure, your Excellency."

"I am."

"Then..." very slowly "...if you are so sure about Ulrika, perhaps you know something you haven't yet told me about someone else...someone who did have something to do with it."

"Yes...that is...you realise we're Russian citizens, Herr Kommissar?"

"No, I didn't realise that. With a name like von Hagen..."

"We're of German stock, of course, but from Estonia."

"I see." The Lieutenant nodded sagely, though clearly he didn't see at all. "And you know who broke into your house today?"

"Not exactly, though I believe I know the name of someone involved."

"And that would be...?" The Lieutenant licked his fingers as he took out his notebook again, manifestly indicating that whatever he was about to hear would be nonsense.

"There is a man called Martinelli...Arturo Martinelli. At least, that's what I know him as. He's supposed to be a dealer in religious statues.

He's in Berlin at the moment. We met him this afternoon by the Spree."

The Lieutenant raised his eyebrows unbelievingly, wrote slowly in his notebook and concluded by drawling the words 'religious statues'. He added a full-stop dramatically and waited with pencil poised to hear more.

"He robbed me once on the Express from Florence to Vienna."

"Florence to Vienna," the policeman repeated punctiliously.

"I don't believe his name's Martinelli at all. And it's too much of a coincidence, running into each other in Paris and then again, here in Berlin."

"So you think," the policeman said slowly, almost derisively, as though trying to follow a most difficult line of abstract logic, "you think, do you, sir, that this man who sells religious statues is in reality a member of a gang of international house-breakers?"

Paul made a visible effort to restrain his irritation while Leonore looked sharply at him. "You must see, Herr Kommissar, this isn't an ordinary case of house-breaking."

The policeman looked indulgently interested.

"Surely, it's obvious! They didn't steal anything! Not my wife's jewelry, nothing from among my business papers…"

"So you said at the beginning, sir."

"They didn't come to steal anything…only to warn us that they are watching us."

"And who would that be…watching you…sir?

"The Russian Secret Police."

"Ahhhhh!" The policeman slowly expelled the air from his lungs and slipped his notebook into his pocket.

"You must know about them. You certainly have Secret Police here, your Prussian…"

"Exactly, mein Herr," the Lieutenant exploded before the name could be spoken openly. "You think, do you, that for some reason the Russian…er…the Russian authorities are interested in your affairs?"

"Isn't it obvious?"

The policeman looked exceedingly embarrassed. "We shall make all necessary normal enquiries," he said, edging towards the door. "But...unofficially, of course...I can't do more than offer you an opinion. In view of the present friendly relations between our two countries..."

"I cannot expect protection from your Government, you mean? As a foreigner, living and working in your country..."

"Please, your Excellency, I am speaking as your friend. If I were you..."

"Yes?"

"What can I say, your Excellency? What I would say to any foreigner in difficulties. Pay a call at your own Imperial Embassy," he said as he bowed and left. He didn't take Ulrika away with him. Neither did they hear from him again. The von Hagen affair might have been stored in a 'Cases Pending' file, a 'Cases Dead' file or the Lieutenant's waste-paper basket.

CHAPTER 17

▼

1891

It was days before the agitation subsided. The pretty little house had been raped—something not easily forgotten. The servants were thrilled by the excitement and revived it as often as possible without being in any way seriously affected. Ulrika became a kind of domestic heroine and found her nervousness very pleasantly appeased. For Leonore, the agitation lasted long—all the deeper because Paul refused to talk about it with her.

"Be reasonable, darling. You must put it out of your mind. We know they were only trying to frighten us—that's all. They can't possibly do anything to us because we've done nothing wrong."

That wasn't enough for her; she either couldn't or wouldn't believe it. Paul tried to break her miserable pattern. He suggested she take the children for a holiday in the Harz Mountains. But the thought of the family being separated for any reason whatever, terrified her even more.

When the summer reached its end, Leonore agreed with Paul that Dorothea should begin her education at a local, socially approved kindergarten. Dorothea was delighted by the idea.

"Can Sonia come too?" she asked.

"No, darling, Sonia's too young. She'll have to wait for another time."

"Then I shall teach her everything I learn," Dorothea declared precociously, and left for school on her first day in a glow of self-importance.

Leonore fell into even deeper anxiety and would only leave the house after the child returned from her lessons. Paul was therefore especially grateful when they heard unexpectedly from Rachel, providing Leonore with a new interest.

Paris,
18th October, 1891

Dearest Leonore and Paul,

I do hope you are all well. I should have written to you long before this to commiserate on your burglary. But if I were to tell you how busy I have been, you just wouldn't believe me. Anyway, I hope you have all been able to settle down long since.

I know it has only been months, but it seems like years since I last saw you and I'm hoping to hold my little nephew in my arms very soon. If I don't hurry, I'm afraid he'll be too old and grown up to tolerate his Aunt making a fuss of him when I do see him. Men can be so very awkward, can't they? I've really no idea at what age they start.

Besides, I have some very exciting news for you but I'm not going to tell you anything about that until you tell me that I may come.

Your Very loving Sister, Sister-in-Law and Aunt,

Rachel Goldfarb

Rachel arrived two weeks later, and when she told them her news, they were confused and not particularly happy. She had left Paris.

"But Warsaw is just the place these days," she insisted repeatedly. "Warsaw gowns are all the rage. Not everyone wants to go so far as Paris, even if they can afford to."

"What about the French themselves," Paul objected. "And I know of men here who send their wives to Paris."

"Oh yes, I know," Rachel agreed with an annoying self-assurance. "And the British and the Americans. But…don't you understand? I want my own business. I'll never manage that in Paris, but I've saved enough to start up for myself in Warsaw."

"You're being ridiculous, Rachel. You haven't thought things out," Paul told her impatiently. "Poles don't like Jews. You're away from all that now, Rachel. You're safe in Paris."

"Oh that, Paul…you worry too much."

"There'll be more trouble there one of these days, Rachel," Leonore told her. "There always is."

"There's trouble in Paris. You know that yourself, Leonore. It's a different kind of trouble, of course."

"But surely…apart from all that, it must be very expensive to start up any kind of business these days."

"Father had barely a couple of kopeks when he started."

"There's no comparison. Times have changed. Surely, you'll need a workroom, a stock of materials, a staff…"

"Machinists, vendeuses, models, advertising," Leonore added enthusiastically and silently tried to think of further objections.

Rachel laughed. "My dears, I shall do everything myself. Oh, I picked up lots of design ideas in Paris, believe me. And I shall be my own machinist, my own vendeuse, and my own model until I can afford someone to help me. As for advertising, I shall do all that myself. I shall be seen everywhere, all the time, looking magnificent. And everybody will be demanding to know who dresses me. And Leonore, I've decided to take one of those large apartments on Sienna Street. That's a very good, mixed area. Remember?"

Leonore nodded dazedly.

"There are quite a lot of well-off people round there, Jews as well as Gentiles. I shall get to know their wives and daughters! Rich people long for the extraordinary, in order to show everybody how rich they are. I shall offer them exceptional style without undue expense."

Paul smiled impatiently. "You've obviously thought it out, Rachel. There's nothing more for me to say, except...genuinely...to wish you success my dear."

"Thank you, Paul."

"Now, if you'll excuse me, I have a business appointment."

Leonore was still far from convinced of the practicality of all this, but when the time came for Rachel to leave, her departure was almost unnoticed. Dorothea came home from school with a running nose, sore eyes and ear ache. Leonore suspected only too easily what the trouble was and summoned Doctor Hartmann.

"I will call again tomorrow," the doctor said complacently, having examined the child thoroughly but not really thoroughly enough to satisfy Leonore. Dorothea was put to bed with a rising temperature and feeling very miserable. The following day Sonia, her constant companion, inevitably displayed the same symptoms. Marie, apart from whining because her sisters were receiving so much attention and she was not, remained healthy. So did Eduard, and Leonore watched them both very carefully. Two days later Doctor Hartmann pointed out a positive rash.

"Open your mouth, my child! Come! Wider than that!" He motioned Leonore to come close. "See, dear Lady? The little white spots inside the cheeks? We have the measles." He regarded her triumphantly, "The other little one, she is obviously developing it, too. Bring her into the same room...it will be easier to nurse them together. Keep the other child right away from them so long as she shows no signs of course...have you anywhere you could send her for a day or two? No? Well, never mind...be sure you keep her well away from these two. And, particularly, keep watch on the boy. At his age the result, if he gets it, could be very serious."

Leonore knew. Measles, Scarlet Fever and Diphtheria were annual events among the teeming children of Zamenhofa Street. Her own family had been comparatively lucky. Only one of her younger sisters had been left deaf, and the eyesight of one of her brothers was considerably weakened. But no one died. Their deaths were held in abeyance, until the Cossacks came.

She was drawn out of this frightening recollection by the doctor's sharp insistence. "You understand, dear lady? The room must be kept dark at all times. Hang a curtain soaked in disinfectant over the door. And there must be a basin of disinfectant outside the door at all times. Everybody coming in and out must wash their hands at all times...everybody!"

All this was horribly familiar to Leonore.

"Above all, watch the little one," he reiterated. "From six to eighteen months..." He shook his head pessimistically. "A dangerous age...a very dangerous age."

In spite of all his mother's prayer and care, Eduard caught the measles, of course. He lay whimpering in his cot, his skin burning and blood red, with no energy to grasp any longer at the world around him. Leonore abandoned her daughters' care to the housekeeper and spent every moment with her son. She even discouraged Paul from visiting the child for fear he might bring in a further infection from the outside world. To pacify her torment he gave in.

Leonore's torment consisted largely of guilt. She knew she was about to lose the little boy who meant so much to her. She had so longed for him. When he came, he was her triumph. For his sake, she felt, she had all but deprived her daughters of the love and attention they deserved. Her sin was pride; outrageous, relentless pride. Now she was to pay the penalty. She sat in the darkened room beside his cot, a wet cloth in her hand, trying to bring down his temperature. Her hair was uncombed, her dress unchanged. Her eyes were red and swollen with crying. She might have been taken by a renaissance master for a study in repentance. But she knew her repentance had come too late.

"Pride goeth before destruction and a haughty spirit before a fall," mocked her from the Proverbs she had been taught in her childhood.

And there was no comfort, either, in the creed of her conversion. "God resisteth the proud and giveth grace to the humble," she was assured. And as she watched her baby suffering in his cot she knew there would be no grace given to her.

CHAPTER 18

▼

1891

Margarethe Behrendorf was also, in her own way, battling with pride. For her, unfortunately, there was no recognition of it and, therefore, no repentance. She was realistic enough to admit to herself that her taking up the Cross of Christ and following her husband to Africa was not entirely altruistic. Her father had schooled her to recognise her Duty, to do it and to be thankful that the Lord had provided it to be done. When, obviously, her Duty no longer lay within Estate Wirsberg, she had looked for another field in which to work and found it under the impetus of panic over her seemingly useless future.

Her duty had always involved being a scourge, and she had come to Africa to scourge it. Her background had encouraged her to make unalterable judgments between right and wrong. In Africa she found loathsome wrongs. In spite of all her tongue-lashings, the men of her husband's flock still went stark-naked, sniggering at the attempt to make them wear Christian trousers. Their womenfolk shamelessly flaunted their breasts, covering the secret parts of their anatomy for the enhancement offered by decoration, rather than for modesty's sake. Their sexual habits appalled her. They lived in physical filth with no idea of what did or did not belong to them. They ignored all her efforts to teach them simple hygiene. Their faith in their centuries-old religious practices and the rituals of their disgusting superstitions were impregnable. Worst of all, they refused to attend the school she was trying to establish.

"Education must be the only way," she pleaded hopefully. "Mustn't it?"

Her husband, seated across the supper table, stared at her as though he recognised her vaguely, but could not quite place who she was. He moved haltingly these days and spoke slowly. All the fire of his first sermons had disappeared and he replied to whatever was said only after a pause, as though it took time either to understand or to decide what to say in reply. They were both aging before their years, their bodies wasted by constant effort in the unforgiving heat, their skins yellowed by recurrent fever. They were like matchstick people, their bones discernable beneath the skin.

"I shall go to Buea," she told him briskly. "I shall see the Governor. He must be told how things are. The government must see how important it is to set aside money for education."

"It's a long way," he said at last, adding nothing more.

He was right. It was a long way and she did get there in the end, traveling slowly, her bones shaken horrendously over roads that were no roads. The Governor received her kindly. He was recently arrived and was still plump and pink-skinned; but he was sweating she noticed with a feeling close to satisfaction. He clicked his tongue sympathetically. Of course he understood that she needed help, but things were difficult here in the capital too. Berlin allotted a criminally limited budget. The price of bananas, rubber and cocoa once they reached the European market fluctuated distressingly. What could he say? Perhaps next year...

She went home despondent, but more despondent over the lack of government organisation and foresight than with her own failure. Why, she asked herself, why were they all here? Why did the government bother to waste any money at all in a territory they either didn't understand or didn't have the interest to develop? Did Germany need colonies in Africa so badly, the world bananas so ardently, her own sacrifices could possibly be worthwhile?

She descended the slopes of Mount Cameron and drove over rutted grasslands where bizarrely leaping deer miraculously found miraculous foothold. After the grassland she entered the jungle. Day by day she had come to hate it more and more. The tall trees held out the sun; what grew at ground level had an abundance of obscenely fat, rich green leaves, many exuding a foul, dead smell. There was little light there and the heat seemed to strike upwards from the dank, mulch-covered ground, as well as pressing down on her from above. Every night it rained. At dusk, all heaven's faucets opened at once, deluging the leaves and soaking everybody and everything beneath. When it touched her skin, it was icy cold; how could it be so cold in such an atmosphere she wondered. When it touched the ground it rose in a haze of dank-smelling steam.

Margarethe didn't fear the jungle any more, even though she knew it hid animals and reptiles and insects that would kill her if they could. She had come to conquer the land for Christ and she was not to be intimidated—not by anything it threatened.

When she reached the Mission, everything was as she'd left it except that now, Pastor Behrendorf had fever. He lay on his truckle bed, his mosquito net over him, writhing and sweating and muttering insanely. She stood for a long time, looking at him. Had she intended to tell him about her trip? She really didn't know. It wasn't important, anyway, whatever she'd done. She heard his irrational mumbling but didn't bend down to hear the words in case they made sense. Her heart was empty for him. She had no feelings at all, neither good will nor bad, love nor resentment. She had tried a long time, but now she had given up. It was impossible for her to feel for his man who had brought her to this depth, this man who had married her and condemned her to a frozen unconsummated union.

CHAPTER 19

▼

1891

Channah had meant what she said. She abandoned the Baron's bed and left his house at the same time. In the shock of it and the darkness, Loff hadn't understood that she was speaking the truth. He thought he was hearing a futile female fancy that would be gone by morning. So he slept well that night and expected to see her, as usual, presiding at his breakfast table next morning. Prince Fermatov was sitting there alone and looking puzzled. There was no sign of Channah, nor of breakfast.

"Fräulein Litvak isn't well this morning, perhaps?" Fermatov asked diffidently.

"No...er...that is...dammit! Where's breakfast?" Loff flung his napkin onto the table, stood up so violently that his chair toppled over backwards, and felt the samovar so roughly with his hand that it fell of its unlighted lamp and cold water gushed all over the cloth. Incident adding by incident to his anger, he stormed out of the room and into the kitchen.

Everyone there heard him coming and, if they couldn't escape altogether, busied themselves with anything at all, eyes down and backs towards the door.

"Karlis!" he shouted, grasping the shoulder of the unfortunate boot-boy who was standing confused and closest to the door. The boy seemed to shrink physically beneath his touch.

"Where's breakfast?"

The boy half turned, fearful. "Fräulein Litvak didn't come, your Excellency. We don't know what your Excellency requires."

Loff released him and recoiled. His anger was dispersed by a vast unease. "Bring bread, cheese and some meat for Prince Fermatov, I suppose. And a hot samovar. And some tea, of course."

The physical relief in the kitchen was manifest when he left. He climbed the stairs slowly, as though delaying his arrival at the top. He shuffled along the landing to what had been Channah's room until she started sharing his own. It was empty. Her bed was unruffled, her cupboard door swung slightly open and he could see from where he stood that all of her few dresses were gone. He sat heavily on the narrow bed. There was a heart-breaking space on her clothes chest where her Menorah had stood when it wasn't being used.

He didn't sit for long. There was a situation to be dealt with. Eating was furthest from his mind, but he returned to the breakfast table. Prince Fermatov was there, gnawing a hunk of bread dipped in a glass of tea, secretly wondering whether it had been wise, after all, to accept the Baron's offer if this were, indeed, the mad house it now seemed.

"Fräulein Litvak…" The Baron paused but because he had a respect for the truth, instilled during his days in the Law he discarded the various convenient excuses that flitted through his mind.

Fermatov looked puzzled. "Gone?" he echoed.

What comment could the Baron make? "Women, you know," he snorted.

CHAPTER 20

▼

1891

There was nothing to be done to help the von Aschenbauers now they were already pillaged. Loff's immediate problem was to defend his own property, and he had not the least idea whom among his people he could trust. The house servants were now virtually strangers; outside, his peasants, like all the peasants in the Principality were changing their attitude.

Their misguided reaction to subtle Russianisation was to feel themselves freed from their landlord's traditional domination. Previously, between them and their God, Pastor Vikkers and those like him said, stood their landlords. That wasn't so said Father Tikhon and those like him.

"Blessed Father in Heaven stands the Tsar, your Little-Father-on Earth, the Anointed One. He loves you, my children. Day and night he prays for you alone. He longs for your happiness.

He talks about you to his Father-in-Heaven, the One we all share and in whom we trust for mercy. He asks for advice how best to ease your burdens and soothe your woes."

Loff knew this was pure politics, and had nothing to do with trying to convert. It was having an effect on the peasants' thought and behaviour, though.

If he got through this night without disturbance—please God!—he would ride to the von Aschenbauers tomorrow to find out what actually had happened. Did the peasants there attempt to save the contents of the barns? Did von Aschenbauer trust them with arms? If he had, could he be sure they would use them? And against whom? They may by now have been so muddled by everything they'd been told as to think the raiders were emissaries of the Little Father in St. Petersburg, come to collect the grain with the sanction of God Almighty in order to ease the suffering among His children elsewhere.

The next morning he decided not to leave the estate after all.

Prince Krasnov must by now have read his letter and realised that his situation was serious. Meanwhile—he couldn't trust Father Tikhon and would never ask his advice—he sent for Semyon Semyonovitch. When the man came, he interviewed him in the hallway—not quite in the house like a trusted advisor but not quite outside like a peasant.

"We have a problem, Semyon Semyonovitch. You've heard about the raid on Count von Aschenbauer's barn, I suppose?"

"Yes, your Excellency."

"What do your men feel about it?"

"Feel about it, your Excellency?" he asked slowly, as though not understanding the question.

"Well yes, man, what do they feel about it? What are they saying?"

"It happened far away. What should they say about it?"

"It happened on the next Estate. Don't they remember the Count locking them in his barn on their way here?"

"Ah." Semyon Semyonovitch nodded as though everything was now clear, but he said nothing.

The Baron was becoming irritated. "The point I'm getting at is, how far could I rely on them if the same thing were to happen here?"

The man looked blank. More annoying, he didn't look away or fiddle with his loose shirt or the buckle to his belt as might have been expected. He looked straight back into the Baron's eyes, but his look was blank.

"What I want to know is, if I issue them with firearms, will they help me defend the place or not?"

The man's pause was long and eloquent. Then he said, his voice quite flat, "I will ask them, your Excellency."

When Semyon Semyonovitch had left, Loff assembled all the men of the household in the hall. They shuffled while he inspected them like a military platoon. By now, it was inevitable; everyone knew the details of Channah's leaving though not the details. The house hummed with rude jokes about her and the Baron. The Baron, they decided, must have heard somebody talking and was about to take his revenge. They were very surprised to find that was not what he was going to talk about.

"You've all heard by now about the attack on Count von Aschenbauer's Estate last night, I suppose?

They mumbled that they had but weren't much concerned, since it didn't directly concern them.

"We can't expect they'll be satisfied with only what they stole from the Count. We must be prepared for them to come here next."

That produced a rumble of anxious exclamations.

"I've written to Prince Krasnov. He'll be sending us a company of gendarmes very soon but, until they come, we've go to see about looking after ourselves."

There was no excited reaction to this—no reaction at all, in fact. There was more shuffling and everyone looked everywhere but at the Baron in the hope of escaping his attention

Personally, the Baron was angry. He had tried reasoning with them, tried to encourage them to feel that this was a common interest—his and theirs. But it was no good. It never was.

The only way to get them to do anything was to bark and swear at them.

"You! You! And you!" he snapped. "You're my captains! Split the rest up into equal numbers. Divide the night between you. I want one squad here in the hall at regular intervals from dusk till dawn. Understand? No excuses! One of the squads on guard in the barn all night long!"

This brought a more positive reaction. The men he picked looked the oldest and, he hoped, were therefore the most reliable. They were now sorting out their men. There was a lot of pushing backwards and forwards but after a few minutes they seem to have sorted themselves out.

"Good! Now! Who's taking first shift?"

The captains looked at each other but were silent, waiting for one of the other two to speak first.

"God in Heaven! One! Two! Three!" The Baron pointed to each squad in turn. "Now you'd all better get some rest. I'll see the first squad here in an hour."

Loff went to the armory, after they'd gone, and unlocked his small store of rifles. He wasn't happy about issuing them, but supposed the noise of loose fire would drive the raiders off.

He certainly didn't want a lot of unnecessary slaughter about the place.

The squads assembled in turn and went out to the barns with him. The nights were cold. A hard frost was upon them, transforming blades of grass into vicious spikes. The land was covered in a white shroud deluged in a dead translucency from the autumn moon hung in a steel-grey sky above them. It was a bright, cold, alien light and the shadows of trees along the track lay across the frosted earth like fallen fence-posts.

On their way to the barn the four men in each squad were quiet, intimidated by the light, the quietness of the night and fear, perhaps. In the barn they spoke at first in whispers. Then, as time passed, their voices grew louder and fretful.

They were cold, tired and uncomfortable. They didn't see any point at all in being there. Loff was disturbed by the change in them. Normally, on meeting him, they were soft-voiced, respectful, monosyllabic. Now they spoke with an insolence born of nervousness. Already, before dawn on the first night, Loff knew he could never defend the place without help from Krasnov's gendarmes.

But there were to be no gendarmes. While Loff was resting next morning, recovering from his sleepless night, Pastor Vikkers returned with Prince Krasnov's reply.

My dear Baron,

Your friend Pastor Vikkers has safely delivered your letter. I have kept him overnight; he was far too nervous to return to you in the dark.

I was sorry to hear of the unfortunate occurrence to befall Count von Aschenbauer—he has not seen fit to send me any notification himself—and of your own perturbation for the future.

My dear friend, much as I sympathise with you in your present circumstances, I cannot send you any reinforcement. What happened to Count von Aschenbauer is, unfortunately, happening all over the Principality. I find myself with all too few men and it would be unforgivably unfair of me to favour one landlord over another.

With warmest memories of your excellent hospitality I am,

My dear Count, Your obedient servant,

V.F.KRASNOV

Loff crumpled the letter in disgust. The man's motive was all too clear; to deliberately weaken German prestige and authority. He groaned, turned on his couch and reconciled himself to a succession of sleepless nights. And he was not to sleep today, either. His next visitor was Semyon Semyonovitch who stood in the hall twisting his cap in his hands and, this time, avoiding his master's eye.

"I spoke to the men, your Excellency."

"Well?"

"They cannot help."

"Ah."

"People say the raiders are Russian, your Excellency. They cannot fight their brothers."

"They would rather see me ruined, their jobs destroyed."

"Your Excellency, while they remain alive they can work…here… somewhere else…to send money to their wives at home. Once they are dead, who will look after their little ones?"

The Baron dismissed him, returned to his couch and tried to put all thoughts of the men's' disloyalty out of his mind. He tried, also, not to think of Channah either. But when he was not vilifying her, the pain of her loss was unbearable. In his present isolation his need of her was overwhelming.

In its own time the moon waned. Loff blundered through two weeks more without Channah, two weeks more of nighttime wakefulness and watching. The weather was changing for the worse. The thin sliver of new moon was hidden by black, charging clouds. Outside the house at night, the blackness was as thick as a wall. Ponds were beginning to freeze and local boys were testing them tenderly, and betting their trifles as to when they would bear skaters.

By now, Loff was exhausted. He stumbled heavily through the darkness, unwilling to show a light in case raiders were in the vicinity. In any case, he was unable to carry a lantern securely, as well as a pistol, in his only hand.

He was on his way from the barn to collect a relief squad from the house. He did this twice a night and they should be waiting for him in the hall. He hardly expected them though.

They also were experiencing the effects of interrupted sleep and after two weeks of nothing having happened, they were impatient.

He anticipated, each time he made the trip from barn to house finding no one waiting.

He had gone just over half the distance when he heard them coming; horses with muffled hooves swishing across the frozen grass like an evil wind. He stopped for a moment to be sure of what he heard. Then he moved forward again, urgently and silently as he could. Thank God! When he went into the hall, the men were waiting.

"They're here," he said softly and "be quiet!" as they began to murmur. "The last squad is still in the barn. Your job now is to get along there as quick as you can. Don't wait for me! I'm coming. Now run!"

He opened the door for them and they left, more eagerly than he'd expected. He stayed in the lighted hallway for a moment, battling with lack of breath and the pain in his chest. Then he went after them; they wee all much younger and he could never have kept up with them. He ran as fast as he could, surprised by the lack of noise from the barn. The moment he reached it he knew why. One man stood holding a lantern while others shoveled his grain into baskets. When the baskets were full, other men came in from outside and carried them away.

Of his own men, there was no sign.

"Yuri! Who's that? Get him out of here!" It was a harsh Russian voice.

"Stop that! What do you think you're doing?" Loff demanded.

There was no reply. Before he had a chance to cock his pistol someone came on him from behind and hit him hard against the side of the head with a shovel. He went down immediately.

Consciousness returned with daylight. He was lying flat on the grass as the frost thawed. His limbs were rigid with cold, his clothes damp with frost. His head hurt appallingly.

He tried to lift it off the ground and was forced to let it fall back while he panted with effort and pain. And yet he had to get up, had to see; although he knew what would be there. The smell of smoke and smoldering wood was unmistakable. They had not only robbed him; they had burned his barn to the ground.

It felt like hours before he got back to the house. He had first to roll over from his back to his front, then to contract his legs till his body rested o his knees and his one arm simian-fashion. He seriously considered crawling back to the house like that but found the courage to torture his limbs his limbs until they supported him upright. He moved forward slowly, and reached the house with his ear throbbing unmercifully.

He wanted to raise his hand to hold it, but he had no hand on that side of him. To reach the other arm across his body unbalanced him but he could hold his hand there long enough to feel a mass of caked blood.

A footman was crossing the hall when Loff went in, wearing his smart uniform as usually, his shoes tapping neatly on the stone-paved floor. He neither looked at his master nor spoke.

All Loff could do was lean back against the doorframe grasping for breath.

He stayed there waiting for someone else to come, but nobody did. One of the maids surely, he thought…Slowly he dragged himself up the stairs, wincing at every step and reached his bedroom. Fully clothed he collapsed on to his bed with a groan mixed of despair, pain and relief. Quite quickly the blessed blackness closed over him again.

It could have been days; it could have been weeks before the door opened. He didn't know who it was, and he couldn't be bothered to open his eyes to look. A female voice, familiar but an unaccustomed element of harshness in it said:

"Wake up, your Excellency. I'll change your bed and clean you up. You'll feel better."

He would still have preferred to be left alone, but curiosity over came him…curiosity and hope. The figure in the bed, dressed all in black and holding a bowl, was well known though he dared no believe what he saw.

"Come along," she said more sharply.

"Channah!" It was more a question than a statement.

"I was staying in town when I heard what happened," she said briefly. "Come along."

She did, indeed, make him more comfortable and allowed him to sleep again. That was the pattern of several days and he knowingly prolonged them, reluctant to embrace reality again. He lay in his clean bed, well-fed, recovering his strength. He deliberately avoided thinking what came next until he knew by her step, by the way she stood by his bed one morning, that his days of indulgence were over.

"We must talk, your Excellency."

"I know. Fetch a chair."

"First of all, about us," she said as she dragged a chair close to him.

He was slightly shocked. This was not the pliant young girl he'd known before. This was a young woman suddenly approaching middle age and thoroughly self-assured. There were lines around her mouth and at the corners of her eyes he hadn't noticed previously.

"It must be understood," she began. "What I said before I left still stands."

He looked at her, puzzled. "Why come back, then?"

"I was in town when I heard what happened. I told you, but I don't suppose you remember. I was trying to decide what to do next...where to go. When I heard, it was obvious. I had to come back."

"Thank you."

"Of course, when His Excellency wishes to make other arrangements and no longer has need of me..."

"You know that's not likely. And Channah, for God's sake, call me by my name. Call me Loff."

She smiled and changed the subject. "You know, of course, your men ran away that night...the ones you were taking down there as well as the ones in the barn."

"I know." He sighed. "I've stayed here too long. I should have dealt with it right away."

"You were too ill. But you'll have to deal with it now. If you don't, they'll think they've won. That mustn't be. What they did was unforgivable."

He said, not yet resolved, "I'll talk to them."

"That's not enough." Her eyes were hard, her voice like a whiplash.

"What do you think, then?"

"Turn them away."

"What?"

"They're not reliable. It's not safe, these days, living in a place like this without people you can trust."

"But…"

"It's the only way."

"It's almost winter."

"All the men and any wives and daughters."

"We can't turn them out like that, Channah. For the love of God! Where will they go? What will they do?"

"They'll have to do like all the rest who are moving into the towns…look for work."

"We can't manage without them here."

"We can manage with fewer than you had before, certainly.

And I've had my eye on several young people in the village we can train up nicely. Oh, and by the way, I've collected up and locked away all the firearms you issued."

In two days the Baron had completed his preparations, made up his account books and collected together the wages that were due. Then Channah ordered one of the footmen—like a condemned man unknowingly building his own scaffold—to arrange a table and a tall, throne-like armchair in the hall. The men were called and stood in a shame-faced huddle. Each had been rehearsing the excuse he would offer if called upon personally to explain.

The Baron glared at them. The men knew they were in for a verbal lashing at least; possibly they would each take their turn on the cross-frame outside the church.

"I don't want this meeting to last longer than is absolutely necessary for all our sakes," the Baron began. "Your behaviour during the raid was inexcusable and I do not intend to excuse it. You all have the rest of the day to collect your personal belongings. I expect you to leave this house at sunrise tomorrow morning and not come back. Now…! Come up as I call your names and collect whatever money is due you.

Those with wives or daughters here, tell them to come up directly after I've finished with you."

They listened in stunned silence, came up as he called them and turned away without a word. They were beaten, and this was far, far worse than the cross-frame. They felt a new strength when the Baron needed them in his crisis. Now the crisis was over. He no longer needed them, and they were powerless once more. For one brief moment they had had him in their hands. It was too late now to wonder whether they should have stayed at the barn risking a couple of cut heads and broken bones to maintain their hold. But they didn't. This was the way things had always been…were always meant to be.

Prince Fermatov came back from Reval to find a whole lot of fresh, blushing, beardless blonde faces tending awkwardly to his needs. Channah was tireless everywhere, superintending in the kitchen, the brewhouse and the laundry, teaching new footmen to polish boots and wait at table; new maids to make beds.

She found plenty of volunteers in the village who imagined working inside easier than working outside. After die Frau Baronin left working for the old Baron, as everyone thought of him, was said to be easy. True, Frau Channah was back with him now, but she was only a Jew and they could soon put her in her place.

The Prince had found suitable premises in Reval, but not without difficulty. Migrants were flooding in and the sort of accommodation he wanted was rapidly being converted to house workers. The Domberg remained a German residential stronghold, but the suburbs below were rapidly being taken over by Estonians. There were even Estonians on the town council.

Loff didn't want to know about such things; didn't want to have to think about change. Everything around him was overturned beyond imagining. He could only wait, passively as any present, for what the future might bring.

Fermatov was keen to leave for Odessa to hire workers for his amber factory. His departure was cheerfully delayed for several days, however, when Paul and his family, accompanied by Ulrika and the official nursemaid suddenly arrived.

"You sounded desperate in your letter, Brother," he said. "How can I help?"

Loff took him to visit the ruins of the burned-out barn and, with Prince Fermatov sitting with them, talked through much of the night. Paul felt uncomfortably as though this were a confessional; Loff had to admit his great fault: he had lost control and feared he would never recover it.

"If Channah hadn't come back, I don't know how things would be, even now. But she doesn't understand. She's trying to organise everything back to being like it was. But that's no longer any good, you see. The time for that is gone."

"I didn't know Channah had been away."

"No, well..." Loff looked embarrassed. "I was taking her too much for granted, I suppose. In the old-fashioned way, you know. I don't understand exactly how or why, but even between Channah and me, everything has changed."

To Loff's uncertainties, Paul could only add his own. "In some ways I feel we should never have left Florence. It was a backwater, I know. But we were safe there. After we went to Paris there was no more peace of mind. It was even worse in Berlin after the break-in. That affected Leonore very badly. She refuses to live there any more."

"You're home for good?" Loff sounded pathetically eager.

Paul smiled affectionately. "Can't do that, brother."

"Not these days. The country's no place to settle a wife and four children and another on the way."

"Another?"

"Leonore's pregnant. Besides...we still have the business to run. I need to be some place where there's money."

"Your brother's absolutely right, Loff Pavlovitch. The old Russia is changing. Everything is industry and commerce now.

The peasants are land-hungry; they always were. They're handling their claims differently now, though, since so many of them are learning to read and write."

Loff turned to his brother. "You think what Yuri Sergeivitch says is true, Paul?"

Paul nodded. We have to consolidate ourselves in industry, brother. There's less and less value in land these days."

"Where will you go, then?"

"Even before we left Florence I started to feel like a rag doll on a long piece of string. And I'm not the only one. I believe we're all on pieces of string. I don't exactly know who's holding the other end, but he's got to be in St. Petersburg...he must be."

"The eye of the storm," Fermatov said softly.

"And that's where you're going?"

"It'll be good for the children...their education. I won't have them tortured by tutors at home the way we were. They're going to school."

"And after that?"

Paul shrugged. "Then it will be up to them," he said.

They broke up soon after, and Paul went to bed expecting to find Leonore waiting for him. The bed was empty. She was in Channah's sitting room, more self-confident that her pregnancy was established and patiently listening like a good, older, more experienced friend.

"I knew I should look foolish, coming back after so short a time," Channah was saying. "But I couldn't stay away...not when I heard what had happened."

"Of course not, my dear."

"We still don't know whether he'll get back his hearing in his left ear."

"He must go to town...consult a specialist."

"They beat him most terribly. I don't know why they had to be so cruel. He's always been the dearest, kindest man to everybody here."

She was on the verge of tears. Leonore patted her hand sympathetically.

"To beat him like that when there was no reason. And to burn his barn. There hasn't been any burning anywhere else. Why did they have to pick him out for special, horrible treatment? Why were they so vindictive, Channah? And why only to him?"

CHAPTER 21

▼

1891

The child got better only very slowly. For days he lay in his cot moaning and burning with fever. Leonore sat beside him, demented. Doctor Hartmann visited the patient twice a day, tutting, shaking his head and moving restlessly about the room. Leonore sought comfort in prayer. The doctor was a modern scientist and an unbeliever. He had no comfort whatsoever, while the child's disease resisted all his efforts. The older children were scolded into silence. Paul was at last allowed back into his son's room. Ironically, at this time of deep anxiety, his financial affairs flourished fabulously. He tried to pray with Leonore, but the despair in his heart drove everything else out.

Sonia was fretful, copying Dorothea's mood. Dorothea was resentful. Eduard was her brother and she hated being kept apart from him. Nobody in the household had time to discuss her feelings except Ulrika whom, in revenge against everyone else, she conscripted into her personal entourage. By Ulrika, she and her devoted Sonia allowed themselves to be placated.

Ulrika took them for walks, generally to the Charlottenburg Gardens. There, she herself only recently from the country, Ulrika disclosed secrets nobody else they knew had ever considered important. She could keep them silent and still, fascinated by watching a statuesque, slate-grey heron until its sudden dive and upward soar with a wriggle of silver in its beak. She taught them to distinguish three species of sparrows, various tits, blackbirds from starlings, rooks and crows from jackdaws. She taught them the names of new flowers and grasses each time they went out. More to Dorothea's curious taste, though, Ulrika knew the names of the different sorts of clouds and what they portended. Dorothea loved to exhibit this precocious knowledge where she knew it would be most appreciated.

"It's going to rain today, Papa."

"Is it my love?"

"Yes."

Paul would look suitable amazed. "And how do you know that?"

"It's a secret."

"Tell me."

"No. I mustn't. It's a secret."

He would sigh. "All right, then. I'd better take my umbrella with me, hadn't I?"

She would suck in her cheeks with pleasure and nod vigorously in her triumph.

Ulrika's ability to keep Dorothea contented during Eduard Loff's illness was a relief to everyone. When the disinfected curtain was eventually taken down from his door and the disinfectant bowl discarded, she continued without any discussion, to look after Dorothea and Sonia, while the official nursemaid attended to the younger ones.

Leonore looked very ill herself, just then. Her hair straggled, her face was the colour of putty, her neck was showing the first signs of scrawn and her wrists were as boncy as Margarethe's had ever been. Paul treated her very tenderly. He begged her to take a holiday with him. He suggested Italy—just the two of them. They could visit the romance of the South; she'd never been there. Their servants were reliable. The children would be well enough looked after in Berlin.

She was adamant in her refusal. The idea of leaving any of her family when fatality was only ever just around the corner was unthinkable. Hour after hour she watched over the nursemaid watching over her son. Suddenly she would lift him up and clasp him to her without warning or reason other than fear. She made ridiculous sounds close to his ear: "Mama's a dog—woof woof!" as gruffly as she could manage. "Mama's a pussy cat—meow meow; Mama's a cow—moo moo." His eyes regained their old sparkle has he turned his face to hers, laughed appreciatively and tried to grasp her nose.

Thank god Doctor Hartmann had been wrong. His hearing wasn't damaged.

At other times she would swing the pink pearl necklace Paul had brought with her from Paris in front of the child's eyes, backwards and forwards, to the left, to the right...those eyes flashed with amusement and followed the pearls—left to right, right to left—and his little fists clenched and flayed out to grasp them.

Leonore watched and thanked her God again. He was all right. Everyone had said it was the eyes you had to watch. Measles could have a terrible effect on the eyes, but Eduard Loff had escaped. Even being sure of it she could never be satisfied and repeated the gams over and over again.

Paul watched her with growing anxiety. He found within himself a hitherto undreamed-of tact and after her second refusal of a holiday said nothing more. But their relationship changed harshly and he became fearful of her and for her. She would sit for hours motionless, huddled in her chair, her eyes gazing at something a long way away, that no one else in the world could possibly see.

"I want to go home. I want to go home," she murmured constantly.

Disregarding everything except what might bring her back to him, Paul knelt by her knees and clasped her hands. "Of course you'll go home, my darling. We'll leave for Warsaw directly when you're feeling better. The end of the week, perhaps."

She turned her head slowly, perplexed. "Warsaw?"

"Yes, my darling, if that's what you want, I'll take you home."

She shook her head gently. "I have no home, Paul. I must stay here with my baby."

Paul remembered the illness in Praga and went privately to see Doctor Hartmann.

"The result of a great anxiety, my dear sir," the doctor said. "You must get her out of the house. Take her to restaurants, the theatre, the opera...Anything to divert her morbid thoughts."

"I can't persuade her to go anywhere."

"A holiday...?"

"I suggested that, but she refuses."

"I could, of course, arrange for her to stay for a little in a sanatorium for...er...nervous conditions. People are coming up with some very interesting ideas in that field just now, you know."

"Never!"

"Then..." The doctor shrugged. Why ask his advice if it were not accepted?

Paul said as though to himself, though longing for the doctor to overhear: "She tells me she is isolated. Even when we're together, talking, she feels alone. It's like living in a glass box, she says. She can hear and see everything going on outside, but she can't make any contact."

The doctor shook his had but said nothing. This was clearly something beyond his experience, though he would not admit it. Meanwhile, Paul longed to tell him everything. He needed to talk, though he too, was isolated. He needed to tell someone how their love-making had changed. Instead of being gentle and receptive when he wanted her, Leonore had become rapacious. It was now she who wanted him. Every night she threw herself upon him, tearing at their nightgowns, kissing him with her tongue buried deep in his mouth. At first, in a turmoil of shock and surprise he tried to satisfy her need, without knowing exactly what it was. But after a little it became impossible. Night after night, this storm of passion was too much—not because he no longer loved and desired her, but because she frightened him into impotence. She wouldn't let him be even then. He turned away but she clasped him back to her, manipulating him, moaning over him the lewd encouragements she knew from the streets of her childhood.

Paul lived in a nightmare. Each day he went to the Bourse, pale-faced and heavy-eyed. He watched his colleagues, men he'd known since coming to Berlin, and speculated about their private lives. What were they hiding, all these men he worked among, going about their duties and pursuing their interests with such clear-eyed confidence?

Then, one day, it was over. He had stopped, as he often did these days, in a little bar on his way home. He had drunk, as he usually did, several brandies. They had little effect. He wasn't drunk. They didn't go any way towards soothing his incomprehensible, unbearable present.

This was not a fashionable bar; he had chosen it for that reason. There was no chance of meeting anyone who knew him. Tonight it was more crowded than usual—a mixture of human beings as varied as pebbles on the seashore of his home. They were mostly men; men with gold watch chains across ample bellies and loud voices, sitting as though they meant to stay all night, while other men glanced nervously at the smoke-browned clock before they drank up hastily and rushed away. Men sat at tables as though cast in concrete, men with pale faces, sad eyes, drooping moustaches and an air of hopelessness.

Moving seductively among the tables were the prostitutes, women from the brassy to the beautiful and men—a specialty of the Berlin scene—from straight-backed military men to others whose beards at this time in the evening began to show beneath the cosmetics on their drawn faces.

Paul drank brandy after brandy with sullen determination to forget his worries. He wished the fat, bullet-headed shopkeeper two tables away would keep his voice down.

"May one share the gentleman's table?"

He sensed that the words were directed at him, and nodded without bothering to look up.

"A beer please, Herr Ober." The voice was that of a youngish man.

"Bring me another brandy. A large one." Paul ordered rudely, before the waiter left the table.

"At once, mein Herr."

Paul glanced across the table incuriously. His companion was possibly a bank clerk, wearing an uncomfortably high stiff collar and a tightly buttoned thick, black suit. The man smiled. Paul nodded once more and looked away.

The young man settled his gaze on Paul and because Paul became embarrassed under the stare, easily captured his attention. "This is a jolly place, isn't it?" he volunteered.

As though to refute this opinion, a girl with a cracked voice and wearing a powder-stained black taffeta dress climbed on to the stage in the corner and began to sing dismally of the pain being in love invariably caused her. A memory flashed into Paul's mind of the first time he'd seen Leonore in a place like this, though in his youthfulness he had judged it less sordid. She, too, had sung of love's anguish.

The young man said, repressing his laughter, "She is terrible."

Paul was glad to have his thoughts invaded. This place was nothing like the Doma, nothing like anything else in the whole of his life, like nothing he'd seen even in Paris. Here, everything was naked: the drunkenness, the avarice, the sex. Perhaps it was the young man's enthusiasm reflecting his own at the same age that persuaded Paul to defy his present pain, and join in with the crowd. All his life he had been an observer, accepting everything on his own terms. It was time to admit that that was no longer the way things were. He remembered his father's injunction the morning he left for St. Petersburg to join the army. He smiled. His father must have been living on another planet.

The young man must have thought Paul's smile was directed at him. He said, "I've never been here before. A couple of the fellows at the bank recommended it. They said it would be fun."

Paul considered whether to move on somewhere else or to stay where he was. Why not stay here? He was comfortable enough. He ordered the waiter to bring him the bottle and an extra glass. The young man's excited glances around the place grew more amusing and touching. He couldn't have been more than sixteen or seventeen. Paul remembered when he was that age, in St. Petersburg, being educated by the ladies on Vasil'yevsky Island.

The young man accepted the brandy. "I come from a village near Magdeburg. There's nothing like this there, of course. My uncle knows one of the directors of the bank. That's why I'm in Berlin." He smiled apologetically for talking too much about himself.

Paul grunted disinterestedly and determined to get drunk.

"My uncle found me a room not far from the Alexander Platz," the young man said. "There are lots of us young fellows working at the bank." He said it smugly, as an indisputable fact. "We'll all be sent off to work in provincial towns soon, I expect. I must make the most of Berlin while I'm here." He laughed.

Paul began to envy this fresh-faced innocence as the evening grew more hazy. He wondered what the boy's name might be and couldn't be bothered to ask. The girl who sang came to their table and, uninvited but optimistic, sat on Paul's knee. She fondled his hair. He grinned in response and grasped her firmly around the waist. The young man smiled with a mixture of interest and innocence. This was life as he had never known it before.

Paul slowly passed through the veil of intoxication. The girl remained on his knee caressing him, her object. The young man looked more animated and talked to the girl. Paul listened but could hardly follow their sentences or their meanings. From time to time he wanted to say something himself, but that wasn't easy. There was something wrong with his tongue; it flopped about in his mouth and made words difficult to pronounce. His eyes grew heavy. All he really wanted to do was rest his head on the young lady's shoulder and sleep.

When he awoke, she had abandoned him as a false hope. The bar was quiet. Most of the tables were empty. He believed his senses to be razor-sharp but he had no control of his limbs.

"Time to go home, mein Herr," his companion said respectfully. He stood up as if to leave and Paul wondered how he himself would get home. He rose and balanced unsteadily against the table.

"A cab," he muttered.

"Shall I get you one, mein Herr?"

Paul was conscious of threading his way between the tables towards the door, grateful for the young man's shoulder to lean on. Then he was in a cab. Then he was climbing a long flight of unlit stairs, with someone behind him, hands on his back, helping him on. Existence had suddenly become a series of unconnected experiences. Next came a raucous female voice screaming. Paul realised that being awake wasn't altogether the same as being conscious.

"Out! Out, the pair of you! The very idea! I've never had this kind of goings-on in my house! Come on! Out you get, Herr Ruttgers, before I call a policeman!"

While he came to himself, more of his situation revealed itself. This was a poorly furnished room with grey light filtering in through thin curtains. He was flying full-length and cramped in a narrow bed. Naked! And, God help him! There was someone in the bed with him! He could feel bare flesh against his back!

A voice said, "Please, Fräu Bischoff, it's not what you think. This is my friend, Herr von Hagen."

"Herr von Hagen," she repeated, accenting the 'von' sarcastically.

"We were out together last night. He...he had a little too much to drink, I'm afraid," the voice explained apologetically. "It was too late to take him home."

"There! You see my dear! It's not what you thought at all," a deeper male voice said.

"Shut up, Willi," the woman snapped. "I told you when you first came here, Herr Ruttgers, I don't allow visitors in the bedrooms."

"No, I know, Fräu Bischoff, but..."

"I must say, I was thinking of female visitors at the time. The thought of this sort of thing never crossed my mind."

"I've told you, it's not what it looks like, Fräu Bischoff."

"No, of course not, "said the man with the deep voice." Herr Ruttgers has explained, my dear. Herr von Hagen was ill."

"Well…" the woman said doubtfully.

Paul turned his head and found himself looking much too closely into the eyes of the young man from the abr. His immediate instinct was to get away, but he was reluctant to get out of bed, to appear stark naked before the woman and her husband.

"It's true, Fräu Bischoff. I couldn't leave my friend alone and ill in the street like that, could I?"

"No, well…" the woman's voice softened.

"And now, please, I must ask you to excuse us. I have to be at the bank."

The couple left without saying anything more. The young man smiled at Paul. "I'm sorry." He slipped out of bed and moved modestly about the room, dressing.

Paul said, "You know my name."

"Yes, I had to look in your pocket book for the money for the cab fare. I didn't take anything else…" His voice rose anxiously. "I swear I didn't take anything else."

Paul looked at him confused, lost for words.

"I saw your business cards. I knew where you lived, but I thought it better not to go there. You were rather drunk, you know."

"Yes."

"Nothing like that has ever happened to me before. I had to bring you here. I didn't know what else to do."

They left the tenement together. The young man waited for the tram to take him back to his bank. Paul wanted to get away as quickly as possible and left him at the stop. He walked through what seemed endless drab streets among drab-faced, drab-clothed people on their way to work. He couldn't find a cab until he reached the rank on the Alexander Platz. Sitting far back, sheltering from the light, he realised he knew neither the young man's name nor his address. He was thankful for it. They would never meet again. He wanted the incident wiped from reality as quickly as possible.

When he reached home, Leonore was at the breakfast table with Ulrika and the children. She greeted him with gentle reproof in her eyes but made no comment on his absence. He was grateful and embraced her fondly, and without fear—for the first time in weeks.

After breakfast she led him into the drawing room and asked him to sit close with her. He obeyed with foreboding, but she took his hand and her eyes remained gentle.

"I don't want to talk about whatever happened last night, Paul, I really don't. There's something much more important I have to say."

He looked at her sharply, but her eyes remained gentle and untroubled.

"I have to apologise to you, Paul. I've been acting like a mad woman."

She paused and he didn't know how to reply. He smiled and hoped she would find that, at least, reassuring.

"I was acting like a mad thing, I know. Perhaps I was mad. Paul…Paul, I'm so sorry. I couldn't help myself."

She did indeed look helpless as she sat there beside him, and he was tempted to put his arms around her.

"We nearly lost our son, Paul. He nearly died."

"I know."

"All the time he was ill, I knew God was punishing me."

"My darling…"

"He was. He was punishing me for my thoughts…my intentions."

"My darling Leonore, what on earth are you talking about?"

"I love you, Paul. I always have, I always will."

"Yes?"

"After Eduard was born, I'd given you your son and I didn't want any more children."

"I see. Well, yes, of course, I realised something had changed between us, but…"

"I avoided you whenever I could. I didn't want you to touch me. When Eduard was ill, I could see how wrong I was. I knew I had to give you another son...you, your brother, the family...that was my duty. I didn't realise it before, but that's what I undertook when you married me. Oh, Paul..."

She crumped against him and he took her tightly into his arms.

"My darling, my darling," he breathed. "If I live to be a hundred, I'll never understand you."

She pressed herself against him and kissed his beard. "I went to see Dr. Hartmann yesterday," she whispered. "Paul, darling, I'm pregnant again. And this one's going to be another son. I know he's going to be another son."

Book IV

CHAPTER I

▼

1891

Paul was light-headed with happiness. There was no doubt about it; this was where he belonged: Saint Petersburg. He enjoyed the brightness of its snow-muffled streets, its ice-capped rivers and canals. He wandered everywhere on foot, in and out, up and down, swinging his cane, savouring its champagne sparkle and being astonished once more by the beauty of its rainbow facades. How could he have stayed so long away from its spires, its domes, its skyscapes, and its beautiful women? Saint Petersburg women were eternal in their beauty, nestling seductive in their sleighs, ravishing glances in restaurants, enchanting in their salons and ballrooms. His only regret was to see them always escorted by splendidly mounted officers in fur hats and gold-trimmed uniforms. He was no longer of their company and when regret came to him from a recess of his mind, sharply, bitterly, he thrust it aside before it could take hold. He was now a staid family man in dark suits and spotless linen.

He loved his children. He adored his wife. In comparison, he felt smugly, the officers he still knew after all these years had not yet, as he put it to himself, "grown up." Even his dear friend Sergei Ouroussoff, now a Colonel in the Preobrazhensky, gambled, drank and womanised as if he were still a new-fledged cadet. He was amusing, though, delighted to see Paul again, enthusiastic to inform him of all the great Saint Petersburg scandals since he went away.

"My dear Paul, you're not seriously telling me you heard nothing of the Merenberg affair?"

"No, nothing."

"But…that's unbelievable."

"Russian news reaching Berlin was carefully filtered, you see, Sergei."

"Yes, but this! It nearly set the world on fire."

Paul laughed whole-heartedly. He was drinking with Sergei at Kuzminsky's and sinking gratefully into the warmth of old friendship and gossip. It was exchanging gossip, after all, that confirmed to a man long absent that he was still a member of the club.

"Everyone was talking. You couldn't go anywhere without hearing all about it."

"And you still can't, apparently," Paul laughed.

"My dear chap, it was very, very important, when you think about it."

"Oh?"

"It all came out when the Grand Duchess Olga Fyodorovna was on her way down to the Crimea. She'd only got as far as Kharkhov when she took pleurisy, had a heart attack and died on the spot." He winked suddenly. Like all Russians, he was masterly at investing the most innocent events with the possibilities of hidden mystery.

"Well…?"

"That was in…oh! Last April, I suppose it must have been. And no sooner was the old lady dead when her son Mikhail Mikhailovitch, you must remember him, married the Countess Merenberg…she only a Countess and he an Imperial Archduke, if you please…" He paused to further dramatise the *coup de grace*, "…without asking the Emperor's permission! And would you believe it, old man…?"—he leaned back in his chair as though the monstrosity of it was entirely new to him, his eyes wide with amazement—"…he wasn't sent to Siberia! That's how much things have changed since you went away, my friend. Now that that kind of behaviour is acceptable, even in the Imperial family, how long will it be before the sky falls in, I ask you?"

He prolonged the puzzlement in his eyes for as long as he could, until it was replaced by embarrassment. He was suddenly remembering. "Looking at you today, I can only say I'm glad I was wrong back there in Warsaw, Paul. You know what I'm talking about, don't you?"

Paul nodded and raised his glass. He didn't want to talk about it. Leonore would be arriving at the end of the week, and he was longing to reunite them and to show off his family. At the moment, Leonore and the children were in Warsaw, staying at the Bristol and visiting Rachel. Her business was becoming successful and profitable. Her premises on Sienna Street, opulent but not ostentatious, was already an essential stop on the shopping round of Jewish and Gentile ladies from Warsaw, Saint Petersburg, Lodz, and Berlin.

It was a few months only since they'd met, but Leonore was finding her sister a harder character than before, and reticent beyond being questioned on anything personal. Leonore, content in her marriage and motherhood, didn't understand her sister's attitude. Could it possibly be on account of a man in Paris, perhaps? Was her dominance over her clients repaying her for the fears of her childhood and the way their parents were murdered?

Leonore was on the point of condemning her sister for being different when she found, to her surprise, that Rachel regularly, once a fortnight on a Friday afternoon, closed the workrooms and the salon early and walked to Zamenhofa Street. She shared her cousin Esther's meal on Friday nights, more lavish now because she had already sent round the food for it. From Esther, Leonore learned that Rachel was paying for her children to attend one of the illegal Jewish schools in the city. She hoped the girls would eventually join her in her business, and that the boys would perhaps become Talmudic scholars.

Rachel was an inexplicable mixture of belief and unbelief and invariably, after the Sabbath meal was eaten, fell into argument with Esther's husband Mordechai. The strongest religious influence in the family was undoubtedly Esther's. Mordechai fulfilled his religious role almost superficially, and only then because he believed it was important for his children to grow up with a Jewish background. "A man needs to know where he stood in his childhood if he is ever to know where he stands in the world when he grows up," he used to say. And Mordechai knew where he stood. In the street he still moved close to the walls of the buildings, his eyes cast down, a typical ghetto Jew. In his heart he was quite different—a fighter. He was a socialist, totally convinced and spending all his time at the print works in the basement, producing tracts and, very often, risking distributing them through the streets.

He had affection for Rachel, but she nonetheless disappointed him. In spite of his socialist instincts—and only because he knew her so well and recognised the sufferings of her childhood—he admired her capitalist instincts. He genuinely admired her enterprise and talent for making money. It would be fine if she could teach his girls to do the same thing. But his boys…he wanted his boys to become professional men, in medicine, in finance, the law. He wanted them to be able, in the years to come, to send their wives to Rachel or someone very like her to be dressed. He wanted them to break out of the ring-fence enclosing Judaism; she wanted them to bury themselves ever deeper within it.

They would discuss the future of his sons when the time came. She seemed, to him, to be so free herself, he couldn't understand her complaint that assimilation was becoming impossible to avoid among the young people, and had to be fought against more fiercely. She abhorred his Socialism and his work in the printing shop as dancing before the Golden Calf.

Rachel's besetting sin, he would tell his wife, was that she would live and die a spinster—an unnatural life. His daughters could work for her; he didn't mind that. It was good for girls to be capable of looking after themselves if they had to. But he wouldn't have her influencing them in anything else.

Leonore reported all this to Paul in her letters. They were amusing letters, subtly indicating how far from her Jewish roots she had strayed. They were reassuring letters, too, full of endearments genuinely reflecting her longing for their being together again.

Paul was longing for that, as well. He quickly tired of his bachelor existence in Saint Petersburg. He spent much of his time with Ouroussoff, being persuaded into revisiting the scenes of their youth, where Sergei boisterously attempted to recapture the magic of those days, re-enacting their boyhood capers. They even visited the ladies on the Vasil'yevsky Island, but both of them found the atmosphere too heavy with cigar smoke and cheap scent, the ladies too thickly covered with powder and rouge to hide the pockmarks of childhood illnesses.

From today, all that would be over. He walked out of the Hotel Moskovskaya for the last time and took a cab to the house he'd taken for them. It was very large, entirely the sort of house any man with trustworthy flecks of grey at the temples should live in, if he wished to be taken seriously in financial circles. It was on the Nevsky Prospekt at the corner of the Fontana and cheek by jowl with the Anichkov Bridge. Paul smiled with deep satisfaction. The Anichkov had been his favourite Saint Petersburg Bridge since he was a boy. He had fantasised about its finely sculptured horses, riding off their parapets and into the sky. How far did these dreams influence him now, to take a house from which he could gaze at them from its windows? From those same front windows, Leonore would be able to see all Saint Petersburg passing backwards and forwards in its ceaseless energy. From her bedroom at the back, she would enjoy the quiet calm of the Fontana. And on her doorstep, along the Nevsky and Liteiny Prospekts, she had all of the very best shops in Russia.

Leonore and the children would be with him to enjoy it all at the weekend. Before then, he had an appointment at the Treasury. He had written to the Treasury because Count Witte was Treasury Minister, and Count Witte was a member of the Baltic Baronage. The Wittes and von Hagens were distant acquaintances; they shared a common inheritance. It was naturally in the Treasury, therefore, that Paul might look for contacts and advice to smooth his way in a new city.

He wasn't granted an interview with the Count himself. Perhaps the von Hagen name didn't warrant that. Perhaps his object in seeking it was too vague; he was simply looking for a door to be opened, a useful name or two. Perhaps the Count was busy. Perhaps he was being discreet. Whomsoever he saw, the interview was bound to be useful. Men of the Baltic Baronage were always soldiers or administrators, always in demand by the Imperial bureaucracy. The constant need of them was the most obvious symptom of Russia's inherent disease, indecision: the impossibility of finally making up its mind whether it belonged to the East or to the West.

"We are delighted to welcome you back to Saint Petersburg, your Excellency," the tall man said. He must have been taller than Paul by half a head and towered over his desk like Gulliver in Lilliput. His hair was grey, thin and plastered close to his scalp. His skin—what could be seen of it above his Tolstoyan beard and moustache—was grey, as well. The beard completely covered the man's cravat, and Paul wondered whether he was wearing one at all. "You've been away from us for…er…let me see…" the man continued, rustling papers on his desk.

"Several years now," Paul told him briskly. "I went to live abroad when I left the army."

"Exactly. The Preobrazhensky, I believe." It sounded like an accusation but he didn't follow it up. Paul said:

"My brother and I are attempting to exploit the resources of our Estate. We are…"

"Yes, yes, we know," the man said rustling the papers once more. He wasn't reading them, though, and Paul had the impression he'd already learned them off by heart. His eyes betrayed no emotion and his voice was flat as a tabletop. "You're employing Russian workers on a shale-oil project. You've just rented premises in Reval for an amber factory. You will be employing Russian workers from Odessa for that, we understand."

"That's right." Paul was astonished that he knew so much.

"Then there's the timber business, and this idea you have for building sea-going barges for the Baltic trade."

"What else can I tell you that you don't know already, Boris Petrovich?" Paul was angry. The man was playing with him, letting him know not only that the authorities had opened all his letters, but that they'd read them and remembered them, word for word.

Boris Petrovich smiled bleakly. "That's all very good, very good indeed, your Excellency. His Majesty's Government is always looking out for landlords like you and your brother."

Paul wriggled on his chair. This was like the days when he handed in his lessons to *Herr Trott* and waited anxiously while they were marked and commented upon.

"His Majesty is entirely of the Count's opinion," the man said, pompously giving the impression that the opinion hadn't originated with the Count at all, but with himself. "We must all make every effort to bring Russia into the nineteenth century, and take no rest until she stands four-square with all her competitors in the twentieth."

"I've spent time in the Paris and Berlin money markets raising capital for our schemes," Paul said.

"Exactly." It was one of his favourite words. "The Count plans to revise the bases of the Russian economy. And then there's the railway. The Count plans to inaugurate a railway from Saint Petersburg and Moscow to Vladivostok. That will allow us to develop mineral resources right across Siberia."

"I see." Paul could think of nothing more to say, and they sat watching each other. Boris Petrovich's office overlooked a busy street, but the double windows admitted no sound from outside. The people and the traffic down there went about their business like ghosts.

382   \ A Country Grown Unreal

"Why have you suddenly decided to return to Saint Petersburg?"
The question was as sharp and unexpected in the grey man's
grey-brown office as a pistol shot.

"Why have you suddenly decided to return to Saint Petersburg?"
The question was as sharp and unexpected in the grey man's
grey-brown office as a pistol shot.

"My wife and I decided to come home..."

"Though Warsaw is your wife's home, is it not?" He waved his right
hand airily. "No matter, no matter."

"My wife and I decided to come home," Paul repeated forcefully,
"because we wanted our children to have a Russian education...not to
grow up like exiles."

"Oh?"

"They'll all go to preparatory schools as soon as they're old enough;
the girls for Smolny, the boys for the Emperor Alexander Lyceum."

"Very good."

"Besides, I find what's happening in Russia at the moment commercially and industrially very exciting. Not only do I want to be a part of
it, I believe that with my experience of how these things are arranged in
the West, I can make a constructive contribution." He hated hearing
himself talk like that; but at least it warranted another of the grey
man's bleak smiles.

"I'm sure you can, your Excellency. And that is the Count's opinion
as well. Naturally, he has issued his instructions for me to act upon as I
see fit. There is a way you could be of great assistance to us, if you
will."

"Don't misunderstand me, Boris Petrovich. It is I who am looking
for assistance."

"Hear me out, please. You are looking to raise further funds for your
projects. You need contacts here in Russia."

"Yes."

"We suggest a place for you in the Russo-Asiatic Bank. That's one of
Putilov's concerns. It has vast concessions in the Urals and the Altai
district. It also has close associations with the French Société Generale.
The contacts you already have in Paris there could come in very useful,

and you will make countless other useful contacts here in Saint Petersburg."

Paul was taken aback. "I must confess, I wasn't thinking about anything like that. I mean…what exactly would I be expected to do?"

"Oh, you mustn't worry about that. They'll certainly find lots for you to do. And there'll be some travelling, of course. Do you know Siberia at all?"

Paul left the Treasury light-hearted and light-footed, walked a little way in the gently falling snow and stopped at a cafe for a brandy. Then he took the number seven tram along Nevsky Prospekt to the Anichkov Bridge. He smiled at everyone in the car and received some very doubtful looks in response. He didn't mind. He was warm. He was very, very happy. And he really was at home.

He was sitting beside a tall, thin woman in a small black hat and black coat. She clutched an umbrella between her knees and sniffed from time to time. She looked steadily out of the window without moving a muscle. Paul had a sudden, innocent urge to put his arm around her and tell her how good life was. He thought better of that, however, but still longed to make cheerful, brotherly contact with her. As a preliminary, he cleared his throat, very loudly. She turned her head slowly and stared at him with dead eyes. He was surprised by the way she looked, so surprised he laughed out loud and couldn't stop. Thoroughly embarrassed, followed by knowing glances from everybody, he got up and jumped off the car as soon as he could. His laughter made him unsteady. He slipped and fell on his back in the snow, still laughing uncontrollably. The tram moved off with the woman still staring out of the window at him. Two women passing on the pavement stopped and stared at him while he made no effort to stand up. One of the women moved as though to help him up.

"Come along," the other one told her sharply. "Don't get involved. Can't you see he's drunk?"

CHAPTER 2

▼

1892

She knew he was dead before she entered the hut. This awareness of death was an instinct honed into infallibility over the years. When she reached him, he was lying on his truckle bed, shriveled like a grey-shelled walnut with empty lungs and a static heart. She drew up a stool and sat for maybe half an hour, looking at him indifferently. Over many months now, he had come to look like a desiccated mummy. Had that been his ambition, he had now reached its apogee.

He would have to be buried immediately, and there was no Pastor within days by foot to conduct the service. She would read a prayer over him herself; he would have hated the idea, and the thought gave her pleasure. Burial with the right words said over the body and a cross raised over the grave was an essential Christian ritual. Pastor Behrendorf was a very ritualistic Christian. Margarethe had watched him since they came to Africa, living life like an actor on a stage, playing a role conceived for him alone, haranguing his flock in his sermons and his God in his prayers.

One of the men from the village would have to dig the grave; she was too weak to do it herself. Directly, she sent for him, and the news was out, streaking through the forest and over the grassland like a wild bird. The grave was dug that afternoon; the funeral would be the next morning. Fires were kept burning in the village all night. From where she lay, cold shocked and sleepless in her own hut, Margarethe heard the villagers' dirges, their attempt to placate the anger of the old gods and to deflect from themselves whatever evil it was that had brought the white man to his death.

It was a relief for her that he was dead. They had married without love. He had needed a wife, she a new duty for which to sacrifice herself. Their bargain had been a hard but honest one. She bore her side of it without complaint because she had no complaint. The fault was her own. She had believed, when she married, that to do one's duty was sufficient. It was not. There also had to be love—deep love of the kind she felt for her brothers, even though she knew she would never see them again.

Her husband, she was convinced, had lived all his life without ever having known that kind of love. The only duty he acknowledged was to himself; the maintenance of his character in other men's' eyes, and the need to impress them with the dignity and holiness of his person while, at the same time, hiding his empty heart so skillfully no one would ever suspect it was a vacuum. She was glad he was dead. The life he had chosen for himself and for which, therefore, only he was responsible, had been a waste. Because it was a waste it offended her all through, as would a barrel of sour beer or a batch of unrisen bread when she was in charge of her brother's household.

Afterwards, she remained alone at the mission; there was nowhere else for her to go. Much as she hated the place, she had no other home, and she felt safe there. There was her little school to run, her dribble of invalids and accident victims to attend to. There was no more pretense of holiness or salvation, only human help and perhaps a little understanding. They were mostly a little afraid of her. Her skin was the colour and texture of sisal, her body hard and narrow. Her black gown grew increasingly shabby because she had no other and never troubled to go to Buea to collect her allowance. Her hands were surprisingly gentle when she attended to them.

Overriding whatever else the villagers felt about her was embarrassment. They watched her working in her garden, growing maize as her staple and cassava to make her bread. To them it seemed she lived poorly, and they were sorry for her. After her husband died, one or the other of them would creep to her hut at night and leave a dead chicken hanging from the rafters of her verandah to relieve the monotony of her diet. Next day it appeared stewed as a treat for the children in her school or the patients in her clinic. They were baffled by this response, but continued their gifts because they felt responsible for her. Had she been one of them she would, as a widow, have moved into the house of a male relative, respected, to live the rest of her life in security and a degree of comfort. The men sometimes joked with each other, playfully demanding that one or the other should take her into their family, as would have been the custom. But she was not one of them. And anyway, nobody had the courage to ask her.

So she remained alone in her hut, living her days as they came, peacefully, though not happily because, perhaps, she had never been taught how to be happy. Her world was a world of black faces and, as she understood them, dependant bodies. It unsettled her certainties when anyone white appeared. From time to time a troop of cavalry called. The Germans had been in the area for less than ten years. They came uninvited and remained unappreciated. To get rid of them, half-hearted tribal uprisings occurred from time to time, prompted by British agents posing as commercial traders. The cavalry's irregular appearances were to discourage such enterprises. They came fairly often to visit Margarethe because it was unusual for a white woman to be living alone like that. Captain Hoffmann, a blue-eyed, long-nosed professional soldier from Mannheim admired the rigidity of her courage, which he described as *echte Deutsche*. Among themselves, his men referred to her as the Crazy Woman. Margarethe thought of all of them as irrelevant, another waste with their tinkling brasses, bugle calls and snorting horses.

"I say it every time you come but you do nothing," she reproved Captain Hoffmann. "You never tell them, do you?"

"They don't look for cavalry captains to make strategic policy decisions, *Frau Behrendorf.*"

"*Ach!* You don't have any trouble with my people, do you?"

"No," he said noncommittally.

"That's because they know I'd be after them myself, if they got up to those sorts of games. People are the same the world over, Captain. They need to know someone's in charge."

He nodded and looked vaguely into the green distance. He might have been one of her pupils. She expounded the same lecture each time he came.

"Why are we here?" she demanded and rushed on not expecting an answer. "Traders come and take out as much as they possibly can while putting back as little as possible. The Powers, as they call themselves, drew their lines all over the map and said this piece was for this one, that for that one...and what was the result of that? Absolutely nothing! Except the British! The British know what to do! They settle. They divide the land within their boundaries, and they settle. The natives have landlords. They know someone's in charge. But here..." She shrugged her shoulders in annoyance, and Captain Hoffmann made up his mind not to come this way any more.

She may have sounded crazy, but she wasn't entirely wrong. She came of a line that had been colonising for six hundred years. Who were these people? Where did Captain Hoffmann come from? Mannheim? What was that? What did men like him know about colonising a country and controlling its people?

Captain Mannheim and his troupe rode away. They would be back, of course, despite what he said. *Frau Behrendorf,* the recluse who lived only among natives but would never herself go native, was a feature of the colony. She may not be seriously noticed, but she couldn't be seriously ignored.

CHAPTER 3

▼

1892

The great V.I. Putilov himself was never to be seen, but everyone he came into contact with at the Bank welcomed Paul warmly. His immediate superior arranged, without hesitation, a loan for the rebuilding work at Estate Wirsberg and urged him to apply immediately for advice and assistance regarding any further development there. While he was away, travelling on business for the Bank, he was assured that his personal financial interests in Saint Petersburg would be assiduously looked after.

Through his colleagues at the Bank, Paul quickly got to know the financial titans of the city. Without exception, they all to some degree liked him at first sight. More importantly, or so Paul thought, they liked Leonore and the house they'd chosen to live in. Among their wives, it soon became general knowledge that she was expecting her fifth baby. That was highly approved of. Five children indicated marital stability and that, irrespective of their own personal circumstances, was considered by all of them, men as well as women, to be a very good thing.

Leonore kept very well throughout her pregnancy. She shopped. She entertained new friends at the house and lunched with them in all the best hotels and restaurants. They were the wives of highly placed civil servantsmany of them from the Baltic Provinces themselves—all of them carefully frivolous and eclectically cultured. Very soon she was no longer "*Frau von Hagen,*" but simply "My dear Leonore" or "Leonore, my dear."

In turn, she dropped their patronymics when they were Russian, calling them by their first names or their titles; their titles, in some cases, indicated even greater intimacy.

What did they say about her when she wasn't there, she sometimes wondered?

"Zhyd, of course."

"My dear, no!"

"My dear, yes! Don't you remember what a scandal there was when he resigned his commission in the Preobrazhensky to marry her?"

"I can't believe it."

"What Olga says is quite true, my dear."

"There! Varvara remembers all about it, don't you, darling?"

"Of course. It caused quite a stir. Many girls had hopes in his direction, you see. He was a shy young man who looked ravishing in that green and red uniform."

"My dear, did you ever see a picture of Prince Albert of England when he was a young man?"

"Lydia, how clever you are! That's exactly right. Beautiful!"

"Then why on earth...?"

"Did he marry her? *Une grande amour,* my dear. Tristan and Isolde, Abelard and Heloise, Romeo and Juliet..."

"Not exactly like the Prince and I," someone said, and everybody laughed.

"She converted, of course," someone else said, as if it were only doubtfully in her favour.

"Roman Catholic," disapprovingly.

"I expect that's why they took that house. There's a Roman Catholic Church just along by them, on the Nevsky."

They loved to talk. Saint Petersburg ladies. They loved to discuss gentle scandal involving their acquaintance.

Disappointingly, with Leonore there was no real scandal, or none that they could discover. She may have been a Jew, but it was only workers and peasants and male extremists who took much interest in that sort of thing these days. Mind you, they did say that the Tsar…but that was another thing altogether and they'd no intention of risking their husband's careers by talking rashly about him! Meanwhile, they found dear Leonore charming, perfectly charming. Of course, gossip was so often unreliable these days you could hardly dare believe a thing you heard. It would be lovely, at some time, to discover who she really was, of course, where she came from, who were her people. But for the moment, her charm was sufficient. She fitted into their circle very well; she was already a dependable member of the Red Cross Committee, and she worked very hard for several other charities.

Leonore never thought about what they might be saying. She was content, more than ever in love with being Paul's wife now that he had what she considered to be a "proper job." There were some disadvantages even to that, of course. He was frequently away on trips to the Urals or the Chinese border, but she was proud of his job. She was thankful for the regularity of it and would do anything to support him in every way she could.

In this new life of hers, she relied heavily on Ulrika, whose place could never be taken by anyone else in Dorothea's affections. The German girl needed much persuading before she agreed to come to Russia; but the truth was, she was as fond of Dorothea as Dorothea was of her. Saint Petersburg was a shock to her when she arrived, however. The Russian she heard all round her was a spittle-swilling menace. In the street, her fears were unbearable. She regarded the hairy men in their fur hats and felt boots and the beshawled women of startlingly large girth as she might lions and tigers in the jungle and poisonous snakes in the desert. She was terrified of going anywhere near them and, to begin with, Leonore had to accompany her, or she would never have had the courage to take the children for a walk.

The dilemma was solved by a happy accident. Leonore noticed that among the other servants in the house, only one seemed in any way to appeal to Ulrika. His name was Anton.

He was short with extremely wide shoulders. His hair was fair, his eyes grey and his moustache not yet quite mature. He attracted Ulrika by making it very obvious that she attracted him. They gazed at each other wordlessly, and it occurred to Leonore to appoint the young man Ulrika's personal bodyguard. As she spoke no Russian and he no German, Leonore acted as go-between. When it was time to take the children out, Ulrika simply had to say—in German or Russian, whichever she wished—"Anton! Come!" Anton was immediately to drop whatever he was doing to go with her. In the street he was to walk closely behind until she felt in any way menaced, when she would say again: "Anton! Come!" And Anton would move forward and walk shoulder to shoulder until the presumed danger was over.

This began early in Lent, early enough for Anton to have taken direct charge of their expeditions in time for the mid-Lent fair, set up in Admiralty Square. The children were enchanted by the actors, dancers and acrobats in their crowded rows of decorated booths.

Very soon, Anton took over the leadership of these expeditions altogether. He showed them the way to the Alexander Gardens and to the Saint Petersburg Park. Sensing they were all children together, differing only in age, all four pelted each other with snowballs until Dorothea and Sonia were nearly hysterical with excitement. When they went home, Leonore was delighted to see them so rosy-cheeked and sparkle-eyed. She tried to persuade Marie to go with them next time. Marie wailed her refusals for the remainder of the day.

In quiet moments afterwards, Ulrika decided that she liked living in Saint Petersburg after all. She also began to feel it might be wise to learn to say just a little more than "Anton! Come!" in this new, impossible language.

One of Leonore's minor but consistent anxieties had been Clementine. Since her marriage, they had maintained a regular and warm correspondence. It was easy. They were genuinely fond of each other. Their physical distancing, however, distorted the value of time and the significance of subsequent events. Clementine had met and married her Sasha, left the Doma, left Warsaw, indeed, and come to live in Russia since they'd last met. Leonore had lived in Florence, in Paris, in Berlin. She had given birth to four children, and now a fifth was on its away. At last, she had come to live in Russia, too. All this made exciting news items in their letters, transmitted and eagerly read, though it had no deep effect. They wrote to each other, addressed each other, thought of each other as they were when they were both young girls. But Leonore was conscious of being a young girl no longer. Inevitably, she was much changed by time and motherhood. The more she thought about it, the more her dilemma grew. When they were last together, Clementine had nursed and supported her through all the anguished indecision as to whether or not she should marry Paul. Somehow—in the manner of a joint though unacknowledged conspiracy—they had both ignored all that ever since. As though none of it had ever happened, they leapt back to the time before Paul, to the time they sang at the Doma, working hard for what little they earned, despising Pan Koblinski for the miser he was and doing their duty, inducing Russian officers to spend as much if not more than they could afford. Except for the letters to and from Clementine, Leonore never thought about those days any more. Did Clementine, she wondered? Did she ever, for instance, think now of her Sergei?

She couldn't let it go on like this. She simply had to write. And she did one morning, on the spur of the moment, while the children were out, without thinking about it too much.

My dear Clementine,

You've been on my conscience so long, my dear—ever since we moved to Saint Petersburg. But you can imagine what it's been like, I'm sure—setting up house in a new place and getting everything straight as quickly as possible, finding suitable servants, arranging for endless changes to be made to the furnishings. Well, of course, you know all about that from when you and Sasha moved to Moscow, but you were always the best at anything practical. I'm sure you arranged everything in the blink of an eye; whereas, it has taken me much longer.

Then there's Paul's job at the Bank. That means we have to do quite a lot of entertaining. And with untrusted servants, that's always a worry. You never know how things will turn out until everything's over. And I'm having to serve on lots of charity committees, as well.

But you won't want to hear about all that and, anyway, I can much more easily tell you about it when we meet. And when is that likely to be, my dear? We have plenty of room here. Why don't you and your husband come to stay as soon as and for as long as you possibly can?

Write to me soon,

Ever your loving friend,

Leonore von Hagen

P.S. It is very nice for me to feel you are so near.

The letter lay on her desk for several days, and she read it again every time she caught sight of it. Somehow it didn't seem at all right, but although she made several attempts she couldn't do any better. Finally, she compromised. She translated it from her rather formal Russian into Warsaw argot, sent it and hoped for the best.

Clementine's reply arrived so quickly that she could hardly believe there had been time for her own to be taken to the post.

Darling Leonore,

So near, you say! And yet, not so very! Sasha tells me it's nearly five hundred miles from Moscow to Saint Petersburg. And I may as well be frank, my dear, that to me that means you might as well be living in Vladivostok! I can't imagine when we will be able to come to visit you. For one thing, we wouldn't have any of the right clothes to wear!

Ha-ha! No, seriously, Sasha almost never has time away from the rail-way yards. Day after day he works from morning 'til night, and there are almost always meetings at home after that. I would never have believed it was possible for anyone to work so hard. But that's not your problem.

Now! What I want to suggest is this: you come to see us here. Really! I mean it! We've lots of room. The flat isn't over-furnished, I must admit. But that's all the better for the children to run about and play. Paul could probably think up some business he has to do in Moscow. And he could always go to the yards with Sasha. He's so proud of everything and so loves to show everything off, even if it's only to me.

Meanwhile, you and I can sit by the stove and talk and talk and talk like a pair of old ladies and putter together in the kitchen and cook for the tribe and have the most wonderful time.

Darling Leonore, the more I think about it the more I know I won't be able to bear it if you say 'no.' Sasha and I long with all our hearts to see you. Please don't disappoint us.

Ever, my dearest, dearest Leonore,

Your loving,

Clementine Schimanska.

P.S. By train it's an overnight journey and wonderfully comfortable, Sasha says.

Paul and Leonore read the letter together. He wasn't happy about her travelling anywhere during her pregnancy, let alone as far as Moscow. Being pregnant, on the other hand, made Leonore all the more eager to go immediately, while her time was still so far off.

"And she and Sasha obviously want to see us all as soon as they can."

The tone of Clementine's letter had given her a quite new confidence in their relationship. She was giving no thought to what she had come to think of as "the years between." She still saw their relationship as it was—unchanged. And although she giggled privately, and other people might find that a little ridiculous, Leonore found it very comforting indeed.

"There's no question of that," Paul was saying. "I can't possibly get away from the bank at the moment."

"Well, then, I shall..."

"You can't manage the children on your own."

"Of course not. But I shall take Ulrika and Anton with me."

"They're hardly more than children themselves, my dear. No! If you really must go—and I'm not too happy about it at all, mind—you'll have to go alone."

Leonore closed the conversation by saying she would think about it. And as she did, it came to seem like a good idea. Paul and she had been apart before, but always it was he who'd gone and she who'd stayed. This time...The idea was titillating. One night to get there, one night back and two days there...she'd be away for less than a week. And Paul would be there with the children and she had great faith in Anton and Ulrika.

She made up her mind quite quickly. She sent Clementine a telegram to say when and where she would like to be met and left before the end of the week.

CHAPTER 4

▼

1892

The roads were clear. Spring sowing was well in hand. Prince Fermatov was in Reval with his amber craftsmen from Odessa. The Russians on the Estate abandoned lumbering and were organised into two groups, one to work the shale beds, the other to mine amber in the blue-clay soil. They were overseen and their production coordinated and distributed by Semyon Semyonovitch.

The Baron's respect for his foreman had markedly increased. During his recovery from the assault and his adjustment to the complexities of Channah's return, Semyon Semyonovitch undertook, quite independently, the reconstruction of the burned-out barn. When the snow thawed and it was time again for routine outside work, the Baron had a new barn built of his own timber, standing in place of the old one and resplendent in thick coats of dark red, iron-based preservative.

Now everything was back to normal, and yet it wasn't quite. Outside the house, in their cold-weather slack times, Estonians had watched the Russians working on the barn. They watched but offered no help. They stood about, stamping their feet and clapping their hands to keep warm. They talked in low voices among themselves, and the Russians couldn't hear what they said. Perhaps they were swapping professional opinions about how barns should be built. Perhaps they were saying something quite different. The Russians suspected the latter to be the case.

Since the discovery of Greta's corpse, whatever friendly relationship that had existed between the two was lost. The murder was an unspeakable Russian atrocity; there could be no doubt about that! Certainly no Estonian could ever possibly have done it. Nobody now doubted that the raiders also had been Russian, and that there must have been a connection between them and the Russians living in the village. The Russian attack, the Estonian debacle, the burning of the barn, and the subsequent shortage of food throughout the winter were all uncomfortably unforgettable and unforgivable. Henceforward there could be nothing but antagonism between them; even Father Tikhon would never be completed trusted again.

On their side, the Russians had never respected the Estonians anyway. That they'd all run away directly after the raiders appeared hadn't surprised them in the least. They were despised for their cowardice, for their primitive language that was more like monkey-talk than anything human, for their heretical religious beliefs, and for the abominable quality of the vodka they drank.

They were certainly an inferior race, but—and this was one of the imponderables of creation—they lived in quite a good land, a land with many possibilities, were they capable of appreciating the fact. The Russians were. They appreciated everything about the place, especially the priest who, while accepting responsibility for the welfare of their souls, allowed that what they did with their bodies was their own affair. Father Tikhon understood that a man must sin well in order to confess and repent satisfactorily. There was no doubt about it! All in all, this Estate would be a good place to live! They had come here first in desperation. It was now time, they were thinking, to make it their permanent home; permanent for themselves and their families.

There was a new feeling inside the house, as well. Had she been questioned, Channah would have answered honestly that she still loved the Baron. But she was no longer the terrified girl he'd rescued while she fled through the woods all those years ago. She was changed, and so was he. He was no longer her knight.

Sitting in her room at the hotel during the days she'd been away, overlooking the market square and gently declining the rosy-cheeked maid's endeavours to make her eat, she explored the taste, the feel, the extent of her sudden independence. It was something she'd never known before, except by hearsay in some of the books she'd read to the Baron. It was, she felt, like being a rock in a stormy sea. He had flung her there like a lost ship. Like all castaways, she needed time to learn how to survive in this strange environment. Nevertheless, when she heard of the raid, she knew she must return, but independently.

Everyone sensed the change in her. The servants obeyed her well enough, but whereas previously they'd tolerated her and scorned her a little, they now resented her outright. They were hostile to her new air of certainty. The villagers, too, smarted at her painful gibes and no longer, even among themselves, called her the Baron's whore.

The Baron himself was circumspect. He understood that she felt herself to have been massively offended by him—betrayed, even—though he never understood why. He meant his gesture in front of the von Aschenbauers to be a public acknowledgement of his respect and affection for her, his need of her. If she was incapable of appreciating that for what it was…He hated having the thought cross his mind, but it was true what people said: "Once a Jew, always a Jew." She was a different breed of animal, though until now only Margarethe had recognised the fact. He decided he would write to Margarethe very soon, telling her he had been wrong and asking her to come home. He would find a parish for that husband of hers…he might even suggest to Pastor Vikkers that it was time for him to retire.

He and Channah now shared space as though their former intimacy had never been. They ate separately, sat separately and seldom smiled. In contrast, her caring of him was more marked than ever and the sweetness of it made the loss of her affection all the more bitter. Channah's new attitude to him was making it hard to drive from his mind that Leonore was one of her race. She had given the family the heir it needed, and he had gone to Berlin and loved her for it. Now he was beginning to be fearful for his brother's future happiness.

The sun shone, the days were warmer. The men began to cough in the dust thrown up as they worked in the fields and mosquitoes, one of summer's abominations, commenced their torment. It was the time for Prince Krasnov, too. He announced an inspection of his territory in order to report to Governor Chakhovskoy on the condition of the land and the spirit of the people after the winter's disturbances. It had been a hard time. Famine and cholera continued to flourish in Russia. There might be even worse to come this year on both sides of the border.

When he received notification of the proposed visit, Loff experienced grim satisfaction. Now was his chance to protest the present policies and attempt a reasonable understanding with the government for the future. Krasnov must be made to appreciate the landlords' difficulties!

"My sister was still here last time they came, Channah, but you can remember all about it well enough, I dare say," he said, holding the Prince's letter in a trembling hand.

"Yes, your Excellency?"

"Food, accommodation…that sort of thing. You can work it all out, can't you? Here, this is his letter."

"Yes, your Excellency."

"And my sister had the maids give the whole place a thorough clean-out," he laughed.

"Your Excellency won't have anything to complain about on that account, I assure you."

"No, well…there's no knowing how many you'll be catering for…how many they'll expect us to accommodate. You remember the Princess, of course."

"I remember her very well."

"And…oh, Channah! Confound it! You know perfectly well what I mean. My sister was here with me last time. You'll manage very well, I have no doubt of it, but my sister found, while I was engaged with the Prince, that the Princess needed constant entertaining."

"Yes. But your Excellency won't be relying on me for that, surely. The Princess wouldn't find a Jew at all an acceptable companion. Neither, if she did, should I have the time to entertain her."

The Baron sighed. Impossible woman! Next day he rode to the von Aschenbauers'. Their house felt cold and uncared for. The Count appeared to be entirely alone. He received the Baron in his study and offered no hospitality other than vodka.

"You've heard from Krasnov, of course?"

"Yes, he's coming here sometime soon, I gather. I wrote back directly when I heard. Told him he'd be welcome…couldn't very well say anything else…but that I couldn't possibly entertain the Princess, as well."

"Oh?"

"The Countess and my daughter are still away, you know. The Countess…very nervous woman…very nervous woman, indeed. Couldn't get over that fright everybody had last winter. Only natural, of course. Nasty business. Very nasty business."

"Won't they be home before the Krasnovs arrive?"

"Unlikely." The Count cleared his throat pointedly. "My daughter has…er…my daughter has particular reasons for being away, just at present."

"I see." He didn't see, of course, but was not going to bite at so obvious a bait. "Pity! I came over to suggest that we might combine forces," he laughed. "You could all have stayed with me while the Krasnovs are here. We could face him together in a joint attack. Besides…for the Princess…I shall miss Margarethe, you know. She was marvelous at that kind of thing."

"No question of that, Baron."

"No, I see…" The Baron shrugged as though it really was of no importance. "They're obviously enjoying themselves, to be away so long," he suggested absent-mindedly.

The Count saw how he might land his fish and tried another cast. "I think they are. They're in Saint Petersburg."

"Really?" The Baron was genuinely surprised. "My brother and his wife have moved there now. They've taken a house on the Nevsky Prospekt."

The Count uttered a noncommittal, "Yes."

"By the Anichkov Bridge. You must tell your wife."

The Count smiled broadly. At last! "They already know."

"Really?" The Baron thought little of it.

"Yes. They've had several narrow escapes, apparently. Well, you know how it is. Ladies take these things very seriously and..." he paused, then added hastily, "...and I'm not the one to say they're wrong to do so, you understand. But for the Countess it would be embarrassing. She wouldn't want people to think she and your sister-in-law are intimate, you see."

Loff left without another word. On the way home, he decided to recall Prince Fermatov from Reval. The Princess would surely enjoy having a Prince to spend her time with. And, as a reinforcement, he would conscript Father Tikhon. The Princess couldn't possibly snub him, with all her pretensions to Orthodoxy.

Fermatov was not enthusiastic. Nothing should come before business, was his opinion and he was needed in Reval. His view was possibly influenced by having already met the Princess there. Father Tikhon, on the other hand, was delighted. The Baron summoned him to be at the house when the Krasnovs arrived, and so was Prince Fermatov. Loff introduced Tikhon, a little patronisingly, perhaps, as "My friend Father Tikhon."

"My friend, too," Krasnov responded cheerfully. "We've known each other for quite a while, eh, Father?"

The Princess greeted the Baron in a flourish of French. Then, turning to the priest, said: "You must forgive me, Father. This is absurd, is it not? We are all slaves of fashion, alas! Why else should we talk French, when our beloved Russian is so beautiful and adequate for everything one could possibly wish to say?" She turned again, smiling to the Baron. "*Dites-moi, mon cher ami, ou se cache-t-elle ma chere, ma tres, chere Marguerite?*"

The question startled him. He couldn't believe she didn't already know. "My sister is away," he told her nonchalantly. "In Africa."

"So!" She nodded gravely, and he offered no further information.

Channah came in to show them to their rooms.

"So!" The Princess said again, this time softly, as though only to herself. She glanced sharply at Channah and looked away immediately; there was no need whatsoever to show interest in this particular creature.

Until dinner that evening, time passed uncomfortably for the Baron. There was an atmosphere of important events and weighty conversations occurring in the house, from which he was subtly excluded. His guests all disappeared, and he had to ask Channah where they where.

Prince Fermatov had taken Princess Krasnova to see the rebuilt barn, because it was such a pleasant day. Prince Fermatov and Princess Krasnova had taken horses to ride to the village. The Princess had newly minted kopeks she intended distributing to the newest-born babies. Prince Krasnov and Father Tikhon were in serious conversation in the courtyard, and when she'd sent Karlis to enquire if they wanted refreshment, they answered rudely that all they wanted was not to be disturbed. Later they ordered Ants to bring out the carriage and take them to find Semyon Semyonovitch. On their way, the Prince would visit the shale beds and inspect the amber diggings.

After his day of solitary wandering, the Baron was further frustrated by having to invite Father Tikhon to dine. The priest's eyes flashed wicked satisfaction before turning down to study the carpet. The corners of his mouth creased in a humble smirk. He dry-washed his hands and shook his head nervously, though he said nothing. There was no need. Prince Krasnov spoke enthusiastically. Of course the Father must stay; they still had much to discuss. That was a charming idea, the

Princess declared gaily. And he could, she added, smiling flirtatiously at the Baron, say Grace for them...if an Orthodox Grace were permitted in a Lutheran house.

The ritual of polite eating, making conversation and exchanging toasts went on too long. When the Baron finally moved restlessly in his chair to indicate that the meal was over, Prince Krasnov smiled helplessly and looked apologetic.

"My dear fellow, I'm afraid I must ask you to excuse me. This has been a long day...very interesting, but very tiring also."

"Of course." The Baron hardly knew whether to be relieved or angry.

"Are you ready, my dear?" The Prince offered his wife an arm. She took it coquettishly, and they both said goodnight and left. Father Tikhon immediately said that he must go as well and, looking humble once more, cringingly thanked the Baron for his hospitality. When he had gone, Prince Fermatov yawned unrestrainedly.

"Do you need me any more tonight, Loff Pavlovitch?"

"No, no."

"What a day! She really is an exhausting woman."

On his way out of the room, he passed Prince Krasnov in the doorway.

"My dear Baron...do you have plans for tomorrow morning...say at about seven?"

"No."

"Splendid. Shall we say at seven, then? In the study? Goodnight." He left, and Loff felt as he had, years ago at University, summoned to his tutor's office.

But it wasn't like that at all. While Loff spent half the night awake, determined not to give Prince Krasnov the initiative when they met, the Prince had obviously slept well and was feeling spry.

"This is early, I know, my dear fellow, but we can enjoy our talk without interruptions, you see. You know what I mean?"

Loff sat down heavily behind his desk—this was his study, after all—and invited Krasnov to take the chair opposite.

"I want," the Prince began without preamble, "you and I to understand each other completely, my friend. That is important."

Loff felt the stirrings of suspicion.

"Above all, we must trust each other without any element of doubt."

The Prince drew in breath sharply and smiled ingratiatingly. "I see I am not yet forgiven. You believe I was not telling you the truth when I said I had no men to spare for you last winter."

"I had expected your cooperation, certainly. It was something of an emergency."

"But..."

"I must speak frankly, Prince. The government's policy of imposing Orthodoxy and Russianisation on us is disastrous. Whether you realise it or not, you are undermining the traditional authority of the Balts here in Estonia."

"Oh, but..."

"Let me finish, please! Authority, you see, has its mainspring in the cities, and the people who administer it are generally incapable of recognising the particular conditions that exist in the countryside. Governor Chalkhovskoy has his headquarters in Reval—a very pleasant place to be, I've no doubt. But the Reval I see today is unrecognisable from the Reval I knew when I was a boy. Everything is changed...totally changed! Here in the country, things haven't altered in the same way. What I see when I look out of that window, ride into the village, go to my church...everything is still the same as it was in my grandfather's day. And that's the way the people want it. They're conservative. You're confusing them with all these new rules and regulations. More importantly, you're encouraging them not to hold their landlords in the same regard they used to do. And at the same time, you are forgetting that their landlords are the ones who administer the country for you, and who keep it peaceful. If we were to go, there would be anarchy."

"You're quite wrong, Baron. There would never be anarchy. To a man, our people are loyal to the Emperor."

"The ones who burned down my barn?"

Krasnov laughed disparagingly. "Come now, my friend. You have to admit, these are abnormal times, with the famine and the cholera." He spread his hands in a gesture of helplessness. "Unfortunately, like everywhere else, we have our criminal class. And they are being misled by these so-called liberals with their absurd propaganda. On the whole, the people are solid for the autocracy…as you are, of course, yourself." He smiled while noticing the Baron's air of dejection. "Don't worry," he continued loudly, optimistically. "We are sending the liberals to Siberia as fast as we can. And I have a fresh contingent of gendarmes coming in case of further trouble."

"I take it, then, in the case of any further trouble, I can rely on your support?"

"Of course, my dear fellow, you can rely on me absolutely."

"Then I also take it that you are now willing to accommodate me in that other matter I wrote you about."

"Other matter?" Prince Krasnov looked genuinely innocent.

"I wrote asking you to remove Father Tikhon."

"Ah!"

"The man has a thoroughly unsavoury reputation. He lived for years with a poor demented creature. He was quite open about it. Everybody in the district knew her as Father Tikhon's whore. Eventually she was found horribly murdered and buried frozen under the snow."

Prince Krasnov looked aghast. "My dear fellow, you're surely not telling me he murdered her?"

"Your man couldn't discover anything positive during his enquiry. But Tikhon behaved with abominable callousness when it came to her burial…"

"I see you have every reason to be upset. Baron, but…"—he shrugged dramatically—"nothing is ever simple, you know. I can only advise you to think no more about him…Father Tikhon, I mean. I'm sure I can speak quite openly to you without giving offense...? So far as you are concerned, Father Tikhon is untouchable...quite, quite untouchable! I can say no more, but I'm sure you understand."

After a short pause: "I see," Loff said grimly.

Prince Krasnov was suddenly elated again. "But why should you and I bother with the Father Tikhons of this world? It's you I want to talk about, my dear friend. All the wonderful things you're doing to develop this Estate. You are just the kind of man we need to bring Russia out of the nineteenth and into the twentieth century. It's all splendid, quite, quite splendid."

The object of this enthusiasm wanted to shake himself like a dog coming out of a pond. He felt tainted by the praise. "You mustn't overlook all that my brother has done," he said stiffly.

"Yes, yes, of course, your brother. He has come back to live in Saint Petersburg, they tell me. Good! Good!"

"He was living abroad only to raise money for our enterprises."

"Yes, well, that's as may be. We're glad...very glad...to have him back. Now, Baron, we must go into detail. My wife received most glowing accounts from Prince Fermatov yesterday about what you are doing. As a result, I've been able to write down a few questions. I would like to hear the answers directly from you. Just simple enquiries, you know..." he laughed. "I know nothing of these things. Treat me very gently, I beg you."

CHAPTER 5

▼

1892

Leonore spent the last hour of her journey examining her face in a small hand mirror. She had never been so anxious as she was at the prospect of meeting Clementine again after all these years. The fears of her childhood weren't anything like this; the cutting edge of this was that she was entirely responsible for herself. The fear and its causes were her own, surfacing like a spring from somewhere deep within her.

It was for only a short period in their lives really, she reflected, that she and Clementine had been so extraordinarily, intimately connected. Without Clementine, at one time, Leonore admitted, she would not have survived. But that crisis was long since over. They parted when it was resolved and now lived quite separate lives. She didn't even think of Clementine very often these days though, whenever she did it was always tenderly. She thought tenderly but never seriously imagined they would ever meet again. But they were going to! Within the hour! Her gratitude had become an urgent, nerve-wracking embarrassment.

The train swayed closer to Moscow, and she continued watching herself in the mirror. Paul hadn't wanted her to come and refused to allow her to bring the children. She had wanted to bring the older, at least, to show them off. She needed them for a defense, evidence of her success, proof of her worth.

The face in the mirror gazed back at her impassively, as though they were not connected. She stared at it, unblinking, trying to decipher its message. It stared back, its meaning hidden. To her, just then, it was like a flat, badly painted portrait. The cheeks were rounded, perhaps a little puffy. Lines round the eyes and mouth were etched in unnecessary detail. The nose was somewhat larger than she remembered it. A flash of white in the black hair disappeared beneath the tight curve of her hat. None of this said anything to her. Would it say anything to Clementine? The style of the hat would surely impress. The grey coat trimmed with black silk, the grey dress beneath it with its little black silk buttons all the way down the front were the latest thing. Had Rachel been visiting after all this time, she could have shown Clementine the clothes—the creation of the little Jewish school-girl she'd been kind to years ago. Clementine—any woman—would have understood in simple terms of taste and fashion. But without her children, Leonore had only her face to show. Could that be so easily understood? Or would it only be seen as a long retreat into nothingness.

Her first sight of Clementine at the station was of a thin, pale-faced woman dressed entirely in black—a black coat that hung unevenly as though designed for someone else, and a round, black, narrow-brimmed hat topped with a few straggly black feathers like a nest. Leonore would not have recognised her had she not waved and stepped forward to greet her. They clasped each other wordlessly for many moments, and Leonore felt the thin black body shaking with silent sobs. When they separated, Clementine turned hastily and, holding Leonore's hand, drew her away, behind the porter carrying the luggage. In the station yard, she stood undecided between horse-buses and cabs. Leonore directed the porter to a cab.

Neither spoke on the way to the flat. But Clementine held Leonore's hand between her own, stroking it gently and from time to time, raising it to her lips.

Leonore looked steadily out of the window, not knowing what to say. Gradually, the pleasures of what she saw overtook her embarrassment. Saint Petersburg was beautiful, superbly conceived and planned—all high art. Moscow greeted her with all the ebullience of folk art. Its colours—reds, yellows, blues, greens—were brash and beautiful, its domes jostled each other in near-vulgar abundance. Its streets were crowded with costumes from all over the Empire, making the people of Saint Petersburg, despite their high fashion, look drab by comparison. Moscow was an oriental bazaar where people came to trade with the boyars; in Saint Petersburg, sober-suited bureaucrats entertained sober-suited diplomatists in their sober-paneled offices, seeking liaisons and protocols in secret conversations. Saint Petersburg was a social minuet; Moscow, a reckless fandango. In spite of all Tsar Peter's efforts, Moscow remained the real capital. Saint Petersburg was Sleeping Beauty, Moscow her Prince.

Clementine's apartment was a shock, scarcely furnished—six rooms with bare floors, few chairs and some scrubbed tables. In what Clementine called their living room, the furnishing was a little more adequate: a couch, two sagging armchairs drawn close to the stove and Pan Koblinski's enormous samovar on a table against one of the long bare walls. Leonore's bedroom was bleak, but comfortable enough. The bed was large, and there was a small Oriental rug for her to put her feet on when getting in and out of it. There was a cupboard cleared for her convenience, a chair, a washstand, and a large mirror on the wall close to the window where the light was good. She sensed that this was Clementine's and Sasha's room and that they'd moved out because they didn't have another they considered suitable for her.

Clementine had tea waiting when Leonore unpacked. "Is everything all right, darling?" she asked, as though continuing a conversation they'd been having for the past year or so.

"Everything's perfect. But I more or less invited myself, Clementine. Are you quite sure I'm not giving you a great deal of trouble?"

"Now you are, sounding like your old silly self." Clementine gave a little laugh, and it sounded very nearly like her laughter in the old days.

"And Sasha?"

"He's longing to meet you, my dear. And I know you'll like each other. Though goodness knows what time he'll be home. I never do."

"But you're happy?" She heard herself uttering the words without intention and hated herself for sounding patronising.

"Of course." Clementine looked as though she had been struck.

Leonore was embarrassed again. "I'm sorry. It shouldn't have sounded like that."

Clementine recovered immediately. "My darling, I've been crying all morning because I am so very, very happy to see you…and looking so well. You're more beautiful than ever. Middle age suits you."

"You, too."

Clementine made a grimace of disbelief. "We must stop this nonsense," she said. "We both know it isn't important, and we've so little time. I want to know everything about everything. Tell me about Paul and the children and your house and…and…"—she gave a timorous, sly smile—"…do you hear anything of Sergei Ouroussoff these days?"

Leonore was pleased to talk. She was feeling confident because the situation between them was the reverse of what she'd expected it to be. Clearly, it was Clementine who needed to make excuses. Leonore didn't understand why, but the feeling deeply troubled her. Clementine had lost her early bloom completely, and her sense of fun. She seldom smiled, even while they reminisced on their times at the Doma, the meanness of Pan Koblinski and their flirtatious exploits with the Russian officers. Leonore had never enjoyed those days herself, but today, for Clementine's sake, she tried hard to believe it had all been fun. The effort brought her near to tears.

The atmosphere lightened when Sasha came in for supper. He was a very tall young man and thin like Clementine. Leonore thought him handsome. He wore his fair hair shoulder length, his face was clean-shaven and his eyes deep brown and sad. His nose was short and straight, his lips full and very red. He greeted Leonore gently in their native Polish and when he spoke his ideas were neatly expressed, his words carefully articulated. During the meal they spoke about Warsaw, recalling the places they all knew and rekindling the faces of acquaintances they might have shared. After they'd eaten, Sasha played his flute, the women sang folk songs, and they all drank vodka.

Their laughter had carried them far from reality, and it took Leonore a long time to fall asleep afterwards. In their laughter she had glimpsed brief snatches of the old Clementine and liked Sasha more each moment because he obviously made her friend happy. Nonetheless, she was discomforted by certain looks that passed between the two of them. Their eyes came together in unbidden, searching contact and the laughter died away. The moment faded almost instantaneously when they remembered that she was in the room with them and it was necessary to continue the happy charade.

When she awoke the next day, Sasha was already away to his railway yards and Clementine guided her around the Moscow sights. She was still cheerful and friendly, but the intimacy of the previous night had gone. She answered noncommittally when Leonore wanted to talk about Sasha and told her they possibly wouldn't see him that evening, as he would probably have a meeting to go to. She was vague as to its nature, and Leonore assumed it would take place at the railway yard or somewhere else outside the flat. She was surprised, then, to hear the door to the hallway open and the tramp of several heavy feet coming in. Clementine sat listening, alert as a bird. She said nothing, listening to various doors banging noisily shut.

"I must take them their tea," she said at last, leaving Leonore alone. She didn't come back for nearly half an hour and, when she did, smiled guiltily and said nothing about the visitors, indicating that she wished for nothing to be said.

The next day was wet and humid. Leonore awoke feeling feverish and would have liked to rest. But Clementine was anxious they shouldn't waste their short time together and insisted on more sightseeing.

Leonore climbed into the Petersburg Express that night with considerable relief. The windows of the long line of coaches were shaded by blinds when the train drew into the Station. Leonore gave Clementine a quick goodbye—the speed of it was taken by Clementine as a cover for her emotion—and followed the conductor to her compartment. Her bed was already made up and she sank onto it gratefully. The going back would be so much easier than the coming. Paul would be waiting for her, to gather her into his arms and make everything normal. The children would be waiting at the house, and Ulrika and Anton, she knew, would be pleased to see her.

Here in the anonymity of the train she knew she would sleep, in spite of the rattling of the wheels beneath her. In Clementine's flat, she was ensnared by something...she couldn't realise exactly what it was, but it soured the happiness they'd tried to refine together. Leonore couldn't give it a name. Perhaps it was exaggerated while she was there because she was there. But she wasn't the only cause of it. She knew it persisted just as strongly now she had left. It was the mainspring, she was sure, of Sasha's well-hidden sadness. It had robbed Clementine's eyes of all their light.

CHAPTER 6

▼

1892

During the hottest of Petersburg summers, the von Hagen's second son—Albrecht Joseph—was born. He was born reluctantly, as it appeared, fighting in his mother's womb to put off the decisive moment for more than thirty-six hours. When he finally appeared, it was generally agreed miraculous that he had lived to struggle so long. His hairless head was huge, his shoulders and hips unnaturally narrow. His eyes were deep blue—naturally enough. But the one on the left had a pronounced cast. His nose and chest were congested with mucus, and he breathed with noisy difficulty.

The doctor advised Leonore to be ready "for anything." Leonore, pitifully exhausted, was ready for nothing. She had given Paul his second son. His birth was nearly unbearable, and now he was troublesome and unattractive. She felt no pleasure at taking him into her arms, but she fed him by the breast because that was her duty. He was a von Hagen boy; therefore, he was important.

Dorothea looked at her new little brother and said only, "eruh!" Sonia, standing close behind her, said "eruh!" too. Then they both left the room, highly disinterested. Eduard was still too young to mind anything either way, but Marie, perhaps recognising something of him in herself, smiled and cooed lovingly.

It was another month before Paul saw his new son. He had been out to the Altai and the Urals on behalf of the Bank. On the journey home from Chelyabinsk, he'd had four days in the train to read and reread Leonore's letter.

My darling Paul,

Our baby has come — another boy. I had the priest here to the house to christen him Albrecht Joseph as we'd decided. I couldn't wait for you, my dear. There was need for haste because, for a time, his survival was doubtful. Now, thank God, the doctor tells me he is beyond risk.

I wish I knew how I should describe him to you. He is not handsome, I'm afraid. Though when children are very young, that's nothing to go by. They can greatly improve as they grow older. But he is not, I must admit, beautiful like Dorothea, Sonia and Eduard. Marie is the only one who shows any interest in him, so perhaps that sums it all up. The three older ones are good-looking like you von Hagens. My poor Marie and Albrecht are like my side of the family — my poor father was a very good man but, oh dear, oh dear, he certainly couldn't claim to be beautiful.

I hope you won't think I'm an unnatural mother, writing to you like this about our baby. He'll grow to be a good child and a wonderful person, I'm sure. I just don't want you to be disappointed when you see him.

My darling, we all long for your return. Dorothea says she hopes you will bring with you a little Chinese brother or sister for her. I certainly hope you do not.

For ever and ever, my darling Paul,

Your devoted wife,

Leonore von Hagen.

Funny creatures, women! When he was young, he had known all about them, understood them in every detail. Now, particularly

Leonore! When he got to Saint Petersburg, he had himself driven straight to a shop on the Liteiny Prospekt and bought a whole cartload of red roses. He directed them to be delivered to the house; then he went to the Preobrazhensky Barracks for a drink or two with Ouroussoff.

When he reached home, he found Leonore radiantly happy and excited to see him. He kissed her—almost perfunctorily—and demanded to see his new son. She took him to the nursery, and he gazed long at the infant while his wife hovered nervously, hoping he would say something yet dreading what it would be.

"My darling, he's beautiful," he told her with boisterous conviction when he judged she'd been kept waiting long enough. "He's a splendid little chap."

He clasped Leonore and his little son to him, ignoring the infant's snuffles. He covered them both with kisses. Leonore's response was what he expected.

"Oh, Paul! Oh, Paul! My darling, darling Paul!" she said with very evident relief, half-laughing, half-crying. The baby took exception to this noisy familiarity and objected healthily with snuffly roars. Paul laughed and laid him back in his cot. "Come now, my love. No more worries about him. You've given me another wonderful son."

They were overjoyed to be together again, and the children were equally overjoyed to have him back, though Dorothea chided him for not bringing her the Chinese brother or sister she longed for.

When he and Leonore went to bed, he took her into his arms most tenderly and loved her so that she thought her heart would break with the happiness of it. Every moment, every action of his expressed his total adoration, his joy at being her subject and her slave. They slept scarcely at all, lying side by side exchanging light kisses like young lovers on the threshold of life, yet remembering, each in their own way, the days, the weeks and the years they'd been together. They were closer now than they had ever been, though it might have seemed to lookers-on that they were living disconnected lives, drifting apart.

Whether they wished it or no, they were now a part of Petersburg society, living self-contained lives after the style of fashionable people. Leonore's days were occupied by her children and her women friends. Any suspicions Petersburg matrons might have entertained about her background were swept aside when she was taken publicly under the wing of Princess Surotkina.

The Surotkins had been wealthy landowners with Estates all over central Russia, their nobility stretching back to Catherine the Great. The Princess was the only sister of three older brothersrogues allwho had fornicated and gambled away practically everything they had. They disregarded the necessity to make good marriages and now lived out their boring days penniless in the country, tweaking the bottoms of chambermaids whenever they had the chance.

Everybody knew the story. Russian aristocracy was still tribal in its universal familiarity, its closeness not a positive defense when almost everybody could climb into an order of ennoblement on grounds of money alone. Everybody knew the story and they respected the Princess because of it, rather than in spite of it. Thy respected her and accepted her protégés into their circle.

Leonore met the Princess almost every day; they served on the same committees, lunched at the house by the Anichkov Bridge quite often, and took tea together in fashionable cafés.

Another member of the circle was Countess Poulanskaya, more pitied than enjoyed, an ardent girl in her early thirties who had waited some time and would marry Sergei Ouroussoff this very afternoon, if only he would ask her. She became devoted to Leonore the instant she heard the von Hagens were friends of his, and bought their children expensive presents embarrassingly often.

Varvara Milyova was approaching middle age, the wife of a naval officer stationed at Vladivostok. She was living her life seven thousand miles away from her husband because she was convinced their children—all now grown up and safely married themselves—couldn't possibly manage without her. Neither, she knew, could her husband. She loved Leonore for listening so patiently to her lamentation of indecision as to who needed her most.

Valentina Popova was a woman of forty-five or thereabouts, stout, short, with bright blonde hair and vermilion-tinted cheeks. She wore a lot of ostentatious jewelry that Princess Surotkina declared could never have been worth more than a hundred roubles all told; in colour, her gowns were invariably blush pink or deepest red. The reason for her acceptance by the others was never acknowledged. It depended upon her husband's being a powerful figure at the Russia and Asia Bank. He was Paul's immediate superior, in fact, and because of his position in the hierarchy would know, they were sure, rather more of their private affairs than they would care to be made public.

Paul's hours were packed with Bank business. The Urals and the Altai were an Aladdin's Cave of minerals for prospectors with large-scale capital to spend. The Great Russian Railway, though still in sections waiting to be joined, gave some access to this untouched heart of the Empire. Siberia was still largely a land of mystery—one of the last and certainly the largest on earth. People talked of it in terms of romance as well as money. There were always whispers about its exciting future, including the dream of a Russian-controlled railway through Manchuria, to take out its treasures as quickly as possible.

With all this on hand, Paul had little free time. The world was becoming aware of the great Russian potential in human beings, as well as minerals. Men with High Hopes came from France, Germany, England, and America, capitalists or their representatives, to be wooed by Paul to put their money into the Bank and all its bound-to-yield-great-dividends projects. Once in St. Petersburg, they were feted and introduced all round, often at Paul's house with Leonore as their hostess. She was always successful with them, popular because she had never been taught the stuffy protocol of most of the people they met there.

Leonore reserved her judgment about most of them. She had been brought up by a father who bought and sold, albeit in a humble way.

She was aware that altruism was never the main incentive and was genuinely horrified when Princess Surotkina told her, as a very great secret, that Paul had persuaded her to invest what little money she had in a gold mine in the Urals.

"How could you, Paul? She's such a nice lady, and so innocent of all that sort of thing."

"What the devil's being nice got to do with it?"

"You know she's not rich."

"Exactly."

"Then why did you do it? If she loses that money she gave you, she'll probably have nothing."

"But she won't lose it."

They were preparing to go to a reception at the Popovs. Leonore heard of the Princess's investment only that afternoon after a Red Cross meeting. She pounced on her husband directly when he came into the house.

"You know she lives like a pauper in that flat of hers. She's sold everything she possibly could, and she still tries to help out those brothers of hers."

"Leonore!" He had never shouted at her like that before, and the shock of it stopped her dead. "What kind of a man do you think I am? Do you honestly think I'd get that woman to invest in anything if there was the slightest chance she'd be the loser by it?"

"No...well...perhaps I was too..."

"Be reasonable, for God's sake! Whether you admit it or not, you were the one, when we married, who complained about my not having a job. Well...I've got a job. That's why we're here...my job. I've got a job, and I'm good at it. I make a lot of money; you can't complain about that. Believe me, I don't need the few kopeks' commission I'll make out of Surotkina. And it wouldn't give me any pleasure at all to see her bankrupt."

Leonore's anger dissolved into guilt. It was all true, what he said. She was responsible for everything, even for his having met the Princess. He knew all of Leonore's friends, of course. He was polite to them all, but he liked Princess Surotkina particularly—as much as he disliked Valentina Popova.

There was good reason for that, Leonore thought. Sergei Ilyich Popov was not the easiest man to get along with. He resented Count Witte at the Treasury because he was a Balt. He distanced himself from Paul for the same reason. The flood of foreigners into Russia, all money-grubbing and self-seeking, confused him. He was a spider of a man, bland-faced with expressionless eyes. He listened without registering on his features what he heard. His lips were thin, his voice almost falsetto.

These two, the Popovs, who were giving tonight's reception, were a pair who might well have emerged from the *Commedia del 'Arte*. At the Bank he was immovable and implacable and, Paul believed, genuinely regretted the supercession of the abacus for double-entry bookkeeping. In a social setting, like tonight, he went through all the motions of courtesy as though powered, inside, by a clockwork motor. Nobody really liked him, yet his parties were always a success. Tonight Count Witte was there, as were several of His Majesty's Ministers. There were quite half a dozen foreign ambassadors, resplendent in State Stars and Sashes, three actresses (which one was the old fox sleeping with at the moment, everyone wondered?), and a host of people who hadn't quite yet "arrived" but who felt certain, for the sake of this evening, that they were close to doing so.

The next morning party time was over, and he burst his bomb. Paul arrived at the Bank early, still sensitive from the argument with Leonore the night before. He was shocked. How could she doubt his honesty and his motives the way she did? Could she not, even after all this time, accept him as an honest man?

When a clerk came to tell him that Director Popov wished to see him immediately, he followed the young man without much interest. It was a usual Popov summons—immediate but for some quite unimportant matter the Director himself couldn't understand. He went in.

"Ah, your Excellency…" Popov sat at his desk, smiling and rubbing his hands. His face betrayed nothing, but Paul sensed trouble. He was generally "Paul" unless something serious was afoot. "There's a little job I want you to do for me."

"Yes, Director?" Paul tried to look interested. Some minute controversy about an account that would waste hours of his time to sort out, he supposed.

"That's right. Oh! Do sit down! You're going to Manchuria."

"Manchuria?" Paul was staggered. He must have misheard.

"That damned frontier should never have been drawn the way it was," Popov said, as though continuing a conversation he was already having with somebody else. "Forces everything we want to move too far north. You can imagine what it's like in the winter. Straight through! That's the way we ought to go—cut out Kharbarovsk altogether—straight through Manchuria."

"Excuse me." Paul was still incredulous. "I still can't understand how any of this concerns me."

"The Far East is where we should be concentrating nowadays. And luckily for us, there are, er…" He brought his hands together with a slight 'plop,' "there are interests…" he said the word slowly, very carefully "…who have the foresight and the necessary financial backing to…help us reach our Destiny, shall we say?"

"Director, I still cannot see," Paul began again but, once more, he was interrupted.

"You will apply for extended leave on personal grounds, which, of course, I shall grant without question. Ostensibly, you will be fulfilling an ambition, leading an expedition from Vladivostok into the hinterland. Your companions will be two American surveyors with experience of building railroads through the Rocky Mountains. Together, you will select the best route out of Vladivostok westwards, across to Harbin and on to the Russian border again and to Chita. We'll cut out Kharbarovsk altogether."

Paul couldn't say a word. What he was hearing was outrageous, the suggestion that he be in any way connected with it, preposterous. Had the man lost his reason overnight? He tried smiling gently to bring him down to earth.

"Sergei Ilyich, I know nothing about surveying, nor about building railways."

"No, but you understand money. Your job will be to convert the figures they give you into hard cash. And look around you generally. Talk to people. Find out what they think about things. But don't say anything about your plans for a railway, of course."

"My plans," Paul echoed weakly.

"Drop whatever it is you're doing at the moment. Get a book about surveying. Oh! And a map of the area. Get some idea of where you're going. I've arranged a preliminary meeting for you with the surveyors at my house tonight. Seven o'clock. They'll be bound to know what you'll need for the journey. I want you away as soon as possible...tomorrow would be ideal."

"But...we can't go yet. The snows will start any day now. They're probably metres deep across Siberia already."

"If we wait till spring, the entire country might be crawling with crowds of people, all with the same idea. We have to get in first, you understand...approach the Chinese Government with a feasible plan before anybody else can get to them."

The man was completely mad!

"We'll need Count Witte's sanction, of course..." It was almost a question.

"The Count already has enough on his mind...the spirits monopoly, the Siberian Railway, putting the rouble on the gold standard..."

"But Director...an expedition like this will cost a lot of money."

Sergei Ilyich laid his hands comfortably palms down on his desk. "I've already explained to you, my dear Paul. Money is no problem. There are...interests."

There was a smug silence in the room until Paul broke it. "I'm sorry, Sergei Ilyich, I can't agree to any of this. And even if I did, I wouldn't be prepared to go at this time of year."

"Ah! Your Excellency is refusing?"

"Positively."

Popov's head shook sorrowfully. His hands flipped over in a gesture of helplessness, and he fumbled in his waistcoat pocket for a key. He opened a drawer in his desk but before taking anything out, looked at Paul again, giving him another chance. "You're quite sure?"

"Quite sure. And certainly not without the Count's knowledge."

Popov drew a fawn folder out of the drawer. "I'm sorry, Paul. I'd hoped never to have to remind you," he said sounding genuinely apologetic.

Paul knitted his brows but said nothing. He had no idea what the man was talking about.

"There was a little incident in Berlin, you'll remember."

Paul remained puzzled.

"A boy...a young man called Heinrich Webber. You picked him up in a bar on...wait a moment, I have the date here...ah yes, you picked him up in a bar and spent the night with him at..."

"How dare you!" Paul was white with fury. "That is a foul, disgusting idea!"

"My dear fellow..." Popov was all open-mindedness and equanimity. "Don't distress yourself. It's true, I'm not attracted to that sort of thing myself, but I'm not here to judge you. Of course," he continued, "if you refuse to oblige me in this instance you may, of course, appeal to the Count...put your point of view, you know. But in that case, I should have to have a word with him myself. That would be only fair, don't you think?"

Paul could still say nothing. Whatever he said might sound like a defense, an excuse, and he couldn't tolerate the idea of it.

Popov snapped the folder closed with mock finality. "Now I suggest you take my advice...read a book...examine a map. And I'll see you at my house at seven. Oh! And you will give my warmest regards to that lovely wife of yours, will you not? I thought, last night, she looked quite charming...quite charming."

CHAPTER 7

▼

1892

Paul walked along the Neva Embankment, head down and twisted against the weather. He felt emptied. It was a physical, not an emotional sensation. His body was a hollow—a skin holding together only his bones and containing none of his organs. He stayed close to the parapet in case he should fall and expected his bones to rattle as he went along. He remembered quite well now, Popov's "incident" in Berlin. He recalled quite clearly the yellow lighting and smoke-filled atmosphere of the bar, though he didn't know it's name and had no idea of its address. He could see again the well-dressed young man, looking like a bank clerk, who sat at his table and spoke to him. He remembered waking up in the morning in the cold, grey room, naked in the young man's bed, berated by a raucous landlady and her husband. But how did Popov come to know about it...all the details, the date, the address, even the young man's name?

He was betrayed, of course, but that hardly mattered now. Someone in the secret police—a friend of Popov's? His agent? It really didn't matter who, had followed him assiduously...for how many days and nights until then? Whoever it was had registered that he was at a low ebb and had summoned the young man to come to the bar. It was a plot to compromise him. And it had succeeded. But no one else was to blame. How could he have been so foolish? How could he have drunk so much, been so beguiled by the vapid conversation of a total stranger?

He allowed the situation to occupy his mind in order to avoid more serious considerations. The trenchant question was, what was best to be done now? Leonore was at the heart of his anxiety. He could agree to Popov's plans. But how, then, could he make believable to Leonore this sudden, secret expedition to Manchuria? If he rejected Popov's plan, he would have to face Leonore's reaction to his indiscretion in Berlin. He had little hope of her understanding. If she believed he was attempting to rob Princess Surotkina, she was capable of believing anything of him. Besides Leonore, there was no doubt that Popov would spread his lie to its most deadly advantage throughout the city.

The wind from the sea tore at the flesh on his face. He was chilled to the bone and longed to sit quietly over a drink, but was nervous of taking one in his present mood. The day was darkening. The clock was hurtling to the moment he would have to make up his mind. And he was still nowhere nearer to knowing whether he would or would not attend the meeting at Popov's house.

CHAPTER 8

▼

1892

Ulrika asked coyly whether she might talk to Her Excellency and Leonore immediately agreed, though with a sinking heart. All the children were so fond of her, Leonore trusted her so implicitly that her leaving would be tantamount to a disaster. She took the girl up to her dressing room sat her down and looked encouraging—more encouraging than she felt. Ulrika said nothing, however. She blushed and wrestled with the handkerchief between her fingers but made no sound. Leonore decided this was not the attitude to be expected from someone about to give up her job. She made a guess at the reason for all this embarrassment.

"Is it Anton, my dear?"

Ulrika blushed even deeper and looked to on the verge of tears. Leonore began to have forebodings. "You'd better tell me whatever it is you want to tell me," she said quite briskly. "We'll never sort anything out if you don't."

Ulrika gulped and somehow managed to dislodge the kernel of whatever it was—embarrassment? shame?—caught in her throat. "He says he wants to marry me. Your Excellency."

What a relief! Leonore leaned forward and clasped the girl's hands, smiling. "And you, my child, what have you to say about that?"

Tears ran down the girl's cheeks.

"Does it please you?" Leonore asked her softly.

Ulrika nodded vigorously.

"Well then, I have to tell you, I think Anton's a very nice boy."

Ulrika looked relieved.

"But Ulrika, I must also tell you, you have to think about this very carefully. You are a German and Anton is a Russian. That means that however much you love each other, however close you are, at some time in the future if you burn your hand, you'll cry out in German and Anton in Russian. You can't change that. Do you understand what I'm saying? You'll give and give and give, both of you; you'll try and try and try till it hurts. But you'll always be different, deep down. There'll always be that little something between you."

Ulrika looked devastated. "It's no good then, your Excellency?"

"I didn't say that, my dear. His Excellency and I are very happy together. He's good to me, as I'm sure Anton will be good to you. He'll never deliberately hurt me, I know. I trust him everywhere…in every possible way. But we're still different—for all that. And the secret of success is…never to be surprised when that difference shows itself."

The girl smiled, still not fully understanding.

"You must expect to be judged—not always charitably—by your husband's family. Anton's parents are still alive in the country somewhere, I believe. Your ways won't be their ways until you've learned to change. The way you make soup won't be as good as theirs. Certainly not the way you bring up babies. And your babies, too. You'll be watching them, in spite of yourself. They'll be an almost perfect mixture but they'll be just that little bit different: this one a little more Russian, that one a little more German."

She suddenly put her arm around the girl and gave her a fond hug. "But it's never easy, my dear, no matter who you are, nor where you come from. But we all manage somehow. And if he really loves you and you really love himm you'll be happy, believe me."

It was only a little after Ulrika had gone away smiling to find Anton, that Paul came in from the office, earlier than usual. He looked weary and distressed and greeted the children abstractedly. Leonore thought he must be sickening…an attack of influenza, perhaps. She was even more perturbed when he called for brandy immediately and sat morosely staring at nothing. She'd never seen him like this before. She didn't know whether to question him about it or wait until he decided to tell her whatever it was himself. Her tension was relaxed when she was called to the telephone. She came back looking happy.

"Paul dear, that was Valentina Yurievska. She tells me you're meeting Sergei Ilyich and some other men at his house at seven. She's asked me to go too. We'll play bezique until you've finished. Then we'll all have late supper together."

When she sat down and concentrated upon him once more, she was startled; his eyes were glazed with horror. "Paul! Paul, dear, what is it? Aren't you well? Shall I send for a doctor? Shall I telephone and say you can't come?"

He rose, waving his hands before him as though parting a curtain. "I…I'm all right, my dear. I have some papers to look at. I must go to my study."

With the door closed behind him he should have felt safe, but he did not. Of course the invitation for Leonore had been Popov's idea, not his wife's. Whichever way he moved now, he would be more firmly stuck in the web than ever. To be frank with Leonore was unthinkable. Even if he managed to convince her tonight of his innocence, in only an hour or two she'd be bound to hear Popov's account. Whether she believed that or not, she would be shattered to the depths of her soul by the scandal. All their Petersburg friends would swallow it like pigs at a trough. They love to elaborate it, embroider it. It would be their revenge on him for being a Balt and on her for being a suspect Jew.

Either way, whatever he did, there would be a price to pay. Either he could lay Leonore open to all that, or he could put himself completely within Popov's power. Henceforward he would have to do everything the man told him to. But to save Leonore so much distress, that was the price he would have to pay.

He found her playing with the children, and asked Ulrika to take them away. "This meeting with Popov tonight," he began, "he wants me to go to Manchuria."

"Manchuria! Why? When? What are you supposed to do there?"

"I'm sorry, my darling, I can't tell you that." He tried to make it sound like a joke. "It's all most terribly, terribly confidential."

She didn't respond to his lightness.

"Don't look like that," he told her, gaining confidence. "It'll be fascinating. I'll enjoy it. An expedition."

"But where will you be? How will I get in touch with you? One of the children could be ill."

"I really don't know." He hesitated. "Our Agent-General in Vladivostok, perhaps." He regretted it the moment he'd said it.

"Vladivostok!" Leonore looked relieved. "Varvara Milyova's husband is in Vladivostok. She hears from him quite regularly nowadays."

"Darling, I won't be in Vladivostok for very long. I'm going to Manchuria as soon as it can be arranged."

Leonore became aloof. Fortunately she had a contact in Vladivostok and Varvara Milyova was more likely than her husband to give her all the information she needed.

"When are you going?" she asked casually.

"Very soon. Within a week, perhaps."

She recoiled. "But it's winter! You can't go all the way out there in the winter. Paul, I can't believe this. It's mad. You can't go now."

"I must. It's urgent."

She tried to hold his eyes, but he turned his head away. "You're not telling me everything," she said accusingly. "Paul, you're hiding something."

"My darling, I'm sorry. I can't tell you any more. It's confidential bank business."

CHAPTER 9

▼

1894

It was a good time for the von Hagens; Loff was happy. The famine was over, and its after-effects were fading into mythology, the personal stories everyone has when times of crisis are over. Trade was improving; von Hagen amber was selling in the smarter shops of Saint Petersburg, Kiev, Moscow, and Warsaw. Government policy was to direct finance into commerce and industry. The first of Fermatov's barges were crossing the Baltic to Stockholm and Helsinki. Close to the boat-building yard at Kohtla-Jarve, they were building a small refinery to produce oil from Estate shale—eagerly bought-up by the innumerable new factories now being established throughout Russia.

Close to home, in the village, Russian incomers were united with their wives; date of arrival of the first baby was now wagered on. The place now was nearly twice its original size, but the Russian houses were all set apart, out along the grass track (with constant use more mud or dust than grass) beyond the barn. Father Tikhon was still using that as his home and church. Other Russians were coming to live in new Orthodox parishes all over the country. Few of them were left long with only temporary churches. Baron Loff made no application to build anything more permanent. And Father Tikhon, perhaps, wouldn't have wanted it. As things now were, he was considered by new priests and settlers to have been something of a pioneer in his time, a reputation he was disinclined to dispel.

With the discovery of Greta's dead body, Father Tikhon has lost much of his influence over the Estonians, and the line between the two races became deeply drawn. The government was building a school in the region, not too far away but far enough for the Estonians to find innumerable excuses for keeping their children away, once they understood the language of instruction was to be Russian.

The Baron was disturbed because, in their indifference to Father Tikhon, the Estonians didn't return to their old dependence on Pastor Vikkers. They attended his services only perfunctorily, and now, as they went into his church, they didn't have to pass the cross-frame outside. Flogging had been abolished by law, and the removal of the frame was proof of how much the old order was changed.

Law was re-established after the burning, but it was clearly government law and no longer only the Baron's. That was the biggest change of all, perhaps. In response to Loff's call for assistance last autumn, Prince Krasnov had now stationed a unit of gendarmes in the region. Their Barracks were well away from the village, but close enough, even so, for the men to come in whenever they were off duty. They spent their pay, courted the village girls and roistered in the tavern. There was a sprinkling of Estonians among them but even so, the Estonian villagers hated them all. They were Russians and alien. Father Tikhon became their chaplain. They supplied him with a mule that lived up to the reputation of its kind. The priest rode it all over the district, slow as a donkey and embracing its neck like a lover. Local boys called after him, protesting that they couldn't tell man from beast. Besides the mule, the gendarmes gave him icons for his church, which the Estonians would dearly have liked to see, except that since the Greta affair, their age-old suspicion of Orthodox paraphernalia had returned.

The Baron had no fear of icons. In his opinion, and of much greater importance, was his unshakeable conviction since he'd learned of Tikhon's association with Krasnov that the priest was an agent of the secret police. He warned everyone and merely gained the reputation of being an old man with a bee in his bonnet. People who didn't write or receive letters would never experience the belly crunching fear of having them opened in transit. People whose imaginations were bounded by their daily work, to adequately feeding their families, having money to buy drink at the tavern and freedom to copulate whenever they had the urge, seldom had revolutionary thoughts and were unaware of the accompanying dangers. The authorities could safely ignore them. Whether they beat their wives, abused their children or killed each other in brawls was left to the Baron to deal with. And that was about all that they did leave to him to deal with.

Loff was only in his forties, but he was now thinking and acting like an old man—an old man edged out, deprived of natural functions. Perhaps, in contradiction, he was feeling useless because his life was easier today than it had ever been and he should have been enjoying it more. Thanks to Fermatov's practical advice and Paul's financial knowledge, the Estate was running at a profit. But Loff had never been brought up to regard money as a main incentive in life. He despised the commercialism that now motivated his actions.

He regretted that the Russians and their families he'd encouraged to come here were now living apart in what the Estonians called "Russian Town." He had no relationship with them and felt any visit he made to be an imposition, though he was still their landlord and their employer. He had no rights with them, no knowledge of them. They shared their thoughts and their problems with Father Tikhon. He was left not knowing what they "thought about things."

Knowing what his people "thought about things" was something he'd always been proud of. Now he didn't even know what his Estonians "thought about things," people whose families had been connected with his for generations. As he saw it now, bringing in strangers had been a terrible mistake. His Russian workers had never been really assimilated; they were urban workers now, while his Estonians were still peasants. Since the Greta affair, the rift between the two was unalterable. Were his Estonians as confused about things as he was himself, he wondered? Or did they know better where they stood with their growing independence in this fast-changing world?

On this particular morning, however, Loff had put all that to one side for a month. He was happy. He was pacing the station platform. It was a very long platform because the town was being developed as a holiday resort and it was hoped that even the Tsar would come one day. The Tsar always traveled in a very long train, so the platform was built very long to accommodate it. So far, the Tsar hadn't appeared. But a famous composer had. Loff read about the visit in his newspaper and, remembering his own musical connections years ago in Saint Petersburg, wondered whether to contact him. In the end, he thought not. There were unsavoury rumours about the man. And, in any case, Loff's Petersburg days were far off. When he came back to the Estate to live, he'd come to a different world. Perhaps, if he'd married Cecile von Aschenbauer things might have been different. He still shuddered at the very thought of it.

Nothing of that kind was in his mind this morning. He paced the platform wondering whereabouts along it the Petersburg Express would elect to stop. The family was coming for the summer: Paul, Leonore, the children and a young couple to look after them all. His eagerness to see them brought him here too early. He waited nearly an hour before the train came in and, when it did, it stopped far away. He saw them rumbling out as he walked towards them—all hurried movement, exuberant voices and unnecessary confusion. Directly when she saw him, Dorothea came running towards him and clasped her arms around his waist. "Haven't you remembered where you left your arm yet, Uncle Loff?" They both laughed heartily, both understanding their private joke and all its implications of special intimacy. Perhaps Leonore equally fathomed the mist that came into his eyes when, after they'd kissed, she looked around and asked:

"Where's Channah?"

"She's waiting for you at the house."

There was no outright embarrassment and he didn't know whether she understood that their relationship had changed. At the house it was hardly noticeable that it had. Channah was as pleased to see them as anyone. Before their arrival she spent much time arranging treats for the children. She made Leonore feel that the visit was really important to her. And no one at all, judging by her constant kindnesses and attentions to Loff, could have imagined that their affectionate relationship was in any way changed.

Count von Aschenbauer came to stay for several days. The Countess and her daughter were still in Saint Petersburg and, the Count told them gloomily, Cecile's interest was now centred on another fortune hunter—someone in the army called Ouroussoff. Nobody added to that conversation, and the Count reverted to his habitual grumbling. Things were no more the same with him than they were at the von Hagens. He despaired because he could see no way forward. His idea of their prospecting jointly for shale had been forgotten since Loff's outburst that day. It was clear now that they had separate aims so he threw himself back into the traditional pattern of estate management.

"He's exactly like the Krimovskys," Paul said disparagingly when he'd gone. "They have a big place in the Kaluga Province…"

"And the Princess brought the children to Petersburg last winter. Their Alexei went to the same kindergarten as our Dorothea, and they became quite attached. It was sweet, wasn't it, Paul?"

"Krimovsky won't admit times are changing either," Paul began again, having waited patiently for Leonore to finish. "Landlords are anachronisms today. These big estates are a thing of the past."

Loff smiled to stifle a sharp disagreement. "I'm afraid you've been away too long, Paul," he said gently. "Petersburg isn't the centre of the universe, you know. There are still plenty of people here who don't want the old ways to change."

"But when you get down to the bottom line, it's the amber and the shale oil and the barge building that keeps all this going, Loff, not your peasants who want to go on making no effort, living in the past for ever."

"If you tell me so, of course I believe you."

"And I'll tell you something else! If ever we need money, I shall raise it more easily on the oil and the amber and the barges than on the land."

He leaned back in triumph.

"Business! Business! Business!" Leonore reproved him, laughing. "Do let's talk about something else, Paul. I don't know whether poor Loff's head is swimming by now; I know mine is."

Generally they avoided business; this was a holiday and not the time for it. During the day they spent little time together. Leonore and Channah had understanding chats. Channah decided that if Paul were so often away on business, this was the time for them to be alone together and undisturbed. They arranged picnics almost every day. The Baron called for Ants each morning, and the old man, still grinning and quite toothless now, letting the reins lie loose in his arthritic fingers, drove them to the sea. They all went crowded in together; the children, Channah, Ulrika and Anton. The Baron shared the box with Ants and complained of their dawdling. It was time, he said, for him to sack Ants and pay the horse instead; it was he that was doing all the driving. Ants laughed and commanded the horse to get on with it. The horse took no notice, wandering from side to side of the track picking succulent greenery to chew on the way.

Whatever they ate at the beach was gritty. The shore was all fine sand with hardly a tide to make any of it damp and stable. Sonia suggested that whatever fish ate must be gritty, too, and that made it acceptable. Loff suggested that as well as eating like fish they might play like fish. He peeled off his top clothes keeping his undershirt on so that the children shouldn't see the stump of his sawn-off arm. Dorothea and Sonia followed him in, whooping joyfully in the shallows. Before the month was out he had taught them both to swim. The boys were too young and stayed with Anton and Ulrika. Poor Marie hovered miserably, screaming every time anyone suggested she should join her sisters. She envied them, but envied more the safely, security and dryness her brothers were enjoying.

Paul and Leonore made the most of their privacy for a time but at heart they were neither of them country people. They were distracted, made uneasy by the solitude. Paul was glad to be free of Popov for a few weeks, but missed the bustle of the bank. This was, admittedly, the season of the year when Leonore's committees were prorogued, but she was worried about what decisions the executives might come to while her back was turned. It might have been better they had gone to the beach with the children but felt they couldn't; Channah and Loff were going to such endless trouble to give them a rest from that sort of thing.

During the first week they made a conscious effort to keep themselves occupied. They rode. They walked. They visited the village, where some of the older men and women responded to Paul's greeting with dour, unforgetting, unforgiving looks. They went into Russian Town and Paul was angered at the state the place had been allowed to fall into. They called on Father Tikhon, who was more hairy and smiling even than Paul remembered him. He all but dragged them physically into his church, still smelling of incense, candle grease and pickled herring. He displayed his new icons and brought out his vodka. He poured generously for Paul and himself. If her Excellency didn't wish to drink, there was nothing he could do about it but bring his shoulders up to his hairy ears and look disinterested. Except for needing to go to bed with them sometimes Father Tikhon had not much interest in women.

"On Sunday you must come to our Liturgy, your Excellency. Such bases we have here now. Marvelous!"

Paul made no commitment. Three or four more vodkas were ritualistically downed and they were allowed to leave. On their ride home, they separately reached the same conclusion: that being together for long with nothing to do simply wasn't enough. The next day, when

Paul asked her what she would like, Leonore said she would rest and read a little perhaps but, of course, he must do whatever he wished. The day after, she had letters to write.

Some days later Paul was walking alone along the shore. The sand was soft and the exercise grueling. His calf muscles were pulling unbearably. Ahead of him he saw some figures splashing in the sea and continued towards them without take much notice. As he got nearer he was conscious of good-humoured male voices. Their cheerfulness was inviting, and he decided to join them and sit down for a rest. Only when he was close—too close to turn away or turn back—two of them waded out of the water and he saw they were both stark naked.

"Hallo."

The voice came from somewhere slightly above him to his left. He turned. The speaker was lying comfortably against a steep-sided dune. He was dressed in the uniform of a sergeant of gendarmerie, hatless and unbuttoned at the neck. He was chewing a blade of maram grass, which he politely took out of his mouth before saying anything else. The two men who'd come out of the water were sprawling unselfconsciously on the sand, rifling through their clothing. They rolled cigarettes, lit them and smoked with great content.

"It's a beautiful day," the sergeant said.

"Yes."

"Why don't you join us, your Excellency? Sit down, make yourself comfortable. A drink?"

Paul shook his head but sat down, not knowing what else to do. His muscles were too painful, now that he'd stopped, to walk away with dignity. He couldn't bear the thought of staggering with all their eyes on him. They were all coming out the water now, in twos and threes, all naked, skins tanned to gold and glistening with droplets of seawater.

"You must be the Baron's brother," the sergeant said.

"Why do you think that?"

The man laughed. "There isn't another gentleman in the district would come striding along the beach like that in this hot sun—as if he owned the place. All right, boys! Back into your uniforms!"

The men moved reluctantly but soon recovered their previous cheerful mood. There was a lot of horseplay—perhaps wrestling was a part of their training, Paul thought—and breeches and tunics flew between them, chased by their loudly protesting owners.

The sergeant laughed. "Fun, eh? Given the chance they stay here and play like children all day. But they're not children."

"You are the gendarmerie my brother told me about, I suppose."

"That's right. Good fellows, aren't they? Look at that one, for instance. Nice lad. Grigory Stepanovitch. Got a wife and three children at home and he's still only nineteen. A bit of a lad when he gets out in the village. Man, woman or dog! They say no one's safe when he's had a drink or two."

The sergeant laughed again. Paul struggled to his feet and stood as firmly as he could, balanced on the shifting sand.

"I don't appreciate that kind of talk, sergeant!"

"No? Well...No offense to Your Honour, I'm sure." He turned to his troop, forming themselves into a neat line. "All right, boys! Off we go! Back to work! I shall be bringing the next lot down soon, your Honour. Have a bit of a rest and then have a dip with them. You'll enjoy that. They're fun, and the water's lovely today." He looked expansively about him, and laughed again. "No one within miles around to interfere."

Paul watched them disappear over the crest of the dune, talking cheerfully among themselves. When they were gone, he sank back onto the sand trying to remember every word the sergeant had said. Was it simply barrack-room buffoonery? He remembered that from when he was in the army himself. Or was there any hidden meaning? If there were, who could have spread ideas of that kind about him so widely that even a sergeant of the gendarmerie could smirk? Who else round here knew? Father Tikhon? Count von Aschenbauer?

The rest of his holiday was a nightmare. He was certain the sergeant had somehow come to hear of his embarrassment in Berlin. Sometimes he was too intimidated to leave the house. On others, he determined to brazen it out and meet as many people as he could. One of his worst moments was when Father Tikhon came—it was on one of his black days—to remind him of his invitation to hear the choir. Paul snapped and refused quite rudely. The embarrassing situation was only worsened by the priest's understanding nod and smile that gave the impression his grounds for refusing were quite well understood. The moment Tikhon left Paul went for the brandy decanter, but Loff held it firmly in place.

"I can't stand by any longer. Tell me what it is, Brother."

"What what is?" Paul blustered.

"We've all of us noticed these moods of yours. And you don't sleep. Leonore tells me you lie on the sofa so as not to disturb her, and that you've never been right since you came back from Manchuria."

"I'm all right."

"You're not. You're certainly not the brother I know."

Paul was silent, breathing heavily. "I must have that drink," he said. Loff sighed and released the bottle. "You want one?"

"No. Paul…"

"All right, all right! I'll tell you!" He gulped the spirit and coughed. "I should have told you about it when it happened. But we weren't meeting very soon at the time, and I couldn't risk putting it in a letter."

Loff sat down calmly. "Well?" he prompted. "What is it?"

"It happened a couple of years ago now…in Berlin…"

Paul told him everything, from the night in the bar until he'd completed the last of Popov's 'special commissions.' Loff grew white-faced as he listened.

"My God, Paul! How could you have been such an idiot?"

Paul's hackles rose. "Now look, Loff, if you think…"

"What the hell does it matter now what I think?" Loff got up from his chair and started pacing the room. "No! I'm sorry! Of course I don't think you had anything to do with the boy. If I did, I'd ask you to leave this house immediately—you know that. But whether you did or whether you didn't isn't important now. They're holding it over your head that you did, and you can't prove that you didn't. Oh! My poor Paul! You gave yourself up to them with both eyes closed, didn't you?"

Paul took another drink. "What can I do?"

"That's just the point. What can you do?"

"One half of me is sure nobody could believe such a thing..."

"And the other half isn't so sure."

"If it got out in Petersburg, they'd all be on to it like pigs at a trough. Loff, if Leonore ever go to hear of this, I swear I'd kill myself."

"There I think you're quite wrong. Leonore would believe you, just as I do. And I think, with a thing like this in the background, she has a right to know what's troubling you. Far better to hear it from you than from anyone else."

"I can't tell her, Loff. I've thought about it dozens of times, and I just can't. I can't think how she hasn't heard about it already."

"Who's going to tell her? It's more valuable as a secret than a scandal, to the people who got you into this mess. As soon as it's public, they lose their hold over you. And that's the answer, of course..."

"What about that sergeant? He knew."

"Nonsense! They've conditioned you into having a guilty conscience—the next thing to inducing you to make a confession. Pull yourself together, man! You're quite safe, so long as you go on helping Popov in all his shady deals. On the other hand..."

Paul's head was in his hands. "Why me? Why pick on me?" he groaned.

"Don't be stupid, Paul! You are influential in financial circles, and you were living abroad at the time—that's always suspect. They looked at your record and decided they could find a use for you some day."

"Who did?"

"Secret police, of course."

"Popov?"

"Perhaps. Or if he isn't one of them, he has influence with someone who is and arranged to have you when you got back to Russia."

"But…that particular evening…that bar…"

"Paul, they could have been watching you for months. That particular evening, circumstances were right for them. You were in the mood to get blind drunk, and they sent in that young man to make sure you did. The woman and her husband next morning were part of it too. If they're not, they'd certainly be called in as witnesses."

"But it was months before I'd thought of coming back. How could they possibly suppose I would be useful?"

"Remember fishing when we were boys? They had you in their keep net till the time was right, Paul. You and hundreds of others, no doubt. When they can use you, they pull you out and you're cooked."

"And they expect me to live like this for the rest of my life…always at their disposal 'til the day I die? Doing underhanded deals for Popov or someone like him? Always terrified they'll make it public?"

"I've already told you, they won't make it public. You're too useful as you are…until you make it public yourself."

"Dear God! You must be mad! I could never do that!"

"Why not? Listen, Paul…they're all 'round us. Father Tikhon's one, I'm sure. The Captain of Gendarmes? Someone among those Russians I brought in? Pastor Vikkers…"

"For heaven's sake!

"Fermatov? You, even?"

"That's ridiculous."

"It's not! They're everywhere, and everybody knows it. Everybody suspects everyone else. Everyone can tell you a tale or two about what they've done to them, or to friends and relatives of theirs. Come out with your story, Paul. Face them! Publish it in the newspaper, and you'll have everyone on your side. No one's going to believe them, whatever they say. And that's their one big weakness—they just aren't credible."

Paul didn't say whether he would or whether he wouldn't. It was easy for Loff to talk. He hadn't a wife and family to think about. And nobody was interested in him anyway, living out here in the country.

He still hadn't come to any decision at the end of the month. Half way through October there came the shattering news that the Tsar was dead—painfully—of nephritis. The death of a monarch is a social and political earthquake. People talk in clichés: the end of an era; the brink of a new (and hopefully glorious) future. Old women cry openly in the streets and bells toll mournfully.

In Russia, it was more than an earthquake—a cataclysm. Russia was an autocracy, like a huge business concern controlled by a managing director without a board. Favoured departmental directors might offer advice, but the last word was always the Tsar's—he was the Big Boss. Now the Big Boss was dead, and nobody could be sure of being in the right place, nor of moving in the right direction anymore; not until the new Big Boss was settled in the managing director's chair. The future was a portent for many individuals.

Alexander the Third had been just the man to pull the country together after the murder of his father...strong...vengeful. Nicholas the Second...? Nobody knew. Nobody knew anything much about him, except that he hated Jews. He used the word *Zhyd* for anybody he didn't like: the Jews themselves, anyone who opposed him, inefficient soldiers, revolutions and the entire English nation, lock stock and barrel.

If not exactly glorious, the future promised to be interesting: favourable for some and disastrous for others. Some advice might no longer be acceptable. Departmental directors clutched their seats in hope mingled with fear.

Petersburg ladies, Leonore among them, saw things from quite a different point of view. They knew nothing of politics, because their husbands didn't encourage them to do so. They were more interested, therefore, in the fact that the new Tsar was very handsome and about to become betrothed to another beautiful grandchild of Queen Victoria of England, the Princess Alexandra of Hesse. They made a beautiful couple. It was a shame the death of the old Tsar should mar their happiness and delay the wedding.

That was the opinion of the Petersburg ladies, and that was the opinion of some of the Petersburg factory workers, ferrymen, street-cleaners, shop assistants, tramway workers, beggars…if ever they bothered to think about it. A change of ruler would bring a brief splurge of excitement into their lives. But it would be only transitory and they didn't expect more benefit from it than that.

At the height of the general excitement, Ulrika asked once more if she might speak to Her Excellency. "It's about Anton," she explained shyly. "He says the new Tsar will be marrying a German lady and what's good enough for him is good enough for Anton. I shall be converted into the Orthodox, and we shall be married as soon as we can. Perhaps on the Tsar's wedding day. That would be nice, wouldn't it, Your Excellency?"

CHAPTER 10

▼

1894

The journey was terrible. The ship heaved and humped every inch of the way and Ida's suffering was horrific. She was sick from the moment they left New York until they reached the calm of the Baltic, only a day or so before Bremen. She was sharing a cramped third class cabin with three other women. They were delayed two days on the way because of the weather, and it was Christmastime. They lamented that they would not now be home for the holiday. An American fellow passenger, fat, red-faced and brash, traveling third class but with a first class opinion of himself and looking to interest a manufacturer in Germany in his plan for an internal combustion engine, demanded to see the Captain. There would be a mutiny among the passengers, he warned, if they were not provided by the shipping line with suitable Christmas celebrations.

Ida's companions spent days discussing what it would be, left her in peace while they went away to eat the banquet, and talked endlessly afterwards about what they'd had to eat and what it had been like. They made Ida feel no better. She prayed earnestly, asking God to let her die.

Her discomfort at the time was considerably increased by anxiety. Had the letter she'd sent to Clementine six weeks before leaving New York got through?

Dear Clementine,

You will be surprised, to hear from me after all this time, I know. Leonore gave me your Moscow address. I hope you won't mind my writing to you now. We were such good friends when you used to visit us at the Convent in Warsaw. I don't know why we lost touch, except for the most obvious reason I can think of. I don't resent it at all. Perhaps things are easier now.

Everything has changed, of course. Leonore and Paul live such a fine life in Saint Petersburg, I gather. He has a splendid job at the Bank, she tells me. Leonore is much too grand for me these days and although we will always be sisters—nothing can ever change that—I can't feel that we would have much else in common. Rachel is making a great success of her life in Warsaw, I understand. I haven't heard a word from her directly since she moved there, though.

And now I need a little help. Isn't needing help always a reason for contacting old friends after a long silence? I hope it won't be a trouble, but if it is, say so—I shall quite understand.

I shall be coming to Moscow quite shortly. As you know, I have never been there. And I'm told there are numerous regulations travelers like me must adhere to these days. Would it be possible for you to meet me when I arrive and help me find my way through them?

I should be truly grateful if you could. I feel my sisters are much too exclusive to know anything about these mundane affairs nowadays. I'm hoping to arrive a few days before Western Christmas, if I can get a berth. I'll let you know the details later.

Please don't think I'm entirely selfish. I am simply longing to see you again. I shall never forget your many kindnesses to me when I was young. And of course, I'm eager to meet your husband. Leonore tells me he's very nice.

Yours ever affectionately,

Ida Goldfarb

Postal censors generally spent hours every day sitting at their desks and reading their newspapers. Occasionally they opened a letter or two.

When the build-up grew too great, they'd let a whole lot down the chute unopened. Except in special cases, letters weren't tampered with overmuch, but they could be long delayed.

Clementine's from Ida was delayed. She handed it to Sasha when he came home from work. He read it slowly and handed it back, looking unconcerned.

"Of course you'll look after her."

"You think I should?"

"Naturally."

"But this has been held up. She'll probably be arriving any day now, and I've no idea when nor where."

"Write to her tonight. Don't say very much. Just tell her we'll be very happy to see her."

"She's very Jewish-looking, Sasha."

"So you've said."

"And suppose she doesn't get my letter before she leaves?"

"As well as writing to New York, you'd better send a postcard to every port she's likely to arrive at in the week before Christmas. Address it care of the ship in each case."

"You're so full of ideas! How do I know the names of the ships to write to?"

"I have friends in Berlin," he grinned. "All you have to say on the cards is 'Welcome Home!' And ask her to telegraph you when she'll be in Warsaw."

"I can't go all the way there…it'll cost far too much."

"The frontier, then. We can't let her come any further than that alone. Tell her you'll meet her at Brest-Litovsk."

Clementine wrote away that night, but the letter didn't reach New York in time, and Ida worried about it all the way across the Atlantic. There was a postcard waiting at Bremen, however.

> *Welcome home, Ida dear. I shall be in Brest-Litovsk for a day or two very soon.*

*Telegraph me the time and the day your train gets there. It would
be fun to meet. Much love, Clementine.*

Ida examined timetables at Bremen Station and decided to stop off
for a night in Warsaw. There were two things she wanted to do there:
go to the Hotel Bristol, where Paul had stayed and bought them such
marvelous cream cakes, and visit Rachel.

She had no luck at the hotel. The restaurant manager told her
brusquely there was no room, though from where she stood in the
doorway to the restaurant she could see there were plenty of empty
tables. At the reception desk, when she asked the clerk to find her
Rachel's number, he snapped quite rudely and looked straight through
her.

She knew Rachel lived in Sienna Street. Any Jew there would help
her if she couldn't find the Salon. She found it quite easily, in fact; the
ground floor of a well-maintained building with a highly polished plate
on the pilaster: "RACHELLE." She went in diffidently and was almost
overpowered by the claustrophobic atmosphere, heavily fragrant with
Eau-de-Cologne.

Several elegantly dressed ladies stood about chatting. Others sat in
ones and twos on tiny gold chairs set against the pale pink walls. Young
women dressed in featureless black, their hair scraped back unattrac-
tively so as to offer no competition to the clients, moved about with
silent concentration. At the centre of all this controlled activity, the
prima ballerina, was her sister.

Rachel was as fashionable now as any of her clients. Her dark hair
fell in soft waves to her neck and was there gathered up and back into a
cluster of curls on the top of her head. Her dress was brown—a rich,
magical brown with faint suggestions of gold and red in it—cut low at
the neck across a cream vestée.

She was holding a turquoise creation in her arms, ready to show it to
a lady sitting against the wall. She moved smoothly across the floor, as
though her feet were on wheels. Suddenly, she saw Ida. Her arms fell
apart with the shock of it and the turquoise gown tumbled to the floor.

One of the young women, seeing crisis, immediately glided across to her assistance and picked up the gown, while receiving her instructions.

Then Rachel came across to her. "Ida, my dear! What are you doing here? Where on earth have you come from? Come into my office." She turned to lead the way, talking quietly over her shoulder. "Why on earth didn't you tell me you were coming? As you can see, my dear, this isn't terribly convenient at the moment. We're exceptionally busy this afternoon."

She closed the door and asked Ida to sit down. The room was as exquisite as its occupant. The desk had delicately carved cabriole legs, and the chair Ida sat in was obviously designed more for its elegant appearance than for ease.

"You really should not have come half way across the world like this without giving me some kind of warning, you know. When did you arrive? How long are you here for? Have you arranged for somewhere to stay?"

Ida smiled a trifle grimly, "Oh yes, don't worry about me. I'm on my way to Moscow."

"Moscow!"

"Some friends in New York have relatives there. They've asked me over to stay with them."

"I see."

"Never mind now. I'll give you plenty of notice next time, and we can spend a few hours together on my way back."

"Darling, that would be lovely."

Ida stood up awkwardly. "I just wanted to know how things are."

"Marvelous, my dear. Frantically busy, as you can see. Now, my sweet, I really must get back, or they'll be wondering what's happened."

"Yes, of course. I thought I'd go to Zamenhofa Street and spend the night with Mordechai and Esther."

"Marvelous. If I possibly can—if I can get away from here early enough, that is—I'll join you later. No promises, though. And give them all my love, won't you."

Ida was surprised to be allowed to go through the salon again, and not to be shown out by some private way. After a miserable walk, she was in Zamenhofa Street. She had started out eager to see how the district had changed. Very soon she was thoroughly depressed by it. She had become accustomed to New York. She herself lived in one of the cold-water walk-up tenements on the East Side that were all most newly arrived immigrants could afford. In spite of the poverty, though, the district pulsated with a rowdy optimism. In the freeze of winter, lives were lived on the landings outside the apartments, the most intimate gossip shouted between neighbours from floor to floor. In the sweltering summers, they swarmed into the streets, hung daringly out of upper-story windows and bawled their news from building to building, or tried to contact people as far away as the next block.

Here all was dead. The snow lay filthy and uncleared in the streets. Passers-by kept their eyes well down as though greetings were too expensive to lavish. There were a few carts in the roadways and whenever they passed their drivers looked away, making their passage somehow surreptitious.

The stairs up to Esther's flat were still the same, smelling of cats' urine, pickled herring and borscht. The handrail was still sticky; surely, no one could have wiped it since the last time she'd fingered it.

She stood several moments outside the door, wondering after all whether to knock or not. When she did, the door opened quite quickly. Esther was there, hair awry, red-faced and work-weary. When she saw who it was, her eyes and her mouth opened wide, and she stood transfixed. Then, as her face creased into the broadest of smiles, she almost screamed:

"Ida!"

She turned away and screamed again, over her shoulder this time: "Mordechai! It's Ida! Oh, my darling, how wonderful…what a surprise...how marvelous...come in, come in. Mordechai! It's Ida! My dear! Oh! I don't know what to say. Come in! Come in!" She tried to draw her into the flat, but was holding her so tightly in the open doorway that neither of them could move. Ida thought the kissing would never stop, and it did only when Mordechai shuffled up smiling, to stand hand outstretched behind his wife.

The welcome lasted a long time. The children were as pleased as their parents to see her, and she decided she must leave money for them when she went the next morning. She was embarrassed at having brought nothing for them from New York—about which they asked so many questions. But family visits had not been uppermost in her mind before she came away.

Esther cooked a meal before she'd allow any of them to relax, and shot the children angry glances when they commented on the quality and the quantity of it. When that was over, she sent them out to read quietly in another room. She saw Ida glancing repeatedly at the clock.

"Don't keep looking at the clock, dear. I don't expect she'll come."

"She never comes nowadays," Mordechai mumbled.

"She can't. You know that very well."

"I know it," he said with a sigh.

"She's good, is Rachel," Esther said. "Since Mordechai's been out of work, she's never let a month go by without sending us some money. I don't like having to take it but...for the little ones. If it was Mordechai and me..."

"Aren't you working, then, Mordechai?"

"He hasn't been able to get a job since this last lot of troubles started."

"But...what about the print shop?"

"They came one day and smashed everything up. Such a waste!" He shook his head sadly. "All right, I admit it. We were illegal. But why did they have to break everything up? They could have taken away the machines and given them to someone else. Such a waste to smash them up like that."

"He hasn't been able to get a job anywhere since. There's nothing going. Still, it's not as bad for us as it is for some."

"The man I worked for—Lev Samuelsson—they took him away. There's been no sight nor sound of him ever since."

"His wife's near out of her mind with worry."

"He's an atheist...wasn't a member of any Synagogue, so they get nothing from the Community. Esther spares them something every month out of what Rachel gives her. I don't know how she manages it. But if she didn't, they'd have nothing. They'd starve."

"It's been bad here too, then, has it?"

"Not so bad as eighty-two, thank God! But down south..."

"Kishinev...that's where it all began," Mordechai said, a flame of anger in his eyes.

"SSSh! Don't let the children hear."

"They know. You can't stop children from talking among themselves. And even if they didn't, it's time for them to know what it means to be a Jew...not just the words and what to eat and what to wear. What it really means."

Esther looked at Ida. "You wouldn't have heard much about it over there, I suppose."

"Oh yes, we heard. But it's all hearsay. It's hard to work out what's true and what's..."

"Don't worry about that. Whatever you've heard, you can multiply it by ten, and it still won't be as bad as it really was."

"Mordechai! You've come back at a bad time, Ida, my love."

"When is it not a bad time for Jews?" Mordechai asked.

"Mordechai lost his parents in a flare-up in the Ukraine," Esther said softly and stood up to put her arm 'round her husband's bent shoulders.

"Flare-up, you call it," he scorned. "Why don't you call it for what it is? Murder! It's legalized murder, and they won't stop it till every one of us is dead." He sank into a gloomy silence, staring into space.

"It's dying down a bit now, though. You'll be safe enough once you get to Moscow. Nothing really terrible ever happens to us there...nor in Saint Petersburg."

"Not since they turned us all out it doesn't. How can it? What do you think? Listen, Ida! I don't know what you've heard, but this is what really happened—the truth! It was just before their Easter last year. Someone asked the local Bishop whether our people had killed a young man to use at our Passover—God only knows how—and he said yes. That's all it took. There wasn't a body. No young man had gone missing. Nothing! The mob went crazy all the same. The police did nothing except to point out any Jewish premises they'd missed on their way 'round. They killed two hundred Jews and wounded thousands of others. Six hundred homes, four hundred shops were destroyed. And the soldiers and the police did nothing for two days...nothing until they were ordered by the Governor to step in and stop it."

He sank into silence again, exhausted by his own bitterness.

"That's more or less what we heard," Ida told him.

Esther said: "You will be careful tomorrow, won't you, my dear? You never know who'll be on those trains these days."

"I'll be all right, Esther, don't worry. I'm meeting a friend at Brest-Litovsk. She'll see me through from there to Moscow."

"Jewish?" Mordechai asked sharply.

"No," Ida smiled. "But she's safe. I've known her for years."

"Why have you come back just now, Ida?" Mordechai's eyes were no longer vacant, and his voice had regained its strength.

"A holiday, of course," she laughed. "I was lonely for you all. I needed to see you again."

"I'm serious," he said, "and I'm warning you. Don't do anything stupid. It's the way things have always been. And a child of a girl like you won't be able to do anything to change it."

Next day was deceptively sunny, but with a chill wind across the snow-banked landscape. At Brest-Litovsk, she leaned out of the window and saw a familiar but much changed woman waiting on the platform. Clementine's joy at seeing her was obvious; Ida's reactions were mixed. Clementine was greatly altered. She looked older than her years, her body wasted by a hard life. Ida felt guilty. Her own life was probably no easier, but she was borne along by natural optimism. Clementine seemed to have lost all hers.

They talked casually on the way to Moscow or sat silent enjoying each other's company. At Moscow, Sasha waited for them on the platform. He greeted them briefly and drew Ida by the hand against the flow of passengers heading towards the exit. They crossed the tracks and went to his office, a hut standing just beyond the end of the platform. They sat down, and he poured them drinks.

"You'll be needing something after your journey," he said, rubbing fingers through his golden hair as though trying to clear his head of some of its problems.

"Thank you, I am a little cold," she said.

He nodded understandingly and looked searchingly at Clementine. She had nothing to tell him. He turned to Ida.

"Ida," he began, "I can call you Ida, can I? You don't prefer to need some other name?"

"No, no, Ida will be quite all right," she assured him, looking slightly uneasy.

"I imagine you haven't come all this way just to see the sights," he said, smiling. "I don't know why you're here and I don't want to know. You're very welcome to stay with us for as long as you need."

"Just for a night or two I'd be grateful. Not for long. I've come to see some people in Bessarabia and the Ukraine."

He nodded. "When you're ready to go, you'd better leave it to me to arrange your tickets."

"Or I can go and get those quite easily," Clementine put in.

"There's only one thing I'd like you to bear in mind while you're staying with us," Sasha continued. "I very often have meetings at home. Railway men, you know…"

"They come for Sasha's advice whenever there's anything troubling them or that they don't understand," Clementine laughed.

"They're all good chaps, but they're simple working men, you see. Some of them still believe what they've been taught since childhood and...well...they don't much care for Jews, I'm afraid."

"Neither does my sister Rachel," she said with a short bitter laugh.

"Well..." Sasha looked uncomfortable. "You must excuse me, I have to do some things in the yards. I'll be back for you in about an hour."

It was nearly an hour and a half before he returned, apologetic. "It'll be all right to go now, I'm sure," he said.

"Sometimes the secret police put an agent in the station to watch who's coming off the international expresses. But it'll be clear by now, I'm sure."

CHAPTER II

▼

1895

"Novosibirsk!"

"Only for six months. A year at the most."

"No, no, no! Out of the question! How can you even think of it?"

"Darling, we don't have a choice. And we'll keep the house on here. You'll have it to come back to afterwards."

"No, Paul! The children need to be settled. And I certainly wouldn't think of leaving them behind. They need their parents. I'm not having them brought up like orphans, the way we were."

"You know the alternative. You're willing for us to live apart for maybe a year, then?"

"Of course I'm not willing. But the children come first. You understand that."

"We could send them to the Estate."

"No!"

"It would be good for them. It's a wonderful place for children."

"I said no, Paul."

"Loff and Channah would be delighted to have them."

"It doesn't matter what you say. I won't change my mind. The children are staying in Saint Petersburg, and so am I."

"I see." He was pained. She was being unreasonable, and he was trapped. The worst part of it was that he couldn't tell her why.

"It's a thoroughly unreasonable idea," she continued implacably. "Sergei Ilyich must have someone else he could ask to go—someone younger than you, without a family."

"The job needs someone senior. I don't know whether or not you realise it, but the lifestyle we have here carries responsibilities with it, my dear. I shall have to go, whether you come with me or not."

"Oh, Paul…Paul, my darling, of course I know how important you are at the bank…how much they need you." She stood poised, ready to embrace him while he stood paralysed by the ghastliness of his situation. "I love you so much." She took him into her arms. "I hate it when we're apart, even for a single minute. We've been so happy since we moved here. Everything's gone so well. If we must be apart for a while, it's a price we have to pay. It's our duty, and we mustn't complain."

He returned her embrace before suddenly holding her at arm's length.

"Leonore…suppose all this had to change." He gently sat her down. "Suppose I were no longer at the Bank, and we could no longer afford this house…"

"Paul, I can't imagine what you're talking about. You're not telling me what you're trying to say, are you?"

"What I'm trying to say, my dear," he began, with a hint of impatience, "is that if you refuse to come to Novosibirsk, we may have to be separated for as long as a year. If you don't agree to that, understand that it means that honestly and truly, I shall leave the Bank."

"You can't possibly."

"You'd leave me no choice. We'd have to give up this house, of course."

"That may not be so bad; Varvara tells me there are some really pretty houses on the north side of the Vasil'yevski Island. We could find one like the one we had in Charlottenburg. Ulrika and Anton would stay with us wherever we went. They seem happy enough. I think they'll stay even after they're married."

"I doubt whether we'd be able to afford one of those houses. The girls won't be going to Smolny, nor the boys to the Alexander."

She paused, her enthusiasm crushed. "Is that really true? You're not just saying it to frighten me."

"It's worse than that. Sergei Ilyich is not the nice man you think him. If I go against him in this and leave the bank, we may as well leave Saint Petersburg altogether."

"What do you mean?"

"He'll take care not to lose face. He's likely to spread God knows what rumours about me."

"But…" she laughed uncertainly. "What stories could be possibly spread about you?"

"Whatever he says won't be pleasant; you're bound to have to live through a scandal of some sort."

She looked frightened, and the conversation died. Fantastic, tormenting thoughts they dared not expressed remained in the minds of them both. In bed that night they lay stiffly, side by side, not touching, not sleeping, each suffering a personal, waking nightmare. When he got up next morning, she kept her eyes tightly closed in case he thought her awake and wanted to talk again.

Arriving at the Bank tired and distraught, his mood was not improved by the approach of a junior clerk with a familiar, insolent grin.

"There's a postcard for you, your Honour," he said. "I thought you'd like to know; I put it to one side so nobody else could read it." He winked.

Paul managed to restrain his instinct to hit the man, grabbed the postcard and slammed his office door before looking at it.

Dear Paul, I am in Moscow, staying with Clementine. I shan't be here for long, but I do want to see you, so come down as soon as you can. Love always, Ida.

He slipped the postcard into his pocket and, without understanding why, suddenly felt cheerful. Without worry or any preparation, he found himself in an unexpected and pleasant situation that somehow eased the tension of his own. His funny little Ida was here. He was the one she particularly wanted to see.

He squared his shoulders and walked into Popov's office with a brisker step. He didn't bother to knock. Popov looked up from his desk, surprised.

"Sergei Ilyich, I've thought about your...offer, shall we call it? I've discussed it at home, naturally, and my wife isn't willing to move the children. I've no intention of going without them, so I'll let you have my written resignation later in the day."

Popov was startled, his smile uncertain. He rose, came 'round his desk to put a hand on Paul's shoulder and guided him into an armchair.

"My dear, dear Paul, what on earth are you talking about? Your resignation? I've never heard anything so absurd. Of course you don't have to go if you don't want. Nobody would dream of making you do anything you don't want." He gazed down with an oleaginous smile he meant to be paternal. "I thought you would enjoy the experience, but of course, I can send someone else to go...of course I can."

Paul relaxed, crossed his legs and tried to look innocent, as though he wasn't enjoying himself. "I'm sorry, Sergei Ilyich, I must have misunderstood you at our last meeting, then. It seemed to me you left me no choice."

"No matter, no matter, my dear fellow, we'll find someone else. You may have a suggestion or two there yourself. I'll still want you to be in overall charge, of course. The Manchuria Railway scheme is simmering now, but it will come to the boil soon, I hope. You're our authority on that, you know. You'd be agreeable to making short trips there from time to time, I presume?"

"Naturally. On Bank business only, of course."

Popov opened his eyes wide, uncomprehending. "My dear Paul," he began but Paul wouldn't let him continue.

"You see…" he laughed in self-disparagement, "you see, Sergei Ily-ich, ever since you mentioned that you knew about that little difficulty of mine in Berlin…"

"Difficulty?" Popov queried firmly, so as not to be silenced. "Some little difficulty you had in Berlin?"

"…I've been a little nervous in case someone else should come to hear about it, as you did yourself. How did you come to hear about it, by the way?"

"I can't remember. I've no idea at all, my dear fellow. You know how these things get about. In any case, stories of that kind are gener-ally absurd."

"Yes, aren't they?" Paul laughed and felt foolish, as though he were reading a script. "But I must apologise to you, Sergei Ilyich…"

"My dear Paul…"

"I didn't know you well enough in those days. I know you better now. I know you're not the man to spread these rumours further."

"My dear fellow…"

"No one else has ever said anything to me about it. And even if they were to do so, I should deny it, of course."

"Of course, my dear chap."

"No one I care about is likely to think me guilty of such a thing."

"How could they, my dear fellow? Not anyone who knew you at all…however slightly."

"You, for instance, Sergei Ilyich, you'd never believe me guilty of sodomizing any young man, would you?"

Popov registered monumental shock. He blushed and perspired, his head was bowed and his shoulders almost met across his chest, so com-plete was his effort to convey absolute trust.

"Besides," Paul continued, releasing his last arrow, "as everyone knows, a secret disclosed has no value any more…not once it ceases to be a secret."

He bought an armful of flowers for Leonore and arrived home in time for lunch.

"I've had a meeting with Sergei Ilyich this morning. I won't be going to Novosibirsk after all. I'm in charge of the operation there, though, so I'll have to make the occasional trip."

"There," she said, looking pleased and a little smug, as though she'd known all the time he was making a silly fuss. "You'll have to change your ways, my darling. You're too anxious to help. You say 'yes' to anything anybody asks you."

"I'll have to be on the Moscow train tonight, though."

"Darling, that's perfectly all right. I'd far rather it were Moscow than Novosibirsk. How long will you be away?"

"I'm not sure."

"Well, do try to make time to see Clementine while you're there, will you? She'd love to see you."

"I'll see, I'll see. I will if I possibly can."

When he got to Clementine's flat, Ida was out.

"She's gone to buy some coffee. She's brought all her American habits with her," Clementine laughed. "She won't be long. And I'm glad to have you to myself for a little. How's Leonore?"

"Wonderful. She sends her love."

"I'm glad."

"How's Sasha?"

"He's wonderful, too. You'll like him. I know you will. You are staying with us, aren't you?"

"I'm staying to meet Sasha, of course. But I have a room at the Metropole." He thought she looked relieved. "And how are you, my dear?"

She laughed again, determinedly. The old glow was returning to her eyes, but in repose her features were almost haggard. "I'm wonderful too. And it's wonderful to see you. What fun we used to have, didn't we, Paul? Does Leonore still sing? She had such a pretty voice."

"No, but the girls do, a little, and it wasn't fun all the time," he told me in mock rebuke. "Not for me, anyway."

"No, I can remember. The way you two went on about each other. Sometimes I felt I was living in the middle of a tragic opera."

"I've never forgotten how much I owe you, Clementine…everything."

"You were meant for each other," she told him softly, with light-hearted seriousness. "And we mustn't get sentimental, or you'll have me in tears."

He was telling her about the children and how wonderful they were when Ida arrived. She ran directly to him and dropped her coffee in her haste. She kissed him hard and moistly, the way she used to when she was a child.

"Oh, Paul…my dear, dear Paul…I'd no idea you be here so soon."

"My dear little Ida."

"Hardly 'little' anymore," she laughed, stretching out her arms to display her ample figure. "I'm fat like my poor Mother. Isn't Leonore?"

"Not particularly."

"She always was the lucky one. And have you seen Rachel recently?"

"No."

"Such a lady of fashion these days. And her salon…! Everything's so tremendously smart. And she looks like she's wearing a steel tube underneath the glamour…all the way down from her neck to her knees."

"Is that naughtiness or jealousy," Clementine asked, scooping up the spilt coffee. No one could imagine that Ida was wearing anything underneath her tight-fitting bottle-green dress…much too tight and revealing, in Paul's opinion. It hugged her until about a foot above her ankles where it flared and swung as she moved in what Paul thought was a somewhat erotic manner.

"I was puzzled when I read your card, Ida. Why didn't you want me to tell Leonore you're here?"

"I'll go and make the coffee," Clementine said.

"Remember how I told you to do it," Ida called.

"I will."

Clementine closed the door.

"She's leaving us alone to talk," Ida giggled.

"Well?"

"Tell me about the children. Are they as lovely as Leonore tells me they are in her letters?"

"Come to Saint Petersburg and see for yourself."

"I didn't bring them anything, I'm afraid. I left New York in rather a hurry."

"Ida, why are you here?"

"Visiting old friends."

"I don't believe you."

"Paul!"

"Why won't you come to see Leonore? It will break her heart if she ever finds out you've been and she didn't see you."

"It's nearly breaking my mind already but I have to do what's best."

"I still don't understand."

"No, I'm sure you don't. But Leonore would, Paul. I know you're a good man; why can't you face it? Things aren't good for Jews just now."

"No, well...there have been rumours."

"It isn't rumour. You know very well what's happening, and I'm not going to get Leonore and the children involved."

"You're her sister."

"And no one in Petersburg knows that, thank God! You're a respectable businessman...good family. Leonore passes, I expect...she always did. What do you want me to do? Come to visit you after it's dark? Come in by the servants' entrance like a parlourmaid?"

"You think we're not involved already, now I've visited you here?"

"Leonore writes to say you're traveling about quite often. Moscow's an obvious place for you to come on business."

"And Clementine and Sasha?"

"That's all right. They understand."

"Oh? What have you told them that you won't tell me?"

"Nothing. Sasha understands…that's all. And now that I've seen you, I'll be leaving tomorrow."

"Where are you going? What are you doing, Ida? Please tell me."

"It's a secret."

Clementine came back with the coffee.

"That smells good, Clementine."

"Keeping a secret can grow a chancre in the heart, my dear."

She seized the tray excitedly from Clementine. "How do you drink your coffee, Paul? With cream? I didn't spill all the cream, did I, Clementine? With sugar or just plain black?"

"If you'll forgive me, Clementine, I won't stay for coffee. There are people at the Bank I ought to see. But I'd like to come back later."

"Of course. We expect you for supper. And afterwards we'll drink a little, and Sasha will play his flute and we'll sing. We'll make it like the old days…remember, Paul? You and Sergei…? I know you and Sasha will like each other."

They did. Paul appreciated Sasha's quiet authority. He was commanding, but not at all pompous. He played country dances on his flute and sang folk songs in a clear tenor voice with smiling enthusiasm. Particularly, Paul admired the air of trust and understanding there was between Sasha and Clementine. Without endearments, without display of any kind, they made as though they were two halves of a single whole and only the greatest force could ever pry them apart.

The evening went so well, nobody was surprised when Sasha put on his furs and galoshes to walk Paul back to the Metropole. Paul protested half-heartedly. He would take a cab, he said. Sasha insisted. The exercise would clear their heads and do them both good.

The night was very cold, and the snow on the pavement crunched under their feet. They walked arm-in-arm through the empty streets like age-old companions.

"Did Ida tell you why she's here?" Paul asked.

"Not entirely. You?"

"No." A few steps in silence. "She's leaving for Kharkhov in the morning."

"She told me she was moving on tomorrow. She didn't say where."

"You know, Paul, I'm not happy about any of it. She looks...well...she looks very Semitic, doesn't she?"

"Very. When she was young, she was always making jokes about it. A cover-up, I suppose."

"Or pride, possibly."

Paul glanced at him sharply. "I'd never thought of that, I must confess."

"No."

"She's...well...she's just Ida. What she looks like isn't important."

"Not to you, perhaps. It might be very important to someone else. A young woman traveling alone at the moment...particularly in the South and looking the way she does, it could be dangerous. I wish I knew why it's so important for her to take the risk."

"All she would say to me is that it's a secret. And she'll never tell us what it is. I know her from years back. She'll never change her mind once she's made it up."

"I'd feel better if I knew she was carrying someone's name and address on her, just in case she gets into trouble...the police pick her up or anything like that."

"The police?"

"It could happen. I can't give her mine, unfortunately. I can't afford to be involved. I..." he laughed softly..."I have my secret, too, you see. But you..."

"Me?"

"You're respectable enough. You're so obviously on their side."

"Their side?"

"Well, yes...aren't you?"

Paul lay in his bed that night thinking...thinking about Clementine and Sasha and their evident, unspoken understanding. "Did he and

Leonore have it?", he asked himself and, in honesty, confessed that he didn't know. Sometimes they did, sometimes not. Did Clementine know Sasha's secret? Seeing them together, he was sure she would know it, even without Sasha's putting it into words. Sasha had a secret and Clementine shared it. She probably had secrets of her own, as well. Ida had a secret. He certainly had secrets. Did Leonore?

He gave Sasha his card to hand to Ida before she left.

Now he lay in his bed, a murky dawn invading the room. Secrets were so often synonymous with guilt—justified or not. Everyone except Leonore had one, it seemed. Was there, then, so little innocence left in the world?

CHAPTER 12

▼

1895

Everywhere bustled with excitement through the winter and the spring. In May of next year, the decencies would have been sufficiently observed, and Nicholas the Second could decently marry his chosen bride—"the Nemka," the German, as they were already calling her in the streets in their ribald jokes. Moscow and Saint Petersburg prepared for the ceremonies, each in their own way. By tradition, the crowning would be in Moscow. In Saint Petersburg, there would be the diplomatic, the international show. These were signaled by the Imperial family's longer-than-usual residence in the Winter Palace. Normally they went off to Tsarskoe Selo as soon as they possibly could.

Paul and Leonore would be required to attend quite often, according to Paul's rank in the scale of nobility. Loff would have to come up from Estonia and partake to an even greater extent. Leonore was already planning what she might do to repay Channah, while she was with them, for all the wonderful holidays she'd given the family. She was concerned to bring her more closely into the making of her arrangements.

"Nonsense! You can get all you could possibly need here in Saint Petersburg, darling."

"I shall write to ask Channah to come down to meet me there. Oh! And I shall take Ulrika with me, too, of course."

"You surely don't intend Rachel's prices for things you'll probably never wear again?"

"Men!" she snorted. "And we can buy Ulrika's wedding dress while we're there."

"One of Rachel's creations for Ulrika?"

"Nothing too fancy. Just something nice. It'll be such a treat for her, Paul. She's very unhappy at the moment."

"If it'll cost that much to put it right, I don't want to hear about it, whatever it is."

Leonore looked at him fondly. "I was hoping you'd have a word with Anton, actually. He doesn't want to wait any longer. Now she's converted, he wants to be married right away."

"That's not unreasonable, surely. Now, after leading him on all these months, she's decided she doesn't want to marry him, after all— is that it?"

"Of course she still wants to be married. But she either wants to be married in Germany or to have her parents here. Only Anton says that will be too expensive and they can't possibly afford it."

"Of course they can't. The girl must be mad."

"Paul, darling, you're wonderful and I love you very much…really I do. But sometimes you talk as if you're the meanest man on earth."

"Call me mean if you must! I am not paying any ridiculous price for her wedding dress. And I am certainly not paying for them both to go, too, and get married in Germany!"

"Oh you!" she laughed. "Isn't it about time you went to the Bank?" He scowled and kissed her before he left; and they both knew that whatever he said, she would do exactly as she wanted.

The children were as excited as anyone. Dorothea and Sonia wanted to play at weddings all the time. Usually, Dorothea played the Tsar and Sonia his bride. Very occasionally, they could induce Eduard to play, too. But he was infuriating! He didn't want anything at all to do with being married and flatly refused to be the groom. Instead, he made a lot of noise, stamping about, flourishing his sword and shouting orders

to an imaginary guard of honour. He was a Colonel in the Preobrazhensky like his Uncle Sergei, detailed to protect the royal couple.

Marie stood aloof, condescending. She already had strong opinions
about the things she knew; and even stronger ones about what she
didn't. At six, she was becoming deeply affected by what she heard in
church and was longing for First Communion.

Albrecht was still tiny enough for Dorothea to heave him like a bundle and plop him down on a cushion on the floor.

"You're our loyal subjects, Albrecht," she explained. "You have to
show how pleased you are and wave your arms and shout 'hurrah' as
we go by."

He did as he was told, enthusiastically. He watched them wide-eyed,
waved vigorously, shouted loudly, and dribbled a lot. Generally, that
lasted only until Marie discovered where he was. She would drag him
away to play with her. They played together a lot. Nobody ever knew
what they got up to when they played together because they'd stop as
soon as anyone else came along. Marie would never tell about their
games, and Albrecht couldn't.

Albrecht was now three years old and didn't yet talk. From the day
he was born, he had never been known to utter a single comprehensi-
ble word. Marie evidently understood his grunts, though no one else
did. The older children laughed and called him cute. Leonore took
him to all the best doctors in town, none of whom suggested a satisfactory reason. They all agreed that he wasn't deaf, there was no obvious
malformation of the larynx, but that she should never expect too much
of him.

She tortured herself with guilt. She could never forget her own
insane passion at the time he was conceived, a mad lust no decent
woman would ever have given way to. She told herself it was because of
the urgency of giving Paul a second son. She did it for the sake of the
family. It was her Duty. Now she knew that it was the devil that was in
her, driving her to do the unspeakable things that made her burn
whenever she thought about them. And this was the price she, or rather

Albrecht, was paying. She was having to watch him every day, knowing the fault and that it was all hers.

Only once, frozen with embarrassment, did she try to talk to Paul about the boy. He was jocular about it—perhaps his way of hiding his true feelings.

"He'll surprise you one of these days, my dear…you'll see. He isn't saying anything yet because he knows he's got nothing interesting to say. Sensible little fellow. You can always trust a man who knows when to keep his mouth shut."

He would never have anything said against any of his children. When they were good, they were paragons. When school reports were favourable, they bordered on genius. And when they were naughty…

"Don't be too hard on them, my love. They're only children, after all. And if children aren't a little naughty sometimes, there's something wrong with them. It's only their fun."

Paul, everyone agreed, was an ideal father. He indulged his children sometimes, perhaps, but they were, on the whole, very well-behaved and not at all spoiled. He had their photographs all over his office and several in his pocket book. He would bore anyone, at the drop of a hat, with his praises. And all their friends were a little jealous when their own children expressed the desire to be able to come and live with him.

Sunday was the special day—the family day in Saint Petersburg like it was in Berlin. In summer, after Mass, there was a walk along the quays near home if the weather was doubtful, and a longer trip to Tsarskoe Zeio or out to one of the islands when it was good. In winter, they had a very formal luncheon together. Paul and Leonore stood to welcome everyone at the top of the stairs. The children and their playmates ascended one by one, Anton at the bottom, Anton in the hallway announcing their made-up names in ringing tones as they went. At the top, Dorothea would sometimes fall back behind Sonia to take Marie's arm.

"This is really my sister's governess but we must be very nice to her all the same. She's a dear little person really."

Doubtless she didn't mean it unkindly. And even if she did, Marie learned to laugh about it eventually. Except for her swarthy skin, and young as she was, Marie reminded Paul uncomfortably of his sister.

Eduard was invariably Colonel von Hagen and saluted his parents smartly when he reached them. Albrecht was carried up by Ulrika— perhaps because he imagined himself a great panjandrum—laughing hugely and grabbing at everybody and everything within reach.

The children and their various friends felt deprived when Paul was away. And he often was away these days—in the Urals, the Altai or, more and more frequently now, in the Far East. He now invariably lengthened his journey in order to visit Sasha and Clementine. There was a deepening intimacy between them. He and Clementine were destined to be fellow-conspirators, it seemed. So far back as their days in Warsaw, Paul had never been sure of himself, and always attributed to Clementine's subtle influence on Leonore's decision to marry him.

Now, they were conspiring against Leonore once more—to save her worry by keeping her in ignorance of Ida's presence. But—and it amazed him now to think of it—his deeper intimacy was with Sasha— an unspoken understanding between two men who had nothing at all on earth to bind them together.

"We stand on opposite banks of a river, Paul," Sasha once said to him. "I can't see whether it's a river of water or of blood but, whatever, there must always be a bridge across it between the two of us."

On many of his visits to the flat, Sasha didn't appear at all.

"Another of his meetings," Clementine would say in a playfully long-suffering way. "But you understand, don't you, Paul?" And whenever she asked him that it sounded like a plea for his discretion.

He did, in a foggy way understand that he was running some kind of a risk in coming here. But the warmth of his welcome was by now an addiction, satisfying something deep within him, even if it was only curiosity. While they were alone, Clementine amused him by mimicking the clients they'd both known at the Doma, and describing them as the girls who'd worked there saw them. Obviously, she enjoyed talking about Ouroussoff too.

"I'm afraid he's desperate, our Seriozha," Paul told her smugly. "For too long he's been used to flirting and walking away. But this time it's not going to be so easy."

"Who is it this time?"

"Cecile von Aschenbauer—the daughter of one of our neighbours at home, as a matter of fact. She's quite pretty; may even be in love with him, though I doubt it."

"Whether she is or not, he doesn't want to marry her."

"He doesn't want to marry anybody. He's in love with the Army. He's exactly the same as he was when you knew him, Clementine...hasn't altered one bit."

"Poor young lady."

"Oh, she'll find someone eventually, I expect. The trouble is, time's slipping by, and the von Aschenbauers aren't as well-off as they were."

Clementine's continuing curiosity about Ouroussoff intrigued him. Surely she couldn't have any deep feelings for him? He could never seriously be compared with Sasha. But Clementine was an impossible romantic, of course. After he'd told her about his brother and Channah, she asked about them every time she saw him. She found their situation extraordinarily erotic, she said. Among the people who came to Sasha's meetings were several she knew who lived together without being married. They excited her too, she said, and he wondered whether, after all, she would prefer not to have married Sasha.

"Of course I always wanted to marry Sasha," she told him sharply. "Not being married is a way to bring about a little change, though, isn't it? It's defiance of at least one of the conventions that suffocate us so. Respectable people won't have anything personally to do with them, of course, though some of them are well-known writers, painters, actors, musicians. People applaud them very loudly for their work, but if they met them on the street, they'd pretend not to know them...and they wouldn't dream of inviting them into their houses."

"We don't know anyone like that in Petersburg," he told her regretfully, "not couples who lived together. Lots of my colleagues keep mistresses, of course, but that's not at all the same thing. No commitment."

"The people I'm talking about are as faithful to each other as anyone could possibly be."

"They keep their mistresses in flats as far away from their wives as they possibly can. They never go out together. Either they see each other on a regular basis, so many times a week, or they make appointments, I suppose."

He laughed, but she laid a restraining hand on his arm. "Don't laugh, Paul. Any one of us might have married the wrong person in the first place and be condemned to spending the rest of our lives regretting it."

"I didn't," he grinned.

"I know." She relaxed. "You know, until the very last moment, I never thought you'd get Leonore to marry you."

"Neither did I," he admitted, "and it's largely due to you that she did."

She shrugged. "When your brother sees how happy you are, doesn't that make him want to marry Channah?"

"He can't," he said lightly, "she's a Jew."

She staggered back in her chair as though he'd struck her.

"You married Leonore."

"It's not the same. I was only a soldier. He's the Baron. Loff and my sister both live up to their moral duty, and it's ruined both their lives."

"You have no moral duty, then?"

"Not really that I can see, beyond caring for my family. And...it's a lesson the Army taught me: to obey without question the last order given me by my superior."

"Horrible! Your son, Eduard. He'll be Baron one day."

"If the system lasts that long."

"Will he recognise his moral duty, do you think? Or will he keep a lady hidden somewhere in a flat in Saint Petersburg?"

"That's not at all the same thing."

"Oh, yes, it is. There may be a difference in your mind, but not in mine. Morality has nothing to do with the system. If the system is justified, it upholds itself by common consent. Our moral duty, whoever we are, lies solely towards our fellow human beings and to them alone."

The next time he went to the flat, he was dubious about his reception. He needn't have worried. Clementine greeted him as warmly as ever, and Sasha was at home, as well.

"I'm on my way to the Far East this time," he told them. "It's this war between the Chinese and Japanese. We're not interested in the fighting. They could have killed each other 'till there wasn't one man of them left, so far as we're concerned. Now that it's almost over, we're extremely interested in the settlement, though—what the Japanese intend to do with Korea and Manchuria."

"Why, for heavens' sake!" Sasha sounded exasperated. "We surely don't want to spread any further east, do we?"

"Not at all."

"Then why...oh, I see. You're not diplomatic; you're commercial. And there's money involved!"

"We're not making it public just yet, Sasha, but since you're a railway man, you could be interested. There might even be a place for you out there if you wanted one."

"The Far East! I think not, thank you very much," Clementine said sharply.

"I'm going out to keep my ear to the ground...see what's happening diplomatically. Putilov and the Bank have the idea for a new railway east from Chita in Siberia, and through Manchuria to Vladivostok."

"For God's sake!"

"Profitable from every point of view: strategic as well as commercial. The Japanese are top dogs at the moment and..."

"And they have to be handled very carefully, don't they? You can't hoodwink them as easily as you can the Chinese."

"We're not hoodwinking anyone. It's simply that if the Japanese take Manchuria…"

"The Bank and the great V.I. Putilov won't make the profits they expect. That's your duty at the moment, is it, Paul?" Clementine's voice was shrill, and Sasha looked at her, surprised.

"Oh, Paul, Paul dear…what's made you change so?"

He wriggled uncomfortably and didn't know what to say. He didn't understand the question.

"You were Leonore's white knight when we first knew you," she went on. "Mine too. You were willing to give up everything for her sake, and I thought that was wonderful. You were alive in those days, Paul dear, truly alive. Now you're dead. You're dead to everything except your smart life in Saint Petersburg and to chasing money."

She stood up suddenly and went to where the table stood with the samovar on it. She lifted the cloth and rummaged in a small drawer. She turned back with a piece of paper in her hand and Sasha uttered a low warning.

"Clementine! No!"

"Why shouldn't he know? They say knowledge is responsibility, don't they?"

She held it out and Paul took it. It was a grubby piece of paper with grease-marks along its folds. It was written in ill-formed letters by a child of twelve or so, he supposed, and in simple Russian.

Dear Friends,

Boris will bring this. I am travelling a lot and have met many friends. So many have died. There is an epidemic spreading everywhere. Some want to go abroad. We have found a safe route for them. It would be too hot for me there. I am busy here. I visit everyone. I write to my pen friends. They send me the money that makes everything possible. Don't worry about me.

Olga.

Paul handed back the letter. "I don't understand. Who's Olga?"

"Drop it, Clementine! He doesn't need to know."

"Why show it to me, then? Who's Olga, Clementine?"

"Ida! Ida, who always pretends she hasn't a care in the world and makes us laugh so much. You never noticed, Paul, but she was much more in love with you than ever Leonore was in those early days."

He could only stare at her, blankly.

"We received it last week," Sasha told him quietly. "A man we trust, a train conductor, fetched it up from the south."

"Who was he?"

"Boris."

"I want to talk to him. Where is he?"

"Impossible!" Clementine snapped.

"If he's seen Ida recently, I want to know where she is…what she's doing."

"You don't know what you're asking, Paul," Sasha told him seriously. "Helping Jews isn't easy, and it's dangerous. Listen! Boris…and I may as well tell you that that isn't his real name…had his story rehearsed in case he was searched. A little girl he got friendly with on the train gave him the note before she got off and asked him to deliver it to her friends in Moscow. Unfortunately, he hadn't written down their name and address at the time and now he's completely forgotten it."

"You think they'd believe that?"

"They always believe the most obvious lies," Clementine said with a cynical smile. "It's their twisted minds. Lies mean so much more to them than the truth."

"We can't tell you anything more than that; Ida was safe and well when she wrote that note. And of course, I don't have to tell you, do I, that by telling you all this we've placed ourselves completely in your hands?"

"Of course not. You won't say anything to anybody, will you, Paul? Not if I order you not to. Remember? Last Orders? Duty? Or aren't I superior enough?"

"That's not fair."

"What's fair? This is life, Paul…for millions of us. Nothing's fair, but at least Ida's trying to do something about it for someone."

"You may as well tell me the rest," he said dully.

"Ida wasn't sent over from New York by a relief group, Paul," Sasha explained. "She's financed by some of the poorest Jews imaginable, but at least, now that they're free, they don't forget their brothers and sisters at home."

"Ida's job is to cover Bessarabia and the Ukraine—where they've had the worst of the pogroms. Looking like she does, she's not too noticeable in the street. But in the train…there's always the chance she'll be pulled off and interrogated."

"She organises as many trips as she can, for those who can't afford to pay their own fare, either to America or Palestine. She communicates with the outside world by a couple of seamen who sail out of Odessa and a few railwaymen who work across the border in Roumania."

"They're all called 'Boris', incidentally," Clementine laughed.

"I was able to tell her some safe names and addresses when she was here."

"You're in it too, then?"

"Not directly. Not in that, anyway. We have our own…" He smiled, embarrassed. "We have our own cause. But Ida's always been Clementine's favourite, and we had to do everything we could to help."

"And she's getting Jews out to America…?"

"And Palestine."

"There's this man Herzl," Sasha began to explain.

"Herzl?"

"Oh, Paul...Paul, darling, don't you know anything?" Clementine laughed at him in the old way and crouched down in front of him with her arms on his knees. "Oh Paul...please forgive me, my dear, I must have sounded like a dreadful bitch to you."

"Yes, as a matter of fact, you did."

"I'm sorry, but you have to understand. We're serious. We're not idealistic students. We're grown men and women, Sasha, Ida...hundreds like us. We know this country has to change. There's too much freedom in the world these days for us to go on existing without it. We know the country has to change and we know how to change it. But we can't do it alone. We need you to help, Paul. You're the kind of man people listen to." She shrugged. "They put us in prison or send us to Siberia when they catch us, but you..."

"You're asking me to be one of your revolutionaries?" he demanded incredulously.

"Oh, I get so angry when you talk so glibly about building your railway," Clementine began, angry again. "Think about it! Just for one moment, think about it! What's it for? Who's going to make all the profit? How many people will you have to turn off their land for them to make that profit? How many workmen will die in accidents or with disease in the building of it?"

She stopped suddenly, and there was an unbearable silence in the room until Sasha said:

"We're not asking you to throw bombs or to shoot anyone, Paul."

"Your influence at the Bank is too important for that," Clementine added.

Paul stared at them both, confused, unable to understand anything.

Clementine stood up and spoke softly, seductively.

"Paul...Paul, dear, you must know that we love you very much, don't you? We believe we're building something beautiful, Sasha and Ida and I and all the rest. We love you so much we want you to be a part of it, to relish the joy of it when it's done."

Paul was still in a daze when Sasha walked him home. On the steps of the hotel, Sasha took him into his arms and hugged him very tightly. Paul felt the warmth of the man, his body, his ideas, flow into him.

Long before he drifted into sleep that night he knew they had captured him.

CHAPTER 13

▼

1895

Leonore forever after remembered it as a Black and Purple period. All Russia—so far as Petersburg society was "All Russia"—swathed itself in a haze of mourning. Society strove to impress itself with its grief. It was an uncomfortable time for everyone. It had to be lived through according to a formula, and because nobody knew quite what that was, everyone tried to outdo everybody else.

In the von Hagen circle, the winter season was unnaturally quiet. Private balls were unheard of. In lilac (black held too many memories from her childhood), Leonore offered her friends nothing more exciting than tea parties, at which the only entertainment was their own closed-circle gossip.

Princess Surotkina came regularly and cried a lot, more on her own behalf than for the Dowager Empress. She had, she sobbed, already lived through so much; she was too tired to make a new beginning at her age. She would never learn to live with the eccentricities of a new regime.

Princess Krimovskaya was frankly bored. Where was the point of being in Saint Petersburg if there was no social life? "I never liked the man when he was alive, and I simply will not pretend I'm heartbroken now that he's dead! The Prince constantly urges me to make more of a show, but…"

Varvara Milyova looked anxious. The old Tsar's death left her tentatively hopeful that the new one would recognize her husband's talents and recall him instantly from Vladivostok. Here in the capital, without a doubt, the Admiral would immediately be recognized as a New Man indispensable for the New Future.

Valentina Popova was as aloof as ever. She put aside her pinks but nevertheless scorned purple or anything like it. She went into deepest black, decorated from head to foot with a carapace of jet that glittered in a most unmournful manner. Her confidence in this armour reflected her confidence in the future of Sergei Ilyich. Nothing was likely to change, so far as he was concerned; he would always be safe.

Countess Poulanskaya was almost suspiciously cheerful. This was a new manifestation of her personality and earned her quizzical glances. What, everybody wondered, could Poulanskaya find so very advantageous to herself in the advent of a new reign?

While Leonore entertained her friends Paul went to the Bank and conducted his business beneath a portrait of the defunct Tsar draped heavily in black crepe. His colleagues, so soon as the weather allowed for traveling, sent their families to perform the less rigorous etiquette of mourning on their estates in the country.

Princess Krimovskaya was among the first to go, grateful for Leonore's offer to have Pyotr Alexeivitch move in with them, to save cutting short his winter term at the Lyceum. Dorothea became suddenly self-conscious when she was told of the arrangement. She abandoned the game of royal weddings. She followed their guest from room to room, hanging on to his every word. Sonia hated him for it.

The men who couldn't yet leave the city locked away their glittering uniforms, closed their offices early every day and spent their evenings in their clubs or with their mistresses. They read their newspapers and complained that nothing was happening, nothing moving. Without direction from the top, indeed, without a top at all, Russia was dropping off to sleep once more. Everyone abroad was very wide-awake indeed, it seemed, and everything was happening over there.

The Germans were about to open their Kiel canal, which would shorten the voyage from Saint Petersburg to the North Sea by three hundred miles. In Italy, Marconi was transmitting sound by radio waves. Roentgen was working on magic rays to lay bare the human bone structure beneath the living flesh. In Vienna, Sigmund Freud was working on psychoanalysis, laying bare the structure of the unknown and seemingly independent life of the human mind within its skull.

None of this much interested Leonore. She was, however, exceedingly disturbed when Paul received unexpected instructions to go once more to the Far East.

"Why Paul? Why now? You said yourself, nothing important could possibly happen until after the Coronation."

"Not here in Russia, I meant. This has to do with the war between the Chinese and the Japanese in Korea."

"They don't expect you to do anything about that, surely."

"Not me alone, darling…a group of us. Now that the fighting is nearly over, and the Japanese have all but won, it'll be our job to see that Russia's interests don't suffer when the peace treaty gets written."

"You're really pleased you're going, aren't you!" She was hurt because it had already occurred to her that these days, they talked from opposite ends of the room, without the need or desire to touch each other any more.

His laughter was sheepish because he knew what she was thinking, and he knew she was right. He was pleased to be going. His frequent trips beyond the Urals were inducing in him a fascination with Far Eastern affairs. Now he welcomed any excuse to go. And his delight was greatly increased when, at the point of departure, he heard that Sergei Ouroussoff was to be one of his travelling companions.

Leonore was not at all pleased by that. For old times' sake, she made Sergei welcome whenever he came to their house but she was nonetheless irritated by his adolescent determination never to take life seriously. She feared that his uncaring attitude would, in the long run, affect her husband, even to the extent of his unworried acceptance of Albrecht's speech problem.

She had the boy on her lap when Paul left for the start of his journey. She greatly revered the Catholic Mother and Child image and never hesitated to use it herself whenever she considered it might have an effect. This time, Paul hardly noticed. He kissed her lightly on the forehead and left. She watched him go, simulating indifference. As soon as the door closed, though, she longed to rush after him, to beg him to come back, but she had no intention of showing weakness. She continued to sit, lips tight, clasping the child more closely than was comfortable for either of them, until there was a gentle tapping at the door. Ulrika came in looking miserable. Leonore could only feel impatience.

Brides traditionally discover the nature of their husbands on the wedding night. Ulrika was learning somewhat sooner than that. They had met when they were little more than children, but Anton had grown up remarkably quickly. The gracefully drooping moustache now bristled, the blonde hair was coarsened and his features were decisive. He was no longer the boy of the snowball fights in Saint Petersburg Park.

Ulrika began to understand what living with a Russian husband might mean. In the early days Leonore could reassure her from her own experience with Paul. Neither remembered that all men are not the same. Paul was a Baltic, Westernised aristocrat; Anton was a Russian peasant. His grandfather had been gambled away as a serf. His mother and two of his sisters had starved to death in the famine of '91. His culture was to value a wife only slightly above the family pig.

"It's the same old trouble, I suppose," Leonore began before Ulrika could say a word. "You don't have to marry him, you know."

"No, my lady." Ulrika uttered a single, dry sob.

"I told you at the very beginning. You have to talk everything through; reach a compromise together."

"Yes, your Honour." The agreement was unconvincing. "He won't have anyone to the wedding, your Honour, neither his parents nor mine."

"Well, yours certainly can't come all the way from Germany, can they? And his...they're from somewhere near Tambov, I believe. My child, they're as far away as yours."

"But if I don't have any family there, I shan't feel I'm properly married."

"Nonsense! His Excellency and I had witnesses off the street. And do stop making that silly noise! I'll be there...and the children...and his Excellency, if he's home. Surely you think of us as your family after all this time, don't you?"

It was polite to agree, but Ulrika couldn't hold back her tears. It was no more than a manner of speech, and the speaking of it brought home to her the depth of her aloneness.

Irritated by the girl's determination to be miserable, Leonore suddenly put Albrecht off her lap and on to the floor. He went immediately on to his hands and knees and she gave him a playful pat on his bottom. He set off immediately, crawling 'round the room on all fours and hooting like a locomotive.

"Once and for all, Ulrika, you must make up your mind, for all our sakes. Do you want him, or don't you?"

"I must, mustn't I?" the girl mumbled through her tears. "What else can I do? Where else can I go?"

"You can go home. If you really don't want to marry Anton, I'll send you home with a little money to get you settled. Then you'll be able to look out for some nice German boy—someone you'll like better, perhaps..."

"But I love Anton, your Honour," the girl moaned, barely above a whisper.

"Then go and find him and tell him so. Tell him you'll marry him at the Tsar's Coronation. That's what you promised all along, didn't you?"

After that, for several weeks, there was a kind of calm happiness in the house. Ulrika didn't cry any more, and Leonore reconciled herself to Paul's absence. The girls occupied much of her time. Dorothea still lay unabashed siege to young Krimovsky. She practised piano whenever he was in the house, rendering *Etudes* with a degree of romanticism Chopin himself might have considered "going too far." On the rare occasions the instrument was free, Sonia perched on the stool and gave her own interpretation of whatever was Dorothea's favourite of the moment. She had a talent for making each of her sister's pieces sound like a military march. If Pyotr Alexeivitch were in the room, he tapped his foot and nodded his head in time with the music. He was careful not to let Dorothea see him smiling at the joke. Leonore shook her head with mock severity.

Sonia was not attempting to attract Pyotr Alexeivitch to herself. She regarded Romance as 'soppy' and didn't approve of Dorothea's being so 'mushy' about a young man and letting him see that she was.

Marie was characteristically scathing and humourless about everybody and everything except Albrecht. Whatever else went on in that little boy's mind, it was clear that he adored being adored. And he was in no doubt that Marie adored him. He was still her chosen playmate at all times. Leonore watched the two of them, but she was out of her depth. She longed for Marie's secret. She herself didn't know what to do with this strange child except to love him. And Marie was evidently better at that than anyone else. He appeared to greet each member of the family with equal delight: with bright eyes and dribbling laughter. With Marie, however, there was less laughter, as though he considered it unnecessary. He would open his pudgy little arms for her to pick him up and, in her arms, jerked his body against her own like a rider urging his horse to carry him away.

Paul seemed to her to be disinterested and Leonore needed some other adult to whom she could express her worries. The friend she found most sympathetic was Varvara Milyova. The child loved her. Whenever she came into the room, he agitated for her to pick him up.

He allowed her, without complaint, to clean his nose and mouth. She caressed him without worrying about stains on her dress. Whenever she held him, her eyes were tranquil.

"He is a special blessing, Leonore. You must thank God for him."

Leonore stared, not knowing what she was expected to say.

"My husband has served the Emperor all over the world. There are people, you know, who believe that to have a child who is…who is in any way different, is a particular dispensation. God wouldn't trust Albrecht with everyone. You were chosen."

The ice in the Neva was cracking pistol shots and the streets were filled with the music of dripping icicles. Leonore still hadn't had a letter from Paul. She hoped, each time she saw Varvara Milyova, that the Admiral might have sent a message about him from Vladivostok.

There was never anything. And this long silence became suddenly sinister when, without warning, Lydmilla Fyorodorovna called at the house and presented her with another worry.

Leonore rushed into the hall as soon as she was announced but stopped still in the doorway, shocked. The painter was unrecognisable. Her hair was now quite white, her face haggard, her shoulders hunched. She was leaning heavily on a stick.

"Lydmilla! Where have you been? Why haven't you written?"

The colourless face attempted a smile that was no more than a grimace. "The government sent me on a little holiday," she said. "Nowhere near as nice as the Crimea, unfortunately. In the East, of course."

Leonore hardly understood, at first, what she was saying.

"Oh, Lydmilla, my dear, I am so sorry. We thought, after Paris, you were probably still in England." She moved to embrace the woman, but Lydmilla waved her away.

"I have to find your husband."

"Paul?"

"They couldn't or wouldn't tell me anything at the Bank."

"My dear…I don't know where he is." Leonore giggled with embarrassment. "It's something to do with the war in Korea. I haven't heard from him for weeks."

"Oh, my God!"

The woman looked about to collapse. Leonore took her firmly in her arms and led her to a seat.

"But I must get in touch with him. You must help me find him."

"I swear, I don't know where he is. But why don't you tell me what it's about? Maybe I can help."

"You!" There was a wealth of meaning in the way she said it, but no affection or respect. "Has he told you anything about…" She paused and shrugged as though nothing mattered now. "Has he told you about Olga?"

"Olga?"

"You don't know anything."

Was she trying to tell her Paul was having an affair? Leonore made a feeble effort to save face.

"Paul meets so many people these days. He tells me who they are, but I can't sort them all out."

"You'd remember Olga. Paul would drop everything if he were here."

"Can she be that important? What are you trying to tell me?"

Lydmilla looked about to struggle to her feet, but was arrested by a new thought. "Your brother-in-law…"

"The Baron?"

"Maybe he can help. And he's married to a Jew, isn't he?"

"Not exactly."

"Olga's a Jew."

Leonore was becoming annoyed. "I don't understand any of this!" she said sharply. "Naturally, for old times' sake, I'll do whatever I can to help your friend. But you can't possibly expect my brother-in-law to become involved."

"She's only a girl. The very thought of her breaks my heart."

Leonore began moving about the room to ease a tightness in her chest. She didn't want to hear anything more about this...this Olga...except to know whether Paul was having an affair with her. And even if he were, it couldn't be a problem for the entire family.

Lydmilla Fyodorovna persisted. "The police have taken her. We must have someone with influence to get her free. She mustn't be left to go through what I went through."

"Lydmilla, I'm very sorry for her, but..."

"She was betrayed, of course," Lydmilla broke in. "Some people will do anything for money...and convince themselves they're doing the right thing."

It was a reproof, Leonore felt. She was being reminded that however far she might travel in her life, her point of departure would never alter. She said:

"If this girl really is important to you..."

"She's important to all of us. You must believe me."

"Then I'll see if I can get the Baron to help, though I can't promise anything."

"You have to get in touch with him right away. It may make all the difference between life and death."

"I must give him a reason."

"I'll tell him everything he needs to know when he gets here. Send a telegram. Say Paul's away, and you desperately need his help. That's all you need to say."

CHAPTER 14

▼

1895

The constant rocking of the cab over pock-marked alleyways was making him feel sick. He grasped his stick until his knuckles were white and would have used it to thrash the driver, had he known where in this benighted place to find another vehicle. The man, he was sure, was deliberately driving from pothole to pothole. The rusty springs creaked. His anxiety became more unbearable with every lurch.

Loff hated travelling these days. Paul and Leonore came very regularly to visit him with the children, and there was no one else he bothered to visit. The thought of travelling to Moscow next year for the Coronation was intolerable to him. And this trip into the depth of Bessarabia was madness. How could he possibly have allowed that woman to talk him into it? And yet, once he knew, how could he possibly have refused. The look in Channah's eyes when she read the telegram left him no option. "These are your family," she told him, simply.

"But what is it she wants? Why doesn't she tell me what's wrong?"

"I'll pack your bag."

"Please come with me."

She shook her head.

When he reached Saint Petersburg, he went straight to the house on Nevsky Prospekt. The children went wild with excitement when they saw him. Leonore kissed him fondly but stood back, looking at him enigmatically. At least she saved them both the embarrassment of small talk, asking about his journey.

"It's an old friend of Paul's and mine, Loff. I don't know the details but, apparently, it's serious."

"You've fetched me down here because of some kind of emergency, and even you don't know what it is?"

"She's out at the moment. She's in and out so much I never know where she is. But...well, wait till you meet her. Then you'll understand. Why don't you rest after your journey? I'll let you know the moment she comes back."

They were equally eager for a polite excuse to separate. Loff went to his room, and an hour later Leonore came in with a tray of coffee, followed by someone else she introduced as Lydmilla Kholchevskaya.

"She is one of my oldest and dearest friends, Loff. Please do whatever you can to help her...for my sake."

Leonore left the room and Loff stared at his visitor's deep-lined, colourless face. Her shabby black coat fell straight to the floor as though the body beneath it had no bulk. She motioned him to sit, and when she spoke her voice was low and rough. Her words sounded somehow inevitable, like opening a once-read book.

"Be patient, *Herr Baron*, I will answer all your questions, but let me talk first. It is an effort, you see. The police have arrested Leonore's sister Ida, but Leonore doesn't know. We must do everything in our power to set her free before she finds out." She smiled grimly. "Once they take you, there's no knowing what will happen. You may come out a wreck, or you may never be heard of again. I am only here because...well...that doesn't matter. For Leonore, you understand, her own sister...it would all be too terrible. Even with a name like yours to help her, our poor little Ida is still a Jew, unfortunately."

"What has she done? I won't help if she's a revolutionary."

"She's not a revolutionary in your sense of the word. She doesn't throw bombs or try to shoot people." Lydmilla gave a dry, weary laugh that started her coughing. "She's with an organisation trying to get Jews out of the country."

"Ida?" He was disbelieving. "Our Ida...?"

"She takes life very seriously since she was in America. She was speaking at a meeting in a small town in Bessarabia. The police broke in an arrested her. She was betrayed, of course."

"Where is she now? What do you think we can do?"

"You must go there immediately. These petty officials...! They can all be bribed, particularly in the South. If they haven't transported her already..."

"And if they have?"

"Then we must pay to find out where they've sent her, go there, wherever it is, pay someone else and someone else...And if you believe in your Lutheran God, pray to Him. The deeper they suck her into their system, the more difficult, the more expensive it will become to get her out."

Loff went south on the night train and took a cab at the Station. The driver was in a bad temper, which he considered justified. This passenger was making a fool of him, and that fact must, inevitably, very soon be known all over the small town.

The man was obviously a gentleman, a man cab drivers addressed without thinking as "your Honour." He was brusque when he was picked up at the railway station, and that was understandable. Gentlemen mostly traveled in their own carriages—certainly when the choice came to branch lines like this one from the capital. He must have a special reason for wanting to get here urgently. Naturally, he was stiff and smut-marked after the journey from Kishinev. But the driver needed to know what was so important to bring him here at this time of night and in this condition. Otherwise, he would certainly lose face. Cab drivers gathered intelligence that all kinds of people were eager to hear and to pay for.

"The police station," the passenger said, without bothering to look at the driver's face. His accent was strange, like nothing remotely local.

"Yes, your Honour, at once, your Honour." The driver saluted with his whip, and his horse made a sullen movement forward. His master, conscious of his responsibility to the rest of the townsfolk, spat companionably and turned his head. The gentleman's order to be taken straight to the police station must be significant. Many men in bug-ridden beds, men sleeping in dirty back rooms, mill-workers, students, railwaymen, road-menders might find in this man's arrival their reason to disappear.

"As quick as I can, your Honour. You'll find Sergeant Isolvsky on duty tonight, I expect."

The man said nothing. Perhaps, the driver thought, perhaps, after all, he was not the gentleman he appeared to be. Perhaps he was some kind of official, on urgent business from the capital, hiding his rank and his purpose in a frock coat instead of a uniform. If he were an official, of course, his business could have serious consequences for anyone or everyone in the whole town. He might even be a member of the Okhrana, God forbid! The driver crossed himself and, deciding he needed time to think, turned his vehicle off the main road and into a maze of narrow lanes.

"There's nothing goes on in our town that Sergeant Isolvsky doesn't know about," he said over his shoulder, encouragingly. "As a matter of fact, he's a cousin of my wife's." His laugh expressed his pride. "In my job as a driver, I very often get to hear things he's very grateful to know about."

"Get on with it, man!"

After a moment's silence: "Would your Honour not like me to drive you to a hotel first? This is a small town, you know, not like the capital. Our hotels are only tiny. They fill and close their doors very early."

"The Police Station!" Loff barked with a hint of menace.

"The Police Station. Yes, your Honour. At once, your Honour."

There were further twists and turns and more moments of silence in the black night.

"There's always my wife, your Honour," the man began again. "She keeps a respectable house, thank the good Lord. You won't find a single bug or louse in her beds, I promise you. And she's great friends with Sergeant Isolvsky. He tells her everything. She may be able to save your Honour the trouble of going to the Police Station at all. It's not much of a place."

The man uttered a sudden squeal, as Loff unexpectedly brought his walking stick down on his shoulder.

"Listen, my friend! Stop this nonsense and take me to the Police Station the quickest way and no more of these ridiculous twists and turns. You won't expect me to pay for all this tomfoolery, of course. And if you want to make a fuss about that, you can wait until I've had my talk with that Sergeant of yours, and we'll see what he has to say about it!"

After that, a single turn of the cab was enough to bring them to the front door of the Police Station. Loff stormed in, banging the door behind him. The office stank with the heat of unwashed bodies and two paraffin lamps hanging from the ceiling. The Sergeant behind the desk looked up with unrestrained respect. A gendarme, sitting on a wooden bench with his back to the wall, hovered, knees bent, undecided whether to stand or remain sitting.

"I'm hoping you can help me, Sergeant," Loff began, politely enough.

"Yes, your Honour, of course, your Honour." He turned sharply to the gendarme. "Get a chair for his Honour, Idiot!"

The man scuttled into a backroom and came back with a chair. When the visitor was seated, the Sergeant resumed his own place, sitting eager and encouraging, finger-tips together.

"I need your assistance to trace the whereabouts of a young woman."

The Sergeant's eyebrows shot up, his fingertips fell apart. He moved briskly to pull a large ledger lying on the desk to a convenient position in front of him. He dipped his pen in his inkwell. "Such goings-on we hear of these days, your Honour. None of these young people know how to behave. And the country is overrun with brigands of one sort or another: Ruthenians, Ukrainians, Turks, Romanians, Gypsies…" He flipped open the ledger and assembled his thoughts for the business in hand. "If I might have the young lady's name, your Honour…"

"I understand she calls herself 'Olga' these days. Her real name is Ida Goldfarb."

The Sergeant dropped his pen, leaving a blot on his page, and looked thoroughly alarmed. He was middle-aged. There was grey hair in his moustache and more grey hair showing under his cap above his ears. The two lower buttons of his tunic were open for the comfortable accommodation of his paunch, and he was in a deep and obvious quandary. Gentlemen like this one didn't come enquiring for Jews. "Perhaps, if your Honour," he began placatingly…

"Your men arrested her at a meeting several nights ago," Loff told him without preamble.

The Sergeant tried not to squirm too obviously. His dilemma was in still not knowing the status of this stranger who had dropped into his office this quiet night. Was he one of the woman's associates? Should he be arrested himself, just in case? He appeared to be a genuine gentleman, but what interest could a genuine gentleman have in a revolutionary Jew? He might even be an official from the capital, on an unexpected inspection of the Sergeant's efficiency.

"She's a Jew, of course," Loff persisted, and added with sarcasm, "That might help your memory."

The Sergeant banged shut his ledger. He had made up his mind. He was by no means a quick thinker, but he knew by instinct that, whatever the circumstance, it was always safest to say nothing. This was a matter best handled, he decided, by his colleague in the morning. For the moment it would perhaps be politic to display his dignity as a government official.

"That kind of enquiry is dealt with only in the mornings between the hours of 10 and 11," he blustered. "You'll have to come back then."

The gendarme on his bench looked at his superior with a new respect. The Sergeant pushed the ledger to a corner of his desk and, with considerable satisfaction, saw Loff rise. He was horribly surprised when Loff cracked his stick across the desk within an inch of his hand. In raising his stick, he had struck one of the lamps, which was set swinging, crazily illuminating the grubby room from corner to corner. The gendarme moved his head in rhythm, wide-eyed and open-mouthed.

"Your name, Sergeant?"

"Isolvsky, your Honour, Boris Nickolaievitch."

"Well, Boris Nickolaievitch, your superiors shall hear about this. I shall make a full report on your conduct when I get back to Saint Petersburg...understand?"

The Sergeant nodded, though he didn't in the least understand. All he knew was that the ramifications of the structure were so many and went so high up, one never knew where was the top; one only knew—and this was rueful—where was the bottom.

"Now! You'll waste no more of my time! Tell me about this young woman! Your men arrested her a few nights ago when she was talking at a meeting of young Zionists. What happened to her after that?"

"Your Honour..." The man flapped his hands weakly.

"Tell me! Count Witte is a personal friend of mine."

Count Witte or Genghis Khan...it was all the same to the Sergeant. "I think I remember the girl now, your Honour," he began, a reluctant swimmer teetering on the edge of a lake.

"What happened to her? Is she here? I want to see her! Now!"

"Your Honour, she was not of the usual run. I remember now, quite well. I myself gave instructions for her to be treated as a Special. I myself saw that she left here as a Special. She wasn't to be treated like the others."

"Where is she?"

The man's face went blank. He said nothing.

"Did you hear me? Where is she?"

"A Cossack patrol, your Honour. It was all arranged beforehand. They were to take them all to Kishinev."

"And then?"

The Sergeant looked desperately miserable. "The prison in Kishinev," he said, his voice rising with anguish.

The driver was still waiting outside the Police Station, torn between his desire to escape and his need to be paid. Obediently, he drove Loff to the best livery stables in the place (promoted to a township since the May Laws, so as to limit its accessibility to Jews).

Loff offered to double the liveryman's fare if he got him back to Kishinev before daybreak. The day was still only at its greyest when Loff stampeded into the Police Station there. This was an important Police Station in an important city. Nevertheless, when Loff explained his business there was the same uncertainty as to how he should be dealt with. It was a commissioned officer who eventually informed him that "the person"—names were deliberately avoided in this place, it seemed—had been tried and condemned to exile for an indeterminate number of years.

"Where?"

The officer shrugged.

"When did she go? Who can tell me?"

Another shrug. "She speaks languages. They'll probably use her as a teacher. But as to when and where she'll go...if she's not already on her way..."

Loff looked as crushed as he felt, but he had the sense to handle his pocket book.

"You must have records, for God's sake!"

"The Court records will already be on their way to Saint Petersburg, your Honour. If she hasn't been transported yet, you might be able to find her at the railway station, though. They have pens to house them there, you know."

Money went from hand to hand.

The pens were guarded by Latvians already sweating in the mild southern air. They housed men, women and children of every race and degree, standing, sitting and trying to sleep even in their abominably crowded conditions. Their clothing was ragged and filthy; whatever of their bodies could be seen showed signs of rough handling. Some acknowledged Loff's presence at the bars by a croaked off-key song or a crude jig, their hands stretched out for money. The stench was sickening.

Loff walked slowly from one end of the pens to the other and back again. He saw no one he knew. On his return, though, he was arrested by a soft call, soft and sibilant like a bird's. He moved close to the mesh.

"Are you looking for Olga, comrade?" It was a young man, swarthy and hairy, with bright black eyes and a grotesque limp as though both his legs had been broken.

"I might be."

"What do you want?"

"I want to see her."

"She doesn't want to be seen."

"If she's my Olga, I want to help her."

"You can't. We're beyond help here, all of us."

"I've come from Clementine and Lydmilla. Tell her I must see her."

"I'll try." The man hobbled away into a cluster of helpless, hopeless human beings, all marked with the scars of the intensest cruelty. He hobbled back again.

"She doesn't want to see you. And you mustn't tell her sisters."

"What's going to happen to her?"

"She and I are lucky. We know languages. We're going to be teachers in the Tobolsk region."

"When?"

The young man shrugged. "Who knows? When the train is ready. But don't worry about her. She's my friend. I'll look after her. Perhaps if you'll tell me your name and where you live, we can get into touch with you eventually."

"That's not good enough. I want to see her now. At least I want to be able to tell her friends she's still alive."

"Alive!" The young man looked backwards over his shoulder. "There! Do you see her? Between that woman in the green headscarf and the man in the blue shirt smoking a pipe. Can you see?"

Loff gulped and fastened his fingers round the mesh of the cage for support.

"She'll be all right," the young man assured him again. "We're friends. I don't know whether they raped her. She can't talk yet. The eye, though…"

There was nothing to say about the eye. There was no eye to talk about. Where Ida's left eye had sparkled, a hideous red hole was all that was left.

Loff paid the guards, but nothing would open the gate.

CHAPTER 15

▼

1895

The War between China and Japan ended satisfactorily for the Russians, who had done no more than gloat during the conflict. When the Treaty of Shimonoseki was signed, she was strong enough to force a rewriting favourable to Chinese (and ultimately their own) interests. China's gratitude led to Manchuria's becoming "a sphere of Russian influence." Saint Petersburg acquired permission to build their longed-for Chinese Eastern Railway and now had strategic access to an all-year-round ice-free harbour at Port Arthur. The line and its branch were to be run, of course, by Russians, who were awarded wide territory along the tracks, virtually an extension to the Imperial Empire. Russian officials would control the system, their wives would shop in Russian stores, their children be born in Russian hospitals and educated in Russian schools. Russian troops would defend the area, and Tsar Nicholas appointed a Viceroy to rule there.

Paul was exhilarated by this national triumph and kept the telegraph wires to Saint Petersburg buzzing. The processes of formal negotiation intrigued him. He attended official meetings and also learned that waiters, doormen and chambermaids would keep him informed of various secret meetings and their outcomes if he paid them enough. He could foresee eventual difficulties with Japan; all sentient Russians could. But that aspect of the settlement didn't bother him just then.

What could these crinkled little yellow men do against the mighty Russian Empire? His reports home were accurate and efficient; nothing more was required of him. His reputation in Saint Petersburg was growing. In the meantime, he set himself to enjoy Japan. Sergei Ouroussoff remained with him, an observer at every military discussion. The two of them shared a paper-thin house on a hill overlooking the sea. In their free time, they explored Honshu together as far north as Tokyo and Kyoto. But he was not, Paul felt, the Ouroussoff of the old days. The man had tempered his high spirits until he was serious, almost lugubrious. He never once suggested they spent an evening at a *Geisha* house. He hardly drank. He read a lot and wasn't recognisable any more as the man who used to roister on the Islands.

Paul longed to ask him what was wrong but felt the old intimacy was lost and couldn't do so. Sadly, neither of them were any longer the young men they had been in the Army. They had unconsciously acquired the shyness, the reticence of middle age. He might never have known except for an unrelated incident the night before he was due to leave. They were sitting in their paper house, tactfully reminiscing and soberly drinking their vodka, both conscious of the barrier between them and wishing the evening would end. Without warning, their confidence in themselves was challenged; each looked sheepishly at the other because each feared he had lost control. But it was not to do with them. The floor on which they sat shuddered twice like a ship in a heaving sea and they felt themselves integral to the troubled world around them. A small ivory doll, intricately carved in the costumed of its day and supposed to be seventeenth century, crashed off a shelf and smashed on the corner of a low table. Paul looked at it regretfully. He knew it was a fake and he'd given too much for it, but Leonore would have liked it.

They stared at each other surprised until Sergei burst out laughing. "Your final Japanese experience, old man, the climax to your stay. A real earthquake! Only a very little earthquake, of course, but something to boast about at home."

"Come home with me, Sergei! You're a better liar than I am."

"Not yet. In fact, to tell you the truth, I doubt whether I shall ever see Petersburg again. A soldier doesn't have a home, you know; he can't allow himself to belong anywhere. You remember that from the old days before...well, before."

"What about the Regiment?" Paul stared. "You're surely not leaving the Army?"

"Good heavens, no! I'm leaving the Preobrazhensky, though. I'm taking a staff job out here."

"Here!" Paul stared.

"I've decided it's time to settle down."

"And you're settling down out here...in this wilderness?"

"I'll have a better chance in Manchuria than among the old crowd in Saint Petersburg. Too many temptations there, eh, old man?"

"But..."

"Besides...I may as well tell you now. All Saint Petersburg will be gossiping about it by the time you get there, I expect. They'll never believe I'm serious, but I am...I need to be saved, like you, Paul. So I'm getting married too."

Paul was genuinely speechless. "Who...?" he gasped.

"Your wife knows her quite well, actually. Princess Poulanskaya. We've known each other for years...been writing to each other for quite a time, and...For heaven's sake, Paul, don't look like that! Of course, neither of us is in the first flush of youth. Would you expect me, at my age, to go running off with some twenty-year-old? That would indeed be madness. But Olga Grigorievna and I understand each other. She doesn't mind leaving Saint Petersburg. She's quite willing to spend the rest of her life in the East, if need be."

Paul scarcely knew the Princess, but he believed he knew Ouroussoff well enough. He remembered his objections to his own marriage. They had no foundation, of course; he had known exactly what he was doing. But now...in Ouroussoff's own case...Should he give his friend the well-meaning advice he so obviously needed? The ground settled itself after two or three more small flickers, and by then he'd decided: better not! They were probably both too old to manage that degree of frankness, now. The evening ended speedily with uncomfortable congratulations.

Leonore was brimming over with news of the proposed marriage when Paul reached home.

"Paul, darling, I'll ask her to come tomorrow evening, and you must talk to her yourself, poor dear. I've tried to warn her, but she won't listen. No one knows Colonel Ouroussoff as well as you do. You must make her listen! She's even planning to travel all that way alone. I've told her that's out of the question. You must make her see sense! A gentleman would come here to collect her, but he doesn't seem to think that's necessary. All she tells me is that he says he never wants to set foot in Saint Petersburg again. They're to be married in Vladivostok, you see. Of course, Varvara Milyova's husband will be there; he's an Admiral in the Far East fleet. But she'll know no one else. And even the Admiral isn't to be invited to the wedding, if Colonel Ouroussoff has his way."

"Poor Sergei! I really don't know why you hate him so, my darling."

"I don't hate him, but I'll never forgive him. In Warsaw he thought of me as…as just another bar girl…or like those women you two used to go with on the Islands. And my being a Jew didn't help. You'd never have married me, if he'd had his way."

"Leonore, darling, that's not true. And even if it were, it was a life-time ago. It's time to forget."

"It was a life-time ago for poor Clementine, too. She can't forget, not even with Sasha for a husband, and she's lucky with him; he's a good man. But your friend treated her exactly as he wanted you to treat me."

Paul changed the subject hastily. Any speculation about Clementine and Sasha would be unsafe.

"What's this I hear about what's been happening at the Bank? Where's Popov?"

Leonore laughed. "Novosibirsk!"

"Popov? In Novosibirsk? But why?"

"Well, my darling…" she smiled spitefully. "With everybody still in mourning, we haven't had much to do this winter except talk…oh, well! 'Gossip,' if you like. The Director has been speculating on his own account, apparently, sometimes with the Bank's money. Of course, he didn't actually steal anything, and his wife put him up to it, of course. She's entirely without principles, that woman!"

"Don't repeat your gossip to me, please!"

Paul was sharp because he was not expecting to be frightened. But he remembered the envelope in Popov's desk, as she spoke, and wondered who had it now.

She was offended by his reaction. "Very well. I won't tell you what I know about you, then."

"What do you know about me?"

"Simply gossip, darling, and I know you don't want to hear any more of that." She laughed again.

It couldn't be anything bad about him, he realised; she wouldn't be taking it so lightly if it were. But her laughter irritated him. As with so many a longed-for reunions, this one was not going well. There was almost hostility between them, as if each was trying to prove that survival independent of the other was possible and not too much of a torment.

He had dreaded it might be like this from the moment he stepped off the train; his own mood changed. A spring breeze from the south brought with it a certain warmth, but also acrid smells and smoke from the Putilov factories. It was too gentle to shift the heavy grey clouds that barely cleared the city's spires, and did nothing to shift the muslin mist drifting in from the river. The city he'd fallen so deeply in love with when he was a boy, gay and glamorous as a beautiful young girl, was now middle-aged, blowsy and reeking of stale perfume.

In the cab from the Station, he tried to adjust himself to being at home, to drive the blue crispness of the coast at Shimonoseki from his consciousness. He imagined the welcome he could expect from the children and began to feel excited. But when he reached the house, they were all at their schools, and his presents to them were now lying unappreciated in the hall.

His disappointment forced him to a quick decision. "It's time for you and the children to go to Estonia, Leonore. We'll start the summer holidays early."

She was startled. "What about their schools?"

"They can go to the government school on the Estate. That won't do them any harm. Do them good, probably. You mollycoddle them too much."

"You can't expect Alexei Krimovsky to go there. And I promised his mother I'd look after him until the summer."

"He can come with us, or he can go to his mother in Kaluga. Or..." he added with a grim smile "...his father can put his mistress to one side for a while, and the boy can stay with him."

"And you? You won't be coming with us, I suppose?"

He shrugged. "Obviously not. I can't get away now that I've just got back...particularly if what you tell me about Popov is true. But Loff will like to have you there."

"I don't know where Loff is."

"What do you mean, you don't know where he is? He's at home, of course. Where else should he be?"

"He was going south somewhere, last time I saw him."

"South?"

"Something Lydmilla wanted him to do."

"Lydmilla? What on earth could Lydmilla possibly want with my brother? They don't know each other."

She told him sourly of Lydmilla's unexpected visit and of Loff's involvement in place of Paul. "They used this house like a hotel," she concluded. "When they'd got what they wanted, they walked out of the door, and I haven't seen either of them since."

Having finally persuaded her, he would not change his mind about their trip to Estonia—"Channah will look after you if Loff's still away"—he spent the afternoon at the Bank. The atmosphere there was as unsettling as at home. He asked, innocently enough, to see Popov's successor and was given no time even to glance through the pile of documents awaiting his return when he was summoned to a man introduced as an aide to Count Witte—a small, plump, pale-featured little person whose body-temperature (it must have been extraordinarily high) misted his pince-nez and necessitated his constantly taking them off to wipe them clear.

"Your Excellency, your Excellency, welcome back after what was—may we say?—a most satisfactory trip."

He shook hands moistly and Paul involuntarily shuddered. He was ushered to a chair.

"I was expecting to meet Director Popov," he lied blandly.

"Of course." The man nodded but offered no explanation. "My name, incidentally, is Serkov. Andrei Fyodorovitch."

"As I said, I was expecting to see Director Popov."

"Of course, of course. But Director Popov is—may we say?—no longer with us."

"I heard a rumour that he was in Siberia."

"Exactly." Serkov put his hands together and nodded meaningfully, as though Paul had been delicately correct.

"May I ask why?"

Serkov looked suddenly serious, more like a man, less like a slug, Paul thought. "Best not to go too deeply into that, your Excellency. Our friend Popov is a person—may we say?—of the past." His expression changed on the instant; he now smiled broadly, his eyes glowed confidently. "His Excellency Paul von Hagen is the Man of the Future."

"I don't understand." Paul had known instinctively that this was not a man to be trusted and glanced across the desk with veiled eyes.

Serkov smiled again and nodded, as though in a travesty of agreement with Paul's hidden thoughts. "Or—may we say?—His Excellency Herr Director Paul von Hagen." He giggled mischievously at his little joke and leaned back. Slowly, his smile faded. The rabbit was out of the hat, but the audience didn't applaud. Disappointed, he opened the file in front of him and, almost sulkily, passed the first of the pile of documents across to Paul. "The Count's Commission," he said dully. "You are appointed Director in Popov's place."

Paul was genuinely startled and had a hundred questions, impossible, at that moment, to formulate coherently.

"It's probably best if you take the file and read it for yourself, your Excellency. The Count makes his instructions perfectly clear, I'm sure. And I shall always be here—may we say?—to offer whatever poor help I can."

Paul ignored the offer and looked at the file. It consisted largely of every one of Paul's communications from Shimonoseki. Each was in date order and authoritatively annotated. Every step in the harvest that might be gathered from the peace negotiations—a harvest entirely to the benefit of Russia and the Bank—was explicitly expressed. Here was the Tsar's prescription for the absorption of Manchuria as a new province of the Russian Empire. Here was a list of names—famous soldiers and sailors, one underlined—signifying the Tsar's choice of Viceroy for the province. Here, even, was a request to the Army Department for the transfer from the Preobrazhensky Regiment of Guards to the new Manchurian Defence Force of Colonel Sergei Ouroussoff. And here, further down the pile, a detailed survey of the Chinese Eastern Railway with its branch to Port Arthur. Attached were recommendations as to route, mileage and cost. Paul read them scarcely believing that these were his own words, and this, his own swirling signature at the bottom of each page.

He wished he could show Leonore why he had been away so long. Unfortunately, each of the documents had a heavy black stamp at the top: STRICTLY PRIVATE!

Popov came at the bottom of the pile. The man was, it seemed, guilty of bribery, corruption and speculation beyond what was acceptable. Now he was humbled to Novosibirsk to do little more than check bills of lading and count each train as it went by.

Paul sat in his quiet office while daylight died in the street outside. He thought deeply about his change of status. Why had someone engineered it? He could find no reason except that somebody, for his own ends, preferred having him sitting here instead of Popov. Flattering, of course, but he would have been more at ease had he known why. He couldn't, nonetheless, avoid a flush of pride. Doubtless "they" knew more of what went on at every level than was easily believable. He would, himself, in the future, have to be very careful.

Meanwhile…he would have been more content had he been able to find the brown envelope referring to himself that he had watched Popov lock away in his drawer. Now he had Popov's keys in his hand and, when he was sure most of the staff had left the building, he searched the desk and, afterwards, the office, as carefully as any common thief. The triumphs of the day became less certain. Someone else, someone unknown, now had that envelope.

CHAPTER 16

▼

1895

Winter in the Tobolsk region had been less severe than usual; the sudden Siberian spring came early. Ice on the Irtysh River cracked with a series of mighty explosions. Sunshine encouraged tiny flowers to bloom under the trees and along the swampy banks of the River.

The village where Ida was to go was far down-stream. It appeared on no map and was never likely to. It was only a few dozen rickety wooden huts caulked with mud. In summer they were like ovens, in winter like iceboxes. Spring was the time when the people voluntarily abandoned their discomfort, reconciled to being viciously attacked by the million mosquitoes that always appeared with the sun. They were starving and thirsting for human blood.

The people living in this place appeared at a glance to be less than human. They lacked the essential for humanity's survival: Hope! That was apparent in their flat, expressionless faces. Everywhere else, Russia was stirring but here, nothing at all was happening. These wretched people were descended from unfortunates here in days long-since forgotten. Now they bred together because they couldn't help themselves. Their couplings produced under-sized and disease-ridden children who, once they could walk, roamed the tundra hunting and gathering. Ida was supposed to catch them there and turn them into pupils.

When the ground was free from frost and flood, their parents grew what they could—potatoes, a few melons, a cucumber or two. Their River was generous when they fished her. In summer, the youngest and strongest of the men sailed her, if they could get jobs on the barges carrying cargoes of everything from the Chinese border to the Arctic Ocean.

They had a priest, this disregarded people, as much a prisoner of apathy as any of them. As a young man he was a Khiyst, dancing through Siberia in religious frenzies that invariably climaxed in sweat-soaked copulation. Ejaculation was clearly the evidence of God's blessing, but after the moment, nothing else ever happened. Nothing was ever changed except that he grew older, bored, disillusioned. Sex held no further hope. He became yet one more wandering Holy Man, always moving, begging off believers no better-off than himself, until he wandered into this village. He never wandered away again; no one knew why.

He gave nothing for his keep, no services, no consolation. He lived on the charity of the poverty-stricken old women who daren't see him starve; he was holy, and his presence assured them of something they needed to believe.

The authorities chose this village for Ida's confinement because it was a dead place, and they wanted her to be dead. Soon they would destroy the record of her name at Kishinev, and then she would no longer exist for them. Her friends in New York would never hear from her again; they too, would conclude she must be dead. Her family would never hear from her either, and they too, reluctantly, would believe her dead. Eventually, she would forget her own existence in another world and she would be dead, even to herself.

Until she first saw it, she hadn't imagined such places existed. By then, although Loff cushioned her for some of the time, she was inured to shock and suffering. Her anguish began the night policemen, shouting to terrify their victims, stormed into her meeting near Kishinev. She had been warned not to hold it. A Zionist comrade said the time and place was known to the authorities. As a Zionist, he was sure the traitor was Orthodox, intent on halting a Diaspora, which they were convinced would mean the disappearance of the only people on earth with whom God had chosen to make a Covenant.

She ignored the warning. Her work was too important and, in any case, she couldn't believe any Jew would cooperate with the police in the persecution of other Jews. Someone did, though!

Ida was taken. The police took her to their station, beat her and shouted questions to which they weren't interested in listening to the answers. When that particular torment was over, they locked her in a dark cell. The door was slammed with metallic finality and she didn't know if they would ever let her out again. The uncertainty of what was to happen to her became the basis of her fear. She believed her physical torment was over. When the door opened, a guard brought her a piece of maggot-ridden meat. She went on her knees before him, pleading for a candle. He told her he knew what she wanted, placed a boot against her breast and kicked her on to the filthy floor. Before she understood his intention and tried to fight him off, he was fumbling through her clothes. She screamed and struggled, but he was too heavy on her. She could not move, and he raped her roughly, penetrating her mechanically, unemotionally. When he had done, he sighed, part contentment, part mockery.

"You're not bad," he told her. "I'll have to tell the others."

That was only the first visit of its kind. They came to her in varying degrees of brutality. In one of these attacks, she kneed the man in the testicles while he undid his belt and let down his trousers. Crazy with pain, he struck at her face with his belt. She lost her left eye. The buckle scooped out her left eye. The pain was searing, indescribable, and her treatment worse than ever. Going with the Jew-whore became a lighthearted sport. Her disfigurement was a comic attraction, and the obscenity of the perversions they practiced on her became increasingly horrendous. She would have killed herself, had she known how.

Eventually their interest was satiated or they received orders. They took her to Kishinev and, after that, to an open-roofed pen at the railway station where she waited with others like animals on the way to the slaughterhouse.

*   *   *   *

Loff got off the train uncertainly, feeling half-spy, half-criminal. He had been told he would be met by a man dressed as a peasant. The man would identify himself as Boris. Sure enough, out of the gloom of the darkening platform, a man came forward to greet him loudly and excitedly.

"Master, master," he bellowed, "here I am, your Excellency...faithful old Boris. Your Honour is back with us at last, safe and sound, thank the good Lord."

He babbled on, the most obvious of old retainers, while they left the station. Then his voice changed completely. He was evidently of the new middle-class, a Russian from the north, professional, perhaps.

"We don't know exactly where she is but if she's still here, she'll be in police cells."

"I'll go there."

"Take plenty of money, though. They won't tell you anything without the usual bribes."

The man saw him into a cab before disappearing into the darkness. The driver was intrigued. Why did he run off so suddenly? And who was this man lounging on his cushions who'd spoken so authoritatively. What was his business at the police station likely to be?

Among cab-drivers it was a tradition, whenever a stranger arrived, to find out all they could about him and to warn anyone who might be at risk. Government spies and inspectors came in all shapes and sizes. This one spoke with an accent that wasn't from anywhere near this part of the country. He behaved like a nobleman, but so many people did, these days, particularly with the power of the law behind them.

Whoever he was, he must have a purpose in coming here; nobody came to a place like this by chance.

There was no doubt in the driver's mind that he had picked up some kind of policeman; the question was, who was he after? He urged the horse forward slowly while he turned to ask over his shoulder: "Is this your first visit to our little town, your Honour?"

"Can't that horse move any faster?"

"Are you certain you wouldn't like me to go to an hotel first, your Honour? You need a room? This is only a little town, you understand. We go to bed early here. This isn't like…er…"

"Get on with it, can't you?"

The cabman understood that this would take some time and turned off the main road. They entered a maze of lanes where it was too dark for Loff to see anything, and the vehicle lurched from pothole to pothole like a drunken ferry.

"This is a good night to go to the police station, your Honour. Sergeant Korsakin, my cousin's husband is on duty. He'll help your Honour with whatever it is you want. Incidentally, if you don't want to go to an hotel, his wife would let you have a room. She'd do it as a favour to me, of course. And you won't find any bugs in her beds, I can assure you."

His laughter ended in a squeal when Loff brought his cane down hard on his shoulder.

"Be quiet"! The police station! At once!"

The driver was subdued; his cabman's social duty didn't go so far as to suffer physical violence. In two turns they were there. Loff ordered him to wait and rushed inside, banging the door noisily behind him.

The office was gloomy, lit by two lamps hanging from hooks in the ceiling. It smelt abominably of paraffin, sweat, and urine. Sergeant Korsakin, lolling at his desk and sweating unstintingly, was adding to the stench. Behind him, a constable sat uncomfortably on a narrow bench, his back against the wall. The sergeant looked up insolently.

His constable, less confident, didn't know whether or not to rise. He was stationary with knees bent, half sitting, half standing.

"Sergeant Korsakin?" There was something in Loff's look and in the fact that his name was known to him that made the sergeant uneasy. He was obviously from somewhere "higher up." He stood, scraping his chair and breathing heavily.

"At your service, your Honour."

"I want to see a prisoner."

"Ah!" This could mean that the sergeant had, without knowing it, arrested someone important. It could turn out to be beneficial for him.

"Yes, your Honour; certainly, your Honour." He turned to the constable who was still half-crouching. "You! Fetch his Honour a chair from the other room." He pulled a ledger across his desk and opened it. "Now, your Honour, if I might have your name, please...for our records, you see."

"Baron Loff von Hagen."

"Baron Loff von Hagen! Yes, I see, your Excellency. And your Excellency wants to see..."

"Ida Goldfarb."

The sergeant looked up sharply. "The Jew agitator?"

"Has she been tried?"

Korsakin looked uncertain. "There was no need, your Excellency. They'll might do that at Kishinev, though it isn't usual in this kind of case." That was an odd question, he was thinking. If this were an official with any rights, he would surely have known how the system worked. "And your reason for wishing to see this young woman?"

"She is my sister-in-law."

Sergeant Korsakin relaxed. You never knew who was who these days. He closed the ledger and pushed it away. "The hours for requesting visits to prisoners are between nine and ten in the morning. Come back tomorrow and my colleague will deal with you."

In an explosion of rage, Loff brought his stick down on the man's desk only millimetres from his fingers. With its upward swing he caught one of the lamps, which now oscillated crazily backwards and forwards, throwing its light from one corner of the room to the other.

Korsakin cringed. "She's not here, your Honour," he spluttered, "truly, she's not here. We sent her to Kishinev earlier this evening."

In Kishinev, negotiations were easier and, Loff felt, cleaner. The policeman there, a Lieutenant smelling strongly of pomade, was immediately forthcoming—for a fee. Ida was in the pen at the railway station, waiting with others for transport. More money changed from hand to hand. She would be going to the Tobolsk region.

Loff went to the Station. The pen was easy to find, at the end of the platform and exactly what it was called: a pen, a stout wire sty open to wind and weather. It was crowded with men, women and children, loosely chained at the waist. He paced up and down outside, and he was not the only one. Other people were there, some seeking loved ones, others entertainment.

It was impossible to recognise any individual in the dirty, huddled crush inside the wire. Some came close, their fingers waving through the mesh like fronds of sea anenomes seeking food. Others sat on the ground, passive, accepting that there was nothing to be done. Loff walked up and down four times and was halfway through the fifth course when he heard a man's voice calling him by name:

"*Herr Baron! Herr Baron!*"

He stopped. It wasn't easy in that mob to distinguish who'd spoken. But he was eventually he was attracted by the stare of someone with fair, wavy hair to his shoulders, a short straight nose, blue eyes, neat lips...a good-looking young man who...Oh, God! Whatever could a young man who looked like that have done to be here? Loff moved to where the young man stood.

"Ida says I must thank you for coming and ask you not to tell anybody what has happened to her."

"Ida? You know Ida? Where is she? I want to see her."

"She doesn't want to be seen, your Excellency. Please. She is alive. It would be kinder if you went away."

"No! Tell her I must see her. I want to help. I'll stay here until I know she's been taken away." The young man sighed and went back into the crowd. He stopped by a bundle of rags on the ground. It was only the gentle curve of the back that betrayed her as a female. He bent down and said something. For a moment nothing happened. Then the bundle stood up, turned and faced Loff full on.

Oh, yes; oh, yes! Loff recognised her at once when he saw her face and that lustrous black hair. But this was not the confident, laughing young woman who left Berlin that summer for New York. There was only one of her sparkling, laughter-loving eyes, glazed now with suffering but...only one! Where the other should have been there was only a gaping, black and bloody hole.

They took her out of the pen two days later, undid the chain and put her on a train. A guard dragged her along the platform, holding her plait, and pushed her into a carriage with five other women. She was too confused even to be thankful that she wouldn't be traveling in a cattle wagon with the others. The women offered her the sympathy of fellow sufferers. They tore strips off their under-skirts to make bandages to cover that hideous hole.

The journey took six weeks, most of it stationary in sidings while more important trains howled by. At Tobolsk, she was taken off and chained and chained again. A guard pushed her into another pen, but only for an hour or two until she was taken, quite gently, to an office in the station building.

"Ida!" The man's voice was low, gentle and distantly familiar. Perhaps this was not another beginning of her torment after all. "Ida, my dear, you can't have forgotten me. You're safe now, my dear."

She looked at him and caught her breath. Loff von Hagen!

He advanced and put his arm around her. "Don't worry. It will never be so bad again, I promise you."

Her body relaxed against his, dry-eyed because she had no more tears to shed. "Does Leah know?" she whispered.

"No one knows but me."

"Please, please, I beg you…don't tell her."

The day unfolded in a succession of surprises; she had never expected to receive human treatment ever again. Loff was there all the time. He had been spending his money wisely, cunningly. Years ago, when he was prosecuting in the courts, there had been rumours and corruption suffered by the young people he worked against. He didn't believe any of it then; his faith in the system was too strong. It all came back to him now, and he knew it had been true. He used his knowledge as wisely as he used his money.

He paid for her place in the railway carriage. He paid for her food on the journey—although she received very little of it. At Tobolsk, he paid the local Commandant to release her from the pen and to his parole. The man struck an expensive bargain, but Ida was to be in Loff's charge until it was finally decided where to send her.

He took her to a hotel where she could bathe for the first time in weeks. He had new clothes brought in. He fed her. He found a doctor to clean her wound. They sat together that evening with a bottle of vodka between them and approached, crab-like but smiling, the subject uppermost in both their minds.

"Well, my little one, things are not so bad, eh?"

"Oh, Loff…" Her shoulders sagged.

"Remember those arguments you had with Leonore and my brother in Berlin…when you insisted on going to America?"

She was pleased to be reminded of times when life had been normal.

"That was when I first admired you, my dear."

"They were right, though. I should have listened. Oh, Loff, when I got to New York…the stories I heard. Those poor people, that was the real beginning…"

"But you didn't have to come back here, surely. You could have helped them in New York, raised money…cared for them…"

"Oh Loff, Loff…" She was surprised to find herself weeping. "I had to do more than that. And once I'd started, there was no turning back."

"You don't think, do you, that you were being used?"

She shrugged. How could she or anyone tell? There were so many individual interests involved in the changes swirling around them.

He began to laugh, embarrassed because he knew it was a question he shouldn't have asked. She was a young person, idealistic as youngsters and as he, to his regret, would never be again. "We haven't exactly beaten the system my dear, but the system hasn't beaten us either, has it?"

"Only thanks to you. And not in the right way, have we?"

"It was money! That's the curse of it! Without money, I could have done nothing. That's the way it's always been."

"And it's got to change. Oh, don't think I'm not grateful to you, Loff…you've given me the courage not to kill myself. But there will have to come a day when people realise that justice is even more important than money…and just as powerful."

That was weeks ago now, and he had stayed with her, caring for her, soothing her in her punishment. Now it was time for him to go home. The track to Tobolsk was clear for a carriage to get through. Ida stood in the doorway of the hut he'd had built for her, surrounded by a group of filthy-faced children who had learned not to be afraid of either of them. Their parents continued to suspect him for being a Baron and inflicting on their children a Jewish schoolmistress. But during the weeks he was there, no other evil occurred. Now he was going. They stood around the hut, watching his parting with Ida. It was cheerful. He left her confident, with promises of a return very soon. The children sniffing and holding her skirts regretted their loss of kopeks in the future.

Finally back in Saint Petersburg, Loff was told that Leonore and the children had already left for the Estate. Paul was in his office, however, and was obviously a little annoyed at this unexpected visit.

"We thought you might even be dead. We'd heard nothing for so long. And now you turn up without warning, just when I haven't much time to spare."

Loff laughed. "That's a sour greeting, brother."

"Didn't it ever strike you that you owed me an explanation in all this time? There have been all kinds of Estate matters to be settled. Fermatov can't decide everything, you know."

"I apologise, Paul. I wasn't near a telephone, and there was no postal or telegraph service."

Paul looked suspicious. Had Loff suddenly discovered a sarcastic humour? "Leonore told me you went away in the company of a very dangerous woman. We'd known her years ago...in Italy. But that's over, long since, and I don't want..." He looked around his office uneasily. "I don't have time to talk about her this afternoon. But she associates with all kinds of political scum, plotting God knows what." He cleared his throat, drew out his watch and glanced at it hurriedly. "Loff, I'm sorry, I have an appointment with the Count in about an hour. It goes without saying that I'll help you out of any trouble you're in, if I possibly can. Meet me later. We'll dine at the Club and talk about how I might help."

"That won't be possible," Loff told him stiffly. "I also have appointments."

"Can't you cancel them? You must tell me where you've been and what you've been doing."

Loff rose. "I can tell you that in a couple of sentences, Brother. I've been to Tobolsk. Ida is near there in exile. She's had a ghastly time. When the police took her, one of them gouged out her eye during a rape."

He left abruptly and hated himself afterwards, when he remembered his brother's stricken face. He left in a hurry. Some of this haste was triggered by guilt and hurt pride. He had expected Paul to receive him as a brother. Instead, he was evidently an irritating interruption, perhaps even a dangerous one.

Certainly, they'd received him at the door of the Bank as a nobleman, albeit a provincial nobleman. A flunky led him along marble corridors to an anteroom where a young clerk took charge. He was announced but had to wait a quarter of an hour before Paul could see him.

Out in the street, he snorted angrily and took a cab to the Ministry of Justice. He was disappointed there, too. He was known by reputation, of course; even the youngest of the clerks were respectful. His was certainly a great name; but a great name from the past, and the past died yesterday. They listened to him politely, but none offered him definite hope of help. The Jews in the south were being very disruptive just now. Why, indeed, should there be so many pogroms if they were not? However, they listened as kindly as courtesy demanded.

"The young lady originates from Warsaw, you say, your Excellency?"

"Perfectly correct."

"Let me see, now…she is a Jew…am I to understand that she is some relation of your own?"

"She is my brother's sister-in-law."

The man sighed. That was regrettable. "From what you tell me, she was holding a radical meeting when they took her. In other words, she is an agitator…a revolutionary."

"That was never proved. There was no investigation…no trial."

"My dear Baron, you must believe me. I deeply regret your anxiety. But neither of us know exactly what happened that night."

"Somebody knows. The police must have records in Kishinev. Get them sent here."

The man's eyes went colder; he bridled and Loff regretted his own peremptory tone; this was no longer the old days—the man was listening to him only on sufferance.

"She's a very young girl," he muttered apologetically. "She'd suffered terribly when I found her."

"Of course, of course…and I am not unfeeling, my dear Baron. But so many of these young people…they come back from abroad and…well…let us say that while they're away they lose all sense of proportion. They truly believe they hold the only key there is to the future. My dear sir…" He raised his shoulders and smiled, "you and I know that's not true, don't we? They give us no credit for also working for reform. But we know, don't we, that shooting and bombing will never take us to Utopia."

Loff took a room at the Moscovskaya and didn't contact Paul again for two days. He spent the time visiting old colleagues. Some of those he would like to have seen were already dead. The live ones listened with varying degrees of sympathy but were all retired and powerless now. No one had the ear of anyone who had any influence. The world had changed much, even in the land of the law. The fact of the matter was evident and, for her, disastrous; Ida was one more dissident Jew, and common sense should have counseled her to stay abroad where she was safe.

The brothers met once more at Paul's club, a lavish institution on Dvortsovaya Naberezhnaya, where everywhere smelt of cigars and rich leather. They talked politely over drinks, mostly about how much Saint Petersburg had changed since they were young men. Paul introduced him to several acquaintances. Throughout their meal he chattered breathlessly about what he'd seen of the Korean War and of how much military techniques had changed since his own experiences in '82. He told amusing stories about international diplomacy; he talked enthusiastically about the new railway and Russia's unrestricted expansion in the East.

"You know, Loff, I really think I should move out there, if I could persuade Leonore to come with me."

"You'll forgive me if I seem to be rude, Paul, but none of this is what I came to talk about. Can we go somewhere quiet?"

Like a man condemned, Paul took him into a snail sitting room. "It's about Ida, of course?"

"Who else?"

"Well?"

"Well! Is that all you have to say?"

"Damn it! What do you want me to say? I'm sorry. Of course, I'm sorry. But how much is my being sorry worth? What good can my being sorry do now?"

"I hoped you would tell me what to do next, Paul…You are a great man now, a Director at the Bank; soon you will be one of the Tsar's Ministers, I'm sure. You know everybody useful to know…"

"That's exactly why I can't do anything about her and please, Loff, neither must you. You're well enough known yourself and as my brother…"

"The von Hagen name used to have some influence. If we have any influence left, we should use it on Ida's behalf, surely."

"We might have in the old days. Now we daren't."

"You used to call her 'your little Ida', remember? You used to be so fond of her."

Paul brought his hand down heavily on the arm of his chair. "Don't do this to me, brother. Face the truth! Russian society has changed. We have what the Americans call Capitalism, now…Capitalism and Capitalists. They're an entirely new class, and they're becoming daily more influential. They'll be running the country without us, if we give them half a chance. Up 'til now, we've managed to keep them under control, and the Tsar's on our side, of course. They resent that, too. If they find out anything against us, they'll use it to bring us down if they possibly can."

"And would they bring us down for trying to help poor little Ida, do you think?"

"Poor little Ida is a criminal, Loff."

"That's not true. Nothing was proved. She was never tried."

"They must have something against her. They must have, to treat her as they did."

Loff shook his head. "You say Saint Petersburg is changing, my dear Brother. I think it is we two who are changing most. In the days when I lived here, even though I sent many little Idas into exile, I still went to bed each night with a clear conscience. Now...now I feel I have lived too long."

"For the love of God, Loff, don't talk like that! All I'm saying is we must be careful. I'll send her some money, of course. They'll let some of it through, I expect. She shan't go short of anything if I can help it. And next time I go east, I'll try to visit her."

Loff sighed with the weariness of total disappointment.

"This is goodbye then. I'm taking the morning boat to Reval."

"What?" Paul laughed. "Everybody goes by train nowadays, it's quicker."

"That's why I'm going by boat. I need time to think. Time to think about what else I can do for Ida. Time to think up excuses for your wife when I see her. She doesn't need to know the truth...not yet, at least."

CHAPTER 17

▼

1895

The trip to Reval was good, but not long enough. He couldn't see how else to help. In historical times, he could have thrown himself at the feet of the Tsar and begged for mercy. But you didn't do that any more. You couldn't. The Tsar was even more hemmed in with unapproachable underlings than his own brother. As for excuses to Leonore…he could think of nothing. She would be bound to ask questions. He would have to tell her whatever came into his mind when he saw her, he supposed. And in the winter, perhaps, he would go back to Tobolsk.

At the Estate, his mood was lightened by breathing the air of home and the children's' rapturous welcome. They were old enough now for each to greet him in their own ways. Dorothea was quite like a grown-up young lady. He said, with a confidential wink:

"I still can't remember where I left my arm, Dora."

She smiled distantly and turned her head away with a slight toss. She was too old for that joke now and a cloud of regret faded the sunshine of his present. She introduced Alexei Krimovsky, who greeted him very formally.

"How do you do, your Excellency. It is a privilege to be staying in your house."

Dorothea pulled him away and the boy was relieved to go.

Sonia, still resenting Alexei for occupying so much of Dorothea's attention, adopted her uncle Loff as her particular responsibility. She pushed him firmly into a chair, where she kissed him heartily and put her arms around him protectively.

Marie, her sallow skin turned by sun and sea air to a golden glow that made her almost pretty, kissed him gently on the forehead and smiled without speaking.

Eduard was more the soldier than ever. He clicked his heels and bowed formally, stirring long-lost memories of a visiting recruiting sergeant that weren't altogether pleasant.

"We've been waiting for you, sir. We've missed you tremendously. Will you take us all to the beach tomorrow?"

"We'll see, we'll see, young man." He was wishing children didn't grow up so fast. It was so much better, somehow, when they were all together in Berlin.

Albrecht waddled forward after a little push from his mother, grinning. He stood in front of Loff, resting a hand on each of his uncle's knees.

"Hallo, my little man. And how are you today?"

The boy, as usual, said nothing, but evidently understood the tone to be friendly. He climbed onto Loff's lap and wriggled himself into a comfortable position, prepared to stay there undisturbed for as long as possible.

Leonore offered to take him, but Loff waved her away.

"It is so good to have you back, Loff. We heard nothing for so long. We were very worried."

He laughed. "And now, you see, I am back safe and sound and very soon, doubtless, you will be wishing I would go away again."

"What did Lydmilla want?"

"Er...how shall I put it? The use of my name, only. Some of her friends were in a little trouble."

"I knew it! She knows some terrible people, Paul says. I should never have let you go with her. I used to be very fond of her, you know, but I don't trust her any more.

"There's no need to worry now, my dear. Everything is settled. And now this young man and I are going to spend the rest of the summer getting to know each other, eh, boy?"

After that, she was content to talk about Paul. He told her what a great man his brother was, and she was delighted to hear him saying it.

"My only regret when I think of him is that Margarethe is not here to enjoy him. She was so fond of him. She would never let him see it, of course. To her, showing affection was a weakness. But why doesn't Channah come to welcome me? Doesn't she know I'm here?"

"Of course," Leonore laughed. "She knew it before anyone. Now she's extra busy in her kitchen because of you."

"I'll go to her, then."

"No, don't. She hates being interrupted. All the children try to help, but she won't let them. Me neither. We're all supposed to be on holiday, she says. And then she bangs about the house complaining of how much work there is to do." She laughed, suddenly pleased. "You know, Loff, she's getting to be exactly like my mother."

Loff didn't meet Channah until after their evening meal. Then, with the children in bed and Leonore in her room, the house was quiet, and he sent for her. She came after a little delay, wearing her usual black and carrying household account books.

"I expect you'll want to see these, your Excellency. You'll find them all in order, I think."

"Oh, Channah! Channah! Of course I don't want to see them. It's you I want to see. Put those down. Won't you welcome me home?"

"I thank God you're back safe and sound, your Excellency."

"I've been away a long time."

"I know it. I expected every day you'd send word."

"Aren't you going to ask where I've been?"

"Your Excellency will tell me if he wishes."

"I do wish, Channah. In fact, I must. There's no one else I can talk to. My brother knows what's happened, but I daren't tell my sister-in-law. You're the only one who will understand. My brother doesn't. Oh, Channah! I've needed you so much...your common sense, your strength. How did I manage without you? If I'd known when I left, I would have taken you with me."

Then he told her everything, forced himself to relive every detail, spared neither of them any of the horror, not even the indifference of his reception when he arrived back in Saint Petersburg. He needed her to know how alone, how helpless he was without her.

She listened without saying a word. When he had done, weary, old and weeping with the misery of it all, she sprang from her chair and pressed herself against him, covering his face with her kisses.

"Your Excellency! Your Excellency"! Oh, my poor, poor dear man. My poor dear Loff. Loff, my dear...what a truly good man you are...what a good man."

He put his arm around her, holding her roughly to him. She felt his shoulders straighten beneath her.

"Why, oh why," she pleaded, "why do you think you have to act like cast-iron all the time when in your heart you must know you're finest porcelain?"

That night they lay together on his bed, willing prisoners in each other's arms. They were fully dressed, and neither slept. But they comforted each other through the blackness and until the grey dawn.

When grey dawn came, it heralded a grey day with a blustery breeze. It was too cold to go to the beach, Loff decided.

"If it's warm enough tomorrow, we'll go for a picnic and swim."

He would visit his tenants today, he decided, and Sonia insisted on going with him. She could ride on a leading rein.

Dorothea and Alexei were off rambling in their usual way, and Eduard rushed off to find the village boys with whom he usually played rough games. Leonore was to help Channah in the kitchen. She was genuinely pleased to see her so much more cheerful this morning. Perhaps Channah would share her secrets.

"What about my little friend here? He's still pretending to be a steam locomotive, apparently." The Baron tried hard to participate in all this, but it was impossible to rid himself of Ida's disfigured face as she waved him goodbye at the door of her hut. With her, he had failed. But with these children...they were all so precious to him, he couldn't fail...he mustn't! He wanted to hold every minute of their day in his own hands, so that no harm could come to them.

"He'll be quite all right," Leonore said. "Ulrika got the blacksmith to make him a little spade. He's fascinated by what he sees the men do at the diggings. Ulrika and Anton take him there most days so that he can work alongside them. You must find time to go there and see him one day, Loff."

Albrecht frequently brought the products of these proud labours; tiny mites of amber and ugly lumps of shale that took his fancy. Leonore and Ulrika treasured them in their own rooms.

Most often Ulrika and Anton would take him along the track— grass no longer—to the Orthodox Church. There was generally a cluster of old women there, gossiping in the sunshine, who willingly minded him while they went inside to pray. Sometimes, Tikhon was outside there with a group of children who should probably have been in school. He was their special entertainment. Today he was flying a kite.

He saw them coming and gave the kite-line to a boy in the crowd. He was particularly fond of Ulrika because she was a convert, though he often upbraided her for not coming to him for conversion, so that he could have put her down on his own meager score!

They had exchanged only a few words when there was a howling in the crowd. The boy with the line had failed them. The kite came crashing to earth. Ulrika and Anton followed the priest to see whether or not it was damaged, but Albrecht was there before them. He snatched it from the boy who held it.

"Man! Man!" he shouted and held it up to show Ulrika. "Man! Man!" he shouted again, while the adults round him all stood astonished. It was indeed a kite in the shape of a man, a man with sausage-like arms and legs, a great fat body and a large round head, all made from sisal-strengthened paper, attached to a rough birch bark cross.

Father Tikhon looked embarrassed. "It is not a very nice kite, I know," he said, "but I was telling the children the story of Christ's Crucifixion and Ascension. They learn quicker when they play."

The old women were not interested. "He speaks," they were whispering to each other. "He never spoke before. It is a miracle. Christ has touched him." And they crossed themselves rapidly, over and over again and some fell on their knees.

The subject of this reverent wonder was pulling at the priest's skirts and shouting like Eduard at his most military moments: "Man fly! Man fly now!"

The priest took the kite, let out the line and raised it high again. Albrecht watched it go, bewitched by the figure soaring above him. "Man fly! Man fly!" he shouted to everybody who would listen. Then he was pulling the priest's skirts again. "Now me," he was pleading. "Now me! Me fly like kite."

Father Tikhon looked down at him, puzzled for a moment. Then he handed the kite line to Anton and picked up the child, who laughed because the long black beard tickled his neck. "We can't fly like Him, little one," he told him softly "Not yet. He was someone special, and something special happened to Him. You'll understand why, one day."

But Albrecht wasn't interested in what would happen one day. Now was all that concerned him. "Me fly! Me fly now!" he ordered, growing angry.

The priest looked indecisive, then moved away from the crowd. "All right. You shall fly, my little one." He turned the boy round in his arms and took his right arm and his right leg in a firm grasp. "All right? I've got you. Are you ready? Now! You are going to fly!"

He held the boy away from him and turned round and round as quickly as he could. Albrecht indeed appeared to be flying, flying waist-high from the ground. He screamed and whooped and shouted in ecstasy until, thoroughly giddy, the priest staggered to a stop.

But Albrecht wouldn't tolerate being ground-based after that. Anton had to fly him, and after Anton the priest again, then Anton...Later in the day, the men at the diggings had to stop their work to fly him. "Me fly! Me fly! Me fly now!" he ordered everyone.

At home, Leonore laughed and protested and puffed that she couldn't fly him herself. But the footmen and the kitchen boy were brought in to do so. And that night, Leonore and Ulrika spent a long time putting him to bed.

"You're sleepy. You're sleepy. Albrecht, say it now. Me sleepy." They repeated it again and again. But Albrecht wouldn't say it. Instead, he closed his eyes reluctantly and yawned.

"No! Albrecht fly," he murmured.

Leonore spent a long time at her prayers that night and wrote to Paul in the morning. She received a telegraphed message in reply.

I TOLD YOU HE WOULD TALK WHEN HE HAD SOME-
THING TO SAY LOVE PAUL

CHAPTER 18

▼

1896

Having discovered speech, Albrecht couldn't be restrained. He became more loquacious every day. The children, with the exception of Marie, made him their new game. They encouraged him to talk because, as yet, he hadn't control over his tones. His voice swooped and rose again like a heron on a fishpond. They thought he sounded very funny. Paul found him amusing, too, but his reaction was better controlled. Both he and Leonore remonstrated against the others making their little brother too much the centre of their attention.

Leonore took him back to the specialists because she feared his gift of speech might not be permanent. The doctors tested him warily, solemnly, unwilling to commit themselves optimistically. He had a grasp of language, they had to admit, though his inflections were hopelessly incorrect. "The little fellow can apparently talk, your Excellency, and you must be satisfied with that." As to his further development, they could promise nothing, but prepared her in their subtle ways to expect to find him, as he matured, deficient in other fields.

Leonore needed more reassurance than that. Assurance for her child's future, she believed, could only be attained through her own gratitude. In her dilemma, she longed for Ulrika's unquestioning faith. The young German had by now plunged deeply into the enigmas of Orthodoxy. Nowadays, when Ulrika entered a church, she had no doubt she stood at a portal to heaven. The shaggy priests were angels anchored to the earth, the gloom beyond the candle-glow the dark before celestial dawn. These were the properties of paradise, and when she died, she would enjoy them through all eternity.

No Jew could easily contemplate conversion to Orthodoxy; social history of the two precluded that. But Leonore believed, with Ulrika, that Albrecht's release from wordlessness was a miracle, and that Christ had worked His will through Father Tikhon. Anton, a life-long Orthodox, was skeptical, but not more so than Paul. They discouraged Leonore from talking about it. She thanked God privately, and as surely as she could, but never felt the Catholic ritual expressed all that was in her heart. She needed to humiliate herself with an almost sexual frenzy, but didn't know how to do so. Her gratitude centred on Ulrika as much on her God. She developed a mystical obsession with the girl and could never fully express her gratitude.

Saint Petersburg thankfully emerged from its lavender mourning to prepare for the celebration of the Tsar's Coronation and marriage. It was a difficult, self-commercial time, demanding restrained acceptance of the necessity to be joyful. Leonore took more serious interest in Ulrika's marriage than in the Coronation and marriage of the Tsar.

She tried to talk to Anton about how she felt, hoping that, as a born-Orthodox, he would be as pious as Ulrika. He made it clear that kind of thing was women's talk. His own concern was quite other at the moment. Ulrika had been intransigent all winter. His sexual fantasies were becoming more and more compelling. The Tsar's Coronation and his wedding would be at the end of May. That was surely too long for him to have to wait. Anton's prayers were that the Good Lord might pity him and create a really important miracle: by bringing forward the regal nuptials to relieve these dreams that gave him no peace day or night.

Paul showed lordly disinterest in the private affairs of his staff, but Leonore was compelled to make him interested.

"We must make arrangements about Ulrika's wedding, darling," she began one Sunday morning, when they were home after Mass. "She doesn't want to be married in Saint Petersburg, you know."

He restrained a sigh, but signified his irritation by pointedly putting down his newspaper. "I'm not prepared to discuss this any further, Leonore. It's nonsense and, I've more important things on my mind. Ulrika should be grateful she's getting married at all."

"I'm not asking you to send them to his parents in the South, dear, nor to pay for them to go to hers in Germany. It's much simpler than that. She now tells me she'd like it to be on the Estate. Isn't that sweet? They feel they're part of the family, especially since…"

"And whom does she think is going to marry her there?"

"Father Tikhon, of course. Because of Albrecht, you see. She feels the Father was responsible and…Paul, darling, we should be grateful to him for that."

"Out of the question!"

She was genuinely surprised. "Why?"

He looked at her steadily and, for the first time in their marriage, she saw a glimmer of dislike in his eyes. "No, well…that's the difference between us. You wouldn't understand, would you? They are not part of the family, and for them to be married by Tikhon is out of the question."

She started back, determined not to cry. "What do you mean…I wouldn't understand?"

"It's a question of tradition, my dear," he said, not meaning to sound so unkind. "You must remember that immemorial usage has to be taken into account. You undertook an obligation to respect that usage when you married me."

"Oh, I never forget I'm your wife…how I'm expected to behave," she said bitterly. "I can't forget I'm Albrecht's mother, too, and that God chose Father Tikhon to bring him out of his silent world. To me, that's more important than anything else."

"You're talking Ulrika's claptrap. Come now, Leonore...you're not like her. You're my wife, not a common housemaid!"

"She was there, Paul. She saw what happened."

"Ulrika's a hysterical, religion-crazed virgin, and if she doesn't settle down after she's married, Anton's in for a very poor time of it!"

"Paul! That's disgusting!"

He took up his paper. "In any case," he added casually, "Loff will be too busy to have us. He'll be making his arrangements to go to Moscow for the Coronation. We're joining him there. He's taken rooms for us all at the Metropole."

Leonore left the room and, that afternoon, wrote to Clementine.

Dearest Clementine,

I'm so much in your debt already, I hardly dare ask you for one more favour. If you can help just this once, though, I'll be grateful. I'd better say first of all that I haven't mentioned my idea to the couple concerned, so if it isn't convenient to you, you only have to say so, and no harm will be done.

Ulrika—I've told you about her and about how Albrecht started to talk largely because of her—is marrying her Anton during the Coronation. She wants the wedding to be on the Estate, but Paul won't hear of it.

Truly, he can be such a pompous prig sometimes!

To save her being totally disappointed, I want to offer an alternative. My plan is that they should go to Moscow. There'll be so many people there, so much excitement, so much to see; it'll be really wonderful for them, with all the celebrations and processions. And we'll be staying with Paul's brother at the Metropole, so we'll be able to look after them, and they won't be any trouble to anyone else.

The reason I'm writing to you, my dear, is to ask whether you could possibly let them have a room in your flat and recommend a local church for the ceremony. They could come down on the night train and get married the morning they arrive—it needs only to be a simple affair—so they'll want only one room afterwards.

Hopefully we'll be seeing a lot of you and Sasha while we're down and can look after the two of them at the same time.

Perhaps you'll have the flat full already. If that's the case, please don't worry; just let me know as soon as you can...or perhaps you'll even know somewhere else they might stay, instead.

My dear, I can't possibly say how much we are looking forward to seeing you again. Paul likes Sasha very much, you know. He talks about him quite often because he's hoping he can persuade him to take a job on the railway they're going to build in China. He thinks Sasha is a remarkable man, and you can imagine how much it pleases me to hear him say so.

For ever and ever with love, my dear,

Your own

L.

The letter was delivered while Lydmilla Fyodorovna was visiting Moscow; she often stayed with Clementine and Sasha these days. For both of them, she was a woman of mystery. She made frequent trips all over Russia but never said why, nor where. Sasha was disturbed by her. Clementine felt they had a mutual loyalty through Ida, and worked hard to establish a dependable friendship. That wasn't possible. Lydmilla Fyodorovna kept her emotions as tightly corseted as the meager body beneath her black dress.

"I must write and tell her 'no,'" was Clementine's immediate reaction.

"I think you should wait 'til Sasha gets home. He may think it's good to have them here."

"We simply can't have them. The others will be here then."

"Exactly! And these two would be very nice, I think. Young lovers...You remember what that was like, Clementine? They'll make everything seem quite different. And, in any case, I've said all along, Boris is wrong. He doesn't need so many comrades here at the same time. It's not a good idea."

When Sasha came home from the railway yards, he was enthusiastic. "This is splendid! Two innocent young visitors from out of town. I myself will take them to see all the sights. We'll be a happy little family all during the celebrations, and we shan't need anyone else at all. I'll tell Boris his friends need not come."

Leonore read Clementine's reply and put it to one side. There would be time enough later to tell Ulrika what arrangements she had made. For the moment, she was occupied body and soul by a sudden, unexpected visit from Rachel.

Rachel was magnificent, quite regal. She was tall and slim, with a beautiful bosom and molded hips that Leonore's friends envied and whispered about as soon as her back was turned. Poulanskaya was no longer their talking-point; Rachel took her place, and Leonore felt like a dumpy, middle-aged Jewish housewife. Rachel felt no need to adhere to the general code of semi-mourning. Her business was adornment, and she adorned herself for this trip in a bottle-green traveling costume with a skirt that fell to the floor in a frolic of gatherings and flounces. Her jacket was tightly buttoned to a degree that left everyone speechless.

Princess Krimovskaya snorted at all the admiration. "When I was young, every woman had a duty to look like that," she said, "and we did."

Rachel had already been to Moscow on business. Now she was in Saint Petersburg to stay with Leonore, so long as it was understood that she was working, would need to be out a great deal, and to return to Warsaw as soon as possible.

"I'd filled my Coronation orders before the strike began. What I'll do for my winter collection..."

"Strike?"

"Surely, even you must have heard about that, darling."

"No."

"It's terrible. All the mills in Lodz and everywhere else are closed...even the English-owned ones. The workers are demanding a fifteen-hour day. Can, you imagine? I'd be happy if I only had to work for fifteen hours a day."

She opened her bag irritably and took out a box of Turkish cigarettes and a long amber holder. As she looked at it, her mood seemed to change. She held it out for Leonore to see.

"I bought this in Warsaw, darling. It's from your brother-in-law's factory. Isn't it marvelous?"

She lit the cigarette. The air was immediately contaminated by a pungency that was foreign and nauseous.

Leonore wanted to tell her to put it out, but she didn't dare. Rachel was not like her younger sister any more, beyond being told what to do.

"I've been everywhere in Moscow trying to buy up stocks, but…my dear…the prices! I don't suppose I'll do any better here, but I must try, I suppose. I should have gone straight to England, perhaps, but just think of the cost!"

Leonore nodded, but could think of nothing to say. She longed for the children to come in—the only card she held to play against all this cold, sparkling glamour.

"Cigarette, darling?"

Leonore shook her head.

"I thought not." The tone was cruelly dismissive. "I'm hoping Paul can help me. Nobody in Warsaw knows anything about anything, of course. But women still come to us for high fashion. If that weren't the case, I'd be back in Paris. Sometimes I think I was a fool ever to have left. Men!" She angrily stubbed out her cigarette and lit another immediately.

The children came eventually, but their Aunt showed no interest in them. She didn't welcome their grubby fingers on her bottle-green velvet. Leonore sent them out of the room and fidgeted, embarrassed, until Paul came home from the Bank.

Then she excused herself. She had to change, she said. She knew it would be a hopeless quest, however long she took, whatever she wore; she would never meet Rachel's standards.

Paul had greeted their visitor warmly and with astonishment, admiration and amusement. She was certainly identifiable as the Rachel of childhood, as much in control of the situation as ever. But wasn't she, perhaps, a little too much so? She had acquired a hardness that was hardly attractive, and a sexual magnetism that was difficult to ignore. She would have been irresistibly desirable to many men, though not to him. He could all too easily see her living in the shadows of Saint Petersburg's smartest laxities.

"You haven't changed in the least little bit, darling," she told him, "except that you've grown even more distinguished, of course." It was a sharply insincere compliment.

"And you, my dear," he began, but she waved him to be silent.

"I'm sorry, darling. I never allow men to flatter me—on principle. They never mean it."

He laughed uncertainly. "How do you know I was about to flatter you?"

"Weren't you?"

He shrugged.

"You mustn't be offended, my dear." She lit a cigarette and went on quickly: "You see? A von Hagen match. A von Hagen holder."

He glanced at them briefly and nodded.

"I often think of you. You never think of me, I suppose. No! Don't pretend. I think about you and that lovely little flat we had in Praga. I sometimes drive by it for old times' sake. It meant so much. That flat was the beginning of my life. Leonore adored you in those days. I hope she still does...? Perhaps I was half in love with you myself."

"I'd no idea."

"Of course not, darling. You had eyes only for Leonore."

"You make me feel guilty."

"Don't be. Women always take revenge, you know. In later life, they invariably hate the men they used to be in love with when they were young. They never forgive them for being the cause of their self-betrayal."

He looked as helpless as he felt, and she smiled condescendingly.

"No, I don't really hate you, and I shouldn't taunt you, should I? Don't worry, darling. If you feel you owe me anything, you can do me a small favour."

"Oh?"

"You know everyone with any influence these days. Paul, this is serious! The government must send in troops to settle the textile strikes. They'll destroy my business if they're allowed to go on, and not only mine! Unrest and unreasonable demands will spread to every industry in the country, if you don't stop them immediately."

"You overestimate my influence, my dear. There is nothing I can possibly do about that."

"You could talk to someone, surely. Clementine said you were one of the Count's favourite young men. You must convince him this strike is only the first of many. Revolutionaries commit outrages in Poland every day. Here in Russia, you don't know how bad things are. These strikers are just as guilty; they'll destroy everything if they're not stopped now."

"It's a dispute between workers and employers, as I understand it. It's not a political affair, and there's nothing the police can do, so long as they don't break the law."

"That's a feeble point of view, Paul. Nothing happens in this country that isn't political. The police should go in with troops to back them up, immediately. Put the ringleaders in gaol. They're all Jews, of course, and the government isn't usually slow to act where Jews are involved."

Paul stared at her, and there was a throbbing silence between them while she smoked with increased vehemence. At last, she said:

"Very well, darling, if you can't, you can't. There is something else you might do for me, though. I gather you often go to the East."

"Vladivostok and Manchuria."

"You're sure to know someone there who can help. Chinese silk, darling. It's hardly used here, and it's hideously expensive, but I have some wonderful ideas for oriental negligees and dinner gowns. Nothing like them will ever have been seen here before. But my hands are tied. I haven't the material in stock, and I can't possibly go to get it."

He laughed. "My dear Rachel, when I go east, I spend all my time with politicians, financiers and railway engineers. None of them would know anything about dress materials, I'm sure."

"Darling..."

"I'm sorry, Rachel, I really am."

"But you must try, darling. I don't know anybody else I can trust, you see. And I can't possibly go myself. I can't get away for more than two or three days at a time, except in the most serious emergency, like this strike. It's caused an absolute famine of materials."

"I really would like to help you, Rachel, but..."

"My business is successful...very successful, I'd say. But it's small. I don't employ many people. That's why it's successful. Nothing happens there that I don't oversee myself. Nothing is done there that I can't do myself. You can't trust anybody, today. And...and of course," she added slowly and coyly, "I would see that you weren't out of pocket."

He stiffened. "I've said...I can't possibly help you, Rachel." He turned to leave and said over his shoulder: "I wouldn't even risk trying to find an agent for you. I wouldn't know how."

When they met for dinner, it was as though they'd signed a joint agreement to say nothing that would distress or embarrass Leonore. They chatted inconsequentially about the Coronation and the forthcoming royal marriage. Rachel could tell them in advance what many of the women there would be wearing; she had put in the finishing touches herself. Paul was bored and speculating how soon he could go to his study. Leonore was fascinated.

Afterwards, in the small sitting room, Rachel gave them news of Esther and her family, though she didn't visit them any more. She'd disagreed with Mordechai about the bringing-up of the children. He was still an out-of-work printer, harassed from time to time by the police. Esther kept them all by cleaning shops and offices in the town. But Rachel didn't make too much of that. Instead, for Paul's sake, Leonore joined her in remembering their life in Zamenhofa Street. They deliberately made it sound like a Yiddish comedy, and Paul was interested and amused. Then they talked about the flat in Praga that, Rachel said again, was the start of everything that was good for them. She recalled their days at the Villa Belleguardo and the odd old Russian émigrés Lydmilla Fyodorovna found to turn her and Ida into socially acceptable young ladies.

"Do you hear anything about her now, darling?"

Paul looked uncomfortable, but Leonore was enjoying her sister's conversation as though they were in private, just the two of them.

"She was here last year, as a matter of fact. Some friends of hers were in trouble with the authorities, and she wanted Paul's help in sorting it out. You were away, weren't you, dear?"

He nodded, sweating to control and turn the conversation, but not knowing how to do it.

"She insisted on my contacting Loff, instead," Leonore continued. "And would you believe it? He actually dropped everything and came. They went off somewhere together...I've no idea where. He didn't come back for months, and I haven't seen nor heard of her since."

The atmosphere between them was warming, the air in the room becoming cloudy with tobacco smoke. They all had brandy at their elbow, and Leonore was grateful, once more, to see signs of the Rachel of old. Their communion wasn't dead, after all. Their reminiscences took them backwards and forwards, here and there, until they settled on Paris and inevitably, at long last, Ida's name was mentioned. Paul silently prayed for something to happen…something to save the situation; a repetition of the earthquake he and Ouroussoff had experienced in Japan, perhaps. He hoped against hope.

"Ida's first love affair. Do you remember, Leonore, with the gorgeous Monsieur Leon?"

"Truly…how gorgeous he must have been, if everything she told us was true," Leonore laughed.

"Her golden knight on a white charger," Paul said gently. "She always was a romantic, our poor little Ida."

"Why do you call her poor little Ida?" Leonore asked, piercingly. "She chose her life."

"Aren't romantics always the ones to be hurt?" he asked innocently. He turned to Rachel. "About that silk, Rachel, I'll try to help if you let me know exactly what you want."

"Oh, darling, that would be wonderful. I'll send you details about colour, quality and design directly when I get home. Meanwhile, I would really love to see Ida before I go. You don't know where she is, I suppose?"

"She's in America, of course. You must remember," Leonore told her, puzzled.

"Of course you must," Paul joined in hastily. "It was all arranged while we were in Berlin together."

"I remember that, of course. But she's been home since then."

"No! She can't have been."

"But yes, darling, indeed! Rachel was irritated, as though they doubted her sanity. "She came to see me one afternoon in Sienna Street. It couldn't possibly have been more inconvenient. I didn't ask her to stay, I'm afraid; I had much too much on, and she'd given me no warning, you see. But she told me she was going to visit friends in Moscow, and she'd see me again on her way back to America."

"I will not believe it."

"It's true, all the same."

"But...when was this? We've never had a word from her for at least two years, have we, Paul?"

"No, darling." Paul gripped the edge of his chair, thankful to have observed professional diplomacy first-hand.

"And who on earth could she possibly know in Moscow? She doesn't know anyone in Moscow, does she, Paul?"

"Someone she met while she was in America, possibly?"

"Oh! It really is too cruel! To be so close and never to come to see us. Really...too, too cruel. And where is she now? Of course, she's the world's worst correspondent, but...Oh, Paul..." She began to weep.

Rachel turned to look at her with a sudden new thought. "Didn't you tell me Clementine lives in Moscow now? She went there after she was married, didn't she?"

"Oh, no!" To Leonore this would be the basest betrayal. "Certainly not! Clementine writes quite often. If she'd seen Ida, she would have told me. But we're going down for the Coronation, and I'll ask her then. But...no!" She wept no longer, and her eyes were puckered in puzzlement. "She definitely wouldn't have gone to see Clementine without coming to see me, too. Oh, Paul, how could she have been so near without coming to see her own sister? *Oy veh! Oy veh!* What is this world of ours coming to, please tell me?"

CHAPTER 19

▼

1896

Everyone, whether optimist or pessimist, agreed that this must be the beginning of a new era. A new century, a new Tsar. New factories, new railways, new money. A new Slavonia in the East, for surely, it was historically only a matter of moments before the tottering Manchu Empire tumbled into Russia's ever-open pocket. In four short years, the eighteen hundreds would be over: Napoleon, the burning of Moscow, the Decembrists' revolt, serfdom, royal assassinations. They would all be far, far in the past.

Optimists believed the new Tsar could only be a reformer, that he would transform the country into the kind of democracy they were familiar with from their travels abroad. Others had no great expectations. In the deep countryside, little was known of anything occurring outside the village. At the poorer ends of the towns, workers had long since abandoned hope. This Tsar would be as distant as the last; why should he feel for their sufferings? The Tsarina was a German. They called her Nemka and murmured dismally that she came to them behind the old Tsar's coffin. Would she arrange for them to work less hard to feed their families? Would she heat their homes in winter, cool them in summer, see they shared in this new money people talked about?

Of course not! They expected nothing but to be mashed as they had always been.

Subscribing neither to optimism nor to pessimism were the delvers into the nature of the years to come. They were mostly wives of the men who were making the new money. Currently, this new money was propping up the ancient institutions to which the makers owed no loyalty. Their husbands told them the autocracy wasn't financially viable; they were all agreed on that. Everything must be financially viable, or it must be disposed of. These hard-headed entrepreneurs rode to their factories and offices with their workers, on the city's tramcars.

Their womenfolk would not have dreamed of such a thing. They overdressed themselves in their social limbo, not yet of the upper class but distanced in every possible way from the lower. They took cabs to the best shops on Liteiny or the Nevsky and bought the most expensive goods they found there. When they weren't shopping, they met at each other's houses to probe the future.

Princess Krimovskaya, a naturally anxious woman, attached herself to these groups of the new rich, the disciples of every quack and charlatan in the city. She attended séances, fingertip-to-fingertip in shaded rooms, hoping for a message from her father on how to deal with her dissolute brothers. She rapped tables and followed open-mouthed the schematic wanderings of the pointer on a ouija board. She read tarot cards and went out to the islands at sunrise or sunset while a sloe-eyed young man recited incantations in a language so old no one in the world remembered anything about it but himself. She learned the significance of every changing facet of the moon. She adorned herself with numerous charms against the coming holocaust, be it fire or flood, the day when gravity would fail and everyone would go spinning off the earth into endless space, against the renewal of the seven plagues of Egypt. She studied the theosophical writings of Madame Blavatsky and wore a large soapstone Buddha on a chain round her neck. It swung on her breast with a life of its own and hit the children in the face when she bent to kiss them.

They found her fun, now, and called her 'Mrs. Buddha' behind her back. Marie was not certain that was a good joke. She wanted seriously to discuss it all with her mother, but Leonore was occupied with preparations for the Coronation and for Ulrika's wedding.

"This is important, Mama," Marie persisted.

"It's nonsense," was her mother's confident rejoinder.

"How do you know?"

"Because...because if there were anything at all to worry about, Father Martin would have told us."

"Maybe he doesn't know. I think Mrs. Buddha knows more than him."

"Marie! That's a wicked thing to say. Father Martin's our Confessor. He knows everything he needs to know."

"I don't think I want to be a Roman Catholic anymore."

"Go away and play, child, and don't be silly!"

"I hate it here. I want to go and live with Mrs. Buddha," Marie retorted, flouncing out of the room.

Her children and Princess Krimovskaya's eccentric behaviour were not Leonore's only problems. Ulrika was unsettled. She spent her mornings praying in the Church of Saint Catherine and came home in a moody mixture of tears and unprovoked laughter. She no longer worked in the house and, with Anton, vacillated between extremes of affection and aversion. Their relationship became the subject of gossip for everyone, and Anton was the butt of ribald jokes questioning his manhood. He performed his duties uncomplainingly, but his eyes lost their zest, staring into an uncertain future.

Leonore was sufficiently worried to try to talk to him about it.

"You don't have to marry her if you're not sure, Anton; certainly not immediately. Wouldn't it be better to wait until she's settled down?"

"That's all right, my lady. I'll see she settles down soon enough once we're married, I promise you." He spoke in a grimly determined tone.

The evening before the wedding, everyone assembled on the platform of the Moscow Station: Leonore, the children, the bride, who was
nominally in charge of the children, and the groom, acting as his mistress's escort. Paul came briefly to wish them goodbye. He was avoiding the wedding and would join them a day or so later. A very late
arrival—the train was about to leave—was Princess Krimovskaya, the
Buddha at her breast bouncing erratically. Albrecht tried to pat it as
usual but it was late in the day, he was sleepy and mistimed the swing.
It hit him on the forehead. It was heavy and it hurt. He set up a mighty
screaming that even his beloved Marie could not quiet.

Leonore spent the first hours of the journey irritated with everyone.
She was particularly annoyed by the Princess, who had developed a
tone of confidentiality and an unpleasant breath odour because of the
herbs she was now consuming. She came too close.

"Those two," she whispered, nodding towards Anton and Ulrika,
who, with the children, were now asleep. "You must stop them, my
dear. You mustn't let them marry, you know."

"That's entirely their own affair," Leonore told her stiffly. "There's
nothing I can do."

"But they mustn't! They shouldn't be thinking about that sort of
thing…not now. Nobody should. I saw it in the sunrise…only yesterday morning. The omens are all fatal."

Leonore pointedly yawned, closed her eyes and pretended to sleep.
She was allowed peace through the rocking of the train for twenty minutes or so. Then she felt bony fingers scrabbling on her arm. She
opened her eyes; the Princess stared at her with terrified eyes.

"Are you really unaware that something terrible is about to happen,
my dear? Really…? When it does, we shall all be responsible, unless we
stop them."

Leonore pushed the anxious fingers aside and pretended to sleep
once more. The train made its first long stop at Novgorod. Leonore
went on to the platform and walked up and down with other restless
passengers. The engine hissed steam around her skirts; she drank scald-

ing tea and thought seriously about Princess Krimovskaya's fears for the future. Certainly, the future frightened her too; it always had, ever since she was a little girl and discovered what it meant to be a Jew.

Clementine and Sasha were at the Moscow station to meet them. Clementine kissed Ulrika like a sister; Sasha embraced Anton like an old friend. Everyone went back to the flat until it was time for the wedding at St. Simeon of the Pillar. Ulrika wore peasant costume from her home district in Germany. Anton wore a spotless white shirt with an embroidered collar, his trousers tucked into high, polished boots. The children were delighted to see them looking so splendid. Leonore shed tears for them while they made their promenade around the lectern; they were so young. Afterwards, everyone went back to the flat, where Clementine and her friends, at Leonore's expense, had prepared a typical wedding meal—course after course, bottle after bottle, toast after toast. To properly celebrate the wedding Sasha had collected men from the yards, huge shaggy creatures who could dance and sing as well as they could drink. The children were amazed and enchanted by the noise and so much happiness. Also, they were exhausted after their journey and were never afterwards sure whether the music, the colour and the laughter were reality or part of a wonderful dream.

Ulrika and Anton sat side-by-side, dazed smiles on their faces. From time to time one of the guests would shout "bitter!" The cry would be taken up by his neighbour and passed up and down the table until it was deafeningly loud when it reached the bridal couple. It was their command to kiss. The shouting wouldn't stop until, blushingly, they joined their lips.

Leonore consulted her watch. It was early evening still, and the party would go on for hours, but she had to take her drooping children to the hotel and put them to bed. The children objected, but with Clementine's help, they were packed into a carriage. At the Metropole, there were no more complaints. They were asleep immediately, once she put them into their beds. For a while she sat alone in great contentment.

She was far away from everybody except her family, and she wished Paul were here to share the intimacy.

The hotel was crowded to its corners; a pageant of smart men and women from every end of the world. Leonore couldn't eat after the wedding feast; neither could she sleep. She went downstairs. There must be a vacant chair in one of the reception rooms where she could watch the passing show. While she was wandering under the chandeliers, trying to hear over the babble of voices what the orchestra was playing, she heard her name called. She lifted a hand, and a page approached with an envelope.

"This was left for you this morning, Madame," the boy said. "But the gentleman said to deliver it this evening."

She took the letter, thanked him and stood uncertain in the crush until she heard her name again.

"Frau von Hagen!"

The speaker was an aging woman in a turquoise gown, so metallic in its sheen as to dazzle. The bodice was cut low, the bare flesh decorated with ropes of pearls and a spatter of diamonds. The grey hair was coiled high towards the back of the head, while tight curls paraded across the forehead with military precision.

"I am the Countess von Aschenbauer," she said. "This is my daughter Cecile."

Cecile curtseyed briefly. She wore her mother's hairstyle, but her gown was simple white. Her eyes were dead, mocking this attempt to perpetuate a youth long gone.

"We have been living in Paris," the Countess told her. "We came back for the Coronation. Cecile has been having such success in Paris, haven't you, darling?"

"Yes, Mama."

"In other days, other circumstances, we might have met in Estonia, my dear. We were close neighbours to your brother-in-law, Baron Loff."

"I know."

"How is the dear man?"

"Very well, I believe. I'm expecting him later."

"You are? There! You see, Cecile? I was certain if we came we would be sure to meet old friends. Everything has changed. One meets everybody these days. Cecile was a great favourite with the Baron before we left, weren't you, Cecile? We had to leave because of the burnings, you know. It wasn't safe any more...not for women and young girls. Well! We'll just have to make sure we meet the Baron while we're here, Cecile. Has he...er...brought anyone with him, do you know?"

"I don't know. I haven't seen him."

"And your husband, my dear. We hear he's one of our up-and-coming young men, don't we, Cecile? We've met so many people who knew you both in Paris, haven't we, Cecile?"

"Yes, Mama."

Leonore changed the subject to relieve Cecile's embarrassment. From what Paul had told her, these two must have swapped characters in Paris.

"And how is the Count?"

"My dear! Didn't you know? Well, no, of course you didn't, or you wouldn't have asked." She paused before adding sepulchrally, "He's dead!"

"Oh! I am so sorry."

The Countess uttered a tinkling laugh to reassure her. "Don't be upset, my dear, it's not your fault. I'm surprised the Baron didn't tell you. The poor man had a terrible stroke and died before they got him to Haapsalu. We couldn't possibly go back to the Estate now, could we, Cecile?"

"No, Mama."

"I believe I've found a buyer...a Jew, of course...an entrepreneur, he calls himself, and..."

"Mama!"

"Oh! Er..." She swung round. "Look! There...over there, Cecile, talking to that woman. Isn't that Prince...oh, dear...what is his name? You know who I mean..."

She hurried away, leaving Cecile standing for a moment, undecided. Then she asked hurriedly, softly:

"Colonel Ouroussoff. He was a friend of your husband's, I think. Do you hear anything of him, Frau von Hagen?"

"Yes. He's in the Far East. He intends staying there, I believe. Princess Poulanskaya went out to marry him."

Cecile stood frozen. Leonore expected her to scream or cry, but her eyes were as dead as ever. There was nothing except a further sinking of the already sagging shoulders.

Leonore had no more heart for watching people. She went back to her room and opened her letter. It was dated the previous day.

Dear Paul and Leonore,

You will have to represent the von Hagen name at the celebrations. Some business I have been working on for some time is about to come to its finality. I've had to go away to settle it, and I don't know when I shall return. I am well. My dear Channah is with me.

Ever your affectionate brother,

Loff von Hagen

Paul arrived the next day. He was puzzled by Loff's letter, but put it aside as not important, and they saw the sights of Moscow as a happy family party.

The culmination of all the crowding and excitement was the Coronation in the Kremlin, at the Cathedral of the Assumption. The von Hagens watched the procession with Clementine, Sasha, Anton, and Ulrika. The only person of their immediate acquaintance in the Cathedral was Princess Krimovskaya, present because she was of the inner circle; she had been a Lady in Waiting to Tsarina Maria Fyodorovna when she first came to Russia. Afterwards, as a foreigner, Paul was allowed to watch the banquet from a balcony; only Russians were allowed at the feast.

The next day, the Princess came to their rooms trembling with triumph.

"Such a sight, my dears. The flickering of the candles made the gold on the walls look like waterfalls. And the music. The singing was heavenly. The Tsar placed the Imperial crown on his own head; well, obviously, no one was worthy of doing that. And then…" she drew closer, lowered her voice and looked serious. "Something quite terrible happened and everyone has been sworn to secrecy so if anyone heard about it from the von Hagens, I would surely end my days in Siberia."

Leonore had had enough of the Princess' scaremongering. "If it's something you feel you'd better not tell us…"

"But I must! I've been trying to warn you something terrible was going to happen. Well, this makes it certain. During the ceremony, the Chain of Office slipped off His Majesty's shoulders. I wasn't near enough to see it myself, but I heard it land on the floor. Everyone did."

"My dear, why torture yourself worrying about every little thing? It was an accident. It didn't mean anything," Leonore told her.

"Oh, but it did! It must have done! I keep telling you something terrible is going to happen. Do you need a more certain omen than that?"

The Princess was alone in her worry. Nobody else seemed to care. Moscow was gayer than ever. People were reluctant to relinquish their holiday.

A few days after the Coronation, it was to be the turn of the little people—the people who weren't noble and didn't have titles. First there would be a great affair for working men and women on Khlodynka Field—an army training ground outside the city. There was to be a banquet provided by His Majesty and, afterwards, everyone would take away presents—tin plates and mugs stamped with the Imperial monogram. The day was to end with a ball in His Majesty's honour.

Khlodynka Field was to be the highlight of Anton and Ulrika's honeymoon, their souvenirs something to be cherished for the rest of their lives in honour of the Tsar and of their wedding. Clementine and Sasha discussed the event ceaselessly beforehand. They talked about it in hushed voices when they were in bed, so that Anton and his bride wouldn't hear.

"Be reasonable, my dear. We'll get them there, and then we'll lose them among the crowd. There'll be thousands there. It won't be difficult."

"I still say you shouldn't encourage them to go. Anything could happen."

"They'll go anyway, whatever I say. It'll be something to remember for the rest of their lives."

"I can imagine."

"And what could be more natural than that we all go together? Nobody's going to think anything of that. And you can stay with them when I fade away, if that'll make you happy."

"What time does the Tsar get there?"

"Nobody knows, exactly. Sometime in the morning. But we have to be there the night before if we're to get anywhere near the front."

"I still don't like it, Sasha. You shouldn't have got involved in the first place"

"Think of Ida. We owe her something, surely."

"I do. I think of no one else for days and days together."

"Well, then…"

"All right, all right. But I don't want you to take those two with you. They don't know what they're risking."

"They're not risking anything, I promise. I won't be anywhere near them when it happens."

When she heard that Ulrika was going to Khlodynka, Dorothea's insistent demands to go, too, were ceaseless.

"I've said 'no,' and I mean 'no,'" her father said. "And if I have any more of this, we'll pack up and go home immediately."

"Why not, Papa? You always say 'no' to anything I want to do. It'll be fun. We'll sleep in the open air the night before, and I'll have Ulrika and Anton to look after me."

"For the last time—no! It won't be the sort of thing young ladies go to. And that's the last time I want to hear about it."

It wasn't the last time. Wherever they were, whatever they were doing, the subject was inevitable. Finding her father adamant, the child attacked her mother. Leonore, worn down, surrendered what she considered to be the first principle of good motherhood and said wearily, "Ask your father!"

Dorothea didn't ask her father again. But when she judged the time was about right the night before, and Sonia was sound asleep in the other bed, she left the Metropole and walked to Clementine's flat. Once she was in the street, she was frightened, but pride forbade her turning back. The crowds were still about, men, women and children. Some wandered, looking at the shops or the stars. Others lurched from side to side on the pavement. Some stroked her face as they passed and told her what a pretty girl she was.

By the time she reached the flat, she was perspiring and panting. Clementine was horrified to see her, alone and in that condition. Without giving her time for more than the most garbled explanation, she dragged her straight back to the hotel. By now she was crying bitterly from fear, from exhaustion, but mostly from realising the enormity of what she'd done. Clementine left Sasha, Ulrika and Anton to make their own way to Khlodynka and said she was would try to find them later. She put Dorothea back to bed and waited for Paul and Leonore to return from the theatre. Paul was furious when she told him what had happened. Leonore had an attack of conscience.

"They all looked to be sound asleep before we left," she said. "It never occurred to me she'd dare do a thing like this. To go out into the streets...at night...alone..."

"She's getting too far above herself, that young lady. She needs a damned good whipping."

"Paul!"

"Don't worry, he doesn't mean it, do you, Paul? What she did was foolhardy…"

"It was very wicked," Leonore put in weakly.

"But it was also quite brave. And, after all, she wasn't actually disobeying you, was she?"

"She knew very well I told her she wasn't to go to Khlodynka," Paul said.

"She wasn't going to Khlodynka, she was coming to see me. Now, you may not have allowed her to do that had you been here, but you were both out…enjoying yourselves," she added tartly. "And she wasn't to know what the streets would be like."

"No, no, that's right, Paul. She couldn't have known it was so dangerous," Leonore agreed eagerly.

Paul grunted. He had intention of whipping his daughter, but resented these women eating away at his paternal authority.

"Anyway," Clementine rushed on, ahead of any more interruptions, "what I suggest is, you let me take her to Khlodynka tomorrow."

"No!"

"Please, Paul, listen to me for a moment. I'll take Dorothea and Sonia too, if she wants to come. All the people—it's bound to be a wonderful sight. We'll watch the crowds, but we won't go anywhere near them. Your children won't ever need bags of free food and tin mugs, thank God! I'll hold onto their hands all the time, and we won't be in any danger at all, I promise you."

"But aren't you going with Sasha and the youngsters?"

"They'll have left without me by now. They have a basket of food for their breakfast, and Sasha is meeting some men from the yards on the way."

There was a long, contemplative silence while Clementine looked from one to the other.

"I swear, I won't let go of their hands for a single moment."

"Well," Leonore began very slowly, "she does want to go very badly, Paul."

Paul shrugged, his meaning clear: he was only the child's father. They must do as they wished.

"I'll be here to collect her at seven," Clementine said, and left before there could be any further argument.

By eight, they were on the field, and it was as Clementine had said: both children were delighted to see the crowds and had no desire at all to get mixed up with them. A continual column was trudging from the city, men, women and children, some walking, others riding on their fathers' shoulders. It was a light-hearted, holiday crowd, generally drably dressed, the greyness relieved here and there by the colourful headscarves of some of the women.

The ground was badly pitted by horses and rutted by army wagons. This was where the training for the military processions and parades in honour of the Coronation had taken place the previous week. At the far end was a long row of booths, their awnings decorated with multi-coloured flags fluttering in the spring breeze. Behind the booths were the boxes of food and the boxes of plates and mugs ready for when the distribution started. The timing for that was a matter in dispute. The Tsar and Tsarina were expected some time in the morning to watch their peoples' gratitude for all this generosity. Something must be left to be distributed when their Majesties arrived.

The people at the front of the crowd, the ones who'd tried to sleep on the hard ground and whose patience was shortened by their aches and pains, were the first to start shouting. Those behind, hearing angry voices at the front, concluded the source was disappointment. The food and tin-ware was already distributed. There was nothing left for them.

They surged forward over the uneven ground, as urgent as a menacing black thundercloud driven forward by a high wind. Mingled with the angry shouts were screams, screams and more screams until the screams were louder than the shouts. Clementine held the children close to her, frozen by the horror of what she was seeing. At the front, bodies were building up into a wall of corpses. At the back, people were still pushing. Soldiers rode out of nowhere, it seemed, splitting the latecomers into small disgruntled groups; they couldn't see what was happening ahead, and they were bitter because, like always, promises from on high meant nothing.

Sonia and Dorothea were sobbing into Clementine's skirts with terror. She pulled herself together and started dragging them back to the city. Dorothea didn't want to go. She wanted to stay to see the Tsar and Tsarina. Clementine told her angrily they wouldn't come, not now. But they did, after the soldiers had thrown as many bodies as they could under and behind the booths so that the royal eyes shouldn't be offended by the sight.

It took a long time to get back to the city. The road was choked by people and vehicles coming and going, by people on foot, in carriages, stopping to relay the news and to spread rumours. Princess Krimovskaya was already there when Clementine got the children back to the Metropole.

She was babbling hysterically. Three thousand people had been crushed to death, they said. Hadn't she told them all along that something terrible was going to happen? And those two dear children! Hadn't she said they oughtn't to get married? She'd known it. She'd known it all along.

Leonore clasped her children to her and thanked God for their deliverance. She and Paul had invitations to the Tsar's celebration ball that night. She refused to go. He tried to persuade her. Not to accept a royal invitation was tantamount to treason, he said. She didn't care. She would never leave her little ones again.

Clementine went back to her flat and waited. No one! She went down into the darkened street and watched. No one! Others watched with her: old folk, sick people who knew they'd never survive the walk out to Khlodynka, the wait and the walk back again. People passed by with snippets of news. The Kremlin was illuminated; the Tsar was giving a ball.

"It's not him," people said. "He'd never do that on a night like this. It's *Nemka*!"

And they hated her a little more because of it.

Nobody came back to the flat. Anton and Ulrika were never seen again. It was presumed they were among the unrecognisable thousands.

Sasha escaped. He was hiding under one of the booths when it happened. The shock of it touched his mind. For three days, he wandered Khlodynka Field like a mad thing. On the fourth, he returned to his wife, his mission uncompleted.

CHAPTER 20

▼

1897

Loff had at last secured a means for Ida's release. For months now, he had written letters and made telephone calls and secret visits to the capital to knock on doors. A Coronation would traditionally have been the time for generous amnesties, but the new Tsar was bitterly prejudiced against Jews. Loff expected no help from him. Instead, he worked deviously, circuitously, from the moment he left Ida alone in the Siberian schoolhouse. He worked with his pocket-book in his hand, for it was only money that could achieve the impossible.

He recruited the assistance of Jews; not Jews of the Pale, but successful Jews—Jews rich enough to be living in the bigger cities, pursuing their interests and increasing their fortunes. They knew influential Russians: Russians whose word could mean banishment or, for the right price, permission to remain. Jews who knew this kind of Russian only too well took Loff's money and negotiated on Ida's behalf. It was another kind of trade.

He sold them the image of Ida as heroine, a latter-day Esther or Judith, perhaps. Her only crime, he assured them, had been in helping young men of the Bilu to leave Russia. Unfortunately, they combined Marxism with their nationalist fervour. Their ambition was to establish a liberal home for Jews in Palestine, where they would maintain themselves as farmers or labourers, eschewing the peddlery and petty trade that was all life in the Pale would offer them.

Rich Jews feared Marxism equally with the Government. They would pay anything to have those radicals shipped out of the country. Ida was working to that end. They were thus combined in their interests. And there was comfort in knowing that Ida wasn't a red revolutionary herself; she hadn't thrown any bombs, nor had she assassinated any Government Ministers. She wasn't the kind to do anything to cause a pogrom. What she did, she had done for the good of all Jewry.

They assembled forged documents for her, with danger and difficulty to themselves. For the last thing, immediately before the Coronation, they visited at the Metropole with an Amnesty Certificate and a Passport in the name of Zara Goldberg. Loff had mortgaged his businesses to pay for them. His land remained entire, though. It had been von Hagen land for centuries. It must remain so. It must continue to feel the footfall of von Hagens long after he was dead. The diggings, the workshops and the shipyard; he had no real interest in any of them. They were a part of the new world; he would live and die faithful to the old. When he told her what he was doing, Channah was silent, but she held him close and he knew that she loved him.

Instead of attending the Coronation events, they traveled together to Tobolsk. After an exhausting trip, he was surprised and delighted to see Ida again. Life in the dramatic climate of Siberia suited her. Her cheeks were healthily flushed, her figure more graciously developed. The children who shouted and scampered around her had life in them he hadn't seen before.

Ida sent them home on an unlooked-for holiday, and the three of them were alone. It was then, quietly and without fuss, that he presented Ida with her freedom. He put the documents on the table in front of her, and she looked at them uncomprehendingly.

"You're free to leave here whenever you want, my dear."

"This wonderful man has moved heaven and earth to get you these," Channah told her happily. "Isn't it wonderful?"

Ida fingered them as though their touch would poison her.

"They're forgeries, but they're good forgeries. They'll get you passed anywhere," Loff assured her.

"I didn't know...I mean...I'm very grateful, of course, Loff."

"You're bowled over, my dear," Channah told her comfortingly.

"I thought I was here forever. That's what happens. They put you away, and you die...eventually. Those women on the train told me. From now on, they said, your life will never change. Day after day after day, it will always be the same." She smiled uncertainly. "Either you come to terms with that or...you go mad, I suppose."

"You came to terms."

"I was lucky. I had the children." Her voice rose with excitement. "Loff, do you remember what they were like when you were here before?"

"Yes. You've turned them into human beings since then."

"They were human all along. Nobody had opened any windows for them before."

"Well, now it's all over," Channah said briskly, trying to make the previous year not to have happened.

"I don't know." Ida was diffident, nervous, embarrassed.

"What don't you know, please, tell me?"

"There are the children here."

"And there are a lot of young Jews out there."

"The children need me."

"So do those boys. Listen to me, my dear! Out of snow you cannot make a cheesecake. You should know that yourself. What are you doing with your life?"

"It isn't easy, Channah. I..."

"What isn't easy?"

"Choosing."

"What is to choose? They are young men who'll grow into good Jews if people like you get them to Palestine. That's your life, Ida.

Here, in this wilderness, you have only little Russians who'll grow up and perhaps be very happy one day to cut your throat."

"They're only children, Channah. They won't grow up evil if some-one shows them a different way."

"So now you're telling me you're a *lamedvavnik*?"

"Oh, Channah!" Ida laughed with embarrassment.

"Now listen to me, my girl! Nobody thinks you're anything special. You're an ordinary Jew, just like me, not one of the chosen few who'll save the world. Be reasonable! This dear man is offering you a new life. You should remember what they say: on the Day of Judgment, we Jews will be called upon to answer for all the things we might have enjoyed and didn't. You're still enough of a Jew to know what I'm talking about, aren't you? Living in New York so long hasn't changed you that much, surely."

For the rest of the evening, Channah sulked and said almost noth-ing. When they were in bed, Loff felt her body stiff, unyielding beside his. He held her gently, understandingly, his arm beneath her neck, his hand caressing her hair. He was silent, hoping her breathing would soften, but his serenity didn't reach her. At last he spoke.

"Channah! Channah, my dear, don't be angry with her, please. She's had a terrible time, remember. We tried to help, that's all. Whether or not she wants what we're offering is up to her."

"Oh, Loff...my dear, dear man." Her body softened, she turned to face him and clasped him tightly with her arms round his neck. "My wonderful, wonderful Loff...you're everything good that anyone could ever possibly be, but...even you don't understand everything, my dear."

He snuggled against her, thankful for this change of mood. It wasn't often she allowed him this degree of soft, almost maternal warmth.

"What don't I understand?"

"It's not your fault. You're not a Jew."

"Can't you tell me, then?"

There was a long pause, and he didn't know whether she was titillating his interest or merely collecting her thoughts.

"It's because of the way we have to live, we Jews. We can't afford your Christian attitude to life. We have to plough our furrows as deep and as often as we can, while we have the opportunity. We don't have your choices."

"Is that why you're so angry with Ida? You think she's behaving more like a Christian than a Jew?"

"Loff, you've offered her a new life. She's choosing to live out a kind of death."

It was his turn to pause. Then he said with some surprise, "I never realised."

"What?"

"You're still a Jew."

"Of course. I'll always be a Jew. That was what I was born."

"I've never really thought about it, I suppose. But gradually, during all these years, I'd forgotten there were any differences between us."

She hugged him. "It's late, my dear. We must go to sleep."

"Can you forgive me, Channah?"

"Forgive you for what?"

"For not remembering what you are…who you are. For not respecting you as I should have done, I suppose, is what I'm trying to say."

She hugged him. "When I answer at the Day of Judgment, my love, I shall be able to say there were no possible pleasures in life that I didn't enjoy, ever since that day you rescued me in the wood." She kissed him and added: "Ida's a good person. I'd like her to be able to say she's been as happy in her life as I have in mine."

By the time Loff completed the long journey back to Saint Petersburg, the Coronation would have been long since over. Nonetheless, Channah pressed him to go back as soon as possible. She would remain, she said, until Zara, as they were trying to remember to call her, made up her mind what she would do. She had little doubt they would soon be following together. Seeing the determination in Channah's eyes, neither had he.

On the train, he mused gratefully that, when he met her again, he could tell Leonore the truth. She had been distant to him ever since he left her house to go south with Lydmilla Fyodorovna. He anticipated more iciness after leaving the Coronation celebrations without warning.

Not wishing to meet her alone, he took a room at the Moskovskaya and telephoned Paul at his office.

"You're still alive, Brother," Paul greeted him sarcastically.

"I'm sorry if I've worried you, Paul."

"Oh, we weren't at all worried. We're used to your sudden disappearances."

Loff ignored the jibe. "We must meet—we two, with Leonore, of course. It's good news, though I think I'd better not say over the telephone."

He entertained them to dinner in his rooms at the hotel and successfully controlled his irritation at Leonore's attitude. She ignored entirely the effort, the risk, the cost of arranging a kind of freedom for her sister.

"Why on earth didn't you tell me the moment you knew she was in Russia?" she demanded.

"Other people were involved."

"What did that matter? I'm her sister."

"It was Ida's wish. She feared causing trouble for others...you, the family, Clementine, Lydmilla Fyodorovna..."

"And you...you knew, I suppose?" She spat the words at Paul.

"I was away at the time, if you remember."

"That's why I was involved. You sent for me yourself," Loff said.

"Naturally, Loff told me about it afterwards, as soon as he could," Paul said, without any apparent embarrassment.

"You know you're not being fair, Leonore. Don't you think there might have been a very good reason for keeping it a secret? When I saw her in that prisoners' pen at Kishinev…"

Leonore stood up and shouted at him. He was glad they weren't in public. "Stop it! Stop this immediately! I don't want to hear…not from you! All I want from you is to know where she is now. I shall go to her at once."

"She's still in Siberia. Channah's with her. She's being well taken care of."

"Channah! You even told Channah before you told me!"

"I needed her help."

"But not mine. Even though Ida's my own sister. Paul, take me home! And you, Loff, I want to know exactly where she is. I shall go to her in the morning."

It took most of the night for Paul to talk her out of precipitous action. They could, he said, she and Ida, quite easily pass each other on trains going in opposite directions.

She satisfied herself, at last, by writing a letter begging her sister to come home; then she settled down to wait. Paul was helpful in reminding her that the children still had not recovered from the shock of losing Anton and Ulrika at Khlodynka. Dorothea, in particular, remembered that she had wanted to be with them herself. He had to be at the office all day…he might even have to take a sudden trip, he said, and there was no one else the children could confidently be left with.

Meanwhile, he still hadn't found the courage to tell her that when they did meet, Leonore would find Ida sadly, shockingly changed.

Ida replied affectionately to her sister's letter, but didn't mention when she would be home. Channah stayed in Siberia until frustration drove her back to Estonia. She ran out of patience. Ida was still floundering in a trough of indecision that none of Channah's very practical arguments could resolve.

In none of the boys she taught, Russian though they were, would Ida recognise a potential sadist or killer akin to the ones who'd raped her, beaten and robbed her of an eye when she was in prison. By not abandoning her children now, she declared, she could prevent them from growing up to become like that. She was glad when Channah left. Without her continuing arguments, she could have spent the rest of her life among those children. But Channah persisted in reminding her of the *Biluin*.

Channah reached home, thankful, more devoted to Loff than ever, possessive and protective of him in every possible way. Summer was ending. Paul and his family were spending their last weeks on the Estate. She was tired, frustrated, and none-too-pleased to see them. On her very first day home, they noticed a marked change in her. She was no longer tolerant of everything they said and did. She constantly called to them to clear up the mess they made, not to bring dogs into the house and to make less noise on the stairs and in the corridors.

Leonore bridled. "How dare she talk to them like that, Paul! Whatever goes on between her and Loff, she's still only a servant, after all."

Paul was embarrassed by the friction and could think of nothing polite to say.

"She forgets they're still not over losing Anton and Ulrika," she complained. "She ought to remember what a shock they've had and humour them."

"Perhaps," he replied bitterly, "it's because she's a Jew and only a servant, she doesn't realise that the loss of Anton and Ulrika isn't the worst thing that can possibly happen to them in their lives!"

Alone again in Siberia, Ida continued struggling with the dilemma of what she saw as her conflicting obligations to the children and to the young men of the *Biluin*. Eventually, the *Biluin* won. She was Jew; nothing could change that.

She walked, one day, along the riverbank the length of the village, to interview the priest in his shack. If she did at some time in the future decide to go back to western Russia, she suggested vaguely, would he agree to take over her school and do what he could for the children? She would, naturally, draw up a scheme of learning for him to follow;

it need not occupy too much of his time. And as soon as she was settled in the West, she would send him a small regular allowance to pay for his trouble.

His eyes gleamed a little when she mentioned money, but mostly he sat smiling, reeking of vodka and onions and nodding his head in time with some rhythmic inner chant. She left at last unconvinced that she could rely upon him for help, but more certain than ever that she owed a duty to her own people. She might work in this one village forever, but was it possible her efforts would make any real difference in this apathy-soaked, crumbling society they called the Russian Empire?

She closed the school as the scrubland around the village was turning scarlet and the ground crackled as she walked over it. She went to Moscow. Clementine's welcome was ambiguous, both warm and cool. She didn't show Ida to a bedroom, but made her as comfortable as possible to rest on a couch in the living room until Sasha came home. She asked detailed questions about the arrest and conditions for prisoners in Siberia. But she pointedly avoided asking about Ida's plans for the future. She seemed to understand, without being told, that this sudden freedom was unofficial.

Ida was feeling her stay in the flat could only be very short. There was no sentiment between them, nothing to show that they had shared a past together. And Clementine noticeably avoided looking at the patch.

With Sasha it was quite different. He came clumping into the flat in his heavy boots and stopped like the final crashes of a symphony. Then he burst the silence and hugged her 'til she could scarcely breathe.

"Ida! My dear little Ida! My brave little girl! When did you get here? How did you get here?" He turned his face to one side. "You haven't let anybody know about her, have you, Clementine? Have you got any papers, Ida? Why are you wearing that thing over your eye? That's the last sort of thing you want for a disguise."

Ida gulped, between laughter and breathlessness. This was Sasha, boyish and jubilant as she'd never known him. He continued to hug her, shooting questions at her one after another.

"She arrived off the train this morning," Clementine said dourly.

"No one must know she's here."

"I'm not stupid."

"Not even the comrades! Who got you your papers, Ida? I suppose you have got papers of some sort?"

"Loff von Hagen." She broke away to show him her passport.

"And it's not Ida any longer. See? I'm Zara Goldberg now."

"You must take off that eyepatch. It's too noticeable."

"I daren't let anyone see me without it. Believe me, that would be just as noticeable. And horrible."

"Why horrible?"

"There's nothing there. Only a hole."

She could talk about it now without her voice quivering. The children at the school had taught her that. It was clear from the very beginning that the patch fascinated them. They knew from their folk tales about witches who were old and ugly and wore patches, but their schoolmistress was not as bad as that. If she were a young witch, she would appear unblemished; being unblemished helped them to work their spells.

It was only a matter of time before someone asked the direct question. She wasn't expecting it from this particular boy. He was normally a quiet, dreamy little lad, and she suspected he must have been either elected or bullied into it.

"Why have you got your eye covered up like that?"

She stared at him not knowing, on the instant, what to say. But she had lived too close to reality all her life to make up stories. She believed that the truth was all children needed to know.

"Because I haven't got an eye there, and it's very ugly."

"No...I don't believe you," someone else called out.

"It's true. It was knocked out by a policeman when I was arrested."

"Let's see, then!" It came in loud shouts from all over the hut.

They wanted to see it, so she showed them, and had never felt any embarrassment about it since. Sasha nodded sympathetically when she told him.

"We'll have to get you something less noticeable…an artificial eye, perhaps. And you'll have to stay in the flat until we do."

"I haven't much money, I'm afraid. Loff left me a little, but I really can't ask him for any more. So if it's going to be expensive…"

"Sasha will see to it," Clementine said, warm and confident now, at last. "There must be something in the funds, Sasha…?"

"We look after our own. Don't worry about it," he said.

"What will you do when we've got you new papers, Ida?"

"Aren't Loff's good enough then?"

He laughed. "Amateurish! All right for bumpkin policemen in Siberia, perhaps. But we work with professionals. And believe me, we work with the best. When you've got your new papers, you'll go back to America, I suppose?"

"Oh, no. Sasha, you know I'm grateful, don't you? I heard a little about the work you do from Lydmilla Fyodorovna. Oh! She wasn't indiscreet, I promise you." He nodded. "But she told me enough to realise that you don't have so much money you can afford to waste it on fugitive Jews."

"Don't worry about the money. We'll spend it on you for what you've done, not for who you are."

"Then…I shan't go back to America. So long as I can persuade them to go on sending me money from New York, this is where the real work is to be done."

"Splendid girl, Ida."

"I haven't made up my mind yet, whether to go back to the South, or see whether I can do more good in Poland…Warsaw, perhaps…or Vilno…"

"For all our sakes, it might be better if you went to Saint Petersburg first, Ida," Clementine said when she'd taken her to her room and was sitting on the bed, chatting like they did years ago. "Leonore has a right to know...at least a little of what you're doing."

Ida nodded, and one shimmering autumn day, Leonore met her at the station in Saint Petersburg. With several hugs and kisses, the events of the immediate past were swept aside, and they were sisters again, happy as they were during those last days together in Berlin, before Ida went to America. They sat close together in the carriage to the house. Ida thought: she's letting herself go terribly! She's becoming old and fat like our mother, and it isn't necessary. Why doesn't she let Rachel dress her? At the same time Leonore was thinking: Poor Ida! So thin! And as plain as ever. In fact...she's getting old, I suppose. What she's been through hasn't helped. And there's something even more peculiar about her face than there used to be.

Ida was overwhelmed by the size and magnificence of the house by the Anichkov Bridge, and Leonore was gratified, too gratified to be entirely tactful.

"You can see Paul is a very successful man these days, Ida. He's a Director at the Bank, but that's by no means all he does. Everyone considers him the Count's specialist on Far Eastern affairs. He's away a lot of the time...on business, meetings with important people all over the place. In fact, he's in Berlin at the moment, so I don't suppose you'll see him."

"Leonore...Leonore, darling, I can't tell you how happy I am for you. Everything's worked out wonderfully. And do you remember that time in Praga when Rachel and I were so angry with you because you wouldn't agree to marry the Captain? And aren't you glad you did?"

Leonore beamed. These were the kind of congratulations that mattered. Her circle in Saint Petersburg accepted her for what she was...as they accepted each other, sheltering under the wings of their husbands. But Ida knew the truth. Ida knew all of the truth. Ida remembered life in Zamenhofa Street. There were still nights when Leonore couldn't sleep, and she'd wake with the smells of Zamenhofa Street in her nostrils.

"Of course," she smiled, "there is a price to be paid for all this. We have to be very very careful."

"Careful?"

"Naturally. Paul moves in the highest Government circles, nowadays. You can imagine. We can't go anywhere and associate with just anybody."

"Be honest, Leonore. Am I an embarrassment?"

"Of course not," Leonore laughed unconvincingly. "What a thing to say! You're my sister."

"But you don't approve of what I do."

"I don't know what you do. And I don't want to know," she added hastily. "All I'd ask you to remember is that Paul gave up everything when he married me. I don't want any member of my family to cost him anything else."

"I see." Ida's response was carefully restrained. "Don't worry, my dear, I shan't be any trouble to you. I don't expect to stay in your house, of course. And I shall only be in Saint Petersburg for a day or two."

"Just as well, probably."

"You don't have to sound so bitter!"

"How do you expect me to sound? How should I feel? You come to Russia and never let me know. You're arrested and sent to Siberia, and everybody knows but me...even Channah. I'm the only one in the dark. When you get back, you don't come straight to me! You go to Clementine! I'm your sister, Ida! How do you expect me to feel?"

"Truly, I'm sorry, Leonore. I suppose it's inevitable. You hurt people when you're trying your hardest to protect them."

Leonore recovered her poise gradually, but sounded as though breathing was difficult for her. They were sisters, she said again, and she would never allow her sister to sleep anywhere other than in her house while she was in Saint Petersburg. She stopped herself in time from saying: whatever anybody else thinks! They made self-conscious conversation until the children came home from school.

None of them remembered Ida clearly, though each politely pretended that they did. Dorothea and Sonia curtseyed most carefully and gave this unknown Aunt token kisses. Marie also curtseyed, but kissed only briefly. She stood for a moment, examining Ida's face like a relief map of unknown territory. Eduard, full of self-confidence as ever, bowed and gave her his smartest military salute. Albrecht stood and stared, fascinated. At last, he said:

"You've got a funny eye, Aunt Ida."

Leonore rushed forward and bundled him, squealing, away. She apologised as she went, but Ida knew the child was right. The mechanic in Moscow who'd made the artificial eye had read or, rather, misread the instructions, or wasn't up to following them. Ida's natural eye was dark brown; the artificial eye a marvelous translucent grey.

"Leonore! Don't be angry with him," Ida called. "He's quite right. I do look odd." She ran after them and snatched the little boy from his mother's clutches. "Of course I look odd. You told me so often enough when we were children. And having a glass eye the wrong colour doesn't help."

After that she discarded the eye and wore the patch again. She was used to it. It was more comfortable than the eye. And lots of people had accidents that cost them an eye, after all. Women with variegated eyes must surely be much less common and just as easily identifiable. At least, she decided, the patch gave her a certain air of mystery; if the police took her up again, she would have to seduce them with that.

Book V

CHAPTER I

▼

1897

Leonore was slow to overcome her hurt. The hurt was there because everyone involved had withheld for so long the truth of Ida's return and arrest. That was wrong. Ida would always be her own little sister. For Ida and Rachel—more for Ida's sake, perhaps—she'd endured those nights singing in the smoke and ribald humour of the Doma. Ever since her parents' death, it had been her first consideration to see that they were cared for. Paul had been marvelous. He accepted them like children, sisters, almost of his own.

They'd all shut her out. That was bad enough. But during that awful dinner at the Metropole, she had behaved very badly, and now she felt that although he'd never betray his real feelings, his faith in her must have been shaken. She had lost all self-control. She had shown herself to be no more than a middle-aged Jewish housewife and fighter for her family. She might just as well never have lived anywhere except Zamenhofa Street. Nothing Paul taught her remained. The artificiality of her life all these years was unveiled, naked.

Paul was marvelous. He never referred to it and continued to treat her with his usual respect. She determined to make it up to him and her life bloomed with a new excitement and vigour. At last she recognised her marriage for what it was: her career. Her acquaintances were mildly astonished by the change in her. She became one of Saint

Petersburg's notable hostesses. She entertained constantly, choosing her guests with the advancement of Paul's career in mind and planning the occasions like battles to be won. Colleagues envied him the social graces of his wife. His reputation reflected the effects of her efforts. The von Hagens, it was agreed were very acceptable people, even though they weren't, strictly speaking, Russian. They spun together on a carousel of success.

"My dear, why don't you and Paul join the rest of us?" Princess Krimovskaya pleaded frequently. She was finished with mystic charlatans, particularly now that Leonore had no interest nor time to accompany her to their esoteric assemblies. She proselytised for Orthodoxy and longed to share its comforts with her friends. "We're not so very different, you know. It would be quite easy for you. I will never understand why you didn't change long ago. You must have your reasons, I suppose, but…"

Leonore had never been specific about her religious background before she married Paul. Her friends speculated. They said Paul must have been Lutheran originally—all those Baltic barons were. He probably converted in order to marry Leonore. Perhaps she was the Catholic or, on the other hand…Princess Krimosvakay disciplined her mind to think no further along those lines!

Aboard a vessel riding a calm sea, Leonore gave her religion no more thought than a Captain his steady compass. Her course was set. The priests at Saint Catherine's, further up the Nevsky, considered her to be a good parishioner. She fulfilled all the Obligations without fail and brought up her children to do the same. In reality, appearances in Church were part of her performance. Not even Ida's reappearance could alter that. Ida was a Jew and, if she stayed in Saint Petersburg, everyone would know Leonore was a Jew as well. She was also a quasi-revolutionary, and though no one was supposed to find out about that, she was an exile on the run. Nothing would alter that.

Leonore had confidence enough now to continue in her own direction undisturbed. It was Marie who shocked her back to reality.

"Mama, what is a Jew?"

Leonore thought as quickly as she could. "Why do you ask, darling?" She would have to say something positive, to all of them. Children with Jewish blood needed to be told in case of emergency.

"The new lady we have to teach us French asked me today," Marie explained. "She's lovely; Mademoiselle Cuvier. She's only just come from Paris."

She certainly could not have been in Russia long, to ask a question like that, Leonore reflected. "And what did you say, my pet?"

"I said I didn't know. But we called ourselves Catholics."

"That's exactly what we are, and she should never have asked such a question. What did she say then?"

"Nothing. She turned round to talk to the girl next to me."

"Don't worry about it any more, darling. Run along and get ready for supper."

"Auntie Ida's a Jew, though, isn't she? I heard you and Papa talking about her."

"Run along like a good girl."

She telephoned Paul at the office to tell him he must come home as soon as possible. He was none too pleased. He had a surprise late meeting with a mysterious woman who'd phoned that afternoon, and he was clearing his desk before a trip to the Far East at the end of the week. Somehow this woman had come to know of it and claimed that he owed her a little help "for old times' sake," as she put it.

"Please, Paul, I must talk to you. This is important."

He grunted and said he would be there if he possibly could. She knew he would come. He trusted her judgment implicitly these days.

This was a problem she deliberately hadn't faced before. When she married, she undertook that any children would be brought up Roman Catholic and had thought that would be the end of the matter. But she had half-known she would have need to face this dilemma from the moment she first held Marie in her arms. The child was raspberry-red like any newborn. But there was something different about her, too.

The first two girls were blonde—as blonde as their father—so blonde that none other than the blood of Baltic Barons might ever have powered their antecedents for centuries. Marie was strikingly different. Leonore had dark eyes and dark hair herself. Marie, in addition, had Levantine skin, a throw-back from who-knew-whom. Leonore could not recall it in any member of her family; none of the aunts or uncles. Her poor, ugly Papa was quite fair by comparison.

In the days when Jews were simply regarded as religious aberrants, killers of Christ, whatever their persecutors chose to call them, their crime was religious. But a man in the West was claiming that they were a Race, a Nationality, and that made their situation far worse. Nowadays, being a Jew was tantamount to treason.

As always in times of crisis, Paul's reaction was irritatingly lighthearted. "My poor darling, what on earth do you intend doing? Sit them in a row like birds on a branch and tell them they're tainted because you and I didn't worship in the same way before we married?"

"Of course they're not tainted. But I was a Jew."

"And I a Lutheran."

"That isn't the same."

"No, and it isn't important. You were Polish; I was Estonian with a lot of German blood in me. Dorothea was born in Italy, Sonia in France, Marie in...damn it! Where was Marie born? I can't remember." He paused, but only for a moment. "I tell you, it doesn't matter. They all speak Russian, French, German, a little Italian, a little Polish...They're all going to turn into splendid citizens. What more can you possibly want?"

"Stop it! Can't you see you're making it worse? What you're telling me is that they're nothing in particular, and they don't belong anywhere."

He took her into his arms as though he meant to waltz her around the room. "I know, my darling. Isn't that wonderful? They're free spirits. No labels. They'll go into the future, citizens of the new century, not of any particular country, and we mustn't say or do anything to interfere with that. Tell them if you must. Tell them whatever you like. But if you do, I'm sure you'll be doing the wrong thing. Now! I have a surprise. I saw an old friend of yours today."

She was worried about the children and, therefore, less patient than usual with his propensity for playing silly games. Whom among her acquaintance in Saint Petersburg could he have seen? Why must he try to make any casual meeting into something so portentous?

"Who was that?"

"A lady. She telephoned and left an enigmatic message. A voice from the past, she said. She certainly succeeded in mystifying my staff."

"And now you are trying to mystify me, I gather."

"Sorry, darling. It was Lydmilla Fyodorovna."

"Lydmilla? Where is she? Here in Saint Petersburg?"

"She'd like to see you, but she's frightened. She doesn't know whether you've forgiven her yet."

"Forgiven her?"

"For the last time you met...when she took Loff away with her."

"What did she want?" Her voice was cold. Lydmilla was obviously well-advised not to approach her directly.

"She has one or two quite interesting ideas, actually. She wants me to arrange a trip for her to the Far East."

"I see."

"As a matter of fact, when she heard I was going on Friday, she asked me to arrange a pass for her on the same train."

"Are you her only attraction out there, or will there be someone else, do you think?"

"You're adopting a very unpleasant attitude, my dear. I don't see why you should."

"Don't you? Don't you remember Paris? That's when you turned me against her. You couldn't think of anything bad enough to say about her and the people she mixed with."

"That was a long time ago. She's had a hard time since then."

"She was having a hard time when we first knew her in Florence, I seem to remember."

"I've told her I would arrange the pass. And one for her assistant, a man named Boris Kharbutov."

"Really? An assistant?"

"She believes there will soon be a roaring market in Saint Petersburg and Moscow for pictures from the Far East…landscapes, you know. Views of Vladivostok—it's quite a spectacular kind of place really—and towns and villages along the Chinese Eastern Railway."

"And this…assistant. What will he be doing?"

"Framing, reproducing, copying—I really don't know. Does it matter?"

"Not to me."

"I have her telephone number. She's staying somewhere over on the Vyborgskaya. Would you like to see her?"

"Not particularly."

The next morning, after a restless night, she asked what his trip to the East was all about, besides providing an escort for Lydmilla Fyodorovna.

"It's…er…sorry, darling. It's big. I can't tell you more than that. But you'll read all about it in the newspapers when it happens."

"You'll have to remember to be equally discreet with your friend, won't you?"

She was very angry with him. All her energies went in tending and extending his reputation for sagacity and here, it seemed to her, he was needlessly, foolishly, putting it at risk. He was equally angry with her. She was jealous. He would have expected her to know, by now, that he would never give her any cause to be.

His opportunity for seeing Lydmilla on the journey was limited. He had taken the precaution of booking her and her assistant into a separate car. They met only during meal stops at the distantly placed stations. These were very public occasions. All the passengers mixed together with the bonhomie of explorers for whom the trail has already been well and safely blazed. Their conversation could only be of the lightest nature. Boris Kharbutov, a well-built, lively looking twenty-year-old with a Julius Caesar haircut and one shoulder slightly above the other, listened to everything they said.

"Isn't this exciting, my friend? Nothing but the densest forests for hundreds of miles. I should never be bored if I lived out here. Boris, my dear, please go and buy us some piroshkis. We shan't stop again before midnight, and I don't want to have to come out again then."

Boris shuffled away, quickly and lopsidedly. She said:

"Could we ever have dreamed at Fiesole or in the Olympia we should ever be here together, in such a place, on our way to Vladivostok?"

He stiffened, not relishing these references to what she had called on the telephone: old times. "Lydmilla Fyodorovna, we have known each other many years. I am now almost an old man."

He stopped, not knowing what else to say without making his train of thought explicit.

"And I?" she queried.

"You...? He smiled. You are as fascinating as ever, my dear."

"You too, my friend. Don't dare talk of being old. You are a great man now, a man of immense power and influence."

"Not at all, really..." He was genuinely embarrassed.

"And here we are, you and I, after all these years, in this enchanted country among all these noisy, fidgety people, on our way to the end of the world. I shall paint pictures when we get there, and you...?"

"I shall be occupied on dreary Government business. Nothing in the least exciting, I assure you."

"That too, but there is so much more, I know. You always intrigued me, my friend, because you said so little when you meant so much. I have no idea, you see, why you're here, why you're travelling on this train, through these endless forests to the sea."

"I'm not going to the sea this time. I shall be leaving the train at Harbin."

"I see." She said it slowly as though, at last, she really did see something that had puzzled her for a long time, something she knew he didn't want her to know.

He shivered slightly and tried to recall their conversation word for word. Surely he hadn't revealed anything important? He shifted nervously from foot to foot and turned his head as though willing the signal for the train's departure to sound.

Fortunately, Boris returned with the purchased piroshkis, and their conversation returned to the entirely general. She enthused upon the wonderful extent of the Empire, of its glorious scenery and of the undreamed potentials that they must find here in the East.

Back in Saint Petersburg, Leonore regretted that she hadn't been more affectionate before he left. She hated these times when they were apart and was determined, as soon as the children were old enough to be left, that he would never go away without her again. Whenever he was away, she fretted about his physical welfare. This time, when it seemed he was travelling on especially important business, she was doubting the validity of his judgment. Whichever way she looked at it, she couldn't fathom why he should have agreed to take Lydmilla Fyodorovna with him. Her burgeoning mistrust convinced her that she should follow her own judgment and frankly explain to the family its background.

Eduard stared straight through the walls of the room, seemingly, into a misty distance where the army of the enemy was assembling.

"Jews smell," he said sharply. "A boy at school told me. And you must never trust a Jew with your money. They're all thieves."

Leonore was expecting the worst, but she was horrified. This son of hers, uttering such evil, was only six! "You surely can't believe that of your Mama, darling."

Eduard appeared to shorten his vision to enclose only the room and his mother's anxious face.

"You're not a Jew, Mama," he told her loyally. "We're Catholics. I had a fight about that the other day. This boy said we worshipped the devil. I said we didn't. We worshipped God like the Orthodox. He said we didn't. We did it all the wrong way. So I hit him. I won too, didn't I Dora?"

Dorothea gave him one of her superior shrugs and didn't reply. Sonia giggled. At age nine, she considered herself a bridge between the older and the younger children. She was convinced she understood them all better than they understood themselves.

"I want to see Aunt Ida," Marie said, solemn as ever. "When is she coming back?"

"You'll see her soon, I expect. She's visiting your Aunt Rachel in Warsaw, I believe."

"I want to see her," Marie repeated. "When is she coming back?"

"I don't really know. Soon, I expect," her mother tried to assure her.

"Aunt Ida's a Jew," Marie explained to the others, "but she doesn't smell. I don't care what that boy says."

"I would trust Aunt Ida with all my money," Albrecht, always Marie's ally, shouted so as to leave no one in doubt. "But I haven't got any money," he finished and glowered at his mother.

"Well, I think we should all go and wash our hands before lunch," Leonore suggested, defeated and anxious to be rid of them.

The subject wasn't referred to again. About a month later, she gathered them 'round her once more to read some of the newspaper. The promised announcement was there! China had granted Russia a lease on Port Arthur. All the details were in the closely printed column, and Paul's name was mentioned there, among a lot of others.

This was good news. Now, when Vladivostok was frozen, Russia had a year-round harbor in the Far East: a Naval Base, an outlet for the Manchurian mines and a reminder to Japan that the Far East wasn't hers alone.

Leonore was proud, glad for people to think Paul's hand in the agreement far more important than it was. Everybody flocked to her for details. It was wonderful; a confirmation of Russia's strength and permanency in a new area of the world. This was, indeed, a new century, a new reign, a new world, almost.

In the euphoria of the moment, nobody took very seriously what the reactions of the Japanese Government might be. Neither did they spend time on an almost hidden paragraph buried in the mass of close, poor, boring print about the founding of a new political party. It proclaimed itself as the Russian Social Democratic Party. Its platform was the establishment of a middle-class constitutional regime, to be superseded eventually by a "classless society."

CHAPTER 2

▼

1900

Bells were ringing all over Russia. It was New Year at last, a New Century. The eighteen hundreds were over. The nineteen hundreds, the new paradise, beckoned with promise of everything good, possible and impossible. Even Orthodox Russia, celebrating the passage of time more sluggishly than elsewhere, dreamt hopefully of the future. The New Century symbolised for everyone the genesis of a New World.

The von Hagen children entertained their friends at a New Year Party—girls from the Institute, boys from the Lyceum. A hired orchestra played for the dancing, and Igor, a Tartar of splendid proportions employed in place of Anton, announced each guest resoundingly in a bizarre accent.

Dorothea was first in the reception line. She was fourteen, tall and developing charmingly, her cheeks reproducing the bloom her Mother had when Paul first met her. Paul already mistrusted any boy reckless enough to show interest in her. His anxiety was uncalled for. The only boy in whom Dorothea might have had any interest was Pyotr Krimovsky, but he had spent so much time in the von Hagen family as to pass for an adopted brother.

Sonia was highly amused by her sister's relationship with Pyotr. She deplored any girl's showing interest in anyone of the opposite sex. It was, regretfully, a common weakness, but she and her sisters were, in every way, remarkable young women—too remarkable for anything like that.

"Mama, you really must tell Dora not to make such a fool of herself with Pyotr Alexeivitch. They're the talk of the town, you know."

Leonore hid her smile. This was from a thirteen year-old, in every way as attractive as her sister and a good deal less innocent, her mother suspected. But Sonia had forsworn men forever. She would be a New Woman in tune with the New Century. Women were vastly superior to men in every way, and she had no intention of relinquishing her independence to one of them.

Marie, third in line was shorter, thin, still sallow-skinned, an altogether unusual-looking member of the family. She greeted each guest unsmiling. She was uncomfortable at parties and unknowingly made everyone else uncomfortable too. She didn't like crowds of people. She didn't like dancing; the weekly class, learning steps and how to deal with partners, was a nightmare. This afternoon she wore a very pretty pink party dress; it might just as well have been a hair shirt.

"Paul," Leonore said, not for the first time, "we must do something about Marie."

"Why? What's the matter with her?"

"Look at her! Look at her now! No wonder she has no friends. She reads too much. That's her trouble. It isn't natural for a girl her age."

Paul laughed as he mostly did when she wanted to discuss the children. "She's all right. Don't worry, darling. She'll grow out of it."

Eduard stood straight-backed, clear-eyed and broad-shouldered, the picture in miniature of an Imperial Guard. His ambition never changed: to follow his father into the Preobrazhensky. He worked hard at his lessons and his military training. Contemporaries at the Lyceum respected him and avoided fights if peace was attainable without losing face.

Albrecht, the end of the line, was articulate as always and restless as Puck. His father said he was the most intelligent of them all. Leonore wasn't convinced. He had so many drollnesses that caused her to doubt. His eyes now were flashing 'round the room as though there was only chaos in his head, and Eduard clutched him from time to time, whenever he looked like wandering away. He greeted the guests as though he'd never seen them before and had no idea why they'd been invited.

"Paul! Will you just look at the way Albrecht's carrying on?" Leonore begged.

"He's an imp, isn't he," Paul laughed. "Of course, all this must be very boring for a little lad like him."

Leonore shook her head and sighed hopelessly.

The afternoon reached a successful end. The night was the grown-ups' turn, with a different orchestra but the same New Year decorations. Igor, still in good voice, announced each guest ascending the staircase. Jewelry flashed, braid glittered. Everyone was gorgeous to match their surroundings. They laughed a lot, but uneasy looks passed between them.

The new reign wasn't satisfying their hopes. They sensed menace in the New Century. The Autocracy was more rigid, less imaginative than ever, the bureaucracy increasingly ossified. Russia was too tired to change with the date on the calendar and could never have been persuaded to do so, were it not for a few of the younger, brighter men like Paul von Hagen.

Von Hagen and men like him were sound; they had an eye to tradition, as well as to the future. Otherwise, what was most new, most progressive, what was shortening the commercial gap between Russia and the West had no sympathy at all with tradition and was out of control. New businesses and factories were starting up everywhere; towns were distended with incoming population; villages were abandoned to the very old and the very young. Prices rose. New people with new money could afford to pay them. But none of the new money was going into the pockets of the old landowners.

They called the new people with the new money "middle class"—a term borrowed from the West. They tolerated them because they had to, but they didn't like them. They resented that there were so many of them at the von Hagens' party this evening. They talked of change, they were loud in their demand for government reforms, but the changes and reforms were to be tailored entirely to their own interests.

Even more frightening were people not at the party, people the von Hagen guests would never contact personally, though they knew they were there. They were restive peasants in the country crying for land. They were workers in the new factories; men and women living like animals in hovels streaming with damp, who had monstrous, deplorable morals and who clamoured continually for ridiculously uneconomic shortened days and higher wages. They too had dreams for the New Century, dreams encouraged by the growing number of hotheads among them preaching impetuous action. They were striking, rioting and murdering all over Russia. Even in far-away Estonia there was so much trouble that Loff decided it was wiser to decline Paul's New Year invitation and to stay at home to take care of the Estate.

Many of their old friends had come tonight, though. General Denisovitch-Komarevsky, grossly fat these days after years of home posting, his waxed white moustaches quivering with the effort of climbing the staircase, clasped Paul fondly. He still wore the red and green of the Preobrazhensky, though his days of military significance were passed. He held Paul's hand in an agonizing grip and kissed him lovingly on both cheeks, peasant style.

"Splendid, splendid, my boy," he growled. "I said you were a fool when you resigned your Commission, but maybe you weren't... maybe not. You are one of the New Young Men, they tell me; perhaps Russia has more need of people like you out in the world." He turned to Leonore and bowed. "Madame von Hagen. Charming, charming, dear lady." He kissed her hand with the panache and verve of a much younger man and merged into the crowd with a mumbled: "We have to talk, my boy."

Music flowed through the room, comforting as warm oil, and guests floated on its lilt. Leonore never danced at her own parties until the last waltz, which she saved for Paul. She considered it her duty to move among her guests, tending to their comfort. She concentrated on the women. The men, when they weren't dancing, clustered in corners or sprawled in the smoking room, discussing matters they considered unsuitable for the ears of their wives. She watched Paul approvingly. He danced with deserted females, working hard at making them feel young again. He considered it important that everyone should go home with at least one pleasant memory of the evening. Leonore's duties as hostess were undoubtedly the more arduous.

"After the last strike, the Government closed the University. They're drafting all those poor young men into the Army. It doesn't bear thinking about, does it?"

Close to tears at Leonore's side was Varavara Milyova, wife of the Admiral who had been stationed in Vladivostok since the beginning of time, it seemed.

"My dear, I've been at my wits' end. Our Kolya wasn't involved in any of that dreadful behaviour, of course—there's no question of that—but the police don't stop to ask questions, do they? He was in the University when they smashed their way in, and because he wasn't in the front with the ringleaders he was trapped; he couldn't possibly get out. You can imagine how I was feeling. The Admiral would never have forgiven me if I'd allowed them to take him for the Army."

Leonore squeezed her friend's arm comfortingly.

"It just has to be the Navy, you see. The Admiral simply wouldn't hear of anything else. Though Kolya isn't at all sure…oh, my dear! I shouldn't be bothering you with this just now, but I really feel I can't stand it a moment longer. If only his father had been here. If only they'd send the Admiral home. Though, with all this trouble in the Far East…they can't spare him because of that, of course. My dear, do you think we'll have a war with the Japanese?"

"I'll speak to my husband about it," Leonore told her vaguely, looking around in the hope of finding someone else needing her assistance. "Why don't you come to see me tomorrow, and…"

Varvara Milyova interrupted tearfully. "Your husband is a great man in the East these days, I know, but I can't believe he could influence the Admiralty so far as my husband is concerned."

"I was thinking of Kolya," Leonore told her sharply.

"Oh, Kolya's all right, thank God. At least, I hope he is. Princess Krimovskaya said I should send him straight away to Berlin. He left yesterday morning, though there was a demonstration of workers in the Belorussia yards at the time. But they got the train away eventually. Kolya's always lived a sheltered life, you know. And now he's alone, in Berlin, and…" She sighed deeply, turning away, her handkerchief to her eyes. "But I mustn't spoil your party with my troubles."

"My husband will do all he can to get Kolya back of course," Leonore told her. Varvara Milyov turned back again, instantly cheerful.

"By the way, the Admiral has come to know a friend of yours quite well. He sees her quite often, I believe," she simpered.

"He shows her the sights of Vladivostok. She's an artist, you see. Her name is Lydmilla Fyodorovna Kholchevskaya, if I remember correctly."

"Oh, yes?"

"The Admiral sent me two of her watercolors, scenes of the Port from a nearby hill. They're quite lovely. I must remember to show them to you."

"She's very clever," Leonore said grimly. "She's here tonight, as a matter of fact. I'll find her and introduce you, if you like."

Lydmilla was there, not because Leonore enjoyed inviting her these days, but because she had acquired prestige in Saint Petersburg society. Her patrons reckoned on seeing her everywhere. Her pictures were the latest craze. Everyone who hadn't seen the phenomenon for themselves—and that was virtually anyone—eulogized on her talent for capturing the pearl-like quality of Vladivostok skies. Her work was constantly on show in a gallery on Sadovaya Street, and a party to launch her pre-Lenten display was now a feature of the season.

She went to the Far East twice a year and was popular with everybody there, too. Quite frequently, she traveled out in company with Paul. Mostly they went by train, but on two unforgettable occasions on board ship from Odessa.

Her landscapes and views from Vladivostok's various hills were as highly prized by the colonists themselves as they were in the West. She also created an easy, uninhibited relationship with the men in the Naval Yards while drawing their portraits and scenes of them at their work. Some she gave to men she used as models; others went to the commercial market.

Leonore was reluctant to revive their friendship to its previous intimacy, but Paul never understood that there had ever been a break. Had it not been for Lydmilla, they would never have known what happened to Ida. They owed her a lot for that.

Leonore saw her in a corner talking with a group of men. The old black simplicity of her clothes was not quite a thing of the past. She still wore black. But she had Rachel design and make her gowns, so there was a vast difference in the cut and the quality of the material. Leonore moved reluctantly towards her, but was rescued, for the moment, by Princess Krimovskaya.

Since the von Hagens had so generously opened their house to Pyotr Alexeivitch, the Princess tacitly considered an unofficial betrothal in place between Petka and Dorothea. In other times, such an alliance would not have been agreeable. The von Hagens were unequal in rank. Nonetheless, he was an up-and-coming name in government and commerce...and could one ever be sure that nobility alone would be sufficient to cope with the practicalities of life in the future? Everyone said the Count thought very highly of him. And rumour had it that the present Baron would never marry, which was much to be said in his brother's favour. Perhaps influence in Government would, after all, be the best insurance money could buy in the new century.

"Dorothea, my love! Such a sweet child. I really must tell you how much more charming I find her every time I meet her."

Leonore inclined her head.

"Pyotr is very much taken with her, too. One can see that all too clearly. These young people!" She laughed condescendingly and favoured her hostess with an intimate pat with her fan. "To tell you the truth, we would all like to see more of the child. Do you think, my dear friend, is it possible? Could you bring yourself to allow her to stay with us in the country, for the whole of the summer, if she would like that? Could you possibly spare her?"

Leonore smiled because she knew that a smile would be awaited; she was by now habituated to the contrived gentility of Saint Petersburg society. She remained enough of the person she was deep down, though, a product of Zamenhofa Street; by Saint Petersburg standards, she was extravagantly protective of her children. How dare this woman, so confident in her family name and her wealth, appropriate Dorothea for her son!

"We couldn't possibly spare her for so long, Princess. We always go to Estonia in the summer. Paul's brother would never forgive us if Dorothea didn't come, too."

The Princess smiled with chill understanding. What airs was this woman from only-God-knew-where abrogating to herself?

Surely, even to her, it should be obvious that it was the husband, not the entire family, who was the desired quarry. "Of course," Leonore continued, smiling, "we could perhaps spare her for a week or two. And afterwards, Pyotr might like to come to Estonia with us. He's been before, if you remember." Her smile contained a razor-edge of accusation. You, his mother, it said, deserted him in Saint Petersburg for months, because you were bored with mourning for Tsar Alexander. We took the poor boy in, gave him a home...!

The Princess's smile never faltered. "Of course, my dear, we'll have to see," she murmured, disinterestedly moving away. Leonore, feeling pleased, watched her go. Trial shots across the bows. On target, she congratulated herself. Only minor damage, but...a successful engagement nevertheless.

Through the crowd she watched Paul following the Colonel Denis-ovitch-Komarevsky into the smoking room. The Colonel looked nervously over his shoulder as they went; he had been young once himself, and knew how adept young men were at escaping the philosophising of the old. Paul von Hagen was his prey tonight, and the old man couldn't be at ease until they could safely concentrate in the safety of tobacco smoke. He clasped Paul's arm with nervous energy.

"About the Japanese, von Hagen!" He paused, expecting that all must be perfectly clear and that Paul would respond.

"Yes, Colonel?"

The old man shrugged. What idiots these young men were. "What are they up to? You should know," he barked.

Paul had learned the honey-tongued talk of diplomacy by now. "What on earth should they be up to, Colonel?"

"Don't play games with me, young man. You know exactly what I mean. We robbed them after their Korean War just as we ourselves were robbed in '82. It doesn't do, you know. It never does. Remember how we felt when they took everything away from us?"

Paul smiled, and he hoped it was a polite smile. "My interests are confined to Manchuria these days, Colonel. I've had no direct contact with the Japanese since Shimoneski. I hear from Ouroussoff now and again, though. You remember him, I expect."

"Oh yes! Ouroussoff! First-rate fellow, but never took anything seriously. He left the Regiment too, you know."

"He's married, now. He and his wife have a baby, he tells me; a little girl."

"Ouroussoff a father! Good God!"

"He takes everything very seriously these days, I believe."

"I'd heard he was in Manchuria. They're giving him some sort of job on the vice-regal staff they've set up at Harbin, aren't they?"

"He and his wife live in Port Arthur now. That's why I haven't seen him for a while. He's doing some intelligence work there, I gather. I don't know what it's about."

The Colonel grunted. "If that's what he's doing, I'm glad to hear he's not the man he was when I had him in the Regiment. Let's hope he knows how to keep his eyes and ears open. We're going to have to deal with those Japanese one of these days. You remember what I'm telling you, now!"

Outside in the salon, the orchestra still played, but the dancers were thinning. Many had gone down to supper. Leonore and Lydmilla Fyodorovna, sitting stiffly, uncertainly, side by side, watched them go.

"You know, Leonore," Lydmilla's voice was warm and low, "if I didn't understand that you must have a great deal to occupy your time at the moment, I could easily believe you didn't want to see me."

"What nonsense."

"Come now, my dear. We two are old friends. We know each other much too well to dissimulate."

"I really don't know what you mean."

Lydmilla Fyodorovna sighed, as though giving up the chase as hopeless. "We were such good friends in Florence," she said sadly. "You were so good to me. Now, whenever I'm in Saint Petersburg, I hardly see you. You invite me to your parties, sure enough, but we never sit together as we used to do in the garden of that villa and just...just talk." She paused and continued more firmly. "You'll never forgive me for Ida, will you?"

Leonore was shocked by her frankness. "I don't know why you want to go back over all that tonight, of all nights."

"Because this is tonight, of all nights. Tonight's the night to put it right, whatever it was that went wrong between us in the past. Leonore...Leonore, my dear...I beg you...please, please, please forgive me."

Leonore wanted to stand up and walk away, but this woman was somehow distilling her strength, and she realised her legs would not support herself. She turned slowly, so as to be face to face with her captor. Startlingly, Lydmilla Fyodorovna looked older than she remembered her, even from a moment ago. But the grey eyes regarded her steadily, with warmth and mildness. Leonore knew that somehow, Lydmilla had a hold over her. She didn't know how it had happened, though it must have been something to do with Florence.

"You're quite wrong, you know. I've nothing to forgive. The fault is all mine, not yours."

"My dear…"

"Really! I'm grateful to you. Without you and Loff, Ida might well have been dead by now. You saved her. I could never have done what you did. For one thing, I didn't have your…"—she paused, finding the word difficult—"…I didn't have your contacts. And, in any case, I would have been too emotional. I know that."

"Leonore…I never meant to hurt you. You must believe that. I didn't want you to know exactly what was happening, in case…well, there might have been no hope for her."

"I'd brought her up since she was quite a little girl," Leonore reminisced, speaking to herself as well as to Lydmilla. "When our parents were killed, she clung to me and screamed, on and on. I couldn't comfort her, couldn't stop her screaming. Rachel was white and stiff and quite quiet. But Ida screamed and needed to be held. I'll never forget it. She's been very special to me ever since. I'd never before been so desperately needed by anyone…I'm not sure I ever have again."

"I can understand…indeed, I do. And you must believe me when I tell you that I wasn't trying to take your place. Leonore, I'd never hurt you for the world."

"You didn't hurt me. Rather, you shocked me. Without realising it, of course. How could you know? I'd spent so much of my life trying to be someone I'm not, and nobody but you ever realised it. I've taken everybody in but you. You can see through me. You know I'm just a stupid, ignorant Yiddish woman, and that where my family is concerned, my heart always rules my head."

They both laughed, grateful that the tension between them was relieved and that neither of them were paying too much attention to the actual words.

"Where is she now? I never hear anything, of course."

"She writes to Rachel sometimes; never to us, though. She can't forgive Paul for working for the Government, I think. She's in Vilna, I believe, working for some Jewish political organisation. She's running the same old risks, but…oh, dear!" Leonore saw a special acquaintance coming towards her across the dance floor. "It's Princess Surotkina. Come along, you must meet her, if you don't already know her, that is."

Princess Surotkina approached twitchily, suspiciously, her eyes darting at the ground and from side to side like a very old bird, in either hope or fear. She wore an old-fashioned grey silk gown with a bustle, and a magnificent necklace of emeralds. Over the emeralds, however, she had drawn a feather boa tightly around her neck. It was thrown over her shoulder and reached almost to the floor behind her. Leonore longed to take it off to wash it.

"Princess! Princess, how very good of you to come to my little party."

Princess Surotkina thrust forward her cheek to be kissed, and Leonore wondered whether she would be better employed in washing the Princess herself. Dirt was clearly to be seen in the powdered wrinkles of her cheeks.

"You must have met my friend, haven't you? My very oldest friend, Madame Kholchevskaya, Lydmilla Fyodorovna, the painter."

Princess Surotkina favoured Lydmilla with a sharp glance and looked away again immediately. "No, I don't know her," she said dismissively. "Leonore, my dear, I must speak to your husband. Every time I attempt to do so, someone else has his attention. It's very urgent. Please be so good as to fetch him for me."

Leonore moved away, and Lydmilla attempted to follow, but she was, for the moment, the Princess's captive. "He's such a good man, such a very good man," the Princess told her, as though they'd known each other for years. "Such a good man. God bless him! And, God love me! I've no idea how I've come to deserve him, I'm sure. He does everything for me; absolutely everything. The trouble is, he's away so often. So, when he's in Saint Petersburg, I have to see him whenever I can. I tell him all my troubles. But it isn't easy. God help me! So many other people need to talk to him as well. Sometimes I tell him it's a plot against me." She laughed. "He only laughs and tells me it's not true. But for me it's serious. He's the only one who understands my situation, you see," she continued confidentially. "Everybody thinks that because I have brothers, I shouldn't be needing anyone else. My brothers…? God help me! Drink and dice, drink and dice, drink and dice! That's all they're good for. Dice and drink, dice and drink. Well, you know what they're like. And where would we all be, I ask you, if I let them manage our affairs, let alone know tell them how much I've got to keep that bit of land around the house and the roof over our heads. They've gambled everything else away. God only knows why He put me on this earth, only to be troubled the way I am, and…"

But Lydmilla heard no more. A roar obliterated everything. The room shook. Windows crashed to the floor, making their own kind of music. Chandeliers tinkled in a different key. Smoke and dirt billowed across the dance floor. Women screamed in terror. Two marble dryads vacated their niches, split to fragments and scattered their parts among the trembling guests. Uniforms, so smart a moment ago, were now ripped and dirty. Faces were soot-stained. Blood flowed over jeweled embonpoints and starched shirt fronts. Princess Surotkina fell against Lydmilla Fyodorovna, almost forcing her to the floor, crossing herself insanely. For a moment it was as if everyone was struck dumb. The hysterical screaming stopped. When it began again, it was a restrained, low sobbing. It was overtaken by a new sound. The groaning of the wounded rose in its own urgency to shatter the eardrums. And the brutality of the outrage, the death it brought, the pain and destruction that followed, were to form an unforgettable bridge between the one century and the next.

CHAPTER 3

▼

1900

"You never heard such a noise, Irina. I thought the house was falling down around us. And when I went out of my bedroom to look, there were dead bodies everywhere."

"My dear...!" Irina Petrovna screwed her handkerchief against her lips to stifle her agitation.

"The screams! Irina, you've never heard anything like it."

"I should have died, I know I should," Irina Petrovna said, thoroughly enjoying herself. "Sonia, you're so wonderfully brave."

"Don't tell such lies, Sonia! You didn't see any dead bodies," Dorothea said, joining them unseen.

"You don't know what I saw, Dora! You stayed in your room all the time. You were too scared to come out at all."

"And you were hardly in the corridor before Igor caught you and brought you into my room. He had you slung over his shoulder like a sack of cabbages..."

"Oh, Sonushka!" Irina was Sonia's best friend and her most passionate admirer at the Smolny Institute. She soaked up her friend's story, eager to be terrified. How she wished Sonia's boring sister would go away. It was too thrilling that the terrorists had actually selected her best friend's house for an outrage. Sonia's Papa was tremendously important, of course; everyone knew that. But to Irina Petrovna, just then, no one in the world could possibly have been more important than his daughter Sonia. Day after day, they sat side by side in class, and Irina breathed in the magic of Sonia's toilet water. Sometimes, Sonia allowed Irina to carry her books. They were inseparable every minute. And, most important of all, they had made a secret pact: they would have absolutely nothing to do with boys for as long as they lived!

"Cabbages!" Dora said again. "That's exactly what you looked like, Sonia: a sack of cabbages. He dumped you on my bed and told me to look after you and be sure you didn't get out again and worry Mama and Papa."

"Your Igor…" Irina's eyes glowed. "How absolutely marvelous! I know he's a Tartar, and they're not always very clean, but…"

"Irina! Remember what you promised!" Sonia reminded her sharply. "He's one of them!"

"Yes, dear." Irina let go the delicious fantasy of being rescued in the arms of the beautiful Igor in a moment of emergency. Fortunately, a bell rang just then and they all went back into class.

In contrast to the garrulous Sonia, Marie refused to talk to any of her friends about the bombing. She had been deeply affected, though. After the noise and excitement had petered out, she left her bed that night and went into the salon alone. The devastation shocked her. Pieces of the dryads still littered the floor; broken chairs were jumbled in preposterous heaps. Ripped as they were from top to bottom, a servant had thoughtfully drawn the curtains across empty windows to keep out the night.

She was shocked afresh next morning by the chaos in the courtyard, as though the house had been turned inside out, she thought. The remains of two carriages stood splintered by the portico, and instead of cobblestones, she walked to the gate over a layer of shattered glass. Two men in baggy shirts and knee boots were attacking the disorder with stiff brooms.

After that, her day was a torment. It was impossible for her to concentrate on lessons, and the teachers held her up to ridicule for her lack of attention. Smolny girls should know what to expect when their Papas rose to positions of distinction. They should also realise that to give way in such circumstances was to allow the terrorists to win. Marie von Hagen was behaving shamefully!

They misjudged her. Her abstraction had nothing to do with nervousness. Her mother told her there had been no serious injuries, though some of the guests had been cut by broken glass. Why did they do it, she asked herself over and over. What had they achieved that couldn't be put right almost immediately by men with brooms and hammers and nails, and women with needles and thread? They had achieved nothing. So much ruination for so little. And who were they? Unknown faces occupied her attention all through French and Drawing and Music and Russian Literature. They were all so beautiful, those faces; young girls with golden hair, delicate and glittering like spiders' webs in early autumn; young blue-eyed boys with golden beards and moustaches beginning to ornament their unblemished cheeks. How did they make their bombs? What did you need to make a bomb? Did all those beautiful people spend their lives in noisome cellars fearing betrayal? Was it possible they could really have meant to hurt anybody that night?

Across town at the Lyceum, Eduard was shamefaced and proud, both at the same time; shamefaced because he'd gone to bed as usual, fallen asleep as usual and had neither heard nor seen anything to boast about until after the explosion. He had known nothing until Igor came into his room with instructions from his father: he was to stay exactly where he was and keep Albrecht quiet. Neither of them was to leave the bedroom for any reason whatsoever. It was an order, and Eduard's duty was to obey it punctiliously.

Back at school, he regretted having so little to tell, but that hardly mattered. The other boys had their own stories of attacks they'd heard about, read about, dreamed about, each more bloodthirsty than the last. They shouted one another down, and Eduard's importance laid not so much in what he had to say as that he was eligible for adoption into their schoolboy mythology.

"Eduard's Papa knows more about Manchuria than anyone," someone said enviously.

"I'll bet he's going there again soon, isn't he, von Hagen?"

"Yes."

"There!" The interrogator smirked at the others, one of whom was still sufficiently unimpressed as to ask why.

"Because of the Chinese, of course, stupid."

"They're fantastic," someone else said. "They go to places where they practice fighting and build their muscles and that…"

"And now they're going round killing all the Russians they can get their hands on."

"Is that why your Papa's going out there, von Hagen?"

"Do you think they'll kill him, too?"

"Of course not, you idiot! He'll have lots and lots of bodyguards, won't he, von Hagen?"

"Oh, shut up, you!"

"Was it a Chinaman who threw that bomb the other night, von Hagen?"

"Did you see any of them hanging about before that? They go around on those padded shoes so you can't hear them coming, don't they?"

"The yellow peril," someone said, and growled like a tiger.

"Everyone knows what they're like. The Chinese and the Japanese. And they all look alike, so you can't tell one from another."

"Von Hagen, get your Papa to take you with him, next time he goes!"

"Yes. Then you can come back and tell us what it's like."

"We already know what it's like. It's crawling with little yellow monkeys."

There was no reply to this. The talk ended in a free-for-all, the boys setting about each other like puppies, for no reason. The tiger-impressionist, growling and clawing, attacked his nearest neighbour, and everyone else joined in.

The question was academic, anyway. Leonore would never have allowed Eduard to go with his father; she would have kept Paul himself at home if she could. He was leaving at the end of the week, and Lydmilla Fyodorovna was going with him, though Leonore couldn't imagine why she should want to. He was duty-bound, he said. Lydmilla Fyodorovna had no excuse except that she was curious to see and perhaps paint some Boxer rioters. On the way, they planned to stop at the Metropole in Moscow to visit Clementine and Sasha.

Before he left, Paul received a longer-than-usual telegram from his brother:

> *We were shocked to hear of the attack on your house stop Suggest you send Leonore and the children to us for safety's sake stop Prince Krasnov now agrees we are worth special protection during the current disturbances stop We are never without a small contingent of his gendarmes in or near the premises stop The Aschenbauer place is a prey to banditry stop He should never have sold out to a Jew stop He has put the whole district at risk stop But Leonore and the children would be quite safe with us stop No news from Margarethe stop Loff and Channah*

"Out of the question," Leonore said, handing the telegram back to Paul. "I may be Roman Catholic, officially. But I'm still a Jew, deep down. And we Jews are a stiff-necked, obstinate people; it says so in the Bible. I will not be driven out of my home by hooligans afraid to show their faces to the light. I had enough of that when I was a child."

Paul took her gently into his arms warm with pleasure. With every passing moment, it seemed, he loved her more deeply. The bravery of the front she showed gently amused him, though he was distressed to see, ever since the bombing, a slight tremble in her right hand.

In Moscow, Clementine and Sasha had heard about the bombing before Paul and Lydmilla arrived. Official policy was now to publish details, as gory as possible, of every outrage. The public was to be shocked into hating as well as fearing the terrorists and left with a message that would act like a scalpel to the mind: "NEXT TIME COULD BE YOUR TURN!" Whatever was seen or heard, whatever suspicions anyone might have should be reported to the authorities IMMEDIATELY!

The four of them, Paul, Clementine, Sasha, and Lydmilla Fyodorovna, sat late into the night in the Schimanski's Spartan living room, drinking the vodka Paul had brought with him and indulging noncommittally in a meandering conversation. No one said what they thought until, as time passed and the level of vodka in the bottle lowered, Sasha became more eloquent. It was important for him to be believed.

"It's a terrible thing, Paul, having your house bombed like that and your friends cut up by the glass." He nodded towards Lydmilla Fyodorovna, whose cheek was badly scarred and would bear the irregular needle-marks of a harassed surgeon's hasty stitching for a long time to come. "Terrible! Don't think I don't sympathise."

"But if you knew who'd done it, you still wouldn't tell me, would you, Sasha?"

"No. All I will tell you is that nobody I know had anything to do with it."

After that, what was there say? Each withdrew into their isolated thoughts. Sasha was truly regretful. He loved this man, but could only see the distance between them growing wider. Clementine remembered Paul from before his hair began turning grey—the Doma, the flat in Praga, apple orchards on the banks of the Vistula.

"He doesn't mean he approves of what they did, Paul..."

"I can speak for myself," Sasha muttered sulkily.

"But why, Sasha?" Paul, like Marie, needed an explanation. "It did no good. Nothing will change because of it."

"Something will change, one of these days. Until it does, people like you have to be reminded," Sasha told him.

"What should I need a bomb to remind me about?"

"What you people always forget," Clementine put in, sounding surprisingly bitter. "As soon as the dust clears, you order your servants to clear the place up. Some of your friends were cut; scars like that heal. I'm sorry, Lydmilla, but it's true. That's your kind of suffering, Paul. Do you want me to say I'm sorry for you? What about all the others...the people you never see or, if you do see them, you ignore because your sort has been taught for generations to look through as though they don't exist? Have you any idea at all, what it's like to work in Sasha's yards? Have you ever been hungry, slept in a tenement doorway, even in the winter?"

"Suppose you had no money to feed those children of yours, Paul," Sasha put in. "Have you ever been inside a company barracks, seen the water running down the brick walls and soaking the mattresses that are the only place the workers have to sleep? Have you ever been paid in dockets that have to be exchanged for goods at the store your employer owns...?"

"And he charges outrageous prices, so that from the moment you start to work for him you find yourself with a debt you'll never pay off as long as you live. Work sixteen, seventeen, eighteen hours a day, you'll never pay off that debt...not even if you work the whole twenty-four!"

"Strike to get him to reduce those hours or dry out your barracks or charge reasonable prices in his store, and he'll bring in the Cossacks and the police to beat you black and blue..."

"That's the kind of thing you need to be reminded about, Paul. That's why they do it," Clementine finished, almost soothingly.

Sasha stood up and extended his hand. "I'm sorry it happened to you, Paul, really, I am. I swear to you as a friend, my group had nothing to do with it."

"I believe you. But whether you'd do it to me or not hardly matters. You'd do it to someone else, wouldn't you?"

Sasha shrugged.

"Sasha! Sasha, old friend, that isn't the way. Can't you see? It does no good; it doesn't make anybody sympathise with you. They fear you and hate you and want to see you exiled or shot."

Sasha half-smiled. "Tell me another way and we'll try it. We're reasonable people, too. But we have no voice…nobody to represent us. Only let us try to hold a public meeting about anything, and we're arrested for unlawful assembly. Nobody listens to us. The Tsar wants us to think of him as our Little Father. He doesn't even realise we exist."

"I can't speak for him, but more people than you know are on your side, Sasha. We want to see a change, just as much as you do."

"Oh, yes…I know…there are a lot of you. You mean well, and it eases your consciences. But you don't speak out. You don't really do anything to help us. When was the last time you went into your posh office carrying a banner?"

Sasha giggled. He was embarrassed by an outburst that was honest, but that he didn't want Paul, his friend, to take too personally.

"It's the vodka talking," Clementine said.

"All right, Sasha. I know. I'm one of the people who doesn't do anything, doesn't say anything…so far as you're aware. But how many of us will have to die, do you think, before you change things your way? Oh yes, I believe you can change things your way, eventually. But if you build your new society on hatred…the thought of it frightens me. How much time do people like me have, do you think?"

Sasha gave no answer—nobody could—but the question wouldn't go away; it troubled Paul all the way across Siberia. His brain didn't finally clear until they reached Chita. In western Russia, there was too much talk. On the train, as well, there was too much talk. Lydmilla Fyodorovna tried to convert everyone to Kropotkin's idea for village communes existing side-by-side, with no need for national government. No one traveling soft agreed that Kropotkin's anarchy was the way forward. But their disagreements didn't mean very much. Nobody anywhere agreed with anybody. Everyone knew something was seriously wrong, but nobody was in accord as to how to put it right. For everybody to be made happy at the same time was an evident impossibility.

Of course, changes were happening—not fast enough for some, too fast for others. Workers were now allowed to join unions—Zubatov Unions—organised and controlled by the police; a very meager freedom, Paul agreed. A radical newspaper, *Iskra*—the Spark—was about to be launched, but censorship was as firmly in place as ever. There was even talk of a new political party, the Social Revolutionaries, radicals of yet another flavour. They were, without a doubt, already infiltrated by the police.

The long journey from Moscow ground Paul's life away like millstones—slowly, inevitably. For days, the train panted across a whitened landscape with its walls of forest on either side of the track. Passengers lost some of their political enthusiasm in the unfailing boredom of a life punctuated only by clustering for tea around the samovar at the end of the car and dashing across icy platforms for meals in station restaurants at every stop. Food was the chief diversion of the day. Between those times, there was a miserable, futile attempt to shut everything out and sleep away the tedious time.

At Chita the atmosphere altered cheerfully. They were too far away now for the rumbling discontents of Moscow and Saint Petersburg to be vital. From here on, talk would ignore political theory in the face of a palpable threat. The Boxers, out of control throughout northern China, were becoming increasingly audacious in their attacks on Russian property and diabolic in their treatment of any Russians they captured. They came out of the night, streaking down on isolated missions, farms and railway settlements to slaughter every man woman and child they could lay hands on. Nobody could tell where it was likely to happen next, so Russian soldiers invariably arrived too late. Afterwards, they would chase the raiders, tracking them in the snow. But they were always gone with time to spare, vanishing into the blackness to wreak havoc the next night, miles away.

These Boxer raids on railway property were Paul's reason for being here at this inhospitable time of year. He was to assess the cost for the directors of the Bank. The Bank needed the information to use as a stick for beating the government. Paul would send a duplicate of his report privately to the Count so the government would be forewarned

Chita was on the Russian side of the Amur River and safe, but who could say how long it would be before Boxer fanatics spilled over the border to provoke the ethnic Chinese and Mongols, who found themselves obligatory citizens within the Russian Empire?

Paul got down from the train and stamped up and down the platform in the forty-below temperature. Lydmilla Fyodorovna walked with him, her arm in his, her body close against him in an effort to keep warm. A sharp wind blew from the north, metamorphosing harmless snowflakes into a kind of buckshot hard-edged enough to draw blood.

Before the train continued on to Harbin, a military escort climbed aboard. Soldiers scaled ladders to the roofs of the cars, swearing and dragging machine-guns with them. Their torment would be to squat unprotected from the blizzard throughout the night, straining into the blackness for an attack that might or might not come. Of course, they complained as they climbed. Their more fortunate comrades were at least beginning the trip in the warmth of the footplate, where they jostled the engineer and his fireman in the cramped space and were cursed and sworn at for being in the way.

The soldiers wore regulation uniforms, earflaps buttoned tight below their chins, scarves over their mouths and noses, already stiff with frozen breath, and darkened goggles to protect their eyes from blindness. Even so, some would finish the journey frozen; dead, perhaps. But the Russian Army was never short of men.

Impatient whistles signaled that the train was ready to proceed; Paul and Lydmilla climbed back on board. The locomotive dragged its load with cart horse patience to the bank of the Amur River and across the bridge into Manchuria. The clatter of the wheels sounded hollow as solid ground fell away on one shore until they picked it up on the other. Paul and Lydmilla looked at each other and she smiled.

"We're across the river. We're here," she said.

"Why?"

"My dear Paul, you surely haven't traveled all this way without knowing why you've come." She laughed, abashed by her own poor joke, but he didn't help her by responding in the same vein."

"I know why I'm here."

"But you're not sure of me. You want me to explain myself. Don't you know me well enough to trust me, even now?"

"I want to trust you. I want to very much," he told her earnestly.

"Very well," she responded briskly, "what can I tell you that you don't already know? I am not a rich woman. But you know that already, quite well. What money I make comes from my paintings. The East is in fashion at the moment. People are hoping I shall paint Boxers for them, dripping with Russian blood, if that's at all possible. That is why I am here, my dear. It's quite simple, you see. I'm here to paint because that's the way I earn my living."

"It's too dangerous for you to be here just now."

She shrugged. "How dangerous anything may be depends upon what you have to lose because of it."

"Your life…?"

She shrugged again.

"Lydmilla…why do we meet like strangers, these days?"

"Leonore," she said lightly. "She will never forgive me for not telling her sooner about Ida."

"It has nothing to do with Leonore. I'm talking about you and me."

Her face clouded, and she turned away. For several moments neither said anything, and the train rumbled loudly in their silence.

At last he said, "You were very important to me all those years ago in Florence. Afterwards, I hoped we'd be together in Paris."

She tried to laugh, but her laughter was false. "That was a long time ago, my dear. We were both young, and when one is young everybody is important; one hasn't learned yet to discriminate."

He ignored her meaning. "The painter with the calm grey eyes," he reminded her, "who lived in a room she would never let me visit, with a husband she would never let me meet…"

"Don't, Paul."

"It's true. You confused me. I didn't know what to believe. But your friendship was important to me, and I was willing to believe…to accept everything. You didn't realise it then. Perhaps you don't realise it now, but you're still important. You still lock me out, though, don't you? You still won't let me know who you are, what you do, why you do it. And I'm afraid for you."

"My dear, don't be."

"You think, simply because you tell me so, that's enough?"

"Paul…! Paul! Listen to me! Perhaps when I was young I was…a little naive. You and I were very close. We were good comrades. And we harmed no one. We were both quite sure about that. But…Paul dear, you have to understand…I had other comrades then. I always have had. And they are not at all like you…you would have no sympathy with them. They are forced to live in a dark world because of who they are and what they believe. But they are not dangerous to you. They're longing for change, the way you longed for change when you were young. I…I can't tell you any more about them…I'm sorry. But they're no threat to you, you must believe me."

His shoulders sagged. "I have no choice, have I?"

"Trust me now, my friend. You always have," she said, and kissed him lightly on the lips.

She left him soon afterwards to fetch them tea from the Goddess of the Samovar, as everyone called the old woman who sat at the end of the car and apparently never slept. She hadn't returned when the uproar began. Paul had been slumped in his corner, his mind in turmoil. In spite of what he had told her just now, he didn't trust her at all. He never had trusted her completely, he realised, not even when he was a young man and half in love with her. He was a fool not to have admitted it to himself long before this, but he needed her; his insurance against growing old and unattractive to women. Why hadn't she let him know where she lived, refused to let him meet her husband? Most probably because when she allowed him to carry home her easel, she parted from him nowhere near her true address. Had she even been married, he wondered? She pretended to be so frightened for her husband's health in their dreadful living conditions. But when Leonore offered them a healthier home at the Villa Belleguardo, she ignored the proposal, and Leonore, feeling snubbed, hadn't renewed it. Why, now, was she so frequently visiting the Far East, spending her days in Vladivostok making paintings of the Port and passing so much time among the men working in the shipyards?

The roar of an explosion somewhere near interrupted his ruminations. The unexpected shuddering of the train to a sudden stop threw him from one side of the compartment to the other. He had hardly recovered when the firing began, rifles from somewhere in the inkiness outside, and retorts from the machine-gunners on the roof. As he struggled to his feet, still shaky, the window by his left ear shattered and the lamp went out. He dropped to his knees and crawled towards the end of the car to find Lydmilla. She was on her hands and knees coming back to him, and they met nose-to-nose.

"Paul? What's happening?"

"I'm not sure."

"What should we do?"

"Keep low."

The firing increased alarmingly, and more glass was shattered. Somewhere in the car, a woman screamed hysterically. Paul and Lydmilla crawled towards their compartment in the dark and stumbled over a man lying on the floor. They expected him to move to allow them to pass, but he was motionless. He was dead.

Paul pushed him to one side and Lydmilla whimpered with shock.

"Paul! We've got to get out."

"No."

"He's dead, isn't he?"

"Yes."

"Let go of me! I've got to get out!"

"Don't be absurd. Even if they don't shoot you, how long do you think you'd last outside in this weather?"

She began to cry and nestled against his body for comfort. He lay stiff, head raised, listening. There were cries and screams from various parts of the train. He heard the crash of a door bursting open, and Lydmilla mewed like a stricken animal and irrationally climbed on to his prone body as though he was her safety. Rifle shots whined through the car from end to end, and a couple nearby began praying loudly together. In the darkness, it was impossible to recognise them nor, from their voices, to distinguish what parts they'd taken in the endless political arguments that had lasted since Moscow. Paul could have laughed, had he not, in those circumstances, feared being accused of dementia caused by fear. All that talk—how absurd it was! Days of unforgiving disagreement over what the new world should be like, when now it appeared that none of them would ever live to see it.

A man screamed louder than anyone, and the rifle fire within the car ceased. Screams are the same in any language, but this one, Paul was sure, had been uttered by a Chinese larynx. He wriggled free of Lydmilla in an effort to see what was happening. All the firing was dying down now and figures, only just discernible in the earliest dawn light, moved upright about the car. A man was complaining peevishly about the cold air gusting through the open doorway.

The light of day gradually strengthened, artificially bolstered by the whiteness of the snow all around them. Shouts and firing could no longer be heard outside the train. Inside, there was some sobbing and groaning, but it was low and didn't disturb the moaning of the wind.

A new commotion began at the end of the car. The conductor entered, swinging a lamp and followed by soldiers, clumping loudly in their heavy boots.

"Olga Stepanovna!"

"Yes?" The answer was uncertain from the end of the car.

"The samovar! Their Excellencies need tea!" The conductor wouldn't have known what a psychologist was, but he prided himself on knowing how to deal with people; and elevating everybody in rank was never a bad thing to do.

"At once, Genardi Georgevitch!" The old woman was grateful for having someone to tell her what to do. The conductor was, under the circumstances, extraordinarily full of confidence, advising and directing.

"Do the same here as you did in the last car, brothers," he ordered the soldiers who followed him. "Make the wounded as comfortable as you can on the benches. See to it that they're warm." He lowered his voice. "As for the others…"

"We know, brother," someone said.

"Keep the wounded as warm as possible," the conductor said again.

As a railway official, Paul felt he should take some part in the arrangements. The conductor knew him, had known the reason for his journey ever since they'd left Moscow.

"Can we go on, Conductor?"

"No, your Excellency…not for a little while. They blew the track, you see. Only a little hole, thank God. And, thank God, the Engineer stopped the train in time. It was a miracle he did, thank God, for he certainly couldn't have seen it for the storm. He had an instinct, he says."

"We can't keep these people here for long in a wrecked train with no windows. They'll freeze to death. Are we near a shelter?"

"No, your Excellency. But this isn't the first time this has happened. The boys are getting very good at filling holes and straightening tracks. They'll have us on our way quite soon, I dare say."

"I'll commend you at headquarters, Genardi Georgevitch."

"Thank you, your Excellency." The Conductor looked proud, and straightened his cap before making his way carefully through the rest of the train. Commendations at headquarters were all very well, but he had a wife and seven children living in Harbin. How long did the Government expect them to put up with this sort of thing night after night?

Paul returned to his windowless compartment. Lydmilla Fyodorovna was there already, crouching on the seat, her teeth chattering. In a gesture of what he hoped she would accept as gallantry—for he was not sure now how much he had upset her during their conversation before the raid—he took off his overcoat and draped it around her shoulders. She gave no acknowledgment, and when he looked intently into her face, he realised that she was not cold, but shaking with shock. There was nothing to do now but to wait.

It was just after mid-day when they clattered over a complicated pattern of points and limped to a stop at a platform in Harbin station. Young Kharbutov was waiting anxiously on the platform, waving his arms and stamping his feet to keep warm in the flurries of snow. Lydmilla Fyodorovna surrendered immediately to his solicitude, and Paul, a little resentful, watched them walk to a waiting rickshaw, the driver wrinkled with age and cold. When they were out of sight, he picked up his bag and found a vehicle to take him to Government House.

He was surprised anew each time he saw it, a child's playing-card kind of a house, with a series of smaller and smaller ascending concave roofs, its pink tiles hidden today under snow and with an icicle hanging from each of its many corners.

He was expected. A Russian clerk shuffled forward to greet him and apologise for not having had him met at the station.

"The trains run so irregularly these days, your Excellency," he simpered apologetically. "The Boxers..." He shook his head reprovingly. "Some trains are attacked, held up, even though there are soldiers to

protect them. I expect you had some soldiers on yours, didn't you?"
There have even been passengers shot to death, I believe."

Paul nodded. "When can I see the Governor?"

"This evening, your Excellency. You're dining with him. We didn't
know at what time you would arrive, you see. The trains…"

"Yes, yes," Paul interrupted tired and by now, irritable.

The clerk registered the reproof. "I'll find someone to carry your bag
and show you to your hotel, your Excellency."

Some time later, after Paul had been asleep in his bedroom for perhaps two hours, there was a loud, impatient knocking on his door.

"Von Hagen! I say, von Hagen! Are you there?"

The voice was familiar, but Paul didn't have to guess who it was,
because the owner didn't wait to be invited in. The door flew open and
Ouroussoff stood in the room, beating snow from his greatcoat and
overwhelming Paul's weariness with his own delight.

"My dear, dear old boy! How are you? They didn't tell me you were
coming out so soon. This is marvelous. I'm delighted to see you, I
really am."

"How did you know I was here, Sergei?"

"The visitors book at Government House. You must get into the
habit, too. Look at it every day, whenever you're passing the desk.
Trains don't run to a timetable anymore. You never know when
they're arriving these days, nor whom they'll bring."

Paul reluctantly abandoned his peace, but was finding it hard to
climb out of bed and focus on his visitor. Sergei clasped him, dragged
him upright and hugged him.

"It's wonderful that you're here. How long are you staying? We're in
a mess, believe me. But you'll hear all about it tonight at the Governor's dinner. I shall be there too, by the way."

"Good. I'd no idea you were in Harbin. I was wondering how I
might get down to Port Arthur to see you."

"Oh, I'm here on a temporary permanency," Ouroussoff laughed.
"This is where all the planning will be done, eventually. You'll meet

the rest of us tonight. Not a bad crowd really, except for Bezobrazov. He's a bit too much of a firebrand, really...looking for influence, trying to make his mark wherever he can. He'll be canvassing you, without a doubt."

"If I don't get down to Port Arthur, Leonore will be very angry. She reproaches me every time I come out for not having seen your wife and daughter. Your wife and she were great friends, you know, and she's worried about them with all this trouble going on."

"You can see them easily enough. They're here in Harbin, as a matter of fact. Elizaveta wouldn't stay alone in Port Arthur, stupid woman. Heaven only knows why she's convinced herself she's one of the Boxers' principal targets." He grinned sheepishly and shrugged. "She's no safer here than she was down there, but...Tell me about Leonore."

"She's fine. And the children. We had a little excitement the other night, though. Our house was bombed."

"Good God!"

"Nobody seriously hurt, thank God."

"Who was it?"

It was Paul's turn to shrug. "Some revolutionary group or another. But tell me about these Boxer chaps. They attacked our train last night."

"That's our biggest problem, the railways." Ouroussoff frowned. "They kill as many passengers as they can, rob them to buy their supplies and...this is the serious part...they're stealing our machine guns."

"That's my chief concern here, the railways, of course."

"Thank God you are here, then! Nobody else seems to know what to do, and if we can't keep the lines open we're done for."

"Railways aren't the only targets though, are they?"

"Heavens, no! They're after everything and everybody foreign. We're getting refugees from settlements all along the lines. And that's not helping, either. But we can't get the men to stay in the countryside to hold them back."

"The cities are safe enough, though?"

"Not really. Though Elizaveta thinks nothing can happen here in Harbin. She's quite wrong, of course. She believes that by paying our servants double the usual rate, they'll love her and protect her if ever the Boxers attack our house. Nonsense! We're all in danger, and there's no way out except by destroying them. Any of our servants could belong to them. We just don't know. They can be kowtowing and calling you 'master' one moment and slitting your throat the next."

Paul found the Governor's dinner that night a depressing affair, made particularly so by the bellicose talk of Bezobrazov and one or two others, who saw their only way to fame in an all-out war. The "Righteous and Harmonious Fists" was not an army to be fought, however. They were bands of brigands in collusion with the Manchu government, scouring northern China and Manchuria of foreigners and foreign influence. They didn't prance on hilltops, pennants playing, for the hated foreigners to shoot at. They moved silently in and out of the darkness, knives and torches ready. They were the nightly terror of foreigners and Chinese alike.

Paul agreed with the majority around the table. Whatever it was, this could never be called a war, and simple bombast would never achieve a settlement.

After the meeting he followed Sergei into the street, expecting *rickshaws* to take them to their beds. There were none to be had, and Sergei laughed at his surprise.

"Even if there were, they wouldn't pick us up at this time of night. If anyone attacked us, their throats would be cut as well as ours for carrying foreigners. Do you have a pistol on you?"

"No."

"I'll get you one tomorrow. Don't go anywhere without it...understand?"

Paul nodded. While they walked, they heard gunfire from various quarters of the town. Paul asked:

"Is that a raid?"

"Russians shooting shadows, I expect," Sergei scoffed. "Everyone's on edge." He guided Paul confidently through streets kept deliberately dark because, it was believed, darkness was a friend to the raided as well as to the raiders. Outside the hotel entrance, he stopped and began awkwardly:

"Perhaps, if you're not doing anything more interesting, you'd care to eat with us tomorrow."

"I'd like that very much."

"Yes…well…"

Sergei moved away and Paul moved with him, sensing that there was more to be said. After some steps, he probed:

"If that's all right with your wife, that is."

He stopped suddenly and turned. He knew that if he could see his friend's face in the darkness, it would be flushed.

"Damn it! Paul, you're going to have to be told before you see for yourself," Sergei broke out. "I was right. All along. All those years, I was right."

"Are you drunk, my friend?" It was a lighthearted question. Paul knew that he wasn't, but was attempting to avoid a cascade of words he feared might drown him.

"I was right, you see," Ouroussoff continued excitedly.

"I'm a soldier. I need men about me…one man in particular…one man to clean my boots, brush my uniform, fetch my meals, put me to bed when I'm drunk…I don't want a wife, I don't want anyone to make a home for me, someone who'll go on loving me when I'm completely unlovable. I can do without a family. Do you understand, Paul? I'm not the marrying kind. But I'm married. Do you understand, Paul? God help me, I'm married."

They were at the corner of the street. He turned, and Paul heard his footsteps hurrying away.

"Oh yes, I understand, Sergei, you poor fool," he breathed.

"God help you. I understand. And God help that poor woman, too!"

CHAPTER 4

▼

1901

"You must think seriously about someone, my dear. Poor Fermatov was a very wise choice; it was easier that time, of course. You'd known him for years. But now that he's gone, poor man, you cannot go on trying to manage everything alone."

Loff looked at her resignedly. "And you really believe Stepan Stepanovich is the answer?"

"You won't lose anything by giving him the chance, now, will you? He knows the Estate as well as anybody. He knows the people here, the Estonians as well as the Russians."

"He's a peasant."

He was a peasant, she had to agree. And because he was a peasant and she was a Jew, he treated her like dirt whenever they met. But she had always managed to put what she saw as Loft's interests before her own feelings. "He was a peasant when you first brought him here, but he's changed a lot since then. You chose him because he was different from the others, and you were right to do so. He's able to control any one of them physically. And there's no doubt about it, he's obviously more intelligent than they are."

"Too intelligent, I sometimes think," he sighed. "And there's some-thing not quite right about his accent. I don't know what it is."

She fought against her laughter. How quickly he was growing old; how early he was becoming set in his way of thinking.

"Isn't it a little late to be worrying about his accent? My dear, the important thing is that you are working yourself to death, and you cannot go on like this. Stepan Stepanovich knows more about the diggings than anyone. He can manage the lumbering. The men respect him, the Estonians as well as the Russians. They don't argue when he tells them what to do. And it'll be good to have someone among them who has positive reasons for being on your side."

"He's so different from the others; I sometimes wonder whether he's a Government agent."

This time she didn't restrain her laughter. "You're not serious! You can't honestly believe they'd employ a peasant to spy on you? Father Tikhon, now, when you told me we had to be careful what we said in front of him, I agreed. But Stepan Stepanovich…!"

He waited, but she had nothing more to say. It was the way she always dealt with their problems, forcing him, ultimately, to make the final decision. "Are you telling me the whole truth, Channah?"

"The truth…?"

"Don't you have something else in mind?"

"Well…I do hear in the village that he wants to be married."

"And you think you'll help him by persuading me to improve his prospects. I don't object to that, I suppose. But there's nothing to stop him getting married already, if he wants to. There are enough young girls in Russian Town."

"He wants an Estonian."

"Good God!"

"He's set his heart on Marika Haava."

"A bit young for him, isn't she?"

"That doesn't matter if they both feel the same way. You know that."

He cleared his throat noisily. "Why doesn't he get on with it, then? He knows I'll give her a good dowry."

"Pastor Vikkers is stopping him."

"Doddering old fool."

"He insists that if Stepan wants Marika, he has to convert before he has her."

"And Stepan says no?"

"He says Marika must become Orthodox. But that will make the Pastor's flock even smaller, you see, with people dying and the youngsters moving away. Numbers are his only justification for being here, after all. Konstantin Petrovich keeps account of things like that in Petersburg."

"Rot! Pobedonostsev has more things to worry about than that, I should hope."

"That's what people believe, anyway. And no one wants to see the Government send the poor old man away."

"Then for God's sake, Stepan must convert. He can't think very much of the girl if he won't agree to do a little thing like that. Hasn't anyone explained the way things are to Father Tikhon?"

"Yes, but he doesn't say anything helpful. He doesn't have to, does he? He sits in that old barn of his and smiles. He knows he'll be the winner in the end."

"Damned fools, the lot of them! I'll ride over to the village in the morning and sort it out with Marika's parents."

"Better than that, my dear, announce that you're making Stepan your new Chief Assistant. The Haavas will push the girl into Father Tikhon's church soon enough after that, I guarantee."

Channah was right, of course. She always was, Loff reflected.

When the Haavas knew of Stepan's promotion, the betrothal was easily arranged. In the summer, Leonore, with the children and Alex Krimovsky, were there for the wedding—the most extravagant the village had ever seen. Marika's dowry was secret, but rumoured to be enormous. Stepan's voice was notably deepened and his girth increased with his new authority. For his wedding, his boots were of the shiniest, blackest, softest leather, his shirt of dazzling whiteness, his trousers of the finest wool. Marika was beautiful. Every woman in the village had added (for good fortune and fertility) a stitch to the glowing embroidery on her blouse and skirt. It was in accordance with traditional patterns, but went far beyond necessity in its ostentation.

At the start of spring, Stepan had organised (and paid for out of his own pocket) the grandest of wooden-framed houses. No one had ever seen one like it, not for a peasant to live in, certainly; the whole district agreed it was fit for a landlord. There were two stories to it: a room on the ground-floor for Marika to cook and for the two of them to eat in; another for them to sit like gentry at the end of the day and after church—certainly not the sort of room for livestock in the winter-time. Above them there were another two rooms for sleeping. That amused everyone: whoever heard of a man and wife needing two rooms for that! And where would the children sleep, (God bless them, they'd come in His good time), if not with their parents? Underneath this magnificent house there was yet another surprise, a room dug deep into the earth where, they said, Marika could keep food fresh for as long as she wanted all through the summer!

This residence—it honestly deserved the name 'residence'—stood midway between Russian Town and the old Estonian village. The nearest neighbour would be Father Tikhon, a jolly neighbour to have, even though he wasn't quite so spry with the children these days, and his black beard had been invaded by grey streaks. Nevertheless, he wasn't visibly failing like Pastor Vikkers.

Father Tikhon welcomed into his church for the wedding anyone willing to ignore the fact that, even here, life should have moved into the twentieth century. He rang his bells, overpowered his congregation with incense and came near to stifling them with the smell of the candles he'd had specially blessed and sent from the Alexander Nevsky Cathedral in Reval. He twinkled in his merry way through a long sermon suitable for nuptials. The bridegroom stood, not caring much about anything except that Marika was pretty and all this ceremonial was in his honour. As soon as this wordy old priest had shut up there was to be a formal meal for Marika's family and his own friends in the kitchen of the new house and a great picnic on the Green—plenty of food and more vodka than they could possibly drink—for everyone in the village, Russians and Estonians together. Musicians for the dancing were coming later from as far away as Haapsalu.

Leaning against her husband, tired of standing so long, Marika was confused and a little frightened, wondering when the Service would be over. She was confused by the ritual, even though it had been explained to her, and felt abandoned because so few of her old friends were in the congregation. It saddened her to know they would at that moment be in Pastor Vikkers' church, listening to a sermon equally long, probably about man's being born shackled in sin from the moment of birth and that very day, in that very village, though unfortunately not in that very church, one of their own dearly beloved was pulling those shackles ever more tightly about herself. He would certainly be screaming the word LUST while men groaned and women sobbed. Marika shut her eyes tightly to stop the tears. What she could not know at the time was that during his Sermon, the Pastor who had christened her and taught her to read and write Estonian in his secret school suffered a stroke. He toppled headfirst out of his pulpit and never spoke again.

In Father Tikhon's church, the von Hagen children were enjoying themselves immensely. It was the first time they'd been to an Orthodox service. Today was a special occasion, because their Uncle Loff insisted that the family attend, and they were all there except for Paul, who was still in Manchuria. They had Alexei to explain what was going on. He was in muffled full-flight when Dorothea clasped his arm, complaining that she felt faint. With whispered excuses, he led her out into the sunshine.

Once she was in the fresh air, she assured him she felt better, and they strolled idly across the meadow to Stepan's house. There was nobody there, and they sat side by side on the steps of the stoop.

"Doesn't all that's going on in the Church give you the strangest feeling, Alexei?"

"I'm used to it. All Orthodox services are smelly."

"No, not that. I mean...getting married."

He thought for a moment and, when he supposed sufficient time had passed for him to appear to have been taking the matter seriously, he said, "I don't know."

"Sonia's never going to be married, she says."

"That's silly. Everybody gets married."

"She won't."

"Then she'll turn into a silly, ugly old woman like...like a governess. You know what they're like."

"Not really. We never had one."

"All right, all right...don't be persnickety! You've got teachers at the Smolny, haven't you? You know what they're like."

"Why?"

"I don't know why. They just get like that when they don't have a husband, that's all."

He was sharp because he was embarrassed. He was seventeen, working hard at University and preparing for a diplomatic career. He thought, though he couldn't be sure, that he understood what the two of them were talking about—understood in a round-about way, of course—what men and women did together. He understood, but did Dorothea, he wondered. Probably not; she was a girl.

His fellow-students bragged about their exploits on the Islands. He had never been with them, and what they told him afterwards was mostly bravado, he supposed. They fantasized about the women they'd met, their figures, their perfumes, their enchanting smiles, and how much the evenings cost them. But they never went into detail about what they actually did together. That sort of thing hadn't concerned him at all yet. He enjoyed meeting young ladies at proper parties; they blushed when he talked to them and never refused to dance. Eventually, it would happen that he would like one more than all the rest. He would tell his parents, who would then speak to the young lady's parents and arrange a marriage settlement and a house. After that there would be a wedding and...

"Men don't get like that if they're not married, do they?"

"Like what?"

"Alexei! Concentrate for goodness sake! Men don't grow like governesses when they're not married, do they? Colonel Ouroussoff didn't get married 'til he was ever so old, and he wasn't like that."

She was beginning to be a little embarrassed because they seemed to be hinting at so much, the pair of them, that she had the feeling they shouldn't be talking about. She escaped into a show of irritation and turned her head away as though she was especially interested in a copse of birches swaying behind Father Tikhon's church. Alexei disregarded the trees and looked at Dorothea, instead. There was a flush on her cheek, highlighted by the sun. His fingers tightened and retracted with a sudden, hard-to-control desire to caress the softness she promised. Warmth flooded over him; he was thrilled as if his body was falling softly, effortlessly, joyfully into a velvet well. He was captivated by this realization of her beauty; he wanted her, he knew, whatever that might mean. His entire body was a throbbing pulse-beat.

"How horrible," she murmured.

"Dorothea..."

"It's so awfully unfair," she went on pettishly, before he was able to think of how to say what he wanted her to hear.

"Because I'm a girl, I have no choice. I have to sit and smile and pretend I like everyone until some man comes along and asks Papa if he may marry me. Then, whether I want to or not, my parents decide. If they can afford his price, everybody says how wonderful, how lucky I am, and I become his for the rest of my life."

"Dorothea..." He tried to touch her, but she pulled away.

"And I must agree to it. If I don't, I may not have another offer, and then I shall grow old and ugly like one of those horrible women at the

Smolny, or like Princess Surotkina. Everybody laughs at her, and it isn't fair. It isn't her fault."

"That won't ever happen to you," he said and took her hand. He became even more excited because she didn't draw away.

"Why not?"

"I won't let it."

She turned and looked at him sadly. "What can you do, Alyosha? You can't stop it, silly."

"Yes, I can."

"How?"

"I don't know. But I will."

She sighed. "You really don't understand, do you?"

"Yes, I do."

"It's not your fault. You're a boy."

"I promise you…Dora…"

"Look!" She pulled away. The first of the women to arrange the last details of the wedding feast were running out of the church. They gathered their skirts above their knees and looked as ungainly as ostriches in a panic.

"I won't let anything bad ever happen to you," he persisted. "I'll always look after you, Dora. We'll always be…"

"Friends?" she prompted.

"No, Comrades."

"Comrades! That's what those revolutionaries call each other, isn't it? I don't think that's very nice."

"Oh, yes, it is. It means more than friends. It means forever, until death."

"Really? I like that. It's beautiful."

They stood up as the women reached them, and their summer from that moment passed in a golden glow. They spent every waking moment together, always joining the others in whatever was suggested, but breaking away as soon as they could. Sonia was seriously concerned about her sister.

"How can you, Dora? Surely you must know by now what men are like."

"I know more about men than you do, I'm sure."

"No, you don't. He's only pretending he likes you because he hasn't got anything better to do at the moment. He's bored, that's all."

"That's not true."

"And what do you think he'll say about you to the others, when he gets back to Saint Petersburg?"

"Why? What should he say?"

Sonia laughed. "He'll tell his friends how he flirted with you all through the holiday, and that you fell in love with him, and how bored he was because you wouldn't leave him alone and, anyway, you were better than nothing."

"Stop it! That's not true! He's not like that."

"They're all like that, my dear. They can't help themselves. It's the way they're made."

Leonore was watching her, too, but with a more practical interest. The young couple was obviously attracted to each other, and she liked the young man well enough. By all accounts, he was doing well at the University and with his family connections would have no difficulty making a good career in the diplomatic service. Dorothea was still very young, of course—far too young to be making any serious plans—but it was, after all, a mother's duty to be looking ahead for her daughter's happiness; one could never begin too soon.

Her regret, tinged with anger, was that Paul wasn't with her. She wanted to talk about it with him. But he was still in Harbin, leaving her entirely alone to worry about the family. He hadn't been home for nearly nine months. She wouldn't admit that she worried about him. Everyone told her the Rebellion was nearly over, and that the Russians had won. If that was really true, why didn't he come home? Didn't he want to?

She wrote a lot in her letters about Dorothea's romance. His replies, shorter by far, hurriedly reported his visits to the Ouroussoffs, dinners at Government House and expeditions to various parts of the Province. Nothing she wanted very much to hear about. What she wanted to know was when he would be home, but he never told her that.

Newspaper reports in Saint Petersburg were, perhaps, like newspaper reports everywhere under the circumstances: over-optimistic. Paul's life was not as easy as he made out in his letters; the Rebellion was by no means finished. His dinners at Government House were a boring torment, entirely male and consisting of arguments that went round and round like a snake swallowing its tail. There was never any resolution because nobody knew what should be done. Kill the bastards! Kill every damned last one of them! That was the thing to do. But how? How could you find out where they were...who they were?

His visits to Sergei were rare and uncomfortable. Sergei was taciturn, Elizaveta Dmitrievna pale-faced and, if possible, less happy each time he saw her. She conversed with him as if she were reading sentences from a foreign language phrase book. There were long silences between each one.

Had he heard from Leonore? Pause. How was Leonore? Pause. How were those delightful children of theirs? Pause. Did he expect to be returning to Saint Petersburg soon? Pause. Would he like her to send for more tea?

On his infrequent nights alone in Harbin, he was happiest sitting in his house reading and, when he had the mental energy, studying Mandarin. It had been easy to find a suitable house. The owner was Russian, and because of the Rebellion, the property had been empty for some time. The landlord, lucky not to have had it burned to the ground by the Boxers, was grateful to have it occupied. He and his family were voluntarily marooned in Tientsin, where it would be easy to take ship if things got too bad. In gratitude, he charged very little rent for the house in Harbin. Paul hired a cook and two other man-servants—Chinese, of course. He employed them against the advice he received at Government House.

"You're mad, von Hagen! You can't trust those fellows—never could. I've been out here longer than you. Take it from me! They'll cut your throat as soon as look at you. And now, with all this Boxer nonsense, they'll congratulate themselves on having done a damned good job!"

Sensible Russians, they said, crowded for safety into Harbin's few hotels. The food was awful and the bed bugs rancorous; but at least the man in the next room would be a Russian, and if you needed any help in the night you only had to shout.

Among the few Russians of their class endeavoring to make a permanent home in Manchuria at that time was Colonel Ouroussoff and his faded little wife. God help her! But Ouroussoff was known generally as an odd fellow; should never have left the Guards. And there was the little girl to think of, too. The best thing he could do with Elizaveta Dmitrievna and his daughter was to pack them off to Russia as soon as he could. Ouroussoff was a career man, of course. He would stay there to look after Russia's interests when the Rebellion was over. Most of them would be going home, except for the Governor and that loud-mouthed Bezobrazov, of course. He had his fingers in the timber business here in Manchuria, along the Yalu River and across the border in Korea. Left to him, Russia would take over the whole area.

Paul ignored them all, so far as he could. He slept with a pistol by his bed and trusted his house-boys implicitly. He didn't believe they posed him any risk. Boys they might be called, but they were bony, bent old men, their hair wispy and grey. Their skin was like parchment, and they moved softly, but too slowly ever to surprise him. And anyway, they had no reason; he paid them well, and he wasn't a hard task-master. They nodded and laughed whenever he spoke to them, and behind his back, he knew, chuckled together at his attempts to speak Mandarin. On the whole, he had the feeling they rather liked him.

Lydmilla Fyodorovna visited him whenever they were in town at the same time. She had arranged—a special concession from the Governor, who was fascinated by her independence—for Kharbutov and herself to range the Province attached to a cavalry detachment, chasing rebels wherever it was supposed they were to be found. Often, it was a bloody business. A burned-out Russian farm, railway station, store or school resulted in the slaughter of any Chinese they could catch for miles around, innocent or guilty.

Riding with the troops, she wore a somewhat masculine wide-brimmed hat, a rough dun-coloured tunic and a skirt that finished high above the ankle. She rode astride, and the handsome young Kharbutov had his work cut out keeping up with her. In the field, he looked after her baggage. In Harbin, his job was to crate her pictures and arrange for their transport back to Saint Petersburg.

Her sales there had begun to be less certain—they were no longer popular as wedding presents—and the owner of the gallery in Sadovaya Street sent anxious messages that she scorned to take notice of. What did that meager-spirited man with his nose buried in account books and his shirt-cuffs at just the right length to impress his female clients know about art or of her life out here in the East? He was a money-grubbing merchant, and he didn't understand anything. Of course, her style had changed radically after all she'd seen when she was with the Russian troops at the siege of the Legations in Peking. Even her most faithful followers in Saint Petersburg began to wonder that her habitual landscapes with their pastel skies, umber-tinted fields and balletic trees on pale blue hills, were now slashed with the crimson of a crumpled figure's wasted life-blood. She stirred consciences and excited emotions they preferred not to have to acknowledge. They continued to buy her work, but more to prove to themselves that she couldn't hurt them than anything else.

"My dear, have you seen the latest Kolchevskayas? We simply had to be buy one. They're the oddest things you ever saw. I've no idea where we can possibly hang it, though."

Others said it was the New Art, representing the degeneracy, chaos and appalling taste artists all over Europe were now displaying. You couldn't make heads nor tails of it at all. Heaven only knew what some of it was supposed to represent.

She wouldn't show Paul her work nowadays and refused to talk about it. It was comforting for her, when she was with him, to ramble back in time to the days when she was still endlessly painting the Ponte Vecchio in Florence. He sensed the deep changes within her and responded as well as he could. He recognised her need for peace when he saw the apprehension in those calm grey eyes. Her fear disturbed and depressed him, because it was the signal that what they'd shared together at Fiesole and in that dusty hotel in Florence—their youth— was far away and gone forever.

"They like to see the blood." She sounded dejected. "To them it's like the Serpent in the Garden—the most beautiful thing imaginable. It touches something deep within them that they've never admitted before. It excites them, and they won't admit why. When they see it in my pictures, they comfort themselves by calling it my evil, not theirs. It's not my evil, though. I've seen too much of it to know whether or not it's mine. I'm finished, Paul. I can't stand any more."

"You must rest, my friend. Go back to Saint Petersburg. As soon as you can. Tomorrow. Learn again how to enjoy yourself. Live with civilized people."

"Civilized? Paul you're not listening to me. They're going to those new motion picture shows now. Have you ever seen one?"

"No. But the children have, of course."

"They're amusing enough. It's the audience that terrifies me. The first two or three times, they're intrigued, satisfied just to see the figures move. Then…it must be human nature…they long to see the girl on the hire wire crash to the ground and break her neck. You can feel it in the atmosphere. They want to experience disaster…but disaster to someone else. When it happens to other people, it makes them feel safer themselves. That's why they enjoy the blood in my landscapes."

"You must go home, Lydmilla—soon…tomorrow. Promise! Blagoveschensk was too much…even for you."

She smiled wryly. "I'm glad I was there, Paul. Destiny, perhaps. Photographers took pictures, but they'll never be published...the Government won't allow it. I saw it all, and it's still in my head. They can't do anything about that, can they? They can't get at it there, and I'll paint it one day, as soon as I can bear to, I swear I will. Three thousand men, women and children driven into the river to drown...because they were Chinese. And it was our soldiers who did it. Can you imagine? They were doing it on our behalf, for you and me and all those civilized people in Moscow and Saint Petersburg who buy my pictures on account of the blood."

After that, she couldn't settle. She was restless for the rest of the evening, unable to relax into their accustomed companionship. She shut him off from her, and he surrendered to her mood because he realised he was helpless. He called a boy to bring a lantern and guide them through the unlit streets. They walked together to her house.

When they got there, the place was dark; no light showed in any of the rooms. She didn't expect Kharbutov to be at home; he had his own social life when they were in Harbin, and she didn't inquire into it. Whatever risks he took were his own. But her servants should have been there. They'd been instructed always to keep lamps burning throughout the house to discourage raiders. They stood a few moments in the garden. Was it an ambush? Lydmilla shrugged her shoulders and went in; she was past caring.

She rented the place from Chinese Orthodox Christians shrewd enough to move far south as soon as the Rebellion began. They were well known in Harbin for their commercial dealings with the Long Noses and expected to be targeted by the Boxers. They left servants in the house, and Lydmilla had no reason to suspect any of them of wishing her harm.

The three of them entered the darkness cautiously, and Paul lit lamps in each room as they went. His house had been furnished with pieces brought all the way across Siberia. Lydmilla's was more beautiful, in the Chinese style, adorned with quantities of fragile, antique porcelain. Nothing was touched, nothing broken. It was as though a gentle breeze had blown through the rooms and wafted away the human beings who should have been there.

Lydmilla sat down on a sofa in the salon without removing her coat or hat, too tired to be curious or frightened. Paul followed his boy through the rest of the house, lighting lamps in each of the rooms as they went.

The last door they opened led into a bedroom. The boy's lantern slanted into the darkness and quivered uncontrollably. Paul heard the man's hissing intake of breath and pushed him aside, taking the lantern himself. He gasped in his turn, turned away and hurried back to Lydmilla. Since he met the young man on Harbin Station, he had had it in his mind that Lydmilla and Kharbutov were lovers. If that were indeed the case, how was he to tell her now that the handsome young man now lay naked on his bed in the darkness, with his head nearly severed?

"You must come back with me tonight, Lydmilla. I'll arrange everything tomorrow," he told her, as though she would divine what it was that had to be arranged. "You can't stay here."

"Is it...?"

"Kharbutov's dead."

"The poor boy."

"I'll let the authorities know. Tomorrow, when you're up to it, you must tell me something about him. There are people who'll need to be told, I suppose. I don't even know his name."

"Hs name was Boris," she told him sadly. "And there's nobody who needs to be told...only me."

CHAPTER 5

▼

1902

Paul didn't come home until late in the spring, and when they met, he and Leonore were shy together like strangers. He came off the morning train, straight from the station to the house. Leonore was preparing to go out.

"I didn't know you were coming home today, Paul," she said, and there was a mixture of reproach and relief in her voice.

"I have a Committee meeting. We're organizing relief for the Russians in Manchuria—poor creatures, they need it after what those dreadful Chinese did to them."

"It's all right, darling."

"We're all knitting as hard as we can."

"I have to go to the Bank, anyway."

Official business at the Bank lasted all day, and he was not sorry. There was a constraint at home. During the past year, he and Leonore had traveled far, but separately. They met now like faithful old friends, fond through habit but embarrassed by not being able to remember their reason for being so. In bed that night, Leonore was relieved when he didn't attempt to make love to her.

The children, also, treated him like a stranger. He'd been gone almost a year—a long time in their short lives. They had grown, developed all the while he was away; like snakes they had shed their old skins.

Dorothea was floating through life in a romantic dream, eager for the advent of puberty, her liberation from childhood. Her body was becoming beautiful, in keeping with the shining world around her. Leonore had told her about men, and she indulged in the pleasure of flirting in order to watch their reactions. She almost flirted with her father.

Sonia was testing her powers, too. She addressed him like a public meeting. She and her friend Irina Petrovna had become enthralled by the magnetism of politics.

"Irina has this friend called Yevgeni Grigoriovitch, Papa. He's at the University reading architecture, but that's only an excuse to be there. He's a member of the Social Revolutionaries, and he says Irina and I must join, as well."

"Now listen to me, my child…"

"They call themselves Social Revolutionaries because they want to change society—entirely. They're working to make everyone equal."

"And that's what you really want, is it?"

"Of course. It's fair. It's the only way for all of us to be truly free, Yevgeni says."

"And you're willing to make the sacrifice?"

"You don't understand. Papa. It won't be a sacrifice…not if it makes everyone happy."

"Perhaps you don't realize how privileged your life is at the moment, Sonia."

"Yes I do. That's why we have to join the Party; we must work to make everyone as happy and comfortable as we are ourselves."

Her eyes were eager and he was forced to resist a desire to take her in his arms, throw her into the air as he used to do and catch her while she screamed with the thrill of it. But that would never do, not now. Even were he physically capable, her dignity would be offended. It was sad how the simplicities of life became distorted by time.

"Now listen to me very carefully, my child, and believe what I tell you. I've never yet given you any reason not to trust what I say, have I?"

"No, Papa."

"It's good to think of other people and try to make their lives better. There are lots of people in this country—many of them here in Saint Petersburg, even—who don't have a decent place to live nor enough to eat. But I warn you! The Social Revolutionaries are not the people to put that right. No matter what your friend tells you, they rob and kill people. The police know all about them, and if you have anything to do with them, you'll go down on a blacklist, too! Do you hear me?"

"Yes, Papa."

"Then you must give me your solemn promise not to have any more to do with them."

She was reluctant to reply.

"Please! You must promise me, Sonia. I'm still your Father, remember? You must know that I want what's best for you. Will you promise?"

"Yes, Father." She said it after another pause and left the room, her shoulders rigid with the dignity of the martyr.

Marie said almost nothing when she met him, but followed his every movement with her large, dark eyes, and stayed as close by him as possible. He was grateful. He felt her love and sensed an understanding of his dilemmas far beyond her years. She would also be a martyr if called upon and, he knew, would make him her Cause. He marveled that the one among his children so much of her mother's race and so little of his own could be so special to him.

Eduard was bombastic as ever, his swagger fortified now by the rituals of boyhood. From the beginning of the Boxer Rebellion, the talk at school was all of the indescribable tortures the Chinese inflicted on their prisoners. Now they were poised and ready to send their millions westwards again, like Kublai Khan and his Golden Horde. People didn't call them the Yellow Peril for nothing! Because he had just returned from living among them on a day-to-day basis for so long, like a big game hunter, Eduard's father was revered and expected to add to their lore of gore. He was a terrible disappointment! He insisted on talking about the yellow devils as though they were reasonable, civilized human beings! And, consequently, Eduard spent numerous sleepless nights concocting imaginary horrors they'd perpetrated, to please his friends and maintain his own status in their hierarchy.

Albrecht was still irritatingly loquacious and had recently astonished everyone by developing a precocious talent for figures. He never stopped calculating! Everything must be turned into a mathematical exercise. Paul told him about the railway across Siberia, now open for single-line traffic all the way to Vladivostok. The boy wanted to know how far away that was, how long the journey took and after only a few moments produced his answer:

"The train went at fifteen miles an hour, Papa." And again, after the shortest pause: "But that isn't right because it must have stopped for water and coal sometimes, and at stations and to let other trains pass it going the other way. It was quicker than that, really."

He said all this in a matter-of-fact voice, confident but disinterested. It was merely information, irrelevant but available.

At the Bank, Paul received a gratifying reception; everyone appeared deeply interested in what he had to say. They assembled 'round huge conference tables and picked him clean, leaving him stripped of facts as a sparrow-hawk leaves its prey stripped of feathers. He understood what they were doing, though he said nothing. Everything word was noted down to be reported later to someone else. He was being absorbed by particular interests to bolster future policies. Cabals would justify themselves according to what he said. And if their plans went awry, they would claim him to have been at fault and sacrifice him without a qualm. He was only a pawn. His disgrace could be easily engineered.

This worried him, but he couldn't share his anxiety, not even with Leonore. She had once more developed self-confidence while he was away, and her success was probably more permanent than his. She was a Hostess in Saint Petersburg society. She could do nothing wrong, and everyone desired to be invited to her parties. Besides, while Paul was in Manchuria, she was promoted to being a specialist on whatever was happening there; it was impossible to believe Paul didn't report it all by letter on a day-to-day basis. He was pleased for her blossoming and couldn't bear to agitate her life in anyway whatever. Instead, he wrote to his brother.

The crux of the matter, Loff, is that we have no policy, no policy at all. Everything here is in the greatest confusion. Our Treaty obligations demand that we withdraw our troops within a given time and cooperate with the Japanese to uphold the integrity of China. We are to keep our land grants along the Eastern Railway; the Japanese are to have the south as their sphere of influence.

Our dilemma stems from our mistrust of Japan and our uncertainty as to whether, if we withdraw, she will do the same. Our hand is weak, but there are two ways to play it, I think: bid for peace and withdraw (the policy favoured by Count Witte and General Kuropatkin); or call our opponents' bluff and maintain our troops in the area, as we are being pressed to do by Bezobrazov and his associates.

Those gentlemen are not financially disinterested. At this very moment, they are raising capital for a timber enterprise along the Yalu River, which will very possibly spill over into Korea itself. They have backing at the highest level, I understand; the Tsar himself holds shares in the enterprise. His Majesty has even gone so far as to talk of establishing a Viceroyalty in place of a Governorship in his new Far Eastern Province, a sure sign that he regards our occupation of Manchuria as a permanency.

That is the situation, dear Brother, and I am afraid for the future. I see no way of avoiding war with the Japanese, and I dread to think what the result of that might be. Japan has all the advantages of western technology at her fingertips, and she is already on the spot. Our lines of communication between Manchuria and the West are impossibly long. To add to our other disadvantages, she will fight with fury. She hates us for, as she sees it, helping to cheat her of all she'd hoped to gain at Shimonoseki.

Enough of all this, though—it can be of little interest to you, happening so far from home. Leonore tells me you have hired Stepan Stepanovich in place of poor old Fermatov. I'm delighted you feel you can trust him sufficiently to make real use of him. I haven't, since Fermatov's murder, given you the support you must have needed, and I'm sorry for it. But my duties at the Bank have overlaid everything else.

I long to see the old place again, but I've no idea when that might be. The impression I get here—though nobody says anything outright; (that's the trouble with Petersburg these days: nobody says anything outright)—is that I shall be going east again quite soon. Somebody will be needed to look after the Bank's interests there in case of war. And there you have my present predicament.

When I first went to Manchuria, it was purely as a servant of the Bank. We were investing a great deal of money in the construction of the Eastern Railway, and it was my job to oversee the estimates of cost...only that. I submitted my Reports to the Board and to Count Witte for whom, it appeared, I had been working unratified ever since I came to Saint Petersburg.

Without my being advised of it, my brief was altered following the Sino-Japanese War. I went to the Treaty negotiations at Shimonoseki as an observer, and my reports were submitted exclusively to the Count; without appreciating all the implications, I became an 'official' figure. Perhaps I was naive. Certainly I was smug. I enjoyed the influence I thought I had.

Now, back in Saint Petersburg, I am regarded by both parties as an authority to be used in order to further their own ends. And when you remember what I told you about the Emperor's interest in the Yalu River Timber scheme, you'll understand that the contest isn't altogether a fair one. At the moment I am neutral; but that cannot last for long. And I see disgrace awaiting me if, as is my inclination at the moment, I do not side with Bezobrazov.

Perhaps I am being indiscreet, writing like this. But I shall put my official seal on the envelope, and I don't think it will be opened. In any case, it is essential I write to explain—justify, if you like—whatever you might hear of me in the future. I fear it will not be much to my credit.

He waited for the reply that never came; an unlooked-for rejection. His disappointment was all the sharper because he knew his time at home must be short. Any day now, having sucked him dry, they would gull him into going back to Manchuria, and he couldn't refuse. At home, he used his time trying to reestablish the old relationship with his family—without success. They knew as well as he that his presence could only be temporary, and held aloof.

Marie was the only one prepared to forfeit her day-to-day life to spend time with him, even to the extent of abandoning her beloved Albrecht. She never refused his invitation to "come for a walk, my love." Sometimes, in the afternoon, they sauntered together along one of the embankments by the glistening Neva. This Sunday, she refused an invitation to a puppet show at the Krimovsky house to be with him. He took her to the Summer Garden, because it was one of her favourite places, and they walked hand-in-hand along sun-splashed avenues between their rows of marble statues. She loved him to tell her stories about timeless characters they depicted.

"Alexander went for a swim one day in a River called the Cydnus," he was saying. "It was much too cold at that time of year, but he was that kind of man, always boasting and showing off. As everyone expected, he caught a bad chill and his doctor, a man called Philip, came into his tent to give him some medicine. Now, only a minute before Philip came in, Alexander received a letter—it wasn't signed, so he didn't know who'd sent it—but it warned him that the Doctor was slowly poisoning him. Now, what do you think he did, Marie? Did he call his guard and have the doctor dragged away to have his head cut off? Well, no, not exactly. He gave the letter to Philip to read with one hand and took the medicine glass in the other. I don't suppose it tasted very nice. The best medicine never does, does it? Anyway, he was just going to drink it, when…"

She interrupted him with a pained voice. "Papa, you're not really going to leave us, are you?"

He forgot his story immediately, horribly shocked. "My darling…" They were suddenly a million miles away from Alexander the Great.

"You're not, are you? Say you're not, Papa," she persisted.

"My darling," he said again, and crouched to take her in his arms. "My darling, why on earth should you worry about a thing like that? You know I have to go away sometimes…that's my work. But I'll always come back to you…you must believe that."

"Sonia says one of these days you'll go away and leave Mama and the rest of us for good; you'll never come back at all. You won't really do that, will you Papa?"

"No, I will not. And I'll certainly find out why Sonia is saying stupid things like that."

"It's her friend Irina Petrovna, really. I've heard her say that being married is like eating people: it's wrong, and we shouldn't do it."

"I see. And what else has this Irina been saying?"

"Next time you go away, take us with you, Papa." He could feel her slender body trembling in his arms and hear the desperate pleading in her voice. He drew her away from the statue to a bench, and they sat in the dusty sunshine.

"I wish I could. But you can't come with me, sweetheart. It's much too far away, and there aren't any good schools, and the houses are very cold in the winter. Only people who work on the railway…men like that…take their families with them at the moment. You'd have no one to play with."

"I don't care." She was petulant. I want us all to be together."

"I want us to be together, too. But we can't all be together there. Not at the moment, anyway. You remember my friend Colonel Ouroussoff, don't you?"

"Oh, yes." She sounded enthusiastic.

"He lives there now, with his wife and their baby daughter. Their home is in a town called Port Arthur, but when I was there they'd had to move into Harbin because of the Boxers. They don't like it at all. They'd much rather be in Saint Petersburg."

"You could find us a nicer place to live, Papa."

"It's the same everywhere, darling. Elizaveta Dmitrievna is really terribly unhappy. She's petrified their Chinese servants might try to harm the baby. She's so frightened she locks herself in her room whenever Sergei leaves the house. You wouldn't want to live like that, would you, my precious? It's almost as bad as being in prison."

She sat for several minutes, staring into a dream world of her own imagining. "When you go again, Papa, you really will come back to us? You promise…?"

"My darling, of course I'll come back. I never want us to be apart. I love you all very much. You're my family, and I never want to be without you."

"Sonia says that doesn't matter any more."

"What doesn't matter?"

"Being a family."

"Sonia evidently says a lot of silly things, child. You mustn't worry about what she says."

"But it frightens me, Papa. I don't know what's going to happen. She makes me feel everything I do is wrong. If that's true, will they come one day when you're not here and take me away? If they take me away, I'll never see you again. You won't know where I am, will you, Papa?"

Passers-by looked at them curiously, the greying man and the dark, sobbing girl on the bench, clasped tightly like lovers. They were oblivious to everything but themselves. Eventually he calmed her, but he knew he hadn't been able to take away her terror.

"Please, Papa," she begged again, very softly. "Please, please Papa, take me with you."

He held her away far enough from him for her to look into his eyes. "Now listen to me, my darling," he said and while he collected his thoughts it flashed through his mind that this was a phrase he was using all too often with his children these days.

"Listen to me! Your Mama will always be here to take care of you when I'm away. She'll never let anything bad happen to you. You must know that without my having to tell you."

He reported her fears to Leonore when they were alone that night, and her response surprised him.

"Perhaps she's right, Paul. Maybe it would be better if we were all to stay together."

"You don't know what you're saying, my dear. You can't come with me. You've no idea what it's like out there."

"And you've no idea what it's like here now, either!"

"I know it can't be easy for you with me away all the time. But to think of leaving Saint Petersburg..."

"You're quite right, Paul. It isn't easy. Everything is changing. Nothing's certain any more. I do what I think is right...but who knows what's right any longer? I try to keep the children happy, I behave as normally as I can with my friends, I sit on committees, I do everything I feel I should, but..." She sighed into silence.

"Don't you think you're all taking Sonia's nonsense too seriously? It's her age. She's got a little independence, naturally. She's mixing with a peculiar crowd, perhaps, and coming home with outrageous ideas..."

"It's not only Sonia. It's all young people. Just as soon as they're out of kindergarten, almost, they're turning into revolutionaries. They boast about it...quite openly. Their ambition is to destroy everything. And they're stirring up trouble among the working people. Every single day, there's a new strike somewhere. And what about all these murders and bomb plots? It isn't safe to go out of the house any more; not that it's all that safe to stay inside the house either, as we very well know! Marie's particularly nervous. She never recovered from the bombing. I sometimes think she'll never be quite right again, poor child."

"The others seem to have got over it, though. Dorothea..."

"You know Dorothea, my dear. Life isn't in any way real for her at the moment. Everything's a dream. She's forgotten what reality is like. Sonia would welcome a revolution tomorrow. She's the one I worry about most. If only she were a little older, I'd say we should send her abroad, but…"

"There are always the von Blomberg relations in Koenigsburg," he suggested, but she wasn't listening.

"Eduard will fight anybody at any time—goodness only knows what he'll be like when he's a little older. And Albrecht's driving us all mad with his figurings. Everything has to be calculated, added up, subtracted, multiplied, divided…"

He laughed, trying to lighten her mood, and she smiled in spite of herself, relieved they were together, to be able to share her troubles with him.

"I'm never away longer than I have to be, you know that."

"I know."

"And just at the moment…Leonore, my dear, I don't want you to worry, but I'm afraid there's going to be a war."

"I know."

"How do you know?"

She smiled and kissed him. "You're still my husband, after all. I know much more about what goes on in that head of yours than you think. I know you're very worried about something. Thank you for telling me that much, at least."

For a day or two, they were supremely happy again. They spent every moment together and he loved her with all the passion of a man half his age. They knew it couldn't last, and they weren't surprised when the letter came; he was to go east again.

This time, the Bank made all his arrangements. All his reports in the future were to be sent exclusively to them—to nobody else.

It was a sad parting. Paul and Leonore felt themselves standing on the lip of an abyss. The children wished him goodbye with varying degrees of disinterest; for them it was never his going away but always his coming home that was exciting. Only Marie seemed deeply affected. There was unshaded reproach in her big brown eyes. She said nothing, however, but begged to ride with them along the Nevsky Prospekt to the Moscow Station.

Included in Paul's travel directions was the request that he visit the Moscow offices to collect their commissions on his way. In fact, there were no commissions. Moscow simply wished to hear from his own lips all that he'd told their colleagues in Saint Petersburg.

He was glad of the detour, though, for personal reasons. As soon as he was free, he telephoned to Sasha and Clementine to arrange a visit. He couldn't tell, from the poor quality of the line, whether or not they were glad to hear from him. Strangely, they didn't invite him to their flat but arranged to meet him at a place in an alleyway off Tverskaya Ulitsa called the Anglia Tavern. Clementine suggested he should leave his cab at least two blocks off and go the rest of the way on foot. It was close to the Belorussia Station when he found it, a run-down sort of place. They were waiting for him. The place was noisy, quite a small room thick with smoke and the stench of liquor, sausage, urine, and sweat. Two young women maneuvered their way among the tables, playing piano accordions and singing. Sasha stood on a chair so that Paul could see him, and Clementine, when he finally made his way to their table, embraced him with an unexpected effusion.

"Look happy! Be sure you keep smiling, darling," she admonished him in an uncontrollable voice.

Sasha hugged him in the old, friendly way. "It's good to see you, Paul," he repeated over and over, and Paul noticed for the first time how his clothes smelt of engine oil from the locomotive works.

They sat him down and pressed drink on him. "Well, we didn't expect to see you here tonight, did we, Sasha?" Clementine shouted. Was she shouting to be heard over the general noise level, or was she drunk?, Paul wondered, surprised and uncomfortable.

"Wonderful to see you," Sasha shouted in his turn. "Have another drink and tell us about the family."

Paul turned to Clementine, who was grinning stupidly at him across the table. He was confused. Why were they behaving like this? Why had he to meet them here, instead of at their apartment?

Against a barrage of lusty singing by the customers, he told them everything they could possibly want to know about Leonore and the children. Clementine's eyes glazed over while he was speaking. Her body swayed gently from side to side, and her head nodded almost imperceptibly, as though she was seriously attempting to unravel the meaning and agree with every single word as he uttered it. Suddenly and disconcertingly, her body slumped forward, and her head sank on to the pillow made by her arms on the table. Paul stared at Sasha. Sasha laughed unconcernedly and shrugged his shoulders. "We'll get her out in a few minutes," he said.

He stood to take her by the shoulders and his movement could have been a signal, so general was the effect. The girls stopped their playing on a dismal wail. The customers stopped singing. Those without a seat remained perfectly still like a roomful of people playing Statues. The silence was uncanny, broken only by a clatter at the door. Sasha caught Paul's eye and flashed a warning. Paul turned to the door. Four policemen swaggered into the room, deliberately knocking against customers and tables as they went and causing what confusion they could. Every now and then, they stopped to demand someone's papers. For a moment, they stood by Paul and stared at Clementine, still sprawled on the tabletop. They gave Sasha an understanding grin before they passed on. A few moments later, they left. The noise in the tavern started again like a gramophone wound up half-way through a record.

Sasha edged once more to ease Clementine out of her seat. "It's all right, Paul, leave her. I can manage," he said. And he did indeed manage; he managed depressingly well and Paul realised that this wasn't the first time. He half pushed and half carried her skillfully through the crush and out of the door. In the street he suggested: "You walk on the other side of her, Paul. It looks more natural that way."

They went through several dingy alleys, passing at that time of night only a few hurriers and shufflers. Paul noticed, as they went, that Clementine was recovering, walking more confidently, though she kept her head down, as though not wanting to be recognised. In a few moments they were at the side of the railway tracks, and Paul followed them, stumbling over sleepers and clinkers, towards a little wooden hut Sasha unlocked when they reached it. Sasha lit a lamp. It was some kind of office with a truckle bed in the corner. Paul stood embarrassed, wondering what would happen next. He half-glanced at Clementine who, amused, had been expecting his look. "Oh, Paul, dear Paul," she said, in a normal voice, "it is so very good to see you...really, it is."

"They know us there," Sasha said. "Everyone sympathises with a man when his wife drinks," he laughed. "They concentrate on that and don't look beyond for anything else."

"And her house-keeping must be terrible, they say. That's why they can't entertain their friends at home," Clementine explained. "They're watching us, of course. And we don't want to implicate any of our friends who aren't sympathetic. It wouldn't be right."

"Sorry you had to come to a place like the Anglia. Railway men use it all the time. I know most of them, and it's good to have friends round you if you need them."

"And the people watching the flat don't think anything of it when they see us there, you see. They know we only go to the Anglia for me to get drunk." She laughed again.

"You're safe enough here, anyway." Sasha fetched a bottle out of his desk. "Now we can talk."

They talked almost all night and, after all this time of having to be careful, Paul relished the luxury of being open and honest with someone he could absolutely trust.

"There has to be a change, Sasha, you were right...I know that now. Although, perhaps, I sympathised with your aims before, I couldn't agree with your methods. I still can't agree with your methods."

"My methods. Not only mine. Suppose I told you little Ida was one of us?"

"Ida!"

"After her spell in Siberia, she realized that shipping Jews out of the country wasn't enough. They must be safe to stay here if they want to. They must have the same peace and freedom we want for ourselves, and they'll have it, just as soon as we do. That's what this Government doesn't realize; by all this senseless persecution, they only make things worse for themselves. Their enemies are all of their own making."

"She's one of our best workers now," Clementine said. "She recruits Jewish members."

"Where is she?"

"All over the place."

"We can usually manage to get in touch with her through Rachel, though," Clementine said.

"Rachel!"

Clementine laughed. "We can't pretend that Rachel's devoted to our cause. But she's interested in the problem. She's a businesswoman, trying to make a living. The Warsaw dress trade suffers now because of all these strikes. Her customers go abroad, where they know the seamstresses won't be on strike, and neither will the trains when they're expecting their deliveries."

"So in her own way, Rachel's looking for change too," Sasha added. "Anything to bring stability back into life."

"Rachel never mentions any of this when she writes to Leonore. Ida never writes at all, of course," Paul told them regretfully.

"The people you really want to hear from never do write, do they?" Clementine was obviously hoping to change the subject.

"We've no idea what happened to Lydmilla Fyodorovna after she left Moscow."

"She was here? Recently, you mean?"

"When she came back from Manchuria. Didn't you know she was coming to see us?"

"No. I was surprised when I got to Saint Petersburg to hear she hadn't been to see Leonore."

"It seemed to me she wasn't at all well, Paul. She stayed at the Metropole a couple of nights while she looked for an apartment. Then she decided Moscow was stifling her, and she couldn't live here after all. Warsaw was smaller, she said, it might be better for her there. In any case, she was longing to see 'her girls,' as she called them, meaning Rachel and Ida, of course. She went off one morning, and we haven't heard a word from her since."

Paul raised his eyebrows. He was perplexed to hear that Lydmilla was calling his sisters-in-law "her girls" and saying she was longing to see them. Her interest in them, right from their days in Florence, had always struck him as practical, rather than emotional.

"She'll turn up again when she's ready," Sasha assured them lightly. "Paul, you said there had to be a change. What did you mean?"

Paul hesitated, but Sasha urged him to say what he meant.

"Come along, old friend. Clementine and I have placed ourselves entirely in your hands, after all. Surely you don't think, whatever you say, we'd report you to the police."

Paul still hesitated, but only briefly. "First of all, suppose you tell me precisely what it is you want yourself."

Sasha grinned. "That's easy enough. We belong to the Social Revolutionaries."

"You're the people Sonia wants to join, then."

"She's only one of a growing number, believe me. More and more of our young people are starting to realize that Russia can't go on in the same old way forever. We're Populists. We believe in Socialism. We believe we can build a national order based on ethical values in the community and liberty for the individual. That's of prime importance, Paul: liberty, freedom for the individual. When you think about it, most of the people in this country now, whether they live in the towns or in the country, are treated like animals. They're horribly hungry, diseased, miserable. And what do you think that does to their spirit? It breaks down the nation, my friend. Whether or not the Government realizes it at the moment, it has no credit in the bank to draw on when it's needed. You know, of course, there's going to be a war?"

"Is there?"

"Oh, Paul! I'm supposed to be your friend. Please don't patronize me."

"I'm sorry. Yes, Sasha, I believe there will be a war. But still, however much I may agree in principle with what you say, I can't condone your methods. Terrorism…"

"Terrorism!" Sasha was shouting now. "What do you know about terrorism? We're not terrorists! If you want to know about terrorism, go and talk to the Secret Police. Have a word with the Union of the Russian People…the Marxists, too, if you like."

"As a matter of fact, I know quite a bit about terrorism—first-hand. We had a bomb thrown at our own house not so long ago, but that's neither here nor there. The Marxists may be more indiscriminate than you, but…"

"Paul! Paul! Paul! Imagine you're driving through a thick wood in the middle of the night, no cottages for miles around, trees close on either side of you and one tree, blown down, right across the road. What are you going to do? You can't drive round it; there isn't any room. But you've got to do something. You've got to reach journey's end."

"I'd turn 'round, of course, and…"

"Exactly! You'd turn 'round and end up precisely where you started, wouldn't you? But that won't get you where you want to go."

"Not at all." Paul tried hard to remain calm. "I'd turn back and find another road."

"There isn't another road," Sasha persisted. "You must get rid of that tree. That's what you've got to do. Chop it up. Drag it away. Burn it. You must clear the road."

"Shoot it? Blow it up? That's what you'd do, of course."

"If necessary. Do you know another way?"

"Sasha, can't you imagine a truly just society that doesn't have to stand with its feet in blood? They exist in other places."

"But they weren't built overnight. And we've run out of time."

"A monarch, of course," Paul continued, as though to himself. "We'd need an independent monarch."

"Independent, perhaps. Arbitrary, no."

"With an elected parliament. Ministers elected instead of drawn out of the air on the monarch's whim, as they are at the moment. Equal secret suffrage for every man and woman in the Empire…"

"Liberty, Equality, Fraternity, eh?" Sasha laughed.

"You may laugh, but that's what the French were aiming for. And even with the French, the most civilized race in the Europe of the time, they began at the top, reasonably, rationally, and still hundreds of people were brought to their deaths on the guillotine in the process. You want to start in Russia at the bottom? Sasha, have you any idea what a bloodbath there would be?"

"All right! We won't do it my way. How will you persuade your tree to get up off the road and let everybody get to where they want to go?"

"First of all, you have to realize that it's the Government who are your tree. They're the real autocracy, not the Emperor. Some friends and I have been talking about it—forming a party to influence the Emperor…a new, democratic party."

"Huh! You should go and talk to Professor Miliukov while you're in Moscow, then."

"I intend to."

Sasha shrugged. Paul's case was obviously beyond cure. "Well, when you're looking for your democratic monarch, don't waste time with Nicholas. We're living in the twentieth century, not the seventeenth. That man still believes all Russians look on him as their Little Father, for God's sake. I ask you! He enjoys being an autocrat; he's obsessed by the idea. He genuinely believes he's God-on-Earth. And apart from that, he's only genuinely interested in playing at soldiers, trying to produce a son for the future of the dynasty and…oh, yes! Chasing Jews, of course."

They parted amiably enough, though both knew that the gap between them was widening. That, Paul admitted to himself, was largely his own fault. When he himself hadn't much minded either way, Sasha's political intensity had amused him. Now, after Manchuria, he saw the need for change. He was seriously interested in politics himself. Sasha's way might be practical, but it was also very frightening.

He was glad, the next day, to be able to talk on purely democratic terms with the gentle Professor Miliukov, and after that he took the Trans-Siberian "Express," as it was already being called. He was halfway across Siberia when the expected letter from Estonia arrived in Saint Petersburg. It was written by Channah Litvak and addressed to Leonore.

"Loff feels it will be better if we write to you instead of to Paul, in view of our news. But first he hopes you will assure Paul that whatever happens, whatever he hears, he will never doubt that his brother is acting with honour and will do everything possible to support him. After his experience with Ida, Loff will never in the future accept anything of that nature without thorough investigation. So far as his brother is concerned, Paul's mind should be entirely at rest and, should war occur, he will do everything possible to support you and the family.

Now for our own news—the reason why this reply has been so long delayed. Two months ago Loff received a message from the Lutheran Missionary Society in Berlin. Margarethe was in hospital there, her mind and body completely broken, as it seemed. Apparently a friendly young officer who scouted regularly in her direction and has been keeping a friendly eye on her since her husband died found her on one of his visits semi-conscious. He took her into a hospital in the capital. It was a hospital run by Bavarian nuns, which didn't much please the Prussian Lutherans here in Berlin, as you may imagine. She was far too far gone physically and mentally while she was with them for the Bavarian nuns to show her the error of her theological ways, so *they were delighted to send her back to Germany as soon as a place on a steamer became available.*

Loff went to Berlin immediately and judged, after six weeks, that Margarethe was strong enough to stand the journey home. So she is here, living with us now. She occupies her old bedroom and sitting room but—although we think she is mentally able to do so—will not communicate with anyone. She has her food served privately and, if the tray is not to end up on the floor, it must be left on the table outside her room. Sometimes she comes out to take it in; very often she does not. The only person she will tolerate near her to clear her room, make her bed and sort her laundry is Marika—Stepan Stepanovich's wife. As a result, they have abandoned their beautiful new home for the time being and are also living here with us. This is certainly a relief for Loff. We had neither of us expected that she would let me do anything for her.

The situation is not easy for me, of course. But after all these years, the prospect of our separation would never occur to Loff, nor to me.

You are neither of you to worry about Margarethe. Marika looks after her very well. But of course, if you would like to visit her, you know that you are all welcome at any time you care to come."

Leonore forwarded this letter to Paul at Government House in Harbin. It was bundled into a train and took its time trundling across the taiga. Far ahead of it, Paul had changed trains on to the Chinese Eastern line at Chita and had crossed the Amur River towards Harbin. On the way between Moscow and Novosibirsk, his train was shunted into a siding to allow the Saint Petersburg Express to pass. One of the passengers on that train was his old boss, Popov, recalled from the wilderness. Closer to the junction, at Omsk, it was Popov's turn for the siding while Paul's letter went by him.

CHAPTER 6

▼

1903/1904

Back at the Bank, Popov called assiduously for reports on everybody and everything—to make himself *au fait* with what had been happening during his absence, he said. He was never so crass as to imply direct criticism of anything Paul had done while he was occupying the director's desk; von Hagen had had more than enough to handle in the Far East, so who could complain if a few things—nothing important, fortunately—had gone askew?

Popov was never popular before his "exile," as the young clerks called it. He was no better liked when he returned. He believed his recall was due to his indispensability, and he never ceased to remind them of the fact. That was infuriating enough. But during his time in Siberia, he had adopted the habit of sucking his tea through a piece of sugar held between his teeth like any common peasant. In Novosibirsk, for the first time in his life, he boasted, he had learned to appreciate the unquenchable soul of Holy Russia and to understand that it was also his. That experience must forever shape his future. His young clerks needed to learn the same lesson; perhaps in Siberia themselves? Behind his back, the young men sniggered over cartoons they drew of him, portly as a porpoise, leaping up to suck the sweetness out of sticks of sugar cane hung high over the table, as was customary in workmen's canteens. He knew they despised him, but there was a secret compensation: they also had reason to fear him. Before Novosibirsk, confident he would one day be back, he hid special files in the Bank archives, pertinent reports on every one of them, reports they would not wish to be made public, reports he intended to use when the time came.

On her return to Saint Petersburg, the wife of this grindingly mundane cog in autocracy's wheel burst on the social scene with the flash and force of an out-of-control meteorite. Always the willing helpmeet in her husband's schemes, she kept him *au fait* with the lives of people who were not recorded in his archives at the Bank.

They rented a house with a flamboyant facade opposite the Tauride Park and gave large parties that Leonore was expected to attend. They were her oldest friends in Saint Petersburg, they insisted, and while Paul was away it was their duty to see she was never lonely. Leonore hated their attention. Madame Popova appeared as a new member of every committee on which she was serving. Incredibly, she became almost overnight, *intime* with Princess Krimovskaya and Princess Surotkina; she was at their houses almost every time Leonore went to see them. She 'dropped in' at the von Hagen house as though it were an annex to her own. She exerted herself to cultivate the affections of the von Hagen children, but only inspired their intense dislike. They called her "Mrs. Buddha" because of the little jade statuette she wore bouncing on her bosom, and they disappeared, pleading urgent schoolwork, whenever she was in the house.

This gushing friendship embarrassed Leonore. Further, the woman's constant questioning about Paul offended her. Had Leonore heard from him lately? Where exactly was he at the moment, did she think? What would he be doing there, she wondered? Did he say he'd recently met anybody interesting? Had Leonore heard from Lydmilla Fyodorovna?

"I didn't realize you knew her," Leonore countered, surprised.

"Who doesn't know the famous Kholchevskaya, my dear? I met her here once or twice, in this house, before we went to Novosibirsk. But you wouldn't remember that. Why should you?"

"No, I don't remember." Leonore refused to sound interested.

"She and your husband must see a lot of each other, I suppose, being such old friends and marooned together in a dreadful place like that." She smiled to convey that this was a secret. Being women, they both understood.

Leonore bristled at the innuendo "They meet when they can, I suppose."

"Oh, my dear...I've offended you. Please don't misunderstand me. Oh dear, oh dear..." she laughed. "I'm always being taken to imply something of which I am truly innocent. And your husband's other old friend Colonel Ouroussoff," she continued hastily, "he's out there too, isn't he?"

"You know the Colonel also?" Leonore's tone was becoming frankly hostile.

"I met his wife here quite often before she married. Such a sad-looking woman, I always thought, but so very nice underneath. But...! The reason I came today, my dear. I must have something to wear for this Ball the Emperor's giving. You have a sister, I remember, a very fashionable *couturiere* in Warsaw. Would she take me on, do you think? Would you plead for me? I should be happy to go to her, of course..." She laughed. "So long as the trains are not on strike."

"She will do what she can, I'm sure. You won't need special pleading from me."

"There's an impossible rush, you see. We're all to go in seventeenth century costume as *boyars* and *boyarinas*, and I haven't a single thing that's suitable." She giggled. "We're supposed to be dancing all the old Russian dances, though who's going to remember any of them, I can't imagine. Oh...but I was forgetting...you're not Russian, are you? But you'll be coming to the Ball, won't you? My dear, it will be fantastic. Such a pity Paul won't be able to escort you himself, but you'll come with us, naturally. Doubtless they have other things on their minds in Manchuria. More serious things. Everybody's talking about a war. Does Paul, in his letters, ever say anything about that?"

Paul never mentioned war, for fear of distressing her. But the situation was certainly serious and masquerading as *boyars* to perform old Russian dances had no appeal for him, nor for any of his acquaintances. Secretly, he was glad to escape the embarrassment of it. A Tsar who could look back over three hundred years to play-act while facing a war that could be truly disastrous inspired nobody in the field with confidence.

When Paul's train finally dragged him into Harbin, Sergei and his wife had already gone home again to Port Arthur. By everyone's account, Elizaveta Dmitrievna had been happier since the end of the Rebellion. They said, with some amusement, she was beginning to trust her Chinese servants not to murder her.

The tensions in Sergei's life were also eased because his wife had met a woman friend she thoroughly liked. Sergei had withdrawn into his own world and offered her less and less sympathy. She needed a receptive ear and, in Lydmilla Fyodorovna Kholchevskaya, she discovered one.

Lydmilla was working hard to satisfy a home market demanding for their drawing room walls the topicality and the magnificence of the Grand Fleet lying in harbour and ever ready to defend the Empire against the little yellow monkeys. While she worked, she stayed with her friend. In between times she was seriously attempting to capture the 'Real China' before the West totally overlaid a civilization of five thousand years. She was planning several expeditions into the Manchu Empire, going so far as the gorges of the Yangtse. She had been to the Great Wall twice, walking quite far in both directions. And besides all this, she was painting—to please Elizaveta Dmitrievna—a large Ouroussoff family group, Sergei standing stiffly behind his wife, she sitting on an uncomfortable-looking chair and holding Lili on her lap.

"It's good to have her in the house, Paul," Sergei said. "She spends almost as much time as my wife, petting and pampering and fussing over Lili. I'd never have taken her for that type myself...not at all. Strange creatures, women, aren't they?"

Whenever they were in Port Arthur together, Lydmilla rambled with Paul through the hills behind the town. They sat on the turf and used Lydmilla's folding telescope to watch the ships in the Bay, manned by toy-sized crews skittering in all directions. Miniature launches puffed to the shore and back, carrying officers with gold insignia glinting in the autumn sunshine. From the Port, a procession of cabs went clip-clopping up the hill to Admiralty House, carrying these gentlemen to conferences about who-knew-what.

"It's so beautiful. I can't bear to think there's going to be a war. All this could be smashed to ugliness in an instant."

"It's inevitable with Bezobrazev as Secretary of State. I hear Saint Petersburg is preparing to send more ships."

"That's what everybody says, certainly. One hopes it's a *canard* put about to frighten the enemy."

"It will take more than a *canard* to frighten off the Japanese."

For a moment, she sat watching the ships. Then she turned to him, "Paul...Paul dear, we trust each other, don't we?"

"I hope so."

"No one with any sense can possibly imagine we'll win a war so far from home."

"It won't be easy."

"Can't anything be done to stop it?"

"Our troops are on call at any time to go into Korea to fight for Bezobrazev's logging business. The Japanese won't tolerate that."

"Something must be done; Paul! You must do something!"

He laughed. "I don't have that kind of influence, my dear. And even if I had...I'm only here because it's my duty. It's what I earn being here these days, not any income from the Estate, that keeps my wife and family in comparative comfort. In Saint Petersburg, there are people ready to use me for their own ends. The only way I can hold them off is by keeping my opinions to myself and making it quite clear I'm my own man. I can't afford to go in for political gambles."

"We didn't always believe it would have to be like this, though. There was a time, when we were together in Italy, I remember, you and I dreamed of changing things."

"I'm still as much a liberal as ever I was. But my family come first, and all I want at this moment is to get back to them."

"That's not gallant of you Paul," she teased.

He punctuated their conversation with his silence. Then he suddenly asked, "Why didn't you visit Leonore last time you were in the West, Lydmilla? She's very fond of you, you know."

"You heard all about that, then."

"Of course."

"Don't read too much into it, my dear. Perhaps I was only looking for another point of view."

"Sasha's point of view?"

"Whether or not you agree with him, give the man credit for believing in something…really believing, I mean. When you go back yourself, isn't it stultifying? Everybody's waiting for something to happen, but they don't know what they want, and they don't have the courage to attempt anything. Shooting their pistols and throwing their bombs without anything particular in view…it's so pointless."

"Why did you go to see Rachel?" If the sudden question was meant to disconcert her, it failed.

"My dear man, why does a woman ever visit her dressmaker? And wasn't it lucky? Ida was there, too. I think she works much too hard on Jewish relief, though God knows they need plenty of that in the South at the moment, after Kishinev."

"Even so, she ought to write to Leonore sometimes. Can you believe it? We don't even know her address! If ever we want to contact her, it has to be through Rachel."

"She's traveling all the time. But you can at least tell Leonore I've seen her and she's fine. She looks marvelous, really. She wears a black eyeshade with a golden lion embroidered on it. It's very striking."

That was their last comfortable conversation. Paul was able to visit Port Arthur less; he was in Manchuria, trying to perform miracles by making the railways there capable of carrying troops. Occasionally, he met Lydmilla in Harbin, but their meetings were troubled by accusations of betrayal he saw, or imagined he saw, in her eyes. Their old comradeship had gone, and their future relationship could well become his most serious problem. Clearly she reckoned on his joining her 'group'—whatever that was—and he no longer felt he could rely on her discretion. Sergei wasn't there to be talked to, even if any of their old intimacy had survived. Elizaveta Dmitrievna was an enigma. She lived like a nun, walled into her family and thinking of no one but her husband and her child. Lili was content—more content than any of his own had been at that age, Paul remembered ruefully. Sergei was as withdrawn as his wife. Paul desperately needed someone to talk to.

All was momentarily quiet between the Russians and the Japanese. Their soldiers lay watching each other from both sides of the Korean border, wary as animals waiting to spar before establishing a bloody coupling. On his travels along the railways, Paul grew more pessimistic. For the Russians, at least, the coupling must be a bloody affair. Nothing he saw encouraged him and, in his depression, he longed for Leonore. His need of her was insupportable. On the pretext of delivering an urgent report, he traveled back to Saint Petersburg to be with her.

He arrived some weeks after the assassination of von Plehve, conservative Minister of the Interior. In his place, the Tsar appointed Sviatopolk-Mirsky—inexplicably because he was a liberal and the Tsar most certainly was not. The new Minister repealed a few of the harsher laws and adopted a slogan—well-sounding but meaningless: 'The Dictatorship of the Heart.'

The liberalism of Sviatopolsk-Mirsky was confounded by the growing influence of Pyotr Stolypin, celebrated and notorious among liberals for founding the Union of the Russian People, with its own secret police, the Black Hundreds. They were there to bait Jews and murder liberals.

Paul was pleased to be home. His reports to the Bank were taken semi-seriously. Everyone knew von Hagen was not a 'war man,' and expected his reports to reflect the fact. Besides, he took pains to let everyone know that the von Hagens were a strictly apolitical family! But with Popov at his old desk, paying lip-service to Sviatopolk-Mirsky while all the time supporting Stolypin, neutrality wasn't easy. Jews were being quietly dismissed. Any man unwilling to join the Union had to have improbably good reasons. "Why, good God man! You must! The Tsar himself is a member!"

Popov welcomed Paul's return with shallow enthusiasm. "My dear von Hagen! Glad you're back. We needed you. Things have gone to the devil while both of us were away. And now von Plehve's blown up...You heard about that?"

"Of course."

"On his way to see the Tsar...regular meeting. Own fault, of course. Never use the same route twice. Lesson we all must learn."

"Perhaps that won't be necessary when the terrorists understand what Sviatopolk-Mirsky's trying to do."

"Oh, you're one of those, are you?" Popov's smile was more of a sneer. "Stolypin's the man to watch, my friend. No nonsense about him."

Before they parted, Paul said he was taking a holiday. "My sister is back from Germany. She's home from Africa, actually, and she's very ill."

Popov nodded vaguely and looked perplexed, as though what Paul set before him was a bowl of *borscht* of an unrecognisable colour. "Be careful, my friend."

"I beg your pardon?"

"You've been out of touch too long. I know, I know..." he adopted his elder statesman tone of voice, "nothing's so pleasant as to work alone in the field. New places. New faces. But the office is always there, remember…always watching."

"What are you trying to tell me?"

"Not a good time to be away. To much change everywhere."

He laughed shortly, and Paul realized it was an effort to cover his own doubts. "You and I," he continued, "fortunate to be still here. Both made mistakes in the past, eh? Present uncertain for everybody. Perhaps, remembering Berlin, it isn't wise to turn your back…?" He shrugged and made a visible effort to change their mood. "My wife and I…giving a little party tomorrow evening…*touts intime.* You must come. Bring that lovely wife of yours."

Paul excused himself as diplomatically as he could. He didn't know, he said, what arrangements Leonore might have made. At home, he found that Leonore had made the same excuse to Popov's wife. There was no escaping the intimate party.

Leonore was delighted by the idea of a holiday. Other members of the family were less enthusiastic.

"Oh, no! I couldn't possibly! I couldn't face it, Papa," Dorothea moaned.

"Nonsense. Whyever not?"

"Mama, whatever should I do there?"

Leonore looked grim. This was a difficult time for Dora, and she was sympathetic. Pyotr Krimovsky was in Germany with his parents, and she had refused to let Dora go with them. "Certainly not! We've no idea when your father will be home, and I want you here when he arrives." Now, she realized, she was being punished.

For Dorothea, at the moment, everything was dull and boring and pointless. Her father was home, and that was that. Pyotr was in Germany, and that was that. And she was here, emotionally midway between the two and under threat of being dragged off to the country where there was not the slightest chance of anything interesting happening and…She sobbed again that she couldn't bear it, and rushed off to her room in tears.

Sonia was eager to go, but only so long as she could take Irina Petrovna with her.

"Why would she want to come? I expect her parents make their own arrangements about holidays," Leonore said.

"Oh, no. No, they don't," Sonia told her earnestly. "They never go anywhere. Her father's only a school teacher, and he earns nothing at all…absolutely nothing. Her mother does translating, but that doesn't pay, either, and they have to live on nothing, absolutely nothing, and…Irina was only accepted at the Smolny because she's so terribly clever, and…"

"I thought I told you I didn't want you to have any more to do with her," Paul said.

Sonia blushed. "But you don't know her, Papa. You've no idea how she has to live, and…I think it's our duty to be kind to people like Irina…give them things…make life more interesting for them."

"And how will our taking her to Estonia make life more interesting for the rest of the hard-done-by family?," her father asked.

"They won't have to feed her while she's living with us, will they?" Sonia's reply was bright and confident. "And she'll be able to talk to the peasants. We both will…find out how they live, what they have to eat…how much money they have…"

"I think not," Paul said. "We won't take Irina this time, anyway."

Sonia's breast swelled as though she would burst, and she followed her sister from the room in tears.

"You'll like to come to the country and see Uncle Loff, won't you, Marie?"

"Oh yes, papa. He's nice. So is Channah. Last time we were there, she promised to show me how to make *knishes* and…"

"What are *knishes*?"

"You don't want to know," Leonore told him hastily.

"Channah says she'll teach me to cook all sorts of Jewish things."

Paul shook his head, signaling Leonore to say nothing. His daughter's ambition to become a Jewish cook secretly amused him; even more so did her mother's horror of the idea.

"Well, Eduard? At least you'll enjoy being by the sea, I suppose."

"Yes, sir." Eduard called his father 'sir' now, because that sounded military. "If any of those village boys start a skirmish this time, they'd better look out."

"You can't take on the whole village," Paul laughed.

"Oh, yes, I can," Eduard said. "You'll see, Sir."

Albrecht was as agreeable to this late holiday in the country as he was to everything else. He immediately converted the distance and journey times into figures.

Paul's chief reason for going to the Estate so late in the year was to see Margarethe. Loff would say nothing about her that could be taken as encouraging; nonetheless, when he went into his sister's room for the first time, he was appalled by what he saw. A very old lady with yellow skin, dressed in a spotted black dressing gown, was hunched in a chair by the window, staring out at the gathering dark. He spoke to her very gently, but she showed no sign of hearing or recognizing him.

"Margarethe! Margarethe, it's Paul." He waited a moment before trying again. "You remember me, don't you? Paul? Your Brother?"

If she remembered, she gave no sign. He drew a chair close to hers and sat down. She allowed him to take her hand in his and let it lie there passively. It was cold, shriveled, claw-like.

"Are you comfortable? Are they looking after you?" The questions were banal, but how else could he reach her? This was only the husk of the woman who'd ruled the Estate and her brothers so rigorously for so many years. The body was painfully diminished, the spirit entirely missing.

He made no more effort to get her to talk, but sat quietly holding her hand until it was quite dark outside. Loff had hoped, without conviction, that she might have responded to Paul. Leonore was certain the sight of her nieces and nephews would rouse her interest. Loff said that for a visit from them to be successful, it would have to be in the company of Marika, whom by now she knew so well. Leonore protested. Who better than their own mother to take them in and make the introductions?

They went in with Marika and came out again totally confused. Who was this crazy, speechless old woman they'd never met before? How could they be expected to take any interest in her? Marika took them in and fetched them out with a barely hidden air of triumph.

To begin with, Marika had been annoyed at having to leave the beautiful new house Stepan had built for her, a real mark of distinction among all the huts around. She was also clever enough to realize, though, that life in the "Big House" would have its own potential. Her duty there was to care for *Frau Behrendorf*, whom she chiefly remembered as a sharp-tongued martinette who terrorized the village children whenever she came near. Now she was a mute, senseless old woman whose only means of self-expression was to throw her dinner on the floor. If she didn't behave herself, Marika would throw her on the floor one of these days!

Leonore and Marika took an instant dislike to each other. Channah ignored her and avoided talking about her, though she did unburden herself in her own room one grey afternoon.

"She orders the servants most shamefully. It hurts me to hear. They've done nothing to deserve it, poor things. To begin with, I tried to explain they'd do more for her if she treated them kindly. It made no difference. And nobody says anything because whatever she does or says is all supposed to be for benefit of the *Frau Baronin*, you see. And she, poor soul, must come first whatever happens. That's only right. It's our duty to look after her, poor woman."

Leonore thought Paul might do something, but neither of them knew precisely what. Stepan Stepanovich had changed since he came to live in the house. Previously he had been a good foreman, reliable, satisfactory in every way. But he had taken advantage of Loff's long absence in Berlin to establish a regime of bullying among the workers.

He had a small group he used as lieutenants to impose his personal authority and now, it seemed to Paul, the men were confused and had quite forgotten for whom they worked. When he and Marika moved into the house, he even imposed his will, subtly, of course, upon the Baron himself. In the first weeks after his return with Margarethe, Loff was too concerned about her condition to care about anything else. By the time he could take the running of things back into his own hands, it was almost necessary to ask permission to ride to his own diggings or to inspect his own fields. But of course, the *Herr Baron* need not be anxious about things like that, mustn't concern himself, mustn't worry about anything. Stepan Stepanovich had everything in hand. "The damnable thing is, he really does have everything in hand, Paul. Everything goes like clockwork."

"Nevertheless, you're still the Baron, Brother."

"What really worries me is that there's something seriously wrong underneath."

"What do you mean?"

"I don't know exactly, and I can't prove anything, but...I have a feeling—a strong feeling—the workers are paying him money for their work."

"Good God!"

"Nobody will say a word—they daren't. But if they want to work, I'm sure they have to pay Stepan for the privilege."

"If that's true, you must turn him out at once."

"How can I? He does a good job. Where would I find anyone to replace him? Besides, if I lost Marika, what would I do about Margarethe? She may not take to anyone else so easily. I can't let her sit in that room for ever, unattended and starving."

"You've never said anything about this to Father Tikhon, I suppose?"

Loff looked at him hopelessly. "Father Tikhon's influence has gone, Paul, and it's as much as he can do to save himself.

There's a new feeling in the air among the people. I call it the love of chaos. What I call chaos, they call freedom. Whatever you call it, it's slowly destroying all of us."

Nobody said anything but all the family was in secret agreement by the time they went home that this was the worst visit they'd ever had. Whatever they were doing, going in or coming out, the high spirits of the children were discouraged by the sight of the wizened old woman in the window watching…watching a world occurring outside her life. Paul and Leonore felt the house no longer belonged to Loff and Channah. The presence of Stepan and his Marika was everywhere like some bittersweet odor.

During the following weeks, Paul toyed with the idea of an immediate return. But that was hardly possible. He couldn't be seen to be running away, neither by Lydmilla nor Popov. It was safer to be on the spot, if Lydmilla were to denounce him or Popov to reveal the contents of that brown envelope. Besides, he was responsible for his family, for their present and for their future that, as their father, he held in trust for them.

He longed to go abroad again, to get them all out of it, but they were no longer babies, to be hauled through Europe like a tribe of gypsies. They'd lived too long in the capital for an easy transplant to the Estate. Yet, whatever else he did or didn't do for them, it was also his duty to share with Loff responsibility for Margarethe and the Estate.

"Of course, darling, we'll go and live on the Estate if that's what you think is best." As always, Leonore was ready to do whatever he decided. She was the dream of all Jewish mothers for their sons; a jewel beyond value, the pearl of great price. Without argument, she would support her husband through bad times and good. She would invariably and in everything place the welfare of her children before her own. She was specially commended every Friday at the Sabbath meal and she was, almost without exception, the most misunderstood woman in the world. That was the price she paid for the rock-hardness of her values which gave her the apparent overconfidence with which she turned her face to the outside world.

"It wouldn't be easy. The children would probably have to be sent away from home for their schooling."

"That wouldn't be necessary, I'm sure. We could find tutors for them, not Prussians like yours, though." She laughed.

"And Margarethe?"

"Margarethe?"

"It's impossible to tell now, how much she remembers from the past. Channah certainly couldn't manage her the way Marika does, but whether that' s luck or whether she remembers how much she hated Channah years ago, I don't know."

"Channah hasn't had much education. She hasn't had any experience outside the Estate and…oh, I know she's been marvelous to Loff, but…"

Paul preferred to ignore the trend of what she was saying. "Loff says Channah couldn't manage her, and I'm sure he knows."

"Channah wouldn't have to…not if I were there. And she'd grow to enjoy the children."

Paul let the matter rest. Looking back, it seemed that too many of his larger decisions weren't his decisions at all; they'd been made for him, and he'd taken them without forethought. Joining the army had been a conscious choice. He could clearly remember soldiering as his earliest ambition; he could recall the rustle and the smell of the snow beneath the runners, the day Ants drove him from home to become a soldier. Possibly, in the whole of his life, he had never made another single conscious decision. Even his marriage—though God knew he loved Leonore dearly and wanted her today as much as ever he did—his marriage happened while he was rushing along on a river of hot blood and youthful fantasies. Now, past fifty, he knew there would never be any more rivers like that. There would be no more choices, only inevitable decisions. They would all have to be their own; and they must all be right.

"I'm taking some more time off," he told Popov, in a voice that left no room for argument. "Family business."

Popov looked at him calmly, trying to control his curiosity.

"Estonia, again?" He asked the question as though the answer didn't in the least matter, nor that he cared about the answer.

"No, Warsaw."

"Ah. Never been myself. Interesting place, though, I expect. The Poles have personality. Then there are all those Jews. Your wife came from there, I believe?"

"She lived there at one point, certainly."

Another unspoken question hung between them. "Well, well, *bon voyage*, then. I'll manage here for both of us, I've no doubt."

Paul expected Leonore to leap at the opportunity to see her sisters. But she wouldn't risk taking the children while the Jewish Bund at Vilna was calling for strikes and disturbances all over the Pale. Neither would she be happy, after the bombing, to leave them at home with only the servants to look after them. She couldn't understand why, when everything was so unsettled, it was necessary for him to go himself. She accepted that it was necessary because he told her so—he had business just about everywhere, these days—and she spent two days chasing the children to write letters to their Aunts which she put into envelopes with her own.

The restaurant of the Hotel Bristol in Warsaw was crowded at this hour in the afternoon. Paul could have held his tea party in his suite, but chose the restaurant as probably being of more interest to his guests. As it turned out, his guests were the focal point of interest for everyone else. All the ladies were familiar with Madame Rachel and her fabulous designs. Rachel moved like a queen from table to table, acknowledging their greetings. More interesting than Rachel, though, was the woman who came with her; a Jew with shining black hair, an obviously Semitic nose and an olive skin, wearing no rouge or other adornment. Her one *hommage* to fashion decoration was extraordinarily striking; a black eyeshade with a golden lion embroidered on it. In contrast with Madame Rachel's splendid afternoon gown, this woman wore a plain white blouse and black skirt. Onlookers wondered who she was and why she could possibly be there, whether she was the guest of Madame Rachel (though that seemed unlikely from the clothes she wore, though the eyeshade might, of course, be one of Madame's new fashions) or of the gentleman they'd come to meet. Of one thing they were certain: had she arrived alone, the manager would have excused himself for having no table available. Their reactions, when Ida returned their stares, amused her very much.

"Oh, Captain," she giggled. "You remembered. After all these years, you remembered. The Hotel Bristol."

"And cream cakes!" Rachel murmured, pushing her own aside.

"You see?" Ida was triumphant. "Rachel's still jealous. But she daren't. Her beautiful figure is her trademark, you see. She is her own best mannequin." Paul laughed, though Rachel didn't look pleased.

"This is lovely, lovely, lovely," Ida continued. "Oh, how good to us you were in those days. I often think. Captain...I know you don't expect to be called 'Captain' today, but...do you remember how happy we were when we lived in Praga, and you were still the Captain?"

He looked at Rachel, laughing yet shaking his head helplessly. "If Ida can tear herself away from the last cream cakes, perhaps we could go upstairs and talk," he suggested.

"Talk?" Rachel sounded ill at ease.

"I didn't come all the way from Saint Petersburg just to buy you two tea—pleasant though that's been, of course."

Every eye in the restaurant followed them to the stairs. Doubtless, later that evening, a multitude of curious stories would be circulating throughout the city, especially about the stout, dowdy young woman with the eyepatch.

In Paul's suite, the sisters settled with some nervousness. This must be bad news, they'd decided. What could it be? Leonore? The children?

"What is it, Paul?" Rachel asked calmly, after a slight hesitation.

"Yes, what is it? You mustn't frighten us like this, you know."

Paul shrugged. "You can't really believe I'm trying to frighten you."

"No matter, no matter. What is it?"

"Perhaps you could tell me, Rachel. Why did Lydmilla Fyodorovna come to see you?"

"Lydmilla Fyodorovna?"

"I know she came. I know she came straight to you from Sasha Schimanski in Moscow. Why was that?"

"I really don't see why I should discuss my clients with anyone else, Paul...not even with you."

"Don't ask Rachel, Paul. She doesn't know anything about it," Ida said quietly.

"You tell me, then."

She shrugged. "What exactly do you want to know?"

"Don't waste everybody's time, Ida," Rachel said. "Lydmilla is a friend of ours, Paul...my client...we've all known her since we were in Florence, remember."

"Yes, we've all known her a long time," Paul agreed. "But Leonore and I probably know her better than you two do. Her judgement...and I admit we didn't know as much about her in Florence as perhaps we should have done, before we put the two of you under her influence...her judgment of people isn't all it might be."

"What does that mean?" Ida was angry. "She doesn't like the kind of people of whom you two approve, I suppose."

"I'm not going into details, Ida. Years ago, in Paris, she was mixed up with a very queer crowd...politically unstable."

"According to you."

"She had to get out of France pretty quickly. She came to us for help."

"And you helped her, and that was very good of you." The sarcasm was plain. Ida's face was flushed and, because of that and the eyepatch, looked artificially constructed.

"She could have gone to prison if we hadn't."

Rachel looked confused and fidgeted with her diamond-encrusted fob watch, as though late for another appointment.

"Paul dear, I really think..."

"No, Rachel, let him say what he's come to say."

"Thank you, Ida." Paul sounded formal and swallowed hard. Despite the passing of the years, he felt very young, like a cadet at attention on a platform to deliver a lecture to his fellows about an advanced tactical exercise. "Lydmilla has revolutionary ideas, I'm afraid. How far she's gone or is prepared to go, I'm not sure. We talked about it in Port Arthur not so long ago, and..." He attempted a smile that was horribly like a rictus..."I disappointed her, because I'm no longer the radical I used to be when I was young." He paused and cleared his throat, feeling for the words to go on.

Ida, feeling a fat trout on her line, would play him for as long as it took, determined not to let him go. "Well?"

"Well!" he echoed. "That is as much as I can tell you about her. But I must warn you, for all our sakes. For God's sake, have nothing more to do with her. I'm in a very difficult position over this. It's dangerous to quote names. I don't like having to use names, but..."

"Why don't you? Either you expect us to take you seriously, or you don't, Paul."

"I still have doubts about Lydmilla, perhaps. Because of what she saw in the Rebellion, she was quite ill when she came back. I was sure she'd go straight to Leonore. She went instead, to Sasha, and then she came here to you. I may have doubts about Lydmilla, but I know exactly where Sasha stands."

"And that's the reason for all this, Paul dear? Simply because she chose to stay first with Sasha and then with us, instead of with Leonore...?"

"No, no, Rachel! If he wants to know so badly, we should tell him. After all, you're still our dear Captain, aren't you, Paul?" Ida left her chair and came to stand by him, her arms round his neck. There was no more sarcasm. "You'll always be my dear Captain, Paul. Nothing can ever change that. I'd trust you with my life, and that, perhaps, is what I am about to do." She kissed his forehead and walked slowly back to her chair. "You're right. We are involved in revolutionary work. You'll understand I'm on oath not to name the others, but since you know about Sasha and Lydmilla anyway...Lydmilla's wonderful. She never loses sight of what we are trying to do. She has influence. Because of her work she knows hundreds of people who wouldn't dream of knowing us." She laughed.

"So you are terrorists." Paul sounded exasperated.

"What is that? We are what we believe in, my dear. We're Democrats. If we must use terror to achieve our democracy, so be it. And I promise you this, my dear. We have plans. When we do what we are going to do..."

"Ida!" Rachel half rose, but Ida was not to be stopped.

"...the whole world will know about it. We won't be limited to a bullet or a tiny bomb. With us, Paul dear, it will be huge, and it will be beautiful."

"Ida! Ida, my darling! Haven't you already suffered enough?"

"Don't ask whether I have already suffered enough, Paul. Ask me instead, will I ever have suffered enough?"

CHAPTER 7

▼

1903/1904

Time flowed over Paul like a sea, the waves sometimes anguished sometimes angry, anguish and anger without exception thrashing against the adamantine folly of his young sisters-in-law. He and Leonore had attempted to have them taught at Florence, to equip them with the accomplishments expected of young ladies. But they were hopelessly untutored in the experience of real life. No young girl was expected to know anything about that, and they were average young girls. They lived in ignorance and dreams, exactly as they should have done. Except that now, their dreams had led them to the edge of an abyss they'd no idea was there.

If—God forbid!—they were discovered, they would be treated by a paranoid State as menacing criminals and, as an impending challenge, they would be disposed of. They anticipated never being caught, of course. That was part of the dream.

Their composure in the face of exile or possible death rested partly on the faith they held in the justice of their cause and partly because they subscribed to the popular opinion of the police. Policemen were drunken, none-too-intelligent officers in grubby uniforms, operating from grimy police stations and notoriously as inefficient as the authority they served.

In crises, these police called for the Cossacks, tribesmen born on horses, people said, whose loyalty to the Crown had been purchased by grants of partial autonomy. During public demonstrations, uniformed policemen faded away, and the streets were free for the Cossacks to gallop through, shouting their war cries and lashing to the right and to the left with their knouts. The noise and confusion they created was effective. So was the sight of the bloody bodies they left on the cobbles when they'd passed.

The starving poor—those, it was thought, who would gain most from the overthrow of the system—mainly stayed in their hovels if there was trouble. They longed for relief, but lacked any ideas or organization to bring it about. Their priests conditioned them to believe that everything would be different if they were good enough to go to Heaven when they died. Meanwhile, they should have faith in the Tsar, their Little Father. He loved them and prayed for them and knew how they suffered. Even for him, they were reminded, life was travail.

The police and Cossacks, in union, each playing their allotted part, could deal with the hopeless. Against the rest, the young idealists who would come on to the streets singing songs of freedom and joyously waving their banners…should they survive the gunfire and the knouts, there was yet another force: the Secret Police.

The Secret Police, men and women, whether working directly for the Government, for Pyotr Stolypin, or for anyone else whose self-appointed destiny was to save Russia from the Tsar's beloved children, were ubiquitous in Russian life; a huge unrecognisable army of people looking and acting exactly like everyone's innocent neighbours. They never revealed themselves until the moment when, for their prey, it was too late. Their paymasters knew them, of course, but nobody else. The manipulators who planned the demonstrations had nothing more than unproven suspicions when they sent the young white hopes to their deaths on the streets.

The only defense against the Secret Police, Paul maintained, was to be as unremarkable as possible—inconspicuous as any flatfish lying on the ocean floor. Lydmilla and Rachel were too well-known for camouflage. According to what she'd told him, Lydmilla's history as a revolutionary went back to before she was married. Now, as the best-known female artist in Saint Petersburg she was beyond concealment, everybody's property, of interest as much to the Secret Police as to the family in the next apartment.

Rachel courted notice for the sake of her business. She needed to display, and she displayed successfully. She was too well-known to pass unnoticed by the creatures with soft voices and cold eyes, sitting in their dark offices and keeping up-to-date their record of wrong-doers. They knew nothing against Rachel yet, he supposed; they knew nothing to his discredit about the Tsar either, but rumour had it that they kept a file on him, too.

And Ida...? Sentenced to Siberia once already, there was no influence on earth could secure her release if they arrested her a second time.

For Leonore's sake, Paul tried to appear as normal and cheerful as possible in the house, but her attitude puzzled him. She hardly mentioned her sisters, and for her, that wasn't natural. Her family was the focal point of her life. Every day, she talked endlessly about them, wondered about them, worried about them. Now, suddenly, it was as though they didn't exist! She read Rachel's infrequent letters and handed them to Paul without comment. He couldn't believe her disinterest was genuine. What was she trying to hide? Was she living a private nightmare on their account, so dreadful she dared not mention it, even to him?

He lacked the courage to inquire into her fears—if fears there were—so despite the weather, it was a relief in December to be ordered to the East. As usual, he went first to Moscow for final instructions. As usual, he arrived early in the morning and varied his normal pattern by taking a cab to the Belorussia Station instead of to the Bank. At the head of the platforms, he stood lost and confused among crowds like a first-time visitor from the country. There were far too many people elbowing by him to pinpoint any one individual. And, anyway, the one he sought might not be there at all; Sasha worked shifts. He thought of walking to the end of the platform to see whether he could find his hut. But that would only attract attention, invite questions. He knew, deep down, he was being as absurd as any young lover hoping for a chance meeting with the object of his desire. He'd had no experience of any of this, though, and he couldn't think o anything else to do.

The second cab he took that morning was to the Bank. His business there lasted barely a day and a half. Most of the time, his mind went wandering off into a private *cul-de-sac*: how was he to contact Clementine or Sasha without putting all of them in danger? Perhaps they would be at the Anglia Tavern; but how would he find it again without asking directions, and with his accent, that might seem suspicious? Even if he took the risk, and the doorman allowed him in, Sasha and Clementine might not use it any more. To inquire for Sasha directly at the Station would be too much of a chance. He could ask the hotel receptionist to connect him with the number of their flat, but he would certainly note it for future reference and listen to the conversation in case it turned out to be useful.

In the evening, he went slowly down to the hotel restaurant, so preoccupied with his problem that he didn't hear his name until it was called a second time.

"Paul! Paul, my dear! What a lovely surprise! What are you doing in Moscow? Come and join us; you must!"

He stared. It was Lydmilla Fyodorovna, her grey eyes sparkling, looking very elegant in a black velvet dinner gown and toque. Wonderful! She was again the old, attractive Lydmilla, and Paul rested his eyes on her with pleasure before glancing briefly at her companion. It came to him that he must somehow see her alone for a moment. She may know how to arrange a safe meeting with Sasha. There would be a risk in asking her, but…That preoccupation was dashed from his mind when he looked again at her companion. He was too old to be a new

Boris certainly, and yet Paul could sense an intangible intimacy between the two of them and, ridiculously, resented it.

More perplexing, there was something familiar about the man with her. The hair and neatly trimmed moustache were an unblemished white, the face plump the body pudgy in its tight, dark suit. His nails were trimmed to a degree of feminine delicacy, and he wore two large diamond rings, one on each hand. Everything about him grew more familiar by the minute and Paul knew that though he could not give the man a name, he himself was recognized in return. The man avoided looking at him directly; his eyes flickered in all directions about the restaurant as though he didn't wish to be noticed.

Lydmilla said: "You were in a world of your own, my dear. I had to call you twice. I half thought you were cutting me. Never mind now, I want you to meet my friend—Signore Guglielrno Martinelli."

Immediately as she said it, Paul remembered the suffocating train compartment and the man with the plaster saints with fantastical painted faces, locked in his suitcase. "We already know each other," he said, nodding without gladness.

"Of course, of course, I remember, too." Martinelli pointed to a chair. "Please join us, Signore. We met at Bozen or, as I still prefer to call it, Bolzano. You remember?" He followed this joke with an effeminate giggle that somehow matched his fingernails and made Paul uncomfortable.

"I wouldn't have thought they allowed your...er...pieces into the country," Paul said, deliberately hostile. There was still the question of the stolen letters to be settled.

Martinelli giggled again. "It is true they do not appreciate we Romans in your Holy Russia, Captain. They do not dislike us as they dislike the Jews, but..." He shrugged. "I am fortunate, indeed. Madame Kholchevskaya is my sponsor." He smiled again and spread his hands happily.

Paul sat down with them.

"It is true, Paul. Catholics are beginning to feel almost as intimidated as Jews; but you must know that for yourself." She had taken charge of their table and their conversation, ignoring the waiter who waited for their order. "Are you staying here, Paul? In this hotel?" He nodded. "That's good. We can spend the evening together. Now, where was I? About Guglielmo's trinkets, I have no religious feelings myself...I never have had. But I feel most strongly that, if they want to, other people should be allowed to indulge theirs."

There was no gentleness in her now. Paul had never known her to talk with such force, at such speed. Did she resent being found with a man he already knew, discovering a relationship between them beyond her control? Was her change from Italian to Russian intentional? Martinelli knew no Russian. He gazed at her fascinated, as though at any moment, she might produce a fluttering dove from between her lips.

She talked on, unstoppable. The waiter wandered away. Paul ceased to give her his attention and let his mind drift back to his problem. When he could suppress the idea no longer, he interrupted her lecture.

"He doesn't speak Russian?"

She turned to smile at Martinelli and patted his fat little hand proprietarily. "Isn't he sweet? So very, very..." She searched for a word and produced it in triumph: "Italian, don't you think? And no, my dear, don't worry. He knows no Russian."

"I'd no idea you knew him."

"No, well, not even you know everything about me, dear Paul. Now...what was it you wanted to say that you didn't want him to understand?"

"I must see Sasha!" He stopped abruptly and looked intently at the doll merchant's face, but the eyes retained their simple, inane, incomprehending smile. "Without careful arrangement, I gather, that could be dangerous for everyone."

She was surprised. "Sasha? But Sasha's not here."

"Not here? Where? Not in Moscow, you mean?"

"I thought you must have known. He likes you. I expected him to be in touch." She laughed awkwardly. "He was transferred to Saint Petersburg weeks ago."

"Saint Petersburg!"

"The Vyborg Station. He's in control of the locomotives on the line to Finland."

The next day on the Trans-Siberian, Paul felt at ease. Had he seen Sasha in Moscow, what could he have said? Wasn't he taking it all too seriously, perhaps? Weren't Rachel and Ida old enough, by now, to know their own minds? Leonore and he couldn't be expected to be responsible forever.

He passed his time being jolted through a winter landscape, making up tunes to the beating of the wheels. Nowhere in any direction was there any break in the miles of snow. Near cities, it was besmirched by the detritus of human living. Fence posts stuck up at unnatural angles like amputated limbs. As the distances between towns lengthened, there was less to defile the snow. There was nothing but its whiteness between the insistent train and the inevitable forest. The sight of it, the emptiness of it, relieved his spirits, and he watched from the window with a certain joy, composing in his head the love letter he would write to Leonore once he reached Harbin.

A letter from Sergei Ouroussoff was waiting for him at at Government House.

We count on you to visit us as soon as you can, old fellow. We plan not to be here much longer. Life on the Staff is hell, and I expect you'll understand why, as soon as you're back. The Tsar has appointed Admiral Alexeyev Viceroy Commander-in-Chief. At the same time, General Koropatkin, the Admiral's senior in rank, has been ordered to 'act on his own initiative, taking as a guide the general indications provided by the Viceroy.' That's the official wording and, I ask you, what could possibly be more open to argument and misunderstanding? I'll leave you to imagine for yourself the friction and confusion we live

*with. We mere mortals, of course, can do nothing whatever that meets
with anyone's approval!*

*So, my friend, I am leaving the Army, and the thought of it makes me
feel like a young man again. Neither Elizaveta nor I fancy life in Moscow or Saint Petersburg. I am, therefore, negotiating for a farm in the
Crimea, where we shall grow oranges, lemons and wine!! Our darling
Lili will grow to womanhood there, in a world as uncontaminated by
people and politics as we can possibly make it.*

*Do come as quickly, or God only knows when we shall see each other
again.*

Paul couldn't get any free time until the end of January. Sergei was
ebullient when he got to Port Arthur and lectured him on viniculture
with all the confidence of the student for whom the door has only just
been opened. Elizaveta Dmitrievna, in the excitement of packing to
escape the straitjacket of military life, frequently forgot herself so far as
to leave her beloved Lili in the sole charge of a Chinese nurse.

It was the most delightful, carefree holiday Paul had known in a
long time. Every day he felt the strings of tension loosen within him,
and every day he promised himself he would leave again for duty the
following morning, but never did. By the beginning of February, his
official conscience was sorely troubled, but on the eighth of the month,
the Admiral's wife was giving a ball. All the naval officers would leave
their ships unmanned—at officer rank—in the Bay, and Sergei and
Paul were, of course, expected to be there, too.

They went up with Elizaveta to Admiralty House, excited like children on their way to a very special treat and feeling hot under the
black, frosty sky. On its hill, Admiralty House shone out like a beacon.
Inside, the ladies' gowns were not, perhaps, equal to those to be seen in
Saint Petersburg, but the gaiety went beyond anything Paul had
known since his youthful days on the Islands.

The ballroom was filled with officers and their ladies, specially
attached in comradeship based on the knowledge that they were members of an exclusive club, holding the security of the Empire in their

hands. They were the Emperor's pioneers, their presence here holding the enemy at bay.

Paul was on the dance floor, holding Elizaveta Dmitrievna in his arms and swirling her breathlessly to the speedy one-two-three, one-two-three of a Viennese Waltz when they heard the first gunfire. It sounded from a distance like fireworks or a pageant involving blank cannon arranged for the occasion.

It was no pageant. It was the Japanese firing at the warships in the Bay. The War had unofficially begun.

EPILOGUE

CHAPTER I

▼

1905

Leonore's heart might have been cast in concrete, remaining in her window immovable as Prometheus splayed upon his rock. Wherever she went, whatever she did, her heart stayed there, scouring the street for hope.

Nowadays the Avenue was crowded with people, as if those who followed Father Gapon to their slaughter outside the Winter Palace on Bloody Sunday were followed in turn by a procession of vengeful phantoms.

What a useless waste it had been—every bit of it! That weekend, before he left for the peace and quiet of Tsarskoe Selo, the Tsar, forewarned by the police of possible trouble, had issued a conciliatory proclamation:

> "...I know that the worker's life is far from easy. There are many
> things to improve and organize; but be patient...In my solicitude
> for the workers, I will take care that everything possible is done to
> ameliorate their condition and to give them the means and power
> to express their new needs as these show themselves."

But a proclamation of royal good will was no longer enough. They had no patience left.

The floodgates of restlessness were opened in the beginning of the year, at the celebration of the Epiphany, the Blessing of the Waters commemorating the Baptism of Christ. The usual pavilion was built on the river-bank outside the Winter Palace, and a hole dug in the ice. The stream was traditionally rechristened *Jordan* for the occasion. In the presence of the Tsar and Nobility, the Metropolitan dipped a Cross into the River and took a sip from its waters, while choirs sang and cannon boomed from the Peter and Paul Fortress on the farther shore. This was the signal for universal rejoicing.

This year there was no rejoicing; horrified silence followed the cannonade. An uncomfortable rush of air across the *Jordan*, and a 'crump' close by quelled all other sound. The guns had been loaded with live ammunition instead of blanks. Fortunately for Nicholas II, the conspirators' aim was hopeless. The symbol of hypocrisy, superstition and oppression remained on his feet; and so did the hated glory of Holy Russia. The only casualty was a policeman standing behind the Tsar, who was blown to smithereens.

It may have been a grand conception and magnificent in its consequences, but instead, everything that was to have been changed remained in place. Patience among the workers was no longer relevant. Now they must be made to fear. To kill an Archduke or two was one thing, but to attempt to kill the Tsar himself...It's true the attempt had failed, but everything was changed, nevertheless.

Leonore, born a Jew, was naturally sensitive to communal tension. She had learned from birth that trouble could come from any direction and in any form! She had no immediate anxiety for Paul; his standing was good and his Democrat friends were all equally respectable men. They talked. They would never go further than that, and it was impossible to believe that they would.

It was for her children she fretted whenever they went out of the house. Dorothea, she knew, had no interest in politics. Her interest was centered on when the longed-for letter from Pyotr would come. She was safe. Sonia, like so many young people, longed for a change to the system and hadn't yet learned reserve. She was ready to preach her dogma to anybody who would listen. Marie's absorption was with alleviating conditions among the Jews. Leonore suspected she was probably Zionist like her Aunt Ida. She didn't approve, but she hoped the child would be safe so long as she was careful to whom she spoke. Jews would obviously be prime suspects for the outrage, and talking indiscreetly to the wrong person might make even gentle Marie a suspect! Eduard was in greater danger than his sisters, even. His Majesty had no more fervent supporter throughout the Empire than this son of hers, and every day she dreaded his fighting with one of the bands of revolutionary young hooligans roaming the streets. About Albrecht she wasn't at all worried. The shock of events had driven him back into silence. He hardly talked at all any more, and there was safety in that.

The situation was out of hand; everybody agreed about that. It was largely due to this beastly War, of course. Russia hadn't wanted a War, but what could she do after those horrible little Japanese, entirely unprovoked—but what could you expect from people like that?—attacked her ships in the Bay at Port Arthur? There was something highly suspicious about that! Who told them which night the Admiral's wife was giving her ball, and that the ships were left virtually without officers? And all those dreadful battles in Manchuria afterwards: who was telling them where and when to attack? Revolutionists, Jews, Catholics—there were enemies on every hand.

Everything was equally out of hand at home, too. Inflation was unbelievable. Some people must have been genuinely hungry, and there were certainly more beggars in the streets. Sometimes the trams ran and sometimes not. The same with the trains, even trains with troops and ammunition for the Front. The telephones were erratic, and the same could be said of just about everything else. The only way to manage was to ignore the situation as much as possible and carry on as normal. That is what Leonore and her friends were determined to do.

It was a great relief to have Paul at home, though in spite of Leonore's pleas not to, he insisted he had to make a sudden business trip to Warsaw directly after Epiphany. Lydmilla Fyodorovna was staying with them at the time, and for some reason there appeared to be some animosity between the two of them; she left directly after Paul, and Leonore was pleased to see her go. Everybody's temper was short at the time, and she had more important things to think about. She was worried about Sergei and Elizaveta Dmitrievna. They'd had no news of them during the siege, and when Port Arthur fell at the beginning of the month, they'd no idea whether they were alive or dead.

Above all else, Dora's birthday ball had been planned for months, and nothing was to be allowed to stand in the way of its success! Day after day, however difficult and dangerous, Leonore continued with her arrangements. When the telephone wasn't working, she traveled all over the city to visit dressmakers and caterers. On her way in and out of the house, she had to force herself to disregard the insulting importunities of the beggars living in the courtyard. In the cab, she sat well back, while the driver inched his way through rabble-ridden streets.

Now it was over. It had gone off splendidly in spite of everything. Ignoring the chaos around them, Dorothea's guests came in their finery and danced until the early hours. Leonore felt proud. Her previous formal receptions had all been 'official,' to support Paul in one way or another. This one was different. This one had been for the family. This was in honour of her own beloved child, her beautiful Dorothea. How she had loved it—the people, the music, the decorations, the flowers, the congratulations, the success. How she had been hoping for its ending with the child's first proposal of marriage!

But...instead...

She could never, now, close her eyes without again seeing those faceless men in their grey cloth coats, surrounding her husband in the hallway and taking him away. Loff followed and didn't come back until long after Father Gapon's two hundred thousand had passed her window. He'd made all the inquiries he could, the answers far from comforting. Paul was in the Peter and Paul Fortress. Later, after 'a thorough interrogation,' he would probably be sent to the Kresty Prison. The charge? She froze when Loff told her: Treason!

Loff stayed with her as long as he could, until Channah's news grew too threatening to be ignored. Disturbances were not confined to Russia alone. There were murders and burnings in Estonia, too. The full force of peasant hatred had been visited quite close, on the old von Aschenbauer Estate. The mob came one freezing night, and neither the house nor its Jewish owner had survived the attack. The streets of Haapsalu and Reval were seized by the revolutionists. The gendarmes were nowhere to be seen.

Leonore urged Loff to go home; there was nothing more he could do for her in Saint Petersburg. Paul's confinement in the Fortress was harsh, but she couldn't believe—during the first weeks, at least—that it was due to anything other than an administrative mistake. They were quite common, and tomorrow, for sure, the authorities would discover their error, and she would see him coming home in the street below. Her conviction of it, strong in the morning, almost petered out as the day faded, retained a flicker of life because of her hope for the morrow.

Eventually, in spite of all Loff's experiences, and advice not to do so, she herself dragged through the snow to the door of the Fortress.

The guard sucked his teeth under a bushy grey moustache and regarded her with no particular interest. She was only one of many.

"What's he in for, lady?"

"It's a mistake, of course. He shouldn't be here at all," she said, after telling him Paul's name.

"Yes, yes, yes. I understand. They're all mistakes. And what particular mistake is this?"

"Treason, they say, but…"

"Treason, eh?" He paused, sucking his teeth even more noisily. "That's serious, is treason."

"It's ridiculous, of course. He's innocent. If only you'd direct me to someone..."

"It always amazes me, how they have the heart to fill a great big place like this with innocent people, all these mistakes," he smirked.

"He is innocent, I tell you. I must speak to someone. Please let me in, just for a minute or two. I can find him, and..."

"Well now, as to finding him...with treason, that may not be so easy. He may not be here at all by now. He may be in the Kresty. Or they may have taken him to the Butyrsky in Moscow. That's where they keep them while they're making up the Siberian transports, you see."

"Oh, please! Please! You must help me. They can't send him away without a trial. At least, if you won't let me in, won't you at least find out for me whether he's still here?"

"On the other hand," the man ruminated gently, "they may have hanged him already. You can never really tell. Yes, lady?" he asked, turning to the woman next in line.

She was frantic in her terror. After Loff left she missed him, particularly because he was somehow able to manage the children better than she could. He eased their fears and interposed himself between them and their mother, lessening the strain of her having to be tranquil and undisturbed when they were together. He persuaded them, for their father's sake, to continue at school as normal. She managed to maintain self-control until the day in spring when an unexpected visitor puffed and panted and grunted up the stairs to see her. It was Colonel Denisovitch-Komarevsky.

"I've seen him, and he's all right. You must try not to worry, my dear," he thundered as greeting.

"You've seen him?" The sound of the words siphoned the strength from her body. She grasped at a sofa for support, and he was instantly and noisily by her side. "Oh, Colonel..."

"I'll ring for someone," he said in his harsh, grating voice. "You need brandy."

"No, no, I'm all right," she protested, while he forced her on to the sofa. "Tell me! For God's sake, tell me! You saw him? When? They let you in to see him?"

The old man chuckled. "Being a Colonel still means something, even today. I came as soon as I heard."

"How was he? Are they feeding him properly? Can you get in again? Would you take him some linen?"

"Take your time, my dear, take your time. I saw him, and I told him I was coming to see you directly afterwards, and...well, you know...he's only a damned-fool soldier like me at heart, and we don't say these things very well. You know. But you know what he was trying to say to me for me to try to say to you, don't you? And now, if you don't want that brandy, I do. Where's the bell?"

He waited until the servant had gone. "They're not treating him too badly at all. He's an embarrassment to them now. They don't know what to do with him."

"Why don't they send him home?"

He smiled. "They won't do that. Not yet. He hasn't actually done anything, but it's guilt by association. He was too friendly with the group who tried to kill the Tsar at the Epiphany Service."

She stood up with the shock of it. "But that's absurd. Colonel, you must tell them. You know him well enough to..."

He eased her down again. "That isn't easy. Please, my dear, you must try to hear me out. Unfortunately, it is quite true; he was involved with the wrong kind of people. And you know them too, I'm afraid."

"No!" She breathed deeply and held her hands before her, as if to fight off the demons he was allowing into the room.

"Your friends in Moscow, for instance."

"Oh, no! Not Clementine and Sasha."

"He was one of the prime movers in the group, apparently, together with an Italian anarchist who traveled with a case full of supposedly religious statues. They were stuffed with gunpowder, but because they were religious, he could get by any Catholic customs officer without being questioned."

She said nothing but sat silently, shaking her head in a kind of rhythm.

"You knew him, I believe?"

"He was an acquaintance of Paul's, I know. I recall meeting him once in Berlin, I think it was."

"Those years you lived abroad…they brought you under suspicion, of course." He grunted and looked embarrassed.

"There was an incident in Berlin, years ago…your husband was compromised. They got that from a man at the Bank…chap called Popov, I believe…But that's not important. What's more impor-tant…there are two other people involved: one intimately, the other, like your husband, by association only. You know who I mean…?"

She refused to meet his eyes and stared at the carpet.

"Your sisters, I'm afraid."

She was completely crushed and began mumbling, senselessly, "*Ave Maria gratia plena Dominus tacum in mulieribus…*" The prayer, if prayer she intended it to be, died on her lips.

"My dear young lady," he shouted, and she turned slowly to look at him. "Pull yourself together. Your sisters are quite safe, thank God. They accuse your husband of warning them in time to cross over from Warsaw to Berlin. The Italian was with them, and he's in Vienna, they presume. Your Moscow friends got over the frontier into Finland. They're safe in the West by now."

"Oh, Paul…Paul, my darling…" She burst into tears and could hardly speak. At last she was able to ask: "Why did he run such a risk? Why did he do it, Colonel?"

"Duty, my dear. Loyalty...Loyalty is Duty, of course. He always was a splendid soldier. I begged him not to leave the Army when he wanted to marry you."

"My Paul..." She sobbed, and she hadn't cried like this since they'd taken him away.

"The police had known about the group and what they were planning for months. A police agent had been friends with your husband for many years, though he didn't know who she was, of course. You knew her, too."

"Who was she?"

"The painter, Lydmilla Fyodorovna Kholchevskaya."

"No!"

"She was a police agent *provocateuse*. Your husband tells me she'd tried several times to get him to commit himself to one revolutionary group or another."

"Where is she now?" Leonore's voice was brittle with hatred. Being able to focus her passion on a particular person was a relief. Her life had assumed a pattern once more.

"Where is she now, Colonel? Do you know?"

"They wouldn't tell me that. They're keeping her address secret. But it must be somewhere here in town. They still need her to give evidence, I understand."

"Telling lies! What evidence is that? You say yourself, they've nothing against Paul."

"He'll be free, my dear, I'm sure of it. And I'll be in touch as often as I can, I promise."

He came regularly after that, and Leonore grew calmer in his confidence. At the end of March, as though it concerned anybody very much any more, the Tsar issued a Manifesto:

> *"The Emperor of all Russia has supreme autocratic power. It is ordained by God Himself that his authority should be submitted to, not only out of fear, but out a genuine sense of duty."*

That enigma again, that word, 'Duty'! How many people comprised the Empire? Two hundred million, perhaps? And did any two of them agree as to precisely what that word 'Duty' meant?

Leonore knew her duty, at least. Her every waking moment was spent keeping the family and the home together until Paul was free. Each day, she forcefully trampled on her doubts and insisted to herself that tomorrow would be The Day. Until she heard that Pyotr Stolypin was made Prime Minister, that is, and for everyone except the most extreme die-hards, life took a turn for the worse. She had not much time to concern herself with any of that. Politics had long-since lost all stability, shifting like the shimmering sea. Today people cheered and threw hats in the air because a vessel with sails of one colour was sighted from the sea wall; tomorrow's ship would have sails of a different colour, but the enthusiasm on the sea wall would be equally wild.

Minute by minute, whether or not he had any faith in his latest Manifesto, the Tsar retreated fraction by fraction. The middle class demanded a representative Duma. He gave them one, albeit short-lived. The peasants demanded land, and were prepared to take it for themselves if the landlords were reluctant to give it to them.

That was the case with the Baron. He was riding home from the diggings one evening. He need not have gone; they were deserted, his workers on strike. He had reached the last of the trees at the edge of the meadow outside the house when a group of what he still thought of as 'his people' came out of the shadows. They were led by Stepan Stepanovich, and they were there for a purpose. They pulled him down from his horse and stabbed him, time after time, with their pitchforks. They left him there, the snow stippled with his blood.

Leonore knew nothing 'til Channah got to her after struggling for three weeks through every kind of civil unrest. She was shown into the drawing room by Igor, handsome, well-built as ever, his looks exaggerating how gaunt and grey-haired Channah had become, and how dead her eyes were—dead and dry as stone.

"Channah, *Shalom.*"

"*Frau Baronin, Aleichem Shalom.*"

Leonore stared, disbelieving. Channah took her two hands in hers, stared unblinking into her eyes, and nodded. "It's true."

"Oh, my poor Loff. How? What happened?"

"Murdered."

She took Channah into her arms and held her close. "Channah! You poor, poor thing. At least thank God you got here. What happened? When? Can you bear to tell me?"

After nearly a month, the shock in the telling of it was blunted. Channah was too exhausted for surface emotion. Leonore was distressed on her own account to hear about Loff. She was even more disturbed when she thought about what effect this must have on Paul.

"We must send for the Colonel," she said. "He must go into the Fortress to tell Paul. He's the only one who can."

"Paul's still in that terrible place?"

Leonore nodded.

"At least Loff was spared that part of it, thank God!"

Channah persuaded her that Paul did not have to be told immediately. There was so much else she needed to know. In fact, it was several days before she knew everything.

"That Stepan Stepanovich is a devil, a fiend. I don't think there can ever have been anyone more evil. Hatred is all he knows."

"That's a madness all the whole world knows these days, it seems."

"It's nothing to do with what's happening at the moment. It goes back years. I was only a young girl at the time, but I can remember. He was one of the young village boys."

"Stepan?"

"Jaan. They came and took him for a soldier. It was the way they did it in those days. Every village had to supply a quota. Jaan had just been married. They probably would never have taken him if he hadn't tried to run away. His wife...you remember her...she was Greta."

"Greta? Father Tikhon's..."

"Who knows? That's what people said. Anyway, Jaan deserted and gradually worked his way back from Central Russia.

By chance, he heard about Loff recruiting down there and got taken on with the others. He was determined to come back, in any case. And when he arrived and saw what a state Greta was in...well, I suppose it was some perverted idea he'd learned in the army...some notion of Duty to his mad wife's honour..."

"You're not telling me he murdered the poor woman?"

Channah shrugged. "He was mad with hatred towards the whole human race. And who else would have done it? It wasn't the kind of thing any normal person would do. After he'd finished that bit of business, as it were, he waited 'til the time was right to take the next part of his revenge. Loff was to blame because he didn't stop the Army from taking him away. He couldn't, of course, but..."

On another day, when Leonore was standing at her window, she turned to find Channah watching beside her. She began, without any prompting, as though the memories in her head could be contained no longer.

"When I heard what had happened, I ran to the village, but not a single man there would help me. So I went to Father Vikkers, poor old man, and he and I together dug a grave as best we could. I took some linen from the house; we hadn't anything else. We wrapped him up and laid him in it, and Father Vikkers said his prayers...I don't know what they were."

There was a long silence. Leonore turned, expecting to see tears, but Channah's eyes were hard and dry as ever.

"I loved him very much," she whispered.

Colonel Denisovitch-Komarevsky promised to take the news to Paul. "What's happening to the Estate now?" he wanted to know. "Paul's bound to ask."

"No!" Leonore clasped his arm tightly. "He has enough on his mind. Don't tell him anything else to worry him, Colonel."

"It's bad, then."

"Ask Channah. She knows all about it."

He looked at Channah enquiringly.

"It couldn't be worse. The Estate's as good as stolen; Stepan Stepanovich is the new landlord. If there's any profit in the place, he'll keep it…though he says he'll divide it among the workers. I don't believe that. He turned out all the indoor staff when he got rid of me."

"All of them?" Leonore asked the question in a daze. "A great house like that! Who's…"

"Marika."

"She won't be able to manage without help. You know that better than anyone."

"She'll have to. She's terrified of Jaan. She has to do everything he says."

"But…Margarethe…"

"That's the worst of all. I begged him to let me stay to look after her, but he refused…wouldn't hear of it. He'll keep her living there—a sort of a trophy of his triumph over the family. Poor woman. I don't know what's going to happen to her. He wouldn't even let me in to say goodbye to her."

"Colonel, there must be something we can do," Leonore burst out. "It doesn't matter about the house or the land or the money…he's welcome to all that if it means so much. But we can't leave my sister-in-law in the hands of a man like that. I shall go and talk to him myself."

"I wasn't allowed to say goodbye to her," Channah reminisced softly. "And there was no one there who wanted to say goodbye to me. I tried to see Father Tikhon. I went to his church, but it looked as though he'd already run away. I passed Ants on the road. You remember him, Leonore?

"Yes."

"Poor old man. So old he couldn't remember how old he really was. He was turned out, too. Pastor Vikkers took him in. They'll manage somehow, between them."

In October, the middle class won. The Tsar granted a second Duma, with real legislative powers and an extension to the franchise. It was the beginning of the end for the Revolutionists, though it did nothing to calm Sonia's impatience for Socialism. She came stamping in from the Smolny one day, bursting with rage.

"They made us all go into the hall today, Mama, and the headmistress said a lady-in-waiting had come from the Palace to talk to us. She was an old girl, apparently…can't remember her name. But she was an authentic lady-in-waiting, I suppose, because she wore the Imperial Insignia. No sooner was she on the platform, silly old goat, than she burst into tears, and we could hardly make out a word she said. It was something about the Tsar granting a Constitution—as though that means anything with this one!—and, of course, 'the Tsar can do no wrong,' she said, as though she didn't believe a word of it, but it was the only way to excuse him. We all cheered, of course, and she went absolutely white—absolutely! She'd have carried us all off to the Peter and Paul with her own hands, if she could have managed it."

"Sonia, please don't joke about that place."

"I wouldn't have minded so much," Sonia laughed. "At least I should have been with Papa, shouldn't I?"

Another day, Princess Surotkina came with a request. The Surotkin house in the country had been burned; the Surotkin brothers were homeless and very, very frightened. They were too frightened to stay in the country, and their sister couldn't possibly house them in her own tiny flat in town.

"I hate asking you a favour at a time like this, my dear, especially when you have trouble of your own."

"Hush! Don't talk to me like that, Princess. Since Paul's arrest, you and Colonel Denisovitch-Komarevksy are the only people in the whole of Saint Petersburg who treat us as though we're not already dead and buried. I'm grateful." She smiled.

"You and your husband have always been so good to me. And I know an old woman can be a nuisance sometimes."

"No more silly talk. Tell me exactly what you want."

"My brothers will be arriving tomorrow afternoon, if the trains are still running, that is. I haven't been able to find them anywhere suitable to live—so many people are coming into town from the country—and I daren't let them to go an hotel because…well, you know, they do have a certain reputation, and…"

"You'll bring them here, of course," Leonore said immediately. "There's plenty of room now that I'm having to let the servants go."

"Oh, my dear!"

"They may not be very well looked-after, but I can promise them plenty of space."

"Of course, they'll rent their accommodation officially." She paused, looking at Leonore like an anxious little bird. "You…er…you won't be offended, my dear?"

Leonore laughed to reassure her, but there was no humour in it. "I was very poor once, as you may have gathered. Princess. I'm not too proud to admit it, now, that I'm poor again. There's no income from the Estate since it's been taken away from us. And nothing from the Bank since Paul's arrest."

Princess Surotkina took Leonore's two hands into her own and smiled. "Don't you worry, my angel. We'll all get through this some-how. You know I'll do whatever I can."

Coming in from school the following day, Sonia said, "Mama, there are three strange old gentlemen downstairs."

"I know."

"Who are they? They're really quite odd. One of them gave me a gold rouble. He pretended he'd found it in my hair behind my ear."

Leonore laughed and kissed her. "What are they doing now, my love?"

"Telling Eduard and Albrecht of their exploits years ago on the Turkish frontier. I didn't believe a word of it."

There was very little about it in the newspapers. It wasn't a very important affair, in comparison with the General Strike at the time that had brought the country almost to a standstill.

> *OUTRAGE AT GALLERY IN SADOVAYA STREET. At dusk yesterday, a motor car drew up outside the Art Gallery in Sado-vaya Street. Three young assailants got out, while a fourth remained in the car behind the driving wheel. The three burst open the door to the Gallery, shot dead the proprietor and, also, Madame Lydmilla Fyodorovna Kholchevskaya, the celebrated painter, who was in the premises at the time. Robbery was evidently not the motive.*

Paul insisted Leonore be told nothing; there was so much that might go wrong. So, when it finally happened, it happened as she'd dreamed it would. It was a day or two after the New Year, 1906. The General Strike was over. The tramcars were clattering up and down the Nevsky Prospekt, and the people on the pavements walked as though with purpose, instead of drifting from incident to incident.

The cab stopped at the courtyard gate, and Colonel Deniso-vitch-Komisarevsky turned to hand out his fellow passenger. The second passenger brushed his hand aside with slight impatience as he emerged, determined to display no physical weakness. From the window, Leonore watched them both, turned without a change of her expression and threaded her way between the beds behind her. She and the girls used this as their bedroom now, as more and more of the house had to be set aside to accommodate lodgers.

She went slowly down the stairs, to be certain her knees wouldn't give way at a vital moment. The door opened. Paul stood framed in the doorway. Behind him, Colonel Denisovitch-Komarevsky waved to her and turned back to the gate. She went forwards towards Paul. Their greeting was slow and long. Neither had any need of words.

Paul was amnestied, not guilty, nor yet innocent. His punishment was to be exile in Minoussinsk on the River Yenisey, south of Krasnoyask. A house would be provided, and a salary to exercise himself in administrative duties. The duration…? At the pleasure of His Majesty. God Save the Tsar!

He was diffident when he told the family, as though arrest and imprisonment had robbed him of trust in every member of the human race.

Leonore, accepting as ever said: "I must pack. When do we go? And we'll take Channah with us, won't we? We can't leave her alone."

Sonia wanted to know what tribal groups lived in that area. "We must find what dictionaries we can before we leave Saint Petersburg. We'll never be able to organize those people if we can't talk their language."

Marie said, "I'll help you. Mama."

Albrecht, voluble again with the joy of seeing his father, was already at the table with pencil and paper ready, wanting to know how far it was to Minoussinsk and how long it would take to get there.

Eduard was delighted by the idea of adventure—wild tribesmen, the Hindu Kush, Mongolia…he clicked his heels.

"*Jahwol, Herr Baron.*"

His father looked at him sadly. "Don't ever talk like that again, my son. That's over. Your Uncle Loff was the last real Baron, but it was when we were living in an unreal time. From now on, we must live in real time…real time with our eyes on the future.

0-595-22689-2